Prai...

"A master of the anc... ...iew

"The godfather of historical novelis...
—*Los Angeles Times*

Charleston

"Sure to lure readers . . . [a] masterly tale . . . [an] extraordinary family . . . during the most violent era of Charleston's history."   —*The Washington Post*

"A great read . . . fascinating historical anecdotes."
—*The Charleston Post and Courier*

"An entertaining saga with plenty of action."
—*The Orlando Sentinel*

On Secret Service

"Draws you back into the Civil War and the wrenching days preceding Abraham Lincoln's assassination. The factual details are simply astonishing: You walk the muddy streets, smell the acrid smoke of battlefields, and experience firsthand the inner workings of a vast conspiracy."—Patricia Cornwell

"[Jakes] gets the big story right, while writing in a clear style, keeping the narrative moving briskly from cliffhanger to cliffhanger, serving up portions of steamy sex in between, and offering us plenty of heroes and heroines to admire and several villains to hate. Even a deep-dyed Civil War buff . . . will find himself turning the pages to see what happens next."
—*Civil War Book Review*

continued . . .

The North and South Trilogy

North and South

"In the history of U.S. book publishing, there's never been a success story quite like that of John Jakes."
—The New York Times

"A panoramic, populous . . . lusty trek through the pages of American history . . . thick as a brick with period detail drawn from extensive research."
—San Francisco Chronicle

Love and War

"A feisty assortment of fictional heroes and heroines."
—People

"Massive, lusty, highly readable. . . . In delicious detail are the wicked and tawdry doings of a memorable cast of characters . . . a graphic, fast-paced amalgam of good, evil, love, lust, war, violence, and Americana."
—The Washington Post Book World

Heaven and Hell

"Remarkably vivid."   *—Los Angeles Times*

"He shows you George Armstrong Custer, Andrew Johnson, Buffalo Bill Cody, and a vast array of historical figures whose contending ambitions control the events . . . but he also shows you what people wore, what they read, and what they drank and ate. . . . What you get is the feeling that this is life. That's art."   *—Chicago Sun-Times*

★ THE ★
LAWLESS

The Kent Family Chronicles

VOLUME VII

JOHN JAKES

With a New Introduction by the Author

Ø

A SIGNET BOOK

SIGNET
Published by New American Library, a division of
Penguin Group (USA) Inc., 375 Hudson Street,
New York, New York 10014, USA
Penguin Group (Canada), 10 Alcorn Avenue, Toronto,
Ontario M4V 3B2, Canada (a division of Pearson Penguin Canada Inc.)
Penguin Books Ltd., 80 Strand, London WC2R 0RL, England
Penguin Ireland, 25 St. Stephen's Green, Dublin 2,
Ireland (a division of Penguin Books Ltd.)
Penguin Group (Australia), 250 Camberwell Road, Camberwell, Victoria 3124,
Australia (a division of Pearson Australia Group Pty. Ltd.)
Penguin Books India Pvt. Ltd., 11 Community Centre, Panchsheel Park,
New Delhi - 110 017, India
Penguin Group (NZ), cnr Airborne and Rosedale Roads, Albany,
Auckland 1310, New Zealand (a division of Pearson New Zealand Ltd.)
Penguin Books (South Africa) (Pty.) Ltd., 24 Sturdee Avenue,
Rosebank, Johannesburg 2196, South Africa

Penguin Books Ltd., Registered Offices:
80 Strand, London WC2R 0RL, England

Published by Signet, an imprint of New American Library, a division of Penguin
Group (USA) Inc. Published by arrangement with the author. Previously published in a Jove paperback edition.

First Signet Printing, March 2005
10 9 8 7 6 5 4 3 2 1

Copyright © John Jakes, 1978
Introduction copyright © John Jakes, 2005
All rights reserved

 REGISTERED TRADEMARK—MARCA REGISTRADA

Printed in the United States of America

In memory of my father

CONTENTS

INTRODUCTION:
ANSWERING THE
#1 QUESTION

In Q & A sessions, writers are repeatedly asked one question above all others: "Where do you get your ideas?" In the case of *The Lawless,* the seventh novel about the Kent family, I can confidently point to several sources.

I've said many times before that I've always relished the history of the American West. It has a place in the novel, in the sequences dealing with Jeremiah's unhappy descent into a life of outlawry.

My admiration for the French Impressionists is longstanding and that, too, is reflected in the book's opening section, which finds Matthew Kent in Paris, hanging around with some of the young, and as yet unappreciated, painters who would profoundly influence modern art. Among them is Matt's unruly friend Cézanne.

Eleanor's early career as an actress in a touring version of *Uncle Tom's Cabin* comes from my lifelong love of the stage. These road company adaptations of Harriet Beecher Stowe's blockbuster were called "Tom Shows," and their performers "Tommers," which I used for a chapter title. Tom Shows remained a staple of American theater well into the twentieth century.

It's possible that Gideon Kent became a labor organizer because, early in my life, my parents and I lived for a few years in Terre Haute, Indiana, under the long shadow of the legendary union organizer and socialist Eugene Debs. At the time I had no interest in Debs; besides, my parents, along with most of Terre Haute, dismissed him as a radical who didn't fit in as a proper citizen of Indiana. Ironically, Debs's home has become a tourist attraction, much as sites in Montgomery, Alabama, connected with the once-reviled Martin Luther King are now embraced by the local chamber of commerce and promoted as important places to visit.

But the most specific answer to the question about ideas can be found in a dark room in a building at the south end of Chicago's Lincoln Park. I visited the room many times as a youngster, gazing with awe and fascination at the scenes re-created in miniature behind glass windows: eight of them, as I remember.

The place is the Chicago Historical Society, one of the nation's finest museums and research facilities. The dark room at the CHS contained a series of dioramas, or models, depicting Chicago at various times in its past. The diorama that drew my interest most often showed the city, under a flickering red sky, being devoured by the Great Fire of 1871. Somehow that scene buried itself in my imagination, to be recalled and used at some unknown moment in the future. This turned out to be the sequence in *The Lawless* that finds Gideon trapped in, and trying to escape from, the Great Fire.

When I started this new introduction, I asked the Chicago Historical Society whether the dioramas still exist. Lesley Martin of the CHS Research Center assured me that they do and in fact were recently featured in a photo piece in the *Chicago Tribune*. I was delighted to hear that not everything I knew and loved as a kid has been washed away by contemporary culture.

Thus, for this second-to-last volume of *The Kent Family Chronicles,* I can, for a change, answer the question about the springboard for ideas. I wish it were that easy for every book I've written.

The Lawless remains one of my favorite novels in the series, because it encompasses so many aspects of history that have always fascinated me, not the least of them that harrowing image of Chicago burning. I thank my friends at New American Library for returning this and all the other volumes in the Kent saga to new life in these excellent new editions.

—John Jakes
Hilton Head Island,
South Carolina

"Pistols are almost as numerous as men. It is no longer thought to be an affair of any importance to take the life of a fellow being."

October 13, 1868:
Nathan A. Baker,
editorializing in
the *Cheyenne Leader*.

"What is the chief end of man?—to get rich. In what way?—dishonestly if we can; honestly, if we must. Who is God, the one only and true? Money is God. Gold and Greenbacks and Stock—father, son, and the ghost of same—three persons in one; these are the true and only God, mighty and supreme . . ."

September 27, 1781:
"The Revised Catechism"
by Samuel Clemens,
published in
the *New York Tribune*.

THE KENT FAMILY

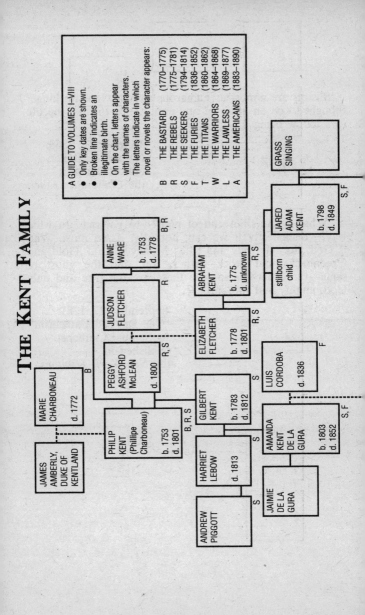

A GUIDE TO VOLUMES I–VIII
- Only key dates are shown.
- Broken line indicates an illegitimate birth.
- On the chart, letters appear with the names of characters. The letters indicate in which novel or novels the character appears:

B	THE BASTARD	(1770–1775)
R	THE REBELS	(1775–1781)
S	THE SEEKERS	(1794–1814)
F	THE FURIES	(1836–1852)
T	THE TITANS	(1860–1862)
W	THE WARRIORS	(1864–1868)
L	THE LAWLESS	(1869–1877)
A	THE AMERICANS	(1883–1890)

JAMES AMBERLY, DUKE OF KENTLAND

MARIE CHARBONEAU
d. 1772
B

PHILIP KENT (Phillipe Charboneau)
b. 1753
d. 1801
B, R, S

PEGGY ASHFORD McLEAN
d. 1800
R, S

JUDSON FLETCHER
R

ANNE WARE
b. 1753
d. 1778
B, R

ABRAHAM KENT
b. 1775
d. unknown
R, S

ELIZABETH FLETCHER
b. 1778
d. 1801
R, S

GILBERT KENT
b. 1783
d. 1812
B, R, S

HARRIET LEBOW
d. 1813
S

ANDREW PIGGOTT
S

AMANDA KENT DE LA GURA
b. 1803
d. 1852
S, F

JAIMIE DE LA GURA
S

LUIS CORDOBA
d. 1836
F

JARED ADAM KENT
b. 1798
d. 1849
S, F

GRASS SINGING

stillborn child

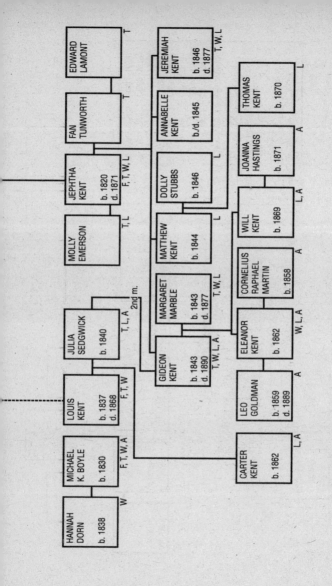

PROLOGUE

THE DREAM AND THE GUN

i

THEY HUNTED BUFFALO and lived in the open, away from the settled places. That sort of life tended to keep a man fit. But sometimes even the most robust constitution couldn't withstand foul weather. So it proved with Jeremiah Kent in April of 1869.

Three days of exposure to fierce wind and pelting rain left him sneezing. Two days after that, he and his companion made camp in a hickory grove. Jeremiah rolled up in his blankets and surrendered to fever. Kola, the Oglala Sioux with whom he'd traveled since early '66, kept watch.

After sleeping almost continuously for forty-eight hours, Jeremiah woke late at night. He saw Kola squatting on the other side of the buffalo chip fire, a dour look on his handsome face. Between Jeremiah and the Indian lay the cards of an uncompleted patience game Kola had started to pass the time. Over the past couple of years, whenever they'd had nothing else to do, Jeremiah had tried to teach his friend all the card games he knew. The Indian liked cards and had learned to shuffle and deal almost as fast and expertly as his mentor.

Jeremiah struggled to rise on one elbow. The fever still

1

gripped him, distorting sounds: the rustle of new leaves in the spring breeze; the purl of water out of a limestone formation behind the grove; the occasional stamp or snort of one of their long-legged calico ponies. From his friend's expression, Jeremiah knew something bad had happened.

He licked the inside of his mouth. The fever made his teeth feel huge, his head gigantic. "You ought to sleep once in a while," he said.

"The sickness has not passed. I will keep watch."

"That all you're fretting about, the sickness?"

The Sioux glanced into the wind-shimmered flame.

"Something's sticking in your craw. What is it?"

The Sioux was three years older than Jeremiah, and his true *kola,* his sworn friend for a lifetime. Jeremiah had found the Indian on the prairie, nearly beaten to death by one of his own tribe; the beating was punishment for adultery. He'd cared for the Indian until he recovered, as Kola was caring for him now.

The young man's bleary stare fixed on the Indian, prodding. "Come on. What?"

Kola sighed. "I did sleep a little tonight. While I slept, a vision came."

The various branches of the Sioux tribe put great stock in visions. Clearly Kola's had upset him. Jeremiah tried to put him at ease with a laugh and a wave. "Listen, I'm the one with the fever and the dreams."

"Dreams of what?" Kola asked instantly.

Jeremiah's grin widened. "Women. Plump women."

Kola grunted. "Better dreams than mine. I dreamed a dark thing."

"Tell me."

Looking at him with eyes that brimmed with misery, Kola said, "I dreamed I saw you with your guns again. I saw the guns in your hands."

Anger and fear started Jeremiah shivering. Almost without thought, he glanced into the dark where the ponies were tethered. His revolvers were wrapped in oilskin in one of his saddlebags. The same bag carried the last of the money stolen in the ill-conceived payroll train robbery up near North Platte over a year ago. He'd been going by the name Joseph Kingston then.

"Well, it must be a false vision this time. I packed the guns away last winter."

I killed eight men and one woman before I came to see that always settling things with the guns was a sickness. A sickness that would whip me one day if I couldn't whip it first.

The faces of the dead whirled through his mind, each vivid and never to be forgotten. Some were faces from the Georgia plantation owned by the man who had been his commanding officer. Before Lieutenant Colonel Rose had died outside Atlanta, he'd begged the young Confederate soldier to leave the beaten army—desert—in order to be of some real use in the last days of the war. He'd implored Jeremiah to head straight for the plantation named Rosewood and help protect it and the colonel's family from Sherman's horde.

Jeremiah had done so. Or tried. At Rosewood, one by one, he'd killed Skimmerhorn, a Yankee forager. Price, a troublemaking ex-slave. And Serena, his commanding officer's daughter. Killing her had given him the greatest pleasure. Hurt him the most, too. Serena had lied to him. Said she loved him when all she really cared about was the Kent money he'd told her about. The money he stood to inherit one day if he went back home, which was impossible after the killings at Rosewood. He fled west.

Some of the faces of the dead were from Fort Worth. A monte dealer who'd tried to cheat him. A law officer who'd tried to arrest him after he used his guns to give the dealer his comeuppance.

There were faces from his prairie wanderings. The busted-luck cattleman, Major Cutright. The major's hired hand, Darlington. A third belonged to a member of Cutright's party whom Jeremiah had foolishly spared and released after the major tried to steal a load of freshly shot buffalo. Jeremiah could still see the terrified, furious face of the boy named Timothy who'd promised to remember him. Remember the deaths. Find him one day and repay him.

Finally there were faces from the Union Pacific railhead where he and Kola had sold the buffalo meat. A sharp named Butt Brown and his dim-witted helper. Those two and all the rest were dishonorable people, deserving death.

But in the end, giving them what they deserved created too many problems. So last year he'd set about overcoming his desire to mete out punishment. He'd taught himself not to need the kind of joy that accompanied killing.

With effort he went on. "Why, hell, I haven't so much as threatened anybody with a gun since we held up the U.P. special in Nebraska and then agreed that kind of thing was too damn dangerous."

Slowly, Kola nodded. "I hear all you say. Nevertheless, I dreamed I saw you with the guns."

"That's *over*!" A bitter smile. "Sometimes I think I'm the only one who believes it. My mother used to talk about a crazy streak in the family. Inherited from someone way back, a grandmother, maybe. Fletcher blood was what she called it. The woman's name was Fletcher. My mother never came right out and said she saw the streak in me. But I know she did. Else why would she have brought it up? I guess what I did at the end of the war and right afterward proves she was right. But I've licked it, Kola. I may have it, but it isn't going to push me where I don't want to go."

He sounded more confident than he felt. Sometimes his mother's words stole into his thoughts and brought a sad conviction that he was a prisoner of something inescapable. He grew vehement again.

"I'm changed for good. The other way makes a man scared all the time. Scared of arrest, scared of every stranger he meets, scared of answering when somebody says an ordinary hello—"

Kola averted his eyes. That angered Jeremiah all the more. "What the hell's wrong now? You don't believe me either?"

"I want to believe you with the fullness of my heart, so you will be free of the hurt those kil—the past has brought you. But—"

"Come on. Say it!"

Kola swallowed, then whispered, "In the dream I also heard a voice."

Jeremiah's spine twitched. "One of the holy voices?"

"Yes, *wakan*, holy. When I woke, I was very careful to recall everything it said." Kola's eyes focused on the dark beyond the fire and his voice took on a singsong quality.

"It said to me, once you take up the guns again, you will never put them down. There will be no end to the killing. The guns will bring great luster to your name for a while, but then it will vanish as swiftly as the light of a winter afternoon. Finally the power of the guns will fade and you will be killed by"—bleak eyes found Jeremiah's—"one of your own."

"*One of*—" He gaped, torn between fright and an urge to guffaw. "You mean, my family?"

Kola's tone was normal again. "I suppose. I only heard the voice say exactly what I told you. There is no more."

Jeremiah wiped his perspiring forehead. "That's the most ridiculous thing I've ever heard. 'Specially the last part. It couldn't happen! My mother's gone and the rest of my family think I'm dead. The only person who knows Jeremiah Kent is still alive is my father's friend Boyle, the Irishman we ran into at the railhead in sixty-six. But he swore never to say a word about meeting me. I couldn't stand to have my father or brothers know the things I've—well, I don't plan to look any of them up. Ever! So it couldn't happen."

Kola ran a finger through the dirt beside the fire. "I hope that is true. I cannot say whether it is. Nothing was explained to me in the vision."

"Then it's a stupid vision! You hear? *Stupid!*"

The strident, fever-dry voice hurt the Sioux, who stared down at the cracked toes of his boots.

Jeremiah's exertions had cost him too much energy. He fell back, dizzy and breathing hard. His voice took on a rambling, sleepy quality.

"I'm through with the guns. People hunt you, put your name up on posters. You've seen those, Kola. I'm all through with that kind of life. It"—he coughed—"it costs too much."

And yet, a taunting inner voice persisted, *there is that indescribable moment when the hand is fused to the gun and the gun becomes part of you, when the bowel-loosening fright spreads in the eyes of the one facing the gun and you feel so powerful*—

"No," he said, "I'm through."

Motionless, Kola contemplated the fire.

Jeremiah's eyes closed. He welcomed the fluffy black of

fever-induced drowsiness. It saved him from thinking about his friend's words. He *was* set on a different course, for good. No matter how poor the season or how meager the profits at the end of it, hunting buffalo was preferable to running and wondering who was pursuing.

"Dream," he mumbled, slipping into unconsciousness. "Dream—was wrong."

He didn't slip away fast enough. He heard Kola whisper with unmistakable doubt, "Perhaps. Perhaps."

ii

In another twenty-four hours, the fever still lay on him. Kola woke him gently. A red sunset light was spearing down, fragmenting in the shade of the grove.

Touching his shoulder, Kola said, "This has lasted too long. You cannot eat, everything comes up. I cannot help you. I must find someone who can."

So dizzy he could barely fight his eyes open, Jeremiah said, "No, that's not safe."

Kola acted as if he hadn't heard. "There is a town nearby. I will find a man who practices white medicine and bring him."

At that moment Jeremiah felt a surge of emotion—love or something very close to it. He was startled to find he was still capable of feeling affection of the kind he'd once felt for his older brothers. Kola was risking much on his behalf. The other man well knew the dangers of riding into a white settlement, one scruffy Indian in white man's clothing. It was especially dangerous in this part of Kansas, which had been plagued by raiding Cheyenne and Arapahoe and Kiowa the preceding year.

"Kola, I don't want you to take a chance and—"

The Sioux pushed him down, interrupting. "I must. I will be safe enough. It will take only an hour or two."

Apprehensive, Jeremiah watched him ride into the blurred red dusk.

He never came back.

iii

On the following Tuesday evening when Jeremiah rode along the Kansas Pacific rails to the settlement, he was still suffering from a slight fever. Although the gusty wind was cool, perspiration gathered under the brim of his low-crowned plainsman's hat. He swayed slightly in the saddle, a tall young man of twenty-three who gave the appearance of being much older.

He had his mother's fair hair and his father's gaunt cheeks and a weathered, pleasant face spoiled only by his mouth, which was so thin it sometimes took on a cruel cast. His good-weather clothing consisted of a collarless cotton shirt, blue once but now faded to ivory; a dirty gray buckskin vest with pockets; checked wool trousers reinforced with buckskin at the places a saddle tended to chafe the worst—the seat and the insides of the thighs. On his boots he wore plain American-style spurs called OKs. The rounded, filed rowels were easy on the flanks of a horse.

Wind blew dust clouds through the darkness and drove the grit into his eyes, making vision that much more difficult. He passed a siding that led to chutes and pens of unpainted lumber. Perhaps nothing symbolized America's resurgent postwar economy so well as the huge herds of Southern cattle beginning to reach Northern railheads. In keeping with the mood of optimism sweeping the nation now that Grant had taken charge in the White House, this town had evidently expected to share in the coming live-stock boom. But something had gone wrong. The new pens contained only little whirlwinds of dust. There were no cattle, and no sign of any.

Sweat continued to accumulate under the band of his hat. He wanted to take the hat off but he didn't. It concealed the one mark which made him easy to identify—the streak of white hair starting above his left brow and tapering to a point at the back of his head. The streak had been white since Chickamauga, where a Minié ball had grazed his scalp. He often disguised the streak with a mixture of dirt and boot polish. Tonight he hadn't troubled; he'd been too preoccupied by worry.

He rode straight up to the tiny frame depot beside the single track. The depot was dark except for an exterior

lantern on the far end. A sign was nailed to the roofpeak
below the lantern:

ELLSWORTH

Ellsworth, Kansas. Not much of a place from what he
could see. A single street with a few pitch-roofed houses
and a handful of commercial buildings of unpainted clap-
board, strung out to the north of some cottonwoods growing on a bluff along the Smoky Hill River. A rutted trail
meandered down to an easy ford.

Only a few lamps glowed in the village. At the far end
of the street, music drifted from one of the largest buildings. A polka, played on a twangy, out-of-tune piano. Despite its raw, impoverished look, Ellsworth was civilized
enough to possess a dance house where a man could have
a rousing gallop around the floor with one of the hostess-
whores such places employed, and while dancing complete
arrangements for later in the evening. Jeremiah saw six or
seven horses in front of the dance house. Trade was light,
but then it was a weeknight.

"Giddap, Nat," he said, barely touching his calico with
one spur. He walked the pony through a billowing cloud
of dust and then abruptly reined in. Light leaking from a
cottage to the line of trees showed him a still form turning
slowly in the wind.

His belly began to feel as hot as his forehead. He rode
close enough to be sure, and when he was, bowed his head.
"Jesus," he said under his breath. "Oh dear Jesus."

He could appreciate what Kola must have felt, reaching
the end so despicably. He could imagine his rage and humiliation. Except for the meanings of dreams, nothing mattered more to a Sioux than a proper death of which the
tribe would be proud to speak for generations. Such a death
had to be met bravely, even flamboyantly, in combat with
fierce and respected enemies. Instead, Kola had died like
a common horse thief.

The anger rising in Jeremiah seemed to banish his fever
and clear his head. He scanned the street to be sure he
wasn't being watched. Then he climbed down and tethered
the calico on the river side of the trees, where the animal
would be hidden from casual observation.

Reaching to his boot, he yanked out a buffalo knife. He scrambled up into the lowest fork of the cottonwood and cut down the hanged Indian.

iv

A sleazy café, the Sunflower, was open, though without customers until he walked in. The old man tending the place regarded him with the familiar suspicion reserved for new arrivals in a small town.

Jeremiah locked a smile on his face. He ordered some food—stew with too little meat and too much chili powder—and a cup of bitter coffee. He sat eating and drinking at one of three rickety tables while the rheumy-eyed, weary old man watched him.

He hated the delay, this pretense. But he needed information. As he lifted the cup to his mouth, his hand was steady despite his sickness. So was his voice when he forced conversation.

"Nice little town you have."

"Glad somebody thinks so."

"I can't be the only one. Someone spent quite a bit on those cattle pens and the spur track."

"Plenty of fools in this town, mister. They're the ones who squandered the money. Even persuaded the governor to lay out a special drover's highway up from Fort Cobb in the Indian Territory. A highway exempted from the quarantine law. We don't need exemption, you understand. We're not in the quarantine zone. But the highway's supposed to show that Ellsworth is interested in Texas trade—"

He wiped his nose. "The Texas boys aren't interested in Ellsworth, though. They won't drive their herds this far north. Too much risk of Indians. Fellow who started the local paper last year, he found out. Printed his sheet for exactly three months, then packed up. He came to understand Ellsworth'd blow away if it wasn't for the soiled doves at the dance house bringing in business. Mostly drunkards from the military reservation."

"Oh, there's an army post here?"

"Fort Harker. East a ways." The man leaned across the

plank counter. "You don't sound like you were in the Union army. You a Southron?"

Yes, you prying son of a bitch. I fought the war we had no chance of winning.

Amiably, he said, "Maryland. We kept no slaves. Our family was loyal to the Union, but my pa was crippled. I had to tend the farm. Cost me three hundred dollars to avoid conscription, but I had no choice. Two months after Appomattox, Pa died and I sold the place and came out west to hunt buffalo. Name's Jason Gray."

The convenient story had served before. It satisfied the old man. After a last bite of stew, Jeremiah added, "I noticed an Indian strung up to one of the cottonwoods."

A shrug. "He should have known better than to walk into the dance house like a white man. I mean, it wouldn't sit well most anyplace but it definitely didn't sit well here. The Cheyenne hit Ellsworth a year ago. After we recovered from that, the K.P. canceled the roundhouse we were promised. Next we got an outbreak of Chinee cholera. And there won't be any cattle trade in the summer. That's all going to Abilene where those scoundrels ignore the quarantine line and bribe the legislature to do the same. The truth is just this, Mr. Gray—and I quote our lately departed editor—Ellsworth is puking to death."

Jeremiah grimaced. "Guess all that trouble would put anybody in a peevish mood. People here took it out on the Indian, is that it?"

"Way I got the story, he refused to leave the dance house when he was ordered. Kept jabbering that he needed a doctor. Sergeant Graves took offense and roused some of the citizenry."

"Sergeant Graves," Jeremiah repeated.

"Yes, sir, from the post. He's down at the dance house most every night. Lends a lot of money to other soldiers. It's a sideline of quite a few noncoms in the Plains Army. Graves charges interest like billy be damned. Must be rich by now."

"And he whooped up enthusiasm for the hanging party?"

"He led it. Tied the noose personally."

"Could your police force have saved the Indian?"

"What police force? All we have so far is a volunteer

chief. And he's away riding the Kansas Pacific half the time. He's a conductor. Off working right now, in fact."

"I see."

"What you don't see is that nobody wanted to stop it. Besides, Graves had every right to do what he did. He lost a brother when Custer took the Seventh Cavalry down to the Washita last year to punish the Cheyenne."

"To massacre them," Jeremiah murmured.

The old man's eyes flickered with suspicion. "In Ellsworth, Mr. Gray, we think Custer did right. It wasn't any massacre. It was protective action. When the Indians broke out of their treaty lands, they raised the very devil all over Kansas. Not twenty miles north of here, they struck Mr. Shaw's homestead on Spellman's Creek. Thirty or forty of them kept Mrs. Shaw and her sister prisoner for most of a day. Subjecting those two poor women to the grossest possible indignity. Over and over, the grossest—possible—indignity." He emphasized the words so his customer was sure to understand.

"Not only did they do that," he went on, "they ruined our cattle business before it even commenced. The Texans won't come here now. When General Custer and the Seventh rode to the Washita, they gave the savages what they had coming."

Jeremiah forced the smile back on his face. "I guess it all depends on who's the killer and who's the victim. If I was to shoot the right person"—the old man started; Jeremiah almost chuckled—"an Indian, for instance—very few in the nation would blame me."

He laid out a shinplaster—one of the pieces of paper money printed during the late war. "Thanks for the meal. I'll be traveling on now."

"Buffalo hunter," the old man grunted, half a question, as Jeremiah received his change.

"That's right." Jeremiah stared. Something in him took pleasure in seeing the old man bite his lip and avoid the unwavering, almost hostile gaze. Amused, he walked out into the dark.

With the dust clouding around him, he comforted Nat. The pony was fretting with Kola's corpse slung belly down over his back.

Slowly Jeremiah unlaced a saddlebag and pulled out the

packet containing the remainder of the proceeds of the train robbery. Two hundred dollars in shinplasters. He held the packet in his teeth and removed the next pouch, and the next. Each contained an army-issue .44 caliber Starr revolver. The second also held ammunition.

He thrust both revolvers into his belt, replaced the two empty pouches and the full one, loaded the guns and said to the calico, "I'll be back soon."

He walked toward the dance house.

You swore never to do this again. You swore you were done with it.

The voice went unheeded as he tramped along in the blowing dust with the cottonwood leaves hissing in the dark on his right flank. He was gripped by a mounting excitement, yet by a certain melancholy too. He'd been a fool to think he could never change what he was. What the war had made him.

He put it all out of his mind composing himself, readying himself for the work to be done. With the barrels of the revolvers gouging his belly at every step, he felt whole again. It was as if a missing part of his body had been miraculously restored.

V

While he approached the dance house, the piano player swung into a mazurka. Loud laughter drifted through the open upper half of a Dutch door. He paused a moment on the dark porch, carefully counting and appraising those inside.

Only four soldiers were present, three quite young. Boys of seventeen or eighteen: new recruits, off duty and unarmed. The fourth soldier was a paunchy veteran.

Next he noted three men in nondescript civilian clothing, and the same number of women in tawdry dresses. Two men were dancing, one young soldier and one civilian, each hauling one of the women around the floor with clumsy, exuberant steps. Another of the civilians, a fellow in a threadbare frock coat, sat by himself at a rear table. The piano player was decrepit, the barkeep round-shouldered with a consumptive's face. Smoke and amber chimneys on the ceiling lamps softened the figures as if they were images in an old, soiled painting.

He suspected his quarry might be present. The paunchy man wore yellow chevrons and was engaged in animated conversation with one of the younger soldiers. Jeremiah buttoned his vest over the butts of the Starrs, noting that the paunchy man had come into town without a sidearm.

He reached for the handle of the Dutch door. Amber-flecked eyes turned in his direction, but just briefly. The monte man was the only one who continued to watch as Jeremiah strolled to the bar, his palms damp and his ears ringing. When the monte man realized the new arrival hadn't come in search of a game, he resumed his concentration on his deck of cards.

Jeremiah ordered whiskey. One of the whores approached. She stood close, so his right hip fitted between her legs. Even with the thickness of her shabby velveteen skirt intervening, he could feel the contour of her. A quiver in his groin reminded him it had been a long time since he'd enjoyed female companionship. But he shook his head.

"Fine thing!" she pouted. "You could at least buy a drink for someone trying to welcome a stranger to our fair—"

Belatedly, she fixed on Jeremiah's eyes. Then her gaze dropped to the almost lipless line of his mouth. The commercial smile faded and a shiver worked across her bare shoulders. She backed away from him.

The dancers whooped and stomped. Their motion stirred the smoke. Jeremiah picked up the dirty glass full of whiskey but didn't drink. He was straining to overhear the paunchy sergeant's conversation down the bar.

"—an' that money's yours till a week from Friday. Then she's due. No leeway."

"Jesus," the young soldier said. "You're worse than a Jew."

The sergeant chuckled. "No, sir. I'm a kind heart. There's your receipt"—paper tore—"just in case you forget how much you owe."

"When I'm handing back twenty percent on it? Jesus."

The young soldier made straight for the card table. The monte man welcomed him with a warm grin and a call for refreshments. One of the whores served them.

Loud enough to be heard by the paunchy man, Jeremiah said to the barkeep, "Pardon me. I'm hunting for a Sergeant Graves."

The barkeep nodded his head. The paunchy man pivoted, beaming.

"Amos Graves? Right here, sir." He couldn't have been over thirty, but the seams in his face and the discolorations on his nose made him look much older. Jeremiah had heard the Plains Army was a haven for men who couldn't control their craving for alcohol.

"Sergeant Amos Graves," the man said, his huge belly jiggling under his dark blue jacket as he approached. A pudgy hand waved a small block of paper. "Unofficial banker of Fort Harker and friend of the needy." He had puffy cheeks, mustachios drooping past his mouth, and a whiskey stink. He planted elbows on the scarred wood next to Jeremiah. "New arrival in Ellsworth?"

"That's correct."

"Well, if it's a loan you're after, I don't ordinarily extend privileges to those passing through, not unless they can offer me some collateral." He surveyed Jeremiah's clothes. "You a Texas boy? Sound a bit like it. Now if you brung a hundred head of cows up this way, I might be willing to—"

"I came to ask about the Indian you hanged."

Despite the music and the thump of boots, most of those in the place heard the remark. One couple halted in the middle of the floor and turned to gape. The piano player missed a beat, mangled the next notes, then quit altogether. In the silence even the hiss of rapidly shuffled cards died away.

Again Jeremiah fixed a smile in place. He didn't want to prod things to a conclusion too soon. He reminded himself to be wary of the barkeep. He suspected the man kept a weapon hidden for emergencies.

Sergeant Graves chuckled in an uneasy way. "You mean that greasy buck strung to the cottonwood?"

"Yes." Jeremiah's smile broadened so Graves would relax. "Just curious about what happened to him."

It worked. Graves waved for a drink, then said, "Why, he marched in here saying he needed a doctor. To treat his pox, I s'pose. All them red men got the pox. When we told him nicely this was a dance house for white folks, he wouldn't leave. Got plain feisty, in fact. That's when me and a couple of the lads took him in hand. I'll give him this. He wasn't armed, but he fought like a catamount."

"You mean to say he came in here looking for help, trusting that someone would give it to him?"

Graves gulped from his refilled glass, grinned. "Yeah, damn fool." A thoughtful pause. "I think he was a Cheyenne."

"He was a Sioux."

Graves' eyes flickered with uneasiness. A yellow jewel of sweat oozed out on his brow, another. Jeremiah thoroughly enjoyed making this drunken whale twitch and wonder.

Quickly he checked the three young soldiers. One was still on the dance floor, one at the card table, one leaning over the bar. He dismissed them as potential sources of danger. He was feeling more exhilarated by the moment.

"You know him?" Graves asked.

To keep the sergeant fretting, he evaded. "I took a look at him and recognized he was a Sioux, not a Cheyenne. Difference in height and in the nose and cheekbones."

Activity in the dance house had come to a complete stop. Jeremiah noted the barkeep's hands hanging in front of his apron, within reaching distance of whatever weapon might lie on an unseen shelf.

"You recognized that," Graves said. "What trade you in, mister?"

"Buffalo hunter. Tell me about the hanging."

Once again a friendly tone lulled the heavy man. He shrugged. "Oh, the whole thing didn't take more than ten minutes. But we did have some mighty good jollification with him before we strung him up."

"Jollification," Jeremiah repeated, unbuttoning his vest.

Sergeant Amos Graves saw the butts of the Starrs and swallowed. His right hand twitched. The whiskey glass fell, rattling and rolling on the bar. The spilled liquor reflected amber light. The smell of the whores' perfume filled Jeremiah's nostrils.

"So you had jollification with him, did you? Let me tell you why he was here: because I was laid out with a fever and he wanted to find a doctor to help me."

"Well, now—look. If you knowed him, why didn't you say—"

"I wanted to hear your explanation first. You murdered an innocent man, Sergeant. My partner."

His right hand moved, crossing over to the left side of his belt. Before Graves could so much as gulp, he was staring at the drawn revolver.

With that odd, lipless smile, Jeremiah flicked his glance toward the barkeep. "This muss is only between the sergeant and myself. You'll be wise to stay out of it."

"All right. Sure." The barkeep nodded. "Anyway, I wasn't on duty the night it hap—"

"Shut your mouth."

Jeremiah returned his gaze to the sergeant. He pointed the revolver at Graves' too-tight belt.

"You killed a fine man. I don't care if you did lose a brother to the Cheyenne. You had no call to do it."

"How—how did you hear about—"

"Never mind."

"I—I dunno what you—what you want now . . ." Graves' voice trailed off.

Jeremiah smiled. "You know."

"Wait. *Wait!*" Fat white hands flew up to protect his face. With the Starr barrel Jeremiah knocked them down. Graves squealed and sucked on a knuckle.

Jeremiah's eyes swept the rest of the customers and employees. "I wouldn't interfere. I don't want to deal with anyone except this dishonorable gentleman. But I will if I must—is that clear?"

A townsman nodded vigorously. No one else moved.

Spittle glistened at the corners of Graves' mouth. "Listen, I'm sorry about your friend. I was liquored that night." He stared at the motionless Starr, then at the unresponsive face behind it. "*Listen!* Nobody out here takes a gun to an unarmed man—you know that. An unarmed man isn't fair game. It's cowardly to—"

Graves yelped as Jeremiah took two long strides backward. The younger man's left hand darted under his vest, yanked the other Starr free of his belt, slammed it on the bar and slid it just hard enough so it skidded to a stop beside the sergeant.

"Now you're armed. You have an advantage my partner didn't enjoy."

"No." Graves' cheeks shone as though covered with oil.
"No, *no*—"

"Pick it up, you yellow bastard."

Seconds ticked by.

Jeremiah's field of vision included an overweight whore
with a hand pressed to her mouth; a townsman with his fist
trembling at the seam of his trousers; the young blue-clad
borrower leaning back in his chair, petrified; the other two
soldiers blinking at one another in confusion; the monte
man with a pale hand locked around his cards, a bemused
spectator's smile curving his mouth.

Amos Graves looked into Jeremiah Kent's eyes and saw
no reprieve. He turned, a clumsy, heavy motion. He practically fell against the molded edge of the bar, slumping over
it and clawing the Starr with both hands. Off balance and
poorly positioned, he tried to pivot back with the revolver.
But he could never have gotten off a shot and Jeremiah
knew it. No man could say his adversary was unarmed,
however.

While Graves was fumbling, Jeremiah fired.

Graves screamed and was lifted off his feet, the Starr spinning up from his jerking hand and thumping on the floor next
to his boots. Someone retched as Graves toppled backwards,
his dark blue blouse wet and smoking. In that instant, the
foolish barkeep stabbed his hands beneath the bar.

What weapon he'd concealed, no one ever saw. Jeremiah
shifted slightly and fired. The barkeep's right temple exploded. Bits of hair and bone spattered on the mirror behind him as his spasming hand dragged down six bottles.

One long step and Jeremiah had retrieved the Starr he'd
thrown to Graves. One glance and the rest of the dance
house patrons knew better than to attempt to stop him.
Graves flopped on his back, still, and Jeremiah hurried
toward the Dutch door, knowing the patrons were all too
shocked and terrified to move very quickly. But the moment he was outside, he sprinted. They'd recover soon
enough.

The café owner appeared against his smudgy yellow window, calling questions into the wind. Jeremiah reached Nat
with no difficulty, swung up from the right, Indian fashion,
and galloped out of Ellsworth.

vi

He rode northwest for seven or eight miles until he located a suitable clump of trees on a hillside well away from the dairy farms he'd glimpsed in the neighborhood. Under the white of the April moon, he used his hands and his knife to break and cut branches and build a platform in a high fork of a tree. Even though pursuers were surely abroad by now—even though he might be caught—there was simply no question about taking the time needed to prepare Kola properly.

As he worked, the cold joy he'd experienced when he shot the two men drained away. He *had* tried to change, but he'd been an idiot to make the effort. There would always be some dishonorable son of a bitch to send him back to the guns.

His tally now stood at eleven. Fewer than the tally of that army scout, Hickok, who'd become the darling of the Eastern press. But Hickok was a Yank, and most of his victims had been former Rebs, which helped him kill with impunity. Jeremiah wasn't so fortunate.

The cynical thought did little to relieve the sadness sweeping over him. Puffing and struggling, he carried his friend up into the tree and gently laid him on the platform. He folded the Sioux's hands on his breast. Then he descended, fetched a buffalo robe from his gear, climbed again and carefully covered the Indian. He tucked the robe beneath the stiffening legs and around the shoulders.

Soon the birds would peck at the dead thing in the tree. They'd tear the robe, the garments, and finally the flesh. The seasons would batter and destroy the body. But all of that was proper. Kola was resting exactly where tribal custom said he should—close to the sky so the ascension of his spirit would be easier, and in the open air so his physical remains would fall back to earth. His body would be reborn in the new buffalo grass that would feed the herds. When his own tribe or another killed and ate the buffalo, his substance would complete the great cycle of the universe and return to his people while his spirit rejoiced in heaven.

Jeremiah wept over his friend's remains. Then he got himself under control, climbed down and searched and listened for indications of pursuit. There were none.

He galloped north, pushing the already exhausted calico much harder than he should. By morning he intended to be far away. Relatively safe and able to stop, sort his thoughts and decide where he should go for sanctuary. East? West? Kansas City? San Francisco? He had two hundred dollars' worth of shinplasters in the saddlebag. Money wasn't a worry.

A memory shook him all at once. For the first time in hours, he recalled Kola's dream.

He tried to laugh the prophecy away but he couldn't. The first part had already become a reality.

Riding fast on the lathering calico beneath the vast, moon-whitened Kansas sky, he couldn't quell a rising fear of the prophecy, or shake a conviction that somehow, in ways he couldn't begin to foresee, the rest of it would come true, including the very last part.

But who among the Kents would want to strike him down? His father who preached the Christian gospel? The idea was ludicrous.

Gideon, then? His oldest brother who had moved his family to the North after the war? According to the Irishman Boyle, three years ago Gideon had still been struggling to make a place for himself in New York City. Was he still there?

Or could it be Matt, the middle brother, who had served on a Confederate blockade runner and then, after Appomattox, traveled to Europe to study painting?

Fiercely he shook his head. Such thoughts were not only morbid, they were foolish. He would never see any of them again. Unless the vision also meant to say the future was decided, no matter what he did.

He couldn't get the prophecy out of his mind.

There will be no end to the killing.

For a while the guns will bring great luster to your name.

Finally the power will fade and you will be killed—

The words sang on the wind whistling past his ears and muttered up from the calico's rhythmic hoofbeats.

Killed by one of your own.

One of your own.

★ *Book One* ★

MATTHEW'S MISTRESS

CHAPTER I

"A DOG'S PROFESSION"

LA VILLE LUMIÈRE never glowed more brightly than in that last spring of the Second Empire.

It was almost twenty years since Louis-Napoléon, nephew of the original Bonaparte, had elevated himself from President to Emperor in the December coup, and begun to re-create the grandeur of half a century earlier. For nearly two decades now, he had succeeded. For nearly two decades Paris had been the most glamorous capital in the civilized world.

There were treasures on view in the remodeled and expanded Louvre. There were delightful public concerts in the garden of the Tuileries palace. There were thousands of lanterns and gas jets to bedazzle the eye on the night of the Emperor's birthday, and the greatest courtesans of Europe stopping at the Meurice and the other fine hotels. There was a wink at financial chicanery, and a forgiving shrug for sexual excess or deviation—and there was plenty of each to be found.

There was an opulent court that moved annually from Paris to Saint-Cloud to Fontainebleau to Compiègne to Biarritz and back to Paris. There was a splendid new look to the central city, which had literally been ripped apart under the supervision of the Prefect of the Seine, Haussmann. At the Emperor's behest, he envisioned and created new plazas and broad new boulevards and installed a much needed new sewer system. He turned a dark, tangled forest into the Bois de Boulogne. Medieval Paris vanished and what replaced it was much finer—never mind the carping of those who said Napoléon III was the worst of dictators, and essential freedoms were gone, and Haussmann had only made the new avenues broad and straight so that Imperial troops could easily rush down them to crush a radical rebellion of the kind which had terrified the bourgeoisie in 1848 and put it in a mood to eagerly accept Louis-Napoléon's discipline. Those on the left used the term repression, but seldom in public.

For those totally uninterested in politics—and Matthew Kent was one—Paris offered a different sort of ferment. The art world was in a continual uproar. Each year's government-sponsored exhibition, the Salon, brought new assaults on the accepted and the conventional. The bemused public didn't know whether to be appreciative of all the new forms of art being displayed, or outraged by them, and so held several contradictory attitudes at once. Thus the shockingly realistic paintings of Matt's friend Edouard Manet could be denounced as "the art of democrats who don't change their linen," or it could be dismissed simply as "nasty," while Edouard himself was treated almost as a celebrity. There were a dozen practicing painters who were intimates in Manet's circle, or on the fringes of it. Matt was privileged to be one of them and to join their gatherings around the marble-topped tables of their favorite café several times a week.

Of these men, some were dignified and some were just the opposite—like Matt's good friend Paul Cézanne, who the critics said "painted with a pistol." Collectively they were rocking and destroying the foundations of established art. They were throwing safe historical and religious and allegorical subjects into the dustbin and painting what they saw in the contemporary world. Peasants tilling a field. An audience awaiting a Tuileries concert. Or just the artist's impression of a light-splashed dirt road in the country. Content was radical, technique was radical, and Matt thought it was the most perfect time in all of history to be in Paris learning to be an artist.

Never mind that Bismarck's ambition lay like a dark cloud over Europe, and that the Prussian generals were perfecting a new, lightning-swift style of warfare based on use of the railroads and the telegraph, two innovations employed for the first time in the American civil war. Never mind that behind the brilliantly lit façades of the public buildings lay seething slums where rats crawled over the cribs of infants. Never mind that angry proletarians held endless meetings in Belleville and quoted the first volume of *Das Kapital* by the journalist and social thinker Marx, or the older but not much less radical pamphlets of Proudhon attacking the concept of private property. The poverty, the fear, the rage went all but unseen in the festive glare of the lanterns and the shimmering gaslights. Napoléon III and his empress, Eugénie, had created a gaudy show to divert the attention of both the French and the world.

But what was unknown to a majority in that last, lovely spring was the fact that the Second Empire had been created fifty years too late. It was obsolete the moment it came into being, and that it had survived for almost two decades was a remarkable piece of luck. Now, in Berlin and Belleville and across the world, forces were moving which would bring it down. Those forces would touch even the Americans who thought themselves safely isolated behind an ocean. They would touch even Matt Kent, who thought nothing could touch him except his two loves—his chosen profession and a young woman named Dolly Stubbs.

Like the Empire itself, one of those loves would be blown away before the winter came.

ii

Out in the stubbled field, the brewer's boy scowled. The stoop-shouldered man crouching on the bare patch of ground glared right back. He gripped the piece of tree limb so hard, his knuckles turned white.

The man's sagging trousers were shiny with grease and daubed with paint. The sun lit a bald spot at the back of his head and the warm wind played with his jutting beard.

Some four feet behind him, Matthew Kent knelt in the dirt. He was supposed to be catching for the game, but right now he was hurrying to finish his sketch. Asking his friend to come along on the regular Saturday excursion had been a disastrous idea. Paul was just not the sort who could function as a member of a team. The game was liable to end in a riot.

"Come on, throw it, you piece of moldering bird shit!" the batter cried, thumping the tree limb on home base and raising dust. The brewer's boy who was pitching bent over and spat on the ground with studied contempt.

"We know you can curse, Paul," he called. "We know you have a large vocabulary of filthy words, and are passionately fond of every one. You don't need to spout them to make me dislike you, though. I already dislike you as much as I could possibly dislike anyone."

Ignoring the scarlet that rushed into Paul's cheeks, the brewer's boy turned his back on him and began tossing the ball up and catching it. One by one, he surveyed his four teammates. Two were in the outer field. One stood close to the rock serving as first base. The other had his pants open and was urinating on third. The three players on Paul's team had returned to their watercolor easels and wine bottles. They had no interest in encouraging the bearded man, even though he was on their side.

Frowning, Matt pushed a strand of sun-bleached brown hair away from his pale forehead. Dolly was returning from her holiday late this afternoon, and before meeting her, Matt wanted some advice from his friend. Paul was certainly the last man on earth to ask about personal relationships, but Matt did respect his opinion of artistic talent, bizarre though Paul's own work sometimes was.

Paul had come up from Aix-en-Provence in preparation for the wedding of his good friend Zola, a pugnacious little journalist who wrote everything from art criticism to melodramatic novels. On the spur of the moment, Matt had invited Paul to join the group of students, practicing artists and working-class boys who tramped out from Montmartre every Saturday for an American-style baseball game. He'd been surprised when Paul accepted the invitation. But then Paul was moody and given to impulses. Matt definitely felt his own impulse had been ill-advised. Paul was at bat for only the second time, and the other team was baiting him unmercifully. Of course Paul's bad manners and utterly foul language begged for it.

"Come on, *come on!*" he screamed.

The brewer's boy glanced over his shoulder. "When I'm good and ready."

Paul gritted his teeth, plainly wanting to rush out to the pitcher and throttle him.

While the deliberate delay continued, Matt's right hand kept moving, making slashing strokes with the lump of charcoal. At least the antagonism of the other team gave him a chance to finish his sketch. It was a recognizable likeness of the batter, but no one would have called it a faithful portrait. It was done in Matt's usual style—a blend of a few graceful, flowing lines and sudden, interrupting angles which perfectly abstracted the essence of the subject and conveyed Matt's highly personal impression of it.

He had put Paul in profile, facing an invisible pitcher. He'd exaggerated the jutting beard so that it resembled a cluster of stiff horizontal wires. Shading heightened the dark quality of Paul's face, and a highlight in the pupil of the eye glowed like a tiny fireball, suggestive of hostility or madness. As drawn, Paul resembled a furious Italian peasant more than what he actually was—an unsuccessful thirty-year-old painter whose father was an altogether proper banker and landowner.

Quickly he put a last shadow on the temple and, at the lower margin, jotted *l'écorché,* wondering if he'd spelled the word properly. He was usually too busy to worry about correct spelling. But he wanted Paul's nickname on the picture. *Man without any skin* was an apt description of his highly sensitive friend.

He added *Paul—June 1870,* and then *M. Kent,* just as Paul bellowed, "If you don't throw that thing, I'll come out there and shove this piece of wood straight up your backside!"

With his left hand, the brewer's boy made a contemptuous gesture. "Your mother is an old whore so ugly the moths nest between her legs!"

Paul screamed another obscenity and started to charge into the field, brandishing the bat. He'd taken two steps when the pitcher threw the ball.

It whizzed past the astonished artist. He stopped and goggled. Matt dropped his charcoal and shot his right hand over his head. The pad slid off his knee as he caught the ball in long, thin fingers.

"Out! Paul? You're out."

Paul spun around. "What does that mean, *out*?"

"I told you the last time you were up and the same thing happened. He struck you out—your turn's over." Matt stood up. The sleeves of his loose white silk blouse flapped in the wind. He waved at the team in the field, all of them clustering around the pitcher as if ready for a fight. "You were the last batter, so that ends the inning and begins a new one with the other team at bat."

One of Paul's own teammates called from his easel, "Ah, he's too stupid to ever understand it."

Matt's friend looked increasingly furious. "I demand to know how my turn can be over. I didn't hit the ball! That turd-eating, lice-ridden little nitwit was distracting me!"

The brewer's boy took a step in toward home base. Matt held up a hand and he stopped reluctantly. "You can be put out on strikes, Paul. We go into the next inning now. They're ahead, two aces to none."

Paul looked at Matt as if he wanted to assault him. Sometimes Matt thought his friend was quite mad. The very names of his dark, troubled pictures suggested it. *The Orgy. The Autopsy. The Strangled Woman.* Even in the circle of friends and acquaintances who'd been christened the Batignolles group, Paul was only marginally accepted—and the group wasn't exactly made up of what could be called conservative men. Still, Matt was absolutely convinced the bad-tempered Frenchman possessed a gigantic talent. He saw it particularly in Paul's paintings of his uncle Dominique.

"You absolutely mean to say I'm finished?"

Matt nodded. He was a slender young man of twenty-six with an oval face said to resemble his late mother's. He had large brown eyes and a scraggly mustache as sun-streaked as his hair. Wide, solid shoulders offset the slimness of the rest of his body and saved him from any hint of effeminacy.

"Yes, Paul, I'm sorry." He started to clap a hand on his friend's shoulder, then remembered Paul despised having anyone touch him.

At the pitcher's mound, one of the other team shouted, "Hey, let's play, uh?"

"A bloody wasted day," Paul grumbled, shuffling away.

The brewer's boy heard. "Come on, thin skin. You had nothing better to do. Certainly your work's just as much of a waste of time."

His teammates laughed and applauded. Paul went rigid. He shoved a hand into the pocket of his soiled trousers.

"You whoresons!" Paul cried, and jerked out a clasp knife. He opened it with his teeth and walked rapidly toward the members of the other team, the blade flashing in the sun.

iii

Panicked, Matt flung himself against Paul and held him back. "Look, it's only a game. I'm sorry I got you involved!"

"Let me pass!" Paul pushed, strong and wild-eyed. "I've had enough of their insults." Which Paul himself provoked, Matt thought sadly. It was almost as if the artist wanted people to despise him, so that he would have proof that he was rejected, isolated, special.

No one on Paul's own team made any move to help him. They clearly wanted him to fight with the five players huddled at the pitcher's position. Two had picked up rocks. Matt shoved at Paul with all his strength, aware of the brandished knife just a few inches from his arm. The members of the other team didn't help matters.

"What's that you're brandishing, sweetheart, one of the tools you use for painting?"

"Oh no"—came another jibe—"he uses brooms and trowels, that's what all the critics say—"

"Everyone, calm down!" Matt shouted. "This has gone too far."

The brewer's boy shrugged. "Tell that to your crazy friend. If he wants to end an inglorious career right here, we'll accommodate him."

Paul let out another enraged growl and shoved Matt's shoulder. As the younger man staggered back, Paul bolted around him. The knife glinted and flashed. Desperate to prevent a brawl, Matt lunged and caught Paul's free hand. He hung on with all his strength, braced his boots in the stubble and yanked.

Paul swung around to curse Matt, flailing wildly. Suddenly he stumbled. He started to fall forward, the knife inadvertently aimed at Matt's midsection.

Only Matt's clumsy leap backward kept the blade from ripping his belly. As it was, Paul gashed Matt's blouse, then toppled to the ground, nearly impaling himself as the knife slipped from his fingers.

In a sudden burst of temper, Matt grabbed the knife and flung it away. Paul seemed to come to his senses and realize what he'd done. Matt glared at him, then at the other team. "I'm the umpire and I say the game's over."

"Splendid!" the pitcher responded. "It's ruined anyway."

"You won, for God's sake," Matt exploded. Then he too began to calm down.

"We'll play again next Saturday, as usual," Matt said.

"All right," the brewer's boy agreed. The thought of the victory seemed to mollify the rival team. "But not if you invite him."

Cursing under his breath, Paul climbed to his feet and stormed off to collect his easel.

iv

For the next few minutes Matt moved among the players, quietly apologizing on Paul's behalf—his friend would never do it himself—and restoring the atmosphere of friendliness that usually characterized the Saturday outings. Soon the players started back across the fields toward Paris, chattering amiably again and leaving a cloud of sunlit dust behind them. Matt's anger with his friend was passing. He knew better than to expect any admission of bad behavior from Paul, even in private.

Ah, well. He'd invited Paul to join the Saturday expedition for a more important purpose than learning baseball or practicing salon courtesies. He needed advice—before Dolly's train arrived.

He walked to where his friend stood motionless in front of his easel. Before the game, the artists in the group had spent an hour working. Paul had begun a study of a clump of alders in the middle distance. Just as Matt approached, he ripped the linen off the frame and flung it out of sight behind him.

"Wretched. Wretched!"

Then he kicked the easel, knocking it over. "Why in Christ's name do I even trouble myself? Camille tries to encourage me to get out of the studio and master this painting in the open air, but I can't get the hang of it. I make botch after botch. This is a dog's profession!"

Matt had an uneasy feeling Dolly was beginning to feel the same way. In the past few months her remarks about the casual, raffish life they lived had grown more and more frequent—and more pointed.

"Here, that wasn't so bad," Matt said as he bent to retrieve the unfinished landscape. "I'll bet your friend Pissarro would agree with me—"

"Leave it alone."

Paul's eyes had that dangerous glint Matt had come to recognize and respect. With a slight lift of one shoulder, he drew his fingers back from the discarded work. Paul shot out his hand.

"Let me see what you did!"

Paul studied the sketch Matt showed him without expression, then handed it back. "I look like Satan." He sounded proud.

Matt helped his friend pack up his pots of pigment, brushes and bottles of diluent. Then he put his own sketch in a lacquered case and fell in step beside the older man. They walked southward, toward the looming butte of Montmartre dominated by the lazily revolving vanes of the oldest of its several windmills, the Moulin de la Galette. The roofs of Paris were largely hidden by the hill on which a drowsy little working-class suburb had grown up in recent years.

Matt wondered what time it was. Early afternoon, to judge from the light. He owned neither calendar nor pocket watch. He was about to raise the question on which he wanted Paul's advice when the latter blurted, "Do you like that silly game you tried to teach us?"

"Yes, a lot of Americans like it. If my country sank into the sea tomorrow, just about the only real loss would be our baseball teams."

"Why don't you ever take part?"

"I used to, but now I'd rather watch. The only way I can draw is to stay out of the game. Paul—did you mean what you said a few minutes ago about painting being a dog's profession?"

"Absolutely! It's insecure, it's scorned by the masses, it's degrading because you live in poverty and it destroys the soul because illiterate critics are constantly showering verbal piss on whatever they don't understand. A dog's profession! I'd give it up instantly, except that every other profession is so much worse." Suddenly Paul's voice grew more temperate, showing an unexpected concern with his friend's state of mind. "Why do you ask? Are you feeling the same way about it?"

"Sometimes," Matt admitted. He couldn't get used to his friend's abrupt swings of mood. But as long as Paul had calmed down, he might as well take advantage of it. "Dolly seems pretty damn unhappy lately."

Paul's face softened even more. "A lovely young woman, Miss Dolly. Is she still in England visiting her parents?"

"She'll be back tonight."

"And she's dissatisfied with the way you're living?"

"I think so. She hasn't said it straight out, but I'm beginning to suspect she'd like me to take up a steady occupation. Maybe I should. I haven't made much progress lately. I've been working on one painting for almost three months but nothing's come of it."

"A painting of what?"

"The woods at Barbizon."

"Why did you choose that subject?"

"Because so many good French painters have done fine landscape work down there."

"Yes, but you're an American, not a Frenchman. Does Barbizon have any special meaning for you? Does it generate any feeling within you?"

"No, but—"

"That's the trouble, then! Paint what you are. Paint what you know! Paint what stirs your heart and excites your eye. Unless you do that, there'll be no passion in your work. No juice of life—"

"Are you saying I should paint something American?"

Paul shrugged. "Perhaps, if nothing else will satisfy the requirements I just set forth."

"Spoke like a teacher!" Matt said with a trace of pique.

Paul didn't take offense. "How is old Fochet, by the way?"

"Just as confused as I am about what's wrong with my work."

"Fochet is good." It was a pronouncement. "An intolerable man as regards his disposition—he's crankier than I am—but he only hectors a pupil to get the best out of him. Tell me, Matthew—why do you hate America so much?"

Matt was unprepared for the sudden change of subject. But he didn't have to ponder his answer. "Because it's become a country of parvenus and social climbers. Because money is all that's important over there. And because of that damn war!" There was a rising fervency in his voice that held his friend's full attention.

"I saw too much of it, Paul. There should have been another way to end slavery, but the leaders on both sides were too stupid and arrogant and self-serving to find it— just like politicians everywhere. So five hundred thousand boys lost their lives while a few profiteers got rich. Half a million boys, Paul! One of them was my youngest brother."

"Ah," Paul murmured. "I never knew that. It explains a great deal."

They walked on in silence, Matt thinking over what Paul had said. As a matter of fact, he *had* grown tired of French subjects—landscapes and the figure models engaged by Fochet, the teacher in whose studio he took instructions and rented space. Fochet sensed his dissatisfaction, but was at a loss to offer a remedy.

Paul's suggestion struck a chord because Matt had been thinking of trying a picture with a subject rooted in his own experience. He'd abandoned the idea because he was contemptuous of virtually everything American, and because such a picture would be too close to lowly genre painting—works depicting everyday life.

Was Paul right? Was he making a mistake by rejecting subjects from his own past? He'd even been having trouble with a small portrait of Dolly. Perhaps there too he was striving for a final effect that was overly refined. Squeezing the juice of life out of the subject, to use his friend's phrase.

Of course that still left the essential question to be answered. He stated it tentatively.

"I guess what worries me most is wasting my time and Dolly's. Wasting good years in a worthless effort. Sometimes I wonder whether I have the ability to justify going on."

"Do you feel you do?"

"Yes."

"Well, I share your opinion. You have a genuine and formidable talent."

Matt felt a knot loosen within him. At least he'd gotten the reassurance he sought, and could face Dolly's occasional jibes with a little less self-doubt. He felt better—but only for a moment. Paul's face grew dour.

"Don't preen and congratulate yourself on having talent, my friend. If you haven't learned it by now, talent's a cruel mistress. She'll bring you just a few very brief moments of supreme happiness, and all the grief you'll need for ten lifetimes. She'll be very demanding, too. If your young lady ever decides to test whether she or your other love is the more important to you, you'll discover how cruel a mistress painting can be."

"Oh, Dolly would never push me to that kind of choice," Matt said, though without great conviction. It seemed to him that over the past few months, she had been tending just that way.

Hoisting his easel to rest it more comfortably on his shoulder, Paul trudged on with his melancholy gaze lost in the golden stubble ahead. Matt followed in silence, grateful that his friend had been willing to offer encouragement. It was just what he needed with Dolly returning this evening. He did love her, and only hoped that after a good holiday with her parents, she'd be her old tolerant self again.

But he found Paul's ideas about what was wrong with his work difficult if not impossible to accept. America meant nothing to him any longer. It was just the accidental place of his birth and the benighted address to which he sent mail for his brother and his father. He would never have any desire to paint American subjects, nor any compelling reason to go home again.

Ever.

CHAPTER II

THE PRUSSIAN

i

PAUL AND MATT climbed the butte and parted company near the summit, Matt turning off toward his quarters while Paul kept on toward the church of Saint-Pierre and the nearby Place du Tertre, where he was to meet his mistress at a café. How the young and pretty model Hortense Piquet could stand Paul's abrasive disposition, Matt didn't know. But he was glad his friend had found at least one person to share his life.

Matt washed, took off the ripped shirt and donned a fresh one, wholly oblivious to the littered state of the two rooms he shared with Dolly. He napped for a bit, then asked his landlady Madame Rochambeau what time it was. Four thirty, she said. He set off down the south slope of the butte, intending to walk all the way to the Gare du Nord. Dolly's train, which had met a channel steamer at Calais, was due at quarter to six.

A lovely panorama of Paris spread before him as he descended the hill. The late afternoon sun bathed the right bank in a mellow light, while in the west, dark clouds sped toward the city, white streaks flickering in their centers.

Matt was unaware of all of it. He was thinking about his
work again.

Matt had been sketching for as long as he could remember. Where he had come by the ability, he couldn't say.
Certainly he hadn't gotten it from his father or mother.

Looking back, he recalled that his earliest experiments
with drawing had been a means of retreating from the turmoil in the Kent household in Lexington, Virginia. That
was before the war, when his mother Fan and his father
Jephtha, a Methodist minister, had differed strongly on
slavery and secession. Their differences finally sundered the
family. After a period of involvement with the Under-
ground Railroad, Jephtha fled for the North.

Matt remained with his mother and his brothers, Gideon
and Jeremiah, in the valley of the Shenandoah. And gradually the sketching became more than a method of escape
from painful reality. It became an end in itself—something
that challenged his mind and hand and prodded him to
search for the essential nature of a subject, then discover
the few lines which would re-create the subject and comment on it at the same time.

In 1859, at age fifteen, he left home. He had his mother's
permission and that of his new stepfather, an actor named
Edward Lamont whom he didn't like very much. He was
poor in school so Fan had agreed to let him go to sea on
a cotton packet operating out of Charleston. He'd taken to
the life at once, and to the vessel's captain, Barton McGill,
a man who seemed to know a good deal about Matt's family but never explained how.

Of course he'd taken his drawing materials along. When
war broke out, McGill shifted to blockade running. Matt
stayed with him. After a dangerous run, Matt was always
grateful for the release he found in doing sketches of West
Indian blacks or stevedores and soldiers in wartime Wilmington. McGill was generous with his praise of the work.

Captain McGill had drowned in a storm in the Gulf in
the last days of the war. The incident shook Matt profoundly and affected his life on two counts.

When the schooner broke apart and went down, Matt
spent several minutes floundering in the black water. He'd
never been a strong swimmer, and for that brief time he
could find no timbers to which he could cling. The storm

growled and screamed and the raging sea was as black as the sky. He realized he was going to die.

Finally he caught a floating spar and clung to it until he was washed ashore. But that time in the water had given him a harrowing sense of his own mortality and made him realize that the only way to beat the game was to create something death couldn't destroy. Most men sought immortality in their children, but he wanted more than that. He decided he could find it in his art.

The second effect of the storm was a radical deepening of his dislike of his native land. The cause was McGill's death.

Despite a pose of cynicism, Barton McGill had impressed Matt as a wise and honorable man. Even though he had believed that the Southern cause was hopeless, and the war itself a grand lunacy, to the very end he'd persisted in making runs under sail from Havana to Matamoras. The more prudent Confederate captains had put their feet up on tables in Cuban cafés and waited for an armistice. As a result, they were alive today—and rich—and McGill was dead. That was the way it went in America, Matt came to believe. The selfish prospered while the virtuous perished, forgotten. The politicians stayed safe and grew fat behind the lines while the young men they sent off to carry out their deranged policies died—just as Matt's younger brother had perished. By the time Grant and Lee met at Appomattox Court House, he was convinced Europe was the only worthwhile place on the globe. And since that was the center of the art world, that was where he would go to learn the techniques of the profession he meant to follow.

Besides, Dolly was in Europe.

It took a while for him to achieve his goal. He spent months on the Texas coast in '65, recuperating from the injuries he'd suffered in the sea. Several bones had been broken.

From Texas he traveled overland to New York, and a surprisingly warm reunion with his father, who had abandoned a temporary career as a journalist and returned to the ministry. Matt's mother was dead. Jephtha had remarried. And while Molly Kent would never generate the special affection he felt for Fan, Matt genuinely liked her.

He found he no longer had any serious differences with Jephtha on the subject of the war. Dolly, whom he'd met in Liverpool while McGill was having a ship built there, had persuaded him the South was wrong on the matter of black slavery. His mounting contempt for the raw, amoral country of his birth had made him an easy convert. Unfortunately Jephtha still believed America had a solid if difficult future. Matt tactfully refrained from identifying that belief for what it was—an illusion.

Jephtha had readily agreed to let his second son have a portion of the California inheritance that would one day be his in full. Matt meant to use the funds to pay for his study. He set out for Liverpool, and Dolly, in a fever of enthusiasm.

Together they laid plans for going to the Continent. For a short time they considered Rome or Munich. Each had a flourishing art colony. Both cities finally lost out to the preeminence of Paris.

They'd convinced Dolly's nervous and proper parents that they would be married before they left England. But they said they couldn't linger long enough to arrange a full-scale ceremony in Liverpool because Matt was expected to report practically overnight to the *École des Beaux-Arts*. The truth was, Matt hadn't even tried to meet the entrance requirements of the renowned state-sponsored school of the French Academy of Fine Arts. He'd made inquiries and found out that the institution's techniques were formal and old-fashioned. Students spent months just copying from paper silhouettes or plaster casts representing parts of the human body. The true adventurer in the field of art studied independently in the atelier of a good private tutor.

Matt and Dolly had arrived in Paris in '66, deeply in love with each other, wickedly in love with the notion of living without benefit of wedlock, and instantly in love with the city of light. Matt found a fine teacher, Étienne Fochet. Dolly soon located a good job which she enjoyed and which gave her the satisfaction of helping with their expenses. Down in the city at a private academy called the École Anglais, she taught English to the children of businessmen and diplomats planning to spend a year or so in England or America.

It had been a wonderful, ideal life for three years. There were quarrels, yes. But they were quickly settled, usually by Matt's ability to bring Dolly to an almost frenzied state of physical arousal. His work progressed reasonably well under Fochet's abusive guidance. *"Do it over, do it over! My God, you won't even be a tenth-rate colorist unless you develop a better palette! Go study Delacroix! And if you can't improve, go home to America!"*

Fochet used it as a threat because he knew Matt was temperamentally unable to go home. Matt's dislike of America had been strengthened by his acquaintance with another American artist, some years older, who visited Paris occasionally.

Jim Whistler was a pugnacious little dandy, just five feet four, and the grandest raconteur Matt had ever met. A failed West Point cadet, Whistler was fond of telling how his military career had come to a sudden end. He'd been asked to step to the blackboard and discuss the properties of silicon. "I began by saying, 'Silicon is a gas.' If it were, I'd probably be a major general."

Whistler claimed he couldn't function in the stultifying, tasteless environment of his homeland. He was a brilliant artist, Matt thought, even if he did bestow curious titles on his paintings—almost as if he wanted to deny that they had subjects. Studies of fireworks exploding in a night sky were "nocturnes." A portrait of his mother Mathilda who lived with him and his mistress in London—a picture he'd been struggling with since '66, he complained—was an "arrangement in grey and black."

Matt now shared Whistler's contempt for the United States. For that reason he rejected appealing subjects from his past whenever they came to mind. Now Paul had suggested that might be a mistake. But he didn't see how he could find good art in bad memories.

He had to do something about his work, though. Even a simple portrait of Dolly was foundering. Was it because there were problems with Dolly?

The change in their relationship had been gradual. He couldn't recall a specific time when it had started. Perhaps, after three years, the novelty of a Bohemian existence had worn off, and Dolly had started to think about the future. He never did that. He seldom even thought seriously about the present. In fact, when he was working, the real world was little more than a peripheral haze. Dolly had begun to let him know that although she understood that, she didn't like it.

Today he was no better prepared to meet her objections than he had been when she left on the holiday. Well, maybe a visit with her parents had relaxed her a little, he thought anxiously as he made his way through the neighborhood near the Gare du Nord.

ii

The storm clouds had moved in, bringing a sudden shower. He wove his way through crowds near the station entrance, first avoiding a couple of street musicians playing a flute and a curious new instrument called a saxophone, then an open-air dentist who was striking his portable chair and umbrella. He jumped off the curb and across the gurgling water in the gutter so as not to interfere with a couple of the Sûreté specials who were becoming more and more visible as street crime increased. The specials were trussing up a howling, kicking man in rags. A purse grabber, probably.

A flower girl who would have been pretty except for the sores around her lips interrupted her chant of "May your love life flourish!" long enough to sell Matt a bedraggled bunch of violets. She glanced into his eyes, then down at his trousers in case he was interested in an additional transaction. He smiled and shook his head but felt an embarrassing physical reaction to the girl's invitation. Problems or not, three weeks was a devil of a long time to be without the woman he loved.

He darted out of the rain into the tumult of the station. In an atmosphere of smoke and noise, people rushed to and fro, knocking against one another like balls striking tenpins. Parisians were constitutional hurriers, he'd discovered. Even a pair of sweet-faced nuns almost bowled him over.

A local train arrived with a scream of iron wheels and an eruption of steam. There were several trains standing on the tracks which ran right up to barricades within the

central area of the station. He didn't know which track
would receive the Calais express, so he sought the schedule
board hanging from iron rafters at one end of the hall.

He found the Calais train and its designated track. As
he gazed upward, he became aware of a man standing just
to his left, rattling off the numbers of all the listed trains,
as well as their arrival or departure times. The man was
speaking accented French and had his back to Matt. But
there was something familiar about his sleek yellow-
brown hair.

A second, gnomelike fellow was copying down the information the first man rattled off. Paris was tolerant of the
eccentric, so no one paid any attention except Matt, who
thought the man might be carrying a watch.

"I beg your pardon—" Matt began. The man pivoted
smartly. Matt recognized him at once, even though this afternoon he was turned out in expensive civilian clothes,
including a tan sack coat with dark brown edging, fawn
spats on his dark brown pumps and, tucked under his arm,
a tan felt hat with a round-blocked crown and wide
brown ribbon.

The man had twice been at the café where Matt and his
friends congregated. The first time he'd evidently come in
by accident. He'd gotten interested in the barmaid, Lisa,
and had come back to see her again. On both occasions
he'd been wearing a uniform of dark blue with polished
jackboots, a sabre and sabretache and a pickelhaube with
an ornate Prussian eagle plate on the front and a wicked-
looking vertical spike on top.

Lisa hadn't been impressed or even slightly interested in
the man's heavy humor, his heavy palm slapping her bottom or his heavy-handed announcements that he was
attached to the Prussian diplomatic mission in Paris and,
therefore, important. Both times, the Prussian had left the
café in very bad humor.

Damn funny crowd, the Prussians, Matt thought as the
fellow removed a monocle from his eye. They'd whipped
the Austrians in '66 by utilizing the railroads effectively.
And here the officer was, boldly copying French railroad
schedules in one of Paris' major depots.

"Well, hello, my friend!" the Prussian said with a lingering look at Matt's mouth. Uneasily, Matt wondered whether the officer was one of those types who found pleasure with persons of either sex.

The Prussian was just a few years older. He had healthy pink cheeks, bright pale eyes and a dazzling grin. "It was the Café Guerbois, wasn't it? You're one of that Batignolles crowd—"

"Good memory, Herr Lepp." Matt nodded, trying to be cordial despite his dislike of the man's mixture of arrogance and smarmy charm. The officer stood with one knee turned out and slightly bent.

"Colonel Lepp." he corrected. "To be quite precise about it, von Lepp. May I ask what you want? I'm rather busy."

Matt burst out laughing. "Doing what? Fixing up an invasion timetable?"

It was meant as a joke, but Lepp lacked a sense of humor. He stiffened, turned red in the face. The gnomish older man hovering near him scowled.

Abruptly, Lepp realized he'd reacted too strongly. He tried to smile. "Oh, no. I'm merely putting together some information for a commercial study."

Matt didn't believe it for a minute. Prussian officers didn't study rail schedules in order to facilitate freight shipments.

"Believe me," Lepp went on, "if there is ever any—difficulty between France and the new, unified Germany, it shall not be Prussia who is the aggressor. But it shall not be Prussia who is the loser, either."

"Look—" Matt raised a placating hand. He forgot he was carrying violets. Lepp snickered. Matt fought to hold his temper. "All I wanted was the correct time. I'll ask someone el—"

Lepp interrupted with a snap of his fingers. The gnome took out a cheap plated watch and showed Matt the dial: twenty-five until six. He was in time.

He murmured a thank-you and started away. Lepp caught his arm, closing his fingers on Matt's sleeve in a way Matt found repellant. Lepp's anise-scented breath washed over him.

"Wait one moment, please. Tell that charming if slightly grubby young woman at the café that I still think of her.

Twice refused, I do not consider myself refused permanently."

A chuckle, a squeeze, and then he let go.

"You must remember Prussia and the Prussian people are accustomed to getting what they want these days. Remind her of that, if you please!" Though he was still smiling, the words had a marked undertone of command.

Matt resented the officer's tone and manner. "Tell her yourself, Herr Lepp. I don't pimp for anyone, Prussians included. Good evening."

Lepp snarled something in his native tongue as Matt walked away. *Damn fool to indulge your temper that way!* he said to himself. But he'd disliked the Prussian from the moment the man had walked into the café, acting as if he owned it.

He turned and saw Lepp studying him, his monocle back in his eye. The officer's expression was not at all friendly.

The Prussian pivoted sharply again and returned to charting the train schedules. Matt hoped he'd seen the last of the fellow, but in view of Lepp's remarks about Lisa, he doubted it.

The Calais train came chugging in at five forty-five on the dot. By then the prospect of seeing Dolly had Matt in a state of physical and emotional excitement. But it was a state tinged with a good deal of tension.

Chapter III

Reunion

i

DOLLY WASN'T AMONG the first passengers who came streaming up the platform. Matt went through an agonizing five minutes as he stared into Gallic eyes and Gallic faces. Had she missed the steamer or thought about their life together and decided she wasn't coming back?

His spirit began to feel as wilted as the violets. Then, suddenly, he glimpsed a round English face and pink cheeks, and large, lovely eyes of a blue that looked lavender in a certain light. He recognized the neat but out-of-date clothing she was wearing: the plush pelisse, the little Windsor cap of straw with its ostrich-tip ornament perched on her yellow curls. She spied him at almost the same moment, dropped her portmanteau, rose on tiptoe and waved.

He started running against the tide of passengers. He had to travel three car lengths to reach her. What he felt as he rushed along—a powerful, soaring emotion that quite eradicated his apprehension—told him how much he truly loved her.

"Oh Matt, Matt love!" she exclaimed, reaching up for him. Her little gray gloves clasped at the back of his neck.

Her cheek, smooth as heavy cream, pressed his darker, sun-burned one. Dolly Stubbs was a head shorter than he. She tended to plumpness, but he liked her plump.

He could feel the swell of her corseted breasts against his shirt. Only a couple of passengers paid any attention as they kissed. He wouldn't have cared if they had an audience of ten thousand. All he wanted to do was savor the sweetness of her parted lips.

"Oh!" she said again, out of breath when they broke the embrace. "Oh, I've missed you so terribly!"

"So have I. My God, Doll, three weeks is longer than I ever imagined."

She understood, laughed and whispered, "Far too long for me. As you'll discover when I get you alone."

He raised his hand, offering the violets. "Not as pretty as your eyes, but the best I could do on short notice." That was said in French. It seemed a more appropriate language in which to frame such a high-flown if heartfelt sentiment.

She inhaled the scent of the flowers, slipped her arm through his and squeezed against him. "Thank you, my darling."

He picked up her luggage. They walked to the clamorous central area of the station. Lepp was nowhere to be seen now, Matt noted with some relief.

"Have you taken care of yourself?" she asked as they started outside.

With a vaguely surprised expression and perfect sincerity, he said, "I don't know. I suppose."

She frowned. "Still having trouble with your work?"

"More than ever."

"Well, we shall have to talk about that. And some other things, too. The holiday was good for me, Matt. It helped me get some of my thoughts in order." It was all said in a very light way. Yet he was disturbed, somehow.

As they left the station, the shower stopped. In the west over a long row of chimney pots, a blue sky worthy of a Constable began to appear between racing clouds.

They walked arm in arm in the newly washed spring evening. An old man selling mussels broke his chant, leaned on the handle of his cart and smiled at them.

"We'll catch an omnibus up to the butte—" he began.

"Nonsense, we'll walk. We're both in good health, and

we don't need to squander our money—even if you will be
a California Midas one day."

He chuckled. He seldom thought about the huge sum he
would inherit when his father died. He had no appreciation
of the value of money, and placed little importance on having more than a few sous in his pocket.

"We've been having unsettled weather, Dolly. Was the
channel rough?"

"A bloody tempest!" she declared with uncharacteristic
vulgarity. "I couldn't so much as nibble a biscuit till we
docked."

"How did you find Liverpool?"

She wrinkled her nose. "Grimy as ever."

"How's your pa?"

"Still at the Birkenhead." Her father was a steamfitter
at the famous Liverpool shipyard of the Laird brothers.
McGill's last steam-driven blockade runner had been built
there, as well as the great Confederate raider *Alabama*.

"Is the rest of your family well?"

"Yes, fine—though of course they think we'll be celebrating our wedding anniversary again this year." She turned to
look into his eyes. "Speaking of that, Peg's found a fellow."

"What? Is it serious?"

"The wedding's planned for October. I told them we'd
be there if we could."

He felt a flare of resentment. He hated even having to
think about taking time from his work to attend such a
meaningless social event. He tried to tell himself it was
important to her, but he wasn't wholly successful in overcoming his irritation.

"Certainly, we'll try." His voice sounded strained. "Your
father had been worrying about your sister's prospects,
hadn't he?"

"Yes, Peg's thirty-three. Well, she's taken care of now.
That leaves only me."

He bent to kiss her cheek. "A poor, benighted twenty-
four."

"Practically an old granny!" Her smile seemed forced.

"As long as your family believes we're married, they
won't fret about—"

"Matthew Kent," she interrupted, stopping by a news
kiosk. "Let us not debate *that* again. You know we don't

agree. I came with you to Paris of my own free will, but that does not change certain facts about our situation. My parents believing we're married and the two of us actually *being* married is not the same thing and never will be. Really"—she gave a little shake of her head—"sometimes you're terribly stubborn. We really must sit down for a serious discussion about this whole situation—and soon."

Right then he would cheerfully have bashed her sister Peg square in the face. The holiday hadn't helped their relationship at all. It had only exacerbated the unhappiness developing in her. His worst fears were coming true—though he was puzzled about one thing. It didn't seem like her to be upset by her older sister finally catching a man and scheduling a wedding. Was there anything else behind her quietly determined statement of a moment ago?

ii

They lived in two rooms in a house on the Rue Saint-Vincent, a pleasant, winding street. The house belonged to Madame Rochambeau, a widow whose husband had been the well-paid manager of one of the gypsum quarries on the Butte de Montmartre. She spoke of the departed gentleman fondly. A lusty spouse, she said, though always with gypsum dust in his pores—the "plaster of Paris" known the world over.

Madame Rochambeau had been left in reasonably comfortable circumstances. She owned the house without debt. But it was still necessary for her to supplement her income by taking in boarders. She fulfilled the duties of concierge herself, thus realizing an economy. She liked Matt and Dolly, but was less enthusiastic about their friends the Strelniks who occupied the other two rented rooms with their infant son Anton.

"Ah, Madame Kent!"

The landlady jumped up from the flowerbed she'd been cultivating and rushed to embrace Dolly. She was a huge breadloaf of a woman with a cheery, mole-dotted face. Matt closed the door to the street and leaned against the wall.

Madame Rochambeau was a militant Catholic, and didn't like a great many modern things, including the land speculators who were invading her little suburb, and the Bohemians who practiced "free love." He and Dolly had felt it prudent to fib about their marital status to her as well. To reinforce the fib, Dolly wore a cheaply plated gold ring on her left hand. Matt had bought the ring from a junk dealer.

"I am delighted to see you home." Madame Rochambeau pinched Dolly's cheek. "Your mama and papa fed you well. There is a little extra under the chin, eh?"

Old meddler, Matt thought, smiling. *Always saying what she thinks!*

"Oh, maybe just a little, just a little—" Dolly acted quite flustered about having a weight gain pointed out. Matt hadn't even noticed.

"There is a piece of mail for your husband," Madame Rochambeau said with an admiring glance at Matt's wide shoulders. "The late post brought it. The quarters have been swept and all the dirty laundry put in a pile."

Ruefully, Dolly looked at him. He was supposed to have maintained the rooms in reasonable order while she was gone but of course had completely forgotten, being occupied with the problems of his work.

"Well, I'm home," she said softly with a wry little smile. "And nothing's changed." She started inside.

Matt swung the portmanteau onto his shoulder and squeezed Madame's arm affectionately as he passed beneath the branches of the old plane tree. The landlady turned scarlet and covered a giggle with her hand. Above the garden, the vanes of one of Montmartre's windmills turned lazily in the fading light.

Their rooms were in the south wing, which they entered from a door directly off the garden. Pattering footsteps ahead of Dolly told Matt the Strelniks' child was romping in the corridor.

"Ah, Anton, you imp!" she exclaimed, bending to pick up the year-old toddler. She laughed and patted the gurgling child. His face curved into an immense, snaggle-toothed smile. She kissed him and rumpled his thick russet hair.

From the doorway across from theirs drifted the odor of boiling cabbage. A woman in her late twenties appeared. She was slender, drably dressed. Her delicately pretty face resembled that of an Italian Madonna, though in fact she was Russian.

"Dolly! Matt said you would be home today!" she cried in halting English.

"And you've been practicing, Leah. That was very good."

The young woman blushed. Because Leah's husband talked about emigrating to America someday, Dolly had volunteered to teach her the language.

Leah dabbed her sweaty cheek with an apron. "But while I was practicing, it seems my son was scampering about naked again."

Dolly handed the little boy to his mother with a particularly fond and lingering look, Matt thought.

Tartly, the English girl said, "Whatever you're doing, you should make Sime tend the baby once in a while."

"Here, don't pick on the poor man when he can't defend himself!" Matt laughed, slipping past her to open their door. He slid the portmanteau in. Bless Madame Rochambeau for straightening up after he left for the station!

A gruff, amiable voice said, "But he is able to defend himself. Welcome back, Dolly."

In French more correctly pronounced than his, she said, "Thank you, Sime."

Matt waved. "Hello, Sime. Figured out how to overthrow the Emperor yet?"

Leah hung Anton from the crook of her arm and put her other hand to her lips. "Sssh! That sort of thing isn't safe to say, even in jest."

Sime Strelnik scratched the front of his wine-spotted shirt. He was a short, overweight man in his mid-thirties. He had round, innocent-looking dark eyes and a beard and hair the color of fire. Strelnik had been born in Russian Georgia and had come to Paris via Berlin, the home of his only living relative, an older brother. Both of them were active in the workingman's movement. Strelnik carried a card in the First International founded in London in 1864. He spent half the day sleeping, the other half reading or writing pamphlets, and most of the night attending meetings with people Madame Rochambeau characterized as "atheistic, unwashed and sinister."

For Matt's benefit, Strelnik had several times tried to differentiate between the various hues and tints of radicalism found in those with whom he associated. There were Jacobins, Proudhonists, Internationalists, Blanquists and several other variations. It was all a meaningless and uninteresting hodgepodge to Matt. But not to his landlady.

"One doesn't need labels to know what they are. It's simple. They're rapists and criminals. Lawless anarchists bent on stealing the wealth of hardworking men and the virtue of decent women. I admit Mr. Strelnik doesn't *look* like that, which is somewhat confusing, but I know he'll show his true colors if the Reds ever stage another insurrection such as the one in forty-eight. I suppose he wants to bring that mad revolutionary Blanqui back from exile in Brussels, too. And where do you suppose he gets the money to send all those thick letters to Berlin and St. Petersburg? The authorities will inquire into that mysterious correspondence one of these days, you mark my word!"

Leah passed the child to her husband. "Kindly see that he gets a diaper before he catches cold. I've supper to fix, you know. Dolly, it really is wonderful to have you home again."

She disappeared. Strelnik dangled the child from one forearm and wedged a cigar stub into his mouth with his other hand. He lit the cigar. The smoke set Anton to coughing. Dolly's eyes narrowed with disapproval.

The paunchy man hoisted the baby over his shoulder and patted the bare rump. "I don't know why you make snide jokes about the Empire, Matt," he said in a rather prickly way. "Of all people, Americans should understand the evils of a repressive government. You fought your way out from under one a hundred years ago."

Matt shrugged. "That spirit's long gone in my country. Now all the people care about is money."

The other man smiled. "Perhaps you'll let me take your place as a citizen, then. I'd love to expropriate and share the wealth of some of those American capitalists."

"Such as my father?" Matt grinned. He genuinely liked the little Russian, but teased him because he found his pronouncements so pretentious. "Sime, I don't think you have the nerve to strip so much as a sou from anyone. You're a man with a conscience."

"Exactly!" Strelnik retorted. "And because I have a conscience, I can't tolerate what I see around me. A worker receiving only two or three francs for a twelve-hour day while that harlot the Countess de Castiglione gets a million francs for giving herself to some English milord for sixty minutes. The only way to redress such injustice is by force! By—" Anton shrieked. The smoldering cigar stub clenched in the corner of Strelnik's mouth had briefly touched the wiggling infant's bare leg.

"Oh my God," Strelnik gasped. Anton howled. The bearded man's eyes filled with tears. "Leah? *Leah, help me!* I've hurt the baby—"

Strelnik rushed into his quarters. Matt shook his head, his smile growing cynical.

"Well, Dolly, there's the marital bliss your sister's leaping into. I'm glad you're not interested in that kind of clerically approved misery."

It was quite the wrong thing to say, nearly as bad, in its way, as his remark to Lepp about an invasion. And it produced the same sort of angry reply.

"I know you and your friends sneer at any kind of convention. But the truth is, I've changed my mind. I am interested in marriage. That's another subject we must talk about. Perhaps it's the most important subject of all."

With an intense glance from those lovely eyes, she hurried into their rooms. Stunned and shaken, he stood staring at the open door. This was worse than anything he'd anticipated. Far worse. Something drastic had changed her while she was away.

CHAPTER IV

DOLLY'S SECRET

i

POOR STRELNIK WAS still wailing for Leah to come to his rescue—which she always did. While he scurried from meeting to meeting, agonizing over political schemes and utopian programs, she provided the family's income by working six hours a day in a laundry which serviced the fine hotels down near the Rue de Rivoli. The moment Leah closed the hall door and took charge of Anton, the little boy stopped crying.

Matt walked into the quarters he shared with Dolly. He'd wanted rooms with northern light but hadn't been able to find any. The large outer room had a slanted skylight facing the southwest. The spring sun cast elongated, slow-moving shadows of windmill vanes on the whitewashed wall at the skylight's east end.

Directly under the glass stood Matt's easel and two small cabinets of equipment. On the easel rested the unfinished portrait. The subject of the portrait had already retired to the bedroom with her portmanteau. He could hear her unpacking.

He walked around several tall stacks of books to the one decent armchair in which Madame Rochambeau had piled the dirty laundry. He flung the laundry on the floor, sat down and glumly stared at the work on the easel.

The painting was done on a linen support he'd prepared with a coarse textured ground. He'd posed Dolly in her best dress—the new realism forbade classical drapery—but the picture still looked stiff and unnatural. So far he hadn't progressed beyond endless repairs on the underpainting.

Dolly returned to the outer room, having put her pelisse and hat aside. She seemed more composed. A scattering of light from overhead created a kind of nimbus around the top of her head. Her face, by contrast, was darker, in shadow. The result was a softening effect that made her features indescribably lovely, and seemed to enlarge and diffuse her eyes, as though Matt were gazing at her under water.

He glanced at the portrait. He'd completely missed the living, breathing reality of his subject.

Her eyes seemed touched with sadness as she sank onto a rickety stool and uttered a little sigh. "Oh, my. The trip was more thing than I thought." She brushed back a stray yellow curl. "I owe you an explanation for what I said outside."

"I'd just as soon wait—or dispense with it entirely."

Firmly, she said, "We can't, Matt. You see what the post brought while I pour some wine. Then we'll talk. It won't become any easier if we wait."

She patted his hand as she walked by. Somehow he felt as if she'd announced an execution.

ii

Dolly rummaged in the little alcove that served as a combination kitchen and dining area. "I can't find the wine. I can't find anything in the middle of these mountains of dirty dishes. Didn't you wash anything while I was gone?"

"My face."

She wasn't amused.

"I forgot about the wine," he said. "Madame Rochambeau borrowed the last bottle yesterday. She had company unexpectedly."

"I'll be right back."

The outer door closed. He was gripped by a feeling of panic. He didn't want to sit down for a talk of the sort she had in mind. What she wanted to discuss was obvious from her remarks about her sister.

He loved Dolly, but he resented this new and unexplained thrust toward domesticity. He was frightened by it, too. He felt as if a trap were closing. He didn't want to be pushed into choosing between mistresses, as Paul put it.

Well, then, he had to get her off the subject. At least for this evening. He decided to try a not unpleasant strategy that had worked before and surely would again.

Nervous, he paced to and fro in front of the easel. He spied the letter lying on a flimsy taboret. The handwriting and the franking registered slowly. From Gideon!

He ripped the letter open, scanned the paragraphs of family news. Gideon's wife, Margaret, was well, and so were the children, eight-year-old Eleanor and the baby, Will, born in 1869. Jephtha and Molly were in good health too, though Jephtha occasionally complained of pains in his chest. He was too busy to see a doctor, Gideon said.

The real purpose of the letter was to convey some exciting personal news. Rather than take a position with the New York *Union,* the highly successful daily newspaper that had come back into the fold after Louis Kent's death in late 1868, Gideon had decided to use a portion of his inheritance and start a small journal of his own. A journal devoted primarily to the cause of the workingman, in which Gideon was vitally interested.

"Oh God," Matt said aloud in disappointment. "Not a Strelnik in the family."

But it was true. The paper would be called *Labor's Beacon.* Gideon planned to buy typesetting and printing on a bid basis, but do the editorial work. His office was to be a small rented loft in lower Manhattan. The family had moved to the island from New Jersey a few weeks ago. Another surprise!

Gideon claimed the times demanded a militant response on behalf of the common man who worked for a living. All such men were exploited by those for whom they worked, Gideon believed. Matt was sorry to hear about his new crusade for two reasons. He considered it wasted effort; Gideon could not hope to pit his opinions against powerful business interests and win. More important, he considered it reckless. Gideon could be hurt—physically hurt—if he offended the wrong people. And he had an established family to think about.

Matt wasn't the only one with that reservation, as it turned out. Just at the end of the letter, Gideon wrote:

> —and I might note, in confidence, that Margaret's reaction to the decision has been odd and not a little upsetting.
>
> As I have so often said before, it was she who brought me to the threshold of the world of ideas, and taught me not to be afraid to enter. It was she who read to me hour after hour in the evening, neither smiling at my inability to understand unfamiliar concepts nor at my clumsiness when I first attempted to pronounce difficult new words which I learned from those readings. It was she who gave me a thirst for knowledge—which in turn generates a thirst to employ that knowledge to some useful end. To accomplish something. Bring about change!
>
> Nowhere is change needed more than in the affairs of the average laboring man. I began to realize that when I worked as an Erie railroad switchman. Margaret used to agree with me—if not outwardly, then tacitly. Now she has begun to exhibit a different attitude. She expresses fear about my establishing the little paper—
>
> Not fear for my safety, though some of that does seem to exist. But her chief fear seems to be that I will become too fond of my endeavor—

Matt was struck by an unexpected feeling of kinship with his older brother. Margaret's reaction to the labor journal sounded much like Dolly's reaction to his painting. Women were not so different after all.

> —too embroiled in producing the Beacon, and thus too inattentive to her, and to the needs of the family.
>
> The fear is unfounded, Matt. I must do my best to convince her.

He started as a shadow fell across his legs. He hadn't

heard Dolly come in. She was carrying two goblets of white *vin ordinaire*. She saw his strained expression.

"Not bad news, is it?"

He folded the letter. "It may be. You can decide for yourself"—he rose and gently lifted the goblets from her fingers—"after we have a proper welcome home."

He bent to kiss her cheek, slipped his left arm around her. She struggled away.

"Matt, we must talk!"

"Plenty of time for that later." He pressed her face with his free hand. A shade too roughly, perhaps, but he was desperate.

"Matthew Kent, I bloody well won't have you trying to get round me this wa—"

He put his mouth on hers. The kiss was long and intense. Her skin smelled sweetly of the lilac water she wore. He ran his fingers up into her blond hair, ruining the carefully created curls.

Her mouth felt cool, unresponsive. He didn't break the embrace. She breathed in—an angry little sound—then pulled back abruptly. Tears shone as she exclaimed, "Oh, you're not fair. Not fair at all."

He kissed her again, ferociously. He worked his right hand behind her, stroking her back while the pressure of his lips bore her head back. She uttered that angry little gasp again, then suddenly went limp against him. With a moan, she flung one arm around his neck. Her mouth opened, eager.

Dolly Stubbs was far from being as starched and proper as all the daughters of Victoria were supposed to be. That was a bounty which had brought him great happiness. Once warmed, her passion was boundless—and this evening was no exception. Her corseted breasts crushed against his shirt as she moved in his arms. When she felt how huge and stiff he was, felt him prodding her through layers of clothing, she moaned again.

He spread his legs, lifting her off the floor and kissing her eyelids. She moaned louder. Surrendering.

He carried her to the other room, and the bed. The room was tiny and without windows. The only illumination came from the fading skylight glow. In moments, he had her outer clothes off, then her corset and undergarments. As he bent to hold and kiss one of her soft white breasts, he knew again that his strategy wasn't mere expediency. He cared for her, deeply.

"Oh, oh," Dolly was exclaiming, arching her bare back. "Oh, you're so damned unfair, Matt Kent. You know how I melt when you do that—"

"I do it because I love you," he whispered, mouth against the warmth of her ear. Her unbound hair tickled his nose.

"You're—a terrible man," she laughed as he spread himself over her, the softness and the roughness of her at once familiar and wondrously new. "A terrible man to make me—so addled—I can't think about what we must—must—oh. *Oh!*"

She brought her body up and forward, a motion urging him to hurry. Eyes closed and clinging to him, she cried, "I love you. *I love you*—"

The end was splendid, as always. And when they rested afterward, the light in the bedroom all but gone, he thought he'd successfully diverted her from discussing domestic matters tonight. He let himself doze off.

Yawning, he woke in response to a gentle tug of his naked shoulder. He heard her whisper, "That was absolutely lovely, Matt. And it told me all over again how much I care for you. But we must still talk."

He'd failed! Feeling trapped again, he sat up in bed. Then came the thunderblow. Her voice affectionate and her hand caressing him again, she added, "It won't take long. I'd just like us to agree to get married."

iii

He was suddenly ashamed of his simpleminded strategy, and of his arrogant assumption that she could be so easily diverted. Sometimes the strength and single-mindedness of the female sex terrified him.

He swung his legs off the side of the bed. "I gathered that was it. You want to exchange all this for an arrangement like Sime and Leah's."

" 'All this?' " she repeated, then gave a short, brusque laugh. "Two rooms in Montmartre and some doubtful prospects for a career as a painter? It's not all *that* magnificent, Mr. Kent! So please don't sneer at me."

He fought to keep the anger out of his voice. "Except for my work, it's exactly what the Strelniks have."

"Oh, no, my dear. For one thing, they have the legal right to give Anton their family name."

He scrambled to his feet. "Dolly, will you kindly tell me what the hell happened to you in Liverpool? Why has a marriage certificate become so damned important all at once? I thought we agreed marriage was nothing but a legalistic fiction. I for one still don't believe the Almighty will smite us dead just because we go to bed without benefit of clergy!"

"No, I don't either," she responded quietly. "On the other hand, certain—changes have put the whole question into a new perspective."

"Your sister snaring some lout and dragging him to the altar, you mean?"

"Don't be cruel," she whispered. "Don't pull that trick you and your friends are so good at—rejecting anything you're not capable of appreciating, or anyone who doesn't think you're doing the most important work since the bloody Creation!"

In the darkened room, heir naked body was a pale blur. She reached for his hand. He was angry enough to pull away but he didn't. She squeezed his fingers.

"I'm sorry, Matt."

Silence for a moment.

"So am I."

"I really didn't mean for this to get so heated. We just have to do some serious thinking, that's all. There is something new to be considered." She drew in a breath. "I'm speaking of a legal name for our baby."

CHAPTER V

STRELNIK'S FLIGHT

i

HALF AN HOUR later, they were seated on opposite sides of a glowing candle set on the taboret in the outer room.

Hundreds of stars spread above the skylight. Somewhere on the butte, a man and a woman argued loudly. The voices faded. A cat meowed in the stillness of the night.

Matt cupped his hands around the warm, fragrant cup of tea Dolly had brewed. But he had no desire for it.

He had put on a shirt and trousers, she an old quilted dressing gown several sizes too large. Her hair was disarrayed, and her cheeks pink from the lovemaking. She sipped her tea and almost fell into a fit of giggling.

"I'm sorry, darling. I really am. But you still look as if the Emperor himself had placed you under arrest."

"That's exactly how I feel." The shock produced by her announcement was slow to dissipate. Certain things were coming into focus, though. The glances at little Anton. Her displeasure at a reference to her weight.

"Well, there's nothing so unusual about a baby. It's only by sheer luck that I haven't gotten pregnant before this. As best I can estimate it, I've been carrying him—or her— for about two months. I saw a doctor in Liverpool to be sure. But I didn't tell my family, Matt. You must believe that."

He nodded, but avoided her eyes.

"I do want the baby to be raised properly," she went on. "I know that may pose some problems in connection with your work. I'm sorry about it, but when a man and woman love each other, and they have a child, the responsibility changes things."

Not for me, he thought, torn by pain. Much as he loved her, he couldn't sacrifice his time and his concentration on the altar of parenthood. He would not give up the life he'd come to Paris to find. Wretched and fraught with problems as the profession was, to be a painter was what he wanted most of all.

And if she'd been with him in that dark, cold water of the Gulf for even one instant—choking, flailing, thinking death was only moments away—she would understand.

She reached around the tiny flame and touched his face. "I don't think I'm asking for anything so unusual, Matt. Just what millions of men and women already share."

Settle for! he thought angrily, but kept silent. Confusion overwhelmed him. He loved her and he loved his work. He was face-to-face with the grim dilemma Paul had talked about. *Which mistress?*

She saw his torment, and relieved it. "We needn't decide tonight. But we will have to decide soon. I must tell you again—this is all my own idea. Not my mother's. Not Peg's. All mine. I do want my child born with a legal name. But if that's not possible—if you don't want the baby—there are women in Paris who can solve the problem."

A shudder of revulsion shook him. "Christ, that's a foul thing to propose! Murder—"

"It's an alternative, Matt."

"A damn vicious one."

She bowed her head. "I know. I'm not proud of it."

A moment later her gaze lifted and locked with his. Her voice strengthened. "But neither am I entirely ashamed of using it to get a commitment from you. A commitment isn't just to my benefit any longer. Oh, I'll gain something if you agree we can get married. Something wonderful—you're a fine, talented man. Not perfect, God knows. But you're exciting to be with, and you're kind and attentive when you think about it. But as I say, I don't have just myself to consider now. I know your family was founded by a bastard, old Philip, but he was an extraordinary chap to judge from all you've told me. Suppose our child's a boy. He might not be as strong. And bastardy is not widely accepted nor lightly tolerated with our dear Victoria setting the world's standard of morality—no, I will not put that burden on any child of mine. So tell me what we're to do, Matt. Get married or—not be troubled by the baby. I want you to tell me by a month from now. July. Surely you can reach a decision by then."

"No, goddamn it! It's an impossible choice."

"Yes," she said gently, and he saw the terrifying strength in her. The strength of womankind, beside which the posings and prattlings of his artist friends seemed puerile. "Yes, it is. But my father always said there were many impossible choices in a lifetime. Being able to deal with them makes you an adult, I suppose. So does dealing with the pain they bring. A month, Matt. I think that's time enough." She finished her tea. "Now shall we go back to bed?"

ii

He left Montmartre about midmorning Sunday. Dolly was accustomed to his disappearing for hours at a time, either to Fochet's atelier or on long walks during which he developed, sorted and rejected ideas about his work.

This morning he could barely think about painting, so full of conflicting feelings was he in the wake of Dolly's announcement. One moment he wanted the child, but the next, he knew it would represent the start of a shackling process which would ultimately rob him of the absolutely vital freedom an artist required.

Pondering, he roamed the right bank from the great triumphal arch at the Place de l'Etoile to the esplanade south of the Louvre, where fishermen dropped their lines into the sunlit Seine. Coal barges moved slowly up the river as he strolled on toward the Île de la Cité and crossed the bridge to Notre Dame. He was not religious in the conventional sense, but he slipped into the cathedral by the door directly

beneath the magnificent rose window and stood in the cool,
vaulted darkness listening to a priest chant the mass far,
far down in the immense nave. Something of the peace of
the church stole into him, and his thinking slowly clarified.

As he walked out he dropped a few sous in the poor
box. He had reached two decisions. He would not give in
to Dolly's demands that they marry, but he would not permit her to do away with the child. He would find some way
to persuade her to deliver the baby out of wedlock. She
really didn't understand all the implications of her threat
to go to one of those women he'd only heard about—old,
frequently unclean women whose instruments helped a
young girl out of a predicament, in violation of the laws of
France and of the Church. He must make her understand
and reject that alternative.

He sat a while in a café near Notre Dame, sipping red
wine in the summer sunshine. He began to feel better, more
confident. He even turned his thoughts to a new piece of
work. Something along the lines Paul had talked about. Not
an American subject—that would be going too far—but
one from his blockade-running days. His mind focused on
an image of a smoky, crowded cantina in the Mexican town
of Matamoras on the Rio Grande. He recalled a dancer
he'd seen perform there. A lovely, dark-eyed wench with
a sinuous body. Soon the organization of a picture suggested itself. Then, excited, he began to expand the mental
canvas to include a few spectators and then the whole of
one side of the cantina. He had never planned anything
half so ambitious.

Toward the end of the afternoon he drifted north again.
Presently he reached the Café Guerbois at number eleven
Grand Rue des Batignolles. Usually the group gathered late
on Friday, so he didn't expect to find anyone—not on a
Sunday evening when the café had no other trade. But
Edouard Manet was there.

The unofficial head of the Batignolles group was in his
late thirties. He came from a bourgeois family just as Paul
did. At that point the resemblance ended. Manet's dress
and deportment were impeccable. His light brown beard
was always meticulously trimmed and combed. Next to his
wineglass lay an expensive walking stick and a pair of yellow gloves. He hardly looked like the sort who would scan-

dalize established authority, but since the early 1860s he had been doing just that with paintings such as *Concert in the Tuileries Gardens, Olympia* and *Luncheon on the Grass,* the provocative study of two gentlemen in conventional daytime attire enjoying a woodland picnic with two young women—one in a diaphanous drapery, the other stark naked.

Manet's infamous picture, so realistic and yet so outrageously fantastic at the same time, had been refused by the jury of the 1863 Salon. Manet and so many other artists had protested so forcefully about the unimaginative rejection of anything the least bit new, Napoléon III had done a surprising turnabout and announced that the rejected works would be shown in a second, unofficial exhibit—the *Salon des Refusés.*

Ever since, Manet had come to be the acknowledged leader of everything revolutionary in French painting. The café group—Renoir, Degas, Fantin-Latour, Monet, Pissarro, Paul and others—drew inspiration from his talent and encouragement from his friendship. Some of Manet's work was even tiptoeing around the margins of respectability. *Luncheon* had been hung in the '69 Salon. But the artist himself was still not acceptable. This spring, Salon jury selection procedures had been revised so that the jury would include practicing painters. Manet's candidacy had been rejected because of his radical views.

"Well—Matthew!" Manet extended his hand, shook Matt's. "How goes it?"

"Not very well," Matt said with a shrug and a grin.

"Pity. I've had the same kind of day myself." He turned and raised his voice slightly. "Lisa?" There was no response from the back, where Matt could hear the splash of wash water and the clink of dishes. "I've been meaning to ask you how you fared in your little experiment a few weeks ago."

Matt pulled a face. "The cocaine made me sick for three days. I don't see why people are convinced it frees the mind. All it did was muddle mine. I have trouble enough turning out work without trying to do it dead drunk or delirious from an injection."

"You sound as if you're having a good deal of trouble right now."

"Nothing's coming out right. I've been tempted to chuck the whole business."

Manet frowned. "That would be a loss. I hope you'll reconsider. Your work is still rough, but it shows great vitality. And unmistakable promise."

A damp hand speared over Matt's shoulder, taking him by surprise. The hand closed on his groin and a coarse, teasing female voice said, "I know something else that shows a lot of promise."

She let go. Matt kissed the reddened hand that smelled of strong soap. Lisa rumpled his hair. She was ten years older than Matt—closer to Manet's age—always disheveled, with her hair falling in her eyes.

She leaned over to set a glass and a new carafe of wine on the marble table. "Eh, Matthew, my Virginia dove"— she pronounced it *Var-ghin-ya*—"why can't you and I ever be close friends?" She caught his head in the crook of her elbow and squeezed him against her blouse and her large breasts. "You know how close I mean."

Manet coughed and examined the ceiling. She released him. "Believe me, if that English girl ever turns her back on you, I'll snatch you away."

"You'll be too busy avoiding all your other suitors, Lisa. I saw one of them yesterday."

She brightened. "You did? Who?"

"That Prussian, Lepp."

"Oh, God. Spare me!"

He described the encounter at the Gare du Nord, including Lepp's promise that he'd be back to see her. At that, she shivered.

"Let's hope not. After he was in here the last time, I made a few inquiries. Some of the—ah—working girls in the neighborhood know a little about him." She proceeded to describe some of Lepp's aberrations. Manet grew increasingly embarrassed, but the barmaid paid no attention. She said Lepp had been heard to boast about a secret pied-à-terre somewhere on the left bank. "He reportedly pays both prostitutes and impoverished students from the Sorbonne to spend an hour satisfying his peculiar needs. I want no part of that fellow, I tell y—"

"I didn't expect anyone to be here!" a bellowing voice interrupted. "Hortense and I have had a terrible fight!"

Matt stood up. "Hello, Paul." His friend looked even more wild-eyed than usual. Manet sat motionless, as if wanting to be inconspicuous. He and Matt's friend didn't always hit it off.

"Lisa, you unwashed slut, get me some wine!" Paul yelled, grabbing a chair and sitting down.

She made a face and told him to get it himself. She flounced out. Paul didn't move.

Manet made an effort to be cordial, extended his hand. "How are you, Cézanne?"

Paul glared. "I do not shake your hand, Mr. Manet. I have not washed for a week."

The other man sighed. "Really, Cézanne, your rudeness is unbelievable sometimes."

Paul fixed the other artist with a murderous eye. "I've nothing to say to you. I'm not intelligent enough to speak on your level. I don't even know why I sit at this table. I don't fit in. I don't dress or speak like a smug provincial lawyer!"

Manet snatched up his stick and gloves. "In one of your insufferable moods, are you? I shouldn't wonder Hortense had her claws out. She'd be happier living with a wild orangutan. Good evening!"

Manet stalked out. Matt stared after him, then sighed in an annoyed way. "Why do you insult everyone, Paul?"

Paul slammed his elbows on the table and covered his eyes with his palms. "Shut up. Just shut up and leave me alone."

It was sensible to give in to Paul's wishes when he was in such a state. Matt slipped away from the table. For a moment he was able to appreciate Dolly's feeling that a normal existence was much more preferable than a career among such emotionally stunted people. It was difficult for Matt to make outsiders understand that outrageous character flaws in a man such as Paul were more than made up for by incredible talent. Indeed, the flaws had probably helped nurture the talent. They were its price.

He was halfway to the arch leading to the kitchen when the front door banged open again. Paul's head had sunk onto his arms and he appeared to be dozing as Matt turned, saw the new arrival, and exclaimed, "Sime!"

Carrying a carpetbag in one hand, Strelnik rushed toward

him. "Thank God. I left the house in such a rush, I didn't have a chance to ask Dolly where you were. I was hoping you might be here."

Matt had seldom seen his friend so agitated. "Sime, what's wrong?"

"I'm afraid I may be in very serious trouble."

iii

Lisa strolled up behind Matt and leaned on his shoulder, absently reaching down with her left hand to tweak his rump. Strelnik couldn't see. He gave the barmaid a suspicious stare, then said to Matt, "I must talk to you privately."

"All right. Excuse us, Lisa."

She shrugged and disappeared again. Matt led the agitated little man to a table against the far wall, six or eight feet from Paul, who was snoring and making maudlin noises.

Strelnik jerked off his shabby cap and twisted it in his hands as he leaned forward. "I have to be gone for a few days, Matt. Will you look after Leah and the baby for me? See that nothing happens to them?"

Matt started to laugh. "What do you mean? What could possibly happen to them?"

"I don't know," Strelnik replied, nervously raking fingers through his bright red beard. "But I fear I've become a dangerous man to know. I want you to be aware of that before you agree to anything."

Strelnik's statements struck Matt as pretentious and melodramatic. Yet what he saw in the Russian's round, dark eyes was the kind of fright that precluded laughter.

"I wish you'd explain that, Sime."

"I'll try. I'm still rather shaky. This afternoon certain—associates of mine sent a coded telegraph message. From Berlin."

Matt was slow to realize the significance. Strelnik blurted, "My brother's been arrested!"

"Your brother? I'm sorry to hear it. But how does that involve you?"

"I'm not sure. But I was advised to go into hiding. You

see, Matt, my brother, Yuri, is allied with certain groups that oppose the monolithic state Otto Bismarck is attempting to build in Germany. Yuri had been trying to discover what position the Premier has taken in regard to the throne of Spain."

Matt didn't understand, and said so. Strelnik cast another anxious look toward the street entrance, then explained.

The throne of Spain had been left vacant after a political upheaval in 1868. It was still vacant because various claimants and candidates were maneuvering behind the scenes. Yuri Strelnik had learned that Bismarck was promoting Prince Leopold of Hohenzollern-Simaringen, a member of the ruling house of Prussia, for that kingship.

Bewildered, Matt shook his head. "Sime, forgive me. I still don't follow."

"No, I realize you don't take politics very seriously, Matthew. But some men take it with deadly seriousness."

"I know. I lost a brother because of men like that. Go on."

"Yuri and his comrades wanted to expose the Hohenzollern candidacy. If it became a matter of public record, France would react violently, since the news would mean Prussia's sphere of influence may soon extend to Spain."

"I never imagined you and your crowd here in Paris were friends of the Emperor, Sime."

"Definitely not! We're interested solely in the people's cause. However, any international friction that embarrasses Bismarck and blunts his drive for power works to the advantage of the German people. Bismarck wants to enthrone William, the Prussian king, as kaiser of a unified, militaristic Germany. By hampering his plan we foster ours, which is the eventual overthrow of Bismarck's regime."

"And your cause is helped by exposure of a meaningless candidacy for a meaningless throne?"

"Believe me, the exposure would not be meaningless. France will not view it that way. The Emperor will consider Bismarck's maneuver to be provocative. And doubly insulting because Bismarck kept the candidacy a secret until the Spanish parliament approved it."

"You don't mean France would declare war over a breach of protocol?"

"Oh, no, certainly not. That would be going too far. But

severe diplomatic repercussions—those are virtually guaranteed."

"All right, Sime, that's reasonably clear. Just explain why you have to go into hiding."

"Because Yuri finally obtained *documentation* of the Hohenzollern candidacy!"

"Have you seen it?"

"I have not. But the Prussians may think I have. Yuri and I correspond all the time. You know that. I'm sure they do too. And the Prussian eagle has talons that reach a great distance," Strelnik declared with breathy emphasis. "A *great* distance."

That much Matt was willing to grant, given the presence in Paris of men such as Lepp. Perhaps Strelnik had good cause for fear, though Matt did find it ludicrous that there could be such furor over an obsolete kingship. On the other hand, Jeremiah had been lost because of hotheaded partisanship for slavery, an outmoded and immoral institution, and for secession, a windy debating platform topic not worth one human life.

"You can count on Dolly and me to watch out for your wife and boy. Don't worry about them."

Strelnik put on his cap and picked up his carpetbag. "I'll try not to, Matt."

"Does Leah know where you're going?"

"No one knows but the people who will be hiding me. I'll come home as soon as I'm told that it's safe. Meanwhile"—he pumped Matt's hand—"thank you from the bottom of my heart. Yesterday you paid me a sort of reverse compliment. Now it's my turn—"

One more swift look at the street door. "You are a decent man, Matthew—even if you do have no comprehension of what powers actually move the world. One of them isn't a paintbrush. That much I'll tell you. I fear that long after the cleansing revolutionary fire has burned out the old order you'll still be standing in the ashes scratching your head and wondering what happened. And you'll never understand why the old order had to die to make way for the new."

"No, I won't," Matt agreed. "In case there's an emergency, I do think I should know where to find you."

"No, you shouldn't!" Strelnik shot back with an alarmed look. "It will be safer that way."

He picked up the carpetbag, paused at the door to look both ways along the avenue, then rushed off into the gathering twilight. For some reason, the little man's last remark made Matt shiver.

CHAPTER VI

IN THE STUDIO
OF THE ONION

i

NEXT MORNING HE woke before dawn, trembling in the spell
of a dream in which he'd clearly seen himself standing before the finished painting of the Matamoras cantina.

The painting had been equally clear—a huge, crowded
canvas conveying a sense of boisterous and bawdy life.
From the central figure of the dark-haired dancing girl to
the dim groupings at the tables around the perimeter, the
images seemed to pulse with a kind of arrested motion. In
the workroom of his dreaming mind, the painting had come
out perfectly. But then Fochet was fond of saying, "Here
is a truth that will prevent disappointment and self-
satisfaction. The picture on your canvas is never as good
as the one in your head."

Details of the dream began to fade almost immediately.
He left the bed quickly. When Dolly murmured and
reached for him, he was already in the outer room. He
lurched about, lighting a lamp and locating paper and a
stick of charcoal.

He began scribbling a series of little scenes from the
dream painting. A fat proprietor with mustachios like opposing horizontal question marks. Three Confederate cap-

tains bent over cards and tequila at one of the tables. A flamboyantly dressed vaquero practically cross-eyed with drink, reaching out to pinch the dancing girl. He finished four sketches before the dream slipped completely away.

In the summer he always slept naked, and tonight was no exception. Though the flat was cool, his body still felt warm from the fever of excitement. His heartbeat was unusually fast, his breathing quick and raspy.

He glanced up at the skylight, saw only brilliant stars against blackness. It wasn't even close to morning. But he knew he couldn't sleep. He dressed, then bent to kiss Dolly's temple.

She lay on her side, snoring lightly again. Gently he touched her upraised hip, as if to bless and protect the unborn baby in her womb. In some curious but certain way, he already knew the child would be male.

How in God's name could he let her even *think* about destroying their son? He couldn't. At the same time, he could not—would not—surrender his independence.

All at once he had what struck him as an inspired idea. Perhaps Fochet would help resolve the dilemma!

The more he thought about the idea, the more he liked it. He was whistling as he passed from the garden into the Rue Saint-Vincent and set off at a brisk pace.

Just as false dawn broke, he let himself into the building which housed the atelier of Étienne Fochet on its second and topmost floor. The building was located halfway down the east slope of the hill crowned by marble-columned Saint-Pierre de Montmartre, the old church which elderly residents of the village said had once been a Roman temple. At the head of the stairs Matt unlocked the outer door of the studio. All the walls on the second floor had been knocked out to create one huge, loftlike room in which he quickly got to work.

ii

By lamplight he hammered a frame together, using scrap lumber Fochet kept for that purpose. The frame was six feet high, nine feet wide. Then he stretched and tacked a huge new piece of linen onto the frame. By nine o'clock, when the other students began to drift in, he had the linen prepared and the frame fitted into two small easels. The top of the frame leaned against the studio's east wall.

Matt stood on a small box, applying the ground with swift, broad strokes. For the moment he'd forgotten everything else: Strelnik; Dolly; the problem of the baby; the fact that he hadn't eaten breakfast; even where he was. The fever, the joyous fever, had claimed him again.

Soon, though, activity in the atelier made it impossible for him to totally shut out his surroundings. Fochet had thirty-one students. About half were present on any given day, the rest off doing copy work at the Louvre, sleeping with their mistresses, recovering from drinking bouts, or just loafing. Only ten of the students were still receiving formalized instruction. They and all the others paid the teacher a small fee which went toward the rent and the wages of whatever model he hired off the street that week. Fochet actually charged nothing for his occasional lectures or for individual instruction. A good thing, too, the students joked. The teacher's usual manner was one of outrage, as if he really hated to be burdened with pupils. The truth was, he preferred teaching above everything else.

Shortly the atelier was in a state of hubbub. Matt kept working away at the ground while the day's first fight broke out. Three students who had been loudly debating the artistic merits of Offenbach's highly popular music decided to settle their differences by punching, kicking and biting each other. Most of the other students paid no attention. Two were guffawing like donkeys over a sketch one of them had done. The picture was a cruel caricature of the pendulous breasts and scraggly pubis of the naked fat girl who sat on a box on the dais in the center of the room. The poor creature looked baffled and vaguely alarmed as she stared out at the ring of young men around her, the clutter of easels and work cabinets, and the combatants tussling and screaming obscenities in the background.

All at once a door crashed open. Fochet stormed in to break up the fight. "Louts! *Farmers!*" He flailed about him, boxing ears. "Get to work or get out of here!"

The three brawlers separated, called him all sorts of filthy names, then went placidly back to their easels. Fochet shook his head in disgust and moved on, stopping here to

observe, there to deliver a scathing critique. He lectured
one pupil for five minutes, seized the brush from another's
hand and made a few swift corrections. No matter how
harsh his criticism or how brusque his manner, the pupils
didn't complain. He was fierce, but he was respected.

Étienne Fochet had come from Limoges, the home city
of a member of the Batignolles group, Auguste Renoir.
Fochet had served an apprenticeship in the decorating
rooms of a Limoges pottery factory, painting eighteenth-
century swains and shepherdesses on an endless array of
plates, jugs and cups. Renoir, coincidentally, had held a
similar job as a boy, though in Paris. Renoir, however, was
still a year shy of thirty. Fochet would never see fifty again.

As a much younger man just come up to Paris with ambition but no training, Fochet had studied with Courbet, who
was almost exactly his own age and already doing revolutionary work. Courbet had rid his own painting of literary
and mythological elements, and taught his pupils to do the
same. He had forever changed the direction of contemporary art by painting subjects from everyday life. In fact,
Fochet claimed to be one of the people depicted in what
was perhaps Courbet's most famous work—*The Painter's
Studio,* his 1855 canvas showing the artist at work in his
crowded atelier. Fochet said he was the bearded man
seated next to a pair of dogs at the extreme left. Matt
had seen the picture several times and didn't consider the
resemblance pronounced.

Courbet had emphasized traditional technique blended
with fidelity to observed detail. Fochet's theory and practice
went one more step. Slavish adherence to old-fashioned
rules of technique was entirely secondary to what the artist
observed. Only that which was optically apparent should
be included in a painting. As he often put it, "The impression, only the visual impression matters! Nothing else is
reality!"

A powerful smell told Matt the teacher was coming up
behind him. Fochet constantly munched bits of stale red
onion which he carried in a pocket of his paint-spotted
blouse. His pupils called him *l'oignon* half derisively, half
affectionately—but always behind his back. He was a short
man, barely five feet, with an immense belly, kinky gray
hair and lively brown eyes that could be fiercely intimidat-

ing. In his youth he'd worn a beard, but it was gone now,
revealing heavily pitted cheeks.

"Well, Kent!" he exclaimed. "A picture in work at last!
Good, good. You haven't done much of anything for the
last six months. In fact I was planning to ask you to move
out so I could replace you with someone actually *interested*
in painting. I had reached the conclusion that you continued to rent space here merely so you wouldn't have to
spend a hard winter on the streets."

Matt was too excited about the new painting to let the
sarcasm bother him. Fochet took notice of the huge frame,
circumscribed it with choppy motions of one hand as he
went on: "Ambitious. I doubt your talent's up to handling
anything that large, but I'm glad you're trying. What's it
to be?"

Matt put his palette aside and wiped his hands with a
rag dipped in diluent. "A café in Mexico."

Fochet brightened perceptibly. "Something you've seen
firsthand?"

"Yes, I drank there quite often when we took cargo up
the Rio Grande river during the war."

"Capital! I've always thought you were an idiot to ignore
all the fascinating subject matter in your personal experience. Not to mention that in your homeland. When I was
younger, Captain Catlin and his Indians convinced me
America was a veritable trove of colorful subjects."

"You mean George Catlin?"

"That's right, the fellow who traveled and painted the
western part of your country twenty or thirty years ago. He
came to Paris in the forties. Exhibited his canvases and a
band of Iowa Indians. My sister was a chambermaid at the
Hotel Victoria, where he kept the savages. She smuggled
me in so I could observe them. The beds were removed so
the Indians could sleep on the floor. The sight of their
sharp teeth gave my poor sister nightmares about cannibals.
But Catlin made quite an impression over here. Quite an
impression on me, too. I sometimes think Frenchmen are
more appreciative of your country than you are, Kent."

"I agree." Matt grinned. "I don't care if I never see
it again."

"Stupid attitude."

Matt stopped smiling, red-faced.

The teacher gestured at the linen half covered with the sand-colored ground. "Tell me more about what you're planning."

"The central figure's to be a young Mexican dancing girl with combs in her hair. Here, I did a few preliminary studies—"

Fochet popped bits of onion in his mouth. He chewed while he examined the sketches. Presently he uttered a few monosyllabic grunts. Matt felt almost delirious with pleasure. Fochet's grunts were virtually his highest form of compliment.

The tutor handed the drawings back, picked a speck of onion from the corner of his mouth and said with mock innocence, "Then I really needn't concern myself with renting your space to someone else?"

"Oh, yes, you still may have to think about that. I don't know how smoothly this is going to proceed. Dolly's given me something besides work to worry about."

Fochet frowned. "Is there trouble between you and your young lady?"

"Yes, I guess you'd call it trouble."

"I can't imagine that. She's always seemed to be a fine sort—for a woman, that is."

"She is a fine woman." Matt nodded. "You know how I feel about her—"

"Don't get too fond of her, Kent! I keep telling you that's very bad for a painter. Sometime, if you wish, you may tell me the nature of your problem." He shrugged as if it didn't matter much. That was his usual way of inviting a student to pour out his deepest woes.

Matt lost no time. "The trouble is, we're going to have a child."

"Unexpected?"

"Yes."

"And you're certain?"

"Dolly says she is."

"Hmmm. Well, I suppose congratulations are in order." He sounded dubious. "Just don't spend too many hours dandling the infant on your knee"—pieces of onion flew as Fochet waved at the oversized frame—"not if you really plan to complete a painting the size of one of Manet's."

"I do. But Dolly wants the child to have a legal name. She wants us to get married."

The teacher's hand stopped halfway to his lips. Then, abruptly, he flung the onion away. "What the devil is the *matter* with women? Do they not understand that it's very difficult to serve the easel and the hearth at the same time? No, not difficult—impossible! Some few seem able to do both, I know. Manet, for instance. On the other hand, you wouldn't call his courtship exactly conventional. He met that Dutch girl, Miss Leenhoff, in 1852—eleven years before the death of his father made it possible for him to ignore family objections and marry her. Someone knocked her up eleven years before the ceremony, too. Very mysterious. Well, at least she wasn't hounding him to surrender to domesticity for all that time. Most women would have reminded him of his moral obligation every hour on the hour—God, some characteristics of the female species are just insufferable!"

Matt was astonished at the vehemence of the little teacher, and even more astonished when Fochet blurted, "I know what I'm talking about! I've had five wives. Did I ever mention that?"

Dumbfounded, Matt shook his head.

"Well, I meant to do so, but you know how my thoughts wander—" That was true enough; Fochet was notoriously absentminded. Again this morning he'd forgotten to button his trousers.

He went on. "Each of the five wanted me to spend more and more time with them, which meant less and less time in the studio. Of course they all launched their campaigns *after* we left the altar. Beforehand, they were very solicitous about my chosen vocation—oh, I tell you they're clever, Kent. When you're courting, they pretend the two of you can reach an accommodation in any disagreement. But after you have stood up before a droning priest, and after the lady has revealed her little treasures in the marriage bed, it's you and you alone who do the accommodating. I'm not blaming them. I believe such tactics are part of their nature. But a man must learn to be wary. Especially a man in this profession. Five times I failed to heed that same advice which other unfortunates had given me. Four times hope triumphed over the warnings of personal experience. And wouldn't you know it? Every one of the bitches loathed onions, too."

After a rueful laugh, Fochet spoke with more kindness than Matt had ever heard from him—and he pitched his voice low so nearby students couldn't possibly eavesdrop. "Has Miss Dolly confronted you with a request that you marry her? Or is it a demand?"

He pondered a moment. "No matter what you call it, the end result's the same, isn't it?"

Fochet nodded in a grave way. "Yes, I suppose you're right. How do you feel about her wishes?"

"Independence is the last thing I want to give up."

"Splendid!"

"But I don't want to give her up, either."

At that, the teacher looked downcast. "Well, I do hope you can work things out without surrendering your freedom. If at all possible, I would like you to be spared the kind of painful choice many painters cannot avoid."

"Paul calls it choosing between two mistresses," Matt said quietly.

"I'm not sure I like your crazy friend's metaphor. It smacks of the vulgar. It's degrading, in fact. Art is a high calling. A priesthood whose members are privileged to show mere humans their common traits instead of their differences. Privileged to show them beauty in a world that has made them weary with its ugliness. Privileged, in short, to help them endure. And you know as well as I do— priests are celibate. For a very good reason. They know they can't successfully serve both God and the flesh. Obviously that's what Cézanne is getting at with his prattle about mistresses. But he's right about one thing. You don't *want* to make a choice between a girl and your career. I've seen such a choice tear many a talented fellow apart. Ruin his composure and his work for months—years—sometimes forever. The secret of avoiding that is to find a young woman who loves to copulate but who is also basically stupid and slovenly. One of those very rare and precious girls who not only don't give a fig for respectability but don't even know what it is."

"I'm afraid it's too late for that, Fochet. I love her."

"And you don't think she would be content to bear the child out of wedlock?"

He remembered the chilling threat about certain women who could *solve the problem.* "No. Once I thought she might, but over the past few months, she's changed. I think she's started to consider the future. When she found out she was pregnant, that convinced her to do something decisive"—a rueful smile—"and so she has. We either marry or"—he hid the worst—"or separate. You know she's a strong-minded girl."

"Yes, I have gotten that impression." The teacher sighed, scratched the tip of his nose. "Let me talk to her. Let me see whether I can convince her it's disastrous to try to fetter someone in this crazy profession—why are you smiling?"

"Because I meant to get around to asking you to do exactly that."

"Of course! Why not? It's logical. I'm older. I know much more of the world than you do. You're just a callow boy—"

"She respects you, too."

Fochet blinked. "She does?"

"Very much so."

The teacher swelled visibly. "I'll definitely speak to her. Just don't get your hopes too high. Women are difficult. However, I can certainly make the effort. And if she does respect me, as you say—"

"She does! You can convince her if anyone can. How can I thank you, Fochet?"

"Very simple. By doing some work for a change."

The moment of sympathy was gone; the tutor was on the attack. "I say again—I believe your ambition exceeds your ability. Prove me wrong if you can. Show me your talent is as big as that"—he waved at the canvas—"expression of your confidence in it. In other words, as big as your ego."

Having thrust the spear in, he turned and walked away, regal as any king. Suddenly his jaw jutted. He broke into a waddling run, headed for the other side of the studio where another fight had erupted.

Matt went back to work, hoping that the teacher might indeed be able to persuade Dolly to change her decision. Soften her attitude.

At least the problem was temporarily out of his hands. He could turn to the Matamoras painting with all his concentration and energy—which was the only way a painter could accomplish anything decent. Dolly had to hear that again.

Hear it and *accept* it—so their son could live.

CHAPTER VII

SOMEONE WATCHING

i

BY MIDWEEK, Matt's work on the Matamoras picture had almost reached a state of frenzy. He was painting for fourteen or fifteen hours at a stretch, sustained only by his young man's strength. But even that flagged eventually, and after the long sessions he went limping back to the Rue Saint-Vincent, totally spent.

Dolly grew short tempered because he wanted to do little more than eat and fall asleep when he got home. He wasn't eager to hear the day's happenings at the English school, or a lengthy account of her first visit to the doctor who'd been recommended to her, a peppery young physician named Clemenceau. He had returned from a stay in Connecticut the preceding year, brought an American wife with him, and set up a Parisian practice. Matt listened with a frown as Dolly took ten minutes to describe how Dr. Georges Clemenceau had examined her and pronounced her pregnant.

She recognized his annoyance and voiced hers. "I should think you'd be interested in the welfare of your own child."

"I am, Dolly. But your sawbones hasn't told us anything we don't already know."

"I suppose you don't worry about poor Sime, either."

"Of course I worry." It was only partially true. In the studio there were long periods when thoughts of the child—or of his vanished neighbor—never entered his mind. He was slightly ashamed of that, but he couldn't change the fact.

He'd told Dolly everything Strelnik had said that evening at the café. She had immediately started spending as much time as possible with Strelnik's wife, to ease her through the tense period. "Has Leah still not heard from him?" Matt asked now.

"No, not a word. She's so upset, she's almost ill."

"I shouldn't wonder. I assume he's all right, though. If he weren't, his friends would have contacted us."

"How very considerate of you to spend a moment expressing that thought!" Dolly's voice was oddly husky. In the light of the candles by which they were eating cheese and drinking wine for a midnight supper, her lovely eyes glowed with resentment. "I mean to say I know how highly you value your time, Matt. When you give up even one precious second on behalf of others, it's deeply appreciated by lesser mortals."

Rage and sadness mingled as he rubbed his forehead. "Oh, for Christ's sake, Dolly. Please don't start again—"

"Start what? It's true. An expression of human feeling is a rare thing from a man whose only mistress is his work."

Matt's eyes grew bleak. "What the hell's gotten into you tonight?"

Suddenly her hostility melted. "I'm frightened. I'm frightened of having a child. I want the baby but there's so much to learn about having one—" She bent her head, tears glistening. "I'm just being bloody bitchy. I do apologize."

"I understand," he said, though he didn't, fully.

Softly, she went on. "It is true about your work, though. If you were in love with another woman, I could fight that. I can't fight a woman like the one you're thinking about every moment these days."

She meant the cantina dancer. He'd been trying to solve a problem of arrangement of the painting's central figure. He'd even been doing some little drawings tonight, before she'd set out the cheese and wine. The pad, charcoal and several discarded anatomical sketches lay at his feet.

For a moment her glance rested on them with unconcealed loathing. He was infuriated by her suggestion that
the problem was unimportant. Before he could say so, she
glanced up from the sketches and sighed.

"No, I can't fight that. Come, let's go to bed. I'm worn-
out, too."

His anger faded. No doubt the pregnancy was upsetting
and tiring her. He supposed that was the case when any
woman had her first baby. But this pregnancy brought a
special burden. She didn't know whether it would go to its
full term.

July was approaching. The deadline she'd set for his decision. There'd been no further discussion of that decision,
but obviously it was much in her thoughts.

*Fochet hasn't spoken to her. When he does, she'll calm
down. Maybe July will come and she'll back off and there'll
be no need for a decision.*

He clung to Fochet as a solution to his difficulty almost
as tenaciously as he'd clung to the spar that had kept him
from drowning in the Gulf—as tenaciously, and with fully
as much desperation.

ii

The remainder of the week went by and the underpainting of the Matamoras scene began to emerge. As he
saw it in his head, in his sketches, and then in broad out-
lines swiftly laid on in black, it would be a canvas full of
sweeping line and swirling motion. The dominant color
would represent a sinister amber lamplight which had
flooded the actual café. He only hoped he could successfully transfer that light from his memory to the canvas.

He'd finally solved the technical problem with the
dancer. The problems with Dolly persisted. She seemed exhausted even when she woke in the morning and was increasingly prone to snap and quarrel over the smallest
imagined slight.

On Saturday he decided to try to do something to make
her feel better. That evening he persuaded her to put on
her best frock, and they ambled up to the Moulin de la

Galette, which had long ago been converted from an actual mill to an open-air restaurant and dance hall.

The spot was one of the most popular in Montmartre. Guests entered through a gate into a deliberately overgrown garden. Then they passed along a narrow hallway in the old house attached to the mill, which some said had first started grinding grain in the thirteenth century. The door at the end of the hall revealed a whole series of pleasing views on the hilltop: beds of daisies and bright morning glories in a broad lawn; an orchard; a vegetable garden. And surrounded by these charmingly rural aspects, there were clusters of white-painted outdoor furniture, a raised dance floor and a small band shell.

To their surprise, they found Paul and Hortense at one table. "Join us, join us!" Paul urged.

Matt and Dolly did so, though not without some unspoken fears about an unpleasant evening. Paul and his mistress had apparently reconciled, however, and both were in quite good spirits. Occasionally Matt had seen Paul completely forget his practiced truculence. Perhaps tonight would turn out to be one of those grand occasions when some curious chemistry took over and released Paul from his need to make people reject him so that he could continue to believe he was special.

The Moulin soon grew crowded. They ordered good, cheap côtes du Rhône in a large pottery carafe with a brown glaze. After consuming two large glasses, Matt all but forgot his difficulties with Dolly.

The lanterns strung in the trees glowed in the summer dusk. The musicians arrived, started exchanging jokes with the guests as they tuned up. Zola dropped in and stayed half an hour, chatting with Paul and the others about plans for his forthcoming wedding. Dolly sent one or two pointed glances Matt's way, to remind him that some who were involved in the arts didn't find it prohibited marriage. He just poured more wine and said nothing.

Auguste Renoir arrived and pulled up a chair. An unusual young man in many ways, Matt thought. Renoir's father had operated a tailoring shop in Limoges, but the business had failed so he'd come up to Paris when his son was quite small. Young Auguste had painted china just as Fochet had, meticulously copying scenes by Fragonard and

Watteau in a dingy warehouse on the Rue du Temple. But to finance his education at the Beaux-Arts, he'd done all sorts of commercial jobs of the kind most aspiring artists scorned. He'd painted figures and ornamental designs on fans, decorated the blinds of shop windows, produced endless copies of coats of arms for important families, and created murals for the walls of obscure little taverns. He was still knocking out commissioned portraits to pay for his living expenses.

Matt believed Renoir had ability equal or superior to Paul's or Edouard's and that his paintings would one day be famous. But the young man from Limoges unconsciously made light of his talent by frittering it away. He incessantly scribbled cartoons and caricatures on anything from napkins to his own paper cuffs. Tonight he started off by surreptitiously doing a sketch of Zola as a dirty, swag-bellied laborer. Renoir didn't care for the journalist or his novels. "He thinks that he fully describes human beings merely by saying they smell," was his comment after the writer had gone.

Auguste Renoir had a tough air sometimes, almost as if he had grown up as a Paris gamin—which in fact he had—and would remain one until the end of his days. Yet mingled with that street-smart cynicism was something pensive and gentle—as now, when he forgot his pique, tore up the nasty cartoon and began another showing some of the Saturday evening celebrants. The Moulin was one of his favorite subjects.

Matt and Dolly waltzed under the lanterns, whirling round and round the raised wooden floor to the melodies of Johann Strauss the younger. The orchestra played the Viennese music with apolitical enthusiasm. At the end of one number, they walked back to the table to find Renoir just completing a cartoon of them pressed close together, as though dancing languidly to some very slow piece. The lines of the drawing were few but eloquent, and there was no mistaking the models he'd chosen.

"Auguste, that's grand!" Matt exclaimed. "You must sign it!"

Renoir ripped the drawing off his pad. "Why? It's trivial." He started to crush the cartoon into a ball. Dolly rescued it from his hand.

"Not to me. It's splendid. May we have it?"

The young man seemed flattered. He glanced down in a modest way. "Of course, if you like it that much." He put his signature on it and handed it to her. She gazed at it with obvious pleasure while they rested during the next few dances.

She really is feeling good tonight, Matt thought when they went back to waltz again. She'd actually shown a liking for a piece of work done by one of his artist friends. Usually her approval was limited to a cool word or two—if that. He often thought she was afraid to display enthusiasm for fear it might imply approval of the profession as well.

Around and around the dance floor they spun, Dolly's eyes sparkling from all the wine and her cheeks pink from the warmth of the summer night. Unexpectedly, he was reminded of the child as he rested his hand on her waist. He seemed to detect a slight thickening there.

Soon the child would begin to change her figure visibly. That would be just the first of many changes in their lives. It was an awesome thing for a man to contemplate the birth of his first offspring. But under the gay lights of the Moulin, it was a happy thing to contemplate, too.

For three short hours, neither he nor Dolly said a cross word. All was right with the world.

Laughing and clinging to one another, they were weaving along the Rue Saint-Vincent as the bell of Saint-Pierre's chimed midnight. Slowly the last tolling died away between the summer stars and the twinkling lights of Paris below the butte. The thickly shadowed street was silent except for the meow of an unseen cat on the prowl.

Matt's curiosity was getting the better of him. The wine he'd drunk finally overcame his caution. In a voice just slightly thickened, he said, "You're in wonderful spirits tonight, Dolly."

"It was a wonderful evening. You know how much I love to dance. I won't be able to do it much long—oops." She slipped on the cobbles. He grabbed her around the waist to keep her from taking a spill.

Giggling, she collapsed against him. Renoir's cartoon rattled in her hand. Her weight pushed him back against a wall two houses down from the one protecting Madame Rochambeau's. Inadvertently his fingers came in contact with the cheap ring she wore. The feel of the metal prodded him again.

"What did Fochet have to say when you spoke to him?"

"The Onion? I haven't set eyes on him since that party at his studio, just before the Salon opened. Was he supposed to be coming to call on me?"

There was something brittle and deceptive in her voice, Matt thought. The ring of pretense.

Or did the wine make him imagine that?

He decided she was telling the truth. Fochet hadn't gotten around to talking with her as yet. Undoubtedly it had slipped his mind. Many other things did.

For a moment Matt was intensely angry at his teacher. Then he realized he was being childish. He knew Fochet's erratic ways. The Onion needed a reminder, that was all.

Well, he'd get one. He definitely would. Dolly had to be persuaded to forget marriage—and *without* mistakenly concluding that he didn't want the child. Only Fochet had the wisdom and experience to make that delicate distinction apparent to her. And if he didn't do it, Dolly might go to one of those women who—

"God!" The very thought brought a shudder of horror.

"What did you say, Matt?"

"Nothing, nothing."

"Well, I asked you whether Fochet was supposed to be calling on me."

"Yes," he said abruptly. "Yes, he was."

"Why?"

He didn't dare reveal that. Trapped, he blurted, "He didn't say. Maybe he's planning another party."

"My, you sound positively grumpy all at once!" She squeezed his hand against her side as they stood in the darkness beside the wall. He knew she didn't believe his explanation. What was he going to say?

Something spared him the need to say anything. He jerked his hand away.

"Matthew Kent, what's wrong with you?"

Quickly he shushed her.

"But it's bloody rude of you to—"

He pointed down the dark street to explain the sudden diversion of his attention. She shook her head.

"I honestly don't understand what you're so worked up about—"

"*Sssh!*" He pressed his mouth against her ear. "Can't you see? There's someone standing across from our gate. In the little alcove beside the fountain. You wait here."

He turned and started walking diagonally across the street toward the spot where he'd spied the pale blur of a face. He was halfway to the alcove—close enough to hear the old fountain trickling—when a figure burst from its deeper darkness. Matt had an impression of a long-skirted overcoat and a floppy hat—curious clothing for a summer night, unless the watcher wanted to disguise his appearance.

The man went racing up the street with one hand clapped to the crown of his hat. "Here, hold on!" Matt shouted. Before the echo died, he broke into a run that would have enabled him to overtake the watcher easily, except that his foot suddenly slipped in the street's drainage channel. He cursed as he sprawled on hands and knees.

He struggled up just as Dolly reached him, the cartoon still flapping in her hand.

"Are you all right, Matt?"

"Fine," he snapped.

"What on earth was that man doing?"

"I think it's pretty plain he was watching the house."

"Our house? For what reason?"

Everything else was forgotten, even their differences, as he answered, "I can't guess the exact one. But I don't think anyone would be interested in the place because Madame Rochambeau lives there. Or because we do, for that matter." With an ominous feeling, he added, "I suspect they're watching it because Strelnik lives there."

He was sober all at once. So was she. They both slept badly.

Chapter VIII

The Callers

i

Another week passed. Summer air lay over the city, breathless and sultry. *Le Figaro* printed reports of damage done by violent thunderstorms along the shores of the North Sea. But no storms rolled down to relieve the late June humidity that oppressed Paris.

Fochet's atelier was an inferno by day and not much better by night. Matt didn't care. The Matamoras canvas was emerging slowly, and he worked on it for as long as eighteen hours at a stretch. During the night he set up half a dozen lamps to approximate daylight, and only concerned himself with details that weren't critical. He worked stripped to the waist with rags tied around his wrists and forehead to catch the perspiration.

When he wasn't working, he slept. One time he arrived back at Madame Rochambeau's at three in the morning and found Dolly asleep in the good chair, her shift plastered to her breasts by the dampness. After a glance at the unfinished portrait, he carried her to bed and stretched out beside her. Tense with the excitement of his work, he couldn't doze off. He rose again at five and started back to the studio, feeling refreshed even though he hadn't slept. The work itself was a tonic.

Twice more he thought he noticed suspicious men loitering in the Rue Saint-Vincent. Twice he approached them with the purpose of asking questions, and both times they hurried away. On Tuesday in the final week of the month he discovered Madame Rochambeau was also aware of the watchers.

He hadn't been home the previous night. He'd worked straight through, completing the hands and clothing of the trio of Confederate captains. The blockade runners formed one grouping in the background of the painting. Along about eleven in the morning, he finished and headed back to the flat for a nap.

He saw no one unusual in the street. As he closed the door in the hall, he heard Madame Rochambeau's voice grating in the corridor outside the rented apartments.

"—sincerely regret to say it, Madame Strelnik"—the landlady didn't sound all that regretful, he thought as he sauntered across the garden, yawning—"but on three separate occasions in the past four days, I have gone outside and seen men one could only describe as layabouts. All of them have been observing these premises. Why, they've been posted across the street like sentries, bold as brass!"

Inside the Strelniks' rooms, Anton cried fretfully. Poor Leah, pale and perspiring, stood in the doorway. She looked miserable, completely at a loss for words. She'd lost weight since Sime had left. Her haggard appearance grew more pronounced every day.

The landlady didn't let up. "Really, Madame Strelnik, I can only conclude that such unsavory persons are hanging around because of your husband's presence. Or should I say his absence? Where is he, pray tell?"

With a desperate glance at Matt, Leah murmured, "I don't know."

"I regret to say I find that difficult to believe."

"But it's true," Matt put in. "Sime talked to me before he left, and he said he was telling no one where he was going."

Madame Rochambeau fixed him with a dour stare. "Did he also tell you the reason for his absence, Mr. Kent, or its probable duration?"

Again Leah cast a pleading look at the young American. He needed no prompting to protect Strelnik with a lie. "No, neither one, I'm afraid."

After a deep inhalation that produced an imposing lift of her bosom, the landlady declared, "Well, my attitude has always been one of live and let live." Matt could have disputed that. "I don't doubt Mr. Strelnik has been forced to go into hiding to avoid inquiries from the Hôtel de Ville. I imagine the authorities want to question him because of his political views and his association with that anarchist crowd."

Matt wanted to tell her the watchers were probably in the employ of Premier Bismarck's government, not the French, but for Leah's sake he again decided to keep quiet.

"In any case, there's a dead fish around here, and it stinks worse by the hour. Well, all right—a stink is unpleasant but harmless. However, if this household becomes involved with the authorities as a result of your husband's dubious activities, Madame Strelnik, I shall instantly ask you to find other lodgings."

She turned and sailed past Matt with a last glance that said he too was included in the warning.

Madame Rochambeau's massive shadow diminished on the floor of the hall. Matt hurried over and clasped Leah's hands in both of his. She rested her forehead against his forearm, close to tears. "Where is he, Matt? *Where is he?*"

"I wish I knew. But he said he'd be in touch when it was safe." He tried to reassure her. "I'm sure he will."

She raised her head, her dark eyes fearful. "I've seen those ruffians who frightened Madame Rochambeau. She's right. They're practically camping in the street at all hours of the day and night. Who are they? What could they want?"

Your husband.

"I honestly don't know, Leah." Far off, summer thunder boomed and reverberated. "Let's not try to find out, either."

ii

He slept for two hours, splashed tepid water on his face, ate a stale croissant, donned a fresh shirt and stood for five minutes examining the unfinished portrait on the easel.

It was too stiff, too formal and lifeless. Even though the Matamoras project was currently occupying all his time, he didn't want to abandon Dolly's portrait permanently though he knew he might have to. He understood the problems, but no solutions came to mind.

Outside, he searched the street but this afternoon saw none of those whom Madame Rochambeau characterized as layabouts. He started for the studio, making an unpleasant face over the motionless, stale-smelling air.

Abruptly he reversed his direction. He'd been working damn hard and he felt like a drink. Several, in fact.

After a brisk walk that left his shirt sodden, he reached the Café Guerbois. He entered and stopped short. Minus his cravat, jacket, gloves and Malacca stick, Edouard Manet was seated opposite Paul Cézanne, who looked particularly antagonistic.

Manet had a platter of assorted cheeses in front of him. The cheeses smelled rank in the heat. The painter didn't seem to mind. He was fastidiously slicing slivers and popping them into his mouth. After each cut he carefully wiped the knife.

Paul shot a hostile glance at Matt, then exclaimed to Manet, "All of you are idiots! The *only* cause to which an artist owes allegiance is the cause of his own life and career. As for everything else, it's so much smoke! You won't find me dying for someone's holy cause. Politicians only create causes so they can savor the thrill of sending other poor assholes off to die for them." Again he looked at Matt in an almost threatening way. "You think I'm right, don't you?"

Paul was being watched by several gaping gentlemen, all fully and respectably dressed despite the heat. Bankers, perhaps. Importers. Brokers of insurance—the sort who had begun to invade the quarter for lunch. Matt ignored them and walked to the table where the other two were seated.

"That's a pretty florid way to put it, Paul. But yes, I do. My older brother's starting a labor newspaper in America. I hate to calculate the grief he'll suffer for the sake of ideas that are probably very noble but absolutely unworkable."

"Old Courbet's going to get himself arrested because of such ideas!" Paul cried. The mention of the famous painter turned heads again. "He's a goddamn idiot to run around proclaiming he's a socialist."

Manet tucked another tiny wedge of cheese into his cheek, dabbed his mustache with a napkin, and only then nodded.

"I agree that he goes to excess. Still, one can't remain entirely neutral. I haven't kept silent on what I consider the repressions of the Imperial government. If it came to a test of loyalties, I know where mine would lie."

"With the Emperor?"

"With the tricolor."

"*Merde,* you'll be a lonely martyr. There's nobody else in our crowd who'd go to war for France."

"You're wrong, Paul. I think Renoir would. Degas. Perhaps Bazille—"

"Well, they'll never put me on the conscription rolls. I'll go into hiding before they can find me."

Manet looked disapproving. He glanced at Matt for support.

"Surely you don't agree with him now, do you, Matt? You fought for a cause in which you believed."

"I was an idiot, just like several million other people." He held up his hand. "My loyalty is right here." He wiggled his fingers. "To what I can put on a canvas. The rest is rhetorical hogwash. Or smoke, as Paul calls it."

Manet sighed and shook his head. "You and your brother must have some lively debates."

Matt shrugged. "I haven't seen him in years."

His flippancy hid a quite unexpected and painful sense of homesickness. He laughed at the feeling silently, and in that way deadened it.

"By the way," he said, "where's Lisa?"

Something unpleasant flickered across Manet's eyes. "In the back." There was a faint undertone suggesting Matt would be wise not to disturb her.

He ignored the warning and walked toward the kitchen; he was thirsty, and he'd never known a bad mood to prevent Lisa from working. He started speaking before he even reached the door.

"Lisa, my love, how about a pitcher of wine for an old and favored—*my God.*"

She was in profile, bent over a tub of water in which she was washing plates and goblets. On her right cheek, held in place by a strip of linen wound around her chin and the top of her head, was a bloody bandage.

For a moment he could think of nothing but the image she presented to his eye. The weary line of her rounded shoulders was reversed and repeated by the line of her breast sagging within a none too clean blouse. Wash water glistened on her red knuckles and forearms. Her hair was so disarrayed, she seemed to be peering at him through strands of a curtain.

There was an air of exhaustion about her, but something more, too. A sadness in her eyes that spoke of her advancing age, and her awareness of it. Of her death and her realization that when it came to her, she would probably still be what she was now—a tavern trull.

He was ashamed of the way he looked at her as a subject instead of a person who'd been hurt. Yet the image still had a powerful impact. His spine was still prickling as he said, "What happened to you?"

"Oh—" A shrug. She dried her hands on her filthy apron. Her smile was wan. "Last evening I was a little too choosy. I refused a gentleman's invitation to go to bed. He demonstrated his displeasure with a sword he pulled out of his cane."

"God," Matt said again. "Who was the son of a bitch?"

He forgot all about the artistic considerations of the meeting when she answered with a sigh, "Your friend Lepp."

iii

Matt put his arms around her. "You mean he did come back after all? Oh, Lisa, I'm sorry."

Her spirits much improved all at once, she snuggled against him, laughed deep in her throat.

"Listen! I guess a little scar is worth it if I get a squeeze like this." Her hand slid below his belt. "Tell me, Virginia. How much of you feels sorry for me? And just what are you willing to do to express that sympathy?"

He disengaged, his cheeks red. She laughed again. He

sat down on an empty wine keg used for a stool. "Where did it happen? Back here?"

"Oh, no. Right out in front. The sword slid out of the cane quick as you please and nicked me just as fast."

"And no one tried to stop him?"

"Don't look so stupefied, my dear boy. A waitress isn't important. She's handy for a laugh and a feel, but she isn't really a person. You understand? Our patrons hesitate to get involved on behalf of a nobody." Her callousness had a false, forced quality, but he said nothing. "Besides, none of my good friends was here. Not Paul. Not you—"

"If I'd been here, I'd have made him goddamn sorry," Matt declared, with only a trace of posturing. He meant what he said. She laughed.

"Here, I thought you avoided crusades and causes!"

"Causes are one thing, friends another."

"I wish you had been here, then. The surgeon who stitched and dressed this"—she touched her cheek—"he said I'll be marked for life. Still, I was lying a minute ago. The wounds to my pride were the worst ones. I got the first wound when nobody tried to stop him, and the second when he strolled out, snickering as if he'd just played a great prank." Her voice began to quaver. "I'd like to make him pay for what he did, the preening whoreson!"

Matt was startled by the sudden change. The coarse but pleasant face grew harsh, the eyes cold, the voice steadily louder. "I'd like to see him dead! Or castrated! No, both! In reverse order!"

iv

Upset by the account of Lepp's cruelty, and in no mood to listen to Manet and Paul debate, he stayed at the Guerbois for only one drink. Then he headed back toward the studio.

As he climbed the butte, a light rain began. He turned and gazed over his shoulder at a rampart of black storm cloud in the west. Relief from the heat might be on the way.

At the entrance of the studio building, he encountered

Fochet coming down the stairs. He decided to say something about the older man's promise to talk with Dolly.

"Hallo, Kent!" Fochet crowded next to him in the tiny
vestibule. He blew the scent of onions into Matt's face and
tried to open an umbrella. The vestibule wasn't wide
enough. Two umbrella ribs touched the wall and bent. It
didn't make much difference since the umbrella had half a
dozen big holes in it.

Outside, the street shone with a greasy look as the light
rain continued. Matt dodged back to avoid having an eye
put out by the end of a rib. Fochet squeezed by. "I'm on
my way to interview that new model I met at the Brasserie
of the Martyrs. If I can just remember the damn address
she gave me!" Fochet's interviews usually consisted of an
all-night visit in the model's bed.

As the teacher left the vestibule, Matt called, "You
promised to speak to Dolly. Did you forget?"

Fochet skidded to a stop just outside. "Now I ask you—
would I forget something so important?" There was annoyance as well as immense scorn in the question, to which
Matt silently answered, *Yes indeed.* By then Fochet was
gone.

Matt didn't chase after him. He thought the reminder
would do the trick.

Upstairs, he worked an hour, completing the detail of
the card-laden table at which the Confederate captains
were playing poker. Tomorrow, when he had daylight, he'd
finish the dancer. She was merely sketched in, a sinuous
figure outlined by thin black brushstrokes.

After cleaning up and carefully closing the case containing the large, clear bottles which held his dry pigments,
he locked the studio and walked back to the Rue Saint-
Vincent, arriving a good half hour before Dolly was due
home. Or so he guessed. It was hard to be sure of the light
on such a day.

The drizzle had stopped. The black clouds had dissipated.
But the sky above Montmartre still had a rainy look, and
the air was hot and saturated with dampness. He noticed
an expensive phaeton standing a short distance beyond the
gate to Madame Rochambeau's but thought nothing of it
because the vehicle was so obviously expensive and the
driver well dressed. It was definitely not the sort of rig that

would be used by one of the layabouts, as the landlady
called them. There were none visible on the street today.

He paused and leaned against the wall, his mind drifting
back to Lisa. He wished he could think of some way to
help her gain revenge without inviting further reprisals. He
couldn't. Lepp no doubt enjoyed diplomatic immunity.
Even reporting the original attack to the police would almost certainly be a waste of time.

An old woman carrying two fragrant baguettes went by,
frowning in disapproval at the young man lounging in the
street with a faraway look in his eyes. Matt never noticed.
His thoughts had turned back to the vivid picture of Lisa
in the kitchen. Another abrupt, unexpected intuition prickled his spine. Somewhere in that compelling image lay the
solution to the problem of Dolly's portrait!

He was absolutely convinced of it. But how, specifically,
would the solution work? How did the older woman relate
to the younger, and how could both be blended into one
composition? He was pondering the questions as he walked
on to the door in the wall and absently lifted the latch. He
was halfway through the opening before he jerked his head
up, realizing he'd interrupted some sort of argument or
confrontation.

"Run, Matthew!"

Leah Strelnik's cry terrified little Anton, who'd been
clinging to her skirt. The boy wailed. On Matt's left, a
burly, bearded fellow in a tight striped shirt jumped forward. The man could only be described with Madame Rochambeau's word: layabout.

He grabbed at the little boy, who darted out of the way
and wailed louder than ever. From behind the thick trunk
of the old plane tree came a voice all too familiar. "Leave
the little wretch alone, Josef. People are used to hearing
brats cry in a residential neighborhood."

All of that happened in a matter of seconds. Matt stood
stunned, beginning to grasp more of the details of the
scene. With them came a consuming sense of physical
danger—the kind of gut-hollowing reaction he hadn't experienced since the war and had hoped in 1865 that he'd
never experience again.

He remembered it now. He *felt* it now, exactly as he had
on nights when McGill's gray painted ship had run into

Wilmington past the rosy glares of Union cannon and the blue showers of Union star shells and the white geysers erupting as the projectiles struck near the hull.

He started to back into the street so he could summon help. A voice on his right barked in accented French, "Don't, Herr Kent."

Matt saw who it was. The gnomelike fellow who'd been copying down train schedules at the Gare du Nord. Instead of a pad and pencil, this time he held a nickeled revolver. It looked gigantic in his tiny hand.

Leah bent to comfort her crying child. Matt hesitated in the doorway. The little man, who wore a derby, shook his head.

"You will stay. Colonel Lepp insists."

The Prussian walked out from behind the tree which had concealed him. His monocle reflected the hazy white sky. He was hatless and elegantly attired in a pearl-gray suit with matching cravat and spats. In his right hand, whirled around and around by supple motion of his wrist, a cane blurred in a circle.

Lepp smiled without humor. "Indeed I do. *Close the door, if you please!*"

The gnome gestured with the revolver. Matt obeyed.

CHAPTER IX

COLONEL LEPP INSISTS

i

ANOTHER LIGHT RAIN SHOWER began suddenly, pattering on the flower beds and the limp leaves of the plane tree. With the slow grace of a cat stalking some smaller creature, Lepp strolled toward Matt. It was eerie to watch the Prussian avoid muddy places without so much as a downward glance.

The gnome and the layabout exchanged smirks of anticipation. Abruptly, Matt wondered about Madame Rochambeau. He glanced toward the door to her quarters. Lepp noticed, stopped and responded with a languid smile, "The landlady? Out on some errand, evidently. If she returns, she'll cause no trouble." He began to slowly unscrew the handle of the cane.

When he had separated the sections, he had a long, needlelike sword in his right hand. He whipped it in an arc in front of Matt's nose. The younger man jumped backward, landing in a bed of poppies. One heel crushed several of them. Lepp laughed and lowered the sword till it was parallel with the seam of his trousers.

"Be so kind as to tell me the whereabouts of your young woman," Lepp said. For the first time in his life, Matt wished he owned a watch. *What time was it?*

His lack of response irritated the officer. Lepp flicked the sword up and rested it against the point of Matt's chin. "Answer me! Where is the young lady?"

"Working." He jerked away from the sharp point. "She won't be home for at least an hour."

He saw Leah react to the lie. But the others were facing him and missed her look of surprise.

The rain fell harder. Clouds darkened the garden. He hoped his face didn't reveal his panic. How soon would Dolly be coming up the street and through the gate? A bad shock could have a damaging effect on a woman carrying a child, couldn't it? Even cause her to lose the baby?

"An hour, eh?" Rain streaked Lepp's monocle. He tossed the empty barrel end of his cane to the layabout, then removed the monocle and slipped it into his breast pocket. "Well, then, we can get on with our business. And let me say this, my young friend—"

The point of the sword darted out again, pricked a bright drop of blood from the back of Matt's left hand before he could move. Again he stepped away. The blood kept oozing as Lepp murmured, "Anyone who wastes our time—who delays and inconveniences us—shall suffer for it."

White-faced, Leah hugged Anton closer to her skirt. The tip of Lepp's tongue moved along his lower lip as he glanced at the thread of blood running down to Matt's fingers.

"You, for example, Herr Kent. You are a painter, are you not? Come, don't look so astonished. You're always with that crowd at the Guerbois. But I know a good deal more about you than that. I know where you study, when you generally come and go around here—yes, a good deal. Let me ask a question." The bright, merry eyes fixed on his. "Could you paint with both hands permanently injured?"

Somehow he found the nerve to say, "You'd enjoy using that sword on me, wouldn't you? Just the way you used it on Lisa."

"Don't mention that unwashed slut! She got what her arrogance earned for her."

"Her arrogance, or just her refusal to lift her skirt for a Pruss—?"

"For God's sake don't bait him!" Leah cried. She was close to breaking. He could hear raw fright in her voice as she leaned against the trunk of the plane tree and begged him, "Let's find out what they want and perhaps they'll leave us alone."

She turned tearful eyes to the poised Prussian; he was idly swinging the sword again. "If you're looking for my husband, he isn't here."

Lepp smiled another of those dazzling smiles. "Yes, madame, we're aware of that. We removed your husband from the place in which his Red comrades had hidden him. We have him right now."

By the end of the sentence, Leah Strelnik's mouth hung open. Her eyes had an hysterical glaze. She made peculiar choked sounds. Lepp was immensely amused.

"In case you don't believe me, Madame Strelnik—"

"I don't either," Matt interrupted. "If you abducted Sime, why didn't his friends report it to us?"

Lepp shrugged. "They've all gone into hiding, too, I suppose. Terrified. Three of them got badly shot up when we took him. Be assured, we do have Herr Strelnik." He snapped his fingers. "Show them, Josef."

From a back pocket, the blue-chinned layabout produced a wad of checked cloth. He shook it out, held it aloft on his index finger and then started to spin it. Matt recognized the shabby cap Sime Strelnik had worn at the Guerbois. Now, however, there was a huge blackish stain on the cap's crown.

Leah Strelnik stared at the dried blood and jammed the edge of her right hand between her teeth and bit down.

ii

Lepp sighed. "Really, madame, these exhibitions are dreadfully tedious. They waste so much time. I insist you get control of yourself. If you'll just give us what we came for, we'll be pleased to leave you alone. We want the correspondence from your husband's brother, Yuri Strelnik, documenting certain confidential political initiatives undertaken by my government."

The Spanish candidacy? They really were concerned that its announcement would create difficulties with the French, then. And the fact that Lepp was conducting a search for the documents meant he was indeed attached to the diplomatic mission, or at least acting as its unofficial agent.

Almost at once, Leah Strelnik began shaking her head. Lepp ignored her. "Naturally your husband claims he has no such documentation. We know he's lying."

"He isn't," Matt said. "But he was afraid you might assume he had letters or papers like the ones you described."

For the first time, Lepp grew nervous. "Did he also describe the information contained in those documents?"

"No, of course not. He didn't have them! He went into hiding because he knew you wouldn't believe that."

The Prussian relaxed. Lifted one shoulder in a broad shrug. "We might expect to hear such lies on your friend's behalf. Well, we shall take you at your word—temporarily." He ran the ball of his thumb along the sword, a slow, almost sensual motion. His eyes strayed briefly to Matt's waist, then back to his face. "When we are suspicious of someone's veracity, however, we have certain highly refined techniques for confirming or denying that suspicion." He turned slightly. "Ah, but perhaps those are best saved for your husband, Madame Strelnik."

Lepp glared, his eyes bright as gas flames. The pale young woman couldn't bear to meet his gaze. She leaned heavily against the plane tree, staring down at her little boy's head in a numb way. Again Lepp switched his tactics from quiet threat to feigned cordiality.

"Of course there'll be absolutely no need for unpleasantness if we find what we want."

Leah screamed, "It isn't here! I don't even know whether it exists!"

Disgusted, Lepp bobbed his head at his helpers. "Get on with the search!"

The blue-chinned fellow ran to Madame Rochambeau's rooms, the gnome to the door on the other side of the garden. Soon, from both areas, there came the sounds of drawers being hurled to the floor, furniture thudding over, crockery shattering. The layabout took special pains to wreck Madame Rochambeau's parlor. He pitched a valuable vase through one of the tall windows overlooking the garden, then tossed out a Madonna she kept near a small altar. The head of the statue broke off and rolled, part of its gilt-edged blue drapery chipping away. The head came to rest with the sad painted eyes turned up toward the rainy sky.

When the statue broke, so did Matt's temper. He lunged forward. Lepp pivoted, bent his right leg at the knee and extended his sword arm full length. He was incredibly fast. Matt nearly impaled himself on the point.

"Yes, do charge in heroic outrage," Lepp said. He put weight behind the sword. The point dug into Matt's shirt. The blade bent into a slight curve. "A grand gesture! And your last one."

Before the point pierced to his skin, Matt pulled away. He snarled the dirtiest epithet he knew. Lepp threw his head back and brayed. In both Madame Rochambeau's quarters and the rented rooms, the sounds of destruction continued.

"For God's sake, Lepp," Matt protested. "You don't seriously think he'd hide anything in the landlady's flat?"

Another shrug. "It's possible. These anarchists are devious."

He seethed. The banging and breaking went on. Four minutes. Five—

Lepp grew bored and began to examine his sword. Three times he swung it in a hissing arc. Matt was literally aching from tension. Facing away from the wall, he kept listening for the rattle of the door latch. If Dolly arrived, he'd only have a second to shout. He had to warn her to stay outside. God knew what these bloody-minded bastards would do before they left.

The layabout, Josef, returned first. He shook his head in a glum way. Then the gnome emerged from the door on the south side of the garden.

"Well?"

"Nothing interesting, Colonel." The gnome folded and pocketed a clasp knife. The tiny eyes flicked to Matt. "Well, nothing except a very nice half-finished portrait. Painted by the young gentleman, I suppose. I fear it'll never be finished now." He giggled as he retrieved the revolver from the side pocket of his coat.

Lepp's ruddy cheeks took on even more color. He executed a crisp right face so that he was again turned toward Leah Strelnik. She had her son in her arms and was practically jamming his head down on her shoulder so he wouldn't cry out. The Prussian transferred the sword to his left hand and kept it pointing in Matt's direction, ready to fend off any sudden rush as he said, "Madame, I insist you answer my question now. *Where is the material from Yuri Strelnik in Berlin?*"

"Insist all you want. I don't have it!" Leah cried. Tears began to streak her cheeks. "There's nothing like that in this house. *Nothing!*"

The Prussian took two long strides to the tree. "I won't tolerate any more lies, you Red whore." He slapped her face so hard, the contact sounded like a pistol shot. But it was Anton, not she, who screamed in fright.

Matt knew he should stand still, but he couldn't. There was no telling what Lepp would order next. A beating? Torture? He started for Leah's side, only to have the gnome cock the revolver.

"I'll shoot you if you take another step, Herr Kent."

Matt halted in midstride. A jaw muscle writhed on the left side of his face. The gnome giggled again.

It felt as if a rope had been wound around his forehead and was being steadily tightened. The feeling of frustrated rage grew and grew. Lepp took a moment to draw out a silk kerchief and dab raindrops from his forehead. Doing that enabled him to get control of himself before he spoke again.

"An impasse has been reached, it seems. Perhaps we need to try a different tack with you, Madame Strelnik. Give you time to reconsider your rash and foolish answers to my questions."

"I don't need to reconsider anything. I've told you the tru—"

"*Be silent and let me finish!* We shall permit you to ponder your ill-advised behavior for the next forty-eight hours. At the end of that time, another of my associates—someone you have never seen before—will call on you to receive the documents. If you fail to surrender them, your husband will be killed."

"My God, why can't you understand? I don't have any documents to give you!"

Now Lepp hammered at her, quietly but without pity.

"Then get them. I know they're somewhere in Paris despite your husband's denials."

"He's telling the truth! *I'm telling the truth!*"

"Nonsense," Lepp whispered.

Leah closed her eyes. While Anton fretted and clutched at her neck, she sank to the ground at the base of the plane tree. She cried in silence.

Lepp retrieved the barrel of the cane from the spot where the layabout had dropped it. He rammed the sword back into the sheath and screwed down the hilt.

"Of one more thing I should particularly warn you, madame. Do not report this visit anytime during the next forty-eight hours." He swished the cane at the plaster head of the Madonna. "Do not report it to the police in this arrondissement. To the Sûreté detectives—to anyone in authority! We shall know if you do. And we shall take immediate, appropriate action."

He extended the cane and used the ferrule to pluck the bloodied cap from the layabout's back pocket. Deftly, he spun the cap through the air. It landed on the hem of Leah's skirt.

Her eyes flew open. She stared at the cap as if it were contaminated. Wide-eyed, little Anton studied the cap too. A radiant smile spread over his face. "Papa's. Papa's!"

"Clever child." Lepp tucked his cane under his arm. "Let us hope he'll have more than a cap to remind him of his father as he grows up. It's entirely up to you, madame."

He barked something in his own language and marched toward the door in the wall. The layabout and the gnome fell in step behind him, almost like trained soldiers. Relief flooded over Matt then. Once the three left the house, he and Leah would have time to think. He kept his eyes on the men, relaxing just a little for the first time in twenty minutes. The men blocked his view of the latch as it moved.

Too late, he realized what had made the clicking sound. The gnome whipped the nickeled revolver toward the door opening inward.

She came into the garden in a rush, her arms laden with packages. Matt's reactions were slow. Before he could make a sound, the gnome jumped sideways, out from behind Lepp. The maneuver gave the gnome a clear target. The revolver leveled, pointing to the center of Dolly's forehead.

CHAPTER X

SHADOW OF DEATH

i

DOLLY STARED AT the gun in disbelief. One of the packages slipped from her hand. The string broke, the paper fell away, and two thick pink chops landed in the dirt of a flower bed.

Matt watched the gnome's finger drain of color as the little man applied pressure on the trigger. He knew Dolly was going to be shot and killed, and the fear he felt was as consuming and profound as his fear had been when he'd thought the Gulf of Mexico was going to pull him to his death.

He started to hurl himself toward her, to get in front of her if he could. His body felt lethargic, his movements impossibly slow. It was as if time itself had been suspended in the garden, the natural laws of the world repealed. When the gnome's mouth opened, a sadistic little grin revealing the gold crowns on his teeth, it seemed to take an hour for the smile to form.

The gnome's finger whitened. One after another, the parcels kept spilling from Dolly's arms.

And he couldn't move fast enough!

But somehow Lepp did, jabbing his cane into the gnome's shoulder. The revolver exploded. The illusion of suspended time shattered. Dolly fell sideways. Matt yelled her name and rushed to catch her.

He bumped Lepp, who shoved him away. Dolly crumpled to the ground. He was certain she was shot, and he knew what an incredible fool he'd been to try to deny how he felt about her.

Lepp seemed momentarily nonplussed by the sight of the fallen girl. Then rage wrenched his face. He shoved the gnome through the open doorway into the street, cursing him for shooting unnecessarily.

The layabout didn't need to be ordered to leave. As the gnome scuttled away in the direction of the phaeton, the blue-chinned man shoved between two elderly women who appeared outside the door. They'd heard the shot. They weren't the only ones. Across the way, shutters banged open. Voices cried questions. Lepp grasped the doorframe, spun and said, "Nothing is changed. Forty-eight hours. He's dead if you say anything."

Then he bolted, savagely kicking one of the women out of the way.

Matt dropped to his knees next to Dolly. She was breathing in a loud, uneven way. Directly above the door, a large pock in the wall showed where the deflected bullet had lodged.

He'd been wrong. She hadn't been hit. But the emotion generated by those moments of utter terror wouldn't leave him. Painters frequently symbolized death as a winged angel. The shadow of that wing had fallen over him for the second time in his life, and also for the second time, the effect was profound.

He slipped his hands under Dolly's neck and shoulder. Her eyes were still half closed. She began to breathe noisily through her mouth. He barely heard the clatter of the escaping phaeton, or the cries of neighbors trying to stop it, or Leah Strelnik's sudden renewed sobbing. As he knelt in the rainy garden, nothing mattered but Dolly. Not the Matamoras painting. Not even Strelnik himself.

"I love you, Dolly" was all he could say. "My God, I never knew how much."

He lifted her head against his shoulder, bending his back as he did so, protecting her from the rain. "We'll get married. We'll give the child a name, I promise."

Her eyes came fully open. For a moment she looked puzzled, as if her mind couldn't hold all that had happened so quickly. Slowly, though, her expression changed, grew more alert. There was an almost ecstatic glow on her face when she reached up with her left hand. Her caress told him she understood what he was repeating with such fervency.

"I love you. I couldn't bear to lose you. We'll get married as soon as you want."

He said it without the slightest reservation.

ii

The next hour and a half were chaos.

More and more residents of the neighborhood arrived at the street door. At first they merely asked what had happened. Matt replied with polite evasions, which were unsatisfactory. The neighbors had heard a gun discharged! The questions grew angry. He heard a mention of gendarmes. Finally he slammed the door in the faces of the people shouting and shaking their fists at him.

During the next few minutes he told Dolly what Lepp had said before she arrived. He put Anton into her care and helped Leah to bed in her ransacked flat. He gave her several swallows of brandy to make her sleep. He also gave her a rash promise that he'd make sure Strelnik came back to her safe and whole.

By then someone else was knocking at the street door—someone with the authority to insist upon being admitted. A gendarme from the local precinct. Matt hustled Dolly out of sight and let him in.

Matt argued heatedly with the young policeman, who wanted to question all the residents of the household. That wasn't necessary, Matt insisted. It was a trivial matter. Yes, there'd been some struggling, a lot of things thrown, even a gun discharged. Still, the cause was merely a quarrel with his girlfriend. Matt said he'd discovered she had a new lover. The gendarme could understand how that enraged a fellow, couldn't he?

Being French, he could. He perched on a bench near the plane tree, prepared a little statement on several small sheets of paper, and Matt signed it. The statement contained the name and address of an entirely fictitious rival lover which Matt had thought up to add authenticity. To verify Matt's story, the lover would be questioned, the policeman promised. Matt hoped the search for the fictitious lover would last at least forty-eight hours.

The policeman left. Ten minutes later Madame Rochambeau arrived, in an overwrought state. Several neighbors had seen her coming up the Rue Saint-Vincent and generously informed her that all sorts of disgraceful violence had taken place during her absence.

When the landlady saw the destruction, she went into a purple-cheeked screaming fit. Even her tiniest facial moles seemed to throb with fury. After she'd bellowed and stormed up and down for several minutes, Matt managed to make her listen to him, and she began to calm down a little.

The calm was temporary. The moment she heard him say the vandals had come in search of some papers they thought Strelnik possessed, she headed for the south side of the garden, bellowing that she didn't care whether Satan himself had kidnapped her tenant, the family had to move out at once—*and* pay for all the damage!

Matt held Madame Rochambeau back physically until she no longer insisted on rushing in and waking Leah. He pleaded, wheedled and finally convinced her Strelnik's wife was in no condition to go anywhere, and that to force her would be un-Christian.

The appeal to the landlady's Catholicism worked. Without going into detail, Matt was then able to communicate a little of the urgency of the situation. He also promised to pay for every bit of damage out of the allowance he received from his father. Why, he'd even add twenty or thirty francs for emotional suffering on Madame Rochambeau's part.

Mollified, she said Madame Strelnik would still have to leave—but not immediately. The landlady picked up the head of the Madonna and flounced into her quarters, where the sound of a broom and little exclamations of dismay were soon heard.

In the disorder of their sitting room, Matt finally managed to get a moment alone with Dolly. He didn't care for the responsibility that was weighing on him.

"I guess I'm the one who must try to find Sime."

Dolly's momentary silence was agreement. Then she frowned.

"Suppose Lepp was bluffing, Matt. Suppose they don't really have him."

He thought about it. They might have gotten hold of Strelnik's cap but not the man himself. In a fight, for example—a fight from which Strelnik had ultimately escaped. There was no guarantee the Prussian was holding anything except that cap, which could easily have been stained with animal blood.

"You could be right," he said with a nod. "But can I take the chance and do nothing? I don't think so. They *may* have him, and he may have only forty-eight hours to live."

"What are you going to do, then? You can't go to the police."

He shook his head. "I wouldn't want to take a chance. Lepp probably has informers inside."

But that wasn't the extent of his dilemma. He couldn't call on any of Strelnik's radical friends, either, for the simple reason that he didn't know who they were or where to find them. Strelnik had never brought a one of them to the Rue Saint-Vincent. Had never even mentioned their names or revealed where he met them in Belleville. Because Strelnik's politics were dangerous—and his associates were presumably scattered after the kidnapping—Matt was alone.

It made him angry. A bit of the anger was even directed at his friend who was in danger, until he realized how shameful that was.

He didn't know where he'd begin his search. Dolly understood that problem as well. "They could have hidden him anywhere in Paris, couldn't they?"

"Anywhere." It had a gloomy sound. A moment later, he enunciated the one idea that had been flitting at the back of his mind. "There's just an outside chance Herr Lepp used someplace which he already had available."

"Is there such a place?"

"I've heard there may be." He sounded distinctly reluctant as he added, "I'm going out for a while."

"Where?"

"To see Lisa at the Guerbois."

He kissed Dolly in front of the unfinished portrait. The gnome had ruined it. Slashed it to tatters.

"But don't be jealous, Doll. It's you I'm going to marry."

For just a moment, while their lips touched, he had an uneasy feeling that by making his promise to her, he'd consigned himself to failure as an artist.

The unfounded pessimism quickly passed. He loved her, and he would marry her if he came out of his imbroglio alive. How Paul Cézanne would snort if he knew Matt had gotten mixed up in politics.

No, that's not really it, he thought as he patted Dolly's arm, glanced at Anton, who'd fallen asleep in a chair, and left the flat. *It isn't really politics I'm embroiled with—it's people.* One of those could be ignored without the slightest twinge of conscience. One, but not the other.

iii

He spoke with Lisa in the alley behind the café. "Do you want to settle with the Prussian?"

She replied with an obscene word. "Do you even need to ask?"

"All right. I need the help of every one of those friends of yours. The ones you call working girls."

"Tomorrow?"

"Tonight."

"Impossible, Matthew. They'll lose business."

"Are they friends or aren't they? Do you want Lepp or don't you?"

Heat lightning flickered in the sky in the direction of the Bois de Boulogne. A bad storm was on the way. Her voice grew harsh.

"All right, go on. What are the girls to do?"

"Help me find that private place you mentioned once—the place where Lepp sheds his public face and amuses himself."

"My God, you're asking to have the whole left bank searched. I don't know that many whores!"

"Ask the ones you know to recruit as many others as they can. The whole left bank needn't be scoured. You said you'd heard that Lepp buys the favors of students."

"That's true. What of it?"

"Have the girls work the Latin Quarter first. The places near the Sorbonne where idlers congregate—the Maube, the Boul' Mich. I know it's a slim chance. But there's no other starting point. If anyone finds Lepp's hideaway by this time tomorrow—this time but no later—I'll pay a hundred francs to the girl and another hundred francs to any informant she uses."

Lisa whistled. "Why didn't you mention those prices before? They're better than what the most popular girl gets for a whole night with some rich man at the Hotel Meurice! We won't have any trouble putting platoons of young ladies on the street. Indeed, I venture to say every slut from here to Marseilles will want to join the search." Her cynical jocularity disappeared all at once. "I shouldn't be laughing. This is urgent business, isn't it?"

"Urgent." He nodded.

"Bad, too, uh?"

"Yes, ugly."

"I thought so. I've never seen you so wrought up—except when you're discussing artistic theories with your colleagues, of course."

"The life of my friend Strelnik may depend on what your girls learn, Lisa." And if Yuri Strelnik's claim that Bismarck was maneuvering to put a Hohenzollern on the Spanish throne ever reached Louis-Napoléon's hands in documented form, the lives of hundreds of thousands of others might be affected by the diplomatic repercussions. The whole basis for Strelnik's abduction still seemed absurd to Matt. Though he found it idiotic and almost inconceivable that some men actually cared about such things as kingships and spheres of influence, his friend's danger was horrible proof that they did.

"One more thing, Lisa. Do you know a shop that sells good secondhand revolvers?"

Gravely, she nodded. "Yes, my Virginia dove. I do."

iv

Lisa's girlfriends spread out through the student section of the left bank before the night ended. By eight o'clock the following evening, one returned with what she said was a reliable address. A tenement in the Rue Cujas just a block from the Boulevard Saint-Michel and the Sorbonne.

The girl had obtained the address from a young Alsatian boy she met in a café. The boy, a philosophy student, had hired himself out to a German. The boy remembered the German well, and bitterly regretted ever agreeing to spend a night in his rooms. He was ashamed of the incident, he said, but he didn't keep quiet about it because he wanted to warn others to stay away from the man, whose name was Gruen. Even by the liberal standards of the Latin Quarter, Gruen had depraved tastes.

Matt paid the young prostitute and gave her the agreed-upon price for the informer as well. Then he set out for the left bank in a heavy rain that had started shortly after his talk with Lisa the preceding evening. The air had turned sharply colder during the day, and still the rain came down. His teeth chattered as he crossed the Seine by the Pont Neuf.

God, how he wished he weren't out on such a miserable night. And on such a dangerous errand. He remembered a letter his father had sent him shortly after he'd arrived in Paris. Jephtha had spoken of the Kents as people of conscience. Cursed if he wasn't right.

Bent against the wind, he hurried on. In one pocket of his shabby overcoat he had a scrap of paper with the tenement address jotted on it. In the other he had a .41 caliber LeFauchaux revolver, model 1861, bearing the mark and identification of the arms company's Belgian works. The revolver was fully loaded.

CHAPTER XI

THE HIDDEN ROOM

i

"NO, I HAVEN'T any tenant named Gruen. Now go away!"

Hard rain pelted the small window in the front wall of the ground-floor foyer. A calèche with its top raised against the storm and its running lamps alight went clattering down the incline of the Rue Cujas toward the Boul' Mich. The concierge, a sour little woman with a flickering candle in her hand, had obviously given Matt the answer she was paid to give.

He decided to try a bluff. He hoped his smile was suitably sleazy. "But he's expecting me. He paid me to come here."

The concierge's old eyes gleamed with rheum. She squinted at him, searching for truth or falsehood in what he'd said. Her candle provided the only illumination in the foyer. Up the stairs lay a darkness full of rustling sounds, creakings, faint cries of passion or pain. The whole four-story tenement seemed astir with unseen life.

Suddenly the concierge said, "He told me it was a young lady—and that she wouldn't arrive till midnight."

Matt kept the lewd smile in place. "Oh, he changed his mind, you see." He winked. "On both counts." With a faintly shaking hand, he slipped a few sous into hers.

"Well—all right. But if there's any difficulty, I'll say you slipped past my door without my seeing you. Do you know where it is?"

"No."

"Top floor. All the way back."

She scratched herself in a vulgar way, turned and began counting the sous as she returned to her foul-smelling room. Lightning whitened the street outside. Thunder rocked the building, loud as huge howitzers firing close by. The concierge's door slammed, blotting out the candlelight. Matt shivered; his overcoat was soaked. He reached into his pocket to grasp the revolver.

During the war he'd carried a pistol for protection in certain ports. On calm days at sea he'd practiced marksmanship off the stern and found he had a fair eye. But shooting at a bobbing barrel for sport was one thing, defending yourself quite another. Never in his life had he fired a shot in anger. He didn't know whether he could.

Reluctantly he started up the stairs in total darkness relieved intermittently by a glow of lightning through the foyer window. By the time he reached the first-floor landing, even a brilliant burst down below provided very little light.

He felt his way around the walls of the landing. He gasped when his right foot struck something soft. A pale flicker from below showed him a ghost's face, a gaping mouth wet with saliva.

His heart pounded. He stepped over the outstretched leg he'd bumped. The derelict didn't stir.

Matt could smell wine in the darkness. But he could hear no breathing. His scalp crawled. Was the man dead? He didn't linger to investigate.

On the next landing he heard a faint squeal and a ticking of claws behind one wall. He touched the walls, damp, springy with rot. The ticking continued. Rats running?

He kept climbing, sickened by the stenches of the place. Rotted meat. Slops. God knew what else. If Strelnik was being kept in another location, could he force the Prussian to tell him where? Was anyone with Lepp this moment? The questions seemed to turn his mind to soup. Sweat broke out on his forehead although the rest of his body still felt cold.

On the top floor, he crept down the hall until he'd gone as far as he could. He found Lepp's door with an outstretched hand, sidled closer, listened.

He thought he heard the Prussian laughing against a curious background noise—heavy rhythmic grunting.

He wiped his wet forehead. Drew the LaFauchaux from his coat. The thunder boomed. The tenement actually shook on its foundations.

As the reverberations died away, he knocked.

ii

The curious rhythmic sound stopped. There was a long interval of silence within the flat. On a lower floor, a woman or a child screamed. Matt rapped again, using the muzzle of the revolver this time.

He heard a whispered colloquy. Two voices, the words unintelligible. Once more he pounded the door.

Rapid footsteps approached. They sounded light, as though someone small were coming to answer. Then he heard the gnome say, "Who is it? Herr Gruen isn't expecting anyone at this hour."

He disguised his voice as best he could, lowering and roughening it. "Tell Lepp to open up. There's trouble."

"Who is that? Who's out there?"

"I said there's trouble. They know we have Strelnik. Open the damn door!"

More conversation. Matt chose an imaginary point in the darkness, approximately where he thought the gnome's head would be, and fixed his eye on that spot. It was a wise precaution. When the door jerked open suddenly, he was prepared—looking straight at the gnome's torso, and the nickeled revolver rising in front of it in the dim light.

Matt shoved the gnome against the doorjamb, pinning his gun hand between his side and the wood. If the little man fired in that position, he risked putting a bullet into his own ribs.

The gnome wriggled, stamped on Matt's foot, squealed, "Colonel, it's the American from the Rue—"

Matt jumped back suddenly. The absence of his weight

threw the gnome off balance. Matt grabbed the little man's stiff collar and dragged him outside. With his revolver he whacked the gnome's forearm twice.

He caught the nickeled gun as it dropped from slack fingers, then laid the barrel of the LeFauchaux against the gnome's temple, stunning and felling him in the hall. He felt only faint guilt over assaulting someone so small. He knew the gnome would have shot him if he'd had the chance.

He darted into the apartment, bolted the door. Then he caught his breath, unprepared for the cleanliness of the place, or the furnishings, or the play of soft multicolored light from paper-shaded lanterns.

Artifacts from China and Japan had become a craze in the West in recent years. Jim Whistler crammed some of his pictures with Oriental objects and costuming, and his fondness for good Chinese porcelain was practically a mania. Someone with similar tastes had decorated this hideaway. There were ornamental screens around the room, low lacquered tables, bamboo mats instead of carpet, and on the walls delicate brush paintings of gardens with willows and lily ponds and graceful bridges.

Matt was still recovering from his surprise when he heard a door open. The door was concealed by a screen standing in front of the wall to his left. The screen fell forward—pushed—and Lepp stared at him.

Matt's belly began to ache. He didn't see Strelnik anywhere. Lepp's bright eyes flicked past him, hunting for the gnome. Then the Prussian darted a look at Matt's revolver.

Lepp was barefoot and clad in a black kimono with two Oriental characters painted in white on the left breast. Through the open doorway Matt glimpsed a bedchamber where layers of sweet-smelling smoke moved slowly. The room's sole illumination seemed to come from a metal statue of a fat little god with a cavity in his belly. Lumps of charcoal glowed in the cavity.

On a pallet, a beefy young man with blond curls and immense forearm muscles lay belly down, his head turned toward the outer room and a drowsy, half-witted smile on his face. The charcoal that made the whole flat insufferably hot put red highlights on the young man's sweaty shoulders and biceps.

"Heaven knows how you found me, Kent," Lepp said at last. "It was rash of you to come here, you know. Rash and stupid."

He took a step toward Matt, his smile blazing suddenly. "I don't believe you'll shoot me. I don't believe you're the sort who can murder an unarmed man."

Desperately Matt scanned the room again. *Strelnik wasn't here!* He was aware of Lepp taking a second step but didn't realize how close he'd gotten until the Prussian gave a hard exclamation and jumped him.

Lepp's hands shot out. Just as he'd predicted, Matt jerked the revolver up in a protective way but didn't fire. Lepp seized the gun, tore it from Matt's hand and rammed his bare knee into Matt's groin.

iii

Lepp uttered a short, self-satisfied laugh as Matt reeled backward. The Prussian pressed his advantage. He crowded the American against the wall and drove his knee in and out again, harder this time.

Matt managed to turn aside and take the third blow on his hip. He was in hellish pain. Everything around him was tilting. The paper-shaded lanterns multiplied and transparent pastel rainbows arched between them—or was that only in his dazed head?

Lepp's kimono came undone. His naked body was hard and muscular, the body of a splendidly conditioned soldier. The beefy young man in the bedroom started asking questions in French, in a surprisingly girlish voice. Lepp didn't answer. His attention was fixed on Matt, who was swaying back and forth, barely able to stand.

Lepp still had the revolver. With a smug smile he dropped the gun on the floor behind him.

Shouts and loud pounding came from the corridor: the gnome trying to get in. Lepp ignored that, too.

With blurring eyes, Matt saw Lepp's guest creep across the doorway, bare butted and with his clothes in his hand. The young man vanished, evidently fleeing through some rear exit. Lepp stepped back. His bare instep came down on the revolver handle. Angered, he bent over and tossed the gun a yard away.

"I don't need that to deal with a foolish person like you, Herr Kent. First, however, I'll show you something."

He paced swiftly to a corner, lifted a wooden framed paper screen aside. Strelnik lay motionless on a mat. Large bruises discolored his face.

"Oh, don't worry. He's breathing," Lepp said. "We keep him pacified with a special draft concocted by a chemist we know. You came to the right place, you see." He stopped smiling. "But you shouldn't have." He still had one hand on the frame of the screen. Without warning, he threw the screen at Matt's head.

Matt tried to keep the thing from falling on him. His fist tore through the paper as he flung the screen off, unhurt.

But Lepp hadn't meant to hurt him, only distract him. The Prussian grabbed Matt's left wrist, whipped him around and hurled him against the wall with terrible force.

Matt shook his head and pushed off from the wall. The collision had started his nose bleeding. Something warm trickled over his mouth to his chin. He tried to focus his eyes as he turned back to face the Prussian.

Lepp was closer than he'd anticipated. The Prussian rammed his knee toward Matt's genitals again. Without thinking, Matt caught Lepp's leg and lifted. The Prussian was unprepared. He tumbled over, landing on his spine with an outburst of breath and skidding on a bamboo mat on which he'd fallen.

Matt staggered toward the glint of the revolver. Hardly a hair out of place yet, Lepp grinned like a white-toothed wolf and snapped over onto his belly. He grabbed Matt's leg in a vise of two hands and used his adversary's own tactics—a lift that sprawled the American on the floor.

The back of Matt's head hit the corner of one of the low tables. Behind his eyes he saw patterns of light like the shellbursts in a Whistler nocturne. He groaned, extended his right hand toward the revolver. The gun was tantalizingly close, but he couldn't quite reach it.

Lepp had regained his feet. He was breathing a trifle roughly.

"Let's see—how you—paint—with a ruined hand—"

Frantically, Matt started to draw his fingers back. Lepp's

bare heel slammed down. He missed Matt's hand by an inch. The impact made the Prussian grimace and scream, "Little *bastard!*" He leaned over, grabbed Matt's hair, banged his head on the corner of the table. Matt's left hand flopped out. Lepp laughed and stamped on it.

Matt didn't want to yell but he couldn't help it. He brought his hand toward his side just as Lepp hammered his heel down again. A miss. The Prussian grew even more enraged. He started stamping with greater force but less control. His knee rose and fell, the foot moving so fast he seemed to be doing some kind of mad dance. Matt managed to keep jerking his hand out of the way.

He shoved his right hand outward again. His fingers brushed the revolver's hatched butt plate. Lepp kept slamming his heel down, *crash* and *crash*. Concentrating on the gun for a moment, Matt didn't pull his other hand away fast enough. Lepp's heel caught him. He yelled. Then his face contorted with rage. He extended his arm until he thought it would tear from its socket. But he caught the butt of the LeFauchaux and brought the gun back across his body and fired upward once, twice, three times.

The first bullet pierced Lepp's left ribs. The second missed. The third tore into his groin. Shrieking, the Prussian was knocked backward. Blood poured over the flapping hem of the kimono. He sat down in a corner, shuddering violently. The light went out of his eyes the moment his spine settled into place.

Matt's right forearm began to shake. He grew aware of voices bellowing in the corridor. Smoke from the revolver floated past his face. For a moment longer he stared at the dead man. The anger in Matt's eyes became disbelief, then consternation.

He rolled onto his stomach and hid his head, fighting sickness. He'd never killed anyone before. And to kill a man as he had—to blow huge, grisly holes in him—God almighty, that was a vile thing, no matter what the justification.

"What's going on in there, Colonel? Who fired that shot?"

The commotion outside wrenched him back to reality. The gnome or someone else was battering at the door. The hinges looked as if they might tear loose from the wood any second.

Matt lurched to his feet. A ringing in his ears diminished. He stowed the revolver in his belt and pushed tangled hair out of his eyes. His left hand throbbed.

In a moment he was kneeling beside Strelnik. He put his ear close to the little man's mouth. He felt faint, warm breath.

"Sime, can you open your eyes? Sime, it's Matt."

He shook Strelnik's shoulders several times and got only a slight groan for his effort. All at once he was unbelievably angry. Who *was* this man who dared to make him feel responsibility he didn't want? He could have died in this room, for God's sake! As it was, the Prussian had come close to destroying his hand, then turned him into a murderer, and he wasn't out of danger yet. Far from it.

The door shivered, struck hard again from the outside. Wood was splintering around the top hinge. The concierge's shrill voice joined the others, howling questions and threats. Fear quickly diluted Matt's shameful anger.

He lifted Strelnik to his feet. Fortunately his friend didn't weigh much. He slipped an arm around Strelnik's waist, then looped Strelnik's arm over his own neck and half carried, half dragged him through Lepp's incense-laden bedroom.

He had no trouble locating the escape route the beefy young man had used. A door stood ajar—a door leading to a short hallway that in turn opened onto the landing of a rickety outside stair. The staircase was attached to the building's rear face.

The stair swayed and sagged in an alarming way as Matt stumbled downward with his burden. Rain lashed his face and made the steps slippery. Several times he almost lost his balance. When it happened on the second-floor landing, he grabbed the rail with his right hand. Rotted wood gave and broke.

He teetered on the edge, gasping, and would have plummeted into space if Strelnik's legs hadn't given out. The dead weight of the little man pulled him backward, out of danger.

Finally he reached the ground. A policeman's whistle

shrilled in the darkness. To his left, lanterns bobbed in a passageway leading back to the Rue Cujas. Strident voices called for him to halt. He yanked the revolver and fired two shots over his head. The voices went silent. The forward motion of the lamps stopped.

Strelnik's free hand plucked at Matt's overcoat. Rolling his head around and gulping air, the little man was waking.

The rain slacked off suddenly. "Come on, Sime, we can make it," Matt whispered, not fully believing it.

He sank to his ankles in mud and garbage as he helped Strelnik stagger through the darkness. All at once a grim thought occurred to him. Now that "Herr Gruen" was dead, his real identity would not remain a secret, nor would that of his killer—the gnome would see to that.

iv

In the garden on the Rue Saint-Vincent, a bedraggled and badly shaken Matthew Kent accepted a glass of wine from Dolly. Leah Strelnik hugged and kissed her bruised husband. Hovering nearby with a lamp, Madame Rochambeau demanded to know what madness was being perpetrated by those who were—forthwith—no longer tenants.

Matt looked like someone who made his living by street robbery. He ignored the landlady, finished the wine and stumbled into the hall leading to his quarters. Dolly followed.

He could barely flex the fingers of his left hand, and the entire back of it was mottled with purple and yellow patches. His spine hurt. So did his arms and his groin.

Yet none of that mattered. All that mattered was the man he'd left dead in the Rue Cujas—a member of the Prussian diplomatic mission.

He made up his mind. "Dolly, pack whatever you need for travel. We're taking the first train to the Channel."

She stopped a pace behind him, looking as if she doubted his seriousness.

"Damn it, I told you what I did to that man! The Prussians will turn this city on its head till the police give them satisfaction."

She hesitated only a moment longer. "All right, love. All right—we'll go."

He slashed the air. "In half an hour! Less, if we can."

She nodded, slipped by him and vanished down the hall. He rested against the wall and rubbed his eyes.

The Strelniks had come in and overheard. Leah said, "You're going to England?"

"Yes, and you'd be wise if you woke Anton and left with us," Matt advised.

Madame Rochambeau's lamp glowed somewhere beyond the garden door. They heard her approaching, asking her repetitious questions. Matt was astonished at Strelnik's reaction to his statement.

"You're right. We'll come."

Leah's eyes widened. "What?"

"Now, now, no objections. Remember, I could be held as an accomplice." He almost sounded pleased.

"Accomplice?" Madame Rochambeau repeated in an alarmed voice. "Who's an accomplice? Me? I insist that someone inform me about the reason for all this commotion!"

But no one did; it wasn't safe. So the landlady lurched into view and stood in the garden door, her expression rather forlorn.

Matt was surprised at Strelnik's ebullience as well as his recuperative powers. The little man looked as if he'd been dragged through the Paris sewers but said he felt remarkably good. On the frantic flight back across the Seine, he'd gasped out the story of his captivity. Part of it remained a mystery. Lepp had refused to say how the Prussians had found Strelnik's original hiding place. There were hints of an informant, but nothing specific.

Once on the Rue Cujas, Strelnik had been subjected to a long and severe beating interrupted by periods of questioning. He thought the questioning had gone on for three or four hours. Finally, when he continued to deny any knowledge of documents dealing with the Hohenzollern candidacy, Lepp had stepped in, slapped him a few times and contemptuously said Strelnik's silence didn't matter; he knew an easier nut to crack: Leah.

"My God, Matt, I thought it was a cheap bluff" was the little man's only comment on that.

After the initial abuse, he hadn't been treated too badly, though he had been forced to swallow endless doses of some narcotic, which kept him pacified. Now that all the horrors were behind him, he seemed happy as a child with candy.

He clapped his younger friend on the shoulder. "I am a man who makes quick decisions in a crisis. I feel like a dead man reprieved. And I don't care to flirt with reversion to the other state." There was an emphatic nod of his head for Leah's benefit. "We're going."

"Going?" Madame Rochambeau bleated from the doorway. Her jowly face was far less truculent now.

Strelnik sniffed. "Precisely, madame. You ordered us to do so."

"In the heat of anger a person sometimes says—"

Dolly poked her head into the corridor, her voice overlapping. "What about your paints and things?"

For the first time, Matt thought of the Matamoras canvas. Leaving that was like leaving a part of himself, like abandoning a precious child of his imagination. It pained him to shrug. "I'll write and ask Fochet to send everything if we get out safely." *Fochet who'd never gotten around to talking with her.*

"Matt, are you sure?"

"Yes! The paints and the pictures don't matter now."

In truth they mattered very much. He hated what had happened tonight. He hated himself for making the choices he'd made, and he hated the necessity of making them, even though he could have made no others. That was the goddamned trouble. He could have made no others.

An uncontrollable bitterness crept in as he added, "Oh, but pack that cartoon of us that Auguste did, will you? After spending several years of my life in Paris, I'd like to take something with me—something besides a hand that may be useless."

With a melancholy look, she disappeared into their rooms again.

Strelnik and Leah rushed away to pack. Matt stood leaning against the wall, studying his numb hand. He heard Anton wake with an anxious cry.

"Leaving," Madame Rochambeau murmured. "I won't have any more income."

He listened to her heavy footsteps retreating across the garden, and her murmured exclamations over the sudden financial calamity. He closed his eyes, thankful just to rest a moment longer.

Little Anton's voice made him think of his promise to marry Dolly. He'd fulfill that promise. Stop wallowing in self-pity; stop speculating about whether things would have come out differently if Fochet had remembered to speak to her. The promise had been given. Besides, a part of him did want to go through with it.

But another part of him felt deep regret—the part that would be squeezed and shorted.

He heard Fochet.

A priesthood.

Priests are celibate for a very good reason. They can't successfully serve both God and the flesh.

I've seen such a choice tear many a talented young fellow apart—

Goddamn it, if Fochet had only spoken to her!

Ah, what was the use? That was past. Finished.

The whole confused situation seemed summed up in two facts. He thought the Matamoras painting was the best work he'd ever done. And he had to leave it behind.

V

Before he and Dolly and the Strelniks set off through the darkness, Matt apologized to Madame Rochambeau for the trouble they'd caused. He gave her half of his remaining money—a decent sum—and she lapsed into maudlin murmurings of regret about their departure. Matt didn't tell her they were going to the Gare du Nord. When the police called, as they surely would, she could honestly deny any knowledge of their destination.

She was so agreeable now, she readily consented to carry a message to a woman who worked at the Café Guerbois. She did say she hoped the message had nothing to do with Mr. Strelnik's subversive interests or the mysterious turmoil of the past couple of days.

"No, it's personal, not political," Matt assured her. "Just tell her I said the obnoxious German customer would never bother her again. She'll be pleased to hear it. She'll probably give you a complimentary carafe of wine."

"She will?" Madame Rochambeau's brows shot up. "Perhaps I'll take my friend Alice when I go."

She dabbed her eyes. "I must say, Mr. Kent, you're really a very—a very nice young man—for an American. But you certainly do get involved in some curious affairs."

He smiled to hide hurt. "I do, don't I? Not always on purpose, though. Goodbye, Madame Rochambeau."

Chapter XII

Sanctuary

i

A NIGHT LOCAL carried them northwestward. Amiens, Boulogne, Calais. Matt was still feeling the physical and emotional effects of the struggle in the tenement. The memory of it was clear enough to start him shivering and bring Dolly's hand over to clasp his.

The two of them were sharing one of the benches in a second-class compartment. Strelnik and his wife sat opposite. Anton was a blanketed bundle in his mother's lap. Both parents were unusually quiet, and Strelnik's face had lost its earlier enthusiasm. Had grown somber, in fact. Matt wondered if the little man was contemplating the family's troubled past or its doubtful future. Either way, he felt sorry for his friend.

Repeatedly, his thoughts returned to the Rue Cujas. To stop it, he rested his forehead against the compartment's outer wall, shut his eyes, tried to doze. It proved easier than he'd expected. Suddenly he was in the midst of a dream fully as vivid as his memories of Lepp's pied-à-terre.

He saw a foul, littered room and a zinc-topped table on which Dolly lay with her skirt twisted above her legs. She wore nothing else below the waist.

A wizened woman in her seventies appeared. She had one filmy white eye and no teeth. She held a knife up near the unshielded gaslight, a huge, triangular-bladed knife that flashed like a sheet of silver. A knife for slicing bread, chopping meat—*or helping girls in trouble*.

Coming half awake, he tried to yell. He couldn't break free of the nightmare. A shadowy assistant grabbed Dolly's wrists, yanked her arms back over her head so she couldn't interfere with the old woman, who first tested the knife's point with her thumb and then pushed Dolly's pale legs apart.

Dolly's mouth came open. She screamed without sound. Matt started to flail. It did no good; no one paid the slightest attention. The old woman held Dolly's legs open with one hand and, with the other, slowly and expertly inserted the knife up into—

Crying out, he bolted upright. He snapped his head away from the wall so hard that he hurt his neck. His eyes felt wet.

Dolly clutched his arm. "What's wrong, Matt? You were groaning and making the most awful faces—a bad dream?"

"Yes, a nasty one."

"What about?"

"Why, ah—" He rubbed his face. "The Prussian."

He apologized to the Strelniks, then looked into her eyes. The compartment lamps had been extinguished, but this far north, there were no more rainclouds, and moonlight flooded through the dirt-streaked window onto her face.

He whispered to her, "As soon as we're in England—the moment we get up to London—I want us to be married."

A curious, apprehensive light filled her eyes. "Are you sure you mean that?"

"Sure," he said after a pause so slight it might not have been a pause at all.

Dolly glanced at Leah Strelnik, who smiled at her almost like an approving mother. Dolly squeezed Matt's hand and leaned against his shoulder as the train rattled on through the silver-and-black night toward the sea.

ii

As dawn broke, a pair of provincial policemen surveyed the passengers boarding the ferry at the Calais wharf. Matt didn't know whether the police were watching for him or for someone else, but he took no chances. He hunched over to minimize his height and walked between Leah and Sime carrying Anton in his arms, just as if they were all part of a single family.

He went up the ferry gangplank, buffeted by the fierce wind blowing off the Channel. He wanted to look back at the phlegmatic policemen standing on the quay, arms folded and short capes snapping at their shoulders. He didn't dare.

Presently the small steamer weighed anchor and turned into the whitecapped water. Matt got violently seasick on the rough trip across the Dover Strait. He still had a bilious countenance when he staggered off behind the others at Folkestone.

He hardly saw the little seaside village with its quaint cottages scattered over low hillsides. Strelnik fetched a pint of beer from a tavern near the rail depot. At first Matt couldn't get any down. The Russian kept insisting it would brace him up. Matt took several small swallows, but it didn't do much good. He was still feeling miserable when the train of sooty cars departed for London.

Once they reached the city Matt planned to head directly for James Whistler's house at number seventeen Lindsey Row in Chelsea. During one of their conversations in Paris, the artist had once extended an invitation: Matt was welcome to drop in if he ever visited England. Certainly the painter wouldn't be expecting four bedraggled people and a child to arrive on his doorstep. But Matt didn't know where else to turn.

They arrived in the big, bustling city about three in the afternoon and located Lindsey Row about an hour later. A charming Irish lass with lovely dark red hair answered their knock. The girl obviously didn't recognize Matt's name. But she smiled, introduced herself as Jo Heffernan, and told them Whistler had gone for a stroll with his friend Rossetti. Matt was familiar with the name of the poet and painter, and with hers as well. She was the painter's current mistress.

Yes, of course she could recommend a clean but inexpensive hotel. Soon the tired travelers were settled in two rooms just off Oxley Street, a couple of blocks north of the Thames and the busy Chelsea Embankment. Matt fell into a stuporous sleep practically at once and didn't awake until noon the next day.

Feeling much better, he shaved, dressed and walked to Whistler's. He received a warm and boisterous welcome from the little American, whose monocle reminded him unpleasantly of Lepp's.

Whistler insisted Matt sit down and share a late breakfast of strong black coffee and stacks and stacks of the artist's favorite buckwheat cakes. Naturally Whistler wanted to know the reason for Matt's sudden arrival. The younger man said he and Dolly had wanted a change of scene. His work had gone stale in Paris; ennui had set in. And Dolly was fretful about the war talk heard so often on the Continent of late.

The little artist, who was thirty-five or thirty-six, jammed a forkful of buckwheat cakes into his mouth, patted his lips with a napkin, and asked, "Is your stay going to be temporary or permanent?"

"Permanent, I think."

"First-rate! We must start hunting for a suitable studio."

Matt was unenthusiastic. "There's no hurry."

Whistler asked about the other couple Jo Heffernan had mentioned. Matt replied with a story about the Strelniks wanting better employment opportunity, here or in America.

The word brought a malicious grin to Whistler's face. "Set 'em straight, Matty. England's the only place. They don't want to emigrate to the land of the free and the home of the gauche. Jo told me they looked like nice, honest people. If that's true, they won't be able to make a damn nickel back home."

When Matt left Lindsey Row, he walked till he located a shop selling Paris newspapers. He bought one, the preceding evening's edition. There was nothing in it about a murder.

Two days later, though—July 1—a brief story appeared.

Colonel Gruen von Lepp, a military attaché connected with the Prussian diplomatic mission, had been found floating in the Seine near one of the piers of the Pont de l'Alma. The information had been released jointly by the Prussian ambassador and the French authorities, which indicated to Matt that the location and all the details of Lepp's death had been cleaned up for public consumption. The concluding paragraph said no suspects were presently in custody, though an unidentified American art student was being sought for questioning.

Shivering, Matt threw the paper into a trash bin. How long would it take the police to follow the trail of his passport and track him to London?

iii

As it turned out, the police and all the other citizens of Paris soon had no interest in cooperating with the Prussians. On the second of July, late editions broke the very story that had led to the arrest of Yuri Strelnik and the harassment of his brother. The Spanish parliament, the Cortes, had adjourned without taking a vote on the candidacy of Prince Leopold Hohenzollern, and through an error on the part of a code clerk, word of the candidacy leaked. Matt often wondered later whether the clerk, like Yuri, was a member of an anti-Bismarck apparatus.

Just as Sime had predicted, the story was a political bombshell. French editorialists reacted with outrage. So did the foreign minister, Gramont. Unbelievably, he went so far as to say there would be a declaration of war unless the Prussians withdrew Prince Leopold from consideration by the Spaniards.

"I told you such matters were taken seriously!" Strelnik said. The young American just shook his head in amazement and horror.

The Prussians didn't deny that Bismarck had been promoting Leopold's candidacy at least since early spring. But the newspapers were soon full of dispatches from Berlin that were obviously designed to minimize the impact of the revelations. The Prince didn't want the throne of Spain anyway, one story stated. He would refuse it unless he received contrary orders from his father, King William. Another dispatch said William was uninterested in the whole question. While London basked in bright summer weather and Matt's memories of the Rue Cujas began to fade, it seemed for a little while that the whole affair might blow over.

Strelnik predicted otherwise. He warned Matt to hurry and write Fochet if he wanted his paints and the Matamoras picture crated and shipped while France was still at peace. "Don't worry about giving the old man your address," he said. "You don't imagine the Sûreté's going to lift a hand to find Lepp's killer now, do you?"

Strelnik himself was agonizing about sending a telegraph message to Berlin. A message asking about Yuri. The little Russian claimed that the arrival of such a message might further compromise his brother. Hence, he hesitated. Matt suspected the real reason for the hesitation was fear of a grim reply.

Matt finally did mail a letter to Fochet. It certainly looked doubtful that the police would pursue him to England, considering the victim's nationality and the comic-opera turns the diplomatic affair was taking.

The French ambassador, Count Benedetti, pursued King William to Ems, where the king was taking mineral bath treatments. Benedetti demanded that the Prussian monarch order Leopold to withdraw his candidacy. Ruffled, William publicly refused, despite widespread press speculation that a private order for the withdrawal would shortly be given if it hadn't already.

Frightened by the specter of a unified Germany with a highly trained army at its disposal, the French weren't satisfied. They wanted not only open apologies but open guarantees that no such plot to expand Prussian influence would be repeated in the future. King William rebelled and refused to grant all the demands, saying they were meant to humiliate the Prussian people. The King even refused to permit Benedetti to continue the discussion in his presence. That was the thirteenth of July.

The worsening crisis finally pushed Strelnik into sending a coded telegraph message to Berlin. The reply was, in a way, good news. Yuri Strelnik's associates did not know what had happened to him. They had been trying to find out for days.

The message closed with mention of a rumor current in Berlin—one that the radicals felt should be communicated to the whole world. A telegraphic dispatch from Ems reporting Benedetti's demands had supposedly been revised and expanded by Bismarck before its release for publication. The purpose was to make it seem as though the French demands had been even more insulting—and insultingly worded—than was actually the case. Thus, said Yuri's friends, the power-mad Premier oiled the Prussian war machine and gave it a big push forward.

On the eighteenth of July a large crate and a second, smaller one arrived at Whistler's residence. The artist put them into storage for their owner, who was vague about when he would remove them. Matt told Whistler that he'd lost interest in his work. The unfinished Matamoras canvas, safe in the large wooden box, no longer meant anything to him.

Whistler didn't mince words. It was all very well for Matt to show this queer lethargy and to rant about giving up painting altogether. But he needed the space. All right, Matt said, he'd claim the things as soon as he found permanent quarters. The thought of searching for a studio was still unappealing, though. He preferred to spend the daylight hours just walking back and forth across the great city, or lounging in some pub, getting drunk. He didn't admit all that to Whistler.

The same day that the crates arrived, a letter from Fochet was delivered to the hotel. First the teacher gave the pertinent shipping information, in case the crates had gotten lost. In his second paragraph he reported that a detective inspector had appeared at the atelier a week ago, inquiring after one of his students without explaining the reason for his interest. Fochet had told the policeman essentially the truth—he never kept track of the whereabouts of his pupils. The inspector hadn't returned. Fochet hoped the foregoing made some sense to Matt, because it made none to him.

Then Fochet went on to talk briefly about the unbelievable political situation. The artistic community was polarized and in an uproar over the talk of war. Wanting to avoid possible conscription, Matt's friend Paul had already left the city with his mistress. Meantime Renoir was telling everyone that he hoped to be drafted, preferably for a cuirassier regiment. Such madness! Fochet said.

Matt agreed. But evidently a great segment of the North European population was afflicted with the madness. On the nineteenth of July, over what some called no more than a matter of protocol, France declared war on Prussia, and the Emperor's troops prepared to take the field against the armies of General Moltke.

Matt and Dolly learned of the war declaration late that night, when they returned to the hotel after a series of frantic visits to various government departments. They had spent the day taking care of the last requirements for a marriage in Britain.

Matt was tired and not in any mood to hear about a war. Europe was no better—no more rational—than his own country. It was disillusioning and even infuriating to realize that.

He was in a bad mood for personal reasons. Certain secret thoughts produced intense guilt feelings. Yet the thoughts persisted. He knew it was necessary to marry Dolly, but he'd lost his enthusiasm for it. And more and more often he found himself thinking of the forthcoming ceremony as some kind of execution. Painless, but an execution nonetheless.

iv

On the twenty-second of July, Matt and Dolly were married by an Anglican priest. The ceremony took place at St. James's, the little Wren church on Piccadilly. Strelnik and his wife stood up for the couple. Whistler and the lovely Jo were present as well.

The newlyweds treated their friends to a fine supper at a splendid fish restaurant in nearby St. James's Street. But they'd planned no honeymoon. It seemed superfluous. Besides, after buying the meal and the wine, Matt was nearly broke. Paying hotel bills and living expenses for the penniless Strelniks had been a big drain on his carefully budgeted allowance. He'd already written his father for an advance on the funds for the next six months. He hoped the money would arrive soon.

Matt saw Dolly was uncomfortable as they left the restaurant and put Whistler and Jo into a hack. He finally got Dolly to admit she was suffering from cramps undoubtedly caused by the pregnancy. He spent his last few shillings on a second hack to carry them back to the hotel. He helped her undress, put her to bed, kissed her forehead and laughingly dismissed her worried statements that she'd ruined the most important night of their lives.

He sat beside her in the twilight until she fell asleep. Then he went downstairs, overwhelmed again by the mental malaise that seemed to be his lot these days.

He found Strelnik seated in the hotel's tiny lobby. The Russian had his hands pressed against his knees and his eyes focused on a blank wall opposite his chair. Matt punched his shoulder.

"Come on, my friend. Even if the bride's sound asleep, we should have some kind of celebration. Let's go around to the Hart and Crown. I'll stand you to a—" Belatedly, he realized why Strelnik's cheeks glistened. "Sime, what happened?"

Slowly, Strelnik wiped his eyes. He drew a wrinkled telegraph blank from out of the pocket of his threadbare jacket. "This arrived while you were upstairs."

Matt unfolded the sheet. The collection of unrelated English words made no sense. "What does it say?"

"It says"—Strelnik's voice was feeble, dry sounding—"it says Yuri was executed the same day I went into hiding in Paris. The same day! And it's taken all this time for the crime to be discovered!"

Gently, Matt gripped his friend's arm and lifted him out of the chair. "I'm sorry. Come out into the air. I'd say we both need a glass of beer."

"Several of them." He snatched the message out of Matt's hand, flung it away. Then he repeated in a fierce whisper, "Several!"

V

As such things sometimes have a way of doing, the future of the Strelnik family worked itself out after Matt and his friend got drunk.

Their drunkenness manifested itself in different ways. Matt grew pensive, then downright melancholy, as if he were the one mourning the loss of a brother. The little Russian grew progressively more angry.

"Bastards. Prussian *bastards*. They're out to swallow the whole world. Room to live—that's all they talk about! I hope Louis-Napoléon crucifies them. I doubt he will, though. That damned Moltke's too good a general. Well, what's left for me in Europe?" A callous shrug. "Nothing."

Matt wiped foam from his upper lip, blinked twice, said in a sarcastic voice, "Why don't you emigrate to America? Hell, it's no worse than Europe now."

"Listen, I've thought about it. Consh—uh—constantly sometimes. I don't see the United States with the same cynical eye you do, Matthew."

"I try not to look in that direction at all."

It was a miserable joke. As miserable as everything in his life lately. Christ, look at him! Spending his wedding night in a London grog shop. On second thought, why shouldn't he drink till he keeled over? He had nothing better to do. Much to Matt's disgust, Strelnik seemed to be growing excited.

"I'd like to go to America. I think Leah would too."

"I gave you credit for more—wait a second. Miss? Refills here."

The serving girl shrieked as he flung his empty glass. She just managed to catch it before it hit the floor. Two dart players gave him sour looks. The owner scowled.

"Matthew, you're drunk," Strelnik whispered. "Drunk and disorderly."

"So what? So are you. To repeat—I gave you credit for more intelligence."

"Come on! At least America isn't run by a gang of bloodthirsty imperialists, the way Prussia is. At least she hasn't got a goddamned skirt-chasing Emperor, like France. In America the workingman gets a fair shake occasionally."

Matt snorted. "Not according to my brother. Oh, but

don't let me shatter your illusions. William Marcy Tweed and his gang will take care of that when you arrive."

"Tweed? Who's he?"

"Oh, just the fellow who sets the standard for public and private morality, that's all. I only know what Gideon tells me about him, but I'll be damned if that isn't enough. Bill Tweed is the political boss of New York City. The Tiger of Tammany—America's greatest spoilsman. You'll find out!"

Strelnik refused to be daunted by the sarcasm. "My family and I must do something soon. We're living on your dole, and that's not right. If I could just find a job, I could earn passage money within a year or two."

Matt sighed. "Hell, I'll loan you passage money when my father sends the advance on my allowance"—that would probably be cheaper than maintaining the Strelniks for an indefinite period—"*if* you're really serious."

"Yes, Matthew, I think I am."

"Then I'll give you a letter to my brother in New York. He's starting that labor paper I mentioned. Maybe he needs some part-time help. At least it's someone to go see when the ship docks."

Strelnik studied Matt a moment, smiled a sad smile and shook his head. "You know, Matthew, for a man who presents a cynical face to the world, you are really quite softhearted."

"Is that a fact! And here I thought I was a ninny scratching my head in the midst of the cleansing revolutionary fires, or some such shit."

"Well, yes, there's that. But you are very generous."

"And you are very sozzled. Finish your beer and we'll go tell Leah you've lost your mind."

He raised the heavy glass which the serving girl had refilled. "To your new homeland. May it give you more than it's ever given me—which is exactly nothing."

vi

In the second week of August, Dolly and Matt accompanied the Strelniks to the train that would carry them to Southampton. The emigrants had purchased space in steerage aboard a vessel sailing directly to New York.

There was a tearful farewell between the two women, fervent handshakes and hugs between the men. Strelnik had carefully packed a letter Matthew had written to Gideon.

"We'll see you in America on your first visit!" Leah exclaimed as the conductor shouted for them to get aboard.

Matt laughed. "I'm afraid you'll be waiting a long time. I don't expect to go back there till I'm buried—if then."

The Strelniks clambered into their compartment. Leah held Anton up to the open window, grasped his arm and waved it. The little boy soon got the idea, waving with great enthusiasm as the train began to move.

The moment it had chugged out of sight, Dolly slipped her arm in Matt's. She had tears in her eyes. "Oh, Matt, did you see their faces? They all looked like children about to be visited by St. Nicholas!"

"I suppose you call that innocence, eh?"

"Or hope."

"Whatever it is, they'll soon lose it over there."

"I wonder. I think they see a great many good things about your country. Genuinely good things you choose to ignore."

"Yes, I'm sure Sime's excited about the so-called freedom of expression he'll find in America. Just wait till he stands up on a crate on some street corner and starts spouting off about dismantling the fortunes of the capitalist warlords. Wait till he says those fortunes should be redistributed to the working class. He'll find himself exercising his freedom of expression in the lockup, maybe for the rest of his life."

Dolly sighed. "I believe that's one of the qualities I hate most about painters. They're so disagreeably cynical sometimes."

Irked, he started to retort. Before he could, she held up a glove. "Darling, forgive me. I shouldn't have started on that subject."

He was astounded. It wasn't like her to surrender.

She drew a deep breath. When his anger abated a little, he noticed the drawn quality of her face. Pregnant women were supposed to look nauseatingly healthy, weren't they? She looked as if worry were wearing her away.

"We have other, more personal things to discuss," she said.

He managed a chuckle. "We do?"

"Yes. Will you take me for a walk along the Embankment?"

"Good God, Doll, it was raining when we came into the station."

"I'd just like to be in the fresh air when we talk."

"Talk about what?"

Looking straight ahead, she said, "About us. Now that the Strelniks have gone, I can do what I've been planning to do for some days now."

He didn't understand the sad, tender expression on her tired face. Touching him, she added very softly, "I'm going to leave you, Matt."

Chapter XIII

On the Chelsea Embankment

i

THEY LEANED AGAINST the stone railing above the Thames. Patches of blue showed in the west—clearing weather—but light rain still dappled the river. There was steady barge traffic. The boats of the watermen scooted back and forth carrying passengers between the public stairs at the bridges. South of the river in Lambeth and Southwark further east, rows of factory smokestacks and great construction cranes jutted into the sky. Vehicular traffic clattered in the road behind them. They neither heard nor saw anything but each other.

"It's goddamned insanity!" Matt cried.

"My dear, that's the fourth or fifth time you've used the same word. But it isn't insanity. The marriage was a mistake."

Dolly seemed very tense, as if keeping her emotions under control only by the greatest effort. Raindrops showed as black dots on her dark green dress, and sparkled in the yellow curls over her ears. Despite the full cut of her skirt, her pregnancy was beginning to show.

"I must be the one to call a halt because you won't," she continued. "Your conscience won't let you. But you haven't done any work since we arrived in London. You haven't even gone to inspect the crates old Onion sent to Jim Whistler's. I know the cause—one silly, mistaken idea that affects you even though it shouldn't. Well, I learned long ago that you weren't perfect, or even sensible all the time. God knows I'm not either—"

"You've lost me. What's my mistaken idea?"

She reached up to touch his cheek. Her wry little smile vanished. "You persist in thinking everything's ruined for you because you have a wife."

"Dolly, that isn't so!" he lied. "I married you because I love you."

"And I love you. I'll never love any man so much. But I do know the real reason you went through with the ceremony."

Her tone was matter-of-fact. A passing waterman leaned on his paddle and waved. She lifted her glove but Matt didn't respond. He stared at her, then blurted, "Why?"

"Because you thought I'd destroy the baby."

He started to deny that, too, then closed his mouth and watched the falling rain and the smoke of the chimneys staining the southern sky like the harbinger of a mechanized, dehumanized world.

"Of course I thought about it," she admitted. "I threatened you with it, and I can only beg you to forgive that. I was desperate. I could never have gone through with it."

He turned to see whether she was telling the truth. Her eyes said yes. Her next words reinforced it.

"Not in a thousand years, Matt. But"—up came her chin; those lovely eyes had a bright glint now—"neither did I want our child to be born without a legal name."

"Our son. It will be a boy."

"You think that?"

Matt nodded. "I know it."

"Somehow, so do I. That makes a legal name important. That's why I can't thank you enough for going through with it."

Humiliated, he slapped his palms on the rough stone railing. His left hand still bore bruises. His face was scarlet as he breathed, "You make it sound like some almighty deed of altruism. I *love* you!"

"I know you do. But I also know how you feel about—

domesticity. You're convinced it has no part in a painter's life. I think you're in error, but I doubt I could ever change your mind, and I'm certain it would be disastrous to try. Yet feeling as you do, you still went through with it. You gave of yourself—the most you could give—and that says a good deal about you, love. I'll be forever grateful. Moreover your chil—your son will be grateful. I'm going to have the baby at my new place of employment, you see."

"Your new . . . ? You mean you've got a job someplace outside of London?"

She was amused. "A good distance outside. I'm leaving England."

"To go where?"

She thought a moment, then chose her words with care. "The Empire is very large, you know. I've secured a position in a rather remote part of it. I've been looking quite hard since I made my decision. Just two days ago, I chanced across an employment bureau that works for the government. The bureau liked my experience teaching English in Paris, and we struck a bargain on the spot. The employment contract's being drawn now. I discovered there's a need for women with some knowledge of literature and grammar at military posts overseas. I'll be teaching the children of officers at—one of those posts," she said with a slight catch in her voice. Inadvertently, she'd almost revealed her destination.

He grabbed her arm with thoughtless roughness. "Listen, Dolly. You've got to tell me where you're going!"

Without any reproof, she glanced down at his hand. Redfaced, he released her. She gave a small shake of her head.

"I don't believe it would be advisable for you to know, Matt. Your conscience might push you into coming after me." She brushed at her nose, tears in her eyes all at once. "Then"—she swallowed—"then think of all the fine paintings that might never be finished."

"Do you want a formal divorce? I don't know what's involved, but—"

"I don't want that unless you do," she broke in.

"No!"

He studied her then, his spirits sinking steadily. He knew what a determined person she could be; underneath her softness was a layer of iron. He thought of a half dozen things to say, all of them inane. All he could do was mutter, "At least let me send you money."

"Absolutely not. I'll be well paid where I'm going. And I didn't marry you because your grandfather owned a California gold mine and your father made you heir to one third of it! If I ever need a little for the baby, I'll get in touch with you somehow. But I doubt that will be necessary."

"I doubt it, too. You're a bright woman—bright and capable and strong—"

"And plump," she teased, laying a palm over her stomach. "I wouldn't have spoken so soon, but I have a long journey, and I must travel before some doctor forbids it—or before there's any danger to the baby. There'll be no danger once I arrive. My destination's quite civilized, I understand. With an excellent military hospital. I'll be sailing in a week, after I've had a visit with my family in Liverpool. I don't know what I'll tell them. I suppose it's best to say we're obtaining a divorce. They'll be unhappy, but much less so than if they thought I was bringing an illegitimate child into the world. Thanks to you he'll be born a Kent."

"But why the hell won't you tell me where you're going?" He felt bludgeoned, nearly as physically stunned as when he'd fended Lepp's attack. His voice grew almost boyish. "Why do you have to leave at all?"

Very crisply, she answered, "So you'll be free. I wanted our child to have a name, but—" Tears brimmed again, unchecked this time. "Oh, I'm so ashamed of this silly crying!"

She flung herself against him, her head deliberately turned outward from the center of his chest so he had trouble seeing her face. "Even before you said you were willing to marry me, I knew I couldn't stay with you. Not as a wife. That would destroy you. It's cruel and sad that you don't want or need what most people do. Affection. Companionship. A family. It's cruel and sad for you, is what I mean to say. But regardless of what caused it, the truth is, you don't need anything except your work. Fochet made me understand."

"Fochet!" Another thunderblow.

"Of course. One night in Paris, he talked to me for three or four hours."

"When? That is—I thought—"

"That he'd forgotten? How could he forget so important a favor for one of his most talented pupils? He just didn't feel it was necessary to tell you everything, that's all."

"When did he speak to you?"

"The night before you took me dancing at the Moulin de la Galette."

"But that night I asked whether you'd seen him, and you pretended to be surprised!" He did remember a suspiciously brittle tone in her voice. "Why did you lie?"

"Because I didn't want to believe what Fochet had told me. I knew it was true, I think, but I didn't want to believe marriage would destroy you. He admitted other men—Manet for one—could handle their work and the responsibility of a family as well, but he doubted you could. He said I might think that was wrong—I do—but I could never undo it. Then he gave me a better sense of the scope of your talent. A sense of all the great work that might never be done if I kept you worrying about patching a roof or paying for baby shoes until you died of misery and a sense of failure. It was bloody cruel of him to put that kind of burden on me! I was still resenting the fact that night when we danced. I got over the resentment—well, somewhat. I now know that most of what Fochet said was true. He thinks you have an immense talent, Matt. And you did make your work secondary when you married me. I can't be any less unselfish—"

Her arm curled around his neck, squeezing as she wept and whispered, "You're free. You're free now."

"I don't want to be free that way!"

She dabbed her eyes. "But it's all settled."

"Nothing's settled. I can't get along without you!"

"Well"—she laughed, not unkindly—"there is a good deal of the helpless boy left in you, Matt. But I think you'll find you can cope with the world on your own. You'll have your work to fill whatever emptiness you feel occasionally. I'll have our son. Actually, I'm rather the luckier one, don't you think? It's not every girl who can fall in love so wonderfully, then give a fine painter to the world, and still have his son too—"

"Fine painter? I'm a dauber, that's all! I'd rather be married to you than paint so much as one more—"

On tiptoe, she pressed her glove against his mouth. "Don't. Say it too often and you'll act on it. Then you'd come to hate yourself for the rest of your life. It's settled."

She tugged his arm again. "Come on, love. Let's walk a little—so people will think all this mess on my face is just the result of rain."

Clouds scudded ahead of a freshening wind from the west. A shaft of sun speared down, gilding a section of the Thames. They walked slowly along the Embankment, both of them too bound up in their love and grief to speak another word.

ii

In the little hotel off Oakley Street, they made love twice that night. It was done a bit clumsily because of her size, and with extreme care. Yet it was concluded more tenderly, more satisfyingly, than he could ever remember. When he awoke in the morning, he discovered the note.

> *My dearest Matt:*
>
> *You will know where to find me for a little while in Liverpool. But please don't because that would merely cause problems with my family. My sister Peg had written to ask whether I would be in her wedding, and now I shall have to tell her I'll be gone. I don't suppose she would want me anyway—by then I shall be swelling like a melon!*
>
> *I don't care about any of that now. There is great happiness in the midst of the sadness I feel over losing you. But then, as I tried to tell you yesterday, I shan't be losing you, really. A part of you will remain with me always. I shall try to make you proud of your son. Please make him proud of you through your work.*
>
> *You have always had the ability to be a fine artist. Now you have the opportunity. To that you must bring the will.*
>
> *Try not to be too disappointed when you experience failures, as you surely will. You have chosen to live with a demanding and capricious and even cruel mis-*

tress. But I know that in the end, she will reward you far more than I ever could.

God keep you, my dearest.

Yours always—

Dolly

CHAPTER XIV

DOLLY'S GIFT

i

HE AWOKE TO find his feet were numb. The quality of the light was all wrong, even for a winter morning. Why was the loft so dark?

Because the sky itself was dark, he realized. Overhead, the glass was wet with wind-driven snow. He watched for a moment or so. A regular damn blizzard!

What day was it? Tuesday? Wednesday? He wasn't sure. He'd worked sixteen hours straight to complete the new picture. When night came, he'd resorted to his trick of finishing less than critical areas by lamplight. He'd worked feverishly because he had an intuition that the picture would be good, and also because concentrated effort helped drain away some of the pain that had been his lot ever since Dolly's departure last summer.

He crawled out of bed. Stamped on the cold floor till his toes began to tingle. Lit one of the four lamps arranged in a semicircle on the floor of his work area. Then he staggered to the old stove and tossed a few lumps of coal onto the embers.

He coughed as he shut the small grilled door. The fumes were abominable. He recalled he'd disposed of some food scraps in the stove a day or two ago. He found the long pole and used it to lift the hinged section of the skylight. Freezing wind tore into the loft. Snowflakes came in as well, whirling on an icy gust one moment, drifting slowly down the next. *What the hell day was it?*

He believed it might be the twentieth of January—or possibly the twenty-first. His head was a muddle—just like the loft with its heaps of discarded clothing and disorderly stacks of books. Dirty dishes stood everywhere. Recent mail was scattered all over the floor.

Wind flowed through the skylight opening and down a wall where Renoir's cartoon hung from a nail. The cartoon rattled. Matt heard the noise but didn't turn. He couldn't bring himself to throw the drawing away because it was such a faithful and touching likeness of Dolly. But neither could he bear to look at it often.

He used the chamber pot in the corner, carried the pot to the kitchen alcove, opened the window and dumped the pot into a howling gray abyss that stretched down four stories. The ground was invisible.

He slammed the window and returned to the main room, passing the scrap of mirror glass he used—infrequently— for shaving. He paused, startled by the unpleasant image in the glass. He saw a man who'd lost weight because he had no appetite and only ate once a day, if then. A man who'd let his beard grow to an incredible tangle. A man with ugly dark circles under his eyes.

He turned the glass mirrored side down on the little shelf.

He sat on the edge of the cold double bed and locked his hands between his legs, pushing his nightshirt down to create a trough where he could generate a little heat for his fingers. His left hand hadn't regained its old flexibility and perhaps never would. But his right functioned normally. That is, it did when his brain was alert enough to provide proper direction. The proof stood in the work area, immediately behind the semicircle of extinguished lamps and to the left of the huge Matamoras painting, which he'd finished in December. The new picture, considerably smaller, had been started on New Year's Day and completed sometime after four this morning.

It was a study of a woman, painted in the new, unromanticized style of the Batignolles group. The woman was washing something in a tub. She was seen in three-quarter view, with the tub indistinct in the lower foreground. The visible sliver of water was done in blue of a dark value, so as to be subdued, like the tub itself.

The picture had several sources. The woman's tired, bent body was Lisa's as he remembered it from that moment at the Guerbois when he'd come upon her with her hands immersed in the dirty dishwater. The clothing was Lisa's, too. So was the straggly hair falling over the eyes, and the faint look of grime. There the resemblance ended.

The woman dominated the right-hand two thirds of the painting. Most of the background was extremely dark, although there was clearly a secondary light source somewhere to her right: an irregularity in the siding of the building in which she was working, perhaps—a gap admitting highly diffused sunshine.

The strongest light came from above and behind the woman's left shoulder. There he'd placed a large open doorway. Outside lay a meadow where two ungainly colts ran in the first radiance of day.

The flanks of the horses glowed with light. He'd used short, overlapping brushstrokes there—a technique with which Renoir and some of the others were experimenting. The effect only worked when you stood a good distance from the finished canvas.

Behind the horses rose blue foothills, quite distant and barely suggested. The splashes of light and the feeling of exuberance in the meadow were meant to contrast with the gloom and tedium inside the imaginary barn, where the woman was trapped by drudge work.

The woman was looking straight out of the picture. Matt fancied that she'd risen early, before anyone else was up, because she had so many chores every day. She was already tired but there was still strength in her arms, and in her back, whose breadth he'd exaggerated slightly. She had a defiant tilt to her chin but a resigned sadness in her large, cornflower-colored eyes.

Dolly's eyes. It was her face.

The meadow, the horses, the hills barely sketched outside—those, too, came from memory rather than imagination. Many times he'd gazed on similar scenes in his home valley in Virginia. After his first reluctant experimentation with the familiar elements, he'd been astonished at how superbly they fitted into the overall composition.

Finishing the picture hadn't purged all of his bad feelings, though. Standing up suddenly, his untidy flannel nightshirt falling down to midcalf, he was at the apex of a triangle whose base points were the portrait easel and Renoir's cartoon. No matter which way he looked, he saw her. It was true even when he was outdoors, or sleeping, or—

Angrily, he shook his head and turned away.

Over the past months he'd located and visited virtually every employment bureau in London. But if any of them had sent a Mrs. Matthew Kent, or a Miss Dolly Stubbs for that matter, out to some godforsaken part of the British Empire, to teach officers' brats to parse sentences and appreciate Wordsworth, no bureau would admit to it. She might have dropped into the pit of hell, for all he could learn.

He thought of the image he'd seen in the fragment of mirrored glass. Might be well to scrape his cheeks clean above the mat of his beard. He rummaged in the litter of books and correspondence, hunting for his razor case. In the search he knocked over a small stack of letters that included one from Gideon. It had crossed the Atlantic on a fast United States mail packet. The letter contained the usual family news and a greeting that had made him feel good:

—*your old friend Strelnik sends you his regards. He is proving to be a splendid part-time helper albeit several shades too "Red" for my taste.*

His bare foot slid past three long letters from Fochet. He stared at them with pensive eyes, wondering whether the Onion was all right—or even still alive. Conditions were frightful in Paris these days. Matt had realized belatedly that he and Dolly were lucky to have gotten out when they did.

Fochet's first letter had been written immediately after the scandalous September 2 surrender of the Imperial forces—and the Emperor himself—at Sedan. The war so

frivolously declared by France had led to that nation's un-
doing in slightly more than sixty days.

After Sedan, Louis-Napoléon had been hustled off to in-
ternment in some German fortress. The Prussian troops
had celebrated their momentous coup by looting all available wine from homes and cafés. Even General Phil Sheridan, accompanying General Moltke as an observer, had
raised an eyebrow at the "sotted" condition of the soldiers,
Fochet said.

Well, they must have been sotted indeed if Little Phil
had been shocked. The former Union cavalry officer, now
an important man in the U.S. military structure, was in
Matt's opinion a ruthless and foulmouthed son of a bitch.
Of course Matt had never met him. The impression was
left over from the war.

Sometimes he was surprised at the potency of his lingering hatred of damn Yankees. The war had been a stupid
and immoral one, and yet he loathed the enemy generals.
It was embarrassing, unsophisticated—and forever a sub-
merged part of him, like the memories of Virginia that had
come filtering through his head and hands to the portrait.

According to Fochet, the Prussians hadn't been too
drunk to scream, *"Nach Paris!"* And General Moltke had
been only too happy to lead them. Soon the French capital
was completely encircled and besieged. There was no
means of escape save a dangerous flight above enemy lines
in a hot-air balloon.

Fochet's other two letters, sent about a month apart by
balloon post, showed the degeneration of the mood of the
Parisian populace. At the start of the siege, Fochet sounded
pugnaciously cheerful. He said there was a spirit of ebul-
lient patriotism in the air, and a resulting widespread optimism despite the city's predicament. The Paris mob had
already proclaimed the repressive Empire dead, and the
Republic reestablished. The political leader Gambetta had
successfully escaped in a balloon basket to set up a government in exile. The "Red" clubs—the Socialist and anarchist
groups with which Strelnik had consorted—were pouring
out a steady stream of courageous, if whimsical, ideas for
breaking the Prussian stranglehold. One Red suggested
dumping poison into the Seine where it left Paris. Another
wanted to unleash all the animals in the city zoo. A third

submitted a design for a weapon similar to a Gatling gun, but with an added musical capability. The gun would lure the enemy into the open by playing Beethoven and Schubert, and then the gunners would blast the Prussians to pieces. The inventor didn't bother to specify how the gun would cause the Prussians to suspend their judgment and leave their fortifications in order to hear the music more clearly.

By the time Fochet wrote his third letter and got it into a pouch on one of the last balloons to leave Paris and sail away over the enemy lines, the earlier pugnaciously cheerful tone was gone:

> —*General Trochu is a lily-liver who stages sorties which fail to break the Prussian grip. The mob grows progressively more ugly as food grows progressively more scarce. The* bourgeois *is hated because he can afford to buy whatever he needs on the illegal market. The* petit bourgeois *grows rich because he sells the* bourgeois *what little is available in his shop. Meantime the* populo, *those from the dark underbelly, growl at both and listen more attentively to agitators from the "Red" clubs who have begun to condemn everything— the provisional government, the Republic—everything except their own dubious panaceas. You wonder whether I exaggerate? Three brief examples will show you how bad things have become. Yesterday I saw a new shop with a sign reading "Feline and Canine Butcher." The famous Jockey Club has begun serving delicacies such as* salmi de rats. *And last week a pundit said, "Civil war is a few days away, famine, a few hours." Be thankful you are not here.*

But he wasn't. He wished he were back in Paris, waltzing with Dolly at the Moulin under the lanterns of summer. Holding her in his arms on a night that somehow would never pale into morning.

Just as she'd promised, he was completely free.

And unhappy most of the time.

For a few weeks after she'd gone and he'd located the loft in Chelsea, the return of that freedom had pleased him. He'd been filled with the excitement of wanting to work again. Excitement had carried the Matamoras painting to completion. Then the passion had cooled, and old emotions had come back.

On occasion he still fell into the frenzy of complete concentration. It had happened yesterday—all last night—when he was finishing the portrait. But that kind of excitement was by no means constant any longer. Oh, he took satisfaction from work well done. But the loft was frigid and lonesome, the bed hard and cheerless, and he had to haunt Whistler's house or sit in the taverns to find a little companionship. A man couldn't paint twenty-four hours a day.

Shivering, he studied the portrait of Dolly. Were a few daubs on canvas worth what he was going through? Worth the chill misery of—

Loud thumping startled him.

"Matty? You in there? Are you dead drunk? Fornicating? Answer me, for God's sake."

ii

"Jim?"

He turned just as the door from the landing burst open. There stood Whistler, snow melting in his handlebar mustache and condensation fogging the monocle in his left eye. Every time Matt saw that monocle, images of Lepp dying flickered in his head.

The painter fairly bounded across the loft. He always moved as if he were in a state of agitation, and he usually was. His friends had to accept the fact that his temper was a bomb with a burning fuse of unknown length. Matt well remembered one of the first times he'd met Whistler in Paris. Whistler had thrashed a street workman who'd spilled plaster on him. A day later Whistler had chanced to meet his brother-in-law, whom he disliked, and had pitched the fellow through a plate glass window.

Whistler was strong, a diligent student of boxing. Other men seldom got the better of him physically. He was quick-witted, too. Judges and prosecutors who tried to punish him for his peccadilloes seldom got the better of him, either.

During that violent visit to Paris, he'd talked fast and gotten off with nothing more than a small fine.

Now Whistler shook snow from his fashionable fur-collared paletot. The heavy three-quarter-length coat was sprinkled with white from top to bottom. He took off his hat and knocked more snow from its broad brim as he said, "Rotten day to be out, Matt. Wouldn't have come, but this looked impor—"

He stopped, spying the portrait. He drew his hand from within his overcoat, where he'd been searching for something. He whistled through his teeth.

"By God that's good, Matty. Insufferably good."

The compliment lifted Matt's spirits a little. He murmured an acknowledgment as the older man marched to the easel.

"Turn up that damn lamp, won't you?"

Matt did so. Whistler dried his monocle on a dry place on his sleeve, fitted it back under his brow and bent close to the picture, examining the brushwork.

"I need to do a little touch-up here and there—" Matt began.

"Hell you do." Whistler pointed with his monocle and issued his decree. "*That* is going to the next Royal Academy Show jury. Bet they'll accept it, too. Now don't argue. You know I punch out anybody who argues with me. Hah-hah!"

He barked the two syllables. Matt was accustomed to Whistler's enjoyment of his own remarks. But some never got used to it, and found it one more evidence of the man's conceit.

Whistler wiggled his monocle at the background area. "What's that stuff? Doesn't strike me it's France."

"No, it's a bit of the Shenandoah Valley."

"Virginia?"

Matt nodded.

"Thought you were dead set against homegrown things in your pictures. Matamoras is on the south side of the Rio Grande, after all."

"You're right. I was opposed to American subjects—for a while. I've changed my mind. No, I guess it's better to say that portrait changed it for me. I've decided I can paint what I know without being a part of it."

"Hell, you can. Not and do it well."

"We'll see."

Whistler shook his head, the final word on the subject. He rooted inside his coat again. As he produced a crumpled envelope, he cocked his head at the portrait. "Got a title?"

"Just *Woman of Virginia.*"

"Pretty damn prosaic."

"Well, I don't think I should exhibit it as 'former mistress of the artist.' "

Whistler barked, "Hah-hah! Caught you, Matty. You said exhibit! You *know* it's good!"

Matt's face reddened. "When I finished, I did feel it was pretty fair—"

"Fair? It's more than fair. It's goddamn fine work! Quit acting like a reluctant virgin! Nobody'll boost your paintings if you don't do it first. Speaking of former mistresses"—he thrust the envelope at Matt—"the hand that wrote this has a decided feminine slant."

Matt snatched the letter. Whistler warmed his hands at the stove and grumped about the snow falling from the open skylight. Matt all but forgot his visitor. On the soiled envelope, *Matthew Kent, Esq.* had been inscribed above Whistler's address. When Matt deciphered the address of the sender, his mouth dropped open.

"*India?* Is that where she went?"

"Don't ask me, sport. I didn't steam it open. Listen, can't you afford more heat than this? Ask your father for a bigger allowance next time you write him."

The voice sounded miles away. Matt tore the envelope open. He was almost afraid to unfold the thin sheet inside, for fear there'd be terrible news.

"Don't suppose you've heard Paris is close to capitulation," Whistler was saying as he bent from the waist and scrutinized various sections of the Matamoras canvas through his monocle. "Don't suppose you care, but the *Telegraph* says there'll be hell to pay. There's talk of Bismarck's jackbooted Dutchmen staging a surrender ceremony in the Hall of Mirrors, maybe. Or parading past the Arc de Triomphe—why, the Reds who claim the resistance was botched will have a field day. And every excuse to take over—Matty? You fall asleep on your feet?"

Matt whispered, "Where's Lahore in the Punjab?"

"Northwest, I think. In the mountains. My grasp of geography's about as complete as my understanding of silicon. Sending you greetings from there, is she?"

Matt nodded. His face glowed with a strange kind of smile. Whistler didn't know what to make of it. His young friend was either in a state of exaltation or about to bawl.

Matt's eyes were indeed a little damp. At last he knew the location of the military post where she was teaching.

But he knew something far more important.

> —*Thomas Matthew Kent came into the world with no difficulty on Christmas Day. He was early by almost a month but shows no ill effects and, oh dear Matt, I do think he already resembles you. You will think so too, one day when the time is right, and you see him—*

But when would that be? Months? Years

"What's that silly grin mean, Matty? It's from Dolly, isn't it?"

"Yes, it is."

"What's it about?"

Wanting to dance for joy, he grinned and handed the letter to his friend. Almost as if he were making a joke, he said, "Immortality."

For once the dapper artist was caught short. He scanned a line or two. "Oh, I see. Guess congratulations are in order. You've got a bastard running around—"

This time it wasn't embarrassment that made Matt redden. "He's my legal son, Jim. Dolly and I are still married."

"Oh, sorry. No offense. Just don't get carried away." He pointed at the portrait. "That's the only sort of immortality that matters, you know."

Less angrily but with complete conviction, Matt answered, "You're wrong. She taught me that much."

But when will I see her again? And when will I see my son? He vowed he would somehow do both.

He put his arm around his friend. "Let me get dressed and then we'll go have something to drink. My treat."

"My Lord, it's only ten in the morning! On the other hand, it's damn fine weather for finding a snug fire and drinking a snootful."

"Sure is."

Matt's voice broke when he thought of all she'd given him. The freedom to think—to create—without responsibility. She'd given him her love. And one other priceless gift every man wanted, deep in some timeless center of himself, when he began to think of the generations that would live after he went to the dark.

All at once he beamed. He sounded almost giddy with happiness.

"I can paint a damn picture any day of the week. But it isn't every day I have a son."

"AND THOU SHALT SMITE THE MIDIANITES AS ONE MAN"

i

ON THE FIRST warm weekend in June of the same year, the Reverend Jephtha Kent relinquished his pulpit to his assistant and traveled down to Long Branch to open the summer house. It was usually referred to as a cottage. The term was applied to all the homes along that increasingly fashionable section of the New Jersey shore, even the most opulent mansion.

The Kent house was no mansion; it had a mere seven rooms. It stood about a hundred yards back from the high-tide line, facing the ocean. It occupied the south end of a row of cottages, and was by far the smallest of them.

Jephtha had bought the place three years earlier, in 1868, feeling that his second wife, Molly, needed a refuge from the stench and clamor of New York summers. Although his duties as a Methodist pastor kept him in town during most of the warm weather, there was no need for Molly to suffer or to risk her health and perhaps her life. All the medical experts agreed disease was carried by the miasmas—the odors of garbage and waste that reached their ripest point in July and August.

On this particular weekend, Molly had decided at the

last moment to stay behind. She was suffering from a bad spring cold. She'd asked her husband to be sure to hire someone to help him with the work. One of the local boys he'd engaged a couple of times before. He murmured vague replies as he left, not lying but not exactly saying he would, either.

Molly worried because Jephtha had been having some pains in his chest for the past couple of years. She'd finally pushed him into visiting a doctor. The physician had delivered a tedious lecture warning him to avoid undue exertion and the cigars which he admitted he puffed on the sly.

Thus her concern over his doing manual work at the summer house was understandable. But when he reached Long Branch, his basically thrifty nature asserted itself and he decided not to hire a helper. It was foolish to squander money that way; money was too hard to come by. At certain times Jephtha Kent was wholly unable to comprehend and accept his status as a millionaire many times over. The weekend was one such time.

He moved most of the summer furniture to the front veranda all by himself. Then, after nipping inside to smoke half of a good Havana, he began taking down the shutters. First the ones at ground level, then those on the upper story. The longer he worked, feeling only minimally winded, the more convinced he became that Molly's fears were groundless, and the doctor's warnings merely the cluckings of a professional hen. Except for the occasional pains he experienced—severe enough, all right, but not very frequent—he felt fit.

He looked it, too. At fifty-one, despite the streaks of white in his long, straight black hair, he fooled many people into believing he was five or ten years younger. His parishioners joked about him resembling an Indian, and for good reason. His mother had been a fine Shoshoni woman named Grass Singing.

As he was removing a second-floor shutter, the pain swept over him suddenly, constricted his chest, crushed it, as though a heavy weight had been dropped on him.

His ears rang. He heard the hissing surf with unusual clarity, smelled the salt spray with unusual intensity. He swayed on the ladder, eight feet above the ground.

He dropped the shutter but barely heard it thump in the

weedy sand. He bent forward, clutching a rung to keep from tumbling off. Although he was frightened, prosaic thoughts flashed through his mind.

You can't do this. Murch is only expecting to take over for one week, and you know he hates preaching. The Reverend Murch was his assistant pastor.

Finally the pain and then his fright passed. He managed to make his way down to the ground. He stood leaning against the ladder, breathing without the tight feeling under his breastbone or the spotty numbness in his left arm.

Three small girls, ten or less, went scampering past the front of the house and on down the beach. They were carrying wooden buckets for crabbing. Their laughter faded. Then out of the sunny haze to the south came drumming hoofbeats. Jephtha saw a light, two-wheeled trap approaching. The mane of a splendid bay horse stood straight out in the wind.

The driver wore a plug hat and duster. A cigar jutted from his mouth. A trail of smoke faded away behind him. Slowly his face took on definition.

The man was in his late forties, with a graying chestnut beard and mustache, and a wart on his right cheek that became visible at closer range. His shoulders were slightly stooped, a trait of those who'd spent a great deal of time on horseback.

Jephtha had met the man at a small reception given last June by one of the wealthier summer residents, the Philadelphia newspaper publisher George Childs. Jephtha had found the guest of honor a painfully shy man, and was somewhat surprised now when the man lifted his plug hat to acknowledge that he recognized Jephtha.

The trap went racing on up the beach, hidden by the veranda. Coming as it did on top of the pain, the sudden appearance of President Ulysses S. Grant put Jephtha Kent in an exceedingly bad mood.

ii

President Grant had chosen Long Branch as his family's summer retreat. The sight or the thought of him usually depressed Jephtha. Of course he was somewhat ashamed of the reaction, but there was good reason for it.

Theo Payne was the alcoholic editor-in-chief of the New York *Union,* the daily paper that was now back in the family along with Kent and Son, Boston, and Payne said Grant was unquestionably lost in the labyrinths of Washington politics.

"He's an honest man and expects others to be honest, which is part of his trouble. He's constitutionally unable to distinguish between true friends and favor seekers who just flatter him. He's the wrong man for the hour. We need a chief executive who's a schemer—or at least can recognize one—because scheming's the style down by the Potomac. Do you know what the cynics call the capital now? The auction room. Every man or woman with his or her price. Every one of them peddling something. Votes, influence, contracts, honor, physical favors—and the whole country's starting to get into the same spirit."

Jephtha trudged around to the veranda. The slight effort tired him, which was both unusual and annoying. He picked up a book from a chair where he intended to do some reading later. He sat down with a loud sigh. It depressed him that he had so little faith in the current administration, since it had come into office on an almost unprecedented floodtide of optimism.

Grant's campaign slogan had been "Let us have peace." People had expected him to end Republican factionalism and the political torment generated by the programs and personality of Andrew Johnson. People had expected him to set new, higher standards of morality in government. People had expected him to run a vigorous, effective administration because his war record proved he knew how to choose able lieutenants and put them to work. Grant would do this. Grant would do that. Grant would do everything and do it superbly.

We Americans do have an unfortunate talent for expecting our chief executives to be kin to the Almighty, he thought. *I'm as guilty as the next that way.*

And like millions of others, he had been cruelly disappointed by Grant's performance to date.

No one doubted the personal integrity of the Union's greatest hero. But Grant's judgment was in question only weeks after his election. He'd packed his cabinet with cronies and incompetent party hacks. Theo Payne maintained there were only two first-class men in major administration posts: Jake Cox of Ohio, who headed the Interior Department, and Hamilton Fish of New York, the Secretary of State.

Last autumn the President's judgment had become even more suspect. Jay Gould, a man who had entertained the President socially, had nearly cornered the United States gold market with the connivance of Grant's own brother-in-law, a lobbyist named Abel Corbin. At the last moment the President had been alerted to the scheme and had ordered Treasury Secretary Boutwell to sell government gold to break Gould's corner. But the national consciousness still held the memory of Black Friday, when the price of gold plummeted and speculators who'd followed Gould's lead were wiped out. Grant had not been shrewd enough to detect the plot on his own.

Lately it seemed to Jephtha that Theo Payne's remark about the auction room was right. It seemed to him that a trend toward dishonesty was accelerating—and rapidly—everywhere from legislative chambers to private boardrooms. But what supposedly concerned the President most? According to Payne and his equally sarcastic colleagues, two things: keeping French cuisine off the White House table and people who told off-color stories out of his presence. Lincoln's fondness for outhouse humor had been an all but unbearable cross for General Grant.

Now, as President, he still knew a great deal about blooded horses, purebred bulldogs and quality cigars. He seemed to know little or nothing about how to control spoilsmen, especially those in his own Republican party.

Of course corruption wasn't confined to the Republicans. Anyone who lived under the control of the Tammany Democrats and their grand sachem, William March Tweed, knew that. For years, New York City and New York County had been bonanzas of boodle. The common council to which Tweed had first been elected had been jocularly referred to as the Forty Thieves. And that was in 1851.

Under the genial Boss Tweed political swindling had been refined to an art, made possible because of the immense power Tweed had acquired. He dominated Democratic politics not only in the county but in the state. His handpicked men occupied the governor's mansion and the chair of the speaker of the Assembly. He himself was a state senator, and it was said that nothing of consequence happened in Albany unless it was first approved in the Boss's seven-room suite there.

But he kept his local positions, too. Commissioner of the New York City schools. Assistant commissioner of streets. President of the board of supervisors. Using all his offices to advantage, Tweed and his cronies had mined a veritable Golconda of graft.

The extent of that mining operation had lately been revealed in the *Times,* with some support from the *Herald* and the *Union.* Theo Payne was contemptuous of the small number of newspapers willing to attack the Boss. Payne said that the silence of at least eighty-nine other papers in the state, both dailies and weeklies, had been bought with fat advertising contracts arranged by Tweed.

Still, certain papers *had* begun to print documentation of Tweed's crimes. Appalling documentation. It seemed the Boss and his "ring" had really begun to function on a truly grand scale two years earlier. The ring's other members were City Chamberlain Peter Sweeney, Comptroller Richard Connolly, and Mayor Oakley Hall. In '69, they had apparently decreed that every invoice rendered to the city or county had to be fraudulently inflated by fifty percent. Lately, it was said, the amount was up to an incredible eighty-five percent. The boodle was divided five ways: one fifth to each of the four ringleaders, with the final one fifth going for assorted political payoffs and favors.

The scope of Tweed's thievery would have been amusing if it weren't so appalling, Jephtha thought. The Boss had long since become a Murray Hill millionaire. He maintained a law office he seldom visited, but prestigious clients such as Jay Gould of the Erie paid the firm huge sums just to assure their right to do business locally. Railroad, insurance and ferry companies were required to patronize a printing house in which Tweed owned an interest. The Boss had become a director of numerous street railway and gas transmission companies without investing a cent of his own money.

And if the newspaper revelations were true, the ring's

masterpiece, and its biggest source of revenue, was the new
county courthouse being built of marble supplied by a Massachusetts quarry owned by—who else?—the Boss. The
town was still agog over one story concerning courthouse
graft. It had been documented that a plasterer named Garvey had routinely submitted bills for wages of $50,000 a
day—and been paid. Mr. Garvey, this "prince of plaster-
ers," as the crusading editors called him, had earned a total
of $2,807,464.06 in a single season of work! It was assumed
that he shared most of his wealth with the ring.

Now, however, a shamed public was beginning to respond to the *Times* stories, and to Thomas Nast's relentless
cartooning in *Harper's Weekly.* There was talk of a mass
meeting to demand legal action. It looked as if Bill Tweed's
heyday might be coming to an end. But that didn't spell
the end of local corruption, Jephtha was sure. It would
continue to flourish with greater subtlety and less flagrant
disregard for the law.

Jephtha's pessimism veered in a new direction as he fingered the book in his lap. It was one of his favorites: *Inno-
cents Abroad,* the surprise bestseller of 1869. The author
was a young Missouri-born journalist who was giving Ar-
temus Ward stiff competition on the lecture platform. He
wrote under the name Mark Twain, a term Mississippi ri-
verboat men used for calling out the depth of water.

More than slightly irreverent, Mr. Twain. Amusing,
though. Jephtha couldn't have admitted it to his congregation, but he relished Twain's comment about the arid Holy
Land. "No Second Advent—Christ has been here once and
will never come again."

Why in thunder couldn't Kent and Son publish authors
of Mr. Twain's obvious talent? He knew the answer. The
editor and general manager, Dana Hughes, was a solid
craftsman. But he lacked imagination and nerve. The Boston book company needed a strong hand and a bold mind
to direct it. The *Union* needed the same thing, because
Theo Payne wouldn't live forever—especially not at the
rate he consumed whiskey.

What the family properties needed was a young family
member in charge! Alas, there was no Kent to shoulder
the responsibility.

Matt was living the dubious life of a Bohemian in Lon-

don. One of his pictures had been accepted by the British
Royal Academy for its annual exhibition, but that success
was balanced by a personal loss. In one of his wretchedly
spelled letters, he'd reported in a casual way that he and
his wife had *brokin up*. Where Dolly was now, Matt didn't
say, but the news of an apparent divorce distressed Jephtha greatly.

And Gideon—well, that was even sadder. Thanks to
God-given intelligence, a bent for self-improvement, and
the encouragement of his wife, Margaret, who had helped
him learn to read and understand difficult material, then
write down his own thoughts in acceptable prose, Jephtha
Kent's oldest son definitely had the ability to guide one or
both of the family businesses, which had been repurchased
from Louis Kent's estate after his death in '68. Unfortunately, Gideon wasn't interested in the daily paper *or* the
publishing house.

After the war, he'd worked for a short time as a switchman in the Erie Railroad yards over in Jersey City. During
a winter storm, a good friend of his had died in a work-
related accident. Gideon had seen the effect of the tragedy
on his friend's family. He'd also seen how reluctant the
Erie owners were to pay so much as a penny of postmortem
benefits. Gideon had finally forced a payment from the railroad, and ever since, the tragic accident and the indifference of the bosses had influenced and directed his life. All
he cared about was the cause of the workingman.

A worthy cause, certainly. But narrow. Dangerous, on
occasion. And almost universally scorned. Jephtha had
never grown accustomed to hearing his own son sneered at
as a Red or an anarchist.

Now Gideon was busy editing a little labor newspaper,
which he'd started with an advance from his inheritance.
Only a relative handful of railroad workers read *Labor's
Beacon,* but Gideon seemed unperturbed. In a way, Jephtha was proud of his son for following his conscience; the
best of the Kents always did. At the same time, he also
hated to see his son squander his talent. By taking a position with the *Union* or even with Kent and Son, Gideon
could promote many worthwhile causes, not just one. He
could reach and influence many millions of people, not just
two or three hundred.

And if ever there was a time in which the country desperately needed men of conviction and principle who were willing to speak out, it was now.

iii

Jephtha's mood persisted throughout the weekend, as he went to worship at a Long Branch church and then returned to the house and threw himself into finishing the spring chores. He got most of them done, leaving only the remaining shutters to be taken down by the boy he hired on the way to the depot on Monday morning.

As he climbed the steps of the coach of the Raritan & Delaware Railroad, the pain struck him again. The conductor leaped forward to steady him.

"Sir, are you all right?"

Obviously he wasn't, but he was too short of breath to reply. He clutched the hand rail and dragged himself up into the vestibule, then inside. He collapsed on a hard wooden seat in the grimy car. The pain persisted for the first twenty minutes of the northbound trip. It had never lasted so long. Never. He was terrified.

When it finally passed, his thoughts focused again on his own mortality—and on the family. The brightest spot in the whole picture was the presence of Michael Boyle, the Irishman who'd served Amanda Kent so faithfully as a clerk and surrogate son.

After Jephtha's youngest boy, Jeremiah, had been lost in the war, he had prayed and pondered and finally willed Jeremiah's share of the California fortune to Michael. He had never once regretted it. The Irishman had immediately taken Kent as his legal middle name, and he was a better member of the family than someone like the deceased Louis had ever been.

Still, Michael would never play an active role in making the Kent family useful to society on a broad scale. The Irishman was hundreds of miles to the west, permanently settled in the town of Cheyenne, in the Wyoming Territory.

He was married to a fine young woman named Hannah, the daughter of a German immigrant. They were raising a family and managing an expanding chain of general merchandise stores along the Union Pacific route. Recently they'd begun to branch out into feeding and finishing Texas beef cattle for the Eastern market.

The Boyles did their share to better conditions around them. Hannah had helped raise money to start a new church in Cheyenne. She'd also worked on a committee that had helped make Wyoming the first state or territory to grant women the right to vote. That had happened in 1869.

Michael was Cheyenne's volunteer fire warden and a member of a club called the Men's Literary Association. He was astute, industrious—the perfect paradigm of a prosperous townsman. Jephtha knew Gideon resented Michael because he wasn't a Kent, and perhaps because he was so successful, too. The gulf between the younger men was another disappointment to which Jephtha had resigned himself.

Presently a slight pain returned. He began to have difficulty drawing deep breaths. To keep his mind off the implications of that, he opened the Bible he always carried in the pocket of his fusty black coat and immersed himself in the search for a text for next Sunday's sermon. Almost unconsciously, he began with the prophets. It was indicative of his feelings that he settled on the seventh verse of the second chapter of Jeremiah:

> And I brought you into a plentiful country, to eat the fruit thereof and the goodness thereof; but when ye entered, ye defiled my land, and made mine heritage an abomination.

An overstatement of the immorality beginning to pervade the nation? He didn't think so.

He knew he mustn't blind himself to positive aspects. In many ways, he and all Americans were living in an undisputed age of miracles.

The transcontinental railroad, the wonder of the century, had been finished at Promontory, Utah, in '69 with the driving of four commemorative spikes—two of gold, one of silver, and a fourth made of gold, silver and iron—into a special tie of polished laurel. Another spike, ordinary iron but wired into the national telegraph system, was hit with a maul to tell the world the oceans had been joined. Now the line from Omaha to Sacramento was carrying passengers and freight on a regular basis.

Petroleum oil to light and heat homes was surging from the ground in Pennsylvania. Bonanzas of silver were being torn from the earth in the far west, and bumper crops were ripening on prosperous farms all across the great midcontinent. Manufactories were churning out marvels of technical ingenuity. Out in Chicago, a city whose tenfold growth in recent years showed the steady ascendancy of the middle west. McCormick's reaper factory could barely keep pace with orders. A meatpacker named Gustavus Swift was reportedly developing a refrigerated rail car that would make long-distance shipment of dressed beef and produce feasible at last. And only two weeks ago, Molly had told him about one more Chicago chap who'd patented a suction cleaning device he claimed would revolutionize the mundane chores of housekeeping. A "vacuum cleaner," the fellow called it.

The miracles were numerous and by no means confined to his native land. The great canal of Suez was now open, materially shortening the passage to India. Cyrus Field's Atlantic cable was in operation, carrying telegraph messages beneath the sea all the way to Europe. Such developments had forced Jephtha to conclude that America could not forever isolate herself from world problems.

And there were problems. Pestilence still ravaged Asia. Political butchery still reddened the cobbled streets of the Continent. The worst excesses of recent years had taken place in Paris this very spring. After the fall of the city, the Prussian conquerors had imposed humiliating peace terms before withdrawing. When the Prussians were gone, the radical elements in Paris reacted—violently. They screamed of incompetence on the part of their own officials, and of betrayal to the enemy. They overthrew the recently formed Republic and proclaimed a new city government called the Commune.

The Commune had controlled Paris for about sixty days. In May the established political machine headed by Adolphe Thiers and operating out of Versailles had sent French troops against French citizens. The Paris Commune had been overthrown with such savagery—so many mass executions—that the country might bear the scars for a century, just as the United States would probably bear the scars of its own civil war.

And certainly the labor radicals would never forget the inspiration of that brief time when the flags of the Commune had flown over the Hôtel de Ville. Nor, despite their own bloody excesses, would they forgive the ruthless extermination of the men and women who had helped raise the solid red banners.

The old men—Jephtha's generation—had consistently blundered. In the United States, they'd racked the land with a war of unbelievable ferocity, and botched the peacemaking afterward. They had carried out a holy crusade to end black bondage and preserve the Union, and had sunk into the squalor of profiteering from the very first day. To make black men and women full citizens, they had passed postwar laws and damned and vilified one another as they did it. They had made pirates like Pierpont Morgan respected members of the best clubs, and tried to hound a well-meaning if sometimes misguided President out of office. They had smashed the machine of democracy and rebuilt it without one of its worst flaws—the inhuman slave system—and in the process they had somehow lost their own souls.

The nation, and the world, needed the leadership of a new generation of strong, moral young men. What was the prospect for the future if America's best political mind belonged to a Grant, and its most successful entrepreneur was a John Rockefeller? Out in Cleveland, the young Baptist businessman, nicknamed the Deacon, was building an oil-refining monopoly. The son of a quack who peddled bogus cancer cures, Deacon Rockefeller apparently saw no conflict whatever between the teachings of Christ, which he studied diligently at an adult Sunday School each week, and driving competitors to the wall with every dishonest economic trick at his disposal. No one seemed especially concerned, or even conscious of the doctrinal paradox. Sometimes Jephtha thought he was the one who was out of step—or crazy.

The times cried out for new young leaders brave enough

to light lanterns of truth in the darkness rapidly covering the land. In that darkness, Jephtha heard certain dominant sounds.

The cynical laughter of lawless men who manipulated or ruined others.

The rustle of currency and stock certificates.

The clink of gold.

Why couldn't Gideon see the darkness falling? Why couldn't he realize he could help roll it back? Would he be forever content to publish a shabby little sheet dealing with just one small segment of the problem? Pondering those questions ruined Jephtha's concentration and put him in an utterly bleak mood by the time he reached the city via a ferry boat which crossed the North River and docked at the foot of Murray Street.

Just before the boat bumped against the pier, he remembered something from Scripture. Filled with a sudden and soaring excitement, he located the passage. He bracketed it with his pencil. Then he wrote on a slip of paper and tucked it in to mark the page.

What he'd recalled was a particular verse from the sixth chapter of Judges. A verse that pertained to the role he thought his son could and should take in the world. Better than anything in Jephtha's own words, it conveyed his vision of his son's potential, and it clarified in precise language the responsibility that went with being a Kent.

It was a responsibility for leadership. Somehow, he must begin to make Gideon understand that.

Using the verse as his guide, he needed to have some long talks with his son. And he needed to do it soon. The prospect was exhilarating.

He drew a deep breath without difficulty and joined the passengers leaving the pier. In just a few moments he'd been filled with a renewed sense of purpose and a heightened, almost heady confidence. That was God's spirit moving, he thought in an awed way. A smile spread over his face as he walked.

He'd taken nine or ten steps along Murray Street when he dropped the Bible, clawed at his coat, gasped for air and fell dead.

iv

Presently Jephtha was identified. Through Molly, his son was summoned to take charge of the body. Gideon broke down and wept when he saw his father's corpse lying on a mahogany bar under the gaslights of a Tenth Avenue saloon, just around the corner from the ferry pier.

He sent a boy off into the summer night to fetch an undertaker's wagon. The barkeep said, " 'Twas the owner, Mr. Callahan, who reached him first. We felt we should move him inside."

"I'm obliged to you."

The barkeep handed over Jephtha's effects wrapped in a handkerchief. "You might be wanting to keep these safe." He gave Gideon the Bible. "This too. It's plain he was a God-fearing man."

"He was a preacher."

"Oh. Protestant, then—"

"Yes."

"Well, it's all the same in the Lord's sight, I suppose," the barkeep said with a shy smile of condolence. He went off to wait on his subdued customers.

Gideon noticed a slip of paper protruding from a page in the Old Testament. He opened the Bible and pulled out the paper. There was something written on it, in his father's hand:

Speak to G.

He saw a verse marked in pencil. He read it once, then again:

> And the Lord said unto him, Surely I will be with thee, and thou shall smite the Midianites as one man.

An eerie feeling pierced his grief. Why had his father wanted to speak to him? Hoping to find a hint, he scanned the page preceding the marked verse. He drew in a loud, sharp breath. The sixth chapter of Judges dealt with a farmer named Gideon who had been threshing wheat by his winepress when the Lord commanded him to lead Israel against its oppressors.

What in the world was his father getting at? What had he meant by bracketing that particular verse in which God encouraged the biblical Gideon?

The eerie sensation continued there in the badly lit saloon whose customers remained quiet in the presence of death. Gideon was certain his father had wanted to speak to him about some symbolism he saw in the verse from Judges. But the essence of the message eluded him. He gazed at the still, suntanned face. Suddenly he exclaimed in frustration, "What is it?"

Heads turned. He paid no attention. Gideon felt that, in his ignorance, he'd failed his father.

"What did you mean to say to me? *What did you mean?*"

Chapter I

NIGHT ATTACK

i

SOMETIMES IT ASTONISHED Gideon Kent that a transplanted Reb could love New York with such fervor. But he had come to love it—the squalor along with the splendor.

He loved the racket of streets such as lower Third Avenue, where he and Sime Strelnik were walking now, just at twilight on a sultry evening in September 1871. The sidewalks were packed with pedestrians chattering in English, Gaelic, German, Italian, Yiddish, and several dialects he couldn't even begin to recognize. The avenue was filled with drays and private vehicles of the sort that made Manhattan one huge traffic jam six days a week. At intersections, telegraph lines leading uptown and crosstown laid black grids against the reddening sky.

Gideon loved New York's raucous energy and the way the city somehow conveyed a feeling that here, indeed, was the place where the nation conducted most of its important business. He loved the beauty of the city's splendidly dressed women and the knock-you-down brashness of its young men on the rise. His affection even included acceptance, or at least tolerance, of certain unsavory aspects: air that reeked of garbage and sewage; hogs that ran squealing on some of the main thoroughfares; sad, sullen slums filled with thousands of men and women too illiterate or too thwarted and weary to rise in the world. That kind of blight needed to be excised. Yet sometimes it seemed almost inseparable from the great mural that was New York.

Gideon loved the city's enthusiasm for innovation, typified by the three-year-old West Side Elevated Railroad which connected Battery Place to Thirtieth Street via Ninth Avenue, and by the great bridge whose first granite piers had been sunk the preceding year. When the bridge was finally completed—fifteen years was the shortest estimate of the time that would be required—it would span the East River from Park Row to Brooklyn. The idea itself was impressive. But even more than engineer John Roebling's concept, Gideon liked the execution of that concept. Roebling intended to keep the span clean and functional, free of the ornamentation which disfigured so many public projects. There was much in New York City that was cheap and meretricious, but Roebling's bridge to Brooklyn was lasting proof that—on occasion—imagination and excellence could carry the day. Gideon had become enough of a New Yorker to believe that no other city in the United States could begin to appreciate—or build—such a marvel.

One recent innovation he didn't care for was the paper tube filled with tobacco that dangled from the lips of his companion. Sime Strelnik had all but given up cigars in favor of the cigarettes that were just catching on in America. Gideon knuckled his blue right eye, coughed and pointed at the cigarette.

"I'm a believer in foreign commerce, Sime. But by God that's one European import we can do without."

At twenty-eight, Gideon still had the soft accents of Virginia. He walked with the unconscious swagger of a cavalryman. A leather patch covered his blind left eye. He'd lost the eye while locked up in a Yank prison during the war.

Although Gideon was Strelnik's employer, the little Russian was seldom intimidated by him. "My boy, don't be provincial. The whole country will be puffing these before long." But he did switch the cigarette to the opposite side of his mouth. "Besides, you're changing the subject."

At Timilty's Twelfth Street Saloon, they'd eaten a cheap supper of oysters and beer before starting back to the office. They'd been arguing about the basic thrust of the labor movement. Strelnik was a disciple of Marx and carried a card in the International. Those credentials plus his experiences in Europe tended to make him pontificate.

"Reformism is failing all over the world. Correction. It has already failed. Can you deny that?"

Gideon shook his head. In America, the three major reform movements of the 1840s and '50s had lost their vigor and most of their spokesmen as well. The cooperators were gone; they had tried to create small industrial plants owned by those who did the work. The associationists—ideological disciples of the Frenchman Fourier—were largely gone along with their plan for creating a sense of mutual need between workers and employers. And the foremost proponent of agrarianism, George Henry Evans, was dead. His scheme to divide all the free land in the West among the working class had never been realized, although his Congressional lobbying had led directly to the 1862 Homestead Act giving 160 acres to any man who would occupy and cultivate it.

All three movements had been well intentioned but contrary to the flow of the times. They were meant to help workers caught in the harsh realities of the expanding industrial system escape from that system. Reformism proposed to substitute life in a pastoral experimental community such as Brook Farm for the day-to-day struggle in a factory. Now, most men actively involved in promoting workingmen's rights had redirected their thinking. The new approach was rooted in reality. It said that to survive in the modern world, workers had to accept and deal with industrialism and industrial bosses.

"Revolution's the only answer," Strelnik insisted. "The trade union movement is failing, too, and our paper should be honest enough to say it straight out!"

"Failing, Sime? I don't agree. The movement has three hundred thousand members!" They crossed at an intersection. Gideon fended off a chestnut seller who nearly ran him down with a pushcart. A drayman blocked by a police van swore elegant oaths.

Strelnik scoffed at the point just made. "And the first time there's a slowdown in production—the first time there's a panic or a depression—they'll quit the unions to scramble for available jobs. And in those jobs, promising *not* to belong to a union will be a condition of employment. All the bosses understand what Jay Gould meant when he said, 'I can hire one half of the working class to kill the other half.' "

True enough, Gideon knew. One of the major problems confronting the movement was a lack of unity and unanimity. The National Labor Union, a loose confederation of trade and craft locals, eight-hour leagues, and groups of last-ditch reformers, had been founded in 1866 with the idea of presenting a common front on behalf of all. It hadn't worked. Craftsmen saw themselves as superior to unskilled laborers. Some workers were against admitting European immigrants—greenhorns, as they were called— to their unions. Almost all opposed the admission of blacks.

Strelnik grew excited, thoughtlessly waving the cigarette in Gideon's face. "I tell you, one of these days you're going to learn a hard lesson! There's only one way to deal with the bosses, and that's ruthlessly. You'll end up doing that, mark my word. The bosses will drive you to it."

"That's nonsense," Gideon began, but the little man bowled right by the objection.

"They will, Gideon. They'll exhaust your patience, your sense of fair play, your strength—everything. They have every resource on their side. Wealth. Public opinion. The willingness to play the hypocrite—why, you know they don't abide by the law, but they always pretend *you* must. That's the way they gain their biggest advantage! How can you even suggest it's otherwise when American workers are still subject to arrest under conspiracy laws if they so much as mention a strike?"

"Sime, if that happens, the arresting officers and the courts that uphold them are breaking the law. The idea that a strike is a criminal conspiracy was thrown out in 1842! The case of Commonwealth of Massachusetts versus Hunt specifically prohibited—"

Strelnik interrupted with a rude sound that made Gideon laugh in spite of his annoyance. "Gideon, I've only been in this country since last year. But don't try to tell me the conspiracy weapon is never used."

"Of course it's used by dishonest judges."

"My very point! The bosses are hand in glove with government—especially the courts. We both know it."

Gideon didn't argue. His companion was right. They turned down Fourteenth to the loft near the East River where *Labor's Beacon* was written and put together twice monthly.

"In fact," Strelnik continued, "the courts are the very instruments by which the owners—and the damned middle class, for that matter—let it be known that they have a strong opinion of the labor movement. Namely—"

He stuck out his thumb and inverted his hand.

"I'll tell you one reason that's true," Gideon retorted. "The public perceives those in the movement as a pack of mad dogs. They reckon we all want to follow Karl Marx's program, and they certainly assume we're the spiritual heirs of the Commune."

"Most of us are, most of us are!"

Gideon shook his head. "Not I."

There was mock ferocity in Strelnik's voice. "Then why have you got an avowed Communard working for you, may I ask?"

"Because you're blessed with a beautiful wife and a handsome son, and no self-respecting Southerner would permit nice folks like that to starve. Also because my brother wrote a fine letter of introduction in which he said you were mostly bark and not much bite."

The teasing infuriated Strelnik, who hated to be revealed as anything less than a practicing revolutionary. More soberly, Gideon went on. "Besides, I like to have you around because your ideas help me crystallize mine. Listening to you, I've decided what I really think about the Commune." He wasn't teasing when he added, "It was a disaster."

"I object! That's the uninformed opinion of—"

"Uninformed, hell. The Thiers government may have committed murder when the Commune was overthrown—"

"They did!"

"Let me finish, will you? The Communards resorted to murder first. To me it makes no difference that the Commune killed *fewer* than the Thiers crowd—or for a supposedly noble purpose. They resorted to murder so they're equally guilty. But even if the Communards were morally

immaculate, I still don't believe in their program. I believe
in capital, and property, and making a profit so long as you
don't exploit others to do it. I believe workers can win their
rights within the system. I don't believe they must tear it
down. Resort to burning and butchery—"

"Wrong," Strelnik declared. Gideon started to argue, but
their arrival at the narrow doorway of the loft building put
an end to the dispute.

Well, no matter. It would continue another time. Arguing
was a fundamental part of their relationship, and in just a
few months Gideon had grown quite accustomed to it. In
fact it was like the wretched stenches that permeated the
city—something that would be instantly missed if it were
suddenly removed.

He disagreed with virtually every point Strelnik had
made. He most especially disagreed with Strelnik's prediction that he would one day become so embittered that he
would resort to violence.

Violence was no stranger, to be sure. Sometimes, as a
matter of survival, he had to resort to it to defend himself
against hooligans hired to disrupt his speeches to workers'
groups. But an act of revenge against one of the bosses?
An act of revenge brought on by failure and frustration?

Unthinkable.

ii

A dark stair led up to the third floor of the commercial
building in which Gideon had rented two rooms now
crammed with old furniture, papers and books. The building was silent. All the other offices had emptied for the
night.

On the solid door facing the landing, the words LABOR'S
BEACON glowed in gilt. The words were separated by a
drawing of a switchman's lantern shooting its beam right
and left. The lantern appeared on the paper's masthead as
well. Having the name and symbol done in gold had been
Gideon's one extravagance when taking the quarters.

He touched a match to a lamp wick, then raised a window to let out the smoke already accumulating. Strelnik
returned from checking something in the other room,

where he kept his desk. He lit a second cigarette from the stub of the one in his hand as Gideon sat down at his own cluttered desk.

Among the scribbled sheets of foolscap, old proofs, invoices, he saw his father's Bible. He frowned. The small scrap of paper was still inserted at the sixth chapter of Judges.

Jephtha Kent had been buried in the family plot at the small cemetery in Watertown, Massachusetts. The message he'd meant to convey by means of the Bible verse still eluded Gideon. He had gotten over the worst of the grief associated with Jephtha's death, but he hadn't gotten over the sense of having failed his father.

To Gideon's left, the wall was covered with bits of paper—ideas, quotations, notes to himself, and a few over-due bills—all hanging from nails. Some of the items were there to remind him to mention and promote certain ideas on a regular basis. One such was an eight-hour workday. The campaign to reduce the working day had been spear-headed by a Boston machinist named Ira Steward, a self-educated man, as Gideon was. Some anonymous poet had put the economic justification for the eight-hour day into a piece of doggerel, and it was this which Gideon had jotted down and stuck on a nailhead.

> Whether you work by piece or work by day,
> Decreasing the hours increases the pay.

Some items were displayed on the wall because they expressed his personal credo far more succinctly than he could. At its 1869 meeting, a small group of delegates to the National Labor Union had enunciated its policy of favoring equality among all workingmen in the form of an address to the convention. The majority of the delegates had refused to endorse the policy by resolution. Gideon had saved a key portion of the address because he agreed with it.

> What is wanted is for every union to help inculcate the grand enabling idea that the interests of labor are one; that there should be no distinction of race or nationality; no classification of Jew or Gentile; Christian or infidel; that there is one dividing line, that

which separates mankind into two great classes, the class that labors and the class that lives by others' labor.

And on a bent nail there was one piece of paper that was Gideon's source of encouragement whenever he was damned as a lunatic and got to wondering whether the battle was worth it.

"Daring ideas are like chessmen moved forward. They may be beaten, but they may start a winning game."
—Goethe

Strelnik puffed his cigarette, awaiting instructions. Finally Gideon said, "What's left to do this evening? I mean besides the impossible task of convincing me that I'll one day be driven to knock the brains out of some capitalist?"

Soberly, Strelnik said, "Don't laugh. You will be."

Gideon stopped smiling. Often there was a curious, sanguinary streak in his assistant's conversation. Strelnik even hinted that he and Matt had been mixed up in some political trouble in Paris, right before the outbreak of the Franco-Prussian War, and that the trouble was the reason the Strelniks, Matt and Dolly had fled to London. Gideon hadn't had a chance to ask Matt about it, since his brother could not be home for Jephtha's funeral.

Gideon had sent a message to Matt on the new Atlantic cable. It was shamefully expensive—the minimum charge was $100—but fifteen words a minute could be transmitted via Newfoundland to the receiving station in Ireland. In the message, Gideon had urged his brother not to feel he must instantly embark for America; even the fastest ship would barely be under way by the time Jephtha was buried.

Gideon did wish Matt would come home for a visit, though. His brother's career seemed to be going well. The British Royal Academy had accepted a painting called *Woman of Virginia* for its exhibition this year—the first public recognition Matt had received. Yet Gideon sensed an underlying melancholy in his brother's occasional letters. Dolly had left him for reasons Matt had never explained. And with every year that passed, he seemed to grow more cynical about his homeland.

"Did you examine the returned copies of the last issue?" Strelnik nodded.

"And you pulled the names off the circulation roster?" Another nod.

"What else is there?"

"Proofing that article about the Crispins." The Knights of St. Crispin had been founded by shoe industry workers in 1867. A revolutionary machine, the McKay pegger, made it possible for factory owners to replace skilled help with greenhorns. The Crispins had organized to resist the trend. Theirs was a secret society, and with that Gideon had no quarrel. But it was also exclusionist. The Crispins openly attacked the notion that all workingmen were equal. To preserve the shrinking number of jobs in their industry, they no longer permitted the advancement of apprentices. They were not really brothers in the cause, but bitter and selfish men desperately trying to deny an inexorable future.

"All right, proof it," Gideon said. "Then you can go home to your son and that beautiful wife of yours. I only plan to stay long enough to finish up the editorial."

Strelnik bobbed his head and walked into the other room, smoke drifting behind him. Gideon reached for his pen but didn't pick it up. The mention of Strelnik's wife Leah had unexpectedly produced a feeling of melancholy.

Gideon had never once let on to his father or stepmother, but for the past eight or ten months he hadn't been going home to his own wife with the joy he'd once experienced. Ever since he'd started *Labor's Beacon,* Margaret had grown more and more critical of his interest in the cause—something he found astonishing, since it was she who had originally encouraged him to study and write and take an interest in the world.

He didn't like to admit it, but he had begun to see certain disturbing signs in her behavior. They made him think of her late father. Willard Marble—the Sergeant, as he'd preferred to call himself—had been crippled in the Mexican War. After that he'd taken to drink. He'd spent his last days in a perpetual stupor.

Lately Gideon had detected the smell of wine on Margaret's breath when he came home in the evening. She normally drank very little. A glass of wine with a holiday meal was usually her limit. He was fearful she was resorting to

the same mind-deadening nostrum that had turned her father into a raving sot. Even though she'd professed a hatred
for the Sergeant's behavior, Gideon had an eerie feeling
she was emulating it, whether she was aware of it or not.

Why? That was the tormenting question. He knew a couple of possible answers. She was upset by his work. And
she was upset by the modest surroundings in which he insisted they live. She found their circumstances particularly
galling because she knew there was so much money available now. When Jephtha died, Gideon had inherited four
and a half million dollars, plus a quarter interest in both
the Boston book publishing firm, Kent and Son, and the
New York Union. Jephtha's will had divided everything
equally between Gideon, Matt, that damned Irishman Michael Boyle, and Jephtha's second wife, Molly, who was
now living permanently in Long Branch.

Labor's Beacon could attract no advertisers. Hence every
issue lost money. But Gideon's fortune was invested and
managed by experts at the Rothman Bank in Boston. Using
investment income alone, he was able to keep the paper
going and at the same time provide a decent home for
Margaret and the children in a good suburb. More ostenta-
tiously than that, he would not live. To have done so would
have created suspicions and doubt among the laboring men
for whom he traveled, spoke and wrote.

Molly nominally operated both the newspaper and the
book company on behalf of all four owners, though in truth
each firm was run by professional managers. Gideon had a
standing offer from his stepmother to move into management of the *Union,* but he'd never even considered it. That
upset Margaret, as did a certain inevitable danger in his
work.

Her displeasure had been making their household very
tense lately. The mention of Leah Strelnik reminded him
that he and Margaret hadn't made love in five or six weeks.
The thought of it produced a stir in his groin, then an
unexpected and slightly embarrassing image in his mind.

Julia Sedgwick. The late Louis Kent's former wife.

Louis, Amanda Kent's only son, had gotten involved with
Jay Gould and Jim Fisk in the '68 Erie stock war. About
that time, Gideon had confronted Gould and demanded
postmortem benefits in the form of payments for the fami-

lies of Daphnis Miller and another Erie worker. He'd managed to bluff the financier into making the payments secretly—just about the only occasion anyone had gotten the best of Jay Gould, Jephtha said later. Gould had needed someone to blame. Apparently he'd chosen Gideon's relative, though there was never any proof of his being connected with what had happened next.

On a street in a dingy section of New York, Louis had been stabbed by an unknown assailant. The attack had left him paralyzed below the waist. He'd slipped into a coma and died during the summer. Gideon had met Julia when she'd come to the funeral with her son Carter; she had gotten custody of the boy when she'd divorced Louis during the war.

Julia lived in Chicago, was wealthy in her own right, and used her money to finance her work as a lecturer for the American Woman Suffrage Association—a cause nearly as unpopular as his. He recalled how impressed he'd been at their first meeting. He'd been taken with her poise, her intelligence, and most especially with her interest in public questions. It was an attitude in sharp contrast with Margaret's. Once Gideon's wife had been much like Julia, but now she was retreating from the world, seeming to want nothing so much as the security of a comfortable life with a husband who was in a prosperous and respectable business.

Yes, Julia had impressed him. And not merely on an intellectual level. She was physically attractive. In a guilty way, he realized the attraction hadn't lessened since that first meeting.

"I say, Gideon—" Strelnik had spoken loudly. "The proofs are marked."

"Good, good," he answered, coming out of the reverie. "Go on home."

"Don't you think I should stay till you're finished?" There was concern in the little man's voice. Despite his arguments with his employer, Strelnik liked Gideon. The feeling was reciprocated.

Gideon shook his head, trying to clear it of pictures of Julia Sedgwick even as his hands cleared a working space on the littered desk. Strelnik objected to the dismissal.

"Listen, it's safer with the two of us here. We got four more in today's mail, don't forget."

With exaggerated significance, he pointed to a small stack of letters on the desk. They totaled twelve now. Only three were signed, and the rest contained threats ranging from mild to maniacal. All the letters had come in response to an editorial Gideon had written in the last issue. He'd criticized the Washington railroad lobby directed by Henry Cooke, brother of Jay Cooke, who headed the huge New York investment banking firm bearing his name.

More and more, it was becoming apparent that the railroad lobby was buying favors and preferential treatment from state legislators and jurists. *Labor's Beacon* printed news of all trades. But the railroads were emerging as the country's most important industry and thus received the most coverage.

Gideon had heard the railroad lobby was deeply mired in a truly spectacular scandal involving the Credit Mobilier, the company which had financed and constructed the Union Pacific section of the transcontinental railroad. He'd unearthed no facts; no one had. But sources he trusted, sources such as Theo Payne, kept telling him Washington would explode like a bomb if the truth about gifts of Credit Mobilier stock ever came to light.

Gideon's editorial had suggested the need for a railroad worker's lobby to offset Henry Cooke and his associates. It had only alluded to potential scandal. Still, the editorial had produced those twelve letters, some quite hateful, and a brief, exuberant feeling that *someone* read his little paper.

"I'll be fine, Sime," he said. "No one's going to show up here."

Strelnik looked dubious but finally shrugged. He lit one more cigarette, blew out the match and asked, "Still planning the trip to Chicago?"

"Yes, the workers on the Wisconsin and Prairie want me to attend their organizational meeting, and I think I should."

"Is Mrs. Kent still against it?"

Gideon nodded. "She hates every trip I take. In fact I think she hates all of this. She's told me several times it was too dangerous."

Well, it wasn't exactly tame. He'd been set on by ruffians three times in other cities, and shot at once. But General Jeb Stuart had taught him how to fight; he held his own. To deal with unwelcome visitors, he kept a loaded Confederate cavalry revolver in the drawer of his desk.

"I heard it's been hot as a furnace out in the middle west, Gideon."

The younger man smiled. "Sime, you needn't hang around to nursemaid me. I'll be out of here in half an hour. Now go home! Tomorrow we'll carry the rest of the issue to the typesetter."

Strelnik cast one more glance at the pile of angry mail, pulled his cap out of his coat pocket and reluctantly left.

iii

Gideon inked his pen, found several sheets of foolscap and printed in capitals at the top of the first one *THE TRAGEDY OF PARIS*.

He chewed the end of the pen. He knew what he wanted to write but he had to phrase it properly. The Versailles government could never be condoned for what it had done in the third week of May; Bloody Week, it had come to be called. In an orgy of fire and shooting that had left much of Paris a corpse-littered ruin, the government had overturned the Commune and executed as many as twenty thousand of its supporters.

In spite of the May bloodshed, public sympathy seemed to remain with established authority. It was the Commune itself, not its overthrow, that struck fear into most Americans. And an obvious but irrelevant connection was still being made between the Commune and American labor. The bosses played up the fact that Marxian Socialists had led the Paris revolt and would, if permitted, lead similar revolts in the United States. There were constant references to the horrors of an earlier French Revolution. The Commune had raised a specter not easily banished, and one that would harm American labor for a long time to come.

Slowly, Gideon began to write:

> The American workingman was ill-served by the late and unlamented Paris Commune. From the outset it must be made clear that although American labor does include within its ranks a few who support the

International, and who would see all private enterprises dismantled and given piecemeal into the workers' hands, such men are in the minority.

The bosses have foolishly tried to make it seem as
though American labor is entirely composed of such
radicals. That is a lie deliberately fabricated to set
back the just cause of workingmen's rights. Most native workers are not Communards in fact or even by
disposition. They have no conflict with legitimate enterprise, and no antagonism to capital, but only desire
to receive a full and proper share of the capital which
their toil creates.

Although certain bosses would wish it, we must not
assume that what was wanted in Paris is wanted in the
streets of American cities and—

Abruptly, he glanced up. Absorbed in trying to get the
editorial to flow smoothly, he'd paid no attention to his
surroundings. Hadn't there been a sound a moment ago?

A sound out on the landing?

He laid the pen down. His palms grew damp. Through
the grimy windows he saw that it was nearly dark.

Voices murmured beyond the door. Two, perhaps three
men. His heartbeat picked up as the door handle rattled.
He'd forgotten to throw the bolt after Strelnik left.

As he leaped to his feet, the door crashed back. Three
ragged, scowling men crowded inside.

"Yessir, here's the one," said the biggest of them, hefting
a short length of lumber in his right hand. "Eye patch, ain't
that right?"

"Right, James," said the second, a wiry fellow with a
slingshot in his fist.

Gideon's heart almost broke; for a moment he was too
sad to be frightened. Here was a perfect example of
Gould's statement that he could use the working class itself
to destroy anyone who fought to improve the plight of the
class. These three men were no criminals but poor, ragged
city dwellers whom all the craft unions barred from apprentice programs, and thus from decent job opportunities.

Men with families, he supposed. Desperate men as yet
unacceptable to the rest of the labor movement. All three
of the men were black.

Sorrowful, he still reminded himself they'd do what they had been hired to do. He eyed the desk drawer where he kept the cavalry revolver. The burly man in charge drew a folded *Beacon* from his sagging trousers. Waved it under Gideon's nose and delivered a message Gideon was sure had been rehearsed.

"Certain gentlemen don't like you printing things about Mr. Henry Cooke down in Washington."

Quietly, Gideon said, "Who paid you? Why are you doing this? You're workingmen, aren't you? I'm on your side."

When they heard his accent, the wiry one sneered. "On our side? Lord God. You hear him, James? He's a Southron an' he says he's on our side! No, Mr. Southron, we ain't *workingmen,* much as we'd like to be, 'cause this old city don't seem to have many jobs for those who ain't got white skin. You come up here after the war just like we did, Mr. Southron? You come here 'cause they wouldn't let you keep niggers as property no more?"

"If it makes any difference, my family never owned a single slave in Vir—"

"No, it don't make no difference," the wiry man interrupted, and lunged.

He swung the shot-loaded sock. Gideon ducked but it grazed his forehead. He grabbed the drawer handle as they surged around him.

He stabbed his hand inside the drawer. Closed his fingers on the butt of the revolver. The leader spotted the gun and kicked the drawer shut. Gideon cried out when the drawer caught his wrist.

"No more stuff about Mr. Cooke, hear?" James said, and slammed the length of wood against Gideon's right temple.

His good eye blurred. He punched the black's belly, but underneath the old shirt the man's gut was rock solid. While the third one held him, the wiry one hit him again. They beat him for three or four minutes and left him gasping and floundering on the floor.

Then they tore up books and papers and, just before they ran off down the stairs, they smashed the office windows. By then Gideon had collapsed, unconscious.

CHAPTER II

BREAKAGE

i

AFTER LEAVING THE precinct house, he had to run to catch the last car of the evening on the Third Avenue Railroad. Every step hurt, and set his head to throbbing. His second-hand frock coat was torn, and because there was no running water in the *Beacon* office, he'd had to clean up with a rag and some bourbon whiskey he kept on hand. So he smelled and looked like a ruffian when he jumped aboard the car. He didn't recognize the conductor.

The man was new on the run, and might have denied him passage except for the peremptory way Gideon slapped the fare into his hand. Gideon sank down on one of the wickerwork seats and stared at the passing street. The conductor clanged the bell. The horse walked a little faster.

It was a long trip north through the country on the eastern side of the island to the growing village of Yorkville, and home. He had ample time to think about the evening's events. He was less concerned about the physical damage to the office, most of which could be repaired, than he was about the prospect of arriving home so late, covered with cuts and bruises. He knew it would cause trouble. And there'd been too much of that in his household of late.

Perhaps he should head off the trouble by telling Margaret he was suspending publication of *Labor's Beacon*. For a few moments he felt like doing just that.

Then he thought of his friend Daphnis Miller.

He closed his eyes. Inevitably, his mind turned back to that winter night in the Erie yards when Daphnis had died, crushed between two freight cars they'd been coupling. Daphnis had slipped on ice while a fierce storm raged. He'd never forget the sound of his friend's scream as the car bumpers snapped his ribs and broke his back. He could still see the sleet spattering Daphnis' wide, lifeless eyes as he lay beside the track like a broken doll.

The memory of that night hounded Gideon like some infernal animal, chasing at his heels and forever making him run faster. He had dreams about Daphnis dying; the sound of his friend's scream or the sight of his dead eyes slipped into Gideon's thoughts when he least expected it. Daphnis had been a decent, nonviolent man of limited learning; he wouldn't even have understood the word Communard. It insulted his memory to say that any effort to take care of his family after his death was a radical conspiracy.

The Daphnis Millers of the world had precious few to speak and fight for them. Gideon would not—could not—diminish the already thin ranks by stepping out. Margaret had taught him to understand what justice was, and to care about it. If it no longer mattered to her, it did to him. *Labor's Beacon* would continue its work.

And damn the consequences.

ii

Dressed in a plain cotton nightgown, Eleanor Kent sang to herself and danced on the worn carpet of the parlor in Yorkville.

She held the hem of the nightgown up around her calves, trying to remember the step one of her school friends had shown her.

She was nine years old. A slim, well-formed girl who already showed signs of growing up to be a beauty. Large brown eyes dominated an oval face. A large mouth revealed dazzling white teeth when she smiled.

Upstairs she heard her mother's voice, raised loudly because Eleanor's baby brother, two-year-old Will, had cried out with a bellyache that had been troubling him since noon. Mama was in a terrible mood tonight.

Of course, Eleanor thought, missing a step and then stopping altogether, that wasn't unusual lately. More often than not, her mother and father seemed out of sorts. They were always arguing, too, about things which puzzled Eleanor.

Papa's safety. Or his traveling too much. Or Mama wanting some particular article for the house and not being able to buy it out of the allowance he gave her. Or Mama simply saying she didn't have everything most wives had.

Eleanor glanced around the parlor. The room was jammed with furniture and potted plants, as current custom dictated. Nearly every inch of space on the papered walls was crowded with knickknacks, ornamental plates and framed pictures. On the tables there were more plants in smaller pots and a Rogers group—one of those highly realistic little sculptures reproduced by the thousands in gray or brown plaster finish. Every well-furnished American home had at least one John Rogers piece: his famous slave auction, or President Lincoln reading a proclamation, or some farmers playing checkers.

They had a lot of things, Eleanor thought. Yet Mama wasn't satisfied. And lately she'd been acting very peculiar. Sometimes she vanished for an hour, and Eleanor would hear rattling in the cellar. A bottle or a jar, she didn't know which. Then she'd hear crying. Finally Mama would reappear, her eyes slightly red and her breath smelling in a strange way. She didn't walk steadily, either.

Once Margaret had lectured her daughter on the evils of drink. She'd used as her example a town idler who could frequently be seen weaving up and down the streets of Yorkville. This evening, quite without warning, it struck Eleanor that her mother's lurching walk was just like the town drunk's. Her cheeks burned, and she felt ashamed of thinking that, but she couldn't help it.

She stared at the parlor mantel. On the wall above it hung an old sword and an equally old musket. Below them stood a green bottle filled with some dry tea, and a glass display case with wooden ends. The case contained a medallion and a piece of tarred rope.

All were things that Eleanor's father said were important to the Kent family—just like the picture in Papa's study showing that ferocious ancestor of hers, Philip Kent.

Tonight Eleanor paid no attention to any of the mementoes. She glanced at the clock. Papa was very late coming home. And Mama had been in a stormy mood ever since the afternoon post brought a letter and a photograph from the Territory of Wyoming.

Mama had examined the photograph with tears in her eyes. She'd angrily refused to answer Eleanor's questions about it, except to say that it had been sent by Uncle Michael's wife. Eleanor knew very little about Uncle Michael and Aunt Hannah except that their last name was Boyle, not Kent, and that Papa didn't like them and said so.

Hoisting the hem of her nightgown again, she began to sing softly.

> Listen to the mockingbird, listen to the mockingbird,
> Oh the mockingbird is singing all the day—

Her feet moved in rhythm. At last she had the step. She kept dancing and singing. She delighted in both.

Papa had taught her to love to sing, and she'd watched street dancers in the city. She loved performing for people, but her practicing was not well tolerated by her mother, who disapprovingly called her a little show-off. In theaters—places she'd only heard about—people were actually *paid* to sing and dance and show off!

Papa had offered to take her to a theater, but Mama disapproved of that, too, even though she had once enjoyed attending plays when she was a young girl in Richmond. Some things about Mama had certainly changed, Eleanor thought. She didn't know why, but she was very sorry about it.

Papa had a fine voice. Sometimes he sang with his daughter—another cause of arguments with Mama. Lately Eleanor had concluded that she didn't want to fall in love and get married if what she saw and heard around her every day was the result. Even though she was taught that girls were supposed to become wives and mothers when they grew up, that wasn't for her if so much quarreling and bad temper went along with it!

She finished the song and turned her head toward the table which bore their one Rogers group, the rustics seated over a checkerboard. Next to it lay the wrapped photograph which had caused so much distress. With a hesitant glance at the darkened hall outside the parlor and an ear cocked to the sound of Mama berating Will upstairs, Eleanor drew in a long breath. She reached for the picture.

Heavy boots on the veranda startled her. Her hand jerked and hit the piece of statuary. As the front door opened, the Rogers group fell off the table. She tried to catch it.

She wasn't fast enough. The plaster shattered.

Horrified, she covered her mouth. There was no possession her mother prized more. She'd nagged Papa for weeks before he finally brought it home as a Christmas gift.

Yet the moment Eleanor turned and saw Gideon, she forgot the damage and the certain punishment that would be hers. *"Papa!"* She hurled herself against him. He was dirty, his coat was torn, and his face was covered by cuts and two huge, purpling bruises. "Papa, what happened to you?"

He managed to grin as he hugged her. "Never mind that, young lady. Why are you still up?"

" 'Cause Will's got the bellyache and he's making so much noise, I can't sleep. Papa, please, please tell me who hurt you!"

He ruffled the lustrous dark hair that hung loose around her shoulders and shimmered in the lamplight. He walked to a chair and collapsed in it, his blue eye looking a trifle glassy. His shoulders slumped as he said, "The same kind of men I've run into before, sweet. Only this time they really took me by surprise."

He sat forward, wincing. "Eleanor stood in front of the pieces of the Rogers group so he wouldn't notice. He probed his side with his fingertips. Oh, how she loved him! He was so handsome and tall, still as dashing as any soldier. She wished he and Mama could be happy together.

He sighed and sat back. "Don't think anything's broken."

Rapid footsteps came down the stairs. Eleanor turned

toward the hall, still shielding the plaster bits by standing directly over them and tugging her nightgown down as far as it would go. The hem was an inch above the carpet.

Her mother rushed in, stricken first by the sight of Gideon slumped in the chair, bruised and dirty, and then by Eleanor's bare toes poking out from under the gown. Margaret Marble Kent was her husband's age, twenty-eight, with brown hair and eyes and a pretty though snub-nosed face. Her bosom and waist had thickened and now had a matronly look.

Flour whitened Margaret's gingham skirt and bodice. Strands of loose hair flew around her shoulders. She let her anger win out over her concern as she turned on her daughter.

"Why aren't you in bed?" She grabbed Eleanor's earlobe, hurting it. Eleanor stumbled, pulled off balance. "I ordered you to your room an hour ag—"

She saw the fragments of the sculpture. Her dark eyes filled with tears. "Oh, no. *Oh, no!*"

She pushed Eleanor aside, knelt and tried to fit two sections of the statue together. Gideon stared at her, a stunned expression on his face. Then color rose in his cheeks. Anger animated his shoulders and arms with a quivering tension.

Suddenly Margaret exclaimed, "You did this, young lady! You broke the only Rogers group we own!" She slapped her daughter's face, and not lightly.

Eleanor reeled back. She was more shocked than hurt. All she could think was, *Mama smells funny again—what's wrong with her?*

"For Christ's sake, Margaret!" Gideon roared, leaping to his feet. Margaret reached for her daughter's shoulder as if she meant to hurt her further. Gideon jumped between them. He pushed Margaret away from the terrified girl.

"Eleanor, go to bed. This instant!"

Eleanor fled up the stairs while Gideon shook his wife by the shoulders.

"Control yourself, Margaret. *Control yourself!*"

iii

She tried, dabbing her eyes with the back of her wrist. "I—I'm sorry. It's been a terrible evening."

"Obviously." He was weary of wondering why her breath smelled as it did. "What have you been drinking? The port from the cellar?"

She looked as stunned as Eleanor a moment ago. Quickly, she backed away. She started to cover her mouth but realized what she was doing and dropped her hand back to her side. Her tone grew defensive.

"Drinking? Nothing!"

The lie shocked him, then filled him with a confused sadness as she faced away and put a hand over her eyes, gasping out her words between bursts of crying, "But it's a wonder I don't drink after all I've gone through. Will's been sick most of the day, and you didn't come home and didn't come home, and Eleanor's so willful, she refuses to go to bed when she's told. All she cares about is practicing her singing and dancing in secret—"

Margaret's eye fell on the shattered statuary. She sobbed harder than ever.

Again Gideon's face showed anger. He overcame it, walked to her, drew her against him. She caught the odor of the liquor with which he'd cleaned up. She wrenched away.

"You're a fine one to make ridiculous accusations about drinking! You smell like a distillery. Were you in a saloon brawl?"

"How kind of you to ask! I thought you were more concerned about the Rogers group than about me. No, I was not in a saloon brawl. The *Beacon* was visited by some gentlemen hired to protest my editorial about the Washington railroad lobby. I managed to survive their tender inducements to stop writing about Jay Cooke's brother."

"I've told you before, Gideon," she breathed. "It's going to keep happening unless you *quit*. Over and over, it's going to *keep happening*. Beatings. People shooting at you on dark streets—"

Staring at her, he was struck by a sudden insight. During their courting days in Richmond early in the war, he'd known little of books, or of the kind of ideas which shaped and moved the world. In terms of those things, he'd been much like an infant barely able to crawl.

After the war, Margaret had helped him learn to walk. She'd read to him at the supper table. Encouraged him to try to read increasingly difficult material on his own, then to attempt to write short paragraphs expressing his personal convictions.

Perhaps she regretted all that, as Jephtha had said parents regretted their children growing to adulthood. Margaret had taught him to walk so he could leave home and, intellectually, he had done so, moving into a deeper and deeper involvement with the world. He was like the grown child who would no longer be directed and controlled.

And she was the parent who would not gracefully let go.

The insight made his scalp prickle. He knew it was right. Didn't she tend to be domineering with her daughter and her son? Her fury over Eleanor's disobedience demonstrated that all over again. Somehow he had become not merely her husband but also another of her children—the most independent one, the most troublesome one. God, why hadn't he thought of it earlier? It explained so much about her recent violent moods.

It disturbed him, too. Profoundly. All at once he craved a drink.

In the regular liquor cabinet, none of the bottles seemed to have been disturbed. He poured a generous shot of bourbon and drank it to ease the aches in his body and the newer one in his mind.

She was staring at him, awaiting a response, her eyes sullen. With all the patience he could muster, he said, "You mustn't take everything so seriously, Margaret. Of course I got hurt a little tonight. But the men didn't mean to do me any permanent injury."

"What about the shooting?" she blazed at him.

"In Baltimore?" He structured a careful distortion. "That was an isolated case. One random shot, late at night. I'm not even positive it was aimed at me." That was an outright lie—to spare her.

"Well—well"—she staggered to a chair, sat sideways in it, her head averted, her eyes closed—"you know what happened to my father in the Mexican War. Then I nearly lost you to the Yankees, and not just once. Manassas. The Peninsula. Yellow Tavern. That damnable prison—"

Her eyes flew open. "Now I'm in danger of losing you all over again. I worry all the time!"

He doubted it, but felt unkind for thinking it.

"—and—and"—half speaking, half crying, she let it pour out—"I'm so sick of it, Gideon. So sick of—the way we live. Grubbing—when there's—so much money—and a job waiting at the *Union*—a high-paying, safe job—if you'll just—speak to Molly—"

He was angered that she brought up the same old requests again tonight. But he fought the anger and went to her side a second time. She recoiled from the touch of his fingers on her shoulder. Forcing himself, he spoke in a calm voice.

"Margaret, I have explained again and again that if we lived any more lavishly, no one would take the *Beacon* seriously."

"Who cares if they do?" she cried softly. "Who cares? I don't!" Suddenly more coherent, she gazed at him, something hard and uncompromising in her dark eyes. "I want you to give it up, Gideon."

I don't want you to grow up and leave me, Gideon.

"You know I can't."

"Won't. You mean *won't*!"

"What's happened to you, Margaret? There was a time—and not too long ago—when you encouraged me. You were the one who taught me to read and write and think, and now you act as if you hate the result."

She whispered, "I do. I made a mistake. A dreadful mistake. Believe me, Gideon, I never would have helped you if I'd realized your main concern in life would turn out to be the welfare of a lot of greenhorns and niggers. Your work has taken you away from me, and I'm facing the very same situation I faced during the war. I'm facing the possibility of losing you. I don't want that. I won't tolerate it. Above everything, I demand that you think about this family and put this family *first*!"

The measured words told him he was right in his assessment of her motives. Deep within her, there was some unhealthy need to be obeyed, some compulsion to be the dominant partner. He tried to reason with her.

"I do think about the family. It's one of my most important concerns—"

"I want it to be the *only* one! I'm sick of being poor!"

"Margaret, please. I try to see that all our needs are met—that we live comfortably. Can you imagine how I'd be received at a meeting like the one coming up in Chicago when word got around that my wife and children were ensconced in a Fifth Avenue mansion?"

She sprang up and Crashed to the wrapped photograph. "But that's the sort of house we *should* have! It's the sort of house I want!. We've been married nearly ten years and haven't lived in a decent place yet!"

He started to protest but didn't. He was alarmed by the near-hysteria in her voice.

"Look what arrived today—from Cheyenne. From the Boyles—"

Gideon stiffened. He hated to hear that damned Irishman's name. Boyle had greedily utilized his portion of the inheritance to build and expand his chain of retail stores. Even Matt, who'd used his share to finance his art studies in Paris, hadn't spent a tenth as lavishly. And Gideon had only drawn on the money to finance the *Beacon* and provide *minimum* subsistence for himself and Margaret.

Margaret thrust a brown-tinted print at him. He saw why she was envious. The photograph, taken from a point some distance from the subject, showed an immense three-story Gothic house with a wide veranda, dormers and a corner tower. The two stiff figures posed on the veranda—the Irishman and his wife, Hannah, the latter with a swaddled infant in her arms—were dwarfed by the huge residence.

"It's their new house, Gideon. Hannah's letter said they've just moved in."

He flung the photograph away. "Damn braggarts."

But he felt a shameful stab of jealousy as he helped himself to more bourbon.

His head was pounding. His whole body throbbed. He wanted to lie down and sleep, and was alternately furious with Margaret and fearful because her nerves seemed in such a precarious state.

"Well, Gideon," she said. It had a forbidding sound of finality. "I believe we might as well thrash this out. And right now. It's time you decided what's important."

He almost laughed in disbelief. Then, abruptly, he hurled the bourbon glass to the hearth, where it shattered. He stalked toward her.

"Three hired thugs beat the hell out of me tonight, Margaret. Three men I dutifully reported at the precinct house, even though I know the police will never find them. Then I crawl home and you deliver ultimatums!"

"Yes," Margaret said in a voice so controlled, his backbone crawled. She pressed a white fist against her skirt. "Because I am tired of scrimping. Because I am tired of being afraid for you day and night—"

Because I am tired of your not doing what I say?

God forgive him, such thoughts were despicable. Farfetched, too. And yet when he looked in her eyes, he wondered.

"I think," she went on in a low voice, "we should draw a symbolic line and see whether you're willing to cross it. Chicago. Let's make Chicago the line. You've been planning another one of your foolish trips. If you want to show me the family comes first, don't go. If you do, you mustn't expect to come home and find things as they were."

"Margaret, you can't ask me to make such a choice!"

"I can and I do, Gideon." She was trembling; even her face was white now. "Your work or this family. The *Beacon* or this family. Chicago or this family."

"No, I refuse. You're being unfair. Three years ago, we agreed I would work on behalf of the movement. We agreed I could do that and we could still have our home life."

He reached out to grasp her arm, hoping an extra measure of gentleness might save the situation and bring her to her senses. It didn't. She wrenched away a third time.

"People *change,* Gideon, and kindly don't touch me again."

"What?"

Something absolutely unfamiliar and terrifying shone in her eyes as she bent forward at the waist, her hands clenched in fists again.

"I said don't touch me. I'm sorry I had your children. I'm sorry I have to bring them up this way. I can promise you there'll be no more children to suffer the way Eleanor and Will suffer."

"Damn it, Margaret, you aren't even making sense now!"

"Yes," she said, "yes, at long last I *am* being sensible. You've made your choice. Don't come to my room or my bed again. Ever!"

Red-faced, he roared, "By God, I won't! I'll sleep in the goddamn shed rather than roll over like a tame dog every time you snap your fingers!"

He stormed past her, deliberately kicking fragments of the broken Rogers group out of his path. Before he limped out of the house, he turned and shouted, "I'm going to Chicago just as I planned!"

He slammed the front door, so stunned and furious he never saw Eleanor's gleaming, frightened eyes watching from between the stair posts.

iv

His father had once told him that if a married couple went to sleep without patching up an evening quarrel, even worse bitterness would result in the morning. He didn't know whether it was actually true, but he'd always acted as if it were and had made sure neither of them said good night still bearing a grudge. He'd always made it a rule to be first to apologize, no matter who had started the argument.

Tonight he broke that rule.

Except for the occasions when he'd been out of town, or she'd been recovering from bearing the children, it was the first night since their marriage that they had slept apart. It marked the real beginning of the trouble between them.

Chapter III

Tinderbox

i

Gideon traveled to Chicago aboard second-class cars of the Erie and Lake Shore and Michigan railroads. Perhaps because he'd slept in so many uncomfortable places during the war, his habits had undergone a change and he could no longer sleep anywhere except in a bed. Since he hadn't paid extra to ride in one of George Pullman's special cars with the unique hinged seats that converted into berths, he was worn out by the end of the trip. Worn out from sitting up all night. Worn out from thinking about Margaret.

The morning after their quarrel, he'd resolved to apologize and had done so. During the hour before he boarded a car for the city, she'd refused to answer him. When he came home that night and tried again, the apology was acknowledged with a slight nod. Her out-thrust cheek had signaled that he could plant a kiss there if he wished.

Damn generous of her! he'd thought. But for the sake of harmony, he'd done it. He hoped to God the turmoil of the preceding evening hadn't really been the product of some emerging need for dominance. He hoped it had only been the result of an especially fatiguing day.

On the night the apology was accepted, he'd returned to

the large bed they shared. Their affection had been perfunctory ever since, and their lovemaking nonexistent. Margaret kept her temper and, as far as he could tell, stayed away from the bottles of port in the cellar. Nevertheless she clung to her position that the trip to Chicago was a symbol of whether he cared more for his work or for his family.

Repeatedly, he attempted to explain that one needn't exclude the other, and that to force a confrontation created pointless pain for both of them. But something in her cried out for a victory, and he got nowhere. They'd had another short, loud argument the night before his departure—and once more they slept apart.

On the long journey west, he thought about his work at some length. Considering what had happened, he did have doubts about continuing the *Beacon*. But the doubts were banished the moment he recalled Daphnis Miller's death.

Strelnik had been right that night on Third Avenue. Reformism was dead as a means of dealing with the juggernaut of industrialism. The masses of workers couldn't traipse off to some bucolic retreat and survive. To put bread in the bellies of their families, they had to reach an accommodation with the factory system and the men who controlled it. And a favorable accommodation only came about through the use of the strength conferred by unity.

Of course conflicts between owners and workers were by no means new in America; study had taught him that. Such conflicts dated to colonial times, when craftsmen had been scarce and wages high for a brief period. The worker never seemed to remain on top for long, though. In 1630, the Massachusetts General Court had set a ceiling on craftsmen's wages and established fines for any employer who paid more. Similar laws had been enacted in other colonies. When all the laws began to be repealed, those punishing overpayment by employers disappeared much more rapidly than those punishing workers for accepting overpayment.

American craft unions had been in existence at least since the 1790s. That decade had seen the organization of the Federal Society of Journeymen Cordwainers in Philadelphia, and of the printers in New York and other East Coast cities. Various trade and craft groups had come and gone since then, some strong and successful, some not.

They were always opposed by owners, and the owners always managed to keep the law and public opinion on their side.

Never had it been more true than in 1806, when eight Philadelphia cordwainers had turned out—struck—for a pay raise of twenty-five cents per pair of boots made. To the alarmed public, the eight were the harbingers of anarchy. To the leather shop owners, they were an economic threat. And to the courts dominated by the Federalists, who drew their political support from the owner class, the eight were men who *had* to be punished. Thus the doctrine of a strike as a criminal conspiracy had first been invoked. The Philadelphia eight had been fined, and jailed until the fines were paid.

As Gideon had observed to Strelnik, the conspiracy doctrine had been overturned in 1842. But it had served for two and a half decades after that as a means of keeping strikes to a minimum, and it was still trotted out whenever some venal judge thought he could get away with it.

Today the cottage industries and the small shops employing a few craftsmen were largely gone. But the conflicts remained—and had even been intensified with the spread of bad working conditions in the dark, dehumanizing factories that made Francis Cabot Lowell's Waltham system a model of enlightenment. In Massachusetts in 1814, Lowell had created the world's first textile plant with all operations under one roof. He had been a hard taskmaster, but a concerned one. As his business had prospered, he had cared for his employees with a paternalism that was now legendary—and obsolete.

Lowell had designed his buildings to admit sunlight; the absentee owners of newer factories crammed their buildings together and shut it out. He had done his best to protect the morals of young girls who worked for him. Recently Gideon had heard stories of men in black-painted wagons cruising the New England countryside to debauch girls and get them into the mills once they were stricken with remorse.

The crimes of profit-hungry factory owners and managers ranged from the horrible to the ludicrous. Gideon knew of seven- and eight-year-old children dying of lung disease contracted in airless, sunless workrooms where textile machinery threw off millions of fiber particles. He had gotten reliable reports of mill owners who tinkered with clocks to make them run more slowly. Of supervisors who flogged employees stupid and trusting enough to confess they had eaten breakfast; a popular theory said breakfast made a worker "langorous."

In the spread of the factory system, he perceived national industries emerging—railroads and textiles and steel to name just three. But he as yet saw no signs of national organizations to effectively represent the workers in those industries. The National Labor Union was really not much more than a debating forum. And he didn't have much hope for the newest of the organizations, the Knights of Labor, either.

The Knights had been founded in Philadelphia in '69. It was a secret society, originally restricted to members of the Garment Cutters Association. The first so-called "sojourner" from another trade had been admitted to membership last year, but the society still seemed to put exclusivity before everything else. Exactly how long it would take for solidarity to replace exclusivity and lead to genuine gains in the labor movement for the skilled and unskilled workers alike, Gideon didn't know. He was afraid it would be a long time.

And with a great deal of violence in the interim.

He could understand Margaret's worries about the risks of his work. He could also understand why she resented their modest standard of living. Since the night of that first terrible quarrel, however, he was convinced something else was at the root of her unhappiness. She resented his independence, which she herself had helped to develop. He had a career while she, by tradition, was required to stay in the home attending to domestic pursuits.

Still, he couldn't change every aspect of society at once. And since marriage was a give-and-take proposition, he felt it was wrong of Margaret to force him to choose between responsibility to his family and responsibility to others. Especially since the element of risk didn't matter to him. One time he'd tried to explain to her that the Kents seldom shrank from doing what needed to be done just because risks were involved. That, too, had been the wrong thing to say.

"Kent, Kent, Kent! I'm sick of that name! I wish our name was anything but Kent! Being a Kent has taken you away from me!"

Yes, her fears were understandable. And he would have borne them, and done his best to soothe them away, except for her desperate new insistence that he *decide* about what was most important in his life. That angered him. The anger was still simmering when he arrived in Chicago.

Perhaps it was the anger that made the memory of Julia Sedgwick pop into mind as the train chuffed into the large and ornate La Salle Street Station. At Louis' funeral, he remembered Julia saying she'd built a home on State Street, within sight of the lake and near the southern limits of the growing city. It struck him that if any human being would understand why he had to continue his work, it would be a suffragist. They were nearly as unpopular as trade unionists.

For a few moments he merely toyed with the idea of calling on Louis' former wife. Finally he decided to do it. It would be refreshing to chat with a woman who cared about something more than the size of her house, or whether a piece of decorative sculpture was broken. Julia had money, but that wasn't enough to satisfy her. She had involved herself in a movement which was trying to change existing conditions—just as he was.

His cheeks reddened as he stepped down from the car. The thought of Julia Sedgwick had produced an embarrassing physical reaction. He swung his shabby portmanteau in front of him. He realized how much he missed the physical affection he and Margaret had once shared so eagerly.

In the jostling crowd heading into the terminal, a ragged old woman fought against the flow of passengers, a beggar woman. She reached Gideon's side, offering withered apples.

"Buy, sir? Only half a dime for three."

"No, thank you," he said with a pleasant smile, and then started. The filthy old woman was scrutinizing him closely, particularly his face and the eye patch.

He walked on. The back of his neck prickled. He glanced around and saw the woman still watching him, not offering her wares to anyone else.

Then he remembered his contact, Nils Ericsson, writing

to say he feared Wisconsin and Prairie management had gotten wind of the organizational meeting and would attempt to prevent or disrupt it. That was one more justification for Gideon's invitation; no regular newspaper in Chicago or anywhere else for that matter would ever carry a story about company thuggery. The large dailies generally thought of unions as instruments of the devil.

From the first, however, Gideon had believed the story could be a good one. An eyewitness account of the struggle to found a switchman's brotherhood. Now there was a hint of trouble. If it occurred, he planned to add material on the lengths to which management would go to oppose a trade union.

The old woman was still staring. He recalled telling Ericsson in his last letter that he could be identified by the eye patch. Had someone read the letter? Or heard Ericsson mention it? There were always spies among militant workers—men paid to feed the bosses reports of disloyal employees with union leanings.

Gideon threw his shoulders back, striding along just as he'd done when he wore a Confederate uniform. The possibility that he'd been observed made him wary, but it lent his arrival a certain zest, too.

More important, it took his mind off the all but insoluble problems with Margaret.

ii

The limited traveling budget that he'd established for himself didn't permit him to stay at a hotel as fine as Potter Palmer's elegant Palmer House at State and Quincy Streets. Ericsson had given him the name of a small, clean establishment called the Dorset. It was located on Jackson, directly south of a squalid area of shanties called Conley's Patch.

At the hotel, Gideon unpacked and napped for an hour and a half. Then he cleaned up with soap and razor and set out to stroll the town.

Last year Chicago had replaced St. Louis as the nation's fourth largest city. Only New York, Philadelphia and Brooklyn were bigger. Chicago had about three hundred and thirty thousand residents, and Gideon thought he met

at least half of them that morning. The streets and sidewalks seemed even more congested than New York's.

It was Friday in the first week of October, an exception-
ally warm day—entirely too warm for autumn. There was
a light haze in the air, and a light breeze carrying a mixture
of odors that included the tang of the lake and the heavier
stench of fresh butchered meat. He presumed the latter
came from the Union Stockyards southwest of the business district.

Cattle, railroads, lumber, grain and the vast McCormick
Harvester Works kept the economy of the city growing.
While still in New York, he had purchased and read a small
Chicago guidebook. He knew there were various nicknames
for the place. Porkopolis. Slab Town. Wild Onion and Bad
Stink—people argued about which of the two was the cor-
rect translation of the original Indian name, which he be-
lieved was spelled Checagou.

The Chicago River and its two branches divided the city
into three districts. He was staying on the so-called South
Side, and would attend the organizational meeting on the
West Side. He spent the rest of the morning roaming the
south section, admiring the courthouse with its imposing
bell tower at Randolph and Clark; the fine retail section
along Lake Street; the one hundred percent fireproof *Chicago Tribune* building at Dearborn and Madison; and some
of the newer businesses on rapidly developing State Street.

Up along the main branch of the river, he saw great
numbers of steam and sailing craft, mostly small but in total
amounting to a huge quantity of shipping for an inland
port. The McCormick works which turned out the reapers
revolutionizing the farming industry, loomed on the river's
north bank. Bridges at main streets pivoted in the center
and swung parallel to the current to permit commercial
craft to pass.

The river skyline was a jumble of wooden office buildings, grain elevators, masts—wood everywhere, Gideon
soon noticed. Strolling southwest again, he observed a great
number of lumber and planing mills, each with its end product stacked in the yard. Close by the south branch he saw
shavings and wood scraps piled up outside small homes
sandwiched between saloons and retail stores. He asked a
newsboy about the scraps and shavings. The boy said thou-

sands of people gathered the waste material of Chicago's lumber industry and stored it on their property for winter fuel.

By two o'clock Gideon's stomach was growling. He decided to omit lunch in order to save money. Like his late father, he often had difficulty believing the California gold fortune was real, and he behaved accordingly. That was another of his traits which Margaret no doubt found annoying.

He walked back to State Street. There, amid the carriages, horsecars and pedestrians, he chanced upon an incredible sight: two houses, resting on rollers and being dragged along by oxen. He asked a policeman what was happening; he'd never seen such a sight in his life.

The policeman laughed and assured him it was common in Chicago. The city had been platted on low, swampy ground. To improve drainage the city council had simply decreed that the grade be raised. Thus, starting in the mid-fifties, the existing buildings had been raised too. Put on pilings, or shifted to new locations.

"Sometimes you see nine or ten houses a day being moved. The Briggs Hotel was jacked four and a half feet, all twenty-two thousand tons of it, and new foundations put in underneath, while it stayed open doing business as usual."

Gideon thanked the officer and moved on. He was impressed again by the ingenuity of the American mind.

A clerk at his hotel had told him Field, Leiter and Company at State and Washington was the city's finest retail store. Gideon headed there now. By the time he'd been in the store ten minutes, his New York chauvinism asserted itself; he silently acknowledged that the store was a good one, but of course it couldn't match Stewart's in Manhattan.

Having carefully counted his pocket change in advance, he bought a bright-colored toy omnibus for Will and, hoping it would help make peace when he went home, a bottle of scent for Margaret.

To find something for his daughter, he went to a nearby row of bookshops. Eleanor was always begging to be taken to the theater. But Margaret no longer approved of that form of entertainment, even though she'd once sighed over the good looks of Mr. John W. Booth and other leading actors when she sat in the gallery of a Richmond theater and watched matinee performances of popular comedies and tragedies. Gideon guessed that Margaret's new dislike of what she termed the immoral theater stemmed from her general retreat from the world. In any case, he hoped it wouldn't cause a fuss if he gave his daughter a little taste of the forbidden fruit. He bought an inexpensive edition of four of Shakespeare's comedies.

Eleanor was only nine, but she was a very bright child. He was reasonably sure she could understand the plots of the plays and all but the most difficult or obscure words in the iambic pentameter. How he loved the roll of that on the tongue! He said it half aloud—"Iambic pentameter!" The clerk peered at him as if he'd committed a public indecency. Gideon didn't care; he was forever trying out new words and terms.

He discovered it was nearly four o'clock. He was sweaty and tired as he started back to the Dorset. On Clark Street he fell in behind a couple of well-dressed gentlemen and heard one say, "—I sent my family up to Wisconsin."

"Don't you think you're being excessively cautious?" the other man asked.

"I do not. How many fires were there last Sunday and Monday? Five, six every night? Small ones, I grant you, but with no more than an inch of rain since July, we're sitting in a tinderbox. Two hundred and fifteen firemen aren't nearly enough to control a really bad blaze if one should—"

The men turned into a building. Gideon recalled all the wood he'd seen stacked in cottage yards, and all the wooden structures in the city. But he forgot about those things the moment he entered the little lobby of the hotel. The clerk signaled him to the desk.

"Mr. Kent, there's a gentleman waiting for you in the saloon bar. He's been here almost an hour."

Gideon wasn't expecting his contact today. But perhaps something had come up. "Ah," he said, "is his name Ericsson?"

"No, sir." The clerk consulted a card. "Florian. Mr. Sidney Florian."

He showed the card. Gideon scowled. Below Florian's name was his title:

ASSISTANT GENERAL MANAGER
WISCONSIN & PRAIRIE RAILROAD CORPORATION

iii

The clerk identified Florian as the tallest, thinnest man
in sight. Gideon found him easily in the saloon bar—a cadaverous fellow wearing a tasteless checked suit and a
derby hat. Florian hunched over the bar, a cane tucked
beneath one arm. He was stuffing raw oysters into his
mouth and washing them down with what appeared to be
schnapps.

Gideon approached warily. "Mr. Florian?"

The other man was four or five inches taller than Gideon.
He turned and peered down. His thin-lipped mouth parted
in an insincere smile that revealed several silver teeth.

"Yes, sir?"

"Gideon Kent"

"Mr. Kent!" A moist, cold hand pumped Gideon's. "The
editor of *Labor's Beacon*—a pleasure, a distinct pleasure!
I've been very anxious to meet you."

"And you knew where to find me. Did you also have
someone at the train station to meet me? An old beggar
woman, for instance?"

Close-set eyes scrutinized him. "I beg your pardon?"

"Never mind." But Gideon did wonder who among Ericsson's associates had taken a bribe. He supposed they'd
never learn that.

"May I buy you a little something to cool you?" Florian
asked as Gideon leaned against the bar. "This blasted
weather dries a fellow out. Damned unusual for so late in
the year."

Gideon figured he might as well end the charade of
politeness.

"I'm not in Chicago to accept Wisconsin and Prairie hospitality, Mr. Florian."

A curt shrug, and Florian was no longer smiling.

"No, you're here to write up what those stupid yardmen
are going to attempt. Write it up and spread it in that
yellow sheet you publish."

Gideon laughed. "I'm flattered my little paper's known to the bosses of your line."

A nasty chuckle. "Of course. We keep stacks in the switch yard privies. The paper may be read, or it may be used. Mr. Courtleigh and I happen to think it's more suitable for the second purpose."

Gideon's jaw clenched. "That would be your president, Mr. Thomas Courtleigh?" He had never met the man, but he knew a good deal about him. Courtleigh had inherited the immensely profitable trunk railroad from his late father. Reputedly the man lived in high style. He also ran one of the most repressively managed lines in the entire country—and bragged about it. When some Wisconsin dairy farmers had protested about exorbitant rates for shipping milk— the W & P was the only railroad in their region— Courtleigh's amused comment for the press had been, "Each man is entitled to the maximum profit he can earn. The farmers milk the cows and we milk the farmers and that's the way it is."

"Correct, correct," Florian said, his long, rather horse-like head bobbing up and down. "Mr. Courtleigh sent me with a message. He wants no publicity about the meeting scheduled for Sunday night."

"Oh, you know about that too, do you?"

"Certainly we know about it. Mr. Courtleigh wants to get it across to Nils Ericsson that the meeting had better not take place—especially not in Ericsson's house."

Sarcasm edged Gideon's voice. "Yes, I don't doubt Courtleigh would like to see it canceled with no resistance."

Florian licked his lower lip. Beneath the brim of his derby, his dark eyes were unfriendly.

"It had better be, Kent, because if it isn't, Ericsson's endangering his family. His family and the family of every man who attends. Do you suppose you could convey that to him?"

"Why doesn't your boss try delivering his messages in person?"

Florian snickered. "Why, Kent, he can't bother with the likes of you or Ericsson. Mr. Courtleigh's an important man! A leader in society in this town. Right now he's involved in planning a ball for his fiancée to be held a week from tonight. He delegates routine matters to me."

To goad him, Gideon smiled and feigned innocence. "I really don't understand, Mr. Florian. If Sunday's meeting is so routine, why do you bother making threats?" Before the cadaverous man could reply, Gideon went on. "Of course I know the answer. The desire of the switchmen to organize and bargain for better pay and better treatment is anything but routine to you and Courtleigh. I should imagine it's got your boss scared to death. Giving the families of yardmen postmortem and injury benefits might mean smaller profits for Wisconsin and Prairie stockholders. A smaller diamond for your employer's fiancée. Or a smaller orchestra for this grand soiree he's planning while his toadies scurry around town doing his dirty work—"

Florian couldn't believe what he was hearing. His eyes were wide with astonishment. Slowly, Gideon reached out and took hold of the tall man's lapel, his smile rigid and his blue eye glaring.

"If I hear one more such threat, Mr. Florian, I will kick you in your bony ass, and keep kicking all the way to the street."

Several customers further down the bar overheard Gideon and stared. Suddenly Florian jerked back, whipped up his cane, flourished it and shouted, "You damn Communard! You'll regret you came to this town. You'll regret you bucked Tom Courtleigh—and Ericsson's wife will regret it even more. You tell him that!"

He shook his cane one more time and stormed out of the bar.

Gideon laughed, but just a bit uneasily. He glared at those who had been watching the altercation. They went back to their own conversations.

"Whiskey!" Gideon snapped to the gawking barkeep. He was unsettled by the encounter, and not at all inclined to laugh off the threats of the Wisconsin and Prairie's president. When he met Ericsson for breakfast, he must tell him what Florian had said and let him make a decision about the meeting. Gideon was glad he'd brought his old LeMat cavalry revolver with him from New York.

As he prepared for sleep that night he unwrapped his night shirt which had protected the revolver in his portmanteau. Far in the distance, he heard what sounded like bells on fire pumpers racing through the streets.

He hefted the revolver and, with the tip of his little finger, removed a speck of dust from the bright barrel. He listened to the clang of the distant bells and abruptly recalled the word used by one of the men he'd walked behind on Clark Street.

Tinderbox.

Chicago was that, all right.

In more ways than one.

Chapter IV

Julia at Home

i

Nils Ericsson arrived at eight the next morning. He was a big, heavy-shouldered Scandinavian with fifteen years' experience on various midwest railroads, and an almost messianic belief in the need for organization. It turned out that he, too, paid his own way to the annual meetings of the National Labor Union, though he and Gideon had never chanced to meet at one of those affairs. Ericsson said he liked to absorb the essentials of the N.L.U. gospel—expansion of the eight-hour day from the Federal sector into the private one; formation of a Federal labor department; elimination of abuses in the child labor system—and then repeat them to any Chicago workingman's group which would have him as a free speaker.

He and Gideon left the hotel and found a restaurant nearby. They ordered breakfast. Only then did Gideon mention Florian's threat. Ericsson didn't take it lightly. But neither was he cowed by it.

"Matter of fact, I'm a bit encouraged, Mr. Kent."

Gideon sipped his coffee. "How so?"

"Well," the other man said in his accented voice, "Florian's visit means Tom Courtleigh is really fretting that we

213

may get enough men together to start a strong brotherhood
and force the W and P to meet our demands."

"They got wind of the meeting, though," Gideon reminded him. "It's obvious you have at least one turncoat
in your crowd."

Ericsson shrugged. "I got used to scabs and cowards a
long time ago. But if you're agreeable, I won't inform any
of the fellows about Mr. Florian's call. I want as many as
possible to show up at my house." The big man took a
moment to use a wooden toothpick from the little china jar
in the center of the table. "How'd Sid Florian strike you?"

"I wasn't overly impressed."

"Don't let his scarecrow looks fool you. He's done plenty
of strikebreaking around this part of the country. Used to
be employed by Pinkerton's. Courtleigh hired him away.
Pays him a small fortune, I hear. When it comes to bringing
grief to the laboring man, there's damn little Tom Courtleigh won't do. Yes, sir—Florian trained under the master.
If he or some of his hirelings should visit us tomorrow
night, we could have a royal scrap on our hands."

Again he didn't sound wholly unhappy; in fact, Gideon
detected a combative glint in Ericsson's eye. That was a
point on which they differed, then. The war had shown
Gideon that violence was not something jolly and sporting,
but a grim, gritty business which always had sad consequences for someone. Sometimes violence was necessary; a
man couldn't permit himself to be walked on. But that did
not mean violence was enjoyable or even desirable.

He thought it wise to remind Ericsson about one specific
part of Florian's threat. "There was a mention of families
being harmed. Your wife, for instance."

Ericsson sobered and shook his head. "That's a grand
demonstration of how much the line knows and cares about
its employees. I'm a widower, Kent. I lost my wife, Helga,
four years ago."

"I'm sorry."

"I do have my spinster sister to look after. She helps me
out around the house."

"Does she live close by?"

"Yes, Sigrid has a flat on Sebor Street. That's just a few
blocks from my place."

"Your letters mentioned a son, as I recall—"

With obvious pride, Ericsson said, "His name's Torvald. He wants to stay for the meeting. I'm going to permit it. He's old enough. Now let me draw you a little map showing you how to reach Taylor Street. It's across the south branch of the river. Not hard to find."

Soon they left the restaurant, Gideon having taken care of the bill. Ericsson glanced at the brass-bright sky. "By damn. Still no sign of rain. It's been a bad summer, Kent. The town's bone dry."

"So I've heard."

Abruptly, Ericsson remembered something: "Ah, but I meant to ask whether you're busy this evening. My sister will be cooking supper at my house. Sigrid and I would be pleased to have you join us."

Gideon smiled. "Very kind of you. But I've already made plans to pay a social call."

"Oh, you have old friends in Chicago?"

"An acquaintance," he replied with a thoughtful expression. "Just an acquaintance."

ii

Shortly before six that evening, Gideon donned a fresh shirt and cravat and walked to the Palmer House. He stepped up to the first hack in the taxi rank and asked the driver whether by chance he knew the State Street address of a suffragist named Julia Sedgwick. He was startled at the vehemence of the reaction.

"The Lucy Stoner who runs around the country spoutin' heathen nonsense about women bein' equal to men? I surely do know her address—been in the *Trib* lots of times. She lives down at State and Twenty-first. The swank neighborhood."

His glance said he thought the last place Gideon would have business was a swank neighborhood. But he asked, "You want to go there?"

"Yes. I'll walk. Thanks for the information."

The cabby was irate. "Looking for some of that free love them godless women practice, are you? She won't fool with your sort, you damn cheapskate!"

Laughing, Gideon walked south beneath the gaslights

glowing in the dusk. His pace grew brisk; his footsteps rapped on the wide plank sidewalks that, together with the softly shining lights, made State Street so up to date and attractive.

His smile faded when he thought of the emotional language the cab driver had used in connection with Julia. All in all, the suffragist cause was almost as badly tarred as the labor movement.

The cabby had called her a Lucy Stoner. The leader of Julia's association had refused to adopt her husband's name when she got married, and many women who followed her did likewise.

He had spat out the word heathen. Most of the country's conservative clergymen opposed the women's movement. The Bible specifically said a wife was required to be submissive and obedient to her husband in all things. This was reflected in the property and divorce laws in effect in most states. It also followed that, given woman's biblically ordained position of inferiority, any attempt to change that position and expand her rights was an affront to God's natural order.

The cabby had also accused Julia of free love; in mixed company the term free association was preferred, since it spared the sensitive. Some members of the movement did boast that they not only condoned but practiced free love. Inevitably, the sins of a few—plus a good many imaginary transgressions—were attributed to any woman crusading for equal rights. It was all wearily familiar to Gideon. *Déjà vu,* wasn't that the French expression?

Soon he began to feel a touch of anxiety. There was no guarantee Julia would be home—or that she'd receive him if she were. Yet he didn't turn back.

Below Sixteenth, the houses grew more imposing, occupying half-block lots and then, after he'd passed Eighteenth, the full block. At a gabled mansion between Nineteenth and Twentieth, a large party was in progress. The place blazed with light, and he heard a string orchestra, and much laughter. Out in front coachmen were tossing dice while they waited for their employers. The men observed Gideon with amusement; he was clearly out of place in this district.

He crossed Twentieth and drew in a sharp breath at the

sight of Julia's house. It was a huge, three-story stone structure with a mansard roof and identical front-corner towers.
Most of the lower windows along the front were illuminated, so perhaps she was home.

But she also had company. A hired carriage bearing the
nameplate of the Parmelee Livery stood in the drive. Again
Gideon drew a scornful look from the carriageman. He
glared until the driver looked away, then marched up the
steps, wiping sweat off his forehead with a kerchief.

He rang the bell. A butler answered, scrutinized him and
started to shut the door.

"Tradesmen or those seeking employment are to go to
the rear entrance."

Gideon shoved his knee against the door. The butler
cried, "See here, sir!"

"My name's Kent," Gideon exclaimed. "I'm—" He hesitated. Did you address a divorced Lucy Stoner as Miss or
Mrs.? "I'm Julia's relative by her former marriage."

The waxy-faced servant sniffed and stepped back. "Your
name again, please?"

Annoyed, he said, "Gideon Kent."

"She is expecting you?"

"No. I just arrived in Chicago and found myself with a
few moments—" He started as the butler shot out his
white-gloved hand.

"Your visiting card."

"I don't have any visiting cards, you stuck-up jackass!"

The butler went white. Gideon shoved the elaborately
carved door all the way open and stalked into a breathtaking foyer, where the crystal pendants of an enormous gas
chandelier scattered brilliant little lights on the walls, furnishings and marble floor. He pivoted and barked at the
butler as if he were addressing a recruit, "You march to
cousin Julia and tell her Gideon Kent's in the hall. Or I'll
give you what Jeb Stuart's cavalry used to give you
Yankees—" He shot out his fist as if it held a sabre and
yelled, "Hah!"

The butler literally jumped a foot. Gideon laughed. The
other man hurried out, mumbling, "She—they—you—may
be required to wait—Cooke—representative—is with—"

Pop-eyed, he disappeared into what appeared to be a
library. Could he have been referring to the banking house

of Jay Cooke, whose brother ran the railroad lobby and who'd personally spearheaded the drive to sell Federal war bonds, becoming a kind of financial hero of the North?

If so, Louis' former wife was traveling in the highest economic circles. Jay Cooke ran a solid and respected bank, and he was the moving force behind the most spectacular railroad promotion of the postwar period—the sale of a hundred million dollars' worth of bonds to finance a second transcontinental line.

The Northern Pacific was to be built along the Canadian border. To move the bonds, Cooke's had even dispatched agents to Europe to set up sales offices in the palaces of the nobility. The war between France and Prussia had undone many of those deals, however. So the banking house had redoubled its efforts at home, had even hired a professional publicist to write about the lush land through which the railroad would run. The publicist's rhapsodies had gotten out of hand, though, and now there were jokes about Jay Cooke's Banana Belt, where orange groves and banana plantations would one day rise from the Dakota flatlands. Still, Gideon knew thousands of small investors trusted both the Cooke firm and the future of railroads, and were putting all their savings into Northern Pacific bonds.

He began to inspect the opulent foyer more closely. Everything about it including its sweeping marble staircase spoke of vast wealth. Julia hadn't taken a penny of Louis Kent's money, that much he knew. She was obviously even richer than he'd thought.

Again he recalled his father speaking of Julia's selfish and willful nature. What had changed her into a fighter on the barricades of social revolution? He couldn't imagine.

He did know a bit about the current state of the women's movement. Earlier in the year, a schism had split it into two groups. One was the so-called Boston group led by Lucy Stone and Julia Ward Howe, the group for which Julia traveled and lectured. Its proper name was the American Woman Suffrage Association. The other group, the National Association, still operated out of New York under the direction of Susan B. Anthony and Elizabeth Cady Stanton.

The split had come about because the leaders of the movement had wanted to start a woman's newspaper to be called *The Revolution.* A sponsor and underwriter was needed, and an eager one happened to be handy—the wealthy and eccentric George Francis Train. Mr. Train dabbled in causes. In fact he dabbled so widely and so uncritically, he'd earned the nickname "the champion crackpot."

Mr. Train had stopped in Paris during the last days of the Commune. He was en route from Britain, where he'd done a jail term for espousing Irish independence, to Japan, where he proposed to sample the pleasures of mixed bathing in the nude. He loved traveling, and wherever he went, he promoted the unbelievable idea that, thanks to modern steam transportation, a man could circle the globe in eighty days or even less. So far no one had.

In Paris, Train enthusiastically endorsed the Commune—a position of which the Versailles troops sternly disapproved. When they closed in on Train at his hotel, he fled to the balcony, draped himself in American and French flags presumably obtained for the occasion, and shrieked at the soldiers to fire if they dared. They hadn't dared, and so Train had returned to the States, where he rushed to the defense of Victoria Claflin Woodhull. Victoria and her sister, Tennessee Claflin, were two of the more flamboyant members of the suffrage movement. *Woodhull & Claflin's Weekly,* which they edited, spoke out for free love—which Victoria cheerfully admitted practicing. When this caused her to be charged with obscenity, Train took up the cudgels so vigorously, he was arrested for obscenity too.

Lucy Stone wanted no financing from anyone that disreputable. Susan Anthony and Elizabeth Stanton were willing to take the needed money almost anywhere they found it. An argument ensued; the ranks were sundered.

The scuff of a shoe brought Gideon's head around. From a rear hallway, a boy of about nine had appeared, holding a toy locomotive in swarthy hands. For a moment Gideon experienced the eerie sensation of gazing at Louis Kent reborn.

But there were differences, as he recalled from the previous occasion on which he'd met the boy. Julia's son was a handsome youngster with dark hair, olive skin and intense dark eyes. His mouth was less petulant than his father's and his demeanor was vigorous and cheerful rather than arrogant.

Gideon strode forward and extended his hand. "Hello, Carter. You don't remember me."

Carter Kent's gaze lingered on the eye patch. "I believe I should, but—"

"It was Boston, after your father passed away. I'm his second cousin once removed—"

"That's right! Gideon Kent."

"Good for you." They clasped hands.

"Of course I remember now," Carter said with enthusiasm. "You're from the Virginia side of the family. You sang all those cavalry songs for me."

"Exactly." Gideon smiled. " 'Jine the Cavalry' and the rest. I'm happy to see you looking so well."

"Gideon Kent?" said a lilting female voice. He turned and his mouth dropped open, and for a moment he was totally unable to utter a word.

iii

Julia Sedgwick was almost as he remembered her: two or three years older than Gideon, tiny, no more than five feet, but beautifully proportioned with well-rounded hips and small, high breasts. What caused him to be so astonished was her costume. She wore pale green slippers and a robe de chambre of emerald silk with collar and cuffs trimmed in white fur.

As she walked forward to greet him, the robe grew taut over her hip. He saw a hint of a whaleboned corset. The throat of the gown was discreetly tied, and the sleeves reached to her wrist. But he could only think of the costume as "advanced." Although it was undoubtedly cooler than a regular dress, proper women simply did not greet callers in attire designed for the bedchamber.

Julia's son probably didn't realize his mother was being unconventional, Gideon thought. From the glow in Carter's dark eyes, it was obvious that he'd have worshiped her if she'd been clothed in rags. Still, Gideon could understand why Julia was something of a celebrity among hack drivers at the city's best hotel—and why one particular driver had classed her with society's withered rose petals, as prostitutes were called in sensational newspapers which dared mention them at all.

Julia glided up to him, glossy dark hair trailing around her shoulders. He sniffed and got another shock. The stubby cylinder trailing smoke from her left hand was a cheroot!

"Gideon, what a happy surprise!" She shook his hand, man fashion.

"Yes—yes—" Somehow her appearance made him tongue-tied. It didn't help to remind himself that suffragists often preferred avant-garde fashions such as Mrs. Bloomer's trouser outfit. It didn't help at all; he felt like he'd wandered into a bordello.

She noticed his discomfort. "Oh dear! I am sorry if the robe puts you off. Poor Mr. Robbins who handles my account with Cooke and Company almost fainted when he first saw it. But I just despise being uncomfortable around home. And life's too short to spend it fretting about outdated conventions." She put her arm around her son and hugged him with obvious affection. "As long as the only man in my life thinks I'm respectable, what do I care about the rest?"

Carter gazed at her fondly. Julia squeezed him once more, then walked back to her guest.

"I'm delighted to see you. I've been home four days and won't be going on another lecture tour for a week. Carter and I get very little company. Have you had dinner?"

"No, but I only planned a brief courtesy call—"

"Nonsense!" Though lightly spoken, the word carried an undertone of insistence. She was accustomed to having her way—with audiences and everyone else, he suspected. "Neither have we. You must join us. Carter—"

"What, Mother?"

"Please run to cook and tell her we'll be wanting something good in about an hour."

With a look at the tall, tawny-haired man who was beginning to recover his composure, the boy asked, "Three of us?"

Julia didn't even bother to glance Gideon's way. There was nothing overtly haughty about that, just a calm unspoken certainty that no one would deny her wants once she'd expressed them. A strong woman, Gideon thought. A mite too strong, perhaps. Yet he found himself fascinated.

"Yes," she said, giving Gideon another warm smile. "Three of us."

CHAPTER V

"THE LUCY STONE BROTHEL, WEST"

i

JULIA TUCKED HER hand around Gideon's arm. "Do come along. I'll finish with Mr. Robbins and then we can have a good chat. I'm curious to know why you're in Chicago."

He felt the firm pressure of her breast against his forearm as she swept him into the library. She introduced him to the portly representative of the investment banking house.

"Pleasure, I'm sure," the Cooke's man said, looking vaguely disapproving of the tall and rather raffish young man who compressed Robbins' limp hand in a much stronger one.

"What remains to be done, Mr. Robbins?" Julia asked.

"Very little, madam. I need your initials on the list of issues which we recommend you buy and sell."

Robbins extended the sheet of paper. Julia released Gideon's arm and signed quickly. "Don't forget the additional five hundred thousand in Northern Pacific bonds," she said.

"Naturally not. I shall telegraph the purchase order before I leave the city."

"And I'll see you again next quarter."

Gideon watched with some astonishment as she took Robbins' arm as commandingly as she'd taken his. She ushered the bank representative toward the door. Just as he left, the soberly dressed banker looked at Gideon with unconcealed envy. As if he thought the younger man was in for an evening of licentious revelry.

Julia shut the library doors. The windows were open. They faced north, to the mansion where the party was in progress. Julia walked to the cold hearth, discarded the stub of her cheroot and took another from a blue and white porcelain jar on the mantel.

"I have precious little time for financial matters," she said. "And not much head for them, either. I let Cooke's handle everything. They're the most solid banking house in the nation, everyone says." Her blue eyes sparkled as she struck a match and lifted it to her cigar. "Does it shock you to see a woman smoking?"

"No, not at all," he lied. "Would you stop if it did?"

She laughed, genuinely amused. "I doubt it. Perhaps I'd honor another woman's request. But never a man's."

He'd never been much good at banter, and he wasn't now. He remained silent as she dropped the match into the fireplace and sat down amid a roiling cloud of smoke. She pointed to a chair opposite hers.

"Do sit down. Tell me how you've been."

"Well enough, thanks." He sat, beginning to wonder why he'd come here—and why he was staying. Dealing with Julia's quick mind and strong will wasn't easy or especially comfortable.

"And how is your very nice wife?"

"Oh"—unconsciously, his voice grew muted—"busy attending to domestic matters. As usual. We have a second child now."

"Do you! That's grand. A boy or another girl?"

"A boy." Briefly, he described Will's birth and some of Eleanor's activities. Julia was smiling in a relaxed, interested way. It put him more at ease. "Margaret does have a terrible fear that Eleanor's outgoing disposition will drive her into something altogether unsuitable for girls."

With a tart smile, she said, "Such as marriage?"

Gideon laughed. "I think it's the theater Margaret fears most."

"Well, I can understand why your wife might believe the theater isn't a proper career for a respectable girl. On the other hand, we live in a changing world. Every woman must be given the right to do what she wants, not merely what she's ordered to do by a parent or a husband—or by custom. I came to that realization a trifle belatedly, I'm afraid. I was dreadfully ignorant when I married Louis. Ignorant and spoiled. I got the first of a series of very bad jolts when I consulted a lawyer about divorcing your late cousin. New York State was and is far more liberal than most. But I discovered that even under New York law, my rights pertaining to property and to custody of Carter were severely limited—and that I only had any rights at all because Susan Anthony and Elizabeth Stanton had worked so hard, and endured so much humiliation, to get amendments passed to the 1848 Woman's Property Bill. I wonder, Gideon"—a slow puff on the little cigar; then a note of seriousness in her mildly sardonic tone—"I do wonder if you or any man can appreciate the profound shock a woman feels when she is first told that, in most states, marriage renders her a nonperson. With no rights to possession of the children she suffered to bear. No voice in the disposition of her own property which became her husband's the moment they spoke the marriage vows. I got a great shock when I began to learn those things. In fact, after I left Louis in '62, what I discovered about the status of women gradually changed my whole existence."

He nodded. "I've always been curious as to how you became a suffragist."

"To really explain it, I have to admit some very unflattering things about myself. And I have to go back to the days when I was still married to your cousin. At that time I divided people into two groups. Those few—a very few!—whom my wretchedly spoiled upbringing led me to believe were my equals, and all the rest—the great majority—who weren't. Let me give you an example of which I'm truly ashamed. My attitude toward black people. Do you know that as a child, I hardly even realized they existed, except in a peripheral way? They existed to wait on me. Hold carriage doors. Fetch and carry my wraps. Then, early in the war I began to grow disenchanted with your cousin. I think it started when I realized Louis could philander without drawing criticism. But his wife? Never!"

Gideon withheld an ungentlemanly question about whether she had wanted to philander and with whom.

"Anyway, when my—devotion to dear Louis began to waver, I started doing things I'd never done previously, including paying attention to the outside world. Just a little at first, but even that was enough to make me aware of the tremendous outcry from the abolitionists. Late in 1861 I consulted an attorney about my rights if I should decide to leave Louis. I got absolutely furious when the lawyer told me I had next to none. Then I thought of the abolitionists. Here were hundreds, even thousands of reformers arguing and propagandizing about setting blacks free—and properly so, I've come to realize—but who was writing and speaking about liberating women? Well, of course there *were* people doing that—and had been for several decades—but it took me a few more years and a great deal of study and soul searching to decide I wanted to join them."

She'd started her journey out of bondage by reading a book, she said. "Margaret Fuller's *Great Law Suit*. Do you know it?" He did, but only by name. "Just what I'd expect from a man! There's never been a greater statement of the conditions forced upon women in this country. Next I went back to old newspapers. I read some of Fanny Wright's lectures—that is, the sections male editors would deign to print! Wright and Fuller were the two who spearheaded the movement in the first half of the century. They were both dead by the mid-fifties, but they'd laid the groundwork. By the time I'd gone through the horrible wrangle of a divorce—and those devastating discoveries about women's property rights—I was leaning toward conversion to the cause. My God, Gideon, do you realize it's barely been ten years since women were acknowledged to be *equal* with their husbands as guardians of their children? And that's only in New York. If Louis had cared the first thing about Carter, I'd never have gotten custody of my son. But Louis never really wanted a family. Children were a bother. In any case, it wasn't until 1866 that I really got over the divorce. It's another shock to the system—and I trust you know it does stigmatize a woman. In any case, five years ago I took another major step. I went to one of Lucy Stone's lectures."

Her blue eyes looked through the smoke, and through Gideon, into the past.

"Such a small, petite lady. But a powerful speaker with

that lovely voice of hers. The crowd was typical, I've learned. Mostly men. Mostly rowdy. Lucy shamed them into silence when she gazed right into the auditorium— right into their faces, one by one—and talked about the night she was born. Her mother described it when Lucy was growing up. If ever there was a story that damns men as unthinking practitioners of slavery, Lucy's birth is it. The night she came into the world, her mother was already in labor when she had to fix supper for a haying crew that was working on the family farm. Lucy's father couldn't lower himself to cook a meal—that was women's work. Then, before she could get on with the business of lying down by herself to deliver a baby, Mrs. Stone had to milk eight cows. But Lucy's mother *accepted* all that. She said it was a woman's duty to submit! Lucy was horrified. From that moment on, she knew she'd spend her life trying to change such stupid ideas."

Julia paused and drew a breath. "I sat in that lecture hall with my spine prickling and my head spinning—and I felt I had to have a part in changing such ideas, too. Because I had lived through a similar proof that a woman's lot is still a pretty miserable one. We're a long way from being as free as the black people, Gideon. At least there were a good many clergymen fighting for abolition. We have almost none on our side."

"That much I know," he said, and added with a wry smile, "Book of Genesis, chapter three."

"Yes!" Julia cried, jumping up and pacing. "The weapon they use against us all the time. 'And thy desire shall be thy husband, and he shall rule over thee.' Lucy says she nearly fell into an apoplectic fit the first time she read that. The Scripture's full of similar remarks. Lucy's learned Greek and Hebrew just so she can examine the original texts and see whether the translators were faithful to them, or only to their male prejudices—oh, but here I am chattering on and on—"

"I find it very interesting," he told her, meaning it. "When did you move to Chicago?"

"In the spring of 1868. I was happy to come. Lucy wanted me to cover the central part of the country, and the East Coast had a lot of unpleasant memories. The contractors finished this house exactly two weeks before Louis died—" With a pitying look, she gazed into the fireplace where she'd thrown the cheroot a bit earlier. "Poor Louis. In a topsy-turvy way, I owe him a great deal. I would never have found my real calling if he hadn't been such a bastard."

She drew another deep breath, managed a smile. "But I've said entirely too much—and haven't even had the courtesy to ask about your business in the city."

"Basically, it's my little newspaper that brought me here."

"Labor's Beacon."

He blinked his good right eye. "You know it?"

"Certainly. The Association keeps track of all liberal-thinking publications. I never knew you had journalistic inclinations, Gideon."

"Inclinations, perhaps, but not much talent. I've had to teach myself to write. Hasn't been easy—"

"When Louis was buried, you were doing organizing work."

"I decided I could reach more workingmen, and do it more effectively, as a writer and editor. You know my father bought the *Union* from Louis' estate—" She nodded. "I now have a quarter interest in it. I could join the staff tomorrow. But I don't think the other three owners would care for me airing my views in the paper. You know how unpopular the movement is."

"Indeed I do. On a par with mine. Go on."

"The *Union* would lose circulation if it took labor's part too openly or too often. I hate to see that kind of compromise, but I know it's a fact of economic life. That's why I've continued on my own. As to Chicago, I was invited to write up an organizational effort by men who work for one of the rail lines headquartered here."

She leaned forward, the green gown pulling taut across the bodice of her corset. "Which line?"

"The Wisconsin and Prairie."

"What? Tom Courtleigh's railroad?"

"You sound surprised. Do you know him?"

She walked to the window. "I most certainly do. He's a dreadful prig, and a hypocrite as well. Prays at the Episcopal church on Sunday and steals right and left Monday through Saturday." She pointed across to the huge mansion brilliant with light. "I have the misfortune to be his neighbor."

Gideon gaped. "That's Courtleigh's place?"

"I'm afraid so."

He rushed to her side so excitedly, he collided with her. His leg touched hers for an instant and he jumped back as if stung. He gazed down at the sweet-smelling luster of her dark hair, experiencing a sharp physical reaction. Julia was gracious enough to keep from looking at him, as if she sensed his embarrassment and didn't want to add to it.

"I really don't know Courtleigh well," she said. "Undoubtedly that's a blessing. When I first moved into this house, I tried to call on him and his mother. She lives with him, you understand. I did the same with all my neighbors—a social courtesy—but Courtleigh's was the only house in which my cards were returned without a reply. In other words, no one in there would speak to me. I understand it's because Courtleigh and his mother are violently opposed to the movement, and consider me no better than a whore."

Gideon almost gasped aloud; the word was never spoken in polite mixed company. Julia went on.

"I've even heard Courtleigh refers to this house as the Lucy Stone Brothel, West." She laughed. "I've considered hanging red lanterns in the windows some evening, to convince Tom and his mama the joke's come true."

Gideon chuckled. "You should hire some shopgirls to parade up and down in their shifts."

"The very thing! I can just see him contemplating a brothel next door. He'd think plunging property values and have a heart seizure—" She giggled uncontrollably for several moments. "Dear me, I haven't laughed so hard in months."

"Nor I," Gideon said, wiping his eye.

She smoothed a palm over her bosom and drew a deep breath. "You say Courtleigh's employees are trying to organize the line?"

"That's right, starting with the switchmen who work in the W and P yards."

She thought a moment, then clapped her hands together. "Do you know, Gideon—I've never attended a labor meeting. I think it would be fascinating. A furtherance of my

education, you might say. You'll take me to your meeting,
won't you?"

Coming as it did on the heels of her use of a forbidden
word, the new request left him speechless again. What an
unsettling creature she was! Perhaps that was part of the
suffragist strategy—to disarm opponents by addling them
with behavior even the most liberal of men didn't expect
from a woman.

His hesitation produced the same glint in her eye he'd
seen when she got rid of banker Robbins.

"Of course you will!"

"No, I don't believe I should."

She was a shade prickly when she said, "Pray tell me
why not."

"Courtleigh has threatened trouble."

In a few brief sentences he described Florian's warnings.
He was again surprised by her reaction. He'd expected
alarm at a mention of danger. It only seemed to exhila-
rate her.

"I insist you take me. And no arguments. I assure you
I'll come to no harm. I can take care of myself—why, I've
been mobbed off more platforms than I can remember. Hit
with spoiled fruit and rocks a dozen times—it's settled."

"Now just a damn—"

The library doors opened. The butler looked in—but not
at Gideon.

"Dinner, madam."

"Thank you. We'll be right along." She smiled up at
Gideon, slipped her arm in his and held it tight, as though
they were longtime friends, even intimates. She was like
some natural force, he thought with mingled irritation and
amazement. She was like a hurricane that blew away whatever resistance it encountered. He'd never met a woman
like her.

She was laughing as she led him out of the library.

"Yes, indeed, we shall go to that meeting. Two scandalous, outrageous, thoroughly immoral thorns in the side of
Mr. Tom Courtleigh. We're two of a kind, Gideon."

Her blue eyes shone as she looked up at him and
squeezed his arm. "I'm so glad you came by tonight!"

ii

They had a splendid dinner, and the longer he was in her presence, the easier it became to carry on a conversation. She had definite opinions on most issues of the day, from Grant's abilities as a chief executive to the debate over greenbacks versus gold. But her willfulness showed only occasionally, and she could listen to conflicting opinions without interrupting—though not without demonstrating impatience with a definite pink cast in her cheeks. By the end of the meal, she'd so charmed him that, in spite of his better judgment, he agreed to take her to Ericsson's the following evening. As she was showing him out, she said softly, "Thank you, Gideon. I knew you would."

He was able to laugh at his own expense. "You knew I would because I'm just a mere man, eh? No match for the Lucy Stoner juggernaut—"

"Nonsense. That isn't it at all." She was smiling, but her eyes seemed full of a peculiarly intense emotion as she gazed at him. Then she glanced away and murmured, "It's because you're very nice."

She reddened again, realizing she'd grown too personal. He was flattered yet uncomfortable: glad to have spent such a delightful evening in the company of a woman who was bright yet feminine; glad at the same time to be starting for the door.

Suddenly a sonorous ringing drifted through open windows. She frowned. "That's the courthouse bell."

She listened to the tolling a moment longer. "It's the fire signal again. I don't know how many more days we can go without rain—well, good evening, Gideon." For the second time she grasped his hand and shook it. "I'll look forward to seeing you tomorrow."

Those frank blue eyes continued to disconcert him, and he knew why. Because she was lovely, and when they'd been talking, Margaret had been forgotten. All too easily.

It made him feel guilty, made him let go of her hand very fast.

"Yes, certainly. Good night."

Her coachman drove him downtown to the Dorset and let him off. The streets around the hotel were packed with people streaming toward the south branch of the river.

Some were frightened, some merely curious. Directly to the west, a bright red glare filled the sky.

"Bad one, looks like," the coachman commented before he turned his rig around and started away. Gideon joined the crowds and walked all the way to the Adams Street bridge. In response to his questions, he was told that a planing mill on Canal Street had caught fire. The blaze had spread to a lumber yard. On the other side of the river, steam pumpers and hose carts went thundering along fire-reddened streets.

The wind had increased; it was blowing briskly out of the southwest. Finally the fire seemed to be contained. He returned to his room at the Dorset.

He found he couldn't go to sleep. The fire might have been contained but it was still burning. The glare illuminated the ceiling and one wall. That kept him awake, and so did memories of Julia.

Her eyes.

Her provocative emerald-colored robe.

Her struggle to educate herself—a struggle much like his.

Her interest in affairs of the world—an interest much like Margaret's before she had begun to change.

He felt guilty about the images of Julia in his mind. But somehow that guilt didn't banish them.

He tried to shut out the firelight by closing the curtains. As he'd feared, that turned the room into an oven. He opened the curtains again, rolled onto his side with his back to the windows and the scarlet sky, and finally drifted off.

The fire burned well into Sunday. It razed a sixteen-acre, four-block area. Hotel guests in the Dorset's dining room at noon spoke of nothing else. The waiters said Chicago absolutely could not tolerate one more such fire. As one put it, overheard by Gideon on his way out, "If Lucifer wanted to bring this town to grief an' make it burn like a cauldron of kerosene, all he'd have to do is toss in one match. No, strike just one spark. That's all. One spark in the wrong place at the wrong time."

It was another hot day, but Gideon shivered as he left.

Chapter VI

Invasion at Ericsson's

i

AGAIN GIDEON WALKED all the way to State and Twentieth.
The meeting was scheduled for eight in the evening, but
Julia had invited him for supper at five.

As he strode south, he began to perspire. The temperature had to be well over eighty, even though the sun was
already setting in a scarlet haze on the prairie west of the
city. A stiff wind blew from the southwest, raising whitecaps
on the lake. The sun put red highlights on the water.

Dinner was elegant, with a game bird bisque, then a
choice of Dover sole or a roast of Texas beef. Carter complained that he liked neither until Julia shushed him. She
took the beef with a Bordeaux, Gideon the fish with a cool
and delicious liebfraumilch. She had to spell the name for
him twice. He wasn't embarrassed; he wrote it down on a
slip of paper so he'd remember it.

The hostess was as elegant as her table. She wore an
expensive-looking summer frock of lavender foulard with
long sleeves that flared at her wrists. Her overskirt bunched
up in back over a French tournure, a device which the
British termed a bustle. In another of the dizzying changes
upsetting the modern world, a woman's appearance from

the rear had become more important than the way she looked from the front.

Again he was astonished by Julia's grasp of political and social matters though the cause to which she was closest came up most often.

"I know it's bad form to speak ill of the dead, but, Gideon, there's just no denying Louis was an absolute rogue. Why, when I think of the calumnies about the movement he ordered published in the *Union*—" She was too exercised to continue.

"Ordered, that's the key word," he replied. "The editor, Theo Payne, had to print that sort of bilge or lose his job. Now that he's running the paper without so much pressure, I hope you've noticed the attacks have stopped."

"I haven't. I quit reading the rag years ago. Along with James Gordon Bennett's *Herald*—my God, *there's* a male supremacist for you! Gordon Bennett, I mean. He once wrote about a member of the movement who—as he put it—formerly ran about to suffrage gatherings but now stays home because she finally got her rights in the shape of a baby. Pregnancy, that's what he considers the proper cure for our mania!"

"Mother really does hate that man," Carter said from his side of the table. He was eating the beef with buttermilk instead of Bordeaux. It was uncanny, the way he resembled his father yet lacked the petulance that had marred Louis' good looks.

Influential publishers who opposed women's rights weren't the only ones who roused Julia's ire. She could quote verbatim—and with scorn—from the British philosopher Herbert Spencer, whose Social Darwinism had become the exculpatory doctrine of the nation's business moguls.

" 'Society is constantly excreting its unhealthy, imbecile, slow, vacillating, faithless members'—that is Spencer exactly, Gideon."

"I haven't read his stuff," Gideon admitted. "I know I should. I tried *Principles of Biology* last year and found it just too damn turgid. Isn't he the chap who's always talking about survival of the fittest?"

She threw him an admiring glance. "Good for you. Somehow people always fancy Mr. Darwin coined the phrase, but he didn't. Survival of the fittest is Spencer's claptrap. Well, I *say* it's claptrap—" A shrug. "I can't confirm or deny its scientific accuracy. Darwin may be correct about the strong surviving and prospering at the expense of the weak in the animal kingdom. But if Spencer's right and that's the way it's to be among human beings in America, I'll move out!"

"But you haven't yet."

"No, because, thank God, despite the climate of corruption in this country, there are still some people who believe the laws apply equally to everyone, and everything guaranteed in the Constitution is guaranteed to everyone, no matter how strong or weak, fit or unfit, popular or unpopular that individual may be."

Gideon nodded to agree. How much alike in their convictions they were!

"I don't doubt all of the President's Wall Street cronies fairly worship Mr. Spencer," she went on. "Whether Grant has ever heard of Spencer is debatable. I'm afraid the only philosophic principle he understands is 'forward—march!' "

"I think he's an honest and well-intentioned man," Gideon replied.

Carter gaped. "How can you say that, Mr. Kent? He whipped the devil out of your side!"

"Carter, no swearing."

"Ma, I said devil, not hell.".

Affection lit her eyes as she teased him, "Yes, but I know what you were thinking." He blushed. She turned back to Gideon. "That *is* quite an admission for an ex-Confederate."

"The war's over, Julia."

"And Butcher Grant hasn't changed. He's still well intentioned and thoroughly naïve. I wish we could get him out of there before the whole country's plundered."

"You're being unfair," he argued. "I imagine Grant's doing the best he can. He never pretended he wanted the position or that he was qualified for it. The Republicans wanted *him*. The hero. He's consistently said he's no politician—"

"An honest admission for a change! He certainly isn't a politician. He's also no president. Any woman could do better."

The disagreement had grown just a little heated, but her last remark took the acrimony out of it; the twinkle in her eye said she was teasing again.

"You?" he retorted.

"Mother would make a fine one," Carter put in.

"Well, I'd certainly like to try it," she admitted. "And I would if I could only figure out how to live to age one hundred and fifty. By then the electorate may be ready for a female in the White House."

Some impulse made him say, "You'd be the prettiest president ever in office, I'll bet."

Carter whooped and applauded. Gideon turned pink. Julia smiled and gazed at him steadily. Then, turning pink herself, she murmured, "Why, thank you, sir." He quickly returned his attention to his silver sherbet dish. He felt as if he'd walked into an oven.

After dinner, Julia kissed her son good night and then led Gideon through the kitchen and out to the carriage house. He was just a bit fuzzy-headed from all the wine, and hot in his frock coat and waistcoat, both of which he would have liked to remove. But the frock coat concealed the LeMat shoved down into his belt near his left hip. He didn't want Julia to know he was going to the meeting armed.

A groom drove a landau out of the carriage house. It was the same handsome vehicle which had returned him to his hotel the preceding evening. He peered around, hunting for the driver when the groom hopped down. Julia tugged on mauve gloves. She saw Gideon's puzzled expression and explained, "Eustace has the night off. I'll handle the horses."

The landau was drawn by a matched team of splendid, glossy bays. Julia hoisted her skirts, not the least embarrassed to reveal sheer lavender hose above her shoe tops. She climbed the front wheel like a teamster. In a moment she was settled on the seat.

He reached for the reins. "See here—you must let me drive."

"But these are high-spirited animals, Gideon."

"All the more reason."

"I assure you I know how to control them."

"Well, damn it, so do I!" he exclaimed, red in the face.

Her smile was sweet but her eyes were mocking.

"Is that because you're a male, and thus instinctively a horseman—while I, being a mere woman, couldn't possibly take charge of such a team?" A sigh. "You do have some fusty, old-fashioned ideas—especially for a trade unionist. We'll have to work on changing those." She patted the seat. "Meantime, climb up."

Redder than ever, he shook his head. "It's a matter of principle. It looks—it looks ridiculous for a man—"

"To ride in a carriage driven by a woman? What utter foolishness!"

Once more she patted the seat. He saw the determination in her blue eyes, and all at once realized how stuffy and traditional his protest made him seem. He burst out laughing. So did she.

"Do come up, Gideon," she urged. "You'll soon get used to it."

Amused, he climbed up beside her.

"And for heaven's sake, stop looking so stricken. Wounded pride isn't a fatal disease, even among men. *Giddap!*"

She flicked the reins over the backs of the bays and smartly turned the landau east to the next street.

ii

Julia had told him she owned the entire block between State and Wabash; the back part of her lot was mostly shrubs and fruit trees, he saw. She turned north on Wabash at Twenty-first, the south side of her property, and the trees and shrubbery prevented them from seeing another carriage swinging into Wabash from Twentieth—prevented them, that is, until they were virtually into the intersection.

Frantically, Julia reined the bays. The second vehicle, a brougham, would have collided with them if she hadn't. Both carriages stopped and the blue-chinned driver of the brougham brandished his whip.

"Watch yer damn team, woman. Better still, leave the drivin' to those who do it right. Menfolk!"

Seething, Julia whispered, "That's Tom Courtleigh's carriage."

Gideon's cheeks darkened. He reached across, snatched the reins and shook them so the bays bolted forward.

"What on earth?" Julia cried as Gideon halted the team again, directly in front of the brougham. The closed, boxy vehicle could not move forward. In the side nearest the landau, a pale face could be glimpsed at an oval window. Gideon tossed the reins aside and jumped down.

"Move!" the other driver shouted at him.

"Not until I speak with Mr. Courtleigh."

Julia folded her hands in her lap, a smile that was half astonishment and half admiration curling her lips. Courtleigh's driver hesitated, not knowing whether to try the whip on such a formidable-looking fellow. By then Gideon had stalked to the side of the brougham and was reaching for the door handle.

He saw that the person by the oval window was a young woman, delicately pretty but with nervous eyes and an unhealthy pallor. He levered the handle. Latched. The woman grew panicky. Beyond her, a much less distinct blur showed where Courtleigh was seated. Gideon could make out no details of the railroad president's face.

"Open up, Courtleigh!" He hammered the brougham's side. The driver warned him off but he paid no attention. "I have something to say to you about your tame dog Florian, so open up." He pounded again.

Even Julia was startled by Gideon's ferocity. A youngster rolling a hoop along Wabash paused and stared at the man beating on the brougham. Suddenly the young woman was pushed aside. Another face loomed in the window: thin, long-nosed, aristocratic. Thomas Courtleigh had wavy auburn hair, small, almost feminine ears lying flat against his head, a narrow and thin-lipped mouth. He was thirty-five, no more.

He leaned in front of his companion—a relative or his fiancée, Gideon assumed—and gazed at the young man with ugly contempt in his hazel eyes. Then he lifted his right hand in the window. He slashed the hand sideways, a sharp gesture of dismissal. Of banishment.

Gideon growled something and started to twist the handle back and forth. Courtleigh raised a cane in his left hand and rapped the ceiling of the brougham. "Well, ye've had fair warning," the driver bellowed at Gideon.

Julia gave a cry of alarm. The whip hissed. Before Gideon could jump back, the lash laid a streak of red on his left cheek.

The insult was worse than the blow itself. He lunged for the driver's arm and missed. The man was already whipping and maneuvering his team around the snorting bays. Within a few seconds, the brougham went clipping away up Wabash, leaving Gideon in a cloud of dust.

Julia got down from the landau and hurried to his side. He pushed her kerchief away. "Don't. You'll ruin it."

"Nonsense." She stood on tiptoe and dabbed at the whip mark. He smelled her cologne as she added in a husky voice, "That was a very foolish thing to do, my dear."

But she wasn't chastising him. Her blue eyes shone with an admiring light as she bloodied the kerchief to clean his cheek, touching him and lingering over the small wound longer than was actually necessary.

iii

The working-class neighborhood immediately west of the Chicago River was inhabited chiefly by Scandinavians, Bohemians and Irish, Julia said as they took a leisurely drive through the Lake Street business district. About half of Chicago's population lived west of the south branch, in fact.

It was dark by the time they doubled back and crossed the river on the Van Buren Street bridge. They proceeded west, then south on Canal to Taylor Street, which ran east and west. The district was a hodgepodge of saloons, woodworking mills and narrow residences set on lots no more than thirty feet wide and four or five times as deep.

Julia brought the carriage to a stop in front of the correct address on Taylor. Gideon tied the reins around one of the three-inch posts supporting the wooden sidewalk. He noticed that Ericsson's narrow lot had two equally narrow cottages on it, one behind the other and both facing Taylor Street. At the far end of the property he glimpsed a barn, the site of the meeting.

He took out his pocket watch. "Quarter till eight. We rambled around town a bit more than I thought."

And he'd enjoyed it, especially after the unsettling encounter with the president of the W & P. The arrogance of the man in the brougham made him doubly glad he'd come to Chicago. No matter what the outcome of this meeting, he'd give Thomas Courtleigh a roasting in *Labor's Beacon.*

Julia took his arm and they started toward the passage which ran between the Ericsson lot and the one adjoining. On the porch of the house fronting on Taylor, a man and a woman, shadow-figures, rocked in wooden rockers. Neither of them spoke. Gideon supposed Ericsson lived in the rear cottage and rented the curbside one. The guess proved right when a skinny ten year old in old clothing waved from the stoop of the second house.

"Mr. Kent?"

"That's right."

The boy ran to them. "I'm Torvald Ericsson—" When he realized Gideon's companion was a woman, he gave her a startled look. "They're waiting in the barn. Not everyone's here yet."

"Thank you, son."

Gideon and Julia moved on through the dark. He caught a whiff of wood shavings, then nearly stumbled into a huge white mound of them at the rear of the second cottage. The whole area had the clean tang of freshly cut wood.

Nils Ericsson was waiting in the doorway of the run-down barn, silhouetted by lamplight from behind. Gideon noted the surprise, then the concern on the railroader's face as Julia became visible. Ericsson tried to conceal his dismay as he said, "I didn't realize you'd brought your wife to Chicago."

"This isn't my wife—" Gideon began, realizing how suspicious that sounded.

Julia intervened. "I'm a good friend and onetime relative. I was formerly married to Gideon's cousin. He's dead now. I'm very interested in your cause, Mr. Ericsson. I live in the city, and when Gideon called on me, I grew positively rude until he gave in and agreed to bring me along. You mustn't blame him for my presence," she finished in a disarming way.

How clever she was, he thought. He blessed her for avoiding the subject of her morally questionable divorce, and for not mentioning her suffragist connections. She had wisely refrained from antagonizing the already suspicious men—a dozen or so—watching them from inside the barn. The men sat or stood, frowning at Julia and her finery. Kerosene lanterns cast a dim light over the men. Several pipes put a fragrant blue haze in the air.

Ericsson gave Julia another doubtful glance and accepted the inevitable. He ushered the new arrivals into the barn. There was an awkward period in which Gideon introduced himself and tried to elicit comments about the switchmen's grievances. Most of the men knew *Labor's Beacon* at least by name, but they were intimidated by Julia's presence, and said little in response to Gideon's questions. Julia sensed the deepening suspicion and withdrew to a gloomy corner. She found a crate, stood it on end and sat down, hoping they'd forget about her.

Gradually they did. They gathered around Gideon, beginning to speak more freely. Then, over one man's shoulder, Gideon saw Julia take a cheroot from her reticule. She studied it a moment and put it away. He was relieved to see that no one else had noticed.

He had already decided to say nothing about his warning from Sidney Florian, or tonight's encounter with Courtleigh. He was particularly afraid that a mention of Florian's threats might dissolve the meeting before it began. But he did offer some heartfelt opinions.

"I don't know Mr. Courtleigh as well as you, but I do know a little. It's quite obvious he's a nabob who lives in style while you and your families lack even the security of a few dollars' income if you're injured on the job or, God forbid, killed. I'm glad you're starting out to change that tonight. I'm glad you're organizing to get postmortem benefits, shorter hours and higher wages. *Labor's Beacon* will be printing the story of your effort—and, I'm sure, its happy outcome."

"Fine, just fine," said a man with an Irish lilt in his voice. "But you won't be printing all our names, now will you?"

There was laughter, loud but nervous. Gideon smiled. "No, I won't be doing that."

"Here's the last of them," Ericsson announced, ushering in two more shabbily dressed men.

"Hallo, Bengt. Hallo, Gunther," the others called. Ericsson's handsome tow-haired son followed the late arrivals into the barn. Again Gideon was introduced. Then Ericsson took a place in the center of the group.

"Fellows, you know there is no official speaker here this evening. Nor any program except us putting our heads together and deciding how we might start a yard brotherhood. I don't think there's much doubt we need one—"

"None," growled the big man named Gunther. Most murmured agreement.

"Good." Ericsson nodded. "I do want to remind you that we have a real honor conferred upon us by Mr. Kent's presence. As he said, he's going to write up the procedures we follow, in the hope they'll be useful to other men working for other railroads around the—"

He stopped and heads turned. They had all heard a team of horses pulling into the alley which ran behind the barn, parallel to Taylor Street. Torvald Ericsson dashed to a back door and peered into the darkness. As the thud of hoofs and creak of axles grew louder, he spun.

"Express wagon, Pa. What are they doing delivering on Sunday?"

Ericsson scratched his graying hair. "I can't imagine."

But Gideon could. As the wagon ground to a halt, he unbuttoned his waistcoat. Someone gasped when he drew out the LeMat and stepped forward.

"Douse those lanterns. I'm afraid Mr. Courtleigh's sent us a few visitors, and I don't think they'll be sympathetic to—"

He didn't have time to finish. The alley door crashed back. One man managed to reach and blow out a lantern, but the rest were staring at the cadaverous figure bending to duck inside. Lamplight flashed on his small plated revolver.

Tonight Sidney Florian wore patched trousers and a castoff black jacket. He swaggered forward, glancing from face to face. The other men fell back. Most recognized Florian and were obviously terrified by the presence of a company man.

Footsteps thudded outside; other men were running along both sides of the barn, surrounding it. Florian's eyes came to rest on Gideon.

"Hallo, Kent. Didn't pay attention to what I said, eh?" His close-set eyes drifted to Julia. "Even brought a doxy with you. She must belong to you because she's too finely dressed to belong to any of these unwashed sods."

He dropped his free hand, licked at a silver canine tooth. "Well, we can figure out something to make her regret she tagged along." He fingered his crotch and grinned. "Damn if we can't."

Gideon colored. Florian laughed loudly, then waved his revolver.

"Toss that gun to me. There are boys behind you. They'll jam their stickers in your back if you don't cooperate."

Gideon's belly ached. He was standing six or seven feet from the main door but facing away from it. Julia was on his left. Her frightened face and glances of warning said there were indeed men behind him, though he had difficulty sorting out the sounds they made; three more burly thugs were entering noisily by the alley door and spreading out around Florian. The W & P workers weren't outnumbered by any means. But Florian's blacklegs had knives and shot-loaded socks, and that made all the difference.

The switchmen showed signs of wanting to break and run so they wouldn't be identified. But if they ran for it, Florian would shoot them down. Gideon decided it might be better to try to seize the initiative; that way, he might be able to help them get away safely.

Florian's horselike face contorted. "Come on, Kent. Hand it over. No? Then I'll take it."

He stepped forward, ducking to avoid a lantern hanging from a beam. His revolver momentarily pointed at the ground.

Gideon nodded as if he meant to give in. Florian saw that and smiled. Gideon raised the LeMat in a swift, smooth motion. Too late, Florian realized what was happening. Gideon shot at the lantern.

The bullet nicked the oil reservoir. Kerosene and glass cascaded on Florian, who screamed like a woman.

"Run!" Gideon yelled. He lowered his head and raced toward Julia. The barn exploded into a bedlam of noise.

He whipped his arm around Julia's waist, then pointed the LeMat at the two hulks who had indeed been poised in the barn door, long dirks in their hands. One of the switchmen dived through an open side window, then another. Someone in an adjoining house yelled a query about the shot. Ericsson was infuriated.

"Kent, we're not going to run from a bunch of—"

Gideon shouted him down: "They *want* you to fight! If one or two get hurt, the rest will never organize!"

He hated saying it, but it was necessary. Ericsson looked baffled and hurt. The rest of the switchmen scrambled out the window while Florian's hirelings waited for orders. The emaciated man signaled for them not to interfere with those who were escaping.

He'd regained his composure. He used a blue bandanna to mop kerosene from his cheeks and forehead. Torvald crouched near the blacklegs in the doorway, tense and angry-eyed.

"You're smart, Kent," Florian said as he put the bandanna away. "Smart or maybe yellow. Either way, we'll let the rest go. But you're going to be an object lesson for them. So are you, Ericsson. You loaned your premises for activities contrary to the company's best interests. Communard activities," he added for Gideon's benefit. He wagged the revolver. "Lads? Chastise Mr. Kent and Mr. Ericsson first. The wench you can save for last. A little reward for a nice piece of work."

The thugs in the doorway nudged one another and started forward. Gideon shoved Julia behind him as, somewhere outside, there was strident yelling.

Florian wet his lips, locked both hands on the butt of his revolver and aimed it at Gideon's head.

"All right, Kent. Crouch down good and slow, and put the gun on the ground."

Gideon obeyed.

"Now stand up. Fine. Boys? Bash him some. Then I'll have my turn with a knife."

Gideon was sure the thugs believed he wouldn't resist because of Florian's gun. So that gave him an advantage, albeit a very small one. The two burly men sidled toward him. One was slightly ahead of the other, tucking his dirk in his belt and balling his right fist for a bare-knuckled swing. Gideon watched the thug's arm for a sign of sudden movement.

With a grunt, the man lunged in, lashing his fist back, then forward. Gideon ducked. The punch missed. He booted the thug in the stomach and shoved him sideways.

Just as he'd hoped, the man stumbled toward Florian and blocked his line of fire. Everyone started shouting except

Gideon, who waited for the second assailant to come darting in with his knife. Before the man got within arm's length, Gideon snatched up the LeMat and fired.

A thunderous explosion—smoke—and the man went shrieking and floundering across the barn, blood streaming down his sleeve. Ericsson jumped another man armed with a knife. Gideon spun toward Florian. The stupefied ringleader shoved the thug who'd ruined his aim, then got off a hasty shot. The bullet chipped a big chunk of wood from a beam above Julia's head.

Gideon was frightened but he tried to do what he'd learned to do in the war—let the fear heighten rather than hamper his concentration. He forced his right hand up, forced himself to take the time necessary to sight, though it seemed forever. Florian wanted to fire again. But Ericsson and his adversary kept reeling back and forth in front of him, locked in a fight for possession of the knife. Gideon finally saw an opening and pulled the trigger.

The bullet struck Florian's right shoulder. The plated revolver dropped between the toes of his boots. With a groan and a dazed look, he sank to his knees, almost like a man praying.

He extended trembling hands toward the ground. The moment his palms touched the dirt floor, his arms gave out. He collapsed on his face, half conscious and trying to crawl toward the alley. He drew his left leg up and pushed with his boot. He pushed a second time. A third. He couldn't move himself forward but he refused to give up. Gideon took no satisfaction from the grotesque sight.

A hurt cry from Ericsson made him turn. Most of Florian's crew had taken a look at their fallen leader and scattered for the darkness outside—a darkness full of a rising clamor of voices. But the man with the knife had gotten Ericsson down, and was hacking at his face. The big man fended off the slashes, taking cuts on the backs of his arms and wrists. Gideon couldn't get a clear shot. Torvald Ericsson rushed to help his father. He grabbed the thug's left shoulder. The man drove his right hand across in front of his chest and plunged the blade into the boy's ribs.

Torvald lurched back, gazing down with round eyes at his red shirt. Then, while his father cried his name, the boy fainted.

The knife wielder jumped up and fled for the door. Gideon fired but missed. He stood shaking while the express wagon rumbled away along the alley. Abandoned by the men he'd paid, Florian kept trying to crawl like some crippled crab. He'd managed to move about a yard, grunting and snuffling and leaving a swath of blood on the ground. But his movements were growing more feeble every moment.

Ericsson and Julia dropped to their knees on either side of the unconscious boy. Gideon's guilt mounted. If he hadn't fired the first time, perhaps Torvald wouldn't have been stabbed. If, if!

Infuriated with himself, he whirled toward the barn door. Why were Ericsson's neighbors shouting so loudly, yet not bothering to rush to the barn? Then he realized it wasn't the fight causing all the commotion. It was a bright, ruddy light shimmering on the walls and rooftops of the cottages facing Taylor Street.

Gideon looked at Torvald. "How is he?"

Pale, Julia said, "I can't tell beyond the fact that he's badly hurt and needs a doctor."

Ericsson's face showed tracks of tears. He gazed at Julia, then Gideon, but saw neither one. "Why did I let him stay? Why didn't I send him to my sister's? Torvald's all I have left—" Impotent rage made him leap up and shriek at the people yelling in the darkness. *"Why are they making so damn much noise?"*

Gideon staggered to the barn doorway. Instantly he felt the strong southwest wind blowing his hair. In the distance someone cried, "It's DeKoven Street. Annie Murray's shed or the O'Leary barn—I don't know which."

The wind tore through his hair and gusted against his face, hot and smoke-stinking. He remembered conversations overheard and had a strange feeling of dread. In a hoarse voice, he said, "There's a fire."

"Oh my God," Julia whispered.

"DeKoven Street," he added. "Where is that?"

Ericsson wiped his mouth, his eyes wild. "Only one block south."

CHAPTER VII

LUCIFER'S MATCH

i

GIDEON SHOVED THE LeMat back in his belt, gently moved the stricken Ericsson aside and lifted Torvald's slashed shirt away from the wound. The cut wasn't wide. But it was impossible to tell how deep it went. Though clotting had started at the ends, blood still oozed from the center.

Gideon raised his head and looked at Ericsson. "Is there a doctor close by? One you regularly use?"

The man shook his head in a vacant way, as if he couldn't hear. It was growing hard to hear anything because of the shouting in the street and the bells of arriving fire equipment. Gideon shook the other man's arm.

"I asked whether you have a doctor!"

New tears filled Ericsson's eyes. "Oh, God—I'm responsible for what's happened to my boy—"

"No! If anyone's responsible, it's Courtleigh. We've got to save your son and then make Courtleigh pay. Now *do you have a doctor*?"

He'd counted on Courtleigh's name jolting the other man out of his daze, and it did. Ericsson wiped his eyes, then shook his head. "A midwife delivered Torvald, and the boy was never sick a day after that. My Helga died suddenly, with no one attending her."

Julia touched Gideon's arm. "My doctor lives in the country. A mile north of the Fullerton Avenue city limits. We could take the boy there."

"Sounds like a pretty good distance, and I'm not sure we should move him at all."

Julia gazed out the door to the sky above the houses. Clouds of sparks were blowing past, driven from the fire site by the wind. She said in an emphatic way, "Well, this place certainly isn't safe. If that fire spreads, we're right in its path. And it *will* spread unless that wind calms down—" She took Gideon's arm. "What if we take the boy and his father as far as my house. Someone can go after Dr. Boling from there."

Bits of burning matter whirled and danced over Ericsson's house. As Gideon watched, several of them fell on its tar paper roof. He realized what the material was: some of the shavings and scrap lumber stockpiled in the neighborhood.

And wasn't this near the scene of last night's fire? Wasn't this a district of lumber yards? Suddenly he remembered another remark overheard at the Dorset. Something about Lucifer setting the town afire with a single match.

He wasn't a superstitious man, but for a moment he had a terrifying presentiment: *This might be it. I think the match has been struck.*

"All right," he said. "Your house. Then I'll go for the doctor."

ii

"Torvald. *Torvald*—"

The sound of Ericsson's renewed sobbing seized Gideon's attention again. The big man was rocking the unconscious boy in his arms. Gideon ran to him.

"For God's sake, Ericsson—don't shake him that way!"

Ericsson kept swaying, cradling his son against his chest, heedless of the blood staining his own clothing. He was beginning to lose control. Gideon's warning came as a shout.

"Don't shake him!"

Ericsson turned his head, seemed to comprehend. He lowered his son to the floor. "What about my sister, Sigrid? She lives in a rooming house near here. Sebor Street—"

"You told me."

"She lives by herself—" Ericsson finally seemed to be aware of the red sky full of flaming wood. "That fire looks bad. I must find Sigrid and make sure she's all right."

"How far is Sebor Street?"

"Just a few blocks north."

"We shouldn't go out of our way, Gideon," Julia put in. "The more bouncing and bumping the boy takes before someone looks after him—"

But Ericsson paid no attention. He turned away from Torvald and, with a curious shine in his firelit eyes, walked out of the barn.

His erratic steps took him toward the back of his cottage. Gideon and Julia exchanged startled looks.

In the yards on either side of Ericsson's property, people were shouting at one another as they hauled furniture from their houses. Sparks were landing on the roofs of almost every building on the block.

Ericsson tottered up the back steps. Julia gaped. "What the devil's wrong with him? *He's going back inside!*"

Gideon ran. He caught the big man just as he opened the cottage door. "Ericsson, don't be a fool. These places will go up any minute. Help me get Torvald into the carriage!"

Ericsson swung around as a foot-long piece of burning wood went sailing overhead. It plummeted suddenly, struck the roof of the barn. Ericsson's lips glistened. His eyes had an irrational light in them. He threw Gideon's hand off. "Leave me alone."

"Listen, you mustn't—"

The big man shoved him. "There are things I have to save! Helga's jewelry. Our wedding photograph. I have no other picture of her."

"There isn't time!" Gideon shouted, trying to drag the man off the stoop. Ericsson let out a deranged howl and clubbed him on the side of the head. Gideon sprawled in the yard. The rear door crashed. Ericsson vanished into the cottage.

Stumbling up, Gideon called his name one more time. Despite the noise around him, he heard Ericsson lumbering through the darkened house, overturning furniture and yelling unintelligible words. Names, perhaps. His son's. His wife's—

Well, first things first. He'd worry about Ericsson as soon as they moved the boy to the landau.

Back in the barn he smelled smoke. Wisps of it curled around the rafters. The roof was catching. The alley door banged in the wind. Gideon pointed at the floor. A snake-like path dampened by blood led to the rear entrance.

"Florian's gone."

"Good heavens!" Julia exclaimed. They both stared at the banging door, then at the trail left by Florian's body. "He crawled out and I didn't even notice."

Gideon shrugged. "Good riddance." He didn't really feel as callous as his words made him sound. A man hurt as badly as Florian would be helpless out in that raging red darkness.

He handed Julia his revolver. "Hang on to it in case we have any difficulty. The street sounds like total bedlam. I need a long piece of your petticoat."

She laid the gun on top of her reticule, lifted her skirt and tore the ruffle from her petticoat hem. He carefully wound the cloth around Torvald's back and chest to soak up the blood. Then he lifted the ten-year-old and put his ear close to the boy's mouth. He felt the warmth of Torvald's shallow breathing. How long they could keep him alive was anybody's guess.

They hurried down the passage between the houses. As they stepped onto the sidewalk, Gideon felt the heat of the wood walk through the soles of his boots. More fire equipment had arrived. Directly across Taylor Street, cottages were burning. Streams of water arcing from the east and west struck the flaming houses, but with little effect. The fire seemed to be consuming the entire block to the south.

People were pouring out of houses along the north side of Taylor. They carried articles of clothing, framed pictures, piles of books, small items of furniture. Most of the people rushed in the direction of the river.

A shirtless hairy man staggered out of Ericsson's rental cottage with a heavy chair in his arms. A wizened woman

followed him onto the porch. The man made straight for
Julia's landau. Miraculously, the vehicle hadn't been stolen
though it obviously was about to be.

The terrified bays stamped and tugged on their tethers,
their rolling eyes huge and red. Julia marched up to the
hairy man as he heaved the chair into the back of the
landau.

"Get that out of my carriage!"

From the first cross street to the west, a four-horse steam
pumper thundered around the corner and slowed to a stop.
A two-wheeled hose cart came rolling right behind.

The hairy man paid no attention to Julia.

"Are you deaf?" she cried. "Remove that chair this instant! We'll take your children if you have any, but we're
not hauling personal belongings." She pointed at Gideon
with Torvald in his arms. "We already have one wounded
youngster to take. And Mr. Ericsson—"

The man eyed Gideon, then looked at Julia again. Her
reticule was in the same hand as the revolver and hid it.
The man scratched his stomach.

"Well, ma'am, I hear what you say. But it don't appear
either of you people can stop me from moving whatever I
damn please. Martha and I got no youngsters. We do have
some valuable pieces which we aim to cart away in that
buggy whether you like it or—"

Calmly, Julia shifted her reticule to her other hand. She
raised the LeMat and pointed it at the man's brow.

"Take that chair out of my carriage or I'll blow your
head away."

The hairy man looked as if he might swoon. He staggered
to the landau, removed the chair and carried it to the cottage porch. Then, with one more terrified glance at Julia,
he shoved his wife through the front door and vanished.

iii

Gideon couldn't suppress a smile as he laid Torvald on
the backseat. Julia didn't notice. She was in the street
studying the sky, turning slowly from one quarter of the
horizon to the next until she'd made a full circle. She
walked back to him.

"Gideon, I'm no expert on such things, but this looks very bad. Just that one block of buildings between here and DeKoven Street is on fire. But the glare is already so bright, I can read the courthouse clock. And it's a good mile to the northeast."

She was right. From a few feet out in the street, the clock numerals were clearly visible. The houses on the other side of Taylor were crumbling and disappearing behind a rampart of flame more white than red. The heat was so intense, sweat poured down Gideon's face. Paint was beginning to bubble on the front of the first Ericsson cottage. More fire equipment swung into the street from the intersection to the east. Soon two more pumpers were directing streams of water on the scorching, wind-tossed bed of embers that had replaced the houses on the south side.

Sparks rained down on Julia suddenly—a whole firefly cloud of them. Gideon leaped to her, jerked her against him, smothered the sparks with his hands. People kept streaming by, carrying everything from tabby cats to chamber pots. There were children fleeing with adults, and some by themselves, their faces confused and frightened. The din was incredible; he had to shout.

"I've got to find Ericsson."

She nodded, then pointed. The roof of the front cottage was starting to burn. "Hurry!"

He ran along the side of the first cottage and in through the front door of the second. He glanced back, appalled at how quickly the fire consumed these wooden structures. Already almost the entire roof of the front house was ablaze—and as he stood in the dark hallway yelling Ericsson's name, a scrap of blazing roof paper floated to the front stoop of this one. Almost instantly, the dry wood smoked, then burst into flame.

He thought he heard heavy trampling in a rear room. *"Ericsson?"*

Wind-driven smoke poured through the house. He coughed as he staggered along a narrow hall and looked in each room. The heat inside the cottage had risen fifteen to twenty degrees in less than a minute. As the flames spread, the smoke took on a cherry glow.

He stopped at the last doorway, on the east side at the

very back. Inside he glimpsed a hulking form holding something white. He swallowed and wiped his stinging eye.

The west side of the house began to burn, the fire leaping out both horizontally and vertically at incredible speed. Smoke poured through open windows on that side, but there was enough light for him to see Ericsson with a silver picture frame under one arm and a yellowed wedding dress in his big hands. As he fondled the lace on the dress, tears streamed from his blue eyes.

"Ericsson, you've got to come out of here!" Gideon yelled as smoke hid the other man for a moment.

"Is that you?" Ericsson shouted.

"What?"

"Is that you, Helga?"

Gideon whispered, "Oh my God."

"Helga, we must go find my sister. She may be in danger!"

Gideon darted forward through coiling smoke, touched the wedding dress—

Ericsson went berserk. He dropped the picture frame and flung the dress behind him. He battered Gideon's head with both fists. Gideon was hurled against an old wardrobe. He struck his temple so hard, he nearly lost consciousness.

Snorting, Ericsson aimed a kick at his groin. It missed only because Gideon pivoted at the last moment. Ericsson's boot hit his calf. Everything—the rosy light, the smoke, his lumbering, demented assailant—grew more blurred. He was afraid Ericsson would land a solid blow and leave him unconscious to die.

But the big man picked up the wedding dress, secured the framed photograph under his arm and blundered back into the hall—just as the lintel of the room opposite burned in half and fell. A heavy piece of it struck Ericsson's head.

He staggered. His hair caught fire, then the wedding dress. Gideon rushed to try to save the other man but flames leaped between and drove him back. Coughing and gasping, he ran to a window on the east side of the house. He leaped through headfirst, nearly breaking his shoulder when he hit the ground. He managed to gain his feet and run toward Taylor Street. Behind him he heard Ericsson screaming his wife's name in a fading voice.

The first cottage on the lot, almost completely burned, was starting to collapse as he passed its rear corner. Its side wall bowed outward, the boards splitting and crumbling into red ash. Gideon leaped out of the way. He bounced against the wall of the adjacent house, which had not yet been consumed. Bits of burning board fell around him but he missed being inundated by the worst of the fiery debris. Guided only by his sense of direction, he finally reached the street. He had to jump over the fire shooting up between the planks of the sidewalk.

"Gideon? Here!"

He followed the cry and, in the center of Taylor Street, saw an incredible sight: Julia standing in front of the landau, reins in one hand, revolver in the other. In the carriage, crowding every inch of space except the seat where Torvald lay, were children from age three to early adolescence. There must have been eight, ten, a dozen, hanging off the back, clinging to the footboards.

" 'Twas the O'Leary dairy barn. I heard that for sure," one youngster shrieked to another as Gideon dragged himself up to the seat and seized the reins. There was no protest from Julia. She took her place beside him. She leaned her head against his shoulder and held his arm.

"I thought I'd lost you. I collected all these temporary orphans, but I thought I'd lost you. I'm so thankful you're all right."

She sounded ready to weep, yet at the same time there was overwhelming relief—even joy—in her voice.

iv

Gideon whipped up the team. Julia brandished the revolver to drive off adults who wanted to take the children's places. They drove a block east, then north toward the nearest bridge. The whole sky seemed alight, though only the area behind them was burning—no, there was a second large fire several blocks north. "That's St. Paul's Catholic going up!" exclaimed a boy in back.

"So it is," Julia said in dismay. "It must be all the airborne debris—good Lord. I just remembered something else. The Bateham shingle mill is within a block of the church. Wood and more wood—"

Gideon veered the team and narrowly avoided a collision with another steam pumper racing in the opposite direction. They fought across a south branch bridge through terrified crowds. It took them the better part of two hours to reach the mansion on South State.

The servants helped unload the children. Some of them had been driven to safety with the permission of their mothers or fathers who had loaded them into the landau and then fled on foot. Others had lost track of their parents in the confusion and had just been plucked up from Taylor Street. Most of the youngsters were laughing and singing as if the whole outing were a lark.

Gideon carried Torvald to Carter's bedroom. Ericsson's son was still alive, but pale and barely breathing.

Returning downstairs, Gideon fortified himself with a good jolt of bourbon. He'd have laughed at Julia's disheveled hair, sooty face and torn dress if the situation hadn't been so grim.

"I've got to fetch this doctor of yours. Will you write the directions for me?"

"Oh, Gideon, it's such a long way—"

"Yes, but the fire's confined to the west side of the river."

"So far."

"Julia, the boy will die unless we get help!"

"All right, all right. I'm being selfish." She avoided his eye as she added, "Thinking of you instead of him. Come into the library."

He left his ruined waistcoat on a chair and rolled up the sleeves of his sweated shirt as he followed her. She sat down and began to write. He consulted his watch. A few minutes after midnight. He was exhausted. Parts of his hair and eyebrows had been singed away. His clothing and his skin smelled of smoke. He'd inhaled so much of it, his lungs hurt.

Suddenly a servant ran in—the man who'd been sent to the highest point of the house, the northwest tower, as a lookout.

"Madam, the fire's leaped the river to the south side."

Julia laid her pen aside. "You're sure?"

"Yes, madam, I can clearly see something burning in the vicinity of the gasworks or Conley's Patch."

And the wind's blowing northeast, Gideon thought. Directly across the route he had to take to the far north side. Well, it would be a devil of a lively story for the *Beacon* if he lived to write it.

While the servant waited, Julia handed Gideon the directions and in the next breath said, "Don't go. We'll find another doctor somewhere close by."

"Do you know any?"

"No, but—"

"And your neighbors who are so fond of you—are they going to rush to help? Of course not."

"But you saw the people in the streets, Gideon. They've gone crazy! You won't get ten blocks."

Quietly: "I will if I take my gun."

Suddenly he responded to an impulse, squeezed her arm and kissed her sooty, sweaty cheek—right there in front of the servant. He murmured, "Don't worry about me."

She closed her eyes and pressed her face against his mouth. "How can I help it?"

How natural and comfortable it felt, being so close to her. But he was aware of the man watching, and drew away. A wry and weary smile hid his apprehension as he said, "I really have no choice about going. You were married to Louis long enough to know the Kents have a passion for lost causes."

Then he went out into a night grown brighter than day.

CHAPTER VIII

INTO THE INFERNO

i

WITH THE LEMAT in his belt, Gideon started up State Street in the landau. The grooms had changed horses, substituting a gray and a graceless but sturdy dapple for the spent bays.

The carriage clattered past Courtleigh's. The place was shuttered and curtained like a fortress. Every window was draped. Only slits of light showed at the edges. A man crouching on the roof with a spyglass kept watch on the fire for his master.

Gideon hawed to the team, driving them on. A few moments after he passed the mansion he was overcome by the shock of all that had happened on Taylor Street, particularly the thought that he'd put a bullet into Courtleigh's assistant general manager.

The shock deepened as he recalled Florian trying to crawl out of the barn. The man couldn't have gotten far on his own. What had happened to him as the fire engulfed the neighborhood? The same thing that happened to Ericsson?

Gideon's arms shook uncontrollably. His head swam. He pressed the sole of his boot against the brake for fear he'd careen the speeding carriage into a fence or gatepost. Then his mind took cognizance of what he had been seeing for several blocks—masses of people running south.

The flight reminded him of what he had to do. He'd worry about the possibility that he'd caused Florian's death if and when Courtleigh raised the issue. It might never happen. Meantime, reaching the north side looked increasingly difficult if not absolutely impossible. Time and again he was forced to slow the landau to avoid the people swarming in the street.

As a boy in Virginia, Gideon had often heard his preacher father refer to Hell. He'd never quite believed in its existence, and his imagination contained only a vague picture of what Hell might be like if somehow it did turn out to be real. Now, just after one o'clock on the morning of Monday, October 9, Gideon beheld the best approximation of Hell he ever wanted to see.

The skyline of the South Side was alight with windblown banners of fire. Clearly the holocaust had leaped the river in more than one place. One immense arm of the fire was burning a few blocks west—the area of his hotel. Where he'd left the gifts for Margaret and the children, he thought with dismay. Further north, he could make out another big section afire, and in the center, the courthouse. That meant the business district was threatened.

The wind still blew fiercely from the southwest. The heat on his left side was scorching. The unbelievably bright sky was full of blazing wood, glowing ash, cinders, occasional clouds of oily black smoke, and great masses of windblown sparks. Gideon had never seen an effect as strange and lovely as that produced by the sparks. It was as if he were caught in a snowstorm in which every flake was lighted from within.

Julia's instructions called for him to get to the north side via a pedestrian and vehicle tunnel running under the river at LaSalle Street. By the time he'd reached State and Van Buren, he was positive the courthouse was burning. He couldn't travel up LaSalle, then. Doing so would take him directly into the worst of the fire.

Van Buren was packed with people, but perhaps he could turn right—east—in a block or two. He remembered his first stroll around the city. He'd seen a swing-bridge over the river at Michigan Avenue. He could go north and use that.

Everywhere the flurry of sparks was touching off new fires. He passed a two-story building with a copper roof, cornice and large windows on the first floor. Suddenly fire eating through the back of the building blew the windows outward with cannonlike force. Men and women around the landau screamed. A rain of glass fell on Gideon, gashing his neck. One fragment narrowly missed his good eye as he fought to keep the team from bolting.

People packed the street, pushing barrows, dragging trunks and mattresses, lugging bundles of personal belongings. Several tried to seize the bits or headstalls of his horses. Others attempted to put their belongings aboard. Finally he had to draw the LeMat to keep them back. He drove with the reins wrapped around his right hand and the revolver in his left.

He made slower and slower progress. Hundreds, perhaps thousands were fleeing south along lower State Street. Although rapidly becoming a prime business thoroughfare, State still had a large number of small frame residences. A man wearing five hats stacked one atop another came running out the front door of one such house. He had a small girl in his arms. He spied the landau, fought his way to it and ran alongside.

"I'll pay you a hundred dollars to hire this rig."

"I'm sorry. I can't do it," Gideon called back.

"Two hundred. Five!"

"No. I need it to fetch a doctor for an injured boy."

Crestfallen, the man limped away. Two of his hats fell off and were snatched up by people behind him.

Gideon maneuvered the landau around the corner to Jackson, heading east. He hoped Michigan would be less congested. He passed several saloons whose patrons were inexplicably celebrating—singing and capering in the street. At one such place, a frantic owner was trying to load his barreled liquor onto a dray. While Gideon drove by, one of the barrels slipped and rolled down the boards laid from the wagon bed to the street. The barrel split open. Whiskey gushed. Floating sparks ignited it. A river of alcohol flowed in the gutter, burning with an eerie blue flame. Revelers at first tried to dance in the stuff. When it set their trousers on fire, they yelped and reeled away.

Behind him, green flames shot from several of the copper cornices he'd seen earlier. The night was turning into a mind-numbing chaos of color and sound. He realized that ever since he'd left Julia's, he'd been listening to a sonorous tolling without quite being aware of it. Now he heard it distinctly. The courthouse bell. Still ringing even though the building was burning down.

He heard boat bells and horns, too: faint clangs and squeaks above the hubbub of the surging crowds. Probably the horns and bells belonged to vessels trying to negotiate the Chicago River to its mouth, and safety.

As he turned the team into Michigan and saw the dark lake rippling with red highlights not far to his right, the earth shook and the sky reverberated with thunderous noise. People shrieked and began to run like animated dolls—without purpose, without direction. Somewhere dynamite was being set off. In the hope of creating firebreaks, Gideon supposed.

And above all the cacophony—bells, horns, detonations, screaming—the fire itself made a noise like a continuous gush of air from a great bellows. All across the downtown, that damnable wind was fanning the flames and creating storms of fire that literally roared.

"Damn!" Gideon said in a despairing voice when some smoke cleared and he surveyed Michigan Avenue for several blocks ahead. It was jammed with people and small mountains of personal items and household goods. Obviously a great number of residents from further west had fled with their possessions toward the lake.

Well, he was cursed if he'd turn back just because the street was impassable. He yanked the reins and sent the landau swaying off the wood paving blocks to the weedy strip of open space between the avenue and the shore of the lake.

The landau bumped and lurched north across the uneven ground. There were piles of household things out here as well, and people camping on them. Gideon maneuvered around one such squatter as a man howled from the street, "It's the judgment of the Almighty! He has seen this city sink in corruption worse than Sodom's. That's why we're all going to die! *The Lord has cursed Chicago!*"

People flung rocks and dirt at the hysterical doom-cryer, probably because they feared he was right. Gideon could almost believe he was.

Three poorly dressed men came slipping up from behind, moving in an oblique line toward the landau's left rear wheel. Gideon's blind spot. He wasn't aware of them until heavy boots thumped on the floorboards and the carriage swayed.

Instinctively, he twisted around to the right so he could have a wider field of vision with his good eye. But one of the men had jumped aboard just behind his left shoulder. The man had a short length of pipe in his hand. Before Gideon saw him, he brought the pipe down on top of Gideon's head.

At the impact, Gideon dropped the revolver. The horses lunged. "Get hold of 'em, Barney!" a man yelled. The one who'd struck Gideon leaped down and dashed in front of the team. He brought the horses to a halt.

Dazed, Gideon was trying to stand. His head rang. Bile rose in his throat. Someone shoved him toward the right side of the seat. A voice growled, "Every liveryman in town's bein' offered five, ten times the normal fare for short hauls." Another shove. "So a couple of us enterprisin' lads"—Gideon tried to punch at the source of the voice but his head was whirling and he missed—"we're enterin' the livery business. Thanks kindly for helpin' us get started."

The unseen man grabbed Gideon's shoulder, tearing his shirt as he booted him off the seat. Swearing, Gideon dropped into the weeds. He hit hard. A rock raked his cheek. He heard the three men laughing and congratulating themselves as they took possession of the landau.

Then, just before Gideon blanked out, one of the men bellowed, "Buggy for hire! Take your personal goods to safety. *Buggy for hire!*"

Gideon's face twisted with rage as he tried to push himself up. The roaring fire and the man's shout blended together. The ground flew up at him and engulfed him in darkness from which all the firelight swiftly faded.

ii

No one bothered him where he lay amid some weeds whose dry stalks rattled in the hot wind. In about twenty minutes he came around. As soon as he regained his feet, he began to think about what he should do next.

On Michigan Avenue, those attempting to escape and those arriving from further west combined to create congestion of unbelievable magnitude. Northward, in the direction of the bridge, he saw nothing but a red-lit ocean of humanity. To try to go all the way to the town limits on foot would take the rest of the night. He'd return to Julia's, saddle one of the bays and try a second time.

Provided the whole city hadn't been razed. Grim-faced, he began to trot south through the scraggly growth along the lake shore.

He ached from head to foot. But he quickened his pace, throwing his head back and gulping the scorching air. He was enraged and humiliated by the loss of the landau. Disgusted that people would take advantage of misery and try to exploit those in peril. He always hoped for the best from his fellow countrymen, and the hope was often realized. Sometimes, though, he was grievously disappointed. Tonight was one such time.

He pumped his arms to help himself run faster. When his chest started to hurt from the exertion, his lungs constricted by the searing air, he didn't slacken his speed. All he could think of was reaching Twentieth, saddling a mount and starting north again.

He staggered into Julia's kitchen by the rear door and collapsed on a stool, his chest heaving. Servants rushed to gather around him. Questions dinned in his ears. Finally he understood one and gasped a reply.

"No, I—don't think the fire will—come this way—not unless—the wind changes." Blearily, he swung his head. "Someone throw a saddle on another horse. Three hooligans knocked me out and stole the landau."

"Oh, Gideon!"

He heard the voice from his blind spot, swung his head slightly to the left. Bundled in the emerald bedroom robe, Julia stood in the doorway. Her blue eyes seemed full of some emotion he was too tired to recognize. He had the odd impression that she would have rushed to him except for the presence of the servants.

"I lost the landau. I'll have to take one of the horses and try to bring the doctor back on—"

He stopped. She was shaking her head. Annoyed, he exclaimed, "Fire or not, I'm going to get him here!"

"It isn't necessary, Gideon." Her eyes brimmed with tears. "About fifteen minutes after you left, Ericsson's boy died."

iii

Afterward, he was never proud of what he did then. His mind filled with a shattering rage in which he seemed to see images of Daphnis Miller and Torvald and Ericsson—and Courtleigh's thugs—all blurred together. He swore, jumped up from the stool and lurched against the table next to it. He overturned the table.

A stack of Spode broke to bits. The servants exchanged alarmed looks. He stormed to the back door and leaned his head against his forearm. "I shouldn't have moved him. I should have gone for a doctor right from Ericsson's!"

Out of his sense of failure, there came a searing new sense of resolve. He would settle with the man who'd caused all this grief. He would settle with Mr. Thomas Courtleigh, who had dispatched hired men to the west side, stayed safe at home himself, and thereby proved the old, sad truths one more time: it was the Daphnis Millers of the world who always suffered, because they had none of the protection afforded by money or position or power. And Margaret wanted him to stop speaking out on behalf of the Daphnis Millers? He beat his fist against the frame of the door.

"Impossible!"

When he blurted the word that made no sense to those who heard it, not one of them scorned his odd behavior. The events of the night had left them almost as shaken and drained as he was.

Weariness sapped his anger and the last of his strength. He was barely aware of Julia reaching his side. She took

his hand and led him back across the kitchen, and out. He
was too exhausted to say a word.

iv

When he was himself again, he found he was sprawled
on a lounge in a bedroom on the north side of the house.
Julia's bedroom? he wondered with a twinge of embarrassment. But he wasn't so embarrassed that he moved; he
was still too damn tired.

French windows opened onto a spacious balcony. Beyond
Courtleigh's rooftop he saw the panorama of the flame-
filled sky. Somewhere a small clock chimed four. He made
a good deal of noise as he sat up.

Julia appeared on the balcony, which extended beyond
the left-hand window. "Gideon? Ah, you're awake—"

He rubbed his throbbing head.

"Would you like a little brandy?"

He nodded. She swirled past him, the robe belling back
from bare calves. The walls and ceiling shimmered with
firelight. He realized no lamps were lit because they
weren't needed.

With some effort, he got to his feet. She handed him a
goblet. He sipped. Raked fingers through his cinder-filled
hair. When he spoke, his voice was hoarse.

"I failed, Julia. In everything I tried to do tonight—
saving Ericsson—saving his boy—getting the doctor—I
failed. And for a finale, I had to lose my temper in front
of your help."

"Please don't talk that way. You did the best you could.
No sane person would expect everything to come out right
on a night like this."

The disgusted growl in his throat said the excuse didn't
satisfy him. He stalked past her to the balcony. He leaned
against the rail of heavy sculptured stone. She followed. He
didn't see her raise her hand near his back, then hesitate.

At last she touched him. He stiffened a little. Once he'd
gotten over his surprise and self-consciousness, he relaxed.
She rested her palm lightly against his shirt between his
shoulder blades. It felt wonderfully soothing somehow.

She nodded toward the northern sector of the sky. "I

think the courthouse has fallen. It's hard to be absolutely sure with so much flame and smoke. Unless they can stop the advance of the fire, the whole business district will go. You can barely see the eighth story of Mr. Palmer's new hotel—it's going to be wiped out, too." A small shake of her head as she took her hand away. "It certainly teaches you not to put too much reliance on the things of this world. They never last."

He hardly heard. "I should have tried locating a doctor in Ericsson's neighborhood—"

"Gideon, stop!" She came around to his side, standing on tiptoe. "Unless of course you enjoy the pose of the martyr."

Her face turned up toward his. The brief anger he saw in her eyes jolted him from the mood of self-pity. Her hair blew against his cheek, driven by a puff of hot wind. Sympathetic again, she touched his chin. "There's no need to torture yourself."

He stood gazing down at her as the wind caught the skirt of her robe and brushed it aside. A bare thigh glimmered red. Her hand moved up his cheek, stroking. She felt the sudden excitement of physical contact and so did he. Her voice broke as she said, "You tried. No man or woman can do more than that."

Later, looking back to that moment, he wondered whether he could have walked away and thus prevented everything that happened as a consequence. Yes—if he'd been less tired, less angry with Courtleigh, less aware of his own fallibility. In short, more of a paragon and less of a man.

Perhaps the excitement of the night contributed, too. During the war he'd heard fellow officers say that thoughts of the perils of combat stimulated their sweethearts and made them less cautious. He recalled a lonely cabin in the Virginia woodlands where he'd saved a young widow from being molested by two marauding Yanks. Quite unexpectedly, he'd spent the night in her bed, and he remembered how passionate she was in the aftermath of danger.

And perhaps he was worn out and needed simple human warmth, and she did too.

Whatever the reason, he found himself staring down at Julia Sedgwick and wanting her.

V

He put his fingers on her shoulders. She reached up with both hands, clasping her wrists around his neck. He had to bend. He did so—quickly—because her blue eyes suddenly spoke of her desire.

They were standing on the open balcony. People were still fleeing along South State. But they paid no attention to the fine houses they were passing. Gideon didn't care one way or another. He swept his arms around Julia's waist. Lifted her off the marble balcony so her mouth would meet his.

She murmured his name, then kissed him, her lips opening. Her tongue stole out and touched his with an ardor he'd never experienced before, not with the widow in the woodland cabin, and certainly not with Margaret. For an instant he was afraid he might not be competent enough for someone so experienced.

Then that didn't seem to matter either. She pressed against him, the belt of the robe de chambre loosening as they kissed. The robe came open. She wore only a light chemise beneath. She was moaning as she kissed his throat, his cheek, his lips. Moaning and reaching for him.

"We'd better go inside to the bed, Julia—"

"No, no, there isn't time—hurry, Gideon—hurry!"

Somehow she helped him free of his trousers. Somehow he left them behind as they stumbled from the red-lit balcony to the deeper shadow of her room. She clasped her legs around him and then they were magically together, she hanging back with her wrists locked around his neck while he braced against the wall.

At the end, clinging to him in exhaustion, she said, "Oh, my dearest. Oh, Gideon darling—that was shameless of me."

"Why—why do you—say that?" He was out of breath. So was she.

"Because—we shouldn't have. It seems that—in a very short time—I've grown hopelessly fond of you. But this is—one of the few times in my life when I'm—a little ashamed of getting what I wanted."

"Don't." He kissed her closed eyes.

"Well"—a small, pained laugh—"you see that I wasn't

so ashamed that I stopped, or am willing to stop now. Make love to me again."

Margaret's face flashed into mind. He thought of the night she'd first banished him from her room. Of how he'd come home to Yorkville, hurt, and three times tried to draw her out of her unhappy mood by touching her in an affectionate, tender way. Three times she'd recoiled from him.

"Please, Gideon. On the bed this time."

The memories faded. "Yes," he said, and crushed his mouth against hers.

Chapter IX

Guilt

i

THEY MADE LOVE twice more that night, each time with greater ferocity and yet greater tenderness than before.

Margaret had never been excessively inhibited in the marriage bed—at least not during the first two or three years—but she'd always insisted on total darkness. Julia did not. Both times he took her by the shimmering light of the sky and watched the gasping delight sweep over her face. The last time, just at the end, someone detonated more powder far off in the blazing city. It seemed a fitting capstone to the incredible experience.

Moments later, when they separated, he was so drowsy he could barely speak. "That was—Julia, that was—"

"What?"

A chagrined chuckle. "I don't know. Beyond words."

She smiled. "I'm glad." She snuggled her small, firm breasts against his naked back as he yawned, then apologized for it. In a moment his eyes shut. He began to snore.

The sound made her laugh softly. She drew back and rubbed his shoulders until she felt him relax. Then her gaze drifted to the open windows. She'd asked the servants to

summon her in the event the fire crossed Twelfth Street.
So far, no one had knocked.

She stared at the smoke and flame in the heavens but
didn't really see any of it. She was pondering the surprising
and incredible joy of what had just happened—what she
had *wanted* to happen since he first called, she realized. He
was a person of principle and determination. A person to
whom failure was unbearable, and whose ambition to
change society in a positive way was as powerful as her
own. He was, in short, a man—in a way poor Louis had
never been.

Yes, she'd wanted him from the beginning. And she'd
gone out of her way to arrange the circumstances so the
want could be satisfied. She'd brought him to her bedroom
when another room would have served equally well as a
place for him to rest. She'd gone to his side when he stood
on the balcony, touched and caressed him.

She could admit all that and be both happy they'd made
love and disappointed in herself. There was a streak of
selfishness left in her from her younger days. She had
learned to suppress and channel it, but she would never
completely conquer it.

What bothered her most—for his sake, really—was the
fact that he was married. When the overwrought state that
had brought them together had cooled, he would feel regret
and guilt and pain. Above all, she didn't want him to feel
pain. His happiness and his hurts were far more important
than hers, and she couldn't recall ever having felt that way
about another human being except her son. Thus Julia
came to realize she was in love with Gideon.

There was a melancholy expression on her face as she
lay staring at the fiery sky, sleepless and wondering what
she could do to ease his inevitable guilt for which she held
herself responsible.

ii

As it turned out, she could do nothing. The instant he
awoke around nine o'clock, Margaret's face intruded in his
memory. This time he found it impossible to banish.

Stale, smoky air tainted the bedroom. Julia was awake

and lying beneath the light coverlet she'd pulled over them.
She read his expression at once, and unerringly.

"Gideon, it wasn't your fault."

"It most certainly was. I'm a married man. The father of
children—"

"And do you still love your wife? I'd be much surprised
if you said yes."

Her directness and candor stunned him. He didn't really
know how to answer her question. The love he'd once felt
for Margaret could never be wiped out as if it hadn't existed; a residue of that love would always remain part of
him. So in that sense he did love her. But not with the
ardor of their first years of marriage.

Was it possible for a man to care for *two* women? One
passionately, and one out of a sense of responsibility? He
didn't know that, either, so he evaded.

"That's beside the point, Julia. What I did was wrong."

"Let me accept the blame! I led you to it. I could have
pulled back—stopped it—half a dozen times. I didn't because I—because I've fallen in love with you." He caught
his breath as she went on. "I know that isn't permissible
in our situation. But I wanted you to make love to me, and
I arranged things so it would happen. You mustn't take the
blame on yourself."

"I must take half of it. I wanted you, too, and I wouldn't
admit it until the very last moment. What the hell are we
going to do, Julia?" Louder, then, almost angrily: "What
the hell are we going to do?"

She kissed the scraped knuckles of his right hand. Then
the palm, and the flesh below the thumb. He was astonished
to see tears in her eyes.

Tears from one so sophisticated? That struck him as im-
probable. But he felt them on his skin as she pressed his
hand to her lips and murmured, "I can't tell you, my
dearest. We can't change last night."

"I know."

"And it may well happen again."

"I know that, too."

"So I can't answer the question. My conscience wants to
reply one way, my feelings another. Whichever answer I
give, don't you see—it will be wrong."

What they did was thrust the whole matter aside and let
the events of the next hours carry them along, divert them
from the dilemma they knew they must eventually resolve.
Gideon concentrated on Thomas Courtleigh, and on what
could be done to make the railroad man pay for the death
of Torvald Ericsson.

From the moment he began to think about that—on
Monday, when the fire was sweeping the north side after
having razed the business district—he knew the Chicago
police and the Chicago courts would be of no help to him.
Even if the police were willing to investigate the boy's
death, he felt and Julia agreed that Courtleigh's influence
would prevent the investigation from reaching a conclusion.

But he intended to do *something* before he left the city.
He brooded about the problem for hours, occasionally falling into such a rage that he entertained thoughts of finding
Courtleigh and attacking him. Only when he remembered
that Strelnik had cynically predicted he'd do exactly that
did he put the fantasies out of his mind.

By Monday night the city's exhausted fire companies had
brought the conflagration under control except for a few
pockets still burning at the northern city limits. In many
areas there was nothing left to burn. On the entire north
side, a returning servant reported, only two houses had
been spared by a whim of wind.

Toward midnight a drizzling rain began to fall. When
Gideon woke beside Julia on Tuesday morning, the vista
from the balcony was an incredible one. A smoky pall still
darkened the sky. To the north, shells of burned-out buildings stretched away like graveyard monuments. The ruins
smoldered and so did the paving blocks of the main streets.
A charred odor permeated furniture, clothing—even Gideon's hair and pores.

On Tuesday Chicago's mayor, R. B. Mason, convened
the city council and issued a proclamation fixing the price
of bread at eight cents per twelve-ounce loaf. To prevent
profiteering, the price was to remain stabilized for the next
ten days. Gideon and Julia learned that earlier proclama-
tions had suspended the sale of liquor and appointed special police to help control looting. Little Phil Sheridan, the

general who commanded the Department of the Missouri from its Chicago headquarters, had telegraphed for two companies of infantry from Fort Omaha.

That same day Gideon and all of Julia's male servants tramped to the smoking ruin of the west side to search for Ericsson's sister Sigrid, and for the body of the man himself. Neither could be found. When Gideon and the servants returned late in the afternoon, dirty and dispirited, they passed the Courtleigh mansion. Gideon noted a couple of derby-hatted men loitering in the drive. One turned his back when he saw Gideon studying him. Gideon couldn't be positive but he thought the man had been in Florian's group Sunday night.

He supposed Courtleigh had the guards on duty to protect his property from the dispossessed who were wandering the streets. Julia seemed to fear no such invasion. In fact, when he got to the house he discovered she'd posted a sign saying campers were welcome on the back part of her property. A dozen or so had already accepted the invitation, he saw.

He went inside and found the kitchen a-buzz with activity. The cook and her assistant were fixing soup, gruel, and hot drinks for the campers. Gideon learned that the head of Courtleigh's household staff had come over while he was away and complained to Julia that granting camping privileges would draw undesirables to the neighborhood.

The cook grinned. "Miss Julia told him to go home or to hell, whichever he preferred."

Tuesday evening, by lantern light, they buried Torvald Ericsson in an oak coffin one of Julia's grooms had hammered together. Gideon helped dig the grave in a clump of apple trees ten yards from the campfire of a homeless family.

Torvald's body had been dressed in one of Carter's outfits because Gideon wanted the boy's blood-covered shirt. Julia had performed the grim exchange. Then she and Gideon had laid the stiff body in the coffin, and Gideon had nailed it shut.

When Julia asked why he wanted the shirt, he said, "As a present for Courtleigh. I'm trying to decide how I'll deliver it."

"Do you really think you should prolong your feud with—?"

"*Feud?*" he exploded. "It's a matter of justice, not a feud. Courtleigh killed that boy as surely as if he'd handled the knife himself."

"We agreed you could never bring him to justice in this town, Gideon."

"I know we did. But the killing isn't going to remain a secret. I can at least make certain of that much."

Now, among the leafless apple trees, Gideon read passages from the New Testament while Carter clutched his mother's hand and gazed at the oak box with rounded eyes. Smoke blew in the darkness. Piles of winter coal were still smoldering throughout the city. The air was foul, bad to breathe.

Gideon found it equally bad to stand there reading from the word of God. He was unfit to do that; he'd taken Julia in adulterous fashion. And while there might be many excuses for it, none was powerful enough to absolve him of guilt. Even granting that Margaret was a wife in name only, the marriage vow still meant something. He had broken it.

Wednesday, Joseph Medill managed to publish his newspaper, though Gideon never found out how; the supposedly fireproof *Tribune* building had fallen victim to the flames. So had the Field and Leiter store, Potter Palmer's hotel, and scores of other fine buildings. The business district as such was gone. Medill's paper sounded a note of challenge:

CHEER UP

In the midst of a calamity without parallel in world history, looking upon the ashes of thirty years accumulations, the people of this once beautiful city have resolved that CHICAGO SHALL RISE AGAIN.

Gideon admired that spirit. But it was clear that the restoration would require a gigantic effort. The toll from the fire was gradually coming into focus.

Property worth more than two hundred million dollars had been destroyed. A hundred thousand people were without homes. Though only two hundred fifty bodies had been found, it was almost certain that thousands had been incinerated in the cottages and tenements, Ericsson and his sister among them.

The fire had leveled an area about a mile wide and five miles long, north to south. The destruction ran from Fullerton Avenue down to Harrison Street, and over the west side as well.

On Wednesday afternoon Julia's grooms repaired a disused pony cart. She and Gideon took their first inspection trip downtown. What they saw was a landscape from a lunatic's nightmare.

Piles of brick and stone rubble lay everywhere. Here and there a section of a wall still stood, some of them surrounding empty window frames. Although the entire commercial section was gone, one man was already back in business. A brand-new plank structure had been erected at Number 89 Washington Street. It belonged to a realtor and was identified by a crude sign:

W. D. KERFOOT'S BLOCK—
FIRST IN THE BURNT DISTRICT

The building hardly qualified as a business block in the accepted sense. But a lounger out in front said all the space had been rented, and the structure had in fact been up since Tuesday night! Near the door hung another sign that made Gideon laugh:

All gone but wife, children and energy!

His laughter faded when he noticed Julia staring at the sign with melancholy eyes. He suspected he knew which words had caused her reaction.

One of the reasons they'd come downtown was to locate the reopened telegraph office. Julia stayed outside the temporary tent while Gideon sent a message to Margaret saying he was safe but would be remaining in Chicago until Friday.

Abruptly he crossed out the last word. He replaced it with Sunday, then went on to explain the delay by saying that unfinished Wisconsin and Prairie business required his attention. In a way that was true. But he turned pink as he

handed the completed blank to the clerk. He was no good
at this business of deception.

Still, he couldn't have gotten out of Chicago without a
good deal of effort. Those railroad lines still operating were
offering free passage to anyone who wanted to leave.

Departing trains were packed to capacity, he'd heard.

Outside the telegraph tent, two men were arguing. One
pounded his palm as he shouted, "Damn it, Jessie, it *is*
bigger than London in 1666—a feller from the fire department told me!"

Gideon smiled. The scope of the destruction had become
a matter of civic pride. He supposed that was healthier
than letting the sights and sounds of the ruined city cause
depression. He was having firsthand experience with depression today. The telegraph message to Margaret, and
the mention of departure, had forced a realization. He must
say goodbye to Julia soon and never see her again.

The smoky streets teemed with sightseers. Gideon maneuvered the pony cart through them to the site of the
courthouse. There Julia pinned a notice to one of several
large message boards erected for government and public
use. She'd listed the names of the nine children she'd taken
in, and noted the address where their parents could claim
them.

Miraculously, four of the children were called for by ten
that night. As Gideon and Julia prepared for bed, she told
him she intended to care for the rest until their parents
appeared. If the parents had died in the fire, she'd work
with Chicago's Relief and Aid Society to see that the children were placed in good foster homes.

Gideon was moved to say, "Do you know my late father
thought you were a very cold and ambitious person? And
now you watch out for stray children as if they were your
own."

"Well, my dear, I suspect that when your father made
his remark about me, it was correct. I hope I've changed a
little. I still plead guilty to being ambitious, although I've
changed the objects of my ambition. Once I used to chase
after invitations to the best society balls. Now I chase after
the franchise."

He laughed. "I'd say that's a considerable change. You're
a remarkable woman, Julia. A very strong woman—"

She bussed his cheek in a wifely way. "Kind of you, sir. May I return the compliment and say the same about you? Anyone must be strong if they have ambition to change the world even a little. The ambition itself is a strength, I've always believed."

He made a face. "I'm afraid my wife considers that kind of ambition to be a weakness—" He realized he'd inadvertently stumbled on one of the reasons he responded so strongly to Julia's personality and intellect.

He patted her derriere and forced a smile. "Permit me to say, madam, that you're sounding like a proper Kent at last."

She laughed and embraced him. "No, I'm just a selfish, shameless lady who wants her ambition fulfilled."

"Which ambition? To vote?"

She put her lips against his ear. "To be taken to bed by a proper Kent—as soon as he can get busy and remove his trousers."

Their lovemaking was intense, yet with a quality of good humor new to their relationship. It added a dimension of comfortable familiarity he'd never experienced before.

But afterward, his conscience tormented him. He was unable to sleep. Finally he touched her shoulder and expressed it in the only way he could—straightforwardly.

"Julia, you must know something. I can never leave her."

"Your wife?"

"Yes. I couldn't hurt her that much."

"I understand. It's just one more reason I admire you. Still—it's difficult for me to curb my hopes completely. You did say yesterday that she's given you cause to think of separating."

"She has. That doesn't give me the right to abandon my children."

An insistent note crept into her voice. "Let's take them, then. They can live with us—"

"*No,* Julia."

It closed a door. She realized it, and sighed.

"You're a decent man, Gideon. Louis would never have agonized this way. It's always the decent ones who suffer."

Decent? Hardly, he thought.

"That said, Julia, I must also say I can't see you again once I leave Chicago."

"I suspected that, too. There's a selfish little girl inside me who's screaming and stamping because of it—" Sadness tinged the feeble joke. She drew a deep breath, collected herself. "Well—this is one time when little Miss Julia won't get what she wants. And she's never wanted anything more than you. Oh, Gideon—I'm hopelessly in love with you, damn fool that I am. You'd better kiss me before I break down and bawl."

iv

While Gideon and Julia slept in each other's arms, Carter was awake and having an illegal pillow fight with two of the homeless boys still living in the mansion. Carter thought his mother and their visitor, Mr. Kent, made a lot of calf's eyes at one another, but beyond that, he didn't concern himself with their relationship. It never entered his head that Mr. Kent could be romantically involved with his mother. Mr. Kent was married, and that automatically ruled him out as a potential suitor. Besides, Carter had never known his mother to be interested in anything except her work. He never kept track of his mother's whereabouts. That plus Mr. Kent's marital status and the presence of new friends all conspired to keep Carter unaware of what was happening just three doors down the long hallway.

v

Mayor Mason had reluctantly concluded that policing the ruined city was beyond the powers of his regular and special officers. Earlier that day he'd voluntarily placed Chicago in the hands of the commander of the Department of the Missouri. General Sheridan in charge meant, in effect, martial law. During the night, telegraph messages summoned troops to Chicago.

Next day the first of the soldiers arrived. Ultimately the city was patrolled by ten regular companies of U.S. infantry, seven companies of Illinois militia, and a specially formed unit of citizens called the First Chicago Volunteers.

With the aid of bayonets, regulated bread prices, and rising spirits, Chicago began to return to normal.

vi

"The hypocritical son of a bitch!"

Gideon flung Thursday's *Tribune* against the wall six feet from the long, polished dining table.

"My," Julia said. "I'm glad Carter's left the room."

The teasing was lost on Gideon. "Murder by night and pronouncements about his own generosity by day—by God that's intolerable!"

His outbursts so rattled the serving girl removing the breakfast things, she almost dropped a tray of dishes as she left. At the other end of the table, Julia refilled her silver-edged cup from an elaborate silver coffeepot. Gideon scowled and slumped in his chair. His eye patch was slightly askew and the nightshirt and old robe borrowed from one of the grooms were much too large.

"What on earth are you talking about?" Julia wanted to know.

"Your neighbor! Florian told me Courtleigh was planning a ball for his fiancée—"

Julia nodded with distaste. "Gwendolyn Strother. Her father's a chum of Philip Armour, the fellow who's getting rich off the meatpacking business. Miss Strother's wealthy in her own right, and reasonably well connected socially. But she's about as robust as a dried thistle. I've heard she has a distinctly nervous disposition. Courtleigh certainly can't be marrying her for her beauty and stamina. Do you suppose he needs more capital?"

Gideon's mouth quirked. "You're a cynic." He was recalling the pale, hysterical face he'd glimpsed in the brougham last Sunday evening.

"A realist," she replied. "I still don't see why you're so exercised."

"Because the paper says he's going ahead with the ball. Tomorrow night!"

"This soon after the fire? That's disgusting."

"Oh, you haven't heard all of it." He jabbed a finger at the fallen newspaper. "Now the guests will be charged a

thousand dollars per card of admission, and everything will
be donated to fire relief. The *bastard*!" he shouted, slamming his fist down so hard, his cup danced in its saucer.
"He can send men to murder a boy one night and pose as
a philanthropist the next!"

"I believe I told you he was like that—" She gasped
suddenly. He'd bolted up in his chair.

"I think I'll go to that ball," he said. "It's the very place
to say what I've been wanting to say to, and about, Mr.
Courtleigh."

"That's insanity, Gideon! You wouldn't dare accuse him
in front of—"

"No?" he interrupted. "You watch."

The furious set of his features told her further protest
was futile. She shook her head, her eyes full of wonder and
admiration that was tempered by a cold knot of fear forming in her stomach.

CHAPTER X

UNINVITED GUEST

i

ON FRIDAY EVENING, Courtleigh's mansion glowed with scores of oil lamps in lieu of the still disrupted gas service. Splendid carriages began to arrive around nine. Soon the smoky October air carried the scrape of fiddlers tuning up and the sweet sound of a harpist practicing runs.

Julia had managed to outfit Gideon presentably by enlisting the aid of all of her servants. She'd come up with a fresh shirt, trousers, cravat and a handsome if slightly worn frock coat, plum colored and only a size too large. He adjusted the cravat and surveyed the fit of the coat in a pier glass.

"Your people are very good to loan me these things."

She smiled. "They're not used to their employer having gentlemen friends. Even if they are a bit scandalized, I think the novelty appeals to them. They've taken to you"— she leaned her head against his shoulder and hugged his waist—"just as I have."

He held her with both arms, totally content. But the peaceful moment soon passed. She stepped back and said in a brisk way, "I may be guilty of repeating myself, my love. But I must tell you again that what you plan to do in that borrowed finery is not only dangerous but absolutely pointless."

Gideon chewed on his lower lip a moment. "I think you're wrong. It'll make him realize I know what he is. Maybe some of his guests will come to realize it, too."

"Gideon, the railroad industry—the entire city—already *knows* what he is. It makes no difference! He has money. Money creates influence, assures friendships and, when necessary, even writes the laws. What weapon will prevail against someone that strongly entrenched? Certainly not a threat of exposure in a penny sheet with a worthy purpose but virtually no circulation. Not biblical wrath eith—good heavens! Why are you staring like that? I'm not making fun of you or demeaning your newspaper—"

"It was what you said. Biblical wrath—" His voice had grown hoarse. "The night my father died, he marked a passage in his Bible. He meant to speak to me about it." He quoted the verse from Judges. "I've never had a clue as to what he meant."

"When he marked the verse, you were already tilting at the railroads, weren't you? And already publishing the *Beacon*?"

"Yes."

"Did he want to encourage you? Was the verse an endorsement of what you were doing?"

Gideon frowned. "I don't think so. If anything, my father might have wanted to discourage me. I know he thought the work was largely futile. Admirable, maybe, but futile. I suspect the verse applies to something altogether different."

"Smite the Midianites," she murmured, pacing. "What do you suppose he meant?"

"I've spent whole nights wondering."

"Do you think he wanted to ask you to—to strike out against someone else? Devote your energy to some other cause?"

He looked surprised, then thoughtful. "You know, you might be right. I can't imagine what it would be, though. There wasn't any variety of injustice that didn't anger my father."

It was annoying to have a possible solution to the riddle reveal itself and by doing so reveal another, deeper riddle at the same time. "Well, in any case"—obviously frustrated, he took it out on his cravat, jerking it one way, then another in front of the glass—"I have Mr. Courtleigh to deal with—despite your scorn for the enterprise."

"Oh, you can be a maddening person! I am not scornful. I admire you. The Tom Courtleighs of this country have to be curbed or we'll be so mired in corruption we can consign the Constitution to the ash bin. But you can't fight Courtleigh and his kind with"—she struggled for a term, then blurted—"theatrical gestures!"

"I disagree. Just on the basis of that *Tribune* story, I'd say Courtleigh is very sensitive to the public impression he creates. If I'm wrong, why did he change the purpose of this little party—and then announce the change?"

She blew out the lamp and they left the bedroom. They started down the staircase, Julia still pleading her case. "You're not wrong in that respect. Appearances count for a great deal with him. So the very thing you're planning will only make him all the more angry—at you!"

"Excellent. Excellent!" Gideon boomed out. She shook her head. The volume of his voice clearly said he was still irked. At the foot of the staircase he turned to block her, and revealed the true reason for his crossness.

"So you don't think much of *Labor's Beacon,* eh?"

"Gideon Kent, I told you I was *not* demeaning your newspaper!"

"Odd, I got exactly the opposite impression."

She stamped her foot. "Are you this difficult with all the women you know, or only those who dare to disagree with you?" He started to retort but she gave him no chance. "I think *Labor's Beacon* is a worthy effort. But by its very nature, it automatically reaches and influences just a small number of people. If you want to have the kind of power necessary to fight a Tom Courtleigh, you must make a great many people listen. You must have an *audience.* The kind"—sudden inspiration quickened her voice—"the kind you'd eventually have if you took that position with the *Union!*"

Gideon saw his father's face. *You don't suppose that's what he meant to say? That the* Beacon *was ineffective? That I could do a better job through an established paper?* He knew how deeply Jephtha had deplored the corruption inundating the land. How he'd preached against it from his pulpit—

And how he'd often said in private that he lacked sufficient reach to do much about it.

Did his father mean for him to broaden his own attack? Was *that* the significance of "smite the Midianites"?

Nonsense. He was reading far too much into a Bible verse and a cryptic message on a scrap of paper. Yet the feeling he'd stumbled onto something stayed with him.

"Julia, I told you that even if I worked myself into a position of responsibility with the *Union,* the other stockholders would never permit me to put the paper strongly behind labor causes. Advertising revenues would dry up. Circulation would shrink. When I first discussed the job with Molly, my father's widow, she made both points and made them strongly."

"Even so, you'd still have a much better platform than you have now. You might write about labor less often. But when you did write, it would carry more authority. And your views would certainly reach hundreds of thousands more than you're reaching today. Can't you see the wisdom of compromising just a little to achieve that?"

He bristled. "The Kents are not known for compromising."

"They're known for stubbornness and fits of pomposity!" she exclaimed. "That much you have in common with Louis!"

Her reaction made him smile. "I guess I did sound stuffy. I'm sorry." He slipped his arm around her. "Are you admitting members of the women's movement compromise their principles?"

"Certainly we do. Every time we lower ourselves to speak to a thickheaded man!"

He laughed, jollied out of his bad mood. She kept her voice light, but anxiety showed in her eyes as she went on.

"Since I can't persuade you to change your mind, please be careful over there tonight. Please come back if there are signs of serious trouble. Frankly, I doubt you'll even get in."

"Oh yes, I will. I'll give 'em a shot of the old Kent pomposity, and they'll fall like tenpins."

Grinning, he kissed her cheek. She watched him disappear into the back of the house and suppressed a little shudder. She knew what he was going after back there.

He called goodbye as he left by the rear entrance. She dashed into the darkened music room, barely aware of Carter and one of the homeless boys whooping and racketing along the upper hallways like wild Indians. From a window she watched Gideon's strong, vigorous figure pass along the north side of the property, silhouetted against the blaze of Courtleigh's house and the line of parked carriages trailing around the corner into Twentieth Street.

After he reached State and disappeared up the mansion drive, she stayed in the music room trying to say a prayer to a deity with whom she was not on the best of terms.

ii

Thomas Courtleigh had withdrawn the guards from his driveway, evidently feeling secure now that small squads of soldiers patrolled the residential streets. A couple of blocks to the north, Gideon saw the wink of bayonets belonging to one such patrol.

Some of the carriage drivers stared, but none attempted to stop him. His mouth grew dry as he mounted the stone stairs to the brilliantly lit entrance. With his elbow he compressed the bundle under the left side of his coat.

An Offenbach melody soared inside the house. He stepped up to the heavy walnut doors with side panels of intricately etched glass. Without bothering to ring, he reached for one of the door handles and walked in.

He slammed the door on the shout of a startled coachman. He was in an immense domed foyer. Three gaping footmen came to life and converged on him. The music and the gay sounds of guests enjoying themselves drifted from an open archway on the left.

As the footmen strode toward him, two couples emerged from the ballroom. The men were in formal attire, the women in dresses with long trains, their hair decorated with jewels. Gideon took another step and the footmen barred his way. The guests spied him, noted his clothes and whispered among themselves.

The oldest of the footmen planted himself in front of Gideon; he was fifty-five or more. The other two weren't much younger. If it came to a physical struggle, Gideon doubted he'd have much trouble with any of them.

He was beginning to feel overwhelmed by the splendor of the house, though. Marble pillars reached up three stories to the perimeter of the stained-glass dome. Veined marble spread underfoot. The air smelled of costly perfume, expensive cigars—and wealth.

The senior footmen extended a white gloved hand. "May I see your card of invitation?"

"I'm not here to attend the party. I have personal business with Mr. Courtleigh."

The footmen exchanged puzzled looks. Their spokesman's tone grew a shade harder. "Mr. Courtleigh left no word that he was expecting anyone from the company."

"I'm not from the company. Look here—" In spite of his nervousness, Gideon managed to smile. It disarmed and confused them. Beyond the footmen, one of the female guests was pointing her fan at Gideon's eye patch and saying something behind her hand. "I have no quarrel with you gentlemen. I'd feel bad if I had to take my fist to any of you." One of the footmen turned pale. "I merely want to see Courtleigh, and I intend to do so. If you'll kindly step aside we can avoid unpleasantness."

"I appreciate what you say, sir." The oldest footman gave a quick nod, clearly not anxious to fight. "But we have orders."

"Then I'm sorry." Without warning, Gideon feinted to the left.

The footmen shifted that way. Gideon's hand shot out, shoving the nearest man. He stumbled. That created a space he could slip through while the other two stared in confusion.

The female guests pulled their escorts out of the way as Gideon walked straight toward the ballroom entrance. Behind him, he heard the oldest footman panting for breath. Then the man cried, "Run and get Cully in the stable. Cully and Jim—they're tough enough to take care of him!"

There'd be roughnecks coming. Well, he hadn't expected to pull this off without a hitch. He stalked by the two speechless couples who simply couldn't comprehend the presence of a tall, tangle-haired young man with ill-fitting clothes, a patch over his left eye and a truculent expression.

Gideon walked into the mirror-paneled ballroom and stopped at the top of three steps leading down to the dance floor. In front of him he saw a blurred panorama of heavy trains swirling, jewels winking, men's black button pumps flashing in time to the music. A young woman near the foot of the stairs was first to notice him. She clutched her escort's arm and stared.

Gideon scanned the ballroom. The orchestra played loudly, Strauss now. The conversation and the music created a din, and except for the one girl, he'd gone unnoticed for the few seconds he stood there.

But every head turned when he shouted, "Courtleigh? Where the hell are you?"

iii

The ballroom's fall, rectangular mirrors reflected the hundred and fifty guests and multiplied their images. A dozen orchestra players all missed a beat; a dozen other violin bows hesitated in midair. The musicians stopped in a disorderly way, the viola and the harp trailing off last of all.

The dancers—some amused, some baffled, one or two frowning—all swung toward Gideon. At last he located Courtleigh. The railroad president had been dancing near the small orchestra stage on the far side of the room. On Courtleigh's arm Gideon saw the pale, panicky creature who had looked at him from the brougham.

From Gideon's left, a white-haired woman veered toward the steps like a warship under sail. Her burden of gems was nearly as large as her bosom. She called to her son, "Thomas, who is this person? Some drunken club-room crony of yours?"

Gideon's hands were trembling at his sides. He thought of Torvald Ericsson and calmed down. He took a deep satisfaction from watching the long-nosed, thin-lipped Courtleigh hurry toward him. Courtleigh was dressed in evening wear that fit perfectly. The wide-eyed Miss Strother hung on his arm and let him drag her along.

"Thomas!" The white-haired woman turned completely around and looked toward her son. "I asked you—"

"Be quiet, Mother." Courtleigh's voice wasn't loud, but it carried because the ballroom had fallen silent. The only other noises were the click of Courtleigh's pumps on the floor and the swish of his fiancée's train. Suddenly there was a clang and a muffled exclamation. Straining to see, the piccolo player had upset his music stand. Courtleigh cast a glance over his shoulder. His eyes were venomous.

He walked to within a yard of the lower step and stopped. His eyes flicked over Gideon's worn coat. The corners of his mouth twitched in amusement. To his mother he said, "This man is a labor agitator from New York. A Communard."

Those close by heard it and passed it on, whispering their shock and horror.

"He came to stir up trouble on the Wisconsin and Prairie." Courtleigh's hazel eyes fixed on Gideon's face and much as he tried, he couldn't control his seething anger. "I rather hoped we might have lost you in the recent disaster, Mr. Kent. How did you get in here?"

"Why, your servants let me in. At the front door."

"I'll crucify them for—" The sibilant words were choked back. He realized his guests were listening closely. He pushed Miss Strother's gloved hand off his arm. She caught her breath and swayed.

Courtleigh planted one black pump on the lower step. He pitched his voice lower.

"If you wish to have a conversation with me, at least do me the courtesy of retiring to my study so my guests needn't be offended by your boorishness."

"Oh, no." Gideon shook his head. "I want your guests to hear all I have to say."

Courtleigh's restraint broke. He took another step up, and Gideon had seldom heard such venom in a voice.

"Very well, Mr. Kent. If it's a public scene you want, it's a public scene you shall have! We'll begin by discussing the disappearance of my assistant general manager, Sidney Florian, in the fire which swept the West Side last Sunday evening. His body has been lost, but I have witnesses who

know how he met his death." Courtleigh shook a finger in
Gideon's face. "Witnesses who will testify that he was
murdered!"

A kind of surflike murmur spread around the ballroom.

"Murder?"

"Who was murdered?"

"What's Tom talking about? Is that fellow a murderer?"

Gideon said, "I'd be happy to discuss it—"

Thunderstruck, Courtleigh retreated to the lowest step.
His smug expression was gone. The Strother girl was pathetically distraught. She looked as if she might faint.

"So long as you first explain how Mr. Florian got to the
West Side. How and why." Gideon raised his voice. "The
man your host is talking about was one of his employees,
and the leader of a gang of thugs who invaded a private
home last Sunday night. Their purpose—"

"Shut up, Kent," Courtleigh whispered. Perspiration
beaded his forehead suddenly. "Shut your mouth."

Gideon didn't even glance at him. He spoke to the silent
throng. "Their purpose was to break up a peaceful meeting
held by a few men who thought Mr. Courtleigh's rail line
was unfair in the matter of wages and benefits. The men
gathered to discuss organizing a protest. To *discuss* it!
That's all! Apparently the Constitutional guarantee of the
right to peaceful assembly is voided when you go to work
for the Wisconsin and Prairie."

The white-haired woman began screaming, "Thomas, silence him. *Silence him!*"

Then there were hisses. Men stepping forward—though
not far—to exclaim.

"Socialist!"

"Communard!"

"Throw him out of here!"

"Break his head open!"

The railroad president looked stunned and confused. He
seemed on the point of rushing up to throttle Gideon. Yet
something—his mother's hectoring, his fiancée's distraught
behavior, the shock of what was happening in his own
home—kept him rooted while Gideon roared over the cre-
scendo of sound.

"Mr. Courtleigh's thugs came calling with guns and
knives. One of them—Florian—shot at me and I fired back.

I wounded Florian and I'll admit that in any court in the land—except the ones Mr. Courtleigh can buy here in Chicago. I too have witnesses, and they'll swear I acted in self-defense."

"What witnesses?" Courtleigh snarled. "That slut of a Lucy Stoner?" He was purple from the humiliation of having Gideon ignore him. But Gideon knew where his audience lay.

"They'll also swear to what Mr. Courtleigh's brave lads did to the son of the man at whose house the meeting took place. A boy named Torvald Ericsson. He was no more than ten years old. This belonged to him."

From where he'd tucked it in his waistband, Gideon drew out the shirt. The garment was stiff with dried blood. The moment he held it up, there was absolute silence again.

Behind him he heard heavy boots hammer, then stop. The stable hands? Evidently so. Courtleigh saw them, hesitated, finally gestured them back.

Gideon held the shirt at arm's length, down where Courtleigh could see it clearly. "One of your thugs put a knife in Torvald Ericsson. He died the same night."

White, Courtleigh could barely croak, "That—that is a foul piece of—character assassination, an—utter lie."

"Now we know how you protect your profits, Courtleigh. By killing children!"

Courtleigh lost control and fairly screamed at Gideon, "You're lying. You're a filthy liar!"

"Of course he's lying," a woman cried. "Tom would never do anything so despicable. The man's mad."

"Mad or a Communard, it's the same thing," someone else yelled. There was more hissing and even some oaths quite out of place in the mixed company.

Courtleigh heard his friends coming to his defense and skillfully took advantage of it. "I don't deny I sent observers to that gathering of anarchists—"

"Observers!" Gideon exclaimed, but now Courtleigh had regained some confidence, and outshouted him.

"They had no orders to hurt anyone, and certainly no orders to hurt children. The very idea is ludicrous!"

"That's right," a male guest bellowed. "Tom's a law-abiding, God-fearing man. Throw that lying Communard out of here!"

Other guests echoed it, surging to the foot of the stairs, their mood ugly. A feeling of defeat began to fill Gideon as he spread the shirt by the shoulders.

Women turned away, covering their mouths with their fans or their gloves. Men cursed him even as their eyes were drawn to the knife slashes in the bloodied fabric.

"I hear what you say, Courtleigh." Gideon pitched his voice low on purpose. It stilled the angry outbursts and brought the crowd forward in macabre fascination. "I'm afraid this piece of evidence speaks louder. You note the size? Clearly a boy's shirt, not a man's. I took this from the body of Nils Ericsson's son. Ericsson himself died in the fire, so you don't have to worry about him. But you do have to worry about me. You can burn this. Bribe all your hired thugs to keep silent. Persuade a few of your fine friends to perjure themselves and testify to your impeccable character—"

Growls from the crowd at that—an ugly, animal sound. Gideon was badly shaken. He hadn't expected all of them to be on Courtleigh's side, but they were.

"Perhaps you can even convince yourself none of it happened. But I know it did. I saw it. And I can't be bought or silenced. *You're a murderer, Courtleigh!*"

Gideon flung the shirt.

Courtleigh leaped back, his eyes fixed on the garment as if it were poisonous. The shirt fluttered down next to the hem of Miss Strother's ball gown. The sight of the ripped and bloodstained fabric was all it took to shatter her. She started moaning, softly at first, then louder. She stabbed her hands into her carefully arranged hairdo, tearing it apart.

Courtleigh shouted, "Get him out of here. Get him out of this house!"

The crowd roared agreement. The stable hands, both burly young men, rushed Gideon from behind.

He turned in time to gut punch one of them. The other slashed the edge of his hand across Gideon's neck, making him stumble and bend forward from the waist with an exclamation of pain. A second chopping blow drove him to his knees.

The two seized Gideon under the arms of his plum-colored coat and hauled him into the foyer. In the ballroom, a roar of shocked exclamations erupted. But loudest of all were two voices.

Courtleigh's fiancée, shrieking as she tore her hair.

And Courtleigh yelling at her, nearly as hysterical.

"Be quiet. What's the matter with you? He's a lunatic. Every word was false! Can't you control yourself? Damn you, be quiet! *BE QUIET!*"

iv

The stable hands dragged Gideon to the front door and booted him down the steps. He landed hard. Coachmen formed into small groups. They stood by the pillars at the driveway entrance as he picked himself up and moved unsteadily toward the street.

One of the stable hands took a threatening step just before Gideon passed. Gideon tensed, ready to defend himself even though he was groggy. The two took note of the glint in his blue eye and decided they'd fulfilled their employer's orders. After a couple of obscene taunts they turned and strolled back to the mansion.

Gideon dusted himself off as he reached the street. While he was crossing Twentieth, the orchestra resumed. Mingled with the melody he thought he detected a woman's screams. But that quickly faded and only the lilting music remained. Hearing it played as if nothing had happened, he felt a stinging sense of failure.

In the ballroom he'd gotten exactly what he wanted—for a little while. He'd gotten an acknowledgment of Courtleigh's guilt through his violent behavior. Gideon supposed no one had ever dared to confront the railroad president that way before—in his own home and in front of friends of his own class.

So perhaps a debt had been discharged in Torvald Ericsson's name. But only a very small one.

The music from the mansion swelled, and he asked himself whom he had persuaded. Courtleigh's friends and cronies would remain that. They would remain the enemies of workingmen.

What had he changed, then? Nothing. His accusation

would have no effect on Courtleigh's power, Courtleigh's style of operation, Courtleigh's determination to resist unions. He had seen Courtleigh squirm, but at best the whole thing was—in Julia's phrase—a theatrical gesture.

And instead of feeling good about it, he remembered the rage and loathing in the eyes of Courtleigh's friends and felt terrible.

He wiped his perspiring cheek. Time to think about the future—and to do it a little more realistically for a change. What if he kept right on just as he'd planned? What if he wrote about Courtleigh's crime in the *Beacon*? Who would believe the charges, or act upon them?

Again the inevitable answer—no one. Courtleigh would find and pay a score of witnesses to prove he'd never ordered the missing Florian to commit murder.

The last of the stormy satisfaction vanished. He felt that he, not Thomas Courtleigh, was the loser this evening. He kept thinking of the hostility of the guests. The words with which they'd taunted him.

Socialist.

Communard.

It was almost inevitable that people in Courtleigh's crowd would believe that of trade unionists. No amount of editorializing would change their minds. But as he trudged up the front steps of Julia's house, he sadly realized the great majority of Americans also held the same opinion. And he'd never change *their* minds or break down *their* prejudices by writing little articles in a paper no one bought.

He lingered on the stoop, thinking about Julia's remarks earlier in the evening. The ends for which he was working might be worthy, but the means were laughable. To change even a few minds about the movement was an immense job. The kind of job which required an instrument of great authority and influence, not a little penny sheet, as Julia so aptly called it.

The answer seemed obvious. The immense task required an instrument like the *New York Union*.

Quite without warning, he felt an eerie sense of his father's presence, a sense of Jephtha being close by and struggling to communicate with him. The Bible verse suddenly came to mind.

*And the Lord said unto him, Surely I will be with thee,
and thou shalt smite the Midianites as one man.*

Insights flooded into his mind with incredible speed. Perhaps Jephtha had marked that verse because he believed Gideon *could* bring about some meaningful changes in society. Perhaps his father had wanted to tell him that.

Speak to G.

And was that the end of it? Somehow, Gideon didn't think so. He had a conviction that his father had believed he must go about his work differently. Julia had been the one to suggest that, just as she'd been the one to suggest the new approach—one which had been in front of him all the time, yet hidden from him by his own narrow frame of reference. It had taken the scene in the ballroom to show him the need for a new means of attacking and overcoming the Courtleighs of America.

He drew a deep, exhilarated breath. The evening might not be a debacle after all. Just the opposite. He rushed inside to find Julia and discuss the idea that was becoming more appealing to him every moment.

As it turned out, Gideon was completely wrong in one judgment which he'd made. The effect of his visit to Mr. Thomas Courtleigh's was not nearly so insignificant as he imagined, though just then he had no way of foreseeing the extent of its profound, even tragic consequences in Courtleigh's life.

And his.

CHAPTER XI

DECISION IN THE RAIN

i

LATE THE NEXT afternoon, Julia and Gideon were taking tea in the second-floor solarium on the south side of the house. Gideon was depressed by the thought of his departure the next day. She felt the same way. Both made a conscious effort to hide their feelings and keep their conversation animated as they discussed his conclusions about his future, and how he meant to implement them.

"I realize you were right last night, Julia. It's better to reach ten thousand people than ten. It's the only way to get public opinion squarely against Courtleigh and his kind."

"Don't be too sure it'll be possible. At least not immediately." He remembered Strelnik's prediction that he would ultimately experience frustration which would vent itself in rage. "I'm not saying the effort shouldn't be made, Gideon. It should."

"Yes, long as I remember one thing." For a moment he saw a lifeless face in a railroad yard besieged by a winter storm. "The man I'm working for."

"The chap you first met on the southbound train after the war?"

He nodded. "Miller."

"I'm sure you won't forget him, *or* what he stands for. You're not the kind to let yourself forget." A moment's silence. "Will you speak to Molly soon?"

"As soon as I put a few things in order. It'll take a couple of months to tie up the affairs of my penny sheet, as you called it." He chuckled. "Did you realize that's what I charge for *Labor's Beacon*?"

"Truly? I confess I've never paid much attention to the price."

"A cent a copy. I guess I'm living in the past. Inflation killed the penny press years ago."

She thought for a moment. "I suppose you realize carrying out your plan won't be easy."

"I've found that very few worthwhile accomplishments are easy, Julia. In fact I can only think of one." A grin. "Inheriting several million dollars."

She laughed. "But you've really marked out a huge piece of work for yourself. Changing careers—"

"I can learn whatever I need to learn." *Even if I don't have Margaret's help and support any longer,* he thought with sadness.

She smiled. "Yes, I'm sure you can."

They looked up as a servant entered carrying a salver with a calling card on it. Julia picked up the card, gave it a casual glance, then sat absolutely motionless. Gideon set his cup on the silver tea cart as she said in a small voice, "Courtleigh."

"Here? I don't believe it."

She showed him the card. Tension tightened his throat suddenly. To the servant Julia said, "Ask him to come up, please."

They exchanged anxious glances during the seemingly interminable time it took the servant to usher their visitor to the glass-enclosed room where October sunlight fell on potted plants, comfortable furniture and the bright surfaces of the tea set.

Julia pulled her lace kerchief from her sleeve, twisted it in her fingers. He knew she was probably thinking thoughts much like his. Suppose Courtleigh considered Gideon's behavior such a gross insult that it could only be repaid with an act of personal revenge. Suppose he'd come calling with a small hideaway pistol.

He rose, patted Julia's arm to reassure her and moved to a place near the expanse of glass overlooking open country to the south. The October light was pale because it was late in the day. A thin haze filled the sky, partly the result of the season, partly of the fire.

Gideon fixed his eye on the solarium entrance. He heard Courtleigh approaching long before the man himself became visible. His tread had a measured, almost sinister steadiness. Finally he appeared.

"Mr. Courtleigh." Julia nodded. She rose and smoothed her skirt. Extended her hand.

Courtleigh made no such effort at courtesy. His hazel eyes flicked over the outstretched hand. "Good afternoon," he said in a curt way. Gideon went rigid.

The railroad president was elegantly turned out in a beige tailcoat, waistcoat and trousers, and a maroon-banded hat and gloves of the same soft shade. He touched one glove to an errant lock of wavy auburn hair.

"I'll stay only a moment. I find merely being in this house extremely distasteful."

Gideon thought he could see Julia's spine stiffen. "Hardly an auspicious start for a social call," she said.

"Not a social call, Miss Sedgwick. An unappealing but necessary visit." For the first time his attention shifted to Gideon, who had rarely seen such hatred in a human gaze. The eyes reminded him of Tillotson, the sadistic Yankee jailer who had blinded him during his wartime imprisonment. "No matter what you term it," Courtleigh went on, "I trust my manners will be better than this gentleman's last evening. He gave a performance worthy of a stage melodrama."

Courtleigh's lips compressed. His gloved fingers closed on the brim of his hat, crushing the rolled edge. "But my house is not a theater, and those at the ball were relatives and personal friends, not gallery hooligans. What you did, Mr. Kent, was insulting, disgusting, and unforgivable."

Gideon had trouble controlling his temper. "Shall we compare it to the murder of a ten-year-old boy?"

Julia could sense the hate crackling between the two men. Perhaps out of instinct, she fell back on the stratagems of the good hostess.

"Here, gentlemen! A little more politeness on both sides. Sit down, Mr. Courtleigh. Let me pour you a cup of—"

"No, thank you. I want nothing from the hand of a woman of your questionable morals."

"You arrogant bastard!" Gideon strode forward. Julia stepped in front of him.

"Let's get this over, Gideon. Clearly it isn't going to be pleasant."

Courtleigh slapped his hat against his trouser leg, squinting into the sunlight suffusing the room. "No, it isn't. I might even manage to overlook your bizarre performance, Mr. Kent—overlook it and chalk it up to the lunatic zeal which affects all those of the Communard persuasion—" Gideon reddened. "I might, that is, except for the unfortunate condition of my fiancée. Your behavior had a most deleterious effect upon her." Every trace of sarcasm was gone now. "Miss Strother has always had a rather delicate, even nervous temperament—"

Just what Julia had said, Gideon recalled. The hazel eyes continued to accuse him.

"And your threatening manner quite undid her. The sight of that rag purporting to be the shirt of some dead boy sent her into a state of complete nervous collapse."

The shrieks he'd heard when the music resumed? he wondered.

"Her parents have dispatched her to a private medical facility up in Lake County. A facility for the disturbed. Quite a fine place, I'm told. Excellent staff, the best physicians in attendance. With a spot of luck she'll be herself in just a few days. But what you did to her—the unnecessary suffering you've caused, the hell you've put her through— that, Mr. Kent, I cannot and shall not forget. Your kind are scum. Rabble bent on destroying every shred of law and order in this country—and the very concept of private property rights!"

"Now see here—"

"No, *you* see here!" Courtleigh retorted. "You hurt the young woman I intend to marry. I pray to God the damage you did to her fragile nature is not permanent, but—"

"A man like you praying?" Gideon scoffed. "That's laughable."

Courtleigh went white. "It's *you* who would be laughable if you weren't so dangerous." He started to draw something from the side pocket of his coat. Gideon tensed until he saw it was merely a piece of paper. He recognized a masthead torn from *Labor's Beacon*.

"You made a serious error in coming to Chicago on behalf of your gutter paper, Mr. Kent. You made an even more serious one when, for some reason I still cannot fathom, you chose me as the focus of your ill will. Not to mention your misguided crusade to see every foundation of society shattered—"

Gideon snorted. "That's the argument you always use, isn't it? You and the rest of the bosses. Anyone who asks for a decent wage, or injury benefits, or shorter hours, or a safe, healthy place to work is automatically out to overturn society. Out to trample the American flag and raise the red one the Communards waved—"

Courtleigh smiled in a frosty way. "Exactly."

"I'll grant it's a fine diversionary tactic. And it does work. But it won't work forever."

The railroad man shrugged again. "I doubt you'll be on the scene one way or another. I predict a very short life for you, Mr. Kent."

Julia stepped to Gideon's side and took his arm. If Courtleigh had raised his voice, or a fist, Gideon might have borne it somewhat better than he did. Instead, Courtleigh kept his tone temperate. Only the hazel eyes showed his loathing for the younger man as he held up the scrap from the *Beacon* and went on.

"But while you're still with us, I am going to crush this rag out of existence." He crumpled the paper and let it drift to the carpet. "I am going to crush your family, and your slut here, and I am going to crush you—though not necessarily in that particular order, and not necessarily at once. But I *will* do it, Mr. Kent. Before God, I will do it all. That I swear."

Trembling but managing a smile, he tipped his fawn hat, about-faced as smartly as a soldier and walked out of the solarium.

ii

Gideon and Julia listened to his footsteps clack down the main staircase. Then came the distant slam of the front door. The venomous hazel eyes lingered in Gideon's mind as he moved slowly to Julia and put his arms around her, feeling her shiver.

Neither of them spoke. At last Gideon leaned down to retrieve the piece of the *Beacon*. He laid it on the tea cart, smoothed it almost as if it were a fragment of a priceless painting.

"Let him try," he said, wanting to sound much more confident than he felt.

"I'm sure we won't have to invite his wrath, Gideon."

"You really think he—?"

She broke in. "I don't think there's any question of it." And again Courtleigh's presence seemed to hover near them, ruining their earlier enthusiasm for talk of his decision to join the New York *Union*.

iii

The eastbound express was arriving. The time had come.

A cold autumn rain poured down on the roofed platform at Englewood Junction south of the city. Wind whipped the rain beneath the eaves, and drove silver needles through the beam of the locomotive's headlight. The locomotive was still a quarter mile from the platform, pouring out steam and wood smoke that added to the murk of an afternoon already dark and dreary. Fast-flying black clouds filled the sky.

Julia's servants had managed to find a closed carriage for the trip. Many eastbound and westbound trains were using the country depot until those in the central city could be restored to full service. Riding through the rain with the wind-lashed lake on their left, Gideon had held Julia's hand tightly and thought about the days just past. The discovery of his love for her was a wondrous experience, though it had now become a saddening one. He was taking the only sensible course, and he hated it.

Still, he knew he dared not prolong the affair. It was

wrong. That seemed a dismal admission to make about something so filled with joy and love, but it was inescapable. What he and Julia had done was wrong in the traditional sense, and memories of his biblical upbringing would never let him forget it. But abstract morality wasn't the most compelling reason for his decision. In his opinion there was a much more practical and important one. The affair was wrong because it carried the possibility of pain and injury for others. For Margaret. For his children, should the liaison ever come to light by accident. For Julia herself if Courtleigh fulfilled his vow.

No, unquestionably, he had to leave her. Perhaps breaking things off would have at least one benefit. He might spare her from Courtleigh's reprisals.

But now, on the platform illuminated by the headlight of the arriving express, it was proving hard to do what was right and necessary. Hard because her mouth was so sweet and eager. Hard because his will wavered.

He lifted her off her feet, kissing her without embarrassment while waiting passengers gaped or made disapproving comments. Because the afternoon was chilly, Julia had worn a little fur-trimmed cape. The fur tickled his cheek as he pressed his face against hers.

"Sometimes I wish this week had never happened."

"I know, dearest. It would be easier for both of us." She drew back. "But what you must think about is—"

A quick glance to see if there were any listeners close by. She saw none. And the express was chugging in, trucks rattling, drivers squealing, steam hissing, bell clanging in a way that sounded mournful, somehow. She formed a word in silence: *"Courtleigh."* Then, aloud, she added, "He'll do what he threatened."

"Yes, you've convinced me of that."

"You must be very careful, darling. Very careful of your family, too." A wistful smile as she wiped rain—or tears—from her face. "Some of my freethinking sisters would drum me out of the movement if they saw me carrying on this way. I—I don't quite know what you've done to me, Gideon. I've fallen in love with you, but at the same time, you've got me fretting about the welfare of the"—she had difficulty saying it—"the woman who's going to keep you away from me. Well, I can't help that. She's important to you and so she has to be important to me. I want her to be safe. Your children, too. You most of all."

She rested her cheek against his chest as the locomotive roared by, shaking the platform. "I'm not so liberal and brave as I pretend. I want to be an independent woman, but all at once, a part of me doesn't. The part that's linked to you for good and all now—"

She was crying. A voice within him insisted, *You've got to say goodbye. Time's running.*

"I think I'd die if anything happened to you, Gideon, I do love you so very much—"

"I—"

Say goodbye. End it!

But the words that were torn out of him weren't the ones conscience and good sense demanded.

"I love you too, Julia."

Unashamed, she let the tears stream down her face. "Oh—dear heaven, that's—the first time—you've told me—"

"I'd tell you a hundred times a day if I could. I love you, Julia. I love you."

The pain of parting consumed them as they hugged each other on the noisy, rain-swept platform. The smeared and dirty windows of second-class cars rolled slowly by, lit from within by hanging oil lamps. Gideon felt dizzy for a moment. He didn't want to plunge into a lifetime of deception, lies to Margaret, silent shame in front of his children. Those were things no decent, rational man wanted or sought.

And yet when he looked down into Julia's blue eyes, so sad and lovely, he knew he couldn't leave her.

Over the train's roar, he exclaimed as he hugged her again, "I've got to see you."

"But—you said—"

"I know what I said. I didn't mean it. Do you want to end it?"

"Yes." She was laughing and weeping at the same time. "Yes, but I can't do it either. Oh, thank you, darling. Thank you, thank you—"

They kissed again, ignoring stares, ignoring mirthful faces behind the streaked windows. Almost out of breath, he said, "It will take me three or four months to close down the *Beacon*. And that's assuming Molly and Theo Payne

will have me on the *Union.* You can write me care of the
Beacon till I send you another address."

"I will, my darling. I'll write you there once a week.
Daily. Hourly! Oh, God, you've made me so happy, Gideon. I know we should stop it. But I don't want to—I don't
want to!"

He picked her up by the waist and whirled her around.
While the other passengers climbed aboard, Gideon and
Julia talked blithely, saying the foolish things lovers say—
things that should never be overheard. He was almost able
to ignore the nagging voice of conscience.

*You damn fool, you should have broken it off. You could
have. This way, you'll gain a little joy, and ten times the
grief a quick parting would have caused.*

Somehow he didn't care. He loved her. That swept everything else aside. In his own way he had become as lawless
as Tom Courtleigh. And if that was sinful, why was he
so happy?

Finally, the conductor's cry broke through his euphoria.
After one last kiss, he raced along beside the moving train
and jumped to the steps of a second-class car. He clung to
a hand rail, overcome with the miracle of his love for her,
and watched her small, strong figure disappearing slowly in
the rain, her head high—confident and unafraid now, as
he was.

Her gloved hand rose and moved slowly, waving in affectionate farewell. He gripped the hand rail and stayed in the
slashing rain until she was lost from sight.

But he knew he'd see her again. Whatever the price,
whatever his punishment.

A SHOOTING ON
TEXAS STREET

i

ON THE NIGHT the Chicago fire began, Jeremiah Kent was sharing in the prosperity of Abilene, Kansas.

His professional wardrobe showed he was doing well. Just within the last three months, he'd purchased a new long-tailed coat, checked trousers, embroidered waistcoat and silk cravat, not to mention the flat-crowned hat in which he kept his hideout gun. After drifting from place to place for a couple of years, he'd finally stumbled into El Dorado.

He'd arrived in Abilene in April, a few weeks before the start of what the locals referred to as the summer season. Everyone told him 1871 would be the biggest year yet in the town's short history as a cattle shipping center. Optimists predicted that six hundred thousand Texas longhorns would move north to the Kansas railheads before winter again closed Jesse Chisholm's trail through the Indian Territory. Of that total, the Abilene stockyards would get by far the largest share.

Ever since the little promoter from Illinois, Joe McCoy, had stepped off the train and seen a profit potential on the empty prairie, Abilene had developed a reputation for enterprise. McCoy and his associates had financed and built pens, chutes and scales, then arranged favorable shipping rates with the railroad.

They had somehow persuaded or paid the governor and members of the state legislature to ignore the quarantine line which made it illegal for longhorns to enter Dickinson County because they were probably carrying spleen fever ticks.

And from the beginning McCoy and all the energetic merchants who'd caught a glimpse of his vision saw to it that the summer visitors were accommodated in every way so that they'd speak favorably of Abilene when they returned home. After all, the war was in the past, Texas was back in the Union, and the drovers and their crews of youthful whites, blacks and Mexicans were not, first and foremost, Southerners or even Americans. They were *customers*. In the true spirit of Yankee enterprise, the customer was Abilene's first and only uncrowned king.

Whatever a trail-weary man wanted—from new red-top boots with stars and crescent moons cut into the leather, to groceries, to a bath, to a woman—he could find it in Abilene. Prostitution operated full tilt in the Devil's Addition, the southeast quarter of town below the tracks. Despite the lobbying of a certain small clique whose piety was bad for business, the City Council refused to vote to drive out the soiled doves. Instead, the Council chose to contain them, since the girls were absolutely vital to the success of a combination shipping point and end-of-the-trail resort.

Strong drink was necessary, too, of course. More than thirty saloons along the Texas Street esplanade provided it. Some of the visitors also liked to buck the tiger. That was where Jeremiah came in. Within four short months, under the latest of a succession of assumed names, he'd made himself one of the best-known gentlemen of Hell Street, as the town's moralistic minority termed the esplanade. He had done it by turning his favorite pastime into a successful profession. He dealt poker, monte, and other games of chance.

In Abilene, he was not far from Ellsworth; it was located just about sixty miles west, beyond the quarantine line. When he had drifted out from Kansas City in the spring, he'd been concerned that he was returning too near the scene of one of his crimes. He stayed alert in case anyone from Ellsworth or Fort Harker should show up and penetrate the various layers of protection provided by his new clothes, new name and new profession. So far, no one had. In fact, after killing the sergeant in the Ellsworth dance house, he'd never seen a sign of pursuit, which convinced him the United States Army thought Amos Graves was unimportant, or that he was. The latter angered him not a little.

Now, in early October, he'd been in Abilene longer than he'd been anywhere else since the war. It seemed an ideal spot for a man of his ability and growing reputation. Besides, the pickings were incredible. And involved next to no risk. Another itinerant gambler whom he'd met in his travels—an older man, wise with experience—had lectured him convincingly about the best way to get rich and, just as important, stay out of meaningless fights. The secret was simple honesty. Not only was cheating dangerous, it wasn't necessary. The odds favored the dealer, and the Texans were usually besotted when they played, further heightening the dealer's advantage. Jeremiah drank too. He'd discovered gin, and put away a pint to a pint and a half every day of the week. But he took care never to be as drunk as his customers.

By cultivating a reputation for honesty, he attracted a lot of repeat business. Of course he had to pass a small percentage of his winnings to the owners of whatever liquor palace he happened to be playing in—the Old Fruit, the Applejack, Jim Flynn's, the Pearl or any of a half dozen other good ones. Even so, he earned enough to dress well, live comfortably, and provide himself with all the female companionship he wanted.

Another aspect of his reputation contributed to his success. Since arriving in town, he'd taken pains to establish that part by dropping casual remarks into card table conversation, and by backing up the remarks with participation in whatever shooting contests or exhibitions the saloon crowd arranged.

Jeremiah never won those contests, never pulled off the most spectacular feats of marksmanship in the exhibitions. His friend the marshal always bested him. No surprise there, though. Abilene's marshal practiced with his pistols for an hour or two every day. Men such as George Custer and Little Phil Sheridan called him the best sharpshooter in the West. The marshal's favorite challenge was to call for a tomato can to be tossed up in the air. No other man Jeremiah had ever met could fire at the can with both pistols, keep it spinning aloft and score nine or ten hits out of twelve rounds—every time. The best Jeremiah had ever done was seven out of twelve rounds. Once.

Nevertheless, he usually ran a good second in the contests, and that lent an air of truth to his smiling, modest answers to questions put to him over cards. Hearing him say certain things about his background, the Texans always seemed to enjoy their game a lot more. Jeremiah knew it was because in the West, murder was not always considered reprehensible. Done at the proper time and place, it could make a man a celebrity. It had certainly done that for the marshal. So he was more than willing to admit to a less than spotless past—without going into detail, of course.

Jeremiah kept track of his family with an occasional letter to Boyle, the Irishman he'd met at the Union Pacific railroad in '66. He always asked Boyle to write him care of a post office. Jeremiah signed a different fictitious name to each letter, but Boyle always knew from the content who was inquiring. During September, Boyle had written to say Jeremiah's father had died of a heart seizure. He'd wept in his room and his tears had made the ink run so that when he went back to read the letter a second time, it was nearly illegible.

The Irishman was certainly doing well for himself. Jeremiah had seen some of his retail stores along the U.P. route further north, and in June, he'd played monte with a man who turned out to be a purchasing agent for Boyle. The man had traveled all the way down from Cheyenne to pick up five hundred prime head to add to the herd Boyle and his wife were building. Jeremiah hadn't let on that he was acquainted with the Irishman. But he was rather proud that the only person in all the world who knew he was still alive was a very prosperous individual, a solid citizen.

Whenever he wrote Boyle, he kept personal details to a minimum. He had a lingering fear of Kola's prophecy, and hence a fear of revealing too much about himself, particularly his whereabouts. Under no circumstances did he want to make it possible for Boyle to slip and accidentally tell one of his brothers where he was. No matter that they were hundreds of miles away—in Matt's case, thousands—he just didn't want to take a chance. So far, every one of Kola's predictions had proved out.

Since Ellsworth, he hadn't put the guns away. And they had indeed given a certain luster to the name he used most often. But Kola had also said the killing would never stop, and that too was turning out to be correct. Once having acquired a reputation, it was periodically necessary to defend it.

So he lived with a nagging fear of the rest of it coming true: the gradual slide back into obscurity, the end of his life as the Sioux had described it.

That, he absolutely couldn't bear to think about. Which was one of the chief reasons he'd grown so fond of gin.

ii

Abilene's commercial establishments didn't observe the Sabbath. Doing so would have eliminated one seventh of a week's profit. So Jeremiah worked that Sunday night as usual. About six forty-five he concluded a blackjack game in the town's largest and finest watering spot, the Alamo.

The place occupied a corner on Texas Street but fronted on Cedar. A good deal of money had been spent to make it opulent. The bar was solid mahogany, the fittings solid brass. A splendid array of pudgy, pink-breasted nudes in gold frames decorated the walls. But the management also believed in appealing to higher instincts. Two musicians sat in a niche playing popular airs on the piano and violin.

Jeremiah had just gotten up from the table and was at the bar, buying drinks for himself and his victim, a gregarious, freckled, tipsy young Texan. He signaled the barkeep.

"Gin for me, Hal. Whiskey for my friend. Ben, I'm mighty sorry to have relieved you of all your wages."

The boy grinned in a fuddled way. "Pleasure— pleasure's mine."

The barkeep put down two brimming glasses. He slid the darker one toward Ben. "Kansas sheep dip. Best in the house."

"Obliged to you," Ben said. He spilled half the whiskey before he got one swallow. He wiped his mouth with his cuff. "Besides," he said to Jeremiah, "I know you did it fair an' square. I don't mind losin' to any man who's good friends with the marshal." The boy belched. "That is the truth, ain't it? You and Wild Bill are pals, ain't you?"

"Bosom companions." Jeremiah nodded, stretching it slightly. "I suppose that's unusual, him being a former Yank scout and me a onetime Reb. But we both like handsome women. We're both students of the picture cards. We both shoot pretty well, although he's the best—" A touch of envy had crept in. He hunched over his tumbler of gin and lowered his voice. "His real name's James, you know."

"Is that right!" The boy glowed. The tidbit of information made him feel intimately connected with the great, which was exactly why Jeremiah used it with all his customers.

"Yes, sir. James," he went on. "James Butler Hickok. I'll tell you one more thing. Jim just can't figure why people out here, and then the Eastern magazines, started calling him Bill. It's a genuine, gold-plated mystery."

"You mean he doesn't know how he got the name?"

With great solemnity, Jeremiah shook his head.

"Think of that," the boy murmured. He drank the rest of his Kansas sheep dip. Most of it wound up on the front of his buckskin vest.

The piano and violin struck up "Just Before the Battle, Mother." One of the barkeeps who had a face as innocent as a divinity student's began to sing the lyric in a clear, lovely tenor. Men at the tables stopped their games. Several soon had tears in their eyes; Appomattox was not that far in the past.

The Texas boy evidently had no strong emotional memories of the war because he kept after his companion.

"The fellers back in camp are gonna be mighty interested to know that about the marshal. They're gonna think it's mighty exciting that I heard it from Mr. Jason Kane, too. That I sat right over yonder and bucked the tiger with Jason Kane. You're pretty famous yourself, you know."

He experienced a moment of complete happiness. "Why, thank you. Thank you kindly."

"But I'd sure like to know one thing, Mr. Kane. That is, if you don't mind?"

He smiled warmly. He knew what the question would be. "Ask away."

"Exactly how many men have you sent to the ground?"

No point explaining he'd killed one woman too; that did nothing for a man's reputation. Jeremiah let his smile thin out a little, till it took on that faintly cruel cast. The Texas boy instinctively stepped away from him. Jeremiah didn't lie.

"Fourteen, and I guarantee you, Ben—every one was a dishonorable person who deserved it."

"Fourteen. Lord God!" Pop-eyed, the boy pumped Jeremiah's hand. "Pleasure, Mr. Kane. Surely has been."

"My sentiments, too," Jeremiah returned, his eyes glowing with good humor. He touched the brim of his oversized hat. "Hope you find work to pay your way home to the valley of the Red." He warmed himself a moment longer in the worshipful gaze of the Texas boy, who couldn't have been more than seventeen or eighteen. At twenty-five, Jeremiah felt ancient by comparison.

When Ben staggered out, Jeremiah finished his gin, called for another and tossed it off with barely a pause. The bartender shuddered.

"Jesus, Jason. You keep drinking it that fast, it'll kill you one of these days."

No, it won't. I know how I'm going to die.

Angered by the intrusion of the thought from God knew where, he slammed the empty glass down, making Hal start and blather an apology. Jeremiah's temples hurt. Why did he have to keep remembering the prophecy? Why did Kola keep reaching out from the dead to spoil everything? He fought his fury and fear, leaned over the bar and gave Hal a magnanimous pat on the shoulder.

"Sorry. Not your fault. I was thinking about something else."

And there's never a day that I don't *think of it.*

A friendly expression returned to his face, forced there. "Pour me another, if you please, and I'll try to follow your advice."

Relieved, the barkeep said, "On the house, Jason."

The smile grew. "Why, thank you. Thank you kindly."

iii

Drink in hand, he walked to the end of the bar, where the night manager, Lester Cross, was seated at a table eating steak and potatoes washed down with beer. If Cross had observed the little altercation, he said nothing. Jeremiah was a good source of revenue, and a dangerous man to anger. Cross knew that as well as Hal did.

Jeremiah greeted the older man, wrote out a chit showing his winnings and the Alamo's percentage, initialed the chit and gave it to Cross along with the specified amount.

"Much obliged, Jason. By the way—before you showed up, there was a fellow in here asking about you."

For an instant, panic made breathing difficult. "Somebody I know?"

"Doubt it. He wasn't familiar with your name. He must have seen you on the street, because he came in and described you and asked who you were. Maybe he saw you hanging out with Wild Bill. Anyway"—Cross chuckled—"your fame's spreading, my boy."

But something nervous was ticking in Jeremiah's mind, steadily worsening his mood.

"You positive you don't know who he was, Lester?"

"No, sir, I never saw him before. He didn't identify himself. He was young, though. And there was no doubt he was a Texas cowpoke—just like those boys."

The manager pointed. He received glares from three summer visitors dining at the next table. He grinned in a crow-eating way Jeremiah found disgusting, then said, "Sorry, boys. Clean forgot that was a dirty word."

Grudging smiles—one more glare—then the Texans went back to their food. The word that had riled them was cowpoke. The newest, greenest hands in a trail crew were the ones who drew the noxious assignment of working at the stockyards when their herd was shipped. The hands used long sticks to prod the reluctant longhorns and drive them from the pens to the freight cars. It was tiring, frustrating, dirty work. In the Texas lexicon a cowboy was someone to be respected, but a cowpoke was scum.

Jeremiah drew a fine cambric handkerchief from his sleeve. Touched it to his upper lip several times. The October evening seemed sultry all at once. Even though the

Alamo's three sets of double doors were folded open, the place was stifling hot.

"Did this Texas fellow want a game?"

"Don't know, Jason. Like I said, all he asked was your name." Cross forked fried potatoes into his mouth. The next words were muffled. "Hell, he didn't look dangerous to me. Or even proddy."

Jeremiah nodded again. "Probably wanted a game, then." But he didn't quite believe it. He'd better stay doubly alert for the remainder of the night.

"Finished for the evening?" Cross asked.

Jeremiah turned toward the ornate wall clock. "Hell no, it's only a quarter past seven. I'll try to rustle up at least one more game. First, though, I thought I'd squander some of my profits in the Addition. This morning Little Mattie brought in four new *nymphs du prairie*. One's about eighteen, with yellow hair and a face that belongs in the soprano section of a Congregational choir."

"Well, you better go get her," Cross said, "because she'll look sixty inside of a year. Give me a report on her, will you?"

"You're married, Lester."

"Why the hell you think I want a report?"

Jeremiah laughed and waved goodbye with his hat, being careful not to dislodge what was hidden in the inner band.

iv

He stepped out of the Alamo and studied the street in both directions. Thunder rumbled in the northwest. He sniffed the wind. A boomer coming. It would put an end to the unusual October warm spell.

He started along Texas Street. All at once he stumbled. A cowhand ambling by let out a snicker. Jeremiah glared as he righted himself. The cowhand hurried on without looking back, but Jeremiah realized the gin had affected him. Maybe Hal was right. Maybe he shouldn't swill the stuff so fast.

He kept moving. The esplanade ran east to west, just north of the Kansas Pacific tracks. It swarmed with cowhands and townspeople on foot and on horseback. The early evening was noisy with laughter, music, the racket of galloping horses and racing hackneys that conveyed visitors to and from the whorehouse district—genial sounds of prosperity occasionally punctuated by the faraway bawl of the cause of it all, a longhorn in the herds bedded down south of the Smoky Hill River.

One noise missing from the hubbub was the crackle of firearms. Early on, the Abilene Council—of which Marshal Hickok was the reluctant sergeant-at-arms, responsible for rounding up equally reluctant members for meetings—had made it a crime for incoming Texans, or anyone, to carry a gun within the town limits. High spirits and fist fights could be tolerated. But a reputation for violence would send the drovers elsewhere.

Thus, as Jeremiah was hurrying along toward the Addition and letting himself relax a little—relax and think of the angelic face of the girl whose favors he was going to buy—one thing for which he was totally unprepared was the unmistakable sound of a pistol cocking.

He was opposite the depot, on a lightless and deserted stretch of sidewalk in front of some shops that had already closed. He'd just passed the black mouth of an alley. Almost the moment the pistol cocked back in the alley, a voice spoke from the same place.

"You, Joseph Kingston. Stop right there."

He leaned forward, shifting his weight in order to run.

"Better not, Kingston. I got a gun on you."

He stopped, hit suddenly by the stunning power of that name from the past. The inside of his mouth instantly parched. He swallowed as he turned and peered into the alley. He could see absolutely nothing.

Who was hiding there? He suspected it was the stranger who'd asked about him. But how had the man tracked him? Waited for him to emerge from the Alamo and then run behind the buildings along the esplanade, parallel to the route he was taking? *And how could anyone know Joseph Kingston?* Perhaps it was all a mistake. A coincidence involving someone else of the same name.

Cold and angry, the voice said, "I finally found you, you damn murderer."

There was no mistake. Jeremiah recognized the voice.

V

The young Texan stepped far enough forward in the alley so that certain details were visible. A Colt's Navy model in his right hand. Chaps and a sugar-loaf sombrero. Then he moved again, and weak light from the depot fell across his face. The features leaped at Jeremiah across a gulf of years.

I should have thought of him when Lester mentioned Texas. And I shouldn't have let him go back in '66.

The boy was older now, early twenties. Jeremiah gazed at him with a mixture of disgust and panic. Would Mr. Jason Kane be brought down by a wet-eared calf? Would that be the end of everything? God, that was impossible. Intolerable!

But he was trapped. And the youngster was nervous, if not downright afraid. Someone in that state, with a gun, was more dangerous than any professional.

The distant depot lantern gleamed on a trickle of sweat on the youngster's neck. He shifted his position; the gleam vanished. The boy was in clear violation of the gun ordinance. Probably he'd kept the revolver concealed under his leather vest. Bear River Tom Smith, the murdered marshal whom Wild Bill had replaced, had been scrupulous about policing the ordinance, even to the point of conducting spot searches of new arrivals. Hickok was more tolerant. He only cracked down when concealed weapons were displayed or, occasionally, used. Jeremiah silently damned his friend for helping to get him into this tight place.

"The first time I seen you was this morning," the Texan said in an unsteady voice, "having breakfast at the Drover's Cottage."

Jeremiah didn't speak.

"This is the third year I've come up to Kansas with a herd. I signed on mostly to find you. Never really figured I would."

I never figured you would either.

"Look here," Jeremiah said. "It's a warm evening. Would you object if I took off my hat?"

The boy thought about it. "All right. But do it slow."

Jeremiah removed the hat and wiped his right sleeve

across his forehead. The streak of white hair showed above his left brow; he no longer colored it.

"I'm not the man you want. My name is—"

"Jason Kane. So they told me at the Alamo."

"That's right, Jason Kane."

"You're famous. We even heard of you down in Texas. I never figured you'd be this easy to take."

You're dead for saying that. He barely kept the rage out of his voice.

"You're changing the subject, boy. I don't know anything about this Joseph Kingston you're—"

"Hell you don't," the boy interrupted. "I'll never forget you murdering my uncle, you and that dirty Indian you was traveling with. You almost killed me, too." The cocked Navy shook as the boy leveled it at the front of Jeremiah's waistcoat. "You should have."

A sigh carried the sound of confession. "You're right." He began to fan himself with his hat. "Years haven't changed you much. Your name's Tom, I recall."

"Timothy. Timothy Stirling of Fort Worth."

"Oh, that's right. Your uncle was from Fort Worth, too, the dishonorable son of a bitch."

"You shut up about—"

"Bullshit," Jeremiah said quietly. "You were in on it. You know what he did. He lost his beeves and tried to steal my buffla so the season wouldn't be a total loss for him. Your uncle got no more than he deserved. But I suppose that won't be of help to me now, will it?"

"N-no."

"You'll go to prison." Jeremiah kept fanning himself in a slow, lazy way. Off across the prairie, lightning flickered and thunder drummed. The boy was momentarily distracted. Jeremiah cast a surreptitious glance into the crown of the hat. The piece in the sweated inner band violated the Abilene gun ordinance too.

Three rowdy horsemen yelled as they galloped past the depot. Drunk, probably. One fell out of his saddle and landed on his tailbone, laughing wildly. His friends rode on without him. No one paid the slightest attention to Jeremiah on the dark sidewalk, nor could a casual observer have seen the young Texan in the alley.

The thunder rumbled away to silence. Jeremiah's palms

itched. Could he reach the hideout gun with his left hand? And use it effectively? Only if he were steady.

To further unsettle the boy, he went on. "Yes, sir, prison for sure. 'Course Marshal Hickok might not permit your case to go to court. He might try you and pass sentence and carry it out himself, if you catch my drift. He's hell on anybody who discharges firearms in this town, let alone kills someone."

He was dismayed at the steadiness of the reply. "That don't matter, Kingston—Kane—whatever it is. Nothing matters except my uncle."

Another sigh. "I'm beginning to see that. You a single fellow, Timothy?"

"No, I got hitched up last winter."

"It's too soon for youngsters, I suppose."

"There's one on the way."

"Then you should reconsider what you're—"

"No."

"All right, all right, don't bust a cinch." Jeremiah did his best to sound as if he were the nervous one. "Do you mind if I put my hat back on before you do what you're going to do?"

Timothy tried to shrug in a casual way. "Go ahead. Slow, like before—"

All the better. He drew the open side of the crown in front of his face. He jerked his left hand up to the hat and jumped a yard to the right. Timothy Stirling swore and shot, but only once. A fundamental mistake.

Jeremiah was breathing fast as he tore the four-barrel derringer out of the inner band of the hat deliberately bought too large. He jerked the hat down. A horse bellowed and fell near the tracks, pinked by Timothy's wild bullet.

Lightning flashed. Timothy saw Jeremiah's strange smile and lost his nerve. He dropped his Colt and dashed down the alley. For an instant Jeremiah gazed at the youngster's back. No one shot a man in the back. And he didn't have to shoot the Texan at all.

Never figured you'd be this easy.

Thunder rolled. "Timothy!"

The shout brought the boy's head around even as he ran. If Timothy wasn't exactly facing him, neither did he have his back completely turned. Jeremiah instinctively observed Hickok's dictum that concentrated and continuous firepower usually brought a man out on top. He used all four shots to blow the running puncher against the wall of the bakery shop forming one side of the alley.

Blood sprayed from a wound in Timothy's neck and ran from another in his left forearm. The two shots in the left side of his vest would be the ones to kill him, Jeremiah thought as he trembled with a feeling close to ecstasy.

By the time Timothy fell down and rattled his last, Jeremiah was surrounded by a crowd of men. Mostly angry Texans who recognized one of their own lying dead. His only hope was that none of Timothy's trail crew was present or close by. He faced the growing crowd of cowhands, Mexican vaqueros and saloon hangers-on. They didn't know his hideout gun was empty.

"It was a private quarrel. I'll accommodate anyone who wants to pick another."

Eyes darted from the derringer to his belligerent face. There were some threatening remarks, but no trouble before the marshal arrived, his usual resplendent and well-armed self.

Jeremiah had never met another man in the West who gave more attention to personal cleanliness and grooming. Hickok kept his drooping mustaches trimmed and his golden-brown, shoulder-length hair combed at all times. He was thirty-four, six feet two and slim, with the light gray-blue eyes legend said accompanied a killer's temperament.

Tonight, as usual, he was fastidiously dressed: an immaculate Prince Albert coat, Irish linen shirt and French calf boots worth at least seventy-five dollars. He was always courteous—even now as he quietly ordered the crowd to disperse, except for two swampers from the Alamo. They were to remove the corpse to the undertaking parlor.

Hickok carried the same equipment he always carried to enforce the peace in Abilene: two .44 Colts strapped to his hips, a Bowie knife visible under his Prince Albert, a sawed-off shotgun in the crook of his elbow—plus, no doubt, the pair of .41 derringers he usually concealed somewhere on his person. He was a terrible walking arsenal. Many of the visiting Texans hated him for that, and for his service in the Yankee army.

He bent to examine the body that now stunk of its own released waste. That was the one thing Jeremiah loathed about death. The dirtiness.

"You killed him, uh?" Hickok murmured.

"Had to, Jim. He was waiting for me when I walked by. He was going to finish me if I didn't get him first. He shot once—" A gesture toward the stricken horse lying in the esplanade. Its sobered owner was gazing at the animal with tears on his face. "Hit that pony."

"What'd he shoot with? I don't see any—oh, there it is." The marshal walked back and picked up the Navy lying near Jeremiah's feet; yards from where Timothy had fallen.

"You really had to drop him, did you?" Hickok asked.

Yes!

Hickok kept examining the Navy, turning it back and forth in his hand.

Jeremiah blurted a lie. "I never saw it fall, Jim. I swear."

"Mmm. Is that a fact. You came damn close to hitting his back." Hickok's tone was faintly accusing. Jeremiah reacted angrily.

"I hit him fair! You know I'd never shoot a man in the back."

"Even so"—the marshal nodded at the derringer in Jeremiah's hand—"you broke the law. Killed a visitor, too. The town depends on the visitors."

"Think I don't know that? Christ!"

"Just laying the hand out for you. The Texans won't like what happened. Neither will the council or the merchants. For your own protection I'd better take you down to the jailhouse awhile."

So that was the verdict. Well, it wasn't nearly as bad as the verdict of his own conscience. Now that the joy was gone, he was ashamed he'd killed Timothy when it wasn't necessary.

And yet, in a way, it had been absolutely necessary. Of all men, Hickok should understand. Hickok had a reputation even more formidable than Jason Kane's.

But Hickok also had a job to protect. And the advantage of being able to maintain his reputation through that job. As a police officer, he was allowed to kill people. Allowed and encouraged.

In his imagination, Jeremiah saw Timothy falling. At the

moment he'd fired, it had made no difference that Timothy was unarmed. *No* difference. He was frightened suddenly. What the hell was happening to him?

"Come along, Jason," Hickok said in a mild voice. Jeremiah fell in step.

vi

Many stared, but no one interfered because of Hickok's weapons and reputation. He was said to have killed forty-three men, not counting Indians shot during his army scout service; Indians were never put in the same class as white men.

Hickok never disputed the total, either. It made splendid copy for the magazines that had turned him into a hero and a legend back East.

At the jail, Jeremiah explained that Timothy's uncle, one Major T. T. Cutright, had attempted to steal a buffalo kill from him five years ago, and he'd shot Cutright and one of his helpers for it. He'd let Timothy go even though the boy had sworn revenge. This evening he'd nearly succeeded in getting it.

Hickok's eyes were emotionless as he surveyed Jeremiah by the light of the lamps in the jail's office area. At the end of the story, he asked, "The boy was with a crew still camped south of town?"

"He didn't say. I presume he was."

Hickok fingered his mustache a moment. "The crew will find out what happened. They'll want your head. We'll have more trouble. Council won't like that."

"Jesus, Jim, I thought you were my friend! Is that all you can say—the council won't like it?"

Hickok looked at him and Jeremiah saw no trace of friendship. "It's the truth. If you stay around, there are liable to be more killings. I can't let personal feelings influence the way I judge a situation. Or the way I do my job."

"Hell, you're just afraid you'll get fired if you take my side against the Texans. Everybody kisses their feet in this damn town."

Hickok blinked his pale, almost sinister eyes. In a voice still devoid of emotion, he said, "I'll act like you never made that remark, Jason." He drew a breath. "You'll have to hide out of here."

"*What?*"

"You heard me. Hide out. Right away."

"There are no more passenger trains tonight!"

"Buy a horse. Bribe your way aboard the midnight freight. I don't care how you do it—just leave town."

"But I'll miss the rest of the season! I won't have enough money to tide me through the winter."

"Should have thought of that before you shot the boy. He was running. The position of his Colt said so. You didn't need to break the law to save yourself. You've got till the sun comes up to get out of Abilene. You made your bed."

In the cold tone and the pale eyes, there was no reprieve.

vii

The thunderstorm broke just as the train of livestock cars pulled out at twelve fifteen. Jeremiah sat in the caboose, listening to the rain pelting the roof and the steers and cows lowing from the head end.

His clothes were soaked. Next morning's beard was beginning to sprout. On the seat beside him lay a brown paper package: the bottle of gin he'd bought at the back door of the Old Fruit before Hickok marched him down to the stockyards siding. Two brakemen had accepted bribes of a gold dollar each to allow him to get aboard with his carpetbag.

One of the brakemen had dropped some kind of cheaply printed newspaper from his pocket as he went out to get the train under way. Jeremiah picked up the paper. The masthead read *Labor's Beacon.* A crude engraving of a switchman's lantern separated the two words. His mouth dropped open at what he saw directly below.

Gideon Kent, Editor-Publisher.

The train gathered speed. Lightning flared above the stock pens, a sea of tossing horns and terrified cattle. Jeremiah found himself knuckling his eyes as he examined the little four-page paper with sadness and envy. Some months ago, Boyle had written to say Gideon was busy organizing groups of workingmen so they'd stand up to their bosses. Gideon was a—a trade unionist, that was the term the Irishman had used.

But Jeremiah hadn't heard about the little newspaper. Imagine! His very own brother, who'd hated books and school as a young man, writing something good enough to be published.

Well, didn't that fit with the family motto that had originated back near the start of the century? His father had repeated the motto many times during Jeremiah's boyhood. *Take a stand and make a mark.* The Kents always did that.

I've done it too. Only I've left gravestones.

Fifteen of them. With Timothy dead, he'd killed fifteen.

The rear door of the caboose crashed open. Rain splattered the floor as the two brakemen came in, complaining about the weather. No, there were three men, he saw. The last one, a bull-shouldered fellow in his fifties, hadn't been bribed. He jabbed a thick brakeman's club at Jeremiah.

"What the hell's he doing on this tra—?"

Jeremiah's motion was sure and smooth. He came to his feet, stepped over his carpetbag and snatched the club with his left hand. He hurled it away. Simultaneously, his right hand blurred across to his left hip and drew one of the Starrs he'd put on after leaving the town limits. He laid the muzzle against the big man's throat.

"Traveling as far as you are, friend."

Eyes frantic, the brakeman still tried to bluster. "The hell—the hell you are—"

The joy spread through Jeremiah like a warm liquid running in his bloodstream. "Want off, do you? Happy to oblige."

He smiled and cocked the Starr with his thumb.

Thunder pealed. The caboose swayed. One of the other brakemen whispered to the man under the gun. "You damn fool, don't you know who that is?"

"No, an' I don't give a shit."

"Well, you better. This here's Jason Kane."

The brakeman's face looked as if it had been greased. "K-Kane?" He could barely speak. "Oh—oh—Jesus—"

Jeremiah's pleasure was almost unbearable. He wanted to prolong it.

"I'll let you finish this run alive if you behave yourself—and if you thank me properly."

He pressed the muzzle into the man's throat so hard, the brakeman could only make choking noises.

"Let me hear you say it, you jackass."

"Th-th-thank you."

"Thank you, Mr. Kane."

"Th-thank you, Mr.—Mr. K-Kane."

A chuckle. He whipped the Starr back so fast, the brakeman almost fainted.

After he'd holstered the gun, he dug down and found another gold piece. He passed it into the brakeman's damp hand. "There. Same as your friends got for keeping their mouths shut. Now I'd be obliged if you'd let me rest and wet my whistle."

"Sure—certainly—any-anything, Mr. Kane." His voice childishly thin now, the bull-shouldered man stumbled to the stove at the head of the car and opened the iron door. Firelight gleamed on his sweating face. He chafed hands that still shook.

Jeremiah's eyes looked sullen all at once—sullen and red in the light of the ceiling lanterns swaying back and forth. The joy was always so fleeting. But at least the guns *had* brought a luster to his name, just as Kola predicted.

He unwrapped the gin bottle, jammed the neck between his teeth and yanked the cork. He tilted the bottle and swilled a hot mouthful of the stuff. Some of it leaked between his lips. He couldn't keep his mind off the prophecy. What if the rest of it came true? What if the power his name invoked began to fade as—how had Kola put it? *As swiftly as the light of a winter afternoon.*

And what if he met death the way—

He could barely force himself to think it.

The way Kola said. At the hand of one of his own family.

Who was the Kent who would kill him? And how would it happen? When? Where?

With a low, almost hurt cry, he wrenched his mind away from the terrible thoughts. He grew aware of his surroundings again. The brakemen gathered at the stove were staring at him as if he were a madman. He felt like laughing. He *was* a madman. At least he was starting to think like one. The questions kept battering his head like crazed, imprisoned birds trying to free themselves.

Who will it be?

When?

Where?

The brakemen were still watching. He let them feel the fury of his eyes. They quickly returned their attention to the open door of the stove. He raised the bottle and slopped down more gin. He realized he'd let the little newspaper fall. It lay beside his carpetbag. The toe of his left boot was resting on the front page. Resting squarely on Gideon's name.

Was it Gideon? His brother was going to kill him?

How?

How?

He wanted to scream that it wasn't so. But he'd said Kola's prophecy was false, and yet it kept coming true. He stared at the newspaper, terror-stricken, as the cattle train plunged on through the lightning-pierced dark toward an unseeable horizon.

★ *Book Three* ★

MARGARET'S
WRATH

CHAPTER I

MOLLY

i

WHEN GIDEON REACHED New York, he enjoyed a certain notoriety. He was a survivor of the Chicago holocaust—an articulate eyewitness to what many called the century's greatest disaster. He was interviewed at length by a reporter Theophilus Payne sent to the office of the *Beacon*. He gave the reporter a good deal of material about Thomas Courtleigh and the disrupted W & P meeting, but he wasn't surprised when none of it appeared in the published interview. Well, he'd take charge of Mr. Payne soon enough.

At home his stories of the fire earned him increased attention from Eleanor for a while. He was happy about that. He loved it when she came to his side in the evening, eager to hear him repeat dramatic parts of the tale. Carefully edited, of course, to screen out any references to Julia.

He began winding up the affairs of the *Beacon*. He composed a letter explaining his decision to those few readers who took the paper on a subscription basis. He didn't immediately show the letter to Strelnik, though.

Relations with Margaret remained strained. They deteriorated even further the night he finally decided to discuss his plan to take a position on the *Union*. He thought that exchanging his current job for a more secure one would please his wife. It didn't. She digested the news and then asked in a slurred voice, "Does this mean I'll see more of you, or less?"

"About the same or a little less for a while."

She wrinkled her nose; the expression was close to a sneer. "I thought so."

She left the parlor, her path a meandering curve rather than a straight line. He'd detected the odor of wine again. He sat with his hands folded under his chin, brooding on what he could possibly do to make her happy.

In the following days, every attempt to be solicitous, or even polite, was met with some sharp remark on Margaret's part. The theme of her anger or sarcasm was always the same. Ignoring the fact that he was doing what she had so long begged him to do, she scored him for being anxious to obtain a position that would keep him away from home for even longer periods. One night the accusation led to another bad quarrel, and he moved permanently into a separate bedroom.

He didn't explain the move to Eleanor, who was old enough to notice that a change had taken place. He wanted to say something to her but he didn't know how to approach her without making it seem as though he was speaking against Margaret.

He began to fix many of his own meals, and came and went without informing Margaret, except by notes left in the kitchen. It would all have been intolerable if he hadn't had thoughts of Julia to sustain him.

Sometimes he believed the trouble at home had been visited on him as punishment for his infidelity. But in more rational moods, he reminded himself the universe didn't operate quite so neatly, and that Margaret had begun her destructive campaign for dominance long before Julia had entered the picture.

One night in late November, after he'd gone home, the office of *Labor's Beacon* was burned out by a fire discovered around midnight. Two other offices in the building were also gutted. Gideon offered to make good on the damage. The landlord promptly accepted, then sent an attorney around to say Gideon's lease had been canceled.

Rather than contest, Gideon found cramped quarters two blocks south. He asked himself whether Thomas Courtleigh was responsible for the landlord's behavior. He was surely responsible for the fire at the *Beacon*.

And for one at the printer's in early December. That fire destroyed the just completed press run of an issue containing a long article about the tragedy at Ericsson's, and a scathing editorial attack on the president of the W & P. Once again Gideon's apologies and a more than generous financial settlement didn't help much. The printer gladly took his money to rebuild the destroyed storage area, but he wanted no more of Gideon's business.

Even during these difficult times, Julia wasn't far from his thoughts. He corresponded with her from each office. Her letters came from all over the midsection of the country: a hamlet in northern Wisconsin; Terre Haute; Louisville; Indianapolis—there, she said, she'd been driven from a stage by rocks hurled with such ferocity that she wondered if the men throwing them had been paid. She reported a pattern of increased harassment. In the past it had happened only occasionally. Now there was some sort of trouble at every lecture.

For this reason, each of her letters urged him to remember one thing above all. If Courtleigh intended to keep after him—and the mysterious fires certainly seemed to verify it—Gideon had to fight back from a position of strength. He wasn't wavering in his determination to join the family paper, was he?

No, he wrote in reply, he was not. He'd prepared a final *Beacon* and carried it to the typesetter's without telling Strelnik it was the last one. Nor had he shown his assistant the editorial which said so. He planned to talk with Strelnik after he spoke to his stepmother—and he was ready to do that now. He promised to let Julia know how he fared.

The last edition was being handled by a seedy print shop just off the Bowery. The night the issue was run, freezing rain struck the city. The printer's roof leaked—or so he said when Gideon called the next day and discovered that the entire run had been ruined.

Yes, the man would be happy to print the papers again if he were paid. But he avoided Gideon's stare when he said it. Gideon looked up at the unusually large hole in the roof. It measured a yard and a half across and hadn't been there the day before. It was much too big to be accidental.

His anger changed to weary resignation. He'd probably never learn how Courtleigh managed to keep track of his whereabouts, but it was obvious how Gideon's suppliers were being turned against him. The printer had undoubtedly been well compensated for letting hooligans smash the roof and pour water over the finished papers.

"Do you want me to run the edition again, Mr. Kent?" the printer asked.

"No. You'll have to be satisfied with the money you got for ruining the first one." He stalked out while the printer protested that he didn't understand.

From that day, Gideon began to see an enemy in every passing face, and a threat in every shadow. He was still feeling that way in the second week of December when he took the train down to the Jersey shore to visit the summer home his stepmother had transformed into an all-year residence.

Except for those times when he'd ridden into battle, he could hardly remember having been so nervous.

ii

It was a blustery gray day, requiring the light of all the parlor lamps. The sea was running high. Great white-crested mountains of water rose out beyond the tide line, then rushed in and crashed apart as new peaks appeared behind them. Gideon came immediately to the point as his stepmother poured tea.

Molly Emerson Kent was approaching fifty. She was a solidly built woman of five feet six inches with a matronly bosom and a wide smile, which revealed a good many teeth and made her plain face radiant. She said she found the size of her mouth embarrassing.

She handed Gideon his cup just as he finished speaking. "So. It's to be the *Union,* is it?" Suddenly she smiled that dazzling smile. "You would have made your father very happy."

"What? He wanted me on the paper?"

"Let's say he considered it a shame for you to stay where you are." She stirred hot milk into her cup as the cottage creaked and whined in the gale. *The verse from Judges,* he thought. *Julia was right.*

"Of course," Molly continued, "I'm pleased too. Newspapering has become intensely competitive of late. It needs young men with vigor and strength. I must say Theo Payne's a fine teacher, though. He's managed to pound quite a lot into the head of an unexceptional lady who once ra.. a boardinghouse—" She sipped tea. "I hope you haven't made this decision lightly, Gideon."

"No, far from it."

"Good. You're not applying for some clerk's position that can be handled with a minimum of effort. If you hope to become worthy of the job of publisher, not just fill it— as I did, out of necessity, when Jephtha died—you'll need to understand every facet of the paper's operation. There are more of them than you've ever imagined. You must also understand the *Union*'s purpose today."

"I'm not sure I follow. Isn't its purpose the same as it's always been?"

"Not at all." She went on to remind him that many newspapers had started as adjuncts of a printing business. It had been that way with the *Bay State Federalist,* Philip Kent's first venture in journalism some eighty years earlier. "In those days, a paper was founded to promote a specific point of view—the owner's, or that of the political party to which he belonged. The pattern held true in the penny press right up through the war. Then, like everything else in this modern world, newspapers began to change. The *Union* is nominally Republican. But it no longer exists for the sake of the party. In other words, like Mr. Dana's *Sun* and Gordon Bennett's *Herald* and a few others, the *Union* no longer automatically endorses everything its party does. You must understand that change to understand the work you want to do. Today the *Union*'s chief product, and its most important and prestigious element, isn't an editorial of the sort you write so well. It's news. Facts. Information, not opinion."

He was deflated to hear her say that. His editorials were his pride, and the main reason for the *Beacon*'s existence. Except for the Chicago article that had died a-borning in the Bowery print shop, he'd never had an exclusive news story of any consequence.

Molly leaned forward, growing more animated.

"This is an exciting time for newspapers. The modern paper exists to give people the facts they need to make sound judgments about local or national matters. It's a mighty instrument for good—or evil, for that matter. Since it appeals to the masses, it can sway them. Its potential power is frightening. Using that power can be an awesome responsibility. I'm sorry if all this startles you—"

"No, it doesn't."

"Fiddlesticks, dear. I can read your face nearly as well as I could read your father's. I'm only trying to prepare you for your first encounter with Payne. I know you've met him."

He nodded. "Twice."

"But you haven't really dealt with him. You two must get along. You won't unless you remember what it is the *Union*'s selling."

Gideon wondered why it was necessary for a stockholder to appease Mr. Payne. But he said nothing.

"I'm sure you can learn that lesson," Molly continued in a reassuring way. "That's always been one of your tremendous strengths, learning quickly. You understand grammar and you've taught yourself to have a facile pen. Now you'll have to master everything from page makeup to the latest advertising techniques—I trust you know both Macy's and Lord and Taylor's broke the tyranny of one-column ads last year? First in the *Times,* then in the *Tribune* and the *Union.*"

He shook his head. He thought that all metropolitan papers still hewed to the single-column, so-called tombstone style presentation of both news and advertisements. Of course he paid very little attention to the advertising content of the leading dailies. He could recall seeing a few ad cuts in the *Union*—trademarks, mostly—but that was it. It made him realize he knew precious little about the family enterprise, other than that it was a morning sheet and sold for four cents, the current price of most of its competitors. He renewed a vow to work hard and base his judgments on the realities of the marketplace, not on some lofty notion of what the idealized newspaper should be.

Seeing how unsettled he was, Molly smiled and tried to cheer him.

"There are scores of things to learn, Gideon, but they're all fascinating. I think you'll find the process a pleasure, not a chore. You'll have to think about features. Poetry, humor—they're relatively new and readers seem to like them, but old-line editors believe they have no place in a news organ. Stunts are becoming quite the thing on some papers. Young Gordon Bennett claims the *Herald* doesn't merely report news—it makes news. And he's proved it by sending his roving correspondent to search for that missing African missionary. He's spending thousands to outfit Mr. Stanley in Zanzibar right now, and should Stanley locate Dr. Livingstone, it will be one of the biggest stories of the decade. Payne grants that, but he still doesn't care for stunts. You'll become involved in more than editorial policy, though. You'll have to make decisions about people—should you hire women as general reporters? Men may resent it. Still, Emily Bettey's doing splendidly at the *Sun*. Then there's the business side—such things as the maximum price we can profitably pay for newsprint. In the last five years it's cost as little as eight cents a pound and as much as twenty-six."

By now Gideon was desperate to show Molly he knew something—anything! Unfortunately he'd left most of the technical details of the *Beacon* to the printer who had handled it for him, and all he could dredge from memory was one meager fact, lamely offered.

"The paper we use is made from old rags, isn't it?"

With a forgiving smile, she said. "Not entirely." His face fell.

She patted the back of his hand. "Don't worry. No one expects you to know everything before you start. There are new inventions called Keller machines. From Germany. They shred wood fiber. For the first time they make mechanical wood pulp an acceptable base for newsprint. The *Union* is now being printed on a sheet that's forty percent mechanical pulp, sixty percent rags. Two months from now, those sheets will be traveling through the Hoe Company's newest and best web-perfecting press."

Thoroughly humbled, he said, "What the hell's that?"

She laughed. "I didn't mean to embarrass you, dear. A web is a continuous sheet of newsprint. A perfecting press prints both sides during a single feed. The presses represent a huge investment, but they're the coming thing. Theo can tell you anything else you want to know."

"Molly, I hate to say it, but I'm getting a mite tired of hearing the editor's name invoked as if he's some kind of god."

Her tone grew a shade less cordial. "In certain circles, he's considered just about that."

"Hell's fire—excuse me—he's only the editor. We *own* the paper."

"But he makes it run. Theophilus Payne is fifty-six years old. He has an uncontrollable drinking problem. He can be irascible and insufferably rude. But in my opinion and the opinion of others much more qualified to judge, he has only two peers among his contemporaries: Horace Greeley and Charles Dana. Payne's lifted the *Union* from an average daily circulation of fifty-five thousand—slightly below the *Staats Zeitung,* which after all is a foreign-language paper—to ninety-three thousand. That's very close to the *Herald,* and only five or six thousand behind the leaders, the *Daily News* and the *Sun.* Payne's a perfectionist. Demanding—sometimes unreasonably so. He's fired career journalists for what you might consider a trivial lapse in grammar. I also know he thinks trade unions are pernicious organizations—"

"But our printers belong to their local, don't they?"

"They do."

"And the typographers belong to theirs?"

"Yes, your father forced that issue and permitted organization in 1866. Payne almost assaulted him, then went on a four-day binge. Now let me finish answering your question as to why he's so important. It's quite simple. He makes a profit for us. And he does it in a way we can be proud of. You don't have to convince *me* to accept you on the *Union.* I'd never deny you a job there. But you'll have to convince Payne. I have absolute faith in his judgment. In fact," she added, very softly, "if he won't have you, I'll back him up."

Gideon sat all the way back in his chair and whispered, "Good God."

Her expression was sober. "I thought you'd be a bit shaken by that. You noticed I delayed getting around to it."

Benumbed, he nodded.

"Would you like a touch of whiskey, dear?"

"No, thanks. Molly—"

"Yes?"

"I hope you won't take offense. This is said in admiration, not criticism. I just didn't realize you'd become such a hard businesswoman."

"I don't take offense. I do take exception. I hope I'm a good businesswoman, not merely a hard one. There's a significant difference. I've only become what I had to, Gideon. You were busy with your own enterprise, and major decisions had to be laid at someone's doorstep. By default they were laid at mine. I've come to enjoy the responsibility. But as I said, I'd be grateful to relinquish it to someone younger. You'll become as hard as I—out of necessity. The New York newspaper industry is ferociously competitive. And you can't change a man's mind about anything unless he buys *your* paper instead of your rival's."

"I'll try to remember that."

"Theo won't let you forget it—if you pass the test."

With another of those shining smiles meant to soothe away his anxiety, she poured more tea for both of them.

"Let's drink a toast to the success of your forthcoming interview."

They did, but it didn't reassure him that he'd succeed with Theophilus Payne.

CHAPTER II

ON NEWSPAPER ROW

i

A WEEK BEFORE Christmas, Gideon took Strelnik to supper at a modest but pleasant tavern on Ann Street, a few steps east of its junction with Broadway and Park Row. They sat at a table by a window. It was just seven o'clock as they ordered veal chops and ale.

The first flakes of a snow began to come straight down in the windless air. Strelnik raised the subject of the letter to subscribers, which he'd finally seen. Gideon was compelled to explain. He finished by saying, "As a matter of fact, I'm going up to the *Union* tonight." He'd been inventing excuses for postponing the visit, no doubt from fear that he'd fail to win Payne's approval.

Strelnik shoved his mug of ale to one side and squinted through the smoke of his cigarette. "And the demise of the *Beacon* is final?"

Gideon nodded.

"Whether the *Union* will have you or not?"

Another nod.

The bearded man snickered. "The worker's paradise is here at last. The boss may be rejected by his own employee. Gideon, I can't believe it. I can't believe you'll go crawling to the editor of that capitalist rag."

"Who hates Southerners, by the way," Gideon put in, hoping to jolly the little man out of his bitterness.. "Molly came up to Yorkville to visit the children last week, and she again confessed Payne isn't as coldly objective as she first led me to believe. He used to despise secessionists, but since that issue has been settled he's switched to hating trade unionists."

Strelnik wasn't amused. He flung his cigarette on the pegged floor and stamped on it. "Isn't that splendid? Well, it's very clear you've sold out."

"Damn it, Sime, I have not!" Heads turned as he raised his voice.

"Yes you have. You've sold out the movement completely."

"I've found a better way to *promote* the movement."

"Pfaugh. I know what happens when a man becomes a boss." The word was supremely contemptuous. "That Mr. Dana who runs the *Sun*—you know how much he likes trade unions."

"He loathes them, just like Payne. What's the point?"

"Twenty or thirty years ago he was a socialist." Gideon gaped. "Ask anybody, it's God's truth. Owning things changes people. Power changes people too. It's done that to you."

Abruptly he stood up. Angry now, Gideon grabbed his arm.

"Don't act childish. I haven't had a chance to give you all the details about the closing of the *Beacon*. I intend to pay you three months' wages to tide you over while—"

Strelnik wrenched loose. "We don't want your charity. Leah does piecework sewing at home. We can survive. Even if we couldn't, I wouldn't touch your money now. Go hobnob with your rich friends. Next time we meet we'll be on opposite sides of a strike line."

"Sime, you're wrong. You'll see."

Strelnik laughed in a scornful way. For a moment more he gazed at his friend with barely suppressed contempt, then spun and walked away. The tavern door made a soft, sighing sound as it closed. Its lower edge was already blocked by a buildup of wet snow.

Gideon looked out the window as Strelnik's bearded figure ghosted by, stirring the falling snowflakes. Strelnik didn't so much as glance his way.

ii

Park Row ran northeast from the intersection of Broadway and Ann. The city's major papers were concentrated along the east side, in a short stretch known as Newspaper Row. It encompassed the blocks from Broadway up to Printing House Square, the tiny triangle where Nassau and Frankfort came in. On the west side of the street lay the snow-covered expanse of City Hall Park.

It was a lovely evening, with the fluffy snow continuing to drift straight down. Gideon was oblivious to the beauty of tree branches and rooftops piled high with white like a winter scene in a book of fairy tales. He was thinking of Strelnik.

He felt wretched about the man's accusations. That was true even though Strelnik could be almost foolishly partisan, and Gideon believed his former assistant was definitely in the wrong this time. Still, he didn't want to lose Strelnik's friendship. He hoped time would heal the rift. He planned to send Leah Strelnik a draft for her husband's severance pay. She was practical enough to accept the money with no quibbles about its source.

Newspaper delivery wagons went racing up and down Park Row in the lamplit darkness. They were traveling at top speed despite the hazardous condition of the street. Gideon was twice bumped by harried men in derbies rushing on some errand or other. Reporters, he surmised. The telegraph helped gather news these days, but there was still no substitute for the reporter's legs.

Soon he began to experience a little of the sense of intimidation he'd felt at Courtleigh's house. Here indeed lay power. The power that reposed in men's minds, and men's published thoughts. The generally nondescript buildings hulking in the snow housed some of the mightiest institutions in the land.

The *Herald*. The *Tribune*. The *Sun. Times. Star. Mail and Express. Commercial Advertiser.* Jay Gould's *World*, acquired as part of a stock deal.

He couldn't think of all the names. But there among them, facing the *Times* and Greeley's *Tribune* on Printing House Square, stood the three-story building with the signboard reading NEW YORK UNION. The board bore the emblem devised by the family's founder—the stoppered bottle partially full of tea.

Philip Kent had adopted the symbol when he started his first printing establishment during the Revolutionary War. He had owned and prized such a bottle. He'd collected the contents when he participated in Mr. Samuel Adams' famous tea party in Boston Harbor. The actual bottle, green glass with the old tea still inside, stood on the mantel in Yorkville. It was one of a number of priceless mementoes of the Kent family's past.

The December night felt almost warm because of the snow's insulating effect. Gaslights blazed all across the second floor of the *Union*—the arched windows of the editorial department.

Gideon gazed at that brilliance and decided his timidity was not only shameful but foolish. Hadn't Jeb Stuart proved time and again that fear never won an engagement for any man or any army? Besides, he was legitimate heir to some of the power on Newspaper Row, and the fact that he didn't yet know how to use it didn't mean he couldn't learn. He could and he would.

His chin lifted. He strode toward the triangular park and saw a number of ragged boys huddling around the base of the statue of the nation's most famous printer, Dr. Benjamin Franklin.

As Gideon's boots crunched the snow in the park, heads came up. Cigarettes glowed beneath the bills of dirty caps. One young face was completely hidden by exhaled smoke. Gideon heard comments exchanged in Yiddish and German. There were about a dozen of the young Street Arabs, as they were called, seeking shelter near the statue. On other occasions he'd seen such boys at the wagon docks of various papers, waiting to be given stacks of the latest edition on consignment. The boys hawked the papers on street corners all over town. And those weren't the only locations they worked. Since his talk with Molly, he had started studying the New York newspaper industry, and he knew the *Daily News* had boosted its circulation to eighty thousand by lowering its price to a penny and sending boys into tenements to tap a completely new market.

He passed the statue and walked on toward the entrance to the *Union*. One of the boys got up and followed. Gideon heard the footsteps. He stopped in front of the building and turned.

Dull light from the frosted windows of the ground-floor press room fell across the face of a startlingly handsome youngster of about twelve. The boy was saved from prettiness by a cheerfully insolent mouth. He wore ragged trousers tucked into heavy black knee stockings, a man's coat with huge holes in it, a scarf and a cap that he dragged off as he asked, "Mister, do you know whether the *Union* will be printing any extras tonight?" Extra editions were a staple of the trade.

"Couldn't say, son. I don't work here."

"Oh, I thought you were a reporter." The boy's voice startled Gideon because it was really two voices, a somewhat nasal adolescent one, and a beautiful adult baritone. The boy seemed unconcerned about the abrupt shifts from one to the other. He started away. "Good evening."

What a remarkable voice, Gideon thought. When it changed permanently, the lad would have all the makings of an orator. Curious, he called to the retreating figure, "Out pretty late, aren't you?"

The boy turned back. "Late?" He grinned. "I thought you were an American, mister."

"I am."

"Then why don't you know that over here, nobody bosses you around? You take charge of your own life, and do what you have to do to make a nickel."

"Where'd you come from?"

"Munich, mister. By way of Bremerhaven. When I was about so long." He measured a foot of snowy air with gloves worn through at all the fingertips. "My father says I lay on my mother's stomach for most of the trip. It cost them the equivalent of twenty-five American dollars to buy two spaces on a mail packet. Two spaces five feet long and two and a half wide, chalked out 'tween the decks. Father says he and Mother got slops for food, and a lot of the newcomers died on the way, but the Goldmans survived, thank you kindly." In a brash and somehow touching imitation of an adult, he extended his right hand. "My name's Leo Goldman."

They shook. Gideon felt the cold of the boy's hand.

"Gideon Kent, Leo."

"Yes, sir, happy to make your acquaintance. You born in America, were you?"

"Virginia."

"Well, I'm only an adopted American, I suppose you could say. But I mean to be a good one. I'm not so rich as a Rothschild yet, and I still live on Hester Street"—the name of a particularly noxious thoroughfare in the lower East Side ghetto—"but I'll change both those things before I'm much older. I'm going to make my fortune here."

Gideon didn't crack a smile. There was a determined look in Leo Goldman's dark eyes, and he had the feeling the boy would punch him if he laughed at the sober, almost passionate declaration.

"An admirable ambition. Do you know how you're going to do it?"

"Not yet, sir. I'll find a way. It's possible to do it in America, you know. Such an amazing country. Every man his own king—every man his own priest. Or in my case, rabbi. Well, good evening to you, Mr.—"

All at once recognition swept over the boy's face. He lost his self-assured air and very nearly stammered.

"Kent, you said. *Kent.* One of the older fellows told me the Kents own this paper." A tattered glove lifted toward the frosted windows and the presses rumbling beyond. "Are you . . . ?"

Gideon nodded.

"Well! You've made your fortune."

"To tell the truth, it was made for me," Gideon answered with a smile. "At the moment I'm trying to learn how to use it properly." He dug in his pocket and produced a one-dollar shinplaster. "Here. You can't carry a stack of papers if your hands are frozen. Buy yourself a decent pair of gloves."

Leo Goldman studied the bill and finally saw its denomination. His eyes grew huge. His voice slid up the scale to a near squeak. "Holy Tammany. I can buy gloves and some bread for my sisters, too."

"How many sisters do you have?"

"Nine. We all sleep in one room, so I camp out whenever I can." He began to unfold the dollar. Then his eyes narrowed, and a suspicious old man looked out from the handsome face. "I don't have to do any—special tricks for this, do I? If I do, I won't take it."

"Leo, it's yours. With no strings on it."

"Thank you, Mr. Kent. Thank you indeed. Good health to you!"

The boy went racing back across the street to the statue of Franklin, where his friends crowded around him to hear of his good fortune. Gideon smiled again. The brief encounter had restored his spirits.

He turned and entered the building. The rumbling presses shook the steps leading up to the editorial rooms. He climbed the steps with confidence, telling himself there wasn't a Yankee born who could stand up to one of Jeb Stuart's own.

CHAPTER III

A HARD TASKMASTER

i

THE EDITORIAL OFFICE was one large room stretching from
the high arched windows at the front to a partitioned telegraph room at the rear. Gaslit cubicles lined the wall opposite the head of the stairs. The hub of the big, dingy room
was a large desk. Two dozen smaller desks surrounding it
were all turned so they faced it. These smaller desks had
tilted tops, and at several of them men in shirtsleeves or
dark jackets were writing longhand copy with pencils, usually amid a litter of notes. Most of the reporters puffed
cigars and wore their hats.

Occasionally one of the men shouted for a copy boy.
There were two working, Gideon observed as he slowly
traversed the room. For all the attention he received, he
might have been a derelict instead of part owner. A few
people glanced at him, but no one said anything.

He watched a copy boy hustle a finished manuscript to
the central desk. The man seated there scanned it, penciled
a few corrections, then wrote something on a separate sheet
and pinned it to the story. The boy ran it to an opening in
the wall—a kind of dumbwaiter—and placed the copy on

a tray. He pulled a cord. The tray started downward. To the composing room, Gideon supposed.

There was continuous, low-level noise in the room, consisting of the rumble of the presses, the chatter of telegraph sounders from the back, and the intermittent buzz of conversation punctuated by yelling or a question called from the central desk. The scene reminded Gideon of a painting done in dark pigments; the figures had a blurred look in the low, smoky gaslight.

His path took him behind the city editor at the central desk. He knew it was rude to pause and peer over the editor's shoulder, but he was curious. He watched the editor print the last of six decks, or headline subheads. The man was working on an important story, then. Only two or three decks accompanied a routine one.

The editor grew aware of Gideon's presence. "What the hell do you want?"

"I'm looking for Mr. Payne."

A pencil stabbed toward one of the cubicles. "Over there. The doorway where you see the young man taking his forty lashes."

Gideon didn't understand the remark until he approached the open door of the office. Inside, a coatless reporter, no more than twenty-one, faced someone hidden by the wall of the cubicle. The reporter turned an old stovepipe hat in his fingers. Gideon heard a grating voice.

"—kindly read the offending sentence, Mr. Mordecai. Aloud."

A hand thrust a proof at the young man. Looking even more nervous, he took it, licked his lips, and read in a quavering tone.

" 'No pronouncements have come from the Treasury Department regarding the Granger position on greenbacks, and none are expected until—until—' "

His voice trailed off.

"You do not deny you committed that rape of the language, Mr. Mordecai?"

"Sir, it was an honest mistake. I was in a hurry to finish."

"Never be in *that* much of a hurry, Mr. Mordecai. If some semiliterate wretch reads your imperfect prose and thereby fixes an erroneous principle of grammar in his head for all time, you have hurt him. You have done him irrepa-

rable harm with your haste. Pick up a week's wages at
the cashier and carry that thought to your next employer,
whoever it is. Good evening."

"But, Mr. Payne—"

"Good *evening*."

The reporter walked out, ignoring Gideon. He jammed
his stovepipe on his head and growled, "Snotty, pie-eyed
little son of a bitch. I'm a journalist, not a bloody
schoolmaster."

Payne heard. "You're both, you ill-mannered oaf," he
called. "The sooner you learn it, the sooner you'll become
a competent newspaperman."

Mumbling oaths, Mr. Mordecai moved away. Gideon
knocked and walked in. He caught the little man opening
a lower desk drawer. The cubicle reeked of whiskey.

Theophilus Payne shut the drawer with a bang. He was
a slightly built man whose feet barely touched the floor
when he was seated. A nose like a large pink radish disfigured his lined face; time, dissipation and daily deadlines
had all taken a toll.

Payne recognized Gideon. He greeted him in an offhand
way, stood up and gave him a limp handshake. The top of
his gray head was on a level with Gideon's shoulder.

"Please be seated, Mr. Kent. Molly told me to expect
you, but I wasn't sure when. Haven't fretted about it much.
I'm not precisely thrilled at the prospect of interviewing a
man who wants to replace me."

Gideon was startled by the editor's directness. Payne
waved and gave him a mordant glance. "Oh, come. Don't
play the innocent. Molly didn't say so, but I'm sure you
fancy yourself as the publisher someday. Should that happen within my lifetime, I intend to see the title bestowed
on a man whose professionalism I endorse. I will not put
a fool or an incompetent on the staff—even if he does own
a quarter of the stock."

Gideon scowled. "It sounds as though you've made up
your mind about me."

Payne held up a hand. "Not yet, sir. Not yet! I'm prepared to do so now, however. If you'll excuse me a moment, I'll adjust my cravat and we'll go for a stroll. This
place is far too noisy for a confidential discussion."

Gideon started to sit in a visitor's chair. Payne coughed.

"Mr. Kent. When I ask you to excuse me, that is a request
for you to leave. Don't you understand the nuances of the
English language? Hardly what I'd call an auspicious
beginning."

Red-faced, Gideon left.

He didn't know whether to laugh at the man or curse
him. And what was all that folderol about Payne fixing his
cravat? He understood when he heard the desk drawer
slide open softly. There was the faint squeak of a cork
coming out of a bottle. A moment later the drawer shut
again.

Soon Payne joined him, struggling into an old frock coat.
What appeared to be graham cracker crumbs speckled the
left lapel. The editor had done nothing to his cravat.

"I'll check with Mr. Staniels to see that all's under control. We're half an hour from locking up the final form, but
it's a quiet night. Excuse me once again, if you please."

And off he went toward the central desk, surrounded by
an aura of authority and a scent of bourbon.

ii

The snow had slacked off. Just a few flakes sprinkled
down to sparkle on the tops of the drifts. Payne's winter
apparel consisted of a plaid muffler, a beaver hat at least
twenty years old, and mismatched gloves.

The two men turned south along Park Row. The news-
boys had left the Franklin statue, presumably taking someone's paper to sell. Payne clasped his hands behind his back
and peered straight ahead.

"I wanted us out of the office so we might speak freely,
Mr. Kent. There is no need for us to act out a farce. You
needn't get my approval for a job on the *Union*. You know
you can force that any time you wish. However"—he shot
a humorless look at the younger man—"this much is true.
If you do join us against my wishes, I can make it damned
difficult for you to get cooperation from anyone. I can, that
is, until such time as you discharge me."

"I wouldn't want that, Payne. And Molly would never
permit it."

A little glint shone in his eye. "I fear you're having sport with me."

"Definitely not. When Mollý deferred to you in the matter of hiring me, it wasn't just a courtesy. She'd rather have you than me."

"Would she! Comforting, very comforting," he murmured, and hiccoughed into his glove. Had Payne known all along that he had Molly's wholehearted backing? Gideon suspected so. Like a good lawyer, Payne might be building a case for his authority a step at a time. He was convinced he was right when the editor said, "If it's indeed true, then it's doubly certain I could make your life miserable—should I choose to do so. Frankly, Mr. Kent—"

"Look here, I wish you'd call me Gideon."

"If ever I think the time is right, sir, I shall. But not until."

Despite his flaring anger, Gideon accepted the rebuke in silence.

"I am not saying I would make things difficult for you. I am not saying that at all. Yet! However, it's questionable as to whether we would get along. I have many opinions to which you might take exception. For example, I have never been able to feel kindly toward anyone who hails from a region populated by former secessionists. No, let's be wholly candid. By traitors."

"Now just a—"

"Be quiet, sir! I have the floor. Or the street, to be precise. Equally high on my list of dislikes is any form of nepotism. Finally, I know what you have been doing prior to this time, and I must inform you I detest trade unions. My loathing was merely increased when your father forced me to accept two of them under our roof. Jephtha Kent was a courageous and intelligent man. But every human being blunders now and then. Your father's blunder of five years ago can only be termed colossal. As I interpret the purposes of trade unions, they ultimately hope to provide a guaranteed wage for everyone, including the man whose work is slipshod. A permanent job for everyone, including the indolent—what's wrong, Mr. Kent?"

Gideon had stopped, fists on his hips. "You, Mr. Payne. Job or no job—you're a goddamned bigot."

He was thunderstruck when Payne laughed. "Very true.

So is any man worth his salt. Bigotry must be confined to the editorial columns, however, not slyly sprinkled into the news. That's a fact you must remember if you come with us."

If. He gave it special emphasis.

Gideon growled, "I'll remember." He kicked a ridge of snow, scattering it. A police wagon passed. Women yelled obscenities from behind the barred windows.

Payne hummed to himself. He acted pleased with his performance thus far. Gideon felt compelled to speak again, regardless of the consequences.

"But I can't accept your definition of the purpose of labor unions. If what you said were true of all of them— or even a tenth of them—I'd quit the movement instantly. But you're wrong."

"Am I, now? I remain to be convinced. And I shall steadfastly refuse to let anyone turn the paper into a labor rag. Sometimes I think we should change the name. But that would be an affront to Amanda, God rest her. She charged me to start a newspaper that would promote the Federal Union when it was in danger of being torn apart. She never realized how a noble word would be perverted. Believe it or not, Mr. Kent, the world does not revolve around the movement which has recently bemused you. Learn that lesson, too, if you please."

What a pompous, obnoxious little wretch he is, Gideon thought. Well, Molly had warned him. The editor's strategy seemed to be based on rattling his opponent. Gideon tried to disarm him with courtesy.

"I realize there are a great many things I'd need to learn—"

Murmured sarcasm: "A considerable understatement."

Gideon finished through clenched teeth, "Commencing with the trivial. Why on earth do your reporters work with their hats on?"

"So the hats won't be stolen, of course. A newspaper is not Saratoga Springs or Baden-Baden. It attracts visitors of all social classes and moral persuasions. And criminality is rampant these days. In fact I believe we are just entering a golden age of peculation and chicane. Do you agree?"

In a strangled voice Gideon said, "I don't know what peculation is. Chicane either."

"Well." Payne halted and gave Gideon a long, keen look. "That's unusual honesty. I like a man smart enough to admit he's ignorant. As for the words, consult a dictionary."

Gideon wanted to whoop. He felt he'd passed a kind of test. Perhaps the decisive one.

iii

They walked in silence to the corner of Broadway. Heavy snow began to fall again. From behind, a couple of street boys came running with early editions of the *Sun*. Payne bought one and thrust it at Gideon.

"Take this home. Read it. Then read it again. Try to figure out why the *Sun* outsells us, and why I'm working like the devil to catch up."

It was true! Payne had accepted him. With unconcealed enthusiasm, he exclaimed, "I suppose one reason is that the *Sun* only costs two pennies, not four."

"Nonsense. In addition to being half the price, the *Sun* has half as many pages. It outsells us because it's livelier and better written. It contains an excellent mix of important news, lurid crime stories and titillating society gossip. As the wags say, the *Sun* makes vice attractive in the morning and the *Post* makes virtue unattractive at night."

Gideon tucked the paper under his arm. The editor continued, "Now as to starting work—shall we say immediately after the New Year?"

"Fine."

"Initially you'll be on a twelve- to fourteen-hour shift, just like everyone else."

"What?" He knew he shouldn't risk throwing his victory away. But this was principle. "That's intolerable, Payne. You know the eight-hour day's the coming thing. The Federal government has adopted it and is demanding its suppliers do the same. A shorter work day is one of the major trade union demands—"

"As long as you work for me, Mr. Kent, you will have to forget about trade union demands and concern yourself with what I demand."

"Well, if I ever take over, things will be different."

"With any luck I shall be dead by then. Spared from

witnessing the pathetic spectacle of a man trying to operate a newspaper on which every employee decides for himself what work he wishes to do, for how long, and for what wage. I can tell you exactly what that kind of paper will be like. It will be called the *Daily Anarchy* and will consist of one sheet. Both sides blank."

"By God, Payne, I'll change your mind before I'm done."

"I doubt it, sir. I sincerely doubt it." But he was studying Gideon from the left side, and the younger man couldn't see a look of grudging respect fleet across the editor's face before he snapped, "Now do you want a job on my terms? You're not going to get one on your own."

Gideon felt bad about compromising his convictions. He tried to remember the larger objective. He nodded in a brusque way.

"I want the job."

There was a practical problem, though. Margaret would abhor the long hours. He needed to find something that would overcome her inevitable opposition. Something to divert her, in some area of their life where he could reasonably effect a compromise.

Should it take the form of a gift? If so, Christmas would be an ideal time to—

"Have you fallen asleep, Mr. Kent? Don't you have more questions? If so, you may state them, but keep your socialistic panaceas to yourself."

Gideon got mad all over again. One moment he liked the prickly little man, the next he loathed him. This was one of the latter moments.

"May I be so bold as to ask how much I'll be making on a fourteen-hour shift?"

"That's a fine question coming from a millionaire."

"I've never relied on the inherited money. I earn my way whenever I can."

"You do, eh? Fancy that." It was not said unkindly. "To start, you'll receive one half the standard reporter's salary."

"But I don't know what a reporter earns. Or an editor, for that matter."

"Reporters receive fifteen to thirty dollars a week, depending on their skill and the generosity of their employer. At the *Union* we pay top men twenty-eight. As to what editors make, that needn't concern you for some time.

Molly said she was placing your career entirely in my
hands. Very well, I'll start you on the dock. You'll unload
shipments of newsprint and load finished papers on the
delivery wagons. Since we're a morning paper, your shift
will begin at four in the afternoon and end around dawn.
For the first few weeks you'll probably go home feeling as
though your back's broken. But if you survive the
experience—"

"I'll survive," Gideon interrupted quietly.

Payne shrugged. "Some don't. In any case, you'll have a
much better understanding of the effort required to create
even one edition of a newspaper." The editor cocked his
head. "Any comment?"

Gideon drew a deep breath. "If you expect a protest,
you'll be disappointed. The dock is fine. I felt I should start
in a menial job."

Theo Payne took the younger man by surprise, and
smiled. Not a cynical smile, but one that was genuinely
friendly.

"Delighted to hear it," he said, "because you don't deserve to start anywhere else, Gideon."

CHAPTER IV

THE HEARTS OF
THREE WOMEN

i

A SUITABLE PRESENT for Margaret suggested itself to Gideon next day. It was one she'd been asking for, at least indirectly, over a period of several years. He spent the remaining days before Christmas touring the town with real estate agents, thought he took a couple of hours out to close the *Beacon*'s last office. By Christmas Eve he had papers covering the first stage of the land transaction in his pocket and was ready to present the gift to his wife.

Light snow began to fall about seven o'clock as the family finished supper. The temperature outside was twenty degrees, and nine-year-old Eleanor begged permission to take her skates to the frozen pond before the snow covered it.

"Excellent idea," Gideon said, laying his napkin beside his empty plate. Eleanor jumped up to hug him around the neck. Across the table, Margaret watched and frowned.

"See that Will's in his bed before you go, would you please?" he added. "Your mother and I must have a chat."

He was smiling as he said it, but the remark brought a look of anxiety to Margaret's face. He was disturbed. He'd smelled something new on her breath when he arrived home. Whiskey. The odor even penetrated the scent of the clove she must have chewed to perfume her mouth. Why was she drinking more heavily? Did she suspect?

No, impossible. He hadn't brought any of Julia's letters home. After he read and reread each one until he'd virtually memorized it, he consigned it to a stove.

"What is it you want to talk about?" Margaret asked when Eleanor was gone. Her speech was slow; thick. "Is it the newspaper? Have you decided it won't be to your liking?"

"Not at all. I'm anxious to go to work."

"Six nights a week." She made a face. "All night."

"Margaret, I explained before—that can't be helped." As they left the table, he put his arm around her. She drew away. He sighed, then said, "Why don't we go into the parlor? I've a little surprise for you."

She shrugged in an indifferent way. For the first time he noticed a faint streaking of white in her hair. Just a few strands—but she wasn't yet thirty years old. The gray hair, the apparent drinking in secret, and her outbursts of anger all combined to bring her father to mind. A man whose sanity had been destroyed by alcohol.

Her obvious misery only intensified his guilt. He touched the side pocket of his coat, as if the paper tucked there was a remedy that would magically restore happiness to the household. In a way, he'd hoped the paper would do exactly that. He feared the hope had been a vain one.

He heard Eleanor clatter down the stairs with her skates, call a cheerful goodbye and hurry out. The parlor was dim and inviting with only one gas fixture aglow. Gideon found a match and began to light the small candles on the fragrant pine tree decorated with cranberry strands and homemade gilt paper ornaments. Soon two dozen tiny flames cast a warm, shimmering light over plump red berries, dark green needles, golden angels. He dropped the burned matches in the bucket of water kept handy in case of fire, then reached to his pocket.

Margaret's distracted expression stayed his hand. She was seated, staring at the table where the Rogers group had stood.

"Margaret?"

Her head turned slowly. "What is it?"

"Please tell me why you're so unhappy. I thought that once I gave up the *Beacon* and went to work at something with a better future, you'd feel better."

The strange, vacant look left her eyes, and they shone with some of the fire he remembered from their courting days in Richmond, when they'd argued about the nature of war.

"I've thought it over and it's my conclusion the *Union* is no different from that sheet you published for those wretched railroad men."

"Wretched? Margaret, Daphnis Miller wasn't just my friend, he was yours too. Our neighbor. Our benefactor."

She waved her hand in a vague way. "That was a long time ago. A very long time ago. This is the present. The *Union* is no different. Oh, perhaps the work's a little safer. For the sake of your children, I'm thankful for that. But essentially you have the same job. One which again proves you place the welfare of others ahead of that of your family."

He hadn't wanted to lose his temper tonight. But he did.

"Damn it, Margaret, you put the most twisted interpretations on everything I do and—"

"Kindly do *not* use filthy language with me, Gideon Kent."

"But I don't know what you *want* of me!"

"The knowledge that you really care about my wishes."

He stalked toward her. "What does that mean? What does it *really* mean? Complete surrender to your whims? A clerk's job in some store? A daily routine in which my most important concern is hurrying home to chop wood or paint the porch trim?"

"Yes." Defiantly, her head came up. "That's exactly what I'd like for a change."

"Well, I'm sorry, but you'll never get me to live that kind of life." A sad smile. "You taught me too well."

"I wish to heaven I hadn't."

"Yes, I'm aware of that feeling."

"Then give up the newspaper business."

More firmly: "It's selfish of you to ask that of me."

"No," she retorted, rising, "selfish of *you* to deny the request. By doing so you're destroying this family. You've already destroyed our marriage. I don't know why I should expect it to be otherwise. You've always put your work first."

"Margaret, you're wrong!" he shouted. "That's a deliberate and wicked distortion!"

How had she developed her sick, destructive need for dominance? He was too angry to care very much. He stabbed his hand into his pocket, yanked out the document and slammed it on a table. "Obviously tonight is an inappropriate time to discuss this."

She stood motionless and gazed at the paper. Unexpectedly, the candlelight lent her face a certain forlorn quality that touched him and cooled his temper.

"What is it, Gideon?"

"A real estate purchase agreement. I've bought a large plot of ground: a corner lot at Sixty-first Street and Fifth Avenue, opposite Central Park. It's prime residential land, and this very afternoon I engaged an architect to draw up plans for a big, comfortable house—" He had been speaking with increasing weariness. His voice was soft as he finished. "If all goes well, we'll spend next Christmas in the kind of place you've always wanted."

She pursed her lips. "How thoughtful. It certainly represents a compromise. I'd concluded that you meant to keep us living shabbily forever."

Ignoring her bitterness, he forced himself to walk to her. To place his hands on her shoulders. This time she let him touch her, but she stiffened as he did. Somehow, he felt like weeping.

A candle on the tree hissed and dripped wax on the carpet. He thought he detected a flicker of movement at one of the lace-curtained veranda windows. Then he decided it was a trick played by the shimmering flames.

With all the restraint he could muster, he said, "I know you've felt I was wrong in refusing to spend the California money on ourselves. Perhaps I was. I admit I can be mule-stubborn sometimes. In any case, to try to make up for that shortcoming, the house is a Christmas gift. I spoke to the architect in terms of a construction cost of a hundred and fifty thousand dollars. The very finest materials and appointments throughout. It will hardly put a dent in the inheritance, and I'd like you to have a home you can live in proudly—"

Again his voice trailed off. Her lackluster eyes and the sour set of her mouth made him drop his hands from her shoulders. He shook his head.

"I thought you'd be just a little pleased."

"Of course I am." She didn't sound it. "I do question your motives. Why are you showing me kindness all at once? What else are you doing that you're ashamed of?"

For one harrowing moment, he was positive she'd found out about Julia. His face turned ashen. "What the devil do you mean?"

She laughed, harshly. "You know very well. Deep down you're ashamed of your selfishness. Ashamed of putting everything—*your* wishes, *your* work, your everlasting need to crusade for something—ahead of this family. You know that kind of behavior is a weakness in your character."

"Some might not consider crusading, as you snidely call it, to be a weakness."

"Who? Your newspaper cronies? Your radical friends? Never mind! Let's stick to the subject of the new house. I recognize it for what it is. A bribe."

"God in heaven—" he breathed. "Margaret, it's a *gift*."

"No. You thought you'd bribe me in the hope it would salve your conscience and change my feelings at the same time."

Guilt pierced him again. There was an element of that in the transaction. But he'd honestly wanted to make her happy, too.

"I'll live in that fine house, Gideon. I'll live there because you owe me that. It alters nothing between us. We'll remain husband and wife for the sake of Eleanor and Will. But it will be a marriage in name only until you put your priorities in order."

"Until I do exactly what you say, isn't that the heart of it, Margaret?"

"Until you put your priorities *in order*!" It came out a soft scream. Her hands clenched at her sides. Her eyes glittered with reflections of the holiday candles. "Until then you've touched me for the last time. You have come into my bed for the last time—"

The situation was careening out of control, flogged by her anger, and by his own that he tried to check but couldn't.

"Oh, I've heard *that* before. Well, no loss. You're no

bargain any longer, Margaret, let me tell you." Suddenly he realized what he'd said. He extended his hand. "I'm sorry—"

It went unheard as she shrieked, "You have experience, then? A basis for comparison? How many, Gideon? How many other women have you had? How many are you keeping? What kind of houses are you building for them?"

"Margaret, I know you're drinking in secret—"

She stepped back, shaken. Was she so muddled that she'd convinced herself he didn't know?

"I think it's affecting your mind. God knows something is. All you have in your heart any longer is venom. Venom and some kind of warped desire to make everyone around you, but especially me, do precisely what you say. I've told you I won't and I tell you again now. Nor am I going to listen to any more of your ranting. Not this evening."

He snatched the purchase offer and flung it at her feet. *"Merry Christmas."*

He stalked out of the parlor. In his haste to escape he knocked over a china umbrella stand in the hall. A moment later his feet hammered the veranda. He disappeared down the snowy street, his hands in his pants pockets and an expression of fury on his face.

ii

When Eleanor reached the pond, she found no one skating. Too much snow had already accumulated. Disappointed, she returned to the house within a few minutes of her departure, her skates tied together by the laces and dangling over her shoulder.

On the steps of the veranda, she paused to pull off her knitted cap and shake melting snow from it. That was when she heard her parents shouting at one another. The strident voices in the parlor brought tears to her eyes, and filled her with a feeling close to physical pain.

She crept along the veranda and crouched down by one of the windows. Heavy condensation on the glass diffused the Christmas candles into blurs of light. She rubbed her mitten against the glass with a circular motion, then stopped as she realized the condensation was on the inside. It was the movement of her hand which Gideon had seen.

The horrible shouting went on and on. Eleanor didn't understand why Papa and Mama couldn't get along. It had something to do with Papa's work and his absences from home. Beyond that, she was mystified.

Eleanor loved her handsome father. She loved his long, light-colored hair and that eye patch, which gave him such a unique and dashing appearance. She loved his gentle hands, and the sound of his fine baritone voice when he sang to her. But he hadn't sung at all lately. He was gone too much. Remembering that brought a flash of resentment.

Resentment of Gideon wasn't an unusual emotion for Eleanor these days. She spent most of her time with her mother. She attended to household chores, which she already found boring, and to little Will's care, which she enjoyed. Without realizing it, in her own mind, she was beginning to take her mother's part. After all, didn't Mama repeatedly say it was a father's duty to make his family happy? Papa was obviously making Mama miserable.

Suddenly he stormed out of the parlor. Eleanor caught her breath. Terrified, she heard his boots thud in the hall. It was too late to run.

Not three yards to her right, the front door crashed open. He came striding out, cursing under his breath.

She pressed against the siding between the parlor windows. Her skates slipped from her shoulder, striking hard on the veranda. But by then her father was through the gate in the little picket fence and striding away down the snowy street. She'd caught a glimpse of his face as he passed. Angry. He was evidently in such a rage, he hadn't heard the thump of the skates.

Once more she knelt in front of a mist-covered window. Inside, her mother moved toward a cabinet where bottles of bad-smelling dark brown liquid were kept. Like the contents of the bottles in the cellar, that liquid made her mama walk unsteadily after she'd had too much. And she went to the cabinet at least once and sometimes twice every morning and afternoon.

Eleanor crept to the front door, made a noise and went inside as if she'd just arrived. Her heart was breaking but she didn't let it show. She seemed to have an ability to put on whatever kind of face she chose. But upstairs, in bed, her self-control melted and she wept into her pillow, wishing the Christmas season would bring just one gift to the household.

Peace.

Love is supposed to make people happy, she thought. *Poems say that. The preacher says it in church. Men and women who fall in love are supposed to be the happiest of all. It must be a lie. Love hurts people. I've seen it for months. I saw it through the window again tonight. Love hurts people. I'll never let it hurt me.*

A seed had fallen in fertile ground, and from that night on it began to grow.

iii

Not quite two years later—September 20, 1873—Julia lay in the bed she'd shared with Gideon on the night they first made love. The bed and the one in which her son was sleeping were the only pieces of furniture left in her mansion. All the other furnishings had been moved out and auctioned for a fraction of their value.

Tomorrow morning she and Carter would move out as well. Then the property would be on the market officially. If she were lucky, a buyer could be found who would pay approximately what she was asking, one hundred and ten thousand dollars. From the proceeds of the sale she and Carter could live and carry on her work for years to come, although in a far less affluent manner.

A day after the panic had started, Gideon had telegraphed to say that his money, handled for him by the Rothman Bank of Boston, was safe. He said he'd provide Julia with whatever cash she needed, and would do it for as long as she required help. She blessed him for making the offer even though she could never accept. No matter how bad her circumstances, she meant to be self-sufficient.

Gideon had been doing well. He'd progressed from the dock of the newspaper through the composing and press rooms to the editorial department, joining two unions en route. A year ago he'd written his first piece of copy—an obituary—then rewritten it three times until the editor,

Payne, said he was satisfied. Gideon's name was now on the masthead as the *Union*'s publisher. Payne remained editor.

Of late Gideon had been trying his hand at editorials and devoting himself to the business side of the enterprise. He'd raised salaries and shortened working hours, thereby attracting better writing talent. His last letter before the start of the panic had been a long and jubilant one. He'd reported that the *Union* had pulled to within two thousand of the *Sun*'s daily circulation. On the strength of that, he had boosted the advertising rate to fifty cents an agate line—or ten cents more than the *Sun* charged. He and Payne had worked for a week on a three-paragraph front-page editorial stating that the *Union* could command a premium because it had a quality readership—men and women who liked the paper and were loyal to it, and would therefore be more receptive to its advertisements. Of course, Gideon pointed out to Julia with a touch of amusement, the same could be said by any paper with a body of loyal readers. The point was, no one had said it before. The strategy had worked, and in one week the *Union*'s advertising linage had nearly doubled.

Then came the fourth of September.

The panic began with the closing of the doors of Jay Cooke and Company at fifteen past noon. Before the day was over, thirty-seven other New York banks and stock brokerage firms had also closed, and the governors of the Stock Exchange had suspended trading indefinitely.

Cooke's was bankrupt, they said. The nation's most solid and reputable financial establishment *bankrupt!* A representative of the house immediately traveled to Chicago to see Julia. It was not Mr. Robbins. He too had lost everything and had put a pistol to his head. The representative had come to do Julia the courtesy of explaining her position. Actually, she had none. She was wiped out.

She didn't understand the representative's roster of reasons for the collapse of Cooke's. He cited railroads expanding too fast in Europe. Currency values inflated there and in America. Overproduction. Feverish industrial growth and subsequent overproduction. Skyrocketing prices for everything, which encouraged investment in highly speculative enterprises such as the Northern Pacific. And lastly, plummeting public confidence in government and business, brought to a climax earlier in the year by revelations that the Credit Mobilier had used gifts of its own, highly lucrative stock to elicit favors from members of Congress.

The representative seemed to comprehend all the interlocking aspects of the disaster. She didn't. But she did understand when he said a depression lay ahead. She understood it even more completely tonight, because tomorrow, she and Carter would be moving to a boarding-house on the rebuilt West Side.

The move should have disturbed her. As evidence of worsening economic conditions, it did. But after she'd gotten over her brief and stormy anger—a vestige of the past, in which she'd expected her life to be perpetual tranquility—she'd begun to view the change as something to which she must and would adjust. She had her son. She had her lover whom she managed to see four or five times every year. And she had her work. She needed nothing else except a little food and a roof to shelter her—and never mind the size or location of that roof.

Odd, the way her role and Gideon's had reversed, she thought as she visualized his face in the darkness. The house was dark throughout, and silent. All the servants had been released twenty-four hours earlier.

When she and Gideon had found one another in the aftermath of the fire, she'd been living in an affluent way while he and his family lived very modestly. Now the publisher of the New York *Union* occupied a splendid new mansion on upper Fifth Avenue—a move undertaken to placate his wife, and one which had not fulfilled its purpose. He said Margaret's behavior was growing more hostile and erratic because of heavy drinking she now hardly bothered to conceal.

Most of Gideon's wealth had been converted to gold bars over a year ago. The Rothman Bank had foreseen a financial crisis on a worldwide scale. Most of Julia's assets had been on paper, and were gone. In two years, nearly everything in her life and his had changed.

Except the most important thing of all: their steadfast and steadily maturing love for one another. He said it was all that sustained him in the increasingly difficult relationship with his wife. And it was all that sustained Julia through the long periods when she was traveling, and facing

increasingly hostile audiences, and thinking of Gideon as
she lay in lonely beds in towns whose names sometimes
blurred together until she could no longer remember where
she was, or in what place she'd last been spat on or stoned.

She heard a peculiar noise from the State Street side of
the house. She rose and drew her emerald-colored robe
around her. It was shabby now. Out of fashion. But she
couldn't afford to discard it.

She walked quietly down the second-floor corridor to
French windows at the front. The windows opened onto a
small balcony. Outside, the September moon was brilliant.
She clearly saw a band of eight or ten men skulking along
the street. They paused in front of her driveway. One
pointed. He'd noticed the deserted look of the house. All
the windows were bare, the draperies gone.

She ran to her room. Breathing fast, she opened the
trunk in which she'd packed the only clothes she planned
to keep. She snatched out a small revolver purchased a few
days ago on the advice of one of the departing servants
who said looters were operating after dark.

She dashed back down the hall and opened the French
windows just as three of the men started up the drive. They
were unemployed, she suspected. Perhaps discharged from
plants that had already shut down, as thousands were shutting down in every state.

She pointed the revolver upward and fired a shot. "Not
this place!" one of the men yelled. He turned and fled. The
others followed.

Carter came racing from his bedroom. "Ma, why did you
use the gun?"

"Nothing to worry about, dear. Some vagrants were
prowling around the house. They're gone."

Carter surveyed the empty driveway below. "You should
have let me shoot. I'd have nailed one of them."

There was no great conceit in the statement, just an assertion of fact. Carter Kent was only eleven but he was
already half a head taller than his mother. His jet black
eyes and hair—so like his father's, yet so different—were
turning him into a handsome young man.

For a moment, though, his confidence deserted him.

"Why is all this happening, Ma? I don't like it much."

She ruffled his hair. "I don't either. But nothing remains

the same for long. Change is one of the few constants in life, and you'll discover that as you grow older. Bad times have come to the country, Carter. Come very suddenly and unexpectedly—"

"Bad times for us too, aren't they? I won't ever get another taste of cook's pecan pie."

She smiled. "You'll survive. So will I." She kissed his forehead. "As long as I have you."

"And Gideon?"

Softly: "Yes, Carter. And Gideon."

After the first time, she'd never again entertained him in her bedroom. They met discreetly, in other cities. But now and then Carter saw arriving mail which included a letter with Gideon's name on it. Once he'd been bold enough to ask whether Gideon was some kind of special friend. That much she had admitted. Probably her son had guessed a good deal more from the way she spoke and looked as she answered. She made it a point not to act embarrassed or ashamed when Gideon's name came up in conversation. She didn't flaunt him to Carter, but neither did she deny his importance.

The boy gnawed his lower lip for a moment. "Ma?"

"What?"

"Would you like Gideon to marry you?"

"Very"—her voice broke slightly—"very much."

"But he can't ever do that, can he?"

"No."

"That's what I figured out. Since he's already married, you'll just be friends for the rest of your life."

"Yes." Her heart ached. "Friends."

Something oppressive seemed to close in around her then—a fear whose source she couldn't immediately locate. She packed Carter back to bed and returned to the front window, opening it and stepping onto the little balcony. She gazed north toward the central business district, where a miracle of rebuilding had taken place since the fire. The brilliant moonlight flooded down on Twentieth Street and Thomas Courtleigh's mansion beyond.

Naturally Courtleigh had survived the panic. He was the sort who would. It was Courtleigh who was the cause of her fear, she realized. He'd harassed her relentlessly during the past two years. At least she assumed he was the one

responsible for the almost constant verbal and physical
abuse she took during her lectures these days. Fortunately
none of the other speakers who worked for the Association
had been harassed in similar fashion. If they had been, Julia
would have quit.

For some reason, Gideon hadn't been bothered since a
brief flurry of trouble right after his return to New York
late in '71. Julia knew better than to think Courtleigh had
forgotten her lover, or forgiven him.

Early in 1872 the railroad president had married Gwendolyn Strother. They'd taken a long European wedding trip.
People continued to say Mrs. Courtleigh was—well, the
charitable used the terms *high strung* or *excitable*. Julia's
servants as well as tradespeople who called at both houses
employed stronger language. They said Mrs. Courtleigh was
not quite right in the head.

In some accounts Julia had heard, Courtleigh's wife was
reputed to have been unstable since childhood. In others,
it was Gideon's visit that was said to be responsible for her
condition. Julia doubted the latter story, though she supposed the melodramatic and by now notorious scene at the
ball hadn't exactly helped the young woman's state of mind.

Julia had seen Courtleigh up close only once since his
call in the solarium. Recent events had kept her too busy
to think of the encounter, but it came to mind now as she
stood in the moonlight and gazed north and then west
across rooftops and treetops toward the Illinois prairie.

Just before the Fourth of July, she'd been supervising
the trimming of some hedges along Twentieth. Courtleigh's
brougham had turned out of his coach yard, and he'd hailed
her from the window. Warily, she'd stepped to the curb.
He'd greeted her with a tip of his hat, though there was
no cordiality in his hazel eyes.

"Good afternoon, Miss Sedgwick—or Mrs. Sedgwick? I
always get so confused addressing a woman like you. Ah
well. I'd like to remind you that I made certain promises—"

"I haven't forgotten them," she snapped back. "The
thugs you send to every one of my lectures make that
impossible."

"Thugs?" He blinked. "I'm afraid I don't understand."
But of course he did, and mirth in his hazel eyes said so.
"I wasn't thinking of you so much as of your—friend." The

pause lent a lascivious quality to the last word. "Remind him that while I sometimes get very busy with other projects, and thus may seem to neglect promises, I do not in fact forget them. I eventually keep every one I make. Mr. Kent should ponder that each night before he goes to sleep. So should you. Good day."

Remembering, she gripped the edge of the balcony rail. For the first time, her confidence in her ability to endure an uncertain future ebbed away.

"I mustn't lose you, Gideon," she whispered. *"I mustn't."*

She shook her head. It did no good muttering to herself. She must write Gideon. Remind him of the ever-present threat Courtleigh represented.

A cloud passed across the face of the moon. The resulting darkness only worsened her fear. She was ashamed of that, yet the fear persisted. Back in her room, she couldn't fall asleep. Wild thoughts went tumbling through her head.

Darkness falling on the land.

Men roaming the streets and roads.

Out of work.

Hungry.

Desperate enough to do anything for anyone who will pay them.

And Courtleigh hadn't forgotten.

"He hasn't, Gideon," she breathed in the stillness. "You don't dare think he has, because that's just when he'll strike."

CHAPTER V

TOMPKINS SQUARE

i

"I HAVE NO business attending a rally conducted by radicals," Theo Payne said as he and Gideon left the *Union* one day almost five months later. "P. J. McGuire is socialist and so is his Committee on Public Safety."

Gideon laughed as they started toward a hack stand on Park Row. It was a mild winter day, bright but cloudy; the thirteenth of January, 1874. "I think you have your verbs mixed up, Theo. McGuire may have organized the rally but it certainly won't be conducted by radicals. The mayor is scheduled to speak. And Johnny Swinton of the *Sun*." Swinton was chief editorial writer for the rival paper.

"That's the sole reason I'm going. I want to watch Johnny reveal his new insanity to the world at large."

There was no point arguing. He could never convince Payne that the hundreds of unemployed men and women at Tompkins Square would be voicing demands that were eminently reasonable. The rally had been arranged to protest the epidemic unemployment afflicting New York and other major cities. Local trade unions wanted the city council to temporarily forbid evictions by landlords, appropriate some money for emergency relief, and start a public works program to create jobs. Payne and many others considered those proposals fully as socialistic as some of the men making them.

Gideon glanced at his watch. They were already twenty minutes late for the start of the program. He'd been detained in a meeting with one of those so-called advertising agents who were popping up everywhere these days. The agents centralized the purchase of advertising space on behalf of a list of clients. Of course they earned a substantial markup in the process, but they offered newspapers a definite advantage. By paying promptly on behalf of their clients, the agent relieved a paper of the burden of collecting from slow-paying or defaulting customers. The agent who'd called on Gideon, a representative of the N. W. Ayer firm of Philadelphia, had placed a large order for space. He therefore wanted the publisher's personal attention and he'd gotten it.

As the two men crossed the square, Gideon gave only slight notice to an unusually tall Street Arab lounging against the Franklin statue. In the autumn just passed, he might have scrutinized the shabbily clad youth more closely. At that time Julia's letter of warning had been fresh in his mind. For a few weeks he was very watchful as he moved around town. Nothing happened. By the end of December he relaxed again.

The story of Torvald Ericsson's death had never appeared in the *Union*. By the time Gideon was in a position to order it put into type, the charges were not only unprovable but stale. He'd had a hot argument with Payne about it. The editor maintained—and correctly, Gideon had to admit once his anger cooled—that Sidney Florian's disappearance in the fire removed the sole source of evidence to support the charges. Without evidence, a statement that Courtleigh had sanctioned murder was only supposition.

"If you want to practice that kind of journalism, Gideon, let's go all the way. Let's pack the paper with accusations against anyone we dislike. We can call your banker a Shylock, my wife a Bowery chippy, President Grant a sot and a spoilsman and do it all with a perfectly clear conscience."

He was only willing to bow to Payne because he felt sure another time would come when Courtleigh would err on the side of repression and get caught at it. Then Gideon would have his hide. In print.

Payne hailed the first hack in line. Gideon called to the driver, "Tompkins Square," and jumped inside. A moment later the vehicle was speeding north along Chatham Street and then into the traffic of the Bowery.

The tall street boy had been loitering along behind them, within earshot. As soon as the carriage sped away, he dashed for a nearby office that transmitted telegraph messages to other points in the city.

ii

Tompkins Square had originally been laid out as a military drill ground. Though still used by militia units, it had now become a park that was being slowly swallowed by the expanding ghetto. The square's northern and southern boundaries were East Tenth and East Seventh Streets. The hack approached along the latter thoroughfare, from the west. Traffic was so heavy, Payne and Gideon were forced to pay the driver at First Avenue, then walk.

A huge crowd had been turned out by the trade unions and socialist clubs. Men, women and youngsters packed the square and spilled into Avenues A and B on either side. As Gideon and his companion pushed their way along the noisy, congested sidewalk in front of Seventh Street tenements, more socialists came parading toward the site of the rally. They marched four abreast to the music of a small band. The winter sky shed a dull light on bare heads and plumes of breath. Most of the marchers wore some sort of improvised red sash over the shoulder or around the waist.

Payne and Gideon took note of three stern New York policemen on horseback near the curb. Elsewhere in the crowd Gideon began to discern uniformed foot patrolmen. All of the police were armed with long, thick wooden clubs.

Payne pursed his lips. "Who turned out so many of our finest, I wonder?"

Gideon shook his head. In the street, another socialist club was marching along from First Avenue. A red beard streaked with white caught Gideon's eye. He stretched on tiptoe.

"Sime?" He waved. "Over here!"

Stepping to the beat of a snare drum, Strelnik swiveled his head. He saw Gideon. He faced front again with no sign of recognition. Slowly Gideon lowered his hand. His face was somber.

"Is the program under way?" Payne asked. His height kept him from seeing much besides backsides on the crowded sidewalk. Again Gideon went up on his toes.

"Doesn't appear to be. The square's full, though. Speakers are on the platform. Oh, there's Frank Jamison—"

Gideon squeezed by an elderly woman in a red sash. Payne followed him to the side of the *Herald* reporter they both knew. "I thought the rally was due to start thirty minutes ago," Gideon said to Jamison.

The *Herald* man was leaning against the corner of a small grocery with a closed sign in its window. He puffed his cigar before answering, "There's been a delay. Some objection from city hall. The mayor isn't going to speak after all. And he's withdrawn permission for the rally."

"You mean all these people are gathered illegally?" Payne said.

With a slow nod, Jamison said, "Only no one's bothered to tell most of them." Suddenly he spied something back along Seventh. He dropped his cigar and pointed.

"Jehoshaphat. Look. Those men are forming up—"

Gideon turned. A whole troop of mounted police was maneuvering into ranks that stretched from one side of Seventh to the other. Near Tompkins Square there were cries of alarm. People in the street scattered. The noses of the police horses gave off streams of vapor. The hazy sun shimmered on polished wooden clubs.

Neither Gideon, Payne, nor any other witnesses saw the signal for the charge that started the riot.

iii

The demonstrators had come in an angry, militant mood. The police were equally militant and equally angry, Gideon realized. He watched with a stunned look as the first mounted rank, then the second and third, swept into the people still unlucky enough to be in the street.

A boy slipped. As he rose, a policeman in the second rank rode by and bashed him with his billy. The boy reeled back, his temple gushing blood down the side of his face.

"My God," Theo Payne exclaimed. "They're going to kill those people."

Gideon said, "Isn't that what they deserve? After all, they're radicals."

The editor gave him a strange, intense look. Jamison of the *Herald* slipped away. There was commotion on the sidewalk, the crowd surging and swaying forward, driven by half a dozen foot policemen swinging clubs.

"Clear the walk. Clear the walk and go to your homes!"

When an elderly man retorted and reached for one of the clubs, two policemen attacked. Gideon heard a crunch of bone, then a cry. The man sank from sight.

What had been a relatively orderly scene quickly degenerated to howling confusion. From all sides, mounted and dismounted police poured into Tompkins Square with clubs flying. Red-sashed marchers broke ranks and either ran or squared off to fight. The speakers' platform began to sway. It quickly collapsed, its supports demolished by the frantic mob.

Buffeted along toward Avenue A, Gideon shouted that he wanted to locate Strelnik. Payne clutched his arm like a frightened child. "Don't abandon me in this sea of lunatics!" Through a break in the crowd, he glimpsed a foot patrolman at the curb. He wedged and shoved till he was facing the officer. "See here, I'm Theophilus Payne of the New York *Union*. Who revoked the order permitting this assembl—"

"Watch out, Theo!"

Gideon's cry came too late. The policeman slashed Payne's face with his club.

The editor pitched backward into Gideon's arms, his cheek bleeding from a break in the skin. The policeman started for Gideon next. Then he took note of his size and ran the other way, swinging his club wildly. Payne could only gasp, "No one has ever—*assaulted* me in—my entire life."

"I expect he mistook you for a socialist sympathizer," Gideon said with a humorless smile. "Here, sop up that blood with my handkerchief."

"But I'm not wearing a sash, for God's sake. I'm doing nothing wrong!"

"Neither are the rest of them, Theo."

Payne gave Gideon another long look. Something seemed to dawn in his eyes as the first of a volley of shots exploded in the square.

iv

Anyone who remained on the footpaths or winter-browned grass of Tompkins Square was fair game for the charging policemen. Gideon helped Payne around the corner to the west side of Avenue A, then down some stairs into a small entrance area belonging to a basement flat. Another young man, dark-haired and rather sallow, had also taken refuge there. He watched the carnage with stricken eyes.

"The radicals brought this on by staging the rally," the man said to Gideon. He was in his early twenties and spoke with a hint of an English accent.

"Sorry. I happen to be on the side of the unions," Gideon answered as he helped Payne sit on a lower step. The editor had a dazed look. He mumbled about needing a bracer.

The poorly dressed young man hadn't liked Gideon's remark.

"So am I, mister. I'm a member of the cigarmakers. But I am not on the side of the socialist fringe that's always pushing for a scrap with the law."

Gideon started to argue. The young man grabbed his arm and pulled him down. A large rock sailed into the entrance area. The rock smashed a narrow window light beside the apartment door. Glass sprayed everywhere.

"You all right?" the young man asked. Gideon nodded. "Guess it isn't the best of places for a debate. I jumped down here fearing for my life."

With good reason, Gideon thought. Back by the corner, someone screamed. The noise and confusion worsened. Out in the square a horseman charged along a footpath. A fig-ure with a familiar red beard ran at the mounted policeman, swinging both fists. The policeman clubbed the man three times and galloped on.

Gideon sprang toward the steps. "Would you watch my friend, Mr. . . . ?"

"Sam Gompers. Certainly will."

He raced up the steps and sprinted into Avenue A. Strelnik lay on the footpath, not moving.

A woman came limping from Gideon's left, hurrying two small, ragged boys away from a foot patrolman who was pursuing them. The older boy had a bruised left eye that was swollen shut. The woman wailed as the officer whipped his club toward the back of her head.

Before the blow landed, Gideon bowled into the man and knocked him down. The woman and children escaped into the melee on East Seventh. Gideon ran into the square before the policeman could rise, but a second unexpectedly grabbed him from behind.

"Clear the area!"

Gideon glanced at the club poised over his head. "Touch me with that and I'll break your back."

The policeman muttered something, lowered the club and went in search of other victims.

There were shouts, screams, moans of pain from all parts of the square. Pairs of mounted policemen started galloping down Avenues A and B in pursuit of escaping demonstrators. As Gideon approached, Strelnik stirred. Gideon helped him up.

Strelnik was groggy; he didn't realize who was grasping his hand. Blood streamed down the right side of his face from a deep scalp wound hidden by his hair.

"Sime, it's me. Come along. There's a safe place over on the side of—"

Strelnik pulled away. "No, thank you, Gideon. I need no help from your kind."

Gideon reached for him again. "Don't be a fool. Take my arm and lean on me."

"Careful, " Strelnik exclaimed, jerking back so hard he nearly fell. "You wouldn't want a workingman's blood on that fine capitalist suit."

"For Christ's sake, Sime, it's time to forget that kind of stupid—"

The paunchy little Russian turned and limped off toward the north side of the square, clutching his middle and weaving from side to side. Blood dripped from the tip of his beard and left bright drops on the footpath.

Gideon followed him for half a dozen steps, called his name. Strelnik never paused. Despondent, Gideon turned back toward the curb. A policeman on horseback rounded the corner from Tenth Street and controlled his prancing horse as he searched the square. When he caught sight of Gideon crossing the street, he broke into a smile.

That was a strange reaction, Gideon thought. All he could see of the policeman's face was a bulbous nose and a large gap where upper front teeth should have been. The man carried no club. Abruptly, he booted his horse into a canter.

Gideon walked faster to get out of the path of the animal. The policeman thrust his hand beneath his dirty tunic and pulled a pistol. Now his intention was unmistakable.

Halfway across the street, Gideon broke into a run. The policeman kicked his horse harder. Its hoofs raised white sparks from the paving stones. On the street's west side, the heads of Gompers and Theo Payne were visible above the sidewalk. Payne yelled. Gideon flung himself sideways.

The policeman's revolver thundered twice. Gideon landed on his shoulder, skidding in a pile of horse droppings. The policeman turned back, his horse looming like some gigantic beast from a nightmare. The horse reared. Slashing forehoofs dropped. Gideon rolled frantically toward the sidewalk. He could feel the air stir as the great weight of horse and rider came down. More sparks shot from the paving.

By firing his pistol the policeman had attracted attention. He saw that, flung the gun away and galloped south across East Seventh before anyone moved to stop him. Gideon gave chase but the man soon swung his horse into an alley and disappeared.

It had all happened with great speed. The shock of it finally struck Gideon. Trembling—and stinking like a stable hand—he walked toward the two men coming up from the stairwell. The young cigarmaker was aghast.

"That was the first policeman I've seen with a gun."

"If he was a policeman," Gideon responded.

"What?" Payne was momentarily confused. Then, in a whisper, he asked, "Is someone after you?"

Gideon managed a smile he didn't feel. "Very possibly, Theo. Very possibly."

"Who, for God's sake?"

"Never mind that right now. Let's get out of here and find a doctor for you."

"Balderdash. I'm perfectly fit. Just a little quivery. It's nothing a few bracers won't cure. I'm going back and write an editorial for tomorrow morning."

"What about?"

"The behavior of the police."

"But they were only clubbing trade unionists. Maybe a few Communards—"

Payne bent down and picked up a piece of red cotton flannel lying beside Sam Gompers' left shoe. Perhaps the scrap had been torn from some marcher's shoulder. A darker patch of red discolored one end.

The editor gazed at the bit of cloth for a moment. Then he tucked it in his waistcoat pocket and looked across a square all but empty of demonstrators. Near the wreckage of the platform, the mounted police troop was forming up again.

"Yes, the victims may have been that," he said in a voice touched by hoarseness. "But they do seem to bleed like anyone else who is beaten without provocation. They do seem to bleed, don't they?"

Hoofs rang on stone. Half a dozen policemen spotted the three men and came cantering along a footpath. Gompers called a hasty goodbye and ran the other way as Gideon quickly shepherded Payne around the corner into Seventh Street.

V

He exchanged his soiled coat for a spare one he kept at the *Union,* then spent an hour at police headquarters. What he'd suspected proved true. From the sketchy description he provided, no one could identify the policeman who had shot at him. A bulbous nose and missing teeth? There were dozens of men on the force who drank too much and whose teeth had rotted out.

The officer to whom Gideon spoke was adamant about one thing. The use of guns had not been authorized for the men sent to clear Tompkins Square. When Gideon asked who had authorized clubs—and why—the officer refused to answer, except to say the socialists were a menace to the maintenance of law and order.

"And are the eight- and nine-year-old children who were beaten also a menace to law and order?"

The other man bit his lip. "I have no comment to make on that, sir."

"You may not, but I do. What I saw in Tompkins Square wasn't a labor riot. It was a police riot."

"I have nothing to say."

"But you'll investigate my charges—"

"Most definitely." The officer's eye was already roving elsewhere. The headquarters building was in turmoil. Flying squads of mounted men were being dispatched to sweep the lower East Side streets of any demonstrators displaying red sashes—or hostility to the authorities.

"Yes, yes, most definitely," the officer said. "We will investigate—"

"As soon as hell freezes." Gideon walked away.

On his way out, he stopped a policeman leaving with one of the flying squads. He asked what law was being broken by the demonstrators the police were going after. All he got for a reply was a hostile scowl. He left the station in low spirits.

The man who'd shot at him would never be found. He suspected the man wasn't even a member of the police department. It was unnerving to realize the hand of Thomas Courtleigh had almost touched him again—and could reach all the way to New York City, could even plant a man in a policeman's tunic right in the midst of bona fide officers.

Who had located him for the assassin? He'd probably never learn that either.

He decided he mustn't say a word to Julia. It would worry her. Nor did he dare tell Margaret. Doing so would only send her into another fit of hysterical anger.

vi

He heard the lamentation long before he reached the pitch-black sixth floor. It was a woman's voice, wailing.

He stood for perhaps five minutes on the landing of the Bottle Alley tenement. The smells of old cooking and urine and dirt all but choked him. Finally he summoned the courage to knock. The wailing went on.

He knocked again. It was Strelnik's five-year-old son who answered.

The glow of candles in the flat—the only illumination—put flecks of light in the boy's damp eyes. But Strelnik's son made an effort to speak without crying.

"Hello, Mr. Kent."

"Hello, Anton. I saw your father get hurt in Tompkins Square this afternoon—" He couldn't go on. There was a heaviness in his belly, a numbness in his fingers. Somehow, he already knew.

But Anton had to confirm it.

"Yes, sir. Papa was hit." He patted the top of his head. "It made him sleepy. After he came home he lay down and he isn't getting up."

Nor would he ever, Gideon thought as he gazed past Anton and saw the body lying on the floor amid candles set in small dishes. A great shadow loomed on one rotting wall. The shadow of a woman swaying back and forth, hands clasped.

vii

Tompkins Square put a new partisan of labor on Charles Dana's *Sun*. John Swinton, the editorialist who had never gotten to deliver his speech. It added a similar partisan to the staff of the *Union*. Long after Gideon had arranged to have Sime Strelnik decently buried, and had borne all the expenses of the funeral and given the widow ten thousand dollars besides, he wondered whether Theo Payne's conversion was worth the little Russian's life. When he remembered Anton's eyes and Leah's grief, he thought it was not.

He wrote a long letter to London, describing Strelnik's death and once again asking Matt to come home for a visit. Once again Matt refused.

CHAPTER VI

IN BOSTON

i

THE OLD SCOLLAY Oyster House did not cheerfully welcome unescorted ladies during the evening. But when Mrs. Henry Blackwell brought a member of her own sex there to dine on chowder and scrod, the proprietors knew better than to complain. In repose Mrs. Blackwell might resemble an angel, but certain restaurant owners who had attempted to bar her from their premises had been known to call her an adder—or worse.

Mrs. Blackwell was in her middle fifties, a tiny woman no taller than the friend accompanying her. Mrs. Blackwell's gray eyes matched her hair. Her dress was a plain black bombazine. She and her companion had come to the Oyster House on an evening in February, about a month after the Tompkins Square riot.

The older woman's eyes sparkled with a youthful enthusiasm as she said, "In spite of the reverses you've apparently suffered, I've never seen you looking happier."

How soothing and melodic that voice was, Julia thought. In a lecture hall it had an almost hypnotic effect. Julia smiled and spooned up some of the delicious chowder. The waiter, a pink-faced young man with thick side whiskers, approached the table.

"Everything all right so far, Mrs. Blackwell?"

The little lady laid her soup spoon aside. "You are new here, are you not, young man?"

"I suppose you'd say that, ma'am. Been in Boston three years, but only in this fine establishment two and a half weeks. I come off the immigrant boat in seventy-one. I learned the hotel an' restaurant trades in Dublin."

"I'm afraid you still have many other things to learn."

He enjoyed the banter. "That so? Pray tell me what."

"It's true that I'm married to Henry Blackwell. But I don't use his name, and that gentleman over there knows it. I imagine he told you to call me Mrs. Blackwell so you'd get in hot water." A glance at the smirking headwaiter confirmed it. "It's not your fault, but I go by the name Lucy Stone."

"And I go by the name Dennis Sheeley," he said with a grin. "Lucy. Now that's one of my very fav—" Suddenly it registered. "Oh. You're *that* one. The one who thinks womenfolk should vote."

"In one U.S. territory, they already do."

"Well," Dennis declared, "it surely won't happen anywhere else—not until the Holy See turns into a musselman an' the Boston summer brings forty inches of snow."

Julia spoke up. "Are you married, Dennis?"

"No, indeed, miss. Would you care to make a proposal?"

"I asked you a serious question."

"All right, here's a serious answer. I am not presently married. But I plan to be when I find the right girl. An' this I guarantee you, ladies. My wife shall know and keep her proper place—which is one step behind me at all times, with an attentive eye upon me so as to detect and accommodate my slightest wish. That's the role women were born to play, an' all this hullaballoo about voting only stirs them up for nothing. I can't speak for present company, but it's generally true that females don't have the head to understand a subject such as politics."

A storm was brewing in Lucy's gray eyes. "Dennis," she purred, "I do believe you had better see to the rest of our order before I bash you with that vinegar cruet. If I don't, Miss Sedgwick will."

Dennis left, rather irked and clearly wondering what he'd

done wrong other than address the infamous lady by her married name.

Lucy sighed. "Sometimes it seems to be such a long, wearying struggle. Americans will rush to embrace any crazy fad from grahamism to phrenology. But when it comes to votes for women—an idea that couldn't be more sensible or fair—you'd think it had been proposed by Satan himself."

"We'll carry the day eventually," Julia replied. "I'm sure of it."

Lucy studied her. "You say that with great conviction. I'm glad. Sometimes I fear women will never help elect a president until long after my life's over. At other times I'm convinced we're close to a complete victory. Perhaps the truth's somewhere between. At any rate, Julia, I'm delighted you could arrange to spend a few days at headquarters. It's a pleasure to see you—especially since you're obviously so happy."

A moment later, she added, "It's a man, isn't it?"

With a warm feeling in her face, Julia nodded.

"I can tell. Frankly, I've been fretting about you lately. I noted your new address in Chicago and decided you must have undergone a financial setback last fall. Was it a serious one?"

"I lost almost everything. Surprisingly, it's been no great hardship."

Because of Gideon—whom she intended to see in New York as soon as her four-day visit to Boston was over.

She was constantly astonished at the secure foundation love gave to one's life. A decade earlier, she couldn't have coped with the changes she'd gone through since the collapse of Cooke's. Now, with barely a qualm, she'd exchanged meals prepared by a chef for stew bowls passed up and down a boardinghouse table. She'd exchanged the finest dresses for bargain merchandise two or three seasons out of date. She'd exchanged a relatively carefree attitude about money for a watchful stewardship of every penny in her small bank account. The State Street mansion had brought her asking price, and at Gideon's suggestion she'd let the Rothman Bank here in Boston invest the principal. It appeared that the interest from those investments might cover what little she and Carter spent.

Carter. She hoped he was doing well at the public school in Chicago. Would he obey the landlady, who was caring for him? He'd promised he would, but he was becoming an exuberant, independent young man. Julia not only loved her son—she admired him.

"That certainly reassures me," Lucy declared as they finished their chowder. "Since the panic, the Association has been forced to operate on a much tighter budget. One of our best girls in the office, Flo Pernell, quit and moved to Colorado when her husband lost his job. We didn't have the money to hire a replacement. Fortunately, we've been able to preserve the travel fund to pay expenses for our lecturers."

Dennis approached to clear away the silver tureens. While he did so, he studied Lucy Stone obliquely as if she were some demon risen from the pit. He shook his head all the way to the kitchen.

Julia decided to raise the subject that had been troubling her conscience for weeks. "Lucy, I've been thinking it might be better if I resigned from the lecture staff."

To her surprise, Lucy didn't act shocked. Her gray eyes met Julia's calmly. "A moment ago, you said the change in your style of life was no great hardship."

"That's right. It isn't money that's prompting me."

"Then what is it? You've never struck me as a quitter, Julia."

"Lately almost every one of my lectures has been disrupted. In Cleveland—my last engagement before I came here—three roughnecks threw some kind of chemical bomb that spread a dreadful odor in the hall, and created so much smoke, the audience went into a panic. A woman broke her leg running for the exit."

Lucy startled her again by nodding. "I've read about some of your difficulties in the newspapers to which the Association subscribes. I hadn't realized we were confronting a new wave of hostility in your part of the country. I thought middle western people were generally open to new ideas—"

"It isn't the fault of the message, Lucy. It's me."

"I don't understand."

"I'm the target, not the Association or its program."

"Our lecturers have encountered hostility before—"

"Not so continuously."

Finally Lucy said, "You're right. That was my reluctant conclusion after an analysis of the newspaper articles. Go on."

"I angered a very important businessman in Chicago. I angered him so badly, I think he's hired men to create disturbances wherever I speak. I'm doing the movement more harm than good. When a lecture's disrupted, no one takes a message away from it. I feel I should resign so the Association's work won't be hampered because of something personal."

"Who is this blackguard in Chicago?" Lucy demanded.

She hesitated, but saw no harm in naming him. "Thomas Courtleigh. He's president of a trunk railroad out there."

The older woman shook her head. "The name isn't familiar. Does Mr. Courtleigh object to your views on womanhood, or is it something else?"

"A bit of both."

"Are you in any serious danger?"

Again Julia paused before answering. "I don't believe so."

"And I don't believe that," the older woman responded with a peppery shake of her head. "Your resignation is refused."

"But, Lucy—"

"Come, my dear, you know as well as I—most women are too poorly educated, or too cowed, to realize they're as cruelly enslaved as the blacks once were. They *need* the Association's message. I won't drive one of our best speakers off the platform by any act of mine." She put her fork down. "However, I do think this might be a good time to broach an idea I've been pondering. We need someone to do a western tour. Nebraska, Colorado—the mountain and plains states. Such a trip might get you out of this Courtleigh's reach for a while."

"That's a wonderful idea!" Then Julia's face grew pensive. "I'll go anywhere except Wyoming."

"What do you have against Wyoming?"

She didn't want to admit it was the home of a man she never wanted to face again. She would forever regret the way she'd behaved with Michael Boyle when Louis was still alive. In '61 she'd flirted with Boyle without really caring for him. Anger and frustration had driven him to a sexual assault—something she'd wantonly enjoyed after her initial fright passed.

She was afraid the act had shamed him. For that, she blamed herself. Gideon had told her Boyle was married now. She didn't want to risk embarrassing him.

"It's really only Cheyenne I want to avoid," she said. She smiled and stretched the truth. "An old love affair. He lives there."

"Well, you can be spared. Wyoming's the one place we don't need to carry the gospel."

In fact the Territory of Wyoming represented the movement's sole victory in the campaign to extend the franchise. Wyoming women had been given the vote almost as soon as the territory was organized in 1869. Wyoming was also proof that, contrary to predictions from assorted platforms and pulpits, the social order didn't collapse the moment women were admitted to polling places.

"I take it you wouldn't object to going anywhere else, then?" Lucy concluded.

"Of course not."

"We have one letter at headquarters that came all the way from California. Two married women asked us to send someone to address a small group in a new gold camp. Would you undertake that kind of chore?"

A western junket meant a long separation from Carter and Gideon. But it also meant a respite from harassment. "With pleasure."

"Some of those camps are very rough places, Julia—"

"I couldn't possibly run into anything worse than what I've encountered lately," she said, not realizing she was quite wrong.

"Splendid. We'll sketch out an itinerary tomorrow. If this junket is successful, perhaps we can make it an annual affair. Two or three months each time—the West is fertile territory, and you can cultivate it more effectively than anyone else who travels for us. Now, where's that benighted blarney thrower who waits on us? I've gotten so excited, I've worked up a fiendish appetite."

ii

Julia scandalized the waiter by requesting a glass of Moselle with her fish. Dennis acted as if she'd violated an eleventh Commandment. When he served the wine, he muttered something that included the word "disgraceful."

By now the young man's attitudes had become less than amusing. With a sweet smile Lucy told him he was a blithering ass. He stomped off. Unconcerned, she launched into an account of her conversion to abolitionism during her college days at Oberlin. In no time at all they'd finished the delicious food, and then it was seven-thirty.

"Good heavens," Lucy exclaimed. "We'll be late to the Howes'. And we must pick up Henry and Alice on the way."

She paid the bill and they went to claim their wraps. Julia had never met the woman who had penned the lyric for "The Battle Hymn of the Republic" after waking in Washington one morning during the war and seeing Federal troops drilling on the misty street outside her hotel. On the few occasions when she had visited the Association's office, Julia Ward Howe had been elsewhere. Tonight Mrs. Howe and her husband Samuel had invited Julia as well as Lucy, Mr. Blackwell and their adolescent daughter, Alice Stone Blackwell, to spend an evening at their home. Mrs. Howe wanted to discuss some new ideas for *The Woman's Journal,* the newspaper which the Association published. Like so many activities of the organization, the paper continually lost money.

The two women stepped into the chilly air outside the Oyster House. The doorman sent a boy for Lucy's carriage. Just as Julia started to speak, movement on the dark sidewalk to her left caught her attention. She blinked.

"Lucy!"

The warning cry was hardly out of her mouth before she pushed the older woman, tumbling her to the plank walk. A big, sharp-cornered brick landed where they'd been standing.

"Jaysus and Mary," the doorman cried.

Down the way, a man whose features were hidden in darkness shouted at them, "Stay out of Scollay Square, ye godless whores. Take yer perverted ideas somewhere else!"

Julia protected Lucy's body with her own as a second brick came flying at them. It struck hard, splintering a plank.

The doorman grew cross as he helped them to their feet. "You ladies shouldn't come here unescorted. The manager's told you that time an' again."

"See here, Martin," Lucy snapped as she brushed her skirt. "Are you blaming *us* for the actions of some"—she turned toward the place from which the bricks had been hurled; the man was gone—"some gutter thug?"

"That's right. I am. Women don't belong out after dark by themselves, not unless they want to be taken for a certain class of female, if you get my meaning."

"I get it and I don't care for it," Lucy retorted.

"I'm sorry indeed, but that's the way it is, Miss Black—Mrs. Stone—ah, who the hell knows what a creature like you's to be called?" He went inside, neglecting his duty when the carriage arrived from the nearby vehicle park.

Julia opened the door for them. Lucy tipped the boy who'd done the running. He bit the coin and pocketed it as Julia followed the older woman inside.

When the carriage was moving, Lucy said, "That really was astonishing. People here have always been reasonably tolerant of the movement. This town's bred and nurtured idealists and eccentrics for decades. If tolerance should flourish anywhere, it ought to flourish in Boston. Of course I've had complaints from the Oyster House about going in alone, but no trouble like that we just—"

"The man threw bricks because of me," Julia broke in.

"You mean he was sent by that fellow who dislikes you?"

"If I gambled, I'd put money on it," she answered with a feeling of despair. Evidently there was no place that offered her an escape from Courtleigh. That meant no place offered it to Gideon, either. "What if one of those bricks had hit you, Lucy? You could have been seriously injured—even killed because of me."

The older woman sensed Julia's distraught state and tried to soothe her. "No need to be all that melodramatic, my dear. I could also stroll down India Wharf tomorrow morning and be killed by an accidental avalanche of whale oil barrels, or by a spar falling from a tea ship. But it hasn't happened. The bricks missed."

"But you just saw one of the reasons I feel I should resign—"

"Julia Sedgwick, I will not hear more." She grasped the younger woman's hand and squeezed it. "The matter's settled. We're going to pick up Henry and Alice and go on to the Howes'. Then you're going out west for us. In fact you're going to remain with the Association for as long as you believe in it and the treasury contains money to pay your travel stipend. As for this fellow conspiring against you, we'll both outlast him. We'll outlast any man who tries to stuff us in a corner with a saucepan in one hand and a baby in the other. The puniest woman is stronger than any man yet born."

Julia laughed, but she only wished banishing the problem of Tom Courtleigh were that easy.

CHAPTER VII

AMONG THE GOLDHUNTERS

i

ON A BRIGHT April afternoon in 1876, a Concord stage-coach drawn by a four-horse hitch headed toward the narrow, mile-long defile leading to the new placer mining camps in Deadwood Gulch. The coach, which was operated by the J. S. McClintock line, led a procession of eleven raffish riders who straggled out behind.

For the trip up from the town of Custer some forty miles south, Julia had been given the place of honor—the seat next to the driver—the better to see the wild, beautiful scenery of the Bad Lands: the majestic rock formations; the immense conifers with patches of unmelted snow surrounding their trunks; the clear, rushing streams that had yielded up traces of gold. The gold was bringing new arrivals into this part of the Dakota Territory every day.

The stage driver, a garrulous old fellow named Fowler, was able to invite Julia to sit beside him because there was no shotgun messenger on the trip. Usually only the outbound coaches were held up, Fowler had informed her. Inbound coaches carried the hopeful, not the rich.

This particular McClintock coach was only four months old, but it already showed signs of wear; this was harsh

country. It was one of the vehicles made by the Abbot-
Downing firm of Concord, New Hampshire. Julia was quite
familiar with travel in Concords. On her two previous trips
west, she'd ridden in dozens of them. She'd learned that
each stage line decorated its coaches according to its own
taste. The McClintock taste ran to dark blue on the graceful
body, vivid yellow on wheel hubs, spokes, and trim, and
sentimentalized portraits of Columbia on the doors.

Julia had come to the Bad Lands on her third western
journey. The initial one, in the spring of '74, had taken her
all the way to California, and from there back to New York
by steamship. Her second a year later had included a
monthlong swing across Texas. She'd grown accustomed to
rough rides on muddy roads, greasy food snatched in railway depots, and hard beds in noisy frontier hotels. But
from the first, she'd fallen in love with the grandeur of the
West. Lucy Stone never had to ask twice to have her
return.

Oh, she ran into the usual rowdy, sarcastic men. But
never were they as vicious as those who'd harassed her in
the East. In fact, after the '74 excursion, there were no
violent disturbances at any of her lectures, anywhere. Gideon too reported that Courtleigh seemed to have forgotten
him. He'd either tired of tormenting them, or was too busy
for it. Welcome as the respite was, Julia suspected it
wouldn't last indefinitely.

The coach rolling toward Deadwood Gulch was packed.
Inside, men jammed the forward, rear and middle seats.
Three more men sat on top, clinging to the low guard rails.
All the way up from Custer Julia had endured masculine
jokes about her foolishness in coming to this godforsaken
part of the country. She'd also been forced to parry quota-
tions from scripture with which she was tiresomely familiar.
Fowler was the best of the lot as a Bible quoter.

"You *know* what it says plain as day in Genesis three,
ma'am. 'And thy desire shall be thy husband, and he shall
rule over thee.' Now just what have you got to say about
that?"

"Three things, Mr. Fowler. I've heard it at least five hundred times. Even the Devil can quote scripture to suit his
needs. Tend to your driving."

At least he chuckled. The men on top guffawed.

The sky was cloudless, with a warm, dry wind blowing. A chinook, Fowler called it. The caravan of mounted travelers who'd been with the coach since Custer started to move up near the vehicle. That was fine with the passengers. They hadn't gotten their fill of goggling at the most celebrated member of the party, the famous scout, law officer, dime novel hero and sometime actor Wild Bill.

It was Bill Hickok who was leading the party of gold-hunters to the new diggings. Julia didn't think much of the gunman. She had no admiration for anyone whose reputation was based solely on the number of people he'd shot to death.

And that reputation was showing signs of age, she thought, like the man himself. In this year of the nation's centennial, Julia was thirty-six. She judged Hickok to be three or four years older. He still wore his hair long, and dressed like a dandy, but twice she'd noticed his hands closing around his reins with arthritic slowness. And sometimes he squinted. If he wore spectacles, he hadn't put them on even once during the trip.

This was not Julia's first look at Hickok. She'd seen him after her trip in '74—across the New York footlights. Gideon had taken her to Niblo's Garden at Broadway and Prince Street. There they'd watched Buffalo Bill Cody perform in a new version of a play called *Scouts of the Plains*.

The three-act drama had originally been created to give the famous scout a vehicle for his stage debut. His self-appointed publicist, Ned Buntline, bragged that the show had been written in four hours. The critics said that fact was obvious. Julia agreed with their opinions, the most charitable of which called the play "very poor slop." But audiences overlooked its flaws and responded enthusiastically to everything from the yelps and barks of the Indian supernumeraries in war paint and stylish short pants to the histrionics of Mademoiselle Morlacchi, the ingenue who played the Indian girl Dove Eyes—with an Italian accent.

After a couple of seasons of trouping, Cody had wooed his old friend Hickok into the cast to pump new life into the show. The night Julia had seen it, the fledgling actor had forgotten many of his lines—no real loss, since the wretched script required him to exclaim such things as, "Fear not, fair maid, you are safe at last with Wild Bill!" To make up for his nervousness, Hickok had diverted the audience by throwing one of his revolvers at a spotlight, and firing blank cartridges so close to the Indians that they shrieked and danced in genuine pain.

On this trip, Hickok had displayed no traces of that fear-induced sadism. In fact he'd remarked several times that he wished he were back in Cincinnati, living unrecognized with his recently acquired wife. Julia thought the protest rang false. There was a peacock quality about the man; he covertly watched others to see whether they were watching him. He liked being admired, as did his fellow scout Bill Cody, whom small boys idolized. Gideon said Cody was a near-alcoholic and a notorious womanizer even though he had a wife and family. Hickok seemed to have neither of those faults.

The mounted travelers had come together solely for mutual safety. Some of them knew one another, but Hickok had several times made clear that he wasn't responsible for the behavior of any of them. There were a couple of really bizarre characters in the group. One Julia liked very much—dapper Charles Utter from Denver. Or Colorado Charlie, as he'd introduced himself at the first station where the horses were changed. He was a gambler by profession, following the latest gold strike. He boasted that he took care of his shoulder-length blond ringlets with a curling iron borrowed from his wife.

The one member of the party Julia disliked was a coarse young woman in her mid-twenties. She was just now riding up beside Hickok, who was on the left of the coach. The young woman annoyed Julia with her foul language and coarse ways.

The girl had a blunt, almost masculine face and coppery hair which she kept tucked up inside a crushed and filthy cattleman's hat. She wore denim trousers, drover's boots and an old Cavalry jacket with corporal's stripes. Hickok addressed her as Calamity, never explaining why. Earlier, she'd tried to make friends with Julia by stating in a somewhat unique way that she believed in female freedom.

"I do whatever I goddamn please. I once lived in a barracks at Fort Laramie just 'cause I took a notion to do it. I was there three weeks 'fore the officers caught me. I never go to bed sober, and lie down for anything in britches so long as the pay's good enough."

Julia did her best to be cordial to Miss Calamity Cannary, but it was hard; she just wasn't that broad-minded.

Letters continued to come to the Boston headquarters from remote hamlets. The letters usually asked for a speaker. Wherever possible, Lucy filled the requests, and she'd done so this time. The letter bringing Julia to the Bad Lands had come from a Mrs. Myrtle Oates, who said she helped her husband operate a hotel for miners. Julia hoped the itinerant prostitute who'd attached herself to Hickok wasn't typical of the audience she'd be facing in Deadwood City.

One thing lessened her worry about the camp's roughness: among the riders was a slender chap who seemed to have taken a fancy to her, though in an eminently polite way. He was about thirty, with a thin mouth and good manners that helped her overlook the puffiness beneath his dark eyes, the unhealthy pallor of his cheeks, and the swollen redness of his nose. He was much too young to be a drunkard but he had most of the characteristics.

Still, his smile was engaging, even if it was accompanied by breath that smelled of the gin he kept hidden somewhere. Julia had never met the man before, yet there was something familiar about him. He seemed to be a friend or at least an acquaintance of Hickok's, though they didn't hobnob much. He'd told her that he, like Wild Bill and Colorado Charlie, was a student of the picture cards. Wandering gambler, she supposed he meant.

The young man had mentioned his name when he'd introduced himself back near Custer. Unfortunately she'd forgotten it. But his name wasn't as important as the brace of revolvers he wore, or the buffalo rifle he carried in his saddle scabbard. She was glad of his protective presence; he was just now jogging up on the right side of the rocking coach.

He pointed ahead into the defile. "Won't be long now, Miss Sedgwick. I imagine you're tired of riding."

"I surely am." Her legs and derrière ached.

He took off his loaf-crowned sombrero and fanned his forehead. A white streak of hair above his left eyebrow lent him a rakish look. "Sun's warm for April. I'm anxious for a bath and a change of clothes." Unlike Hickok, he was

dressed in worn cowhand's garb. "Might attend your lecture, too. Never heard someone of your persuasion speak
before. Where's the talk to be given?"

"In the dining room of a hotel called the Miner's Rest."

"Oh," Fowler said, "that's a grand establishment, that
is." His tone said otherwise.

She was about to question him on it when Hickok, who
was leaning out of his saddle to hold a match to Calamity's
cigar, suddenly straightened. Julia had given up the cigar
habit because the smoke made Carter cough, and he said
that anything so noxious had to be bad for you. He was
probably right.

Hickok raised a hand to indicate half a dozen motionless
figures silhouetted against the sky atop a rock formation
about a half mile away. As Julia gazed at them, she was
aware of Hickok drawing one of his revolvers.

The watching men stepped backward across the top of
the rock and vanished. But not before Julia had a distinct
impression of feathers jutting from their hair.

Hickok kept his gun drawn while he studied the shadowy
pines on either side of the narrowing road. There was a
hard set to his mouth and a disappointed expression on his
face. Finally he slid his gun back in the holster.

"Those were Sioux," said the younger man on Julia's
right. He continued to remind her of someone, though she
couldn't place who it was. He had a soft, musical voice.
Perhaps he'd been born in the South.

She nodded. "I assumed they were."

From the left, Hickok said, "Going to be war in these
parts. The braves have been getting ready all winter. I
heard Bill Cody's old outfit, the Fifth Cavalry, may be
hauled up here from Arizona. General Merritt wants Bill
to quit playacting for a while and come back and scout
for him."

"I'm not surprised there's going to be trouble," Julia
said. "When General Custer marched in here two years
ago, he did so illegally."

Hickok clearly didn't like the statement. She recalled that
he'd served in the army. Been one of General Custer's
favorite scouts, in fact.

"Well," he said at length, "the hostiles better not ask for
war because they'll get that and a lot more. They'll get

scorched earth. People are sick of the tribes standing in the way of progress."

Annoyed, Julia said, "I thought the Sioux were standing where they're legally entitled to stand. Isn't this area guaranteed to them by treaty? Isn't it sacred ground?"

"Yes, indeed," said the young man on the right. "But gold's a lot more sacred to the white man."

"You can't stop progress," Hickok insisted.

"Progress or robbery?" she replied. "Last year the treaty commission offered six million dollars for all the disputed land up here. Of course that was hardly a fair price. If there's a bonanza of gold in the ground, the land might ultimately be worth ten times as much."

The young man chuckled. "Red Cloud and Little Big Man and Spotted Tail got so insulted they countered with a demand for a hundred million, then walked out of the powwow. Now the government looks the other way while prospectors come in"—he grinned in a cynical way—"as well as those of us who mine the prospectors."

"No disrespect to either of you gentlemen," Julia declared, "but I think the government's policy is muddled and despicable."

"The devil it is, woman!" Hickok growled. "Let me tell you which land belongs to the white man. Any land he needs and can take. That's why the army's getting ready for war."

Hickok's attitudes infuriated her, but she decided it was futile to quarrel. She turned to the younger man.

"Since we're almost to our destination, I must make a confession. You've been a very pleasant companion, but I've completely forgotten your name."

Hickok snickered, then spurred ahead. The young man reddened. "Jason Kane," he said. He spelled the surname and stared at her as if expecting a reaction.

Puzzled, she replied, "Thank you, Mr. Kane. I won't forget a second time. You remind me of someone, but I can't—wait." She clapped her gloved hands together. "It's a friend of mine in New York City."

In a strangely hoarse voice, he repeated, "New York?"

"That's right. You don't resemble him physically. But your voices are quite a bit alike. My friend's a newspaper publisher—"

What in heaven's name was wrong? The young man looked as if he'd been struck.

"Tell me your friend's name," he whispered,

"It's Kent. Gideon Kent. Do you know him?"

For a moment the young man was too stunned to answer. Then an opaqueness came into his dark eyes. He jammed the sugar-loaf hat on his head. Then came another abrupt and mystifying change: a touch of sadness in his expression.

It was quickly gone. "No, never heard of him." He touched his hat brim and rammed his spurs into the flanks of his calico, making the horse leap ahead. He cantered away in front of the coach.

"My," Julia said softly. "First I angered Mr. Hickok, and now I've offended him. In the latter case, I don't have the slightest idea what I did."

Fowler stuck a wedge of tobacco into his cheek. "I 'spect he was peeved that you forgot his name the first time. He's just like—" A sly movement of Fowler's eyes indicated Wild Bill. Lowering his voice, he went on. "Jason Kane ain't no Hickok, mind you. In a lot of ways, he's worse."

"I can't believe that, Mr. Fowler."

"Don't be fooled by those la-de-dah manners. He can lay it on for the ladies if he wants. But he's nasty as a rattler when he's riled, and it don't take much to rile him. He's half slopped with drink most of the time."

"How do you know so much about him, may I ask?"

"Why, I been hearin' tales for two or three years. Wild Bill told me about the drinking. He said Kane downs a glass of spirits with his morning eggs."

"I see. Hickok told you. That explains a good deal."

Fowler missed the sarcasm. "I think they used to be pals, don't you see. But I kinda get the impression they fell out at one time. Kane may fool you with his smile"—if what Fowler said was true, the young man had done exactly that—"but he's killed plenty of men. Plenty." He shook the lines over the four-horse hitch. "*Hah!* Come on, you slowpokes! Let's hurry on home!"

"Goddamn right. I'm in danger of expiring from sobriety," the coarse-faced Calamity yelled, quirting her horse. She too went racing down the narrow road ahead of the coach, hallooing to announce the caravan's arrival.

ii

Deadwood Gulch was a long, rock-walled canyon bordered by a noisy stream. Several mining camps had been established along the stream. Julia's destination, Deadwood City, was the largest. As the coach pulled in behind those who'd ridden ahead, she quickly surveyed the camp. Her face fell. She'd seen many a raw new town between the Mississippi and the Pacific. But she'd never set eyes on any place as appallingly primitive as this.

Deadwood City was a hodgepodge of lean-tos and tents with a few unpainted pine buildings mixed in, the whole straggling out in the trampled mud without observable plan or pattern. The camp's winter population had been a few hundred. Fowler claimed there would be twenty or thirty thousand present by summer's end.

Her first look at the Miner's Rest Hotel showed her why the coach driver had been sarcastic. The hotel was not one of the camp's four or five wooden structures, but a huge canvas tent. A secondary sign advertised UPSTAIRS ROOMS. Evidently a second floor had been built into the tent's upper portion.

The Concord creaked to a halt in the mud, right in the center of the camp. Grubbily dressed men swarmed around the coach from all sides. They divided their attention between Hickok, who stayed in the saddle and basked in his celebrity status, and Julia, whom the miners apparently presumed to be a new addition to one of the Gulch brothels. Jason Kane couldn't protect her; he'd disappeared.

A bearded fellow reached up to squeeze her leg through her skirt. She boxed his ear. From the left side of the coach, Calamity shouted, "Here, mister. You want to feel somethin', make an arrangement to buy me a drink. That there's the lady who come in to give a speech tonight."

"The suffrage lady?" yelled another man in the boisterous crowd. "Oh, boy. Lute Sims has a real fine reception waitin' for you, woman."

"Who's Lute Sims?" Julia called, but the man wouldn't answer.

She uttered a short, impatient sigh, hoisted her skirts and climbed down the wheel with an assist from Charlie Utter.

Pistols visible beneath his frock coat kept merriment over his curls at a minimum.

"Let me help you with your valise, Miss Sedgwick," he said, "so you make it to the hotel safely."

"But it's only just over there, Mr. Utter."

"Yes, but I hear this is a rough camp." As if to punctuate the point, a shotgun boomed somewhere along the stream behind the tents and buildings.

Julia looked around while Utter claimed her valise from the coach boot. She said, "Someone was supposed to meet me."

"Must have gotten delayed."

Frowning a little, she thanked Fowler for letting her ride beside him, then took the gambler's arm. Most of the other miners had formed a circle around Wild Bill, who'd dismounted and was absently stroking his long hair as he announced that he'd be happy to have someone stand him to a drink. And could anyone tell him the best place to gamble?

As Julia and Colorado Charlie labored through the mud to the tent hotel, she noticed a second tent standing ten yards behind the main one. A sign on the rear tent read, MINER'S REST DINING ROOM. So that was where she'd be speaking. Good Lord.

But where was the woman who'd written to Boston? Julia had clearly stated her day and time of arrival in a letter sent weeks ago. She was beginning to feel this part of her tour was hexed.

Colorado Charlie lifted the front flap of the big tent. He put Julia's valise inside and bid her good day. A stout, gray-haired woman with a mole-dotted face stood behind a lobby counter consisting of a plank laid across two barrels. The woman eyed Julia with an expression close to dread.

Trying to act unconcerned about the decidedly strange reception, Julia walked past a shaky-looking stair to the second level. The gray-haired woman began twisting her apron. Though it was still daylight, the tent's interior was dim, and it took proximity to the counter and a lantern hanging from the low wooden ceiling to finally show Julia there were tears in the woman's eyes. Instantly, she curbed her annoyance.

"Mrs. Oates?"

"Oh—oh, yes, ma'am, I'm Myrtle Oates. And I know you're Miss Sedgwick. I heard the coach pull in. I was too ashamed to meet it. Your lecture's got to be canceled."

"Canceled?" As kindly as she could, she went on. "I've come a hundred and fifty miles out of my way to speak here. Why in the world would you want to cancel the moment I arrive? Don't you expect anyone to show up?"

"Oh, yes, we'd have an audience." Mrs. Oates nodded. "Six or seven—uh—ordinary ladies, and a bunch more of the chippies."

"That's all right with me," Julia said, struggling to keep a snappish tone out of her voice. Something was frightening the gray-haired woman. "The Association doesn't draw moral distinctions between its various sisters. Others may, but not—"

"You don't understand. I found out there'll be men showin' up."

"That isn't a problem."

"Men showin' up to cause a muss!"

Courtleigh's name flashed into her mind. She laughed silently at the reaction. It was preposterous; his reach wasn't that long, nor his interest in her that consuming these days,

"Don't worry, Mrs. Oates. It happens frequently. I've been mobbed, punched, showered with rotten fruit, had an audience of eight hundred stampeded by firecrackers, another one panicked by chemical smoke—if a possible disruption is all you're fretting about, we must certainly go ahead. I won't be offended if there's trouble, and I'm sure I can deal with a few rowdy miners."

The woman lowered her head, whispered, "One of them's liable to be worse than rowdy."

"Who is that?"

"A terrible, vile-tempered man named Lute Sims." Julia recalled hearing the name shouted just after the stage stopped. "Back in Ohio his wife got hold of a pamphlet by one of the leaders of your movement. I don't rightly know which lady. But after Lute's wife read it, she ran off and I guess that affected him pretty bad. In his head, I mean."

The tired, red-knuckled woman looked close to breaking down. "What I'm trying to tell you, Miss Sedgwick—while I apologize to you in the humblest way I know—is that I'm scared to death for you to speak in Deadwood City. For three days Lute Sims has been going up and down the Gulch telling everyone he'll cause trouble if you show your face. Real trouble. He's been saying he'll hurt you. We've no law here yet. And Lute's the type who doesn't just jaw. He'll do what he says. He's a crazy man."

Julia shivered. It might be wise to heed the warning and—

No. That would make the entire side trip to the Bad Lands a waste of time and the Association's money. It would be cowardly to boot. She'd be hanged if she'd retreat.

She tried to reassure Mrs. Oates with a smile.

"I'll bet this Sims won't even appear. He's probably nothing more than a braggart."

"Miss Sedgwick, you don't know—" The woman's attempted protest was feeble.

"We'll conduct the meeting even if he does attend. Even if he shows up armed to the teeth."

"Miss Sedgwick!"

"I am going to conduct the meeting, Mrs. Oates. I can deal with troublemakers. Nothing will happen—to me or anyone else."

But her stomach suddenly hurt as she said it.

CHAPTER VIII

DEATH IN DEADWOOD

i

THE MEETING WENT far better than Julia expected—at least for the first half hour.

Myrtle Oates' husband had moved the tables out of the dining tent and rearranged the benches auditorium style. Then he'd rolled up the tent's canvas sides and tied them, so the audience could enjoy the spring breeze blowing along the Gulch. Oates was a huge, docile man who dutifully posted himself outside the tent to check on each new arrival. The one he was waiting to intercept, Sims, hadn't shown up by the time Julia rose and began her lecture. She'd wanted Mrs. Oates to introduce her but the older woman was too nervous.

Julia's audience consisted of fifteen women and the same number of men. Oates had relieved one of the miners of a quart of forty rod, and his wife had shushed two of the prostitutes who wouldn't quiet down voluntarily; there were nine such women present, all young, all homely, and all dressed in their best gowns. Neither the girls nor the miner caused any serious trouble. Julia spoke from behind one of the dining tables, on the side of the tent nearest the stream. Four lanterns lit the airy enclosure. And although the men smirked at her, and nudged one another, they paid attention.

As usual, she began with a brief history of the movement in the United States. She spent a few moments on the careers of Margaret Fuller and Fanny Wright, then moved on to the first woman's rights convention in Seneca Falls, New York, in 1848. She came eventually to the work of Susan Anthony, Elizabeth Stanton and Lucy Stone.

Her eyes sparkled as she launched into the story of Lucy's birth. She was always nervous at the start of a lecture, and had been tonight. But the feared interruption by Mr. Sims hadn't materialized, and she was beginning to feel increasingly sure of herself because she had attentive listeners. The women genuinely wanted to hear her message. The men were content to scoff in silence while they gazed at a fancified Eastern woman. On her trips west, Julia had learned that it paid for her to lecture in her best dress and a fancy hairdo. It helped keep the men distracted.

"—and from that time forward," she said as she finished the story about Lucy, "the lady who has been called the morning star of the women's movement has dedicated her life to the fight to free the one class in this country still truly enslaved."

"Oh, jeez, come on," one of the miners groaned. Some of the ladies shushed him but he paid no attention. "My old woman don't feel she's enslaved, Miz Sedgwick."

Julia smiled. "Is she here to verify that statement?"

"No, she's back home in Missouri, waitin' for me to hit the pay dirt."

"Maybe she's never told you how she feels. Have you bothered to ask?"

"Ain't necessary. I already know she's content to do woman's work. Care for the cabin. Plow our acreage. Raise our eight boys—I know *that* satisfies her."

"It does?" Julia seized the unexpected opportunity to use one of Elizabeth Stanton's best rejoinders. "What a pity. I never met a man worth repeating eight times."

Loud laughter—from all except the miner who'd interrupted. But even he had a grudging smile after a moment. Julia was about to resume when she heard boots plopping in the mud on the far side of the tent.

Standing guard back there, Mr. Oates turned toward the

noise. Myrtle Oates, seated on one of the front benches, craned to see. Julia drew a tense breath. Was Sims showing up at last?

She was startled when the new arrival came strolling out of the dark. It was Jason Kane.

He was hatless, freshly barbered, and wearing clean gray trousers, a bottle green frock coat, a linen shirt and flowing cravat. A bulge under the coat showed he'd brought at least one revolver.

He saluted her with a small wave, and smiled a rather bleary smile. He headed for a seat at the back but stumbled over the bench before sitting down. Evidently he'd gotten over his pique about not being recognized; perhaps spirits had helped him.

She smiled to acknowledge his presence, but she wasn't sure he saw, because his eyes closed briefly. When they came open, it seemed to take him a moment to focus them.

She continued her presentation with some comments on antiquated state laws which permitted husbands to assume virtually complete legal dominance over their wives. She described the difficulties women faced in obtaining divorces from brutal spouses. "The situation is only slightly better in New York State, where certain amendments to—"

She stopped. Heads were turning to the left. A yellow-haired chippy in an orange silk dress tugged her companion's arm. The second girl's rouged mouth rounded into a startled O. All at once Julia saw the cause of the concerned expressions.

Outside the tent, a man had planted himself at the edge of the lamplight. A short, thin, undernourished miner in a stained gray work shirt and jeans pants stippled with mud. He had thin brown hair lying close to a balding scalp, bad teeth, and needed a shave. He held a shotgun in hands that were none too steady.

Myrtle Oates' husband jumped to his feet at the back of the tent. The miner pivoted to glare. Julia's palms turned cold.

Like everyone else, Oates saw that the new arrival was seething. After a moment's hesitation, he tried to do something about it, though his voice was none too strong.

"Lute, you're not welcome here when you're in such a

state. Point that scattergun at the ground before it goes off. Then go home."

Sims ignored him. He gave Julia a venomous stare. "This meeting's over."

He was about fifty, she judged. A worn-out man. She felt sorry for him. Yet she couldn't permit him to take control.

She glanced at the shotgun. How much resistance did she dare offer? No way to tell. And she wasn't the only person who could be hurt if he started shooting. She didn't want to be responsible for a massacre.

She was uncomfortably aware of heads turning back her way to see what she would do.

ii

A moment later Julia addressed Lute Sims in a firm but polite voice.

"No, the meeting is not over. You're welcome to find a seat and listen to the rest of it."

The man's stubbled face wrenched with rage. He swept the audience with the shotgun, jerking it from left to right in a menacing arc. One of the chippies shrieked softly and clutched her ears.

"Lute, for God's sake put that thing down!" Oates pleaded. "If your finger gets a mite nervous, someone could be mortally injured."

Again the embittered, rheum-filled eyes sought Julia. "That's exactly what'll happen unless this sinful affair's brought to a halt." A couple of miners ducked when Sims brandished the shotgun again. "Go back to the hotel, woman. Go back to the East with your wicked, deceiving gospel."

A fanatic, Julia thought. He angered her unreasonably, as fanatical men always did. Despite the risks of the situation, she spoke out.

"Nonsense, Mr. Sims. I've heard about you. I don't intend to let your threats stop me from talking to these ladies and gentlemen. I've never liked boors or bullies, and you're both. Now sit down or leave!"

Sims' tired, ugly eyes reflected the flame of a lamp. "Hell,

I will. If you know about me, I guess you know what happened to my missus back in Ohio. She read one of your
damn sermonettes—"

"Not mine, sir. I don't write pamphlets."

"Then it was written by one of your scarlet sisters—
you're all the same. My Carrie read it, and it gave her crazy
ideas. Damn shame her pa permitted her to learn readin'
at all. She took every sinful, blasphemous word to heart
and one night just up and ran away."

"I can certainly understand why."

Several people snickered. Julia instantly regretted the
sally. Sims' glower became even more ferocious.

"You shut up!" Spittle flew from his lips. "You're
through talking here tonight. It's because of the notions of
people like you that my Carrie ran off. She thought she
had to be free. Thought she had to be equal to a *man,* for
Lord's sake. Even thought she should have the right to vote
for presidents, can you believe that?"

She'd seldom been so infuriated by an antagonist. She
shot back, "I not only believe it—I agree."

The miners applauded and whistled, enjoying themselves
at Sims' expense. Julia knew she should walk out of the
tent to prevent the situation from getting worse. Before she
could, Sims screamed at her.

"You're just spoutin' a lot of damn godless *shit!*"
Silence.

The breeze snapped a piece of tent canvas back and
forth. The respectable women looked ready to faint. Oates
took a step forward, eyes on the shotgun. Julia was growing
frightened. Hoping to force Sims to strain to hear her, and
thereby distract him, she pitched her voice very low.

"Mr. Sims, I don't believe further argument would serve
any purpose."

Where was Kane? Evidently he'd slipped out of the tent
some time ago, unnoticed. Perhaps he'd been bored. She
wished he were still there. Her knees trembled under her
petticoats as she continued in a near-whisper.

"I don't think I can change your mind about—"

"Anything!" he cried. "The Bible says a woman's supposed to submit to her husband!"

"Yes, I'm familiar with that shopworn—that argument."
Restraint did no good. Sims fulminated at the audience.

"Why are you listening to her? Can't you tell what she is? She's one of that free love crowd." He jabbed the gun in her direction. The violent motion made her start. "Isn't that right? Don't you believe in free love too?"

"Mr. Sims," she said, "the Bible states that the essence of God is love—" She tried to signal Oates with her eyes, to urge him to get behind the miner and attempt to disarm him while she kept his attention diverted. Oates was too upset to understand the signal. His eye remained on Sims' trigger hand.

"And I don't believe in a woman giving herself away like a piece of cheap yard goods. But if two people love one another, I see no reason why they require a piece of paper contrived not in heaven but on earth just to sanction—"

"You're a whore!" Sims screamed, triumphant. Myrtle Oates lowered her head and sobbed into her hands. *"A whore preaching a whore's doctrine!"*

Terrified, Julia realized that her attempt to create a diversion had only enraged Sims to the point of total irrationality. Something close to glee shone in his eyes. He licked wet lips and went on. "I knew that. But I wanted you to admit it"—the shotgun came up, leveling at her stomach; men and women dived for the dirt floor—"so I'd have justification for blowing you to—"

"Shut up and turn around, you son of a bitch," said a voice from the dark behind him.

iii

For a moment Lute Sims acted confused, as if he couldn't believe he'd heard correctly. Then the voice sounded again, pleasant yet with a hard edge to it.

"I said turn around. You've annoyed these good people long enough."

Slowly Sims pivoted, straining to see into the darkness. By then Julia had recognized the voice. Jason Kane took two steps forward, into the light.

His right hand held back the side of his coat so the butt of his revolver was in the open. Kane hadn't left out of boredom, she realized, but because Sims had shown up and he wanted to get around behind the miner—exactly as she'd hoped Oates would do.

She was immensely thankful, then abruptly disturbed by the amusement in Kane's dark eyes. His body was tensed, hunched slightly forward. And by contrast, Sims no longer looked menacing, just scrawny and pathetic. He even seemed to handle the shotgun clumsily, as if he were unfamiliar with it. He tried to intimidate the younger man.

"Who the hell are you?"

"Name's Jason Kane."

Several of the miners and chippies obviously knew the name. So did Sims. He nearly dropped the shotgun. His Adam's apple bobbed and sweat broke out on his forehead despite the breeze. As soon as Kane reached out and disarmed him, the danger would be ov—

Julia's hand flew to her mouth. Kane's right hand was moving with fluid grace toward the ivory grip of his holstered gun. Sims gaped, fumbled with the shotgun and stained the crotch of his jeans pants all at the same time.

"I want you to remember the name when they ask who sent you to hell." Kane smiled, the revolver out and aimed from the hip.

The shot missed.

Sims yelped and dropped his shotgun into the mud. Kane's face contorted with anger. Sims ran. Two staggering strides. Three.

His face almost as maniacal as his victim's, Kane shot.

Shot again.

Again.

Sims shrieked, lurching to the left, then to the right as the bullets hit. Kane's revolver kept roaring. Finally Sims fell face-first, a torrent of blood pouring from the holes in the back of his work shirt.

Jason Kane lowered the revolver. His hand was shaking. His eyes had a peculiar glint. It faded, and the cruel set of his mouth softened. He took one deep breath and looked around, waiting for the crowd to come to him with congratulations.

iv

He was disappointed. Perhaps it would have been different if his first shot had hit the mark. But the miners and
the women were subdued by the sight of Sims' corpse with
four wounds in its back. The people left the tent in silence
and passed Kane without so much as a word. Only Oates
went to his side, stepping on Sims' shotgun and then his
outstretched arm, half submerging both in the mud as he
pumped the young man's hand.

Men streamed from the street, drawn by the noise of the
fusillade. Myrtle Oates was the last to gain her feet. She
dried her eyes with the worn lace at the wrist of her gown,
then extended her hand to Julia by way of apology. But
Julia was hurrying toward Kane. When he saw her coming,
he shoved Oates aside to be ready to receive a compliment.

He failed to get it.

"I don't mean to sound ungrateful, Mr. Kane, and I suppose I will. We do owe you our thanks for stepping in when
you did. There's no telling what that man would have done
with that shotgun—"

"Quite right, Miss Sedgwick." He sounded testy; he saw
no friendliness in her eyes.

"But he was beaten. He was running. You didn't need
to shoot him in the back, did you?"

She was shocked at the way he shrugged and said, "He
was worthless. Besides, I enjoyed it."

She could smell the gin on him. And something worse.
Corruption. He had no comprehension of what he was
saying.

"*Enjoyed* it? How is that possible? Were you angry because your first shot missed?"

From his sudden scowl, she knew she'd inadvertently
struck the truth. She retreated a step, fearful he might take
his hand to her. Or his revolver.

Fear—that must be why he'd done it, she thought. Kane
had a reputation similar to Hickok's. Missing an easy target
would probably be frightening to him. Might make him
wonder whether his prowess was fading. Might goad him
to prove it wasn't.

Still, that couldn't justify cruelty. And she didn't care for
the way he'd reacted to what she said.

"Don't look so contemptuous, Mr. Kane. I'm not the one who did the shooting. What kind of man are you?"

Red-faced, he said, "Obviously not the kind who's good enough to be a friend of yours. I hoped we might get better acquainted. I had some questions I wanted to ask about—about conditions in the East. I won't waste my time. Good night, Miss Sedgwick."

He spun away, waving and shouting, "I'll buy the first round!"

A crowd of miners surrounded Sims' corpse. At first none of them responded to Kane's offer. Finally, one man with the look of a derelict separated from the others and tagged along, a sycophantic grin on his face.

"Sure enough, Mr. K., sure enough—it'll be my pleasure to join you."

In the crowd around the corpse, someone muttered, "Leroy drinks with anybody."

Julia didn't know which of her emotions was the more powerful—the loathing she felt for Kane as he swaggered off with the shabby man, or the pity. How could someone ever take pleasure in killing? How could a man bring himself to shoot an unarmed man in the back?

Slowly, the miners and the chippies and the merchants' wives straggled away. Oates began to extinguish the lamps in the dining tent. Canvas snapped in the night wind, like echoes of Kane's revolver.

Through a break in the crowd, Julia saw him glance back at her. A scathing glance at first. Then it softened and, for a moment, grew sad. He faced away again. Clapping his arm over the shoulders of the derelict, he vanished out beyond the Miner's Rest. That was the last time she saw him in Deadwood City.

V

Oates attended to the removal and burial of Sims' body. The following evening Julia repeated her lecture for a larger audience, completing it without incident. The women and a few men who'd come in from other camps along the Gulch listened politely, and gave her a solid round of applause at the end.

Next morning she descended from her canvas-walled cubicle on the second floor of the Miner's Rest, said goodbye to the owner, and departed on the regularly scheduled southbound stage. Just before she took her seat in the Concord, she heard the driver say to his shotgun messenger, "—the drink's besotted him, Joe. They say he missed with that first bullet, and then shot his victim the coward's way. If it's true, Jason Kane ain't the man he once was."

As the coach got under way, she couldn't get the killing—or Kane—out of her thoughts. Kane's voice bore an uncanny resemblance to Gideon's, but that was merely a distracting coincidence. What preoccupied her—angered her—was Kane's character, and her own failure to read it correctly. She felt deceived, defrauded by his initial politeness and seeming gentility.

True, old Fowler had warned her all that was a sham. How right he'd been. She'd never seen anything so callous as the shooting of Lute Sims, unless it was Kane's behavior afterward.

The anger faded at last, once more replaced by pity. The coach rolled on toward Custer, passing majestic stands of sweet-smelling pine. She saw only Kane's white-streaked hair. Dark, sad eyes. Cruel mouth.

The civilizing tide of settlers, schools, churches, stores, town councils, and police forces was sweeping westward with great speed. She'd seen that on her three journeys. Soon even freewheeling camps like Deadwood City would disappear, and the men who populated them—the parasitical men who contributed nothing, built nothing—would have no haven except the big city slums. Is that where a Jason Kane would ultimately go?

And what could a man of his stamp look forward to except having his own life cut short as brutally as he'd ended that of the miner? What did the Bible say? Live by the sword, perish by the sword.

An almost occult feeling gripped her for a moment. It was as if she knew that the end of Kane's life had already been ordained.

She wondered whether he knew it. He struck her as unredeemable. Unworthy of compassion. Yet she couldn't be completely unforgiving. She hoped he didn't sense what was waiting for him. A man's awareness of his own inevitable movement toward a violent death would, in itself, be a destructive force in his life. And worse punishment for his sins than anything a court of law could devise.

Thank God, Kane only reminded her of Gideon in a superficial way. It would have been unbearable for someone as humane as Gideon to have a doomed brute like that for a brother.

CHAPTER IX

HOUSE OF ANGER

i

IN NEW YORK, that spring began as a particularly exciting one for Gideon. There was an important family celebration to anticipate—Eleanor's birthday on May thirty-first. He could also look forward to being with Julia again; sometime during May, she was due back from her western tour.

And beyond those personal considerations lay a public one. It was the spring of the Centennial.

Despite the gloom generated by recent events, the nation's one hundredth birthday seemed to infuse the country with a new sense of pride and confidence. Virtually every citizen who could afford it planned to attend the great Centennial Exhibition in Philadelphia. President Grant was scheduled to open the exhibition on the tenth of May.

In Gideon's view, enthusiasm over the exhibition, and over the celebration itself, would help to offset the widespread disillusionment which had been chiefly caused by those in and around the Federal government. If many of the nation's leaders had failed to live up to the standards of honorable conduct envisioned by the founding fathers—and they had—at least the standards themselves had survived; that was one encouraging message of the Centennial.

Grant's aura of heroism had failed to carry him successfully through two terms. The man himself remained relatively untainted by the assorted disasters and scandals of
the past seven years. But his once-lauded talent for administration, and for selection of first-rate subordinates, had
been proved a myth. His powers of judgment had been
found wanting again and again.

The attempted '69 gold corner and the Credit Mobilier
scandal of '72 had been followed by the Whiskey Ring revelations of '75. Two hundred and thirty-eight people—
distillers and bureaucrats including Grant's own personal
secretary, General Orville Babcock—had been indicted on
charges of conspiring to defraud the government of alcohol
tax revenues.

The current year had brought another bombshell—the
discovery that Secretary of War Belknap had been taking
bribes in return for awarding trading post franchises in the
Indian Territory. Belknap had been impeached in the House
on the second of March and had resigned on the same day
to avoid trial in the Senate.

All in all, the President's tenure had been marked by
unprecedented corruption. Gideon suspected the former
general might be enshrined, if that was the word, as the
worst chief executive to date, even though few ever claimed
he was personally responsible for anything but his own
blindness to the cupidity around him.

Gideon believed Americans wanted to celebrate the Centennial, not only as an antidote for the corruption in Washington, but for the country's continuing economic woes.
The panic of '73 touched off by the collapse of Cooke's
had spread into the worst depression in American history.
People who had managed to hold on to their jobs had now
returned to a reasonably good standard of living. But at
least a million men were still unemployed. And millions
more existed on starvation wages as employers ruthlessly
cut costs to keep the doors of factories and offices open.
Only on the farms was there any prosperity.

In the cities, hard times had revealed—and swollen—a
dark, diseased underbelly of society. Month after month,
thievery and murder increased in every major population
center as unemployed men resorted to crime to keep their
families from starving. The slums grew increasingly restive.

They were spawning a new and vicious phenomenon—gangs of adolescent criminals who roamed at night, searching for victims to rob or terrorize. New York's worst youth gangs were the Forty Little Thieves and the Baxter Street Dudes.

In the open country between the overcrowded cities, unemployed men roamed the roads in search of work at any wage. Those who lived in remote areas locked their doors after dark, for like their urban cousins, rural dwellers saw a potential danger in the tramps, as the wandering workers had been christened.

What bothered Gideon most, perhaps, was the havoc the depression had caused in the labor movement. All the trade and craft unions together barely had fifty thousand members left. Competition for a shrinking supply of jobs had destroyed union solidarity and, very nearly, the movement itself.

Protectionist organizations such as the Knights of St. Crispin had been swept away. So had all attempts to improve the relationship between owners and workers. There had been a notable one in '74. Mark Hanna, an enlightened owner of a bituminous coal mine out in Ohio, had realized it was far more productive to sit down and struggle for an agreement with his workers than to refuse to negotiate, and thereby pave the way for strikes, violence and shutdowns that produced neither coal nor pay envelopes. Hanna had persuaded his fellow mine owners in the Tuscarawas Valley to join him at the conference table. But the negotiations had taken a turn he didn't expect. The other owners voted to reduce the miners' pay. And that was the end of a brilliant idea.

The union movement had received another devastating blow because of the Molly Maguires. The secret, pro-labor society operated in the Pennsylvania anthracite regions. It was supposedly an offshoot of Ireland's Ancient Order of Hibernians, the organization which had fought so hard against the British landlords. In Pennsylvania, the Mollies had been accused of everything from beating up mine owners to dynamiting the mines themselves. No one was ever sure how many acts of terror members of the Mollies were responsible for, but the society's reputation loomed larger than the facts. People everywhere shuddered when they spoke of the "murderous Molly Maguires." After a turbulent strike in late '74, the Pennsylvania mine owners decided the Mollies had to be rooted out and destroyed.

The instrument was at hand in the form of a private agency run by Allan Pinkerton. Its purpose was to provide "industrial protection" for businessmen. The term was really a code for organized spying and anti-union terrorism, with Pinkerton supplying the thugs and undercover operatives. He selected his best agent, an Irish Catholic named James McParlan, to go into the coal fields under an assumed name and infiltrate the Mollies.

On McParlan's evidence, twenty-four alleged Mollies had been arrested and indicted. The *Union* reporter who covered the trial was no partisan of the labor movement. But even he said McParlan's testimony linking the defendants to acts of terrorism and, at the same time, to the secret society was flimsy and unsupported.

That didn't prevent guilty verdicts—or the hanging of ten of the defendants. There was serious doubt that all of them were guilty, but even if they were, they'd been convicted on slim evidence. Such cavalier justice enraged Gideon, and he said so in an editorial.

The editorial was clearly counter to the mood of the times, however. The night after the piece ran, the *Union*'s office was stoned. And a couple of days later, at one of the clubs to which Gideon belonged, he bumped into Charles Dana of the *Sun*. Dana was just going in to dinner with two other members. He paused long enough to say gruffly, "Read your editorial on the Mollies. Fine prose but a false premise. Dynamite throwers don't really deserve justice, do they? Reading what you wrote, a person might suppose you'd sold your stock in your paper and joined the anarchists."

The implication that Gideon was a traitor to the class of men who owned newspapers stung and depressed him for days afterward.

Yes, the last few years had indeed been troubled and disillusioning. Yet as Gideon examined America's past and speculated about its future, he saw many bright aspects, not the least of which was the essential honesty, decency and common sense he found in most ordinary citizens.

Again and again, he wished he could also find some tan-

gible way to express his positive feelings about America.
His faith in the worth of the principles on which it was
founded; his belief in the goodness of most of its people;
his confidence in its future despite the turmoil of the immediate past.

He wrote a Centennial editorial on the subject, but it
wasn't one of his better efforts, and it didn't satisfy his
craving. He asked Payne for ideas, but since Payne didn't
know precisely what he was after, the editor could be of
little help.

Well, Gideon didn't know what he was after either—
except that he wanted a way to make a positive and personal statement about his homeland. Good ideas about how
to do it continued to elude him as the spring wore on.

ii

By age thirty-three, Gideon had acquired a few gray hairs
at each temple and a reputation as one of the rising talents
on Park Row. As the encounter with Dana had shown,
his fellow owners disapproved of his loyalty to the labor
movement. But no one denied that Theophilus Payne had
taught him the trade, and done it well.

Working in tandem with Payne, Gideon had slowly
begun to exert a stronger and more personal influence over
the *Union*. When asked whether his paper supported the
Republicans or the Democrats, he liked to answer, "Sometimes one, sometimes the other, but we always support
those who have nobody else to support them." Daphnis
Miller and Sime Strelnik were usually in his mind when he
made the remark.

The *Union*'s masthead now showed him to be the publisher, and he occupied a cubicle next to Payne's. He supervised newsroom policy, watched over the paper's financial
condition, wrote editorials and from time to time traveled
out of town to cover a key story and, not coincidentally,
meet Julia.

During the past year, he and Payne had begun experimenting with the paper's makeup. They had tried expanding the headline area of important stories to two or
even three columns. That wouldn't have been possible in

the days when the actual type went on the press in a curved form. Then, the individual columns had to be held in place by vertical rules. But stereotyping, a process borrowed from the book industry, replaced the form with a solid metal plate that reproduced the type exactly. With the vertical rules gone, stories could be expanded beyond one column just as advertisements had been.

Illustration was becoming more important on daily papers. The *Union* began to run two or three pictures a week, each drawn by the staff news artist. To supervise production of the pictures Gideon hired a Frenchman who had experience with the zincograph process perfected in Paris in the late fifties. Line cuts, acid-etched on metal, were much faster to prepare than the older wood engravings, which had to be laboriously hand carved. Woodcuts remained better suited to the illustrated weeklies, which had longer deadlines.

In the matter of news policy, Gideon had a reputation for being much more of a radical than he actually was. Despite tiresome jokes about the name of the paper, he hadn't turned it into a labor sheet. Certainly his sympathies still lay with the movement. But guided by Payne, he had begun to see that all causes, from the eight-hour day to female suffrage to matters of political partisanship, had to be subordinated to a newspaper's one supreme cause—the pursuit of truth.

Of course he retained a certain inevitable interest in railroads, and a bias against railroad owners, perhaps the most powerful class of industrialists in the country. He hadn't seen Thomas Courtleigh since 1871, and had long since stopped worrying about the man's threats. He wasn't even sure the harassment of late '71 could be laid at Courtleigh's door; there had been no repeat incidents.

Gideon continued to live in the mansion at Sixty-first and Fifth Avenue only because his children lived there. Will was now a stocky, brown-haired and rather phlegmatic boy of seven. He struck Gideon as timid, unwilling to try anything new for fear he'd upset his mother, with whom he spent most of his time. On Sundays, Gideon took his son on jaunts into the country or down to the piers. But a father was no substitute for an older brother with whom a boy could exchange confidences, and Gideon knew it.

Eleanor was his pride. She would be fourteen on her birthday. Her figure was filling out, and many people mistook her for a girl of eighteen or nineteen. She was enrolled in Miss Holsham's Academy for Young Ladies, Margaret's insisted-upon alternative to a public school, but she despised it.

Further, she had taken a fancy to things theatrical. She'd been in a playhouse only once, four years before. Gideon had taken her. From that time on, Margaret had raised objections about the godlessness of the theater—another of the peculiar ideals generated by her drinking.

To keep peace, Gideon bowed to her wishes and never again invited his daughter to a play. But there continued to be friction on the subject. Eleanor's slightest reference to it would send Margaret into a tirade. Her daughter would have nothing to do with the theater! She'd better resign herself to accepting the traditional role of wife and mother! She was to prepare for it by enrolling in Vassar Female College in Poughkeepsie at the proper time. Eleanor stated just as firmly that she would not. There the impasse rested.

Gideon's reaction to Eleanor's interest was ambiguous. He was not particularly scandalized by the Bohemianism of actors and actresses—but he did not want a child of his, especially a daughter, drawn into that kind of life. Once when he tried to express his confusion to Theo Payne, the editor laughed and said he understood perfectly.

"Men worry about daughters more than they worry about sons. It's the nature of the creature, I think. Being father to a growing girl, and wondering what sly seducer lurks in your parlor, turns any man into a conservative. I speak from experience thrice over."

So while Gideon never would have denied Eleanor permission to attend a matinee if Margaret had agreed, something in him feared her developing a passion for plays.

Gideon and Margaret hadn't slept in the same bedroom, or done more than touch in a perfunctory way, for nearly five years. Lately he'd even started to think Will and Eleanor were growing less fond of him. Less demonstrative. He wondered whether Margaret had a hand in that.

Sometimes he considered his suspicions despicable as well as far-fetched. At other times he didn't. His wife

hardly resembled the girl he'd courted and wed in Richmond. She had put on thirty pounds, seldom wore anything
except the plainest of dresses, left the house only when
absolutely necessary, had no friends, and—most annoying
of all—refused to keep her hair neat. He didn't exactly
know why that outraged him, but it did. Perhaps it was
because it called attention to her slatternly state.

Repeatedly, he had urged her to see their physician and
ask him to help cure the drinking that had now become an
integral part of her life—and her means of flight from its
problems. Repeatedly, Margaret denied she drank to excess, though she could no longer claim she didn't drink at
all. Her erratic step, slurred speech, and occasional outbursts of bizarre thinking were evident to all those in the
household. Even the children.

Gideon continued to feel responsible for her state. Sometimes he wished he could give in to her demands. Could
leave the *Union* and become a business dilettante, unin-
volved and unconcerned about the world. It was what she
wanted as proof that she was the dominant partner. It was
the one thing he could not give.

He didn't know whether she suspected his liaison with
Julia. He did his utmost to keep it secret. He no longer
loved Margaret, but he couldn't bring himself to hurt her
intentionally. She needed no one's help in order to suffer,
he often thought sadly.

But he saw Julia as frequently as possible.

In April of that year a new and disturbing element intruded into Gideon and Margaret's relationship. It first
manifested itself one evening at dinner. He was home,
seated under the gaslights at one end of their enormously
long dining room table. Margaret was at the other end.
Spring rain tapped the windows overlooking Sixty-first
Street, to their right. In a few minutes Gideon planned to
drive back to the paper and finish an editorial objecting to
the government's de facto theft of the Indian treaty lands
in the Dakota Territory.

He sipped at the hearty red Bordeaux which Matt ordered for him, and shipped from London in case lots.
Matt's paintings of American life, done from memory, were
finding their way into an increasing number of prestigious
exhibitions and private collections. He'd shown canvases at

the last three Paris Salons, and had submitted another for the collection of American art to be displayed at the Philadelphia exposition. The painting—his largest yet—had been accepted.

Matt's wretchedly spelled letters referred to a procession of mistresses in London, and only rarely to Dolly. She was apparently prospering as a teacher in India, and continued to bear the responsibility for raising their son Tom.

Matt had a new passion ideally suited to his talent for making quick freehand drawings. His friend Whistler had taught him how to do etchings by working directly with a needle on a wax-covered copper plate. The process was called drypoint. Matt had purchased an old star-wheel press so he could produce the plates himself, and Gideon now had one print on the wall of his office—a superb study of a London costermonger done with Matt's usual economy and memorability of line.

Every time Gideon gazed at the print, he wished he and his brother could work on some joint project. Perhaps a volume of Matt's drawings—published by Kent and Son. The Boston book house over which Gideon had no direct control was barely meeting expenses by reissuing old titles. The volumes were handsomely produced. But as Molly herself said, Dana Hughes was not an especially imaginative editor. Kent and Son needed at least one big success to revitalize it.

All these associated thoughts of Matt whirled through Gideon's mind as he sipped the Bordeaux and wondered whether his brother might return to see his painting on exhibit. He'd submitted it at Gideon's urging, and said he had no interest in attending the show in person. Perhaps some way could be found to lure him to Philadelphia.

Recalling the city brought something else to mind. Gideon set his wine goblet aside. "Margaret?"

She glanced up from her untasted food. In the gloom of the April twilight, her sallow jowls looked even more unhealthy than usual.

"What is it?"

"Just a reminder," he responded gently. "I don't want you to forget I'll be going to Philadelphia early in May."

"Philadelphia?" She shook her head. "You never told me that."

For an instant he was tempted to snap at her. Instead, he forced patience into his voice.

"I respectfully beg to say I did. More than a month ago. I'm going to do a feature on the opening of the exhibition. Don't you recall I told you Emperor Dom Pedro of Brazil would be there along with President Grant?"

Again she shook her head, her gaze drifting toward the rain-speckled windows. "No, I don't recall that at all. You never mentioned it."

He shivered then, genuinely alarmed. Was she only trying to aggravate him? Or was her mind succumbing to the damaging effects of too much alcohol, exactly as her father's had succumbed years before he died?

"You said nothing about a trip to Philadelphia to me," she repeated. Then she focused moist brown eyes on his face. "When are you going to take me to the exposition, Gideon? When are we going as a family?"

"Later in the summer, I promise. I can't say exactly when I'll get away, but I assure you we'll go."

"That's good to know," she murmured, glancing away again, her eyes sleepy.

He left the house a few moments later, deeply troubled by her lapse of memory.

iii

The moment Margaret heard Gideon's carriage depart, she hurried upstairs, her anger mounting with each step she took.

How *dared* Gideon pretend he'd mentioned a trip to Philadelphia when he hadn't! It was just another of his attempts to degrade her and make her feel miserable. Well, she had her own weapons in *that* little game.

Even though she'd taken nothing to drink for nearly two hours, she felt good all at once. Her face lost its puffy, lethargic look. Her eyes grew alert, thoughtful.

Lately she'd become convinced Gideon was humiliating her with another woman. She didn't know who the creature was, nor did she have any concrete evidence that she existed. But a man his age didn't practice enforced celibacy without a complaint—or without a reaction.

Well, let him have his slut. So long as he lived, he was never going to put a hand on her naked body again or enter her bedroom, which she always kept locked. Those were only two of several methods she'd devised to punish him for denying her wishes.

iv

"Blow, winds, and crack your cheeks! Rage! Blow! You cataracts and hurricanoes, spout till you have drench'd our steeples, drown'd—"

Scowling, Margaret thrust the door of Eleanor's bedroom open. At once the imitation basso voice—Eleanor trying to sound like a man—went silent.

Dark-eyed and full-figured, Eleanor turned a startled face toward her mother. Cross-legged on the floor at Eleanor's feet, Will lifted his chin from his hands. He looked terrified, as if he'd been caught doing something indecent.

Eleanor tried to hide the small leather-bound book behind her. Margaret lunged and snatched it from her hand.

"I have told you a hundred times. You are not to read and quote playscripts in this house!"

Eleanor's slightly oval eyes flashed back the gaslight. "Mama, I was reciting from *Lear*. Shakespeare. It's fine literature—"

"It comes from the immoral and godless theater, and I won't have any part of that under my roof. Now get to your French. I want to see your exercises the moment you finish them."

While she yelled, Will huddled against the end of Eleanor's bed, as if seeking protection from the shrill voice. Eleanor bit back a retort.

Margaret brushed at a loose strand of hair and said more quietly, "Now. If we have an understanding about this filthy book, perhaps I can convey a message. I asked your father when he planned to take us to the Philadelphia exhibition."

Will brightened. Eleanor remained red-cheeked and resentful. Margaret pursed her lips in a pastiche smile.

"He informed me he is going to Philadelphia for the newspaper. Alone. He'll have no time to take us there as a family."

Will's lower lip jutted. He jumped up. "But he said he'd show me the Corliss engine! And Uncle Matt's picture—"

Eleanor calmed a little. "Yes, I distinctly remember him saying that."

"Well, he's changed his mind. You children must realize that your father completely submerges himself in his work. He has no spare time—and no consideration—for any of us. Perhaps I can arrange to take you to Philadelphia. I'll certainly try."

She gave them a hug. Eleanor acted unresponsive, Will downright fearful. But Margaret was too pleased with herself to notice.

Carrying the Shakespeare, she started out of the room. Will's face changed even as she watched. So did Eleanor's. Her son looked hurt, and her daughter annoyed—though now for quite a different reason. If Margaret's little strategy had worked, Eleanor would no longer be thinking about the confiscated play, but would be directing all her anger at her father.

Or so Margaret fervently hoped.

V

She went straight along to her bedroom. The thirst was goading her. She unlocked the door and slipped in. The chamber was dark. She kept it that way, the curtains perpetually closed.

She lit one gas fixture, then flung the little playbook into the grate. Filthy thing! It would be burned up on the first cool evening that required a fire. She relocked her door and hurried to the cabinet where she kept the bottles of wine and whiskey. She chose the latter. Poured half a glass, shivering and breathing in a noisy way. She shouldn't have waited so long. Her nerves felt horribly jangled; her palms itched.

She drank the whiskey straight, accustomed to the raw, hot feeling it produced. In a moment the effect became one of soothing warmth. The shivering subsided. Her breathing slowed.

Blinking, she filled the glass halfway again and carried it to an expensive and capacious rosewood secretary under the dim gas fixture. She reached into the pocket of her skirt for a second key and unlocked the secretary.

Inside, she kept the diary she'd started a few months ago when her need for companionship had nearly driven her berserk. She sat down, placed the whiskey glass in front of her and readied her pen. She thought a moment. Then, with a faint smile, she began to write:

> *Apr. the 21st. A dark day, much rain. Gideon again cruelly pretended my memory has failed, dear friend—*

The term appeared in almost every entry. Margaret had quickly come to think of the diary as a person, an intimate and very real confidante.

> *But I objected and he left for the evening, his face showing vexation and puzzlement.*
> *Ah, how he delights in hurting me! He is going to attend the opening of the great patriotic exhibition. He says he is to report on it for the paper, but I am sure that is merely a pretext. He will see HER there. God protect me from ever learning who SHE is, for I might be tempted to KILL her—*

With slashing strokes, Margaret underlined all three of the words printed in crooked capitals. She was breathing hard again. She took a big swallow of whiskey. Sweat glistened on her forehead.

> *But no, dear friend, I shall never do anything so lacking in subtlety. I have more delicate ways to attack and punish him for refusing to put me ahead of all others. I asked him whether he would take us to the exposition as a family. He said he would. But after he had gone, I told E. and W. that he had said just the opposite.*

Her cheeks had a mottled, mealy look as she hunched over the desk under the feeble light of the gas. She drank again, laughing and clucking softly to herself. Her pen moved faster.

> *He has turned against me. He no longer feels remorse*

or pain when he denys my wishes, but he WILL feel pain—

More furious slashes beneath the capitalized word.

—because, before I am done with my various plans, and this account of them to you, my only true friend, I will make both his children loathe his face and despise his name and he will never know why they HATE him so!

Oh, it was so pleasing to write that. She drained the glass, already thirsty for more. It was even more pleasing to put down the final lines of the entry:

I have been at work to that end only a few weeks now. But already I see small signs that I am succeeding. More and more such signs will follow from now on. More and more and MORE.

CHAPTER X

FREE SPIRITS

i

"—AND MAKE SURE you start back the moment you've bought everything. Lower Manhattan isn't safe any longer. Too many foreigners. Too many Jews."

"Yes, Mama," Eleanor called, clutching her hat and hurrying down the rear service stairs to escape the hectoring voice.

The one thing she couldn't escape was the tyranny of the clock. It was already fifteen past three. She was a quarter of an hour behind the schedule she and Charlie Whittaker had worked out when she found she'd be permitted to go downtown to shop this week.

What if there were delays in traffic? What if Charlie failed to appear at the meeting place, or went on to Fourteenth Street without her? Fifteen minutes could cost her everything.

She rushed into the coach yard that opened onto Sixty-first and a vista of weedy vacant lots to the south. It was a gray Saturday afternoon at the end of the week in which Margaret had told the children Gideon couldn't promise to take them to Philadelphia.

Eleanor's shoes, yellow-dyed fabric with elastic side pan-

els and a small yellow rosette decorating each, fairly flew
over the bricks of the yard. Mills, the coachman, waited on
the seat of the calash. He glanced at the sky as Eleanor
lifted the hem of her Parisian frock of yellow silk trimmed
with ivory lace. In a moment she'd settled herself beneath
the folding top of the two-wheeled vehicle.

"Rain looks likely again, Miss Eleanor," Mills said.
"Would you care to have me switch Pete to the
brougham?"

"No, no! Let's be on our way."

Mills flicked his whip lightly over the horse's ears. "Giddap, Pete." The calash swung out of the yard, turned right
and then left again into Fifth Avenue, heading south.

Eleanor sat back and tried to breathe slowly and normally. She couldn't. She was much too excited over the
prospect of seeing Salvini—

If she were in time.

Naturally she and Charlie would have preferred to see
Edwin Booth. But he and his whole company were doing
a grand tour of the South. Salvini was an acceptable substitute, though. In one way he was a better choice because
his interpretation of the role of the Moor was thrillingly
wicked—quite unlike Booth's respectable portrayal.

Anxiously she peered around the coachman for signs of
excessive traffic. She so seldom got out of the house by
herself on weekends, and she just couldn't have anything
go amiss today. Especially when so many things seemed to
be going wrong around home.

Eleanor loved her father. But she was very much aware
that lately he'd been paying less and less attention to his
family. The neglect had visibly affected her mother. She
was shunning all daylight and growing sallow and sickly.
And she was drinking to excess—her tonic, she called it.
Eleanor knew it was liquor. It caused Margaret to have
lapses of memory and periods of almost violent anger directed at Gideon.

Eleanor wished she had the courage to ask her father
why he quarreled with her mother so often, or what the
children could do to make things smoother. But Gideon
was seldom home. And when he was, he was tense and
tended to snap in response to even the most casual question. Slowly, and almost against her will, Eleanor was com-

ing to believe that for all her mother's faults, Margaret might be right about Gideon no longer caring for them.

Was it really his work causing that? Or did he have a female friend? What was the word for it? Oh, yes. Mistress.

She knew what a mistress was because she knew what men and women did together. The girls at Miss Holsham's discussed it endlessly—which would have made Margaret faint and then withdraw her daughter from that supposedly refined academy.

When men and women removed most or all of their clothing and did that together, and were not married, it was said to be *illicit*. Somehow her father seemed too nice to be involved in something *illicit*, but what other explanation could there be for his lack of interest in things at home?

Eleanor had already formed definite opinions about the act itself. She was curious about it. She thought it might be interesting to experience, but she suspected it was dangerous, too. That is, she had a feeling the consequences were dangerous. After all, the act was part of the tangled web-work of actions and emotions which went by the name love. And love, she had concluded, merely got people into dreadful difficulties. She'd read about it time and again, in plays such as the one in which Salvini was appearing. She'd heard even more compelling evidence from behind closed doors in her own house. She'd heard quarrels so violent they made her weep.

Of course love in the form of an act performed by two people who cared for one another was evidently necessary to make more people in the world. And there was no denying it provided dramatists with some of their best material. But on a personal level, it seemed to her that love—and, therefore, the act of love—merely brought pain. The sort of pain she'd be wise to avoid as she was growing up.

She did realize that might be hard to do. Lately she was full of strange impulses and longings she only half understood. Her body was changing visibly. Right this moment, beneath her dress and her chemise, her growing breasts ached from the bouncing of the calash. And she was full of contradictory feelings. Why, for example, did she sometimes yearn to have a boy touch her, then recoil from it when it happened by accident?

She didn't understand all the changes within herself, nor all the terrible happenings at home—and together, they made her fiercely afraid of all that was meant by *love*.

The calash clipped along between the green vistas of Central Park on the right and undeveloped plots of land on the left. Her father believed the city would spread north, and that the Kent mansion would one day be in the heart of the best residential district. It certainly wasn't now. She read the society columns in the *Union* and all the competitive papers that came into the house. She knew a man as rich and important as her father should have owned a home in the area the calash was just now entering—Fifth Avenue from the Park down to Washington Square. "Two miles of millionaires," people called it.

Of course it was possible to have a mansion there and still be called a Shoddyite. That was the case with A. T. Stewart, the owner of the store toward which the calash was heading. Stewart had just died, and everyone said he was worth millions. He owned an immense house at Thirty-fourth and Fifth. But those at the top of society—the Astors, the Vanderbilts, the other old families—looked down on him as a Shoddyite. A man who could not enter the best circles for a generation, perhaps more. Stewart had had the misfortune to have new money, and be "in trade."

Charlie Whittaker's father was in trade, too. He sold medicines at wholesale and made plenty of money. But the Whittakers were still Shoddyites. So were the Kents.

Eleanor didn't care, though. In the shining world to which she aspired, such false and arrogant distinctions were of no importance. The theater was not only a beautiful place, but a democratic one.

It was the blight of Eleanor Kent's life that, during her nearly fourteen years, she'd only been permitted inside a playhouse once. Her father had taken her to Booth's, down on Twenty-third Street and Sixth Avenue, in celebration of her tenth birthday. That was in 1872, when they were still living in Yorkville.

Even that long ago, Eleanor's mother had spoken out against the theater. Margaret claimed that attractions today were nothing like the wholesome ones she'd enjoyed as a girl in Richmond. The New York playhouses had become the province of Satan. In the last decade, a veritable flood of immorality had been undammed within them. The actress Adah Isaacs Menken had dared to appear in *Mazeppa* clad only in a Greek chiton and, beneath, all but invisible flesh-colored tights. Niblo's had booked an extravaganza with interpolated songs, *The Black Crook,* in which a chorus of young women wearing black tights displayed their calves and thighs—to packed houses.

But on Eleanor's birthday four years ago, the play at Booth's had been both a thundering hit and eminently respectable. It was *Julius Caesar,* with spectacular scenic effects representing not drab Julian Rome, but the more colorful Augustan period. The famed actor-manager Edwin Booth played several different parts during the run of the show. When Gideon took Eleanor to see him, he was playing Marc Antony.

Although Margaret had been sick in bed with a spring cold at the time, Eleanor remembered that her father had felt it necessary to fib about where they were going. A travel lecture, he said. Eleanor too had been sick the night before the excursion, though for another reason. Sheer excitement.

Even today, she could vividly recall the evening. Booth's Theater had three stone towers. A flag bearing the name of the establishment flew from the central one. She'd never seen anything more magnificent, especially with the calcium lights playing over the exterior.

Gideon had purchased the most expensive seats—a front box—and to reach it they had to climb the impressive main staircase. Halfway up, they paused before the marble bust of the celebrated actor who had trained three sons to carry on the family tradition. Gideon explained that in his day, Junius Brutus Booth had been famous all over the world. Eleanor's eyes were huge as she gripped her father's hand and hung on every word.

Booth Senior had been afflicted with a fondness for liquor, Gideon said. And he suffered from mental instability. Perhaps that explained why one of his sons, John Wilkes, had committed a terrible act of murder at Ford's Theater down in Washington. Still, Eleanor had never beheld such a noble countenance as she saw on that pedestal.

Nor had she ever seen or heard anything that made her spine prickle the way Edwin Booth's performance did.

As Antony, he hit his peak when he denounced the traitors. He punctuated his oration with an abrupt leap from the rostrum. The startling bit of business made the audience gasp. When the speech was over, Booth got an ovation.

The magical images of the towers, the flying flag, the staircase, the painted scenery, Booth's burning eyes and spellbinding personality all blended together to form one shining memory which Eleanor treasured like a gem.

She couldn't forget the aftermath, either: the screaming match four days later. Searching her father's coat pockets on some pretext or other, Margaret had found a crumpled playbill, and had confronted him with it.

From that birthday came Eleanor's fascination with all things theatrical. Her father had never again taken her to a performance, because Margaret was so adamantly opposed to it. The upper tiers of New York playhouses now had liquor bars, and Margaret claimed the denizens of the galleries were all licentious sots. A strange accusation to come from one addicted to mysterious "tonics," Eleanor thought. But she didn't argue the point.

Her friend Charlie Whittaker had attended the theater dozens of times. He gleefully admitted to having sat right up there among those gallery denizens. And yes, they *did* do sinful, hair-raising things during a performance, though he wouldn't reveal specifics. But of course, he concluded with a worldly shrug, only the performances and not the morality of the players or the audiences mattered.

Enforced isolation from the theaters only heightened Eleanor's interest. At Miss Holsham's she asked to be assigned Shakespeare's comedies and tragedies, then other dramatic classics, as extra reading in literature. In 1874 she'd devoted a good many weeks to thinking about her future, and had finally decided she would study to become an actress.

She began practicing a variety of parts, declaiming them for Will or for her mirror until her mother found and confiscated each playbook, as she'd done this week with *Lear*. Then Charlie, who was the older brother of one of her classmates at Miss Holsham's, would buy her another with money Eleanor provided from her allowance.

She really wished she could understand the basis for her mother's objections. Margaret didn't deny she'd enjoyed

plays as a young woman. Eleanor often asked herself
whether Margaret's change of heart could have something
to do with Eleanor's own paternal grandmother—Gideon's
mother—Fan Kent of Virginia, and her second husband.

After bearing three sons and then divorcing their abolitionist father—Grandpa Jephtha, the cigar-smoking minister Eleanor remembered dimly—Fan had remarried. She'd
wed a Southern actor named Edward Lamont. Eleanor had
heard Papa discuss Lamont once or twice. But not in detail,
and never with a smile. Lamont had died during the war.
Papa never said how. Had there been tragic circumstances
which had somehow influenced her mother? Eleanor supposed she'd never know. She usually had nerve when the
occasion required it, but she'd never have enough nerve to
ask Margaret about Lamont.

Still, there *was* an actor in the family, if only by marriage.
She could take that as an encouraging sign.

It had also occurred to Eleanor that the approval an
audience expressed through applause was nothing less than
a form of love. A very safe form. It was at once intense yet
distant, without the potential for hurt that people evidently
experienced when they fell in love with one another. The
love that poured across footlights at the end of a play could
be a highly acceptable substitute for romantic love, she'd
decided. All the more reason to build a career on the stage.

Raindrops splattered against her cheeks, drawing her out
of her reverie and making her aware of the congestion of
carriages and delivery vehicles all around. She recognized
Broadway, a little below Madison Square. They weren't
even close to Union Square, and it must be past four already. She'd never arrive in time!

The calash stopped frequently, Mills shouting at the
stalled conveyances ahead. He wasn't the only one. Dozens
of other carriage and hack drivers filled the air with demands, pleas and oaths. The avenue was redolent with the
odor of manure. At one point, a large heifer wandered
between the stalled calash and a dray just ahead, the cow
lowing and clanking her bell.

Eleanor fidgeted. Finally they got under way again. After
being caught in three more hub-to-hub jams they reached
Tenth Street, and the north entrance of A. T. Stewart and
Company, the city's best retail establishment.

"I'll find a boy to hold Pete," Mills said. "Then I'll meet you right over by those doors. It'll take me no more than five minutes."

"Mills, if I delay one second longer, I'll never get through the shopping list Mama gave me. You must let me go by myself."

The coachman nearly fell off the seat. "By yourself? Why, Mrs. Kent'd flog me."

She jumped down.

"She'll never know if you don't tell."

"Now see here, I can't—"

Eleanor had been rooting in her handbag. She had found a ten-cent piece. "Have a bucket of beer, Mr. Mills. You like beer, don't you?" She knew he did; she smelled it on him often. She laid the coin on his knee. "Have a cool drink and I'll meet you by this very same door when the store closes."

Flabbergasted, Mills stared at the coin and then at the slender, dark-haired girl who in his opinion would be a genuine beauty when she grew to full womanhood. But she was also far too independent for her own good. Fancy inviting a grown man to have a growler of beer!

He craved the beer, right enough. But to have it purchased for him by a mere child—and one he was supposed to be looking after—

"No, Miss Eleanor, I absolutely cannot—"

Too late. She'd already whirled and raced across the sidewalk and vanished into Stewart's. He snatched the dime off his knee so it wouldn't fall and be lost in the gutter. He'd done all he could. And waste was a sin.

ii

Stewart's dry goods store occupied an entire city block bounded by Ninth and Tenth Streets and Broadway and the Bowery, the extension of lower Fourth Avenue. Eleanor fought her way through the crowded aisles and reached one of the doorways on the Bowery side. She strained for a glimpse of Charlie Whittaker waiting in the vestibule. Suddenly she felt like crying.

He wasn't there.

He'd gone ahead without her. She dashed a few tears from her eyes and stamped her foot. Crying was weak-kneed. And it certainly wasn't fair to blame Charlie because she was so la—

She caught her breath. Charlie was outside! The crowds had hidden him. He was pacing up and down, alternately studying the sky and his handsome railroad watch.

"Charlie, here I am!" she cried as she rushed to him.

"*Well!* I was just about to leave for the Academy. I'd come to the conclusion that your mother had penned you up again."

Each sentence was declaimed rather than spoken, with breathy emphasis added in unexpected places and punctuation supplied by sweeping gestures. For Charlie Whittaker, age sixteen, every moment and every commonplace conversation was an opportunity to create drama.

Charlie was a soft, round boy with a pale skin, a likeable, cow-eyed face and cowlicked hair that refused to stay in place no matter how much Macassar oil he applied. He snatched Eleanor's hand.

"Come along, for heaven's sake, or the matinee will be over and Salvini gone before we get there. You're so damned *late,* I shouldn't tell you my good *news.*"

Man of the world that he was, Charlie frequently chose to jolt his sister's schoolmate by employing selected profanities. He got the desired effect with his use of damned. Eleanor's oval eyes grew huge.

Charlie played to that shock. "For heaven's *sake,* Eleanor! What are you going to do when you take a role someday and it requires that you *speak* a curse word?"

"Women's parts don't require that, Charlie."

"Just you wait. The way the playwrights are starting to treat modern subjects—it won't be long." He tugged her hand again, but she protested.

"I have to start on the shopping list before I go."

"I'll help you when we get back. Promise. Now come *on!*"

He sounded not merely dramatic but a trifle angry. Yet she hesitated.

Eleanor looked up to Charlie as someone far more expe-

rienced and knowledgeable. He was two years older—
practically an adult—and his parents actually encouraged
his interest in acting.

But Margaret would be furious if she failed to obtain all
the items on the shopping list. She'd question Eleanor
about the reason for the failure until Eleanor confessed.
Eleanor had never been able to lie successfully. She knew
it was wrong, and on the rare occasions when circumstances
pushed her into trying it, her eyes and her red face always
gave her away.

This time Charlie's insistence won out over fear of her
mother. They hurried north along the Bowery to Fourteenth, then turned east toward the looming façade of the
Academy of Music in the next block. Eleanor was nearly
out of breath, Charlie walked so fast. She finally remembered to ask, "What's your good news? You said you had
some."

She could actually see his chest inflate. "Indeed I do.
The Booth Association has accepted me for *membership*."

"Oh, Charlie!" She squeezed his arm, overjoyed.

He turned pink. One thing in which Charlie Whittaker
did not seem interested was familiarity with the opposite
sex. It actually appeared to embarrass him. Generally, Eleanor was glad of that. She was with him often, and thus
didn't have to worry about him trying to drag her into
fumbling embraces. On the other hand, his very predictabil-
ity made him somewhat dull. Charlie never aroused those
curious and shameful sensations the sight of other young
men—perfect strangers!—could sometimes generate within
her.

"I'm so happy for you, Charlie," she went on. "When
will you go to your first meeting?"

"Next Tuesday night." He pointed north along a cross
street where they paused. "The group rents Hutter Hall,
just two blocks up Irving Place. I've only met the president
and vice president. But if the others are just like them, it
will be a grand group."

"Did you ask about female members?"

"They have none."

Eleanor uttered a tiny "Oh."

"Don't *despair*. They invite young ladies of talent to attend meetings and fill feminine roles. You're welcome to come as my guest any time."

It was the chance she'd longed for—entrée, however modest, into theatrical activities. She could barely contain her enthusiasm.

"Do you mean that, Charlie?"

"Most assuredly, young lady. You must come and read. And not merely something from the Bard, or those wheezy old Greeks. A *modern* role. Something by that fellow Ibsen, perhaps. The latest gossip from Norway says he's all through writing poetic trash like *Peer Gynt* and is planning some totally new kind of drama that will scorch an audience right out of its seats. That's what we want, eh?"

"Oh, yes." Her eyes shone again. Then the corners of her mouth turned down. "But Mama would never let me go out on a weekday evening. Not the way she's feeling lately."

He was dismayed by her hurt expression. "Maybe she would, Eleanor. At any rate, you mustn't give up. You have a first-class talent. And remember, people in the theater are free spirits. They're not bound by the laws that shop girls and ribbon clerks have to obey. Free spirits can always find a way to escape from a cage."

Smiling in an encouraging way, he flung his chubby arms around her and gave her a quick, brotherly hug. Charlie didn't mind physical contact with a girl when he initiated it for purposes of friendship only. Eleanor was cheered by his reassurance, but she felt nothing else—certainly no excitement.

She was truly pleased for him, though. He'd gotten into one of the best amateur acting associations in New York. Small, but with a fine reputation. A great many such clubs flourished in rental quarters all over town. They usually restricted their membership to males. Their occasional productions were done with minimal scenery, or none at all, and were financed by members' dues. Most of the associations were named in honor of popular actors.

Charlie pointed to the line of carriages at the Fourteenth Street curb in front of the Academy of Music. It had originally been constructed as an opera house, but New York wouldn't support a full season of such heavy fare, so con-

certs and limited engagements by famous theatrical person-
alities were required to keep the auditorium lit.

"The hacks and carriages are already here," Charlie said.
"That means we arrived just in the nick. Follow me to the
actors' entrance. I know right where it is. I've been here a
hundred times."

The declaration was emphasized by a gesture that nearly
knocked her hat off. Eleanor was sure Charlie had exaggerated. It was a forgivable fault, but she wondered whether
it was common to most actors.

Excitement mounted within her as they crossed Irving
Place. She glanced toward the main doors and noticed a
boy of seventeen or eighteen watching her.

He had black hair, and one of the handsomest faces she'd
ever seen. It was redeemed from prettiness by his cocky
smile. He wore a duck jacket with the name of the hall
stitched on the front; he'd been sweeping the walk with a
cornhusk broom. Now he was inspecting her—and not
merely her face. His gaze wandered down her throat to her
breasts. What he saw, he approved.

The cocky smile spread warmth through her middle. It
thrilled her and frightened her at the same time. But it
really wasn't polite of him to stare at a girl so brazenly.
Probably he was a Latin, like the hot-blooded Tommaso
Salvini.

The boy suddenly gave her a big wink. She gasped.

"What's wrong?" Charlie asked; he'd been looking
elsewhere.

"Why—why"—the main doors of the Academy abruptly
opened outward; the boy with the broom darted to one
side as a rush of theatergoers emerged into the gray
afternoon—"you were right about the time," she finished
in a lame way.

The boy was quickly hidden by the departing patrons.
Many were scowling. Eleanor wasn't surprised. The attraction at the Academy was a three-week run of *Othello*
with the celebrated Italian tragedian, Salvini, in the title
role.

The same production had been staged in '73, and had
caused a sensation. During the climactic murder scene, Salvini's staging called for him to seize his leading lady, Signora
Piamonti—no American actress would play Desdemona op-

posite him—hurl her on a low bed and fall on top of her, snorting and growling while she writhed beneath him. Every critic in town had been outraged. Charlie said the *Tribune* had called Salvini's initial production "carnal," and Eleanor knew the *Union*'s drama writer, William Dawes, had attacked the revival as "a degrading and unprincipled exhibition of unbridled lust performed solely for profit." Naturally, with notices like that, both the first run and the revival had done turnaway business—though it was clear many members of the matinee audience had been angered by what they'd seen.

Charlie led her to a cul-de-sac behind the Academy. The actors' door was at the end. The narrow space was already filled with well-wishers. And the crowd grew. All at once Eleanor realized she had nothing on which Signor Salvini might sign his name.

Charlie was better prepared. He'd brought an old handbill from Wallack's Theater. He tore it in half and said he'd share his pencil.

"Here they are!" someone screamed. Eleanor thought she'd faint with excitement as the great actor emerged. He was incredibly good looking, with a mane of dark hair, deep-set eyes and a blazing white smile.

Salvini walked slowly and majestically down four steps into the throng of admirers. All of them were clapping and shouting his name. They began thrusting bits of paper and pencils at him. Eleanor got elbowed and stepped on. She didn't care. She was mesmerized by the actor's handsome face—so enraptured, she never noticed the wrinkles at the corners of his eyes, or the bulge of fat at his waist when he swept his cloak back over his shoulder, the better to sign his name.

Despite Charlie's appearance of softness, he was determined, nimble, and, on this occasion, ferociously strong. He elbowed the bellies and ribs of older men—and women— till he got the actor's signature. Then, shrieking, "Take it, Eleanor! Give me yours!" he performed a miraculous exchange of papers in the surging crowd and secured a second signature for her.

None too soon, either. Salvini waved, abandoned twenty or thirty other autograph seekers and escaped into his carriage at the end of the cul-de-sac.

"Next to Edwin Booth's performance, that was the most thrilling thing I've ever seen!" Eleanor clutched the signed scrap of handbill to her breast. "Thank you, Charlie. Thank you!"

"It's nothing," he said with exaggerated magnanimity. "I'll take you to a real matinee if you can ever get out of the house long enough to—"

They stopped, face-to-face with the dark-haired young man with the broom. He'd evidently followed Eleanor and now, grinning at her, he said in the most beautiful baritone voice she'd ever heard, "Thought Signor Salvini was pretty handsome, did you? Well, I work here, and I can tell you for a fact, around the middle he's big as a whale. He wears a corset."

"See *here*!" Charlie said, inadvertently wriggling his eyebrows. "No one asked you for any comments."

"No, but I thought the young lady might be interested." The boy hardly took his eyes off of her. That queer, tingling sensation started in her hands, then in her legs. She found herself thinking, *He's as good-looking as Salvini.*

A panicked knot formed in her throat even as her breasts began to feel tight inside her clothing. These reactions were dangerous. *Dangerous.* She need only remember the quarrels heard through closed doors at home.

Charlie gripped her elbow and said in a pompous way, "Eleanor, come along."

"Eleanor?" the older boy repeated. "That's a pretty name. But then you're a pretty girl. My name's Leo Goldman. Do you like the theater?"

"Very much."

"So do I. That's why I took a job at the Academy. I've decided acting is the fastest and easiest way to make a fortune in this country. I hear managers are clamoring for actors with nice features and good elocution."

"They're not clamoring for anyone as conceited as *you,* sir!" Charlie huffed. He walked away very quickly in case the dark-haired boy took offense.

He didn't. Eleanor reluctantly followed her friend. She was unexpectedly sorry to have the conversation end. She glanced back and saw Leo Goldman walking toward the theater entrance. His face was glum.

"He was only trying to be friendly, Charlie—"

"With you, not me."

"Don't be silly. Why did you take such a dislike to him?"

"I don't trust *anyone* that good looking."

"But he seemed very nice."

"Too cocky, Eleanor. A slum type. I can tell them every time. His pretensions to an acting career are lamentable."

"I wouldn't say so. He has a lovely voice."

"But he's a Jew."

"I don't see what difference that makes." She was growing annoyed.

Charlie compressed his lips. "You're *impossible*. A naive *child*. His kind would *never* be admitted to a club like the Booth Association. I say amen. Let's forget about him. Got your list?"

"Oh my." Panic set in. The boy named Leo had completely driven the shopping from her mind. "Yes, and we'd better hurry. I must buy linens, and oodles of thread—if I don't get it all before Stewart's closes, Mama will have my hide."

"I said I'd *help*, didn't I?"

Charlie led the way through the traffic on Irving Place, jerking Eleanor somewhat roughly as a brewer's wagon bore down on them. She suspected Charlie was irked by her interest in the other young man.

Well, jealousy was ridiculous. She'd never see the boy again. Besides, that sort of interest only led to trouble.

Still, her feelings had been delicious when—

No.

The brewer's wagon veered. Charlie had to give her a second tug to get them safely to the curb. The wagon went by, rumbling toward another couple a half block up Irving. The object of quite a few Manhattan drivers, it seemed to Eleanor, was to crush as many pedestrians as possible.

When they were on the sidewalk and moving at a brisk pace, Charlie begged for more applause. "I trust seeing such a famous actor was a tonic and an inspiration for you."

"Oh, yes. Thank you again for bringing me. I couldn't have come alone."

"No, that's right," Charlie declared with that ponderous air which came so easily. "Wouldn't be safe. Now I know you love and respect your mother—"

Don't say that word, she thought. *I don't love anyone, and I mustn't.*

"—but I do hope you can find a way to visit the Booth Association as soon as I'm settled in."

"I'll be there, I promise."

"Good, good. An amateur acting society is the *only* place a respectable young woman can learn the fundamentals of the profession."

"I'll find a way to visit you, Charlie," she said with sudden fervency. "Believe me, I will."

CHAPTER XI

THE MAN IN
MACHINERY HALL

i

PHILADELPHIA WAS PACKED with visitors and dignitaries who'd come for the opening ceremonies in Fairmount Park beside the Schuylkill River. Hotel space was at a premium, but Gideon had made an advance reservation for two rooms, on separate floors. Julia confessed in a letter that she didn't think the subterfuge would fool a boy as old as Carter, but at least she was trying to maintain the illusion of propriety.

On the night before the exposition opened, she stole down to Gideon's room and they satisfied the intense physical hunger a separation always produced. Afterward, as they lay in each other's arms, she said in a quiet way, "Will you tell me what's bothering you?"

"What do you mean, bothering me?"

"There, you see? You're snapping again. You've been doing it ever since you met us at the depot. What on earth's happened?"

"Nothing."

Silence followed the vehement denial. It lasted five or six minutes. Several times Julia was tempted to speak, but thought it wiser to be patient and wait for him to continue. She was virtually certain he would.

Sure enough, he began to pour it out in a halting monologue. Things were not well at home. Margaret was not only hostile, but beginning to behave in a way that made him worry about her sanity. Even his two children seemed to be turning against him. He feared his son was growing up spineless, and his daughter becoming a partisan of his wife.

Julia stroked his chest lightly. "It's good that you got all of that out. Now that you've identified the problems, the next thing to do is to look for the causes."

"In Margaret's case I needn't look any further than the liquor cabinet or the wine racks in the cellar. She turned me out years ago—at least figuratively. That doesn't mean I want to see her suffer. I've begged her to see a doctor about the drinking. She absolutely refuses."

His voice had grown agitated again. Julia kept her hand moving on his skin in a soothing way as she said, "Perhaps she can't do anything else. We all find our own ways to cure pain. If I hadn't found Lucy Stone after I left Louis, I might have picked up a bottle of whiskey instead. I was hurting. I'm sure your wife is too."

"Well, there seems to be no real remedy for it. I've given up. I'm about to give up on my children, too."

"Oh, Gideon, no—"

"Yes. I'm losing them, Julia. I don't know why. I give them every advantage. Everything they want—within reason, anyway."

Softly: "How much of yourself do you give?"

"What?" He thought a moment. "I see them whenever I can"—a pause—"although I admit that isn't very often. Since Margaret started acting peculiar, I think I've invented excuses to stay away from home."

"There, you've found the heart of the problem. Think back. When did you last talk to your children at any great length? Or look in to wish them good night?"

His voice was faint all at once. "It's been longer than I care to remember."

He turned on his side. Laid his palm against her cheek gently. "You're an astonishing person—do you know that? Most women in your position would be scheming to break my ties with my family, not trying to help me repair them."

"I must admit there are times when the former would be more to my liking. To the liking of the old Julia, anyway. She's still present from time to time, I'm sorry to say. But contrary to what that poor murdered miner said in Deadwood, I really don't want to be a home-wrecking harlot. I don't think I am. What—damage there is in your marriage began to occur long before you and I met in Chicago. Still, I can't stand by and see you run so far from your wife that you also lose what you care about most—your children. Think about trying to give them more of your time, Gideon. More of yourself." She kissed the corner of his eye. "I know what a wonderful gift that is."

He was quiet again. Then, at last, he grew a bit more cheerful.

"Yes, I think you've seen what I couldn't. I've been neglecting them. I'll start doing something about it the moment I get back to New York."

"Good."

He planted a kiss on her lips. "You're a wise and loving woman. Thank you."

"Think nothing of it. It's merely a part of the complete service provided by your surrogate wife"—she touched him, and her voice grew husky—"who craves you shamelessly again."

ii

Few material things moved Gideon Kent any longer; he had become a lover of intangibles. Words. Ideas. But he was moved to awe and admiration by the scope of the Centennial Exhibition whose gates opened to waiting thousands at nine the next morning.

He had an admission card for a roped enclosure near the Main Hall, a section set aside for reporters. He'd gotten tickets for Julia and Carter in an area of special guest seats. And a good thing, too. By ten past nine, every unreserved inch of ground near the Main Hall and the equally mammoth Machinery Hall adjacent to it was packed with people eager to see the President of the United States and the Emperor of Brazil.

Because their places would be held, he and Julia felt free

to walk a while. She took his arm as they strolled. "It's simply marvelous, isn't it?"

"It is. I wish I'd found some way for the *Union* or Kent and Son to contribute to the celebration."

In a sympathetic way, she asked, "Oh, dear, are you still fretting about that, too?"

"Endlessly. I haven't had a single good idea."

"Well, sometimes good ideas pop up when and where you least expect them."

"That's true." But he didn't sound hopeful.

As they walked on, Julia said, "My, this is a huge exhibition."

Gideon was ready with the facts; Payne had put one man to work assembling them for the benefit of all *Union* reporters who would be writing stories in Philadelphia during the summer.

"Four hundred and fifty acres. Almost two hundred buildings. The exhibition was funded by capital stock issued by the Centennial Board of Finance. Other contributions came from Congress, the states and territories, the—Julia, why the devil are you laughing?"

"I'm sorry. It's just that I made a remark and you launched into a lecture. Mr. Payne has really infused you with a passion for spreading knowledge."

Gideon turned pink. "Evidently he has. I didn't mean to rattle on."

"Where's the Corliss engine, sir?" Carter asked.

"In Machinery Hall. We'll see it right after the opening ceremony."

The boy's question reminded Gideon that on several occasions his own son had asked about the engine, the exhibit which thus far had generated the greatest interest among press and public. Will had also asked when Gideon would take him to see it. Julia had been absolutely right last night. Because he wanted to avoid Margaret, he'd also been neglecting the children. He'd start putting that to rights the moment he got home. He'd arrange a family outing to Philadelphia.

"I'm anxious to see your brother's painting," Julia said, clinging tightly to Gideon's arm so as not to be buffeted by the crowds on the footpaths. Most of the opening day visitors were Americans, but Gideon also saw some whose faces or accents clearly identified them as representatives of foreign governments. Nearly every major nation had built a pavilion. For an admission price of fifty cents, a visitor could sample not only a century of American culture, but the cultures of Europe and Asia as well.

"It's in the Art Hall," Gideon said, leafing through a guidebook he'd purchased in advance. "That direction—no, wait. I believe Matt wrote that his picture would be in the Art Annex. The Art Hall is that pseudo-Renaissance palace. It will stay here after everything else comes down. American artists aren't being shown there, however. They've been relegated to the Annex. Matt was sore about it."

Gideon was intensely proud of his brother's growing reputation. He had never seen Matt's immense painting, which had been crated and shipped directly from London. He did know the picture was titled *Wilmington*. Another letter from Matt had said that the nature of the teeming dockside scene, the uniforms on some of the figures, and the fog gray funnel of a steamship towering in the dark background would make it clear to any spectator that a slightly different title would have been more accurate:

"Wilmington—War Time" would be better but Im told this exposition is suposed to unite not divide the contry so I'll leave the tittle what it is. I dont care one way or another whether I serve the cause of the "Union" no Pun meant there Gideon, I have no strong feelings for the contry. I take that back I have strong feelings of dislike. Let "Union" go hang. I submited the Wilmington picture because it came out well. Its a war scene but I can only paint what I remember of America, and I remember that dam wasteful war a lot better than I care to, almost as much as I remember Dolly god bless her. She made the picture posible. She made all of them posible, she is in evry one of them. Someday I will explain what I mean, but I cant take time now, a very handsome creatur the Duchess of T. is waiting for me.

iii

The three visitors were soon caught up in the exciting sights and sounds of the exhibition. The colorful pavilions were encircled by a special narrow-gauge railroad on the perimeter of Fairmount Park. Visitors could ride around the entire exhibition for only five cents. The Pennsylvania line had built the narrow-gauge. Gideon sourly supposed that Tom Scott, the bandit who presided over the Pennsylvania, would somehow find a way to make his exposition railroad pay just as handsomely as his regular line did.

"Isn't there a woman's building on the grounds?" Gideon said as they started back toward the Main Hall. Julia put the tip of her tongue in her cheek.

"Oh, you remembered. Indeed there is. After you go back to New York, I plan to spend a week working there. The pavilion has its own printing office. A newspaper for women will be written and published right on the premises all summer."

Carter's handsome face broke into a grin. "How soon are we going to the woman's building? Right after we look at the Corliss engine? I want to see the butter statues."

Gideon pulled a face. "Surely you're not serious."

"Don't snicker so!" Julia said. "The head of a milkmaid done in butter might be quite attractive."

"And if it isn't, think of the people it will feed." She pretended to hit him with her gloved hand. He laughed and went on, "Butter sculpture. Matt doesn't know the meaning of avant-garde."

The opening ceremonies began at ten fifteen, near the lagoon in front of the Main Hall. First the orchestra ran through a short program of airs. During one of the numbers Gideon scribbled a reminder. He needed to locate and look at the portion of the huge copper-clad statue which was being paid for by the French people as a gesture of friendship. The statue was the work of the sculptor Bartholdi. Liberty's forearm, hand and upraised torch had been rushed to completion and shipped to America for the exposition, although it would be years before the entire 151-foot-high work would be finished. Where it would finally be erected, no one yet knew.

Wild cheering broke out. Gideon looked up. A reporter

near him sneered, "The grand panjandrum himself. Or should I say the chief thief?"

Stocky, plain-faced President Grant had just appeared on the platform. From all the applause and shouting, no one would have guessed he had a tarnished reputation.

Soon the formal program started. The orchestra played a special march composed for the Centennial by Richard Wagner. Then came a new hymn by John Greenleaf Whittier and John Paine. This was followed by speeches, and then a cantata by Southern poet Sidney Lanier and Northern composer Dudley Buck—nice symbolic touch, Gideon thought. Finally the President delivered a brief, banal address which concluded, "I declare the international exhibition now open."

A gigantic flag was unfurled on the front of the Main Hall. And when the choir began the "Hallelujah Chorus," even the cynical professionals around Gideon grew quiet. At the end of the chorus, the artillery boomed and the spring breeze caught the flag and Gideon felt tears in his eye and a prickling along his spine. *It was* a strong and good country. It had survived a devastating internal war and all the other calamities of the past, and come through to show its strength and pride by means of this grand, glorious—and occasionally gauche—festival. It was a strong and good country despite the scoundrels who tried to pervert its principles and take advantage of the freedom it offered.

If only he could think of some tangible way—some project or piece of writing—to express his convictions. But his mind remained a blank.

iv

Machinery Hall was designed to display American technology, from small sewing machines to huge howitzers. The featured exhibit was a gigantic, 1500-horsepower steam engine with two vertical walking beams standing parallel.

At the conclusion of the outdoor ceremonies, people began to stampede toward Machinery Hall. They ignored the hundreds of police and militiamen who attempted to funnel them to the doorways in an orderly way. Shortly the police and militia cordons were disrupted. Gideon found himself fighting as hard as the next person to jam through an entrance in order to be present for the start-up of the Corliss engine. He searched for Julia and Carter but couldn't locate them. They'd agreed to meet immediately after the indoor ceremony.

At last he squeezed inside. He joined a stream of reporters rushing to a special press area marked off by velvet ropes. President Grant and the bearded Emperor of Brazil were already on the steam engine's control platform. The platform was raised several steps above the floor of the hall. A man with a proud expression—the designer and engineer, Corliss, Gideon supposed—stood close to the presidential party.

Gideon tilted his head back. The top of the mammoth machine looked three stories high. As yet he had no statistics on the Corliss; he was supposed to gather those and bring them back to New York.

For a newsman, the faces of those present were almost a more interesting study than the engine itself. Gideon saw wonder on nearly every countenance. It was apparent that the Corliss would be the fair's number one attraction. He had guessed wrong, then. He'd thought the most popular exhibit would be an astonishing new device called a telephone, which was to be demonstrated by its inventor, Alexander Bell.

He was busy making notes when he had a sensation of being watched. He glanced up. He was so surprised, he almost dropped the little block of paper. From the other side of the Corliss platform where he stood among a group of equally well-dressed visitors, a man was indeed watching him.

It was Thomas Courtleigh.

The auburn hair had grayed slightly. The face was a shade paler than he remembered. But even at a distance, Courtleigh's hazel eyes had a compelling power. They almost refused Gideon permission to glance away.

Five years, he thought. It had been nearly that long since he'd stormed into Courtleigh's mansion. And what had that act of bravado accomplished? Exactly nothing.

Gideon had yet to catch the railroad man committing

any crime of which he could be convicted. Twice he'd dispatched a trio of reporters to Chicago to look into Courtleigh's personal and public life. Both times they'd returned empty handed. There were rumors in plenty, but no facts. If Thomas Courtleigh broke the law—and most business tycoons did, one way or another—skilled attorneys and intermediaries covered the track very well.

Both times, Gideon had recalled Strelnik's prediction that he'd become so frustrated attempting to curb a man like Courtleigh, he'd finally resort to violence. Both times, he did feel something close to that kind of frustration. But of course having the impulse wasn't the same as doing the deed.

He hadn't thought of Courtleigh's threats for months. He'd assumed the railroad president had forgotten them. Yet now Courtleigh was staring at him with a fury as great as that which Gideon remembered from just after the fire. Odd.

"Are you both ready? Then, Your Majesty, will you be so kind as to turn that handle?"

Gideon wrenched his gaze back to the dignitaries. Dom Pedro, resplendent in his imperial uniform dripping with gold epaulettes and frogging, turned the indicated handle. Slowly, with a hiss of steam that grew increasingly louder, the first of the parallel walking beams began to move.

Down, then up. Down, up. The shaft sank into the ground far beneath the building, then rose from it again.

An ovation shook the hall. People whistled and stamped. Corliss' great machine would provide the power for all the other, smaller machines on display.

"Now, Mr. President—will you turn your handle, sir?"

With a nervous smile, Grant complied. The second beam started its slow downward motion. Soon the rhythm quickened. With both walking beams in operation, the floor of the hall vibrated. Another, louder ovation burst forth. The opening ceremonies were over.

Gideon tried to jot a few descriptive phrases, but he kept thinking of Courtleigh. When he glanced back to the spot where the W & P president had been standing, the group had rearranged itself. Courtleigh was no longer visible.

Soon the crowd began to disperse to take in the exhibits.

Gideon headed for the rendezvous point he and Julia had agreed upon—the soda fountain located near the bandstand in the Main Hall.

As he walked along, he still had the uneasy sensation of being observed. And some key detail of Courtleigh's expression or appearance troubled him. But the detail remained elusive no matter how hard he thought about it.

V

Late in the day they took a crowded horsecar back to their hotel on Walnut Street. Julia and Carter went to their room; Carter said he was tired. Gideon used a desk in his room to arrange his notes and begin writing his opening paragraphs. He had to take his dispatch to the telegraph office by ten-thirty. Theo Payne was holding space on tomorrow's front page for an account of the opening day.

He met Julia in the lobby at half past six. She looked refreshed. She said Carter wouldn't be joining them for dinner. He'd worn himself out tramping through the exhibits and was still asleep.

In the dining room, over grilled sole and the liebfraumilch she'd taught him to enjoy, he asked her whether she'd seen Courtleigh in Machinery Hall. She hadn't. News of his presence clearly upset her.

"Why would he be here, Gideon? His line has no official connection with the Exhibition, does it?"

"No, but it is opening day. Anyone's free to come."

"I suppose you're right."

"He also has contacts to maintain in the railroad community. The industry's in a turmoil these days. Mullins, one of our men who covers business news, keeps bringing in rumors that some of the trunk lines intend to meet secretly to form a pool."

"Form what?"

"A pool. A group composed of several cooperating lines. Usually a pool's organized to fix freight rates and otherwise squeeze out any competition the pool members don't want. Sometimes those in the pool fund a war chest any of them can dip into if they have trouble with a strike. The fund usually pays for blacklegs. Strikebreakers. For months,

Mullins has been hearing that a new pool's to be started. And wages cut on every line involved."

"When is it supposed to happen?"

He shrugged. "No one knows. This year. Next. Courtleigh might be involved, though most of the rumors have originated here in Pennsylvania." He took a bite of fish. "In any case, Courtleigh hasn't made good on his earlier threats, so it's pointless to worry about him. I just wish I could remember what struck me wrong this morning."

"How do you mean, wrong?"

"Something was out of place when I saw him. Something in the way he looked. I haven't been able to—" Abruptly, he drew in a breath. "Now I remember. He was with a party of well-dressed men and women. But his wife was missing. It wasn't the presence of something that threw me off—it was the absence."

"Oh dear," Julia murmured. "I meant to tell you and in all the excitement, I quite forgot."

"Tell me what?"

"Courtleigh's wife died six weeks ago."

Gideon's palms turned cold. "Are you positive?"

She nodded. "It was in all the Chicago papers. The *Tribune* got hold of it first, and evidently Courtleigh didn't act in time to quash the story."

She was confusing him. "Julia, people don't conceal the death of a spouse."

"No, certainly not the death itself. I'm referring to the circumstances. At the time Gwen Courtleigh passed away, she was a patient in a private asylum in Lake County. The same one to which her parents sent her after you visited the ball in her honor. She'd been locked up there for more than a year, hopelessly insane, and apparently showed no signs of ever recovering—*Gideon*." Her hand closed over his. "You mustn't look that way. I know Courtleigh made foolish accusations about your responsibility for her condition five years ago, but they were just that. Foolish. Don't start believing them now."

Gideon's blue eye was grim. "It doesn't matter a damn whether I believe them. It only matters whether he does."

Stricken silent, Julia waited for him to continue.

"In the past, I did a lot of thinking about Tom Courtleigh's motives, and how his mind must work to permit him to behave as he does. I believe I understand him. Look at life from his point of view. He has money, and power, and those two things will give him almost anything he wants—with little or no opposition. They also provide virtually complete protection against the buffetings of everyday life. The Courtleighs of this world live a sequestered, unreal existence. Ordinary people are more accustomed to bad luck. To blind chance interfering with their affairs. Courtleigh avoids that sort of thing year after year after year. Then comes something like his wife's insanity. He can't order it to heal itself. He can't write a draft and pay some flunky to make it vanish. I'm not trying to be clever when I say he probably found her condition maddening. Trying to undo it, he might come close to going mad himself. And when he discovered he couldn't undo it, I'm sure his anger would demand something on which to place the blame."

She whispered, "Don't you mean someone?"

Slowly, he nodded. "I think that's what I saw in his eyes this morning. He remembers he's never carried out his promise to punish me. And now he has greater reason than ever to do it."

Chapter XII

Vision of America

i

AFTER A NIGHT'S sleep, Gideon felt he'd been an alarmist. He and Julia returned to the Exhibition next day, turned Carter loose, met him again at sunset and had an altogether marvelous time. Gideon saw no sign of Thomas Courtleigh.

He'd sent only a relatively short dispatch to the *Union* the preceding evening. Out of the day's notes he prepared a longer piece, and started for the telegraph office just after ten o'clock. Julia was tired, but she'd promised to meet him in his room when he returned.

He was only a few steps from the hotel on still-busy Walnut Street when someone called his name.

He paused and looked across the street. A man waved. "Over here, Mr. Kent!" He was a small, nondescript fellow. Gideon didn't recognize him. "I've a message for you."

Suspicious, Gideon hesitated at the edge of the plank sidewalk. He didn't dare waste too much time before sending his dispatch. And he absolutely didn't know the man, who was hanging back near one of the darkened shops as if to avoid the gaslights of a restaurant entrance close by.

A carriage clattered past at a fast clip, momentarily concealing the man as he shouted, "Please, Mr. Kent. It's most urgent."

Curiosity overcame Gideon's wariness. He glanced at the hotel doorman who'd been watching the exchange, shrugged and stepped down into the street. He was a third of the way across when a hack drawn by two lathered horses came plunging onto Walnut from the cross street to his left. The horses and the hack rushed at him like a juggernaut.

The hotel doorman cried, "Watch yourself, sir!" Gideon flung up his left arm and hurled himself backward. As he fell, he had a distorted view of the bobbing, wild-eyed heads of the horses, and of the slouch-hatted driver whipping them. The street shook.

He landed on his side, his arm outflung. He jerked his arm back just in time to keep it from being trampled by sharp hoofs and crushed by heavy iron tires.

The doorman ran into the street, shaking his fist at the hack. "Slow down! No furious driving allowed in this district!"

The hack careened out of sight around a corner. The doorman rushed to help Gideon to his feet.

"Any serious damage, sir? Doesn't appear to be—just some dirt on your clothes. Damn cabmen. No respect for the law."

The two moved slowly toward the sidewalk. Gideon had twisted his left ankle, and limped slightly. But he'd already decided he mustn't upset Julia by telling her of the incident.

A few onlookers resumed their strolls. The doorman was still fuming. "Don't know why that idiot was traveling so fast. He had no fare."

Gideon stopped. "You're positive?"

"Yes, sir, the cab was empty. No passengers that I could see." Suddenly the ruddy face puckered into a frown. "And where's that bucko who was hollering at you?"

"Gone," Gideon said, well before he turned to scan the far side of the street. He was right. There was no trace of the stranger.

The doorman shrugged. "Well, it's the cabman I'm exercised about. Driving much too fast, without so much as a reprimand. Where are the police when you need them? Always somewhere else. You could have been badly injured—killed, even. Nobody cares about the law any longer. He whipped around that corner on two wheels and never saw you. Didn't care who was in the street."

"No, I'm sure he didn't," Gideon lied, thinking of Court-leigh's eyes in Machinery Hall, and of his wife dying in an asylum. Did Courtleigh still see the bloodstained shirt landing at her feet? Did he still hear her terrified shrieking?

Gideon felt incredibly tired as he limped away toward the telegraph office. The armistice was over. The war was resuming.

ii

Most newsmen agreed that they got some of their best ideas at unexpected moments. Julia had said much the same thing, and Gideon could verify it. Sometimes he solved a problem he was having with an editorial, or with a department of the paper, at the end of an uncomfortably sleepless night, or while he was stropping his razor, or even while he was sitting on the jakes with a bellyache. So it happened that night. He was on his way back from the telegraph office, still shaken, when he passed a book shop in whose window various souvenir and commemorative volumes were displayed against red, white and blue bunting.

SPECIAL CENTENNIAL EDITIONS read a small hand-lettered placard. He wished Kent and Son were represented in that window even in a small way. But the family firm had produced no book in honor of the hundred years of—

Instantly, the whole idea was there.

A book called *100 Years*—an expensive book produced with the finest typography, paper, and binding. There'd be a minimum of text. He'd attempt to write it himself, but if he found he couldn't do an adequate job, he'd hire someone better qualified. The real focus of the volume wouldn't be the words anyway. It would be—he searched the window and saw nothing exactly like it—one hundred plates. One hundred wood engravings telling the story of the republic's achievement since its founding in this very city a century ago.

The illustrations in the book wouldn't be the hackwork people were accustomed to seeing in newspapers or magazines. They'd tell a story, right enough, but they'd be fine art. They'd be cut by the best wood engravers Kent and Son could find.

But they'd be based on a hundred sketches by his brother Matt.

If Matt could possibly be persuaded to undertake the project, he would easily complete a hundred of his quick freehand drawings in just a few months. Then a staff of craftsmen would transfer them to blocks of boxwood as faithfully as the medium allowed.

A further thought struck him. Perhaps from the best twenty or twenty-five sketches, Matt would prepare a limited edition of etchings. The whole thing was unbelievably exciting.

Now what about the book's content? Historical subjects would be included, certainly. A battle or two. Breed's Hill where his ancestor Philip had fought. The Alamo mission where Amanda Kent had nearly lost her life during the struggle for the independence of Texas. And there had to be a depiction of at least one engagement from the late war, so Americans would never forget the horror of fighting against their own. Perhaps the subject should be Gettysburg, when the South's high tide had crested against a seawall of steel and fallen back.

But Gideon wanted more than war to be represented in *100 Years*. Much more. He wanted to create a panorama of the nation's territorial expansion, and of its agriculture and industry. He wanted the sweep of a corn field dark with the shoulders of a sunburned harvesting crew. He wanted the crowded aisles of a textile factory; the contrast of white fiber and black men in a Carolina gin house; the bottom of an anthracite mine lit only by miners' candles; the inside of a retail store with its wondrous array of goods and products; the crowded patterns of city telegraph wires crisscrossing an Eastern sky; and the isolation of a sod house jutting against a sky in the West—he wanted one great book that would capture the panoply of American life as it had developed in astounding variety since Philip Kent's time.

And he'd make sure not only the famous were portrayed, but the people who were the land's real backbone: the common people. *100 Years*. It was the project for which he'd been searching—and the very thing he needed to take his mind off Courtleigh.

He could hardly wait to tell Julia. She was as excited as he, so excited she never noticed he was limping a little.

"It's a magnificent idea, Gideon—especially having your brother create the illustrations. But a hundred of them?"

"Sketches, remember. He can do it. Before he was twenty, he used to turn out eight or ten a day. They were some of his best work. Brilliant art created around a kernel of realism. Of course there'll be more to this than merely making the drawings. He'll need to research the subjects. He'll have to travel the whole country—the Pacific, the Canadian border, Texas—we'll underwrite his expenses. He should jump at the challenge."

Provided I can present it the right way.

Delighted to see him so happy and enthusiastic for a change, Julia hugged him.

"Darling, I think you've just turned into a book publisher without realizing it."

iii

A day after his return to New York, Gideon took the train to Boston. Dana Hughes of Kent and Son was enthusiastic about the idea. He promised to have a preliminary list of one hundred subjects ready within two weeks.

Down at the Jersey Shore, Molly was equally enthusiastic—although she recognized that thousands of dollars of capital might be ventured in financing Matt's research, and none of it recouped if the book failed.

"After all, Gideon, by the time it's on the market, the centennial will be over."

"Have you looked at some of the souvenir books being sold right now? Junk. They'll be forgotten by New Year's Day. We'll make *100 Years* such a fine book, the delay won't make any difference. Why, with Matt doing the pictures, the damn thing will wind up in museums."

"That's a commendable goal," Molly agreed. "I'm with you. Of course it matters to me if the book fails and we lose the investment. But it will matter far less than the fact that the Kents published it, and did everything in their power to make it succeed. Are we in agreement?"

"We are!" He gave her a hearty kiss on the cheek, and danced her around the parlor till she begged for mercy.

iv

The fourth and final draft of his long letter to Matt concluded by saying:

> I know you have no feelings for this country save a justifiable contempt for its venality. So I won't cloak the project in a patriotic appeal. I present it to you instead as a creative challenge—for what American artist has dared to attempt so vast a labor? One which, simultaneously, wants to be the finest art, yet suited to the popular taste?
>
> If you should consent to undertake it, I would only ask that you do so with an open mind. That is, I would not want you to approach the book from the standpoint of devastating caricature like Tom Nast's. I would like to see representative Americans in the pages—the handsome along with the ugly—and contrary to what you might have come to believe since your exile, we do have a few handsome specimens around. Good God, you're one yourself. But I expect you are honest enough to understand what I am saying—that our states are not peopled exclusively by greedy grotesques. (It merely seems that way sometimes!)
>
> Finally, I see 100 Years as the potential salvation of the publishing house. I am not directly involved in the management of Kent and Son, but both of us draw income from it—or should—and therefore if your mind and heart aren't stirred by the proposal, perhaps I can fall back on family loyalty and beg you to do this one thing for the sake of membership in the Kent clan. Kent and Son was once a proud imprint but it is third—no, tenth-rate now. Between us, we might alter that. Forgive me, but if the possibility of a reversal of its fortunes exists, I think duty compels us to make the attempt.
>
> And although you'll probably mock me for saying

this, Matt, a well done book of the kind just proposed might also change a few of the conditions you find so deplorable. At least it might sweep away some of the fear and cynicism currently pervading America.

Can a mere book do that? Yes, I think so. I have immense faith in, and respect for, the printed word. Citizen Tom Paine, Gen'l. Washington's propagandist, rallied an indifferent populace and turned apathetic men into zealots of liberty. Mrs. Stone's novel, so detested in our part of the world, was nevertheless a watershed of social change.

We may not achieve such memorable results. But I believe the effort itself is worthy—though perhaps I have now ensnared myself, since I suspect such appeals are not compelling to you.

I cannot omit one final one which I confess also plays a part in my proposal. For years I have been trying to find a way to induce you to come home for a good, long visit. I hope I have at last discovered it.

I beg you to send me your answer quickly. I pray it will be a favorable one. I shall await it with great eagerness.

Meanwhile, I remain, as ever, your affectionate brother—

G.

Chapter XIII

House of Hurt

i

"ELEANOR." WILL TUGGED her skirt as she fussed in front of the mirror. "Eleanor!"

"Will, for heaven's sake. Quit that or you'll pull my bustle out of place. Oh, this pesky, ridiculous hat!"

She couldn't get it on at an angle that satisfied her. Will ignored her plea and gave another yank. She swiped at him with her fist. He ducked back, laughing. Her cheeks turned scarlet. Brothers could be the most infuriating creatures in the whole world.

What had come over him this evening? Why had he chosen to act up tonight, of all nights? Most of the time he was quiet and unassertive, afraid to make a peep around the house. Eleanor knew she was the only person to whom he dared show any natural enthusiasm—but blast him, he had no sense of timing. She was in a frightful rush, and all he did was pull her skirt, or leer.

"Who are you meeting at Martina Whittaker's, Eleanor?"

"The Latin tutor, you ninny. Same as last week."

"Oh, fizzlejig." He stuck out his tongue to show his skepticism. "I'll bet it's some boy. Girls don't get that het up over Latin. Every Tuesday you start acting dizzy by the middle of the afternoon."

The hat still wouldn't go on properly. She smacked it against her skirt. "Listening to you blab is going to make me later than ever, Will Kent. You know the tutor gets to the Whittakers' at seven. It's already seven—I heard the hall chimes. Mills is waiting and I still don't look halfway decent—"

Will made another face. "I'd never fix up for some old Latin teacher. Girls are stupid."

This time it was Eleanor who stuck out her tongue. Will retaliated by poking his thumbs in his ears, wiggling his fingers, crossing his eyes and making rude noises—all at the same time.

"Oh, you're a frightful boy. A brainless brat!" she cried, though without any real animosity. Since her father had returned from the opening of the Centennial Exhibition two weeks ago, things had taken a new turn at home. Papa had with him an armload of souvenirs for each of them. Jewelry and lace for her, toys and a small lead model of the Corliss engine for Will. He'd brought presents for Mama as well, though she'd barely thanked him, and had put them in the closet almost immediately.

Still, Papa seemed to be making a special effort to be kind to Margaret. To all of them, in fact. He was almost his old self, sitting in the evening with Will on his knee and Eleanor at his feet as he described the sights of the exposition. He'd even started singing again—rousing choruses of "O Susanna," or renditions of "My Old Kentucky Home" in which he and Eleanor feigned great sorrow, and laughed uproariously afterward.

Eleanor didn't completely understand the change in her father's behavior, but she knew it had something to do with a book project for which he expressed great enthusiasm. Uncle Matt, whom Eleanor had never met, was involved in the project too—or would be if Papa received the right sort of reply from London.

Uncle Matt was becoming a well-known painter in Europe. Eleanor felt a powerful sense of kinship with him. Her father tolerated her interest in the theater, but she didn't think he really understood it. She felt Uncle Matt would understand perfectly. He was an artist. In the past year or so, he'd become a kind of dream hero to her. She imagined him as very wise. Unfailingly kind. Good-humored. Tolerant of others. And of course daringly Bohemian.

For more than one reason, she fervently hoped her father would get the reply he wanted. If he did, Uncle Matt would come home and she could meet him. And the book project might keep Papa in a good mood. It had certainly made a big difference the past couple of weeks. Most evenings he was around the house instead of down at the *Union,* although tonight he'd rushed back after dinner because a messenger had arrived to report a breakdown in one of the huge presses.

He hadn't wanted to go, though. He'd said that when he kissed her cheek just before he hurried out. She thought he was sincere. He seemed like a changed man. He'd even promised several times that the family would travel to Philadelphia to see the exhibition. Mama was the one causing a delay now. She couldn't make up her mind as to when the trip should be scheduled.

Another thing brightening Eleanor's world was what she liked to think of as the Tuesday scheme. She'd concocted it with the help of Charlie Whittaker. At first she'd felt she just couldn't deceive her mother. Then practical considerations took over, and she reminded herself that if Margaret actually knew where Eleanor was going every Tuesday evening, she'd automatically withhold her permission. So in the face of certain rejection, Eleanor had resorted to a whole collection of untruths.

She was getting punished for them, though. She went through torture every time she was forced to fib to one or both of her parents.

Will continued to make faces, but he prudently stayed out of her reach. She struggled with the hat until she had it in a position that was acceptable. Then she picked up her reticule and rushed into the upstairs hall.

She nearly collided with her mother. She stepped aside just in time. Will came rocketing out the bedroom door, an impish gleam in his eyes.

"I'm gonna yank your bustle again, Eleanor. I'm gonna yank—"

He saw Margaret's open hand flashing at his face, but

not soon enough to pull back. Her palm struck loudly. He cried out.

"I've told you a hundred times, Will Kent. You are not to make that kind of noise in this house!"

Instantly, Eleanor was her brother's partisan. "If he can't make noise in his own house, Mama, where can he?"

"Keep out of this, young lady." Her wrathful gaze turned on the boy. He shrank against the wall. "Any more outbursts like that and you'll be locked up in your room for a week, do you understand?"

All the sparkle had faded from his eyes. Very faintly, he answered, "Yes, Mama."

Eleanor would have defended him again, but she knew it would do no good. Her mother was in another of her moods. She'd been wearing the same dress for the past three days. Strands of hair hung down near the outer corners of her eyes. She reeked of the so-called tonic she kept in an unlabeled brown bottle in her pocket. When she wasn't visiting the regular liquor cabinet, she took sips from the bottle—right in front of anyone, including the servants—and said in that hoarse, slurry voice she'd acquired that it was medicine prescribed by the family doctor.

Eleanor fretted as her mother's brown eyes drifted toward her and attempted to focus.

"Where are you going?"

"It's Tuesday evening, Mama."

"Tuesday?" Margaret shook her head. "Is that suppose to mean something?"

Eleanor thought her mother was being difficult on purpose. Then she looked into Margaret's eyes again, and saw how pathetically vacant they were. Her spine crawled. She felt like crying, but she managed to say, "Yes, Mama. Don't you remember I told you Martina Whittaker and I were both having trouble with Latin declensions?"

"No. I don't recall that."

Eleanor bit her lip. "You don't recall the Whittakers hired a tutor? And that every Tuesday evening I go over to their house to work with him, and with Martina? I didn't go last week because I had that touch of influenza, but we've discussed the tutor I don't know how many tim—"

"This is the first I've ever heard of it," Margaret interrupted. "The very first."

Frustrated and conscious of the rush of time, Eleanor let her voice grow too shrill. "You've forgotten. Mills has driven me to Martina's on three different Tuesdays. He drops me off at seven o'clock and calls for me at ten-thirty."

Margaret stepped toward her. "Eleanor, don't dispute me. No one has told me anything. Not you, not your father—I know *nothing* of these sessions." In the gloom beyond her mother's weaving figure, Will watched from the door of his bedroom. He was round-eyed and pale.

"You told your father but you didn't tell me," Margaret continued with exaggerated self-pity. Tears sprang to Eleanor's eyes. Margaret's shoulders slumped suddenly. "Gideon's just keeping things from me again—"

Then, with a small, resigned shrug, she turned and wandered away down the corridor, passing right by her son as if he didn't exist. Eleanor's stomach hurt from pity and fright. *Why* did Mama have to be in such misery all the time?

Margaret stopped at the last door on the right—her room. Just a few steps beyond, her bedraggled figure was dimly reflected in a tall window at the end of the corridor. She reached into her pocket, fumbled and produced the key to open her constantly locked door. Once Margaret was inside, Eleanor heard the lock click again.

"Eleanor?" With a listless step, Will approached. She wiped her eyes as he asked, "What's wrong with Mama?"

There was agony and confusion in her soft answer. "I wish to heaven I knew."

Will shook his head in a baffled way. "She acts like we don't even belong to her, like—no one loves her and she doesn't love anyone back."

There it was again. That hateful word. The source of so much misery. Eleanor was more determined than ever that love would never entangle her. She wanted no part of the sorrow it caused.

The situation in the household was still dreadful, and she'd deceived herself into thinking otherwise. That made her angry. She began to search for a target for the anger. A certain logic led her straight to Gideon. She was furious that he'd fooled her so completely.

"I thought things had gotten better since Papa came

home from Philadelphia," Will said. "He's laughed a lot, and sung songs the way he used to. He's been extra nice to Mama—"

Scathingly: "When we're around. When they're alone, he must be acting horribly. Things must be worse than ever between them. And he must be the cause."

Somehow she hated making the assertion. But how could she deny the evidence of her senses?

Will hated to hear it, too. "Oh, Eleanor, don't say—"

"Look at them!" she broke in, her hands in fists again. "Look at Papa. Then look at Mama. That tells you which one's hurting, and which one's causing it. *That* tells you who's in the wrong. Now leave me alone. I'm late!"

She rushed past Will and ran down the stairs.

ii

Mills drove to the Whittaker town house at breakneck speed. The Whittakers lived on London Terrace between Twenty-third and Twenty-fourth Streets on the West Side. It was another fashionable enclave of new money, the residences occupied mostly by merchants and other types of businessmen.

The Whittaker town house always had an exotic aroma, a blend of the various nostrums Charlie's father sold in wholesale lots. There were always free samples to be had of Dr. Helmbold's Extract of Buchu, or Drake's Plantation Bitters, or Radway's Ready Relief, or Dr. Bellingham's Stimulating Unguent, which Mr. Whittaker enthusiastically claimed had helped President Lincoln grow his beard.

"See you at half past ten," Eleanor called as she jumped out of the calash. Mills drove away and she hurried up the steps. Charlie yanked the door open before she reached it. He snatched her hand and practically dragged her inside.

"You're nearly a half hour late! You *know* how long it takes to drive to Irving Place. And tonight we're going to read the play from the stage!" He paused long enough to look into the parlor. "Goodbye, Mater, goodbye, Pater."

Eleanor called a quick greeting as Charlie dragged her on. The elder Whittakers answered with a cheerful hello. Charlie's mother and father knew nothing of the deception being practiced on Gideon and Margaret. They thought Eleanor came over every Tuesday evening just so Charlie could escort her to the meeting of the Booth Association. It was only proper that she have an escort, New York being as rough as it was after dark. Margaret never encountered the Whittakers socially, so there was little chance of exposure that way. Eleanor was thankful she didn't have to stumble through weekly lies in front of Charlie's parents, whom he now affectedly called *Pay*-ter and *May*-ter.

In the Whittaker carriage racing back across town, Eleanor did her best to explain the reason for the delay. The explanation calmed Charlie's melodramatic wrath and brought forth a sympathetic "How awful. Why is your poor mother so distracted?"

She drew a breath, a bit hesitant to tell her friend so much that was personal. But she wanted to share her anguish with someone.

"I can only guess Papa treats her abominably when they're alone."

"I've just met him once, but he didn't seem like the sort."

"No, he doesn't," Eleanor admitted. "On the other hand, there's one thing you learn from the theater. Some people are very good at pretending. There just can't be any other explanation for Mama's condition. Not any that I can understand, anyway. Sometimes I think Papa must have a mistress."

"What? Are you sure?"

"No, it's just a guess. But it would explain a lot."

"Mmm." Charlie rubbed his chin. "You could be right. I've heard newspaper people practice free association the way actors do. I imagine I'll have a mistress by the time I'm twenty or twenty-one."

That depressed her even more. "You won't fall in love with her, will you?"

"Why shouldn't I?"

"Because you'll feel wretched if you do. Love hurts people, Charlie. But it's never going to hurt me."

Her vehemence shocked him. He quickly sought another topic.

"Before I forget—you have an unpleasant surprise waiting for you at the Association. Last week, when you were

laid up, a new member showed his face. You'll never believe who it is."

"Who?"

"Remember that Jew we saw pushing a broom at the
Academy of Music?"

"Yes!" He frowned at her surprising enthusiasm. An
image of a handsome, cocky face flashed into her mind.
Unexpectedly, she felt a tightness in her breasts. She was
ashamed of the sensation. It was uncontrollable, and it con-
tradicted the declaration she'd just made to her friend. "I
thought you told me the Association didn't admit Jews. I
think that's silly, but—"

"Oh, they admitted *him*," Charlie interrupted. "Last
week he walked in and announced that he'd heard the
Booth Association was the best amateur club in town, so
that's the one he was joining. I found out afterward why
Donald and Percy"—they were the Association's president
and vice president—"practically begged the rest of us not
to blackball Goldman when he stepped out of the room
and we voted. If you can *conceive* of this, Eleanor, Mr.
Goldman of Hester Street—*Hester* Street, the *worst* slum
in New York—spoke to Donald and Percy in private. He
said he'd hold the two of them responsible if he wasn't
admitted. He said he'd bash their faces in. They claimed
he wasn't testy about it, just very—factual. Did you ever
hear of such a thing?"

"No," Eleanor answered. She was tempted to laugh de-
lightedly at Leo Goldman's nerve. She didn't dare or she'd
offend Charlie.

But she admired anyone who confronted obstacles in a
determined way, and did whatever was necessary to overcome them. That was exactly what she'd done in order to
attend meetings of the Association. For that reason, and
others she didn't fully understand as yet, it would be far
from unpleasant to see the dark-haired boy again. Of
course she didn't dare mention that to Charlie, either.

The rest of the trip seemed to pass in an instant. The
coachman delivered them to Hutter Hall at two minutes
after eight.

CHAPTER XIV

AT THE BOOTH ASSOCIATION

i

AFTER FOUR SPEECHES, Charlie stopped them.

Leo Goldman cleared his throat and peered at his hand-written side. Eleanor had a similar sheet containing the lines and cues for her role. Sides were necessary because no printed text of the complete play was available.

She was standing next to Leo on a low platform which served as the stage. The only piece of stage furniture was a wooden box about two feet square.

She had never been in such a state of nerves. The misery of life at home had been completely driven from her thoughts when she walked into Hutter Hall.

The moment she'd arrived, Leo Goldman had hurried over and greeted her warmly. He'd seized her hand, shaken it, and given her a direct but not discourteous look that nevertheless made her blush.

Leo's clothing was noticeably poorer than that of the other members. It consisted of heavy work shoes, old wool trousers, a cotton jacket from which the dark blue dye had faded in several places, and a dingy gray flannel shirt. Every item was clean but shabby.

Yet Leo's good looks and confident smile seemed to

overcome that. He moved with an intensity, an energy, altogether lacking in the more affluent boys who didn't have to scramble for a living. His physical proximity only increased Eleanor's nervousness—as did the fact that they were the first couple asked to read. They'd barely started when Charlie called a halt.

Leo glanced toward the wooden chairs arranged in semicircular rows in front of the platform. Charlie was seated among eleven boys whose ages varied from fifteen to nineteen. In addition, three other girls were present as guests. All were at least three or four years older than Eleanor but the difference wasn't pronounced; she looked as mature as any of them.

The girls were quite taken with Leo, she noticed. She resented that, though she didn't know why she should; she disliked her own, quite uncontrollable interest in him. She wanted no part of him—or any boy. Yet she frequently found herself glancing in his direction.

Behind the seats stood a crate draped with a piece of green velvet. On the velvet lay an old polished gavel, and a copy of the Booth Association's constitution. On the rear wall hung a litho portrait of Edwin Booth which, like the platform, was put up and taken down every Tuesday evening.

"Let's start over, Goldman," Charlie called. "Give your character a little more—a little more *tension.* If you can."

A boy behind Charlie snickered and whispered something to a girl next to him. Leo scowled. Eleanor could have punched the club members for being so condescending. They were just jealous of Leo's good looks and fine voice.

Charlie Whittaker could be faulted for his faintly snide tone, but not for offering criticism. The Association prided itself on advanced methods, and tonight Charlie was acting as director of staging, a job that was just finding its way into professional theaters.

In the past Eleanor knew from her reading, stage business and acting technique had been left largely to the discretion of the actors, and thus to chance. If the cast was competent and happy, a fine production resulted. If they were incompetent, or so jealous that they intentionally blocked one another's positions or jumped one another's

lines, the result could be chaos. Stage directions were supposed to take charge, plan the performance and prevent
that sort of thing.

"And, Eleanor—"

"Yes, Charlie?" She felt every eye on her, including
Leo's. His, at least, was friendly.

"When you and Goldman are exchanging your remarks,
don't stand upstage of him. That's a fundamental lesson
you must learn. Position yourself next to him on an imaginary line from stage right to stage left. Otherwise, don't
you see, you force him to turn too far. We lose his face.
Also, you make him speak too loudly. Professional acting
no longer consists of a continuous shout. Booth made it
acceptable for an actor to vary the intensity of his voice.
But Goldman's forced to shout if you make him face the
upper wall."

Her cheeks felt fiery, but she accepted the criticisms with
a meek nod. "All right." She couldn't be thin-skinned if
she wanted to learn. She was glad Charlie had corrected
her; she hadn't even been aware of moving a few steps
upstage of Leo.

Charlie snapped his fingers. Leo began the scene again.

"Pearl, what does this mean?"

"Oh, it's only a little cloud that I want to clear up for
you." As Eleanor read, she was conscious of the reedy
sound of her voice in contrast to the richness of his. She
had to get control of her nerves or she'd botch everything.

"Cloud?" he went on. "How? Where?"

"Don't I tell you I am going to tell you? Sit down here
by me."

She managed to lower herself gracefully onto the wooden
box. She heard a murmur in the gaslit hall, but didn't dare
look to see whether it signaled approval or scorn.

She and Leo Goldman were reading from one of the
most successful plays of the melodrama genre—Augustin
Daly's *Under the Gaslight*. The famous author-manager had
written and produced the drama during the 1867 season.
One of the elements contributing to its immense popularity
was a sensational spectacle scene in the third act. Daly's
original mounting at the New York Theater was still talked
about for its realism; men had cringed and women had

fainted as a train seemed to rush at the audience, then roar by.

The scene Charlie had chosen came from the play's first act, which got the needed exposition out of the way. Pearl's remarks to Ray contained a revelation about the past of her cousin Laura, who was Ray's sweetheart. Caught up in the dialogue and anxious to make it sound realistic, she soon forgot her surroundings. The scene only contained thirty-one speeches before Pearl's exit. They were at the end almost before she realized it.

She swung into Pearl's last few lines, trying to develop volume without resorting to the bombastic yelling that was passing out of fashion.

"Mother made me promise never to tell anybody this, and you would have known nothing had not Laura made me speak. You see, she would not conceal anything from you. Ray, why don't you speak? Shall I go after Laura? Shall I tell her to come to you?"

Leo's mouth opened and closed in a decent approximation of shock as she went on.

"Why don't you answer? I'll go and tell her you want to see her. I'm going to send her to you, Ray!"

And with a last challenging look at her partner, she turned and stalked away, the sheets of the side clattering noisily in her fingers.

She nearly stumbled and fell off the platform when she heard one or two of the members applaud.

ii

Charlie Whittaker didn't join in. Since she was his guest, that would have indicated undue favoritism. But even one of the other girls was clapping. So was Leo Goldman. His applause was the loudest of all.

Eleanor turned pink. *The most wonderful sound in the world,* she thought.

In a moment Charlie stood up. Eleanor felt warm and content as she took a seat. Leo followed and sat close by, though he left one chair between them. He smiled at her. In the euphoria of the moment, she returned the smile.

Then, flustered, she glanced away, realizing he'd think she was encouraging him.

Charlie's voice interrupted her thoughts.

"All right, time for a critique." A hand went up. "Shad?"

"I thought Goldman mugged horribly."

The criticisms ranged from substantial to petty. Eleanor tried to evaluate each one without emotion, to see whether it contained some bit of helpful information. Leo Goldman fared worse than she did, although she honestly thought he had a more natural talent. His good looks helped him create strongly masculine characterizations with hardly any effort.

In any case, she believed he drew an unfair share of criticism. His eyes tended to flash when the boy named Shad Conway spoke; he was an especially sarcastic sort. But Leo accepted the other criticisms without visible annoyance, and wrote several of them on a little tablet. Eleanor looked over at the tablet and was oddly touched by the block capital heading:

WAYS TO IMPROVE

That told her Leo Goldman not only had the looks a leading man needed—he also had the ambition.

Other couples read the same scene and received a critique. All of the young ladies had a chance to try the role of Pearl. Shad Conway's remarks were uniformly merciless. At one point he made a disparaging comment about the dress a girl was wearing. Leo jumped up and called him a cad—a popular word these days. Conway sneered and started to turn away, saying Leo was too outspoken for a "newcomer" but his brashness was understandable since he was a "Hebrew." At that Leo rushed forward, grabbed Conway and invited him to step into the street without his coat.

Conway turned white. Charlie and Donald Brace, the president, stepped in to make peace. They forced the glowering adversaries to apologize to one another. Additionally, Conway mumbled an apology to the girl whose dress he'd criticized.

"Shake hands," Charlie insisted. They did. Leo's grip

must have been powerful, because Conway turned whiter still. Eleanor relished every moment. She was not only learning how to move and speak onstage, she was receiving valuable lessons in how to behave with other actors.

Once the readings were over, the boys rushed away to cluster beneath Booth's portrait—all except Conway, who sat and sulked. Charlie was grinning when he returned to make an announcement whose purpose Eleanor couldn't guess. At the other meetings she'd attended, only a group reading, with everyone seated in a circle, had taken place.

"Members present have voted," Charlie said. "We declare the following point totals for those guests who essayed the role of Pearl." He consulted a chit. "Miss McDuff, four points, Miss Bartholomew, five points."

Leo grinned in an encouraging way. Eleanor caught her breath. She couldn't believe it when Charlie beamed and read the fourth and highest score.

"Miss Kent, eleven points."

A splatter of applause and some whistles. Leo Goldman silently repeated the name *Kent,* surprised by it, somehow. Conway peered at the toes of his boots and pouted. Charlie raised his hand for order, then continued officiously.

"Now before all you charming ladies rush pell mell to the offices of the various producing managers, I must remind you in my role of stage director for the evening that the club's evaluation scale consists of twenty points. So even an eleven is only about halfway to perfection. The aim of the Booth Association is to promote practice and improvement. We shall repeat the same scene next week, with Mr. Farnsworth as director of staging."

The president whacked the gavel. The meeting was adjourned.

Eleanor was still happy over her surprising success. And for nearly two hours she'd quite forgotten the real world, including her parents and the pain of living with their hostilities. No wonder actors loved the theater.

As she collected her bonnet from the cloak room, Leo Goldman followed her in.

"Congratulations, Miss Kent."

"Thank you, Mr. Goldman. The success of the scene was due as much to your efforts as to mine."

How handsome he is, she thought, almost against her will. His dark cheeks gave off the strong but pleasant smell of homemade soap. He leaned in the doorway.

"I didn't realize your last name was Kent. I used to run newspapers from Printing House Square, and I once met a gentleman there who had the same name. He was connected with the *Union.* Handsome chap. Wore a leather patch—" He touched his left eye.

"My father."

"Your father! What a coincidence. I thought it might be an uncle or something—"

It had the sound of idle conversation. Leo's dark eyes kept darting here and there, watching the others coming and going in the cloak room. Eleanor didn't understand his nervousness until a moment later, when the club's vice president and one of the girls walked out with their wraps and she and Leo were left alone.

He rushed forward, shielding her from observation by standing between her and the doorway. A strong hand, the back lightly matted with black hair, closed on her forearm. He lowered his voice.

"I want to see you again. Call on you in proper fashion. Bet you've never had a beau from the ghetto. I won't be there forever, though. One day I'll be as rich and famous as any man in America."

"Wait, wait!" she exclaimed, both amused and appalled. "You can't call on me, Leo—"

"Parents won't allow it? I'll speak to your father. I can persuade him."

All at once she was terrified by his confidence. Over his shoulder she saw Charlie waiting and watching them. She blurted the first objection that came to mind.

"I'm not old enough to have a beau."

"You're seventeen or eighteen, aren't you?"

"Fourteen the end of May."

"Come on!"

"It's true. I don't have beaux and"—she remembered the misery at home, and slowly choked off the excitement produced by the touch of his hand—"and I don't want any, thank you very much."

She started to pull away. His chin thrust out. "You're fibbing to me. I can tell. I don't know why you're doing it, but I'll find out. When I want something, I don't give up."

She managed to free her hand, and wave. "I'm coming, Charlie. As soon as Mr. Goldman stops talking."

She threw Leo a sharp look and brushed by him, still tingling from the physical contact and telling herself it was wrong.

Leo Goldman's expression grew angry as he watched her leave Hutter Hall with Charlie. Then the annoyance faded, replaced by a look of determination.

iii

"Charlie, that was absolutely grand."

The carriage was hurrying them back to London Terrace, where she'd creep in the back door of the Whittakers', dash out the front and return with Mills to that dreadful house. How she wished she didn't have to do that. How she wished she could lose herself in a performance every night. If only she were as old as Leo Goldman thought, she'd be free to do whatever she wanted. Free to pursue a career.

"Didn't I say you had a first-class talent?" Charlie replied. "The members endorsed my view. Say—what did that Jew want in the cloak room?"

"You mustn't keep calling him a Jew in that tone of voice. If you do, he'll have every right to call you the son of a quack medicine peddler."

Charlie bristled. "Taking his part pretty hotly, aren't you?"

She was aware of warmth in her face again. She struggled to keep her tone casual.

"I'm only trying to be fair."

"You didn't tell me what he wanted."

She shrugged. "He was just paying a compliment."

"Yes, I *saw* him rolling his damned eyes at you all evening!"

"Now, Charlie, don't carry on. Leo means nothing to me."

The falsehood put scarlet back in her cheeks. Shameful images filled her head all at once. Her mouth against Leo's. Their bodies touching, without clothing, in some idyllic,

sun-bright glade where, together, they sank down to perform the mysterious act she'd only heard about—

Stop. That sort of thing only brought pain. She must remember that.

She calmed down, maneuvered the conversation in a different direction.

"I decided something tonight, Charlie. I'm definitely
going to be an actress."

"You mean you weren't sure?"

"Not entirely. Not until I read that scene."

"Well, I'd say you have an *excellent* chance to fulfill your
ambition. Maybe we'll even appear together one of these
days." Then, adopting that man-of-the-world tone, he
added, "Tell me, how soon do you plan to leave the family
fireside and take up trouping? Tomorrow? Next week?"

Lamps on a passing carriage cast a harsh glare in Eleanor's oval eyes for a moment. Her face lost its soft quality.

"Don't joke that way. Things are terrible at home. I
promise you this. I'll leave as soon as I can."

"Really?"

"Yes." She pressed her gloved fist against her skirt. "As
soon as I can."

Charlie retreated into puzzled silence. Eleanor had the
mercurial temperament of an actress, right enough. Her
declaration just now had been almost as strident as the one
she'd made while they were on their way to Irving Place.

He didn't understand why she felt as she did, but it was
very evident violent emotions were churning within her.
Charlie liked Eleanor Kent. He hoped those emotions—or
the unhappy situation with her family—wouldn't bring her
to grief.

Chapter XV

The Birthday

i

THREE DAYS BEFORE Eleanor's fourteenth birthday, Gideon again spent the evening at home. He was doing it more and more frequently of late. Around eight thirty he finished reading Will a section of a new Mark Twain book *The Adventures of Tom Sawyer*. Then he lifted his son off his knee and shooed him to bed. He went upstairs ten minutes later to be sure Will had followed instructions.

Will was in bed with the sheet pulled up to the collar of his summer nightshirt. Gideon sat down on the edge of the bed and mussed his son's hair affectionately. How sober his eyes were. More appropriate to a man of eighty than a boy of eight.

"Will, do you ever give any thought to what you want to be when you grow up?"

"Some," Will admitted. In that reply, as in everything he said or did, he was hesitant, as if he might be criticized or punished.

"Can you tell me?"

Another pause. "I'd like to join one of the volunteer fire companies. But I don't think I'd better. I think I should pick something quiet."

Gideon almost burst out laughing until he saw the seriousness of his son's expression. There was something so
timid about Will, something so cowed and so contrary to
the normal exuberance of boys, Gideon's heart almost
broke with guilt.

"Why do you say that, Will?"

With perfect logic, the boy answered, "Mama likes quiet
children. You don't get yelled at or whipped when you're
quiet."

"But boys need to whoop and holler once in a while.
It's allowed."

"Oh"—he nodded—"I do that over in the Park. By
myself."

*What have we done to him, me with my inattention and
Margaret with her bad moods?* His voice was hushed. "I
see. Well, good night, Will."

"Good night, Papa," The boy's hug was unashamedly
loving.

Gideon turned out the gaslight and left. He walked down
the corridor to bid Eleanor good night before she finished
her studies and made ready for bed. Like Will, she too
represented a problem, though a different one. Of late
she'd started to treat him with a cool reserve he found
upsetting.

Oh, she was never disrespectful. And deep in her eyes
he thought he detected affection struggling to break free.
But she would permit no tangible demonstration of it.

He entered her room quietly. She was bent over her
Latin grammar. He murmured, "Good night, Eleanor," and
reached down almost shyly to touch the back of her hand.
One did no more than that with a maturing girl, he'd discovered. Physical contact with parents seemed to embarrass them.

The moment his fingers brushed hers, she jerked her
hand to her lap. She forced a smile at once nervous and
insincere.

"Good night, Papa. Before you go, may I ask you a
question?"

"Certainly." It was unexpected—but far better than
indifference.

"Do you know a boy named Leo Goldman? He said he
met you once down near the paper."

"Goldman. I don't believe—"

"He's two or three years older than I am. From the lower East Side. He said he used to deliver newspapers."

"Oh, yes, now I remember. It was five or six years ago. He stopped me at the door of the *Union* and asked a question about an extra edition. Good-looking youngster, as I recall—" Memory made him smile. "Struck me as a cheeky sort, but in a nice way. His voice was changing. He was very excited about the opportunity in America. His parents were immigrants, and he said he planned to make a fortune here. I recall thinking he probably would. Where on earth did you run into him?"

"Oh, he's a friend of Martina's brother."

"Of Charlie Whittaker's?" Gideon recognized a fib. His daughter wasn't good at deception, thank heaven.

He didn't press the issue, just murmured to acknowledge that he'd heard. But he meant to stay alert for any further inquiries or signs of interest. He didn't want Eleanor involving herself with some streetwise slum boy, not at her age—not at any age, for that matter.

All at once he saw an opportunity he'd been wanting—chances to converse with his daughter were very few these days.

"Since I answered your question, will you answer one of mine?"

Her response was a shrug. "Of course."

"Why are you so annoyed with me lately?"

"I'm not."

"I'm sorry, but I don't believe you. Is it because of the trip to Philadelphia? That's all settled now. We're going next month. I've booked the suite of rooms. More important, your mother has finally agreed to the departure date."

The trip was scheduled for the eleven-day period between the Republican nominating convention in Cincinnati and that of the Democrats in St. Louis. The *Union*'s chief political reporter would be doing daily stories from both conventions, but Gideon planned to attend a few sessions of each as an observer and editorialist.

Eleanor turned in her chair and exclaimed, "I know—Will's already in a tizzy over the trip. He's driving me absolutely wild."

Gideon chuckled. "Well, I'm glad to see a response, even

if your brother does catch the worst of it. Things are entirely too grim and listless in this house. I'm trying to change that. I hope the excursion will help."

She gave him a hard stare. "I thought you liked things the way they are, Papa."

He suppressed sudden anger. "May I ask what you mean? That's a rather impertinent remark for a girl your age."

"Yes, I'm sorry," she said, and turned back to her grammar. Her tone clearly said she didn't think she'd done wrong. Somehow he was being cast in the role of the family's chief sinner.

Who was doing that? Margaret? She was barely civil any longer. And sometimes, despite the alcohol haze in which she lived, she gazed at him in a most peculiar way. Almost a calculating way.

He hoped to God she wasn't attempting to influence the minds of the children against him. The thought was a sorry climax to his aborted effort to come to some understanding with Eleanor. She didn't even glance up as he left the room and softly shut the door.

Well, it was only a small defeat. He mustn't let it ruin his determination to improve conditions in the family. Will needed the companionship of a brother or, lacking one, of a father. Gideon needed to start teaching his son to play checkers. He ought to buy a bat and ball for them to use in the vacant lot on the other side of Sixty-first.

And despite Eleanor's hostility, he wanted to make her birthday a happy one. As yet he'd gotten no present for her. Time was running out, but he'd been unable to think of the right thing.

He wanted to make the gift a special and important one. The celebration itself was shaping up that way. Cook had drawn up an extra-good menu. And Margaret had surprised Gideon by suggesting she write Molly in Long Branch and invite her to come up and spend the night, a proposal he'd enthusiastically seconded.

So far, he'd done no more than scribble a list of ideas for a gift. Downstairs in his book-lined study, he turned up the gaslight and tugged the list from a waistcoat pocket. He ran his eye down what he'd written.

Brushes.
Combs—moth. of prl. inlays.
Perfume.

There were six other items, equally pedestrian.

What could he get that would excite Eleanor? The obvious answer was something connected with her developing interest in the theater. Did he dare buy a book of some sort? A Shakespearean text? Much as Margaret disliked the New York theaters, she surely couldn't object to a printed play.

He'd search the better bookshops starting tomorrow morning. He would, that is, unless he could think of something even better before then.

He sat down at his desk. He took out pen and tablet to compose a message for the Atlantic cable. He'd had no response to his letter to Matt. He was beginning to think his brother hadn't received it, or had received and dismissed it. In case the latter was true, Matt at least owed him the courtesy of a refusal.

Abruptly he gnawed the end of the pen. The street boy—Goldman. Where had Eleanor met him?

He still didn't believe the explanation about Charlie Whittaker. Had she encountered Goldman in some kind of theatrical activity? He hoped not. Reading plays was fine. Harmless. Becoming personally involved in the seedy, amoral world of the theater was something else again. It was a possibility that, as a father, he couldn't tolerate.

He recognized that he was in effect creating a double standard—one for his children, and one for himself—and Julia. But more and more, he was coming to look at things from a father's perspective. And if a double standard was required to protect a daughter, so be it. Damn what anyone might say about hypocrisy.

He glanced up at the sound of the study door opening.

"Margaret!"

A surprised smile spread over his face. It vanished when he took note of her sullen eyes. How white and weary she looked. For a moment he felt a stir of the old affection. Or was it merely pity?

There was almost a whine in her voice as she said, "I wanted to let you know I saw Dr. Melton today."

Good God. He hardly dared take a breath. Had she realized at last that the drinking was destroying her?

As if to confirm it, she added, "I've been having some problems—"

Careful. Don't upset her.

"What sort of problems, Margaret?"

"Why, feminine ones. The kind a woman doesn't discuss even with her husband." That was unexpected; it jolted him, then brought a feeling of discouragement as she went on. "Dr. Melton gave me a tonic that's different from the one I'm taking now."

The one that's rotting your mind and ruining your life?

Sweat broke out on his forehead. He fought to keep from shouting at her. She continued. "He gave me some other preparations as well. During the next ninety days, he wants me to rest as much as I can. I wanted to tell you at once, because going on the trip to Philadelphia will be quite impossible now."

He tried to conceal his hurt. "I could still take the children—"

A touch of hostility: "It was planned as a family outing, was it not?"

"Of course, of course." He was anxious not to agitate her. "As soon as you're feeling up to it, we can discuss new reservations for the fall. The exposition will be open until the tenth of November. It'll be cooler then. I suppose I'd better tell Eleanor and Will—"

"I've just done that. Will was upset, but Eleanor was very understanding. I'm glad you're taking the same attitude, Gideon."

She turned to leave, her step slow and her face disturbingly blank. In truth, he was furious over the news.

After she was gone he raked a hand through his hair, then picked up the pen with which he'd been about to write to Matt. Suddenly he snapped the pen in half.

"God*damn* it," he said softly as tears of disappointment welled in his eye.

ii

An hour later, Margaret committed her latest coup to the pages of her diary. She chuckled and cooed to herself as she wrote behind drawn drapes and a locked door in the dank bedroom. By her hand stood an unlabeled brown bottle from which she drank occasionally.

> —and he accepted my lie. Tomorrow I shall speak to E. and W. I told G. that I had already done so, but that is not true. Should he chance to discuss the matter with them before I do, I shall plead a misunderstanding. I do not think he will do it, though, as he was exercised, and appeared to accept my word as final. When I talk with the children I shall tell them it is their father who has once again found it impossible to make the journey to Philadelphia. I shall say his work has again taken precedence, and they will hate him. And why not, dear friend? The blame for all the woes of this household is HIS—

She slashed lines beneath the capitalized word. Unlike the underscorings at the start of the book, the ones on this page and those immediately preceding were distinctly uneven. Jagged, Z-shaped lines.

She lifted the brown bottle. Drank. Then, after using her little finger to dab spittle from a corners of her lips, she continued writing.

> Next, if at all possible, I must find a way to make it seem he has intentionally ruined Eleanor's birthday celebration.

iii

Next morning, Gideon awoke angry. He was sure Margaret had gulled him last night.

He'd wanted to exhibit patience with her. Be sympathetic and kind when she needed it. So he'd swallowed her story whole. He awoke doubting it—and her honesty.

He suspected her alleged feminine problems were fictions, invented to once more disrupt the off-again, on-again trip. That angered him, and so did the frustration of being unable to verify her story. The only way he could do it was to go to Melton's consulting rooms and ask vulgar questions about a subject which—as Margaret herself said—husbands seldom if ever discussed with their wives. She probably knew he wouldn't set foot in Melton's office for that purpose.

The suspicion that she'd once again spoiled things in order to create friction stayed with him as he commenced his trip downtown. As had happened before, a time of turmoil unexpectedly produced a good idea. He got an inspiration for Eleanor's gift, and realized with impatience that he wouldn't be able to speak with the *Union*'s drama critic, Billy Dawes, until midafternoon. The editorial people began to drift in then, although certain staff writers who did most of their work in the office reported earlier to prepare and polish filler material.

During the morning Gideon occupied himself with the previous month's financial statement. He met with his chief bookkeeper before going to lunch with Payne at the tavern on Ann Street where he and Sime Strelnik had parted company that winter night in '71.

Gideon had brought along a thick folder of copy. Eight articles prepared by Salathiel Brown, the *Union*'s correspondent who traveled west of the Mississippi. Each article dealt with some aspect of life in a growing city or town in that part of the country. Gideon showed Payne the minor changes and suggestions he'd noted on each of the first seven features. Then he pulled out the last one. The front page bore the title *Paris of the Prairie*.

"Telegraph Sal to try this one again, Theo. That is, if you agree we're not in the business of glorifying card sharps."

"Indeed we aren't," Payne said between bites of a cutlet. "Haven't read the piece yet. What's wrong with it?"

"Mr. Brown chose to focus on the Kansas City tenderloin. Specifically, on the downfall of one man who's been drawn there by boom times in the city. Some fellow named"—Gideon thumbed the copy—"Kane."

"Not Jason Kane?" Payne spelled the last name.

"Yes. You've heard of him?"

The editor nodded. "He's killed his share, like Hickok

and some of those other desperadoes. What'd he do to get in trouble in Kansas City?"

"The same thing for which he says he was wrongfully run out of Deadwood Gulch. He cheated. He was caught, tarred and feathered."

Payne winced at the painful thought. Gideon went on. "The point is, Sal portrays him as a kind of pathetic hero. A victim of his fondness for the bottle"—that just slipped out, but Payne didn't act offended—"and of his need to maintain a fierce reputation. According to Sal's view, this Kane had no chance to succeed after the war because he was a Reb. All he could do was take up a career as a gambler. I don't accept that. Choices are open to every man. Hell, I was a Reb and I swam upstream in the biggest city in the North for years afterward. But I didn't drown."

With a melancholy smile, Payne murmured, "Some of us are not made of such stern stuff, Gideon."

Then pink spots appeared on his cheeks. "I'm sorry. That was self-pitying and unkind. You're a good friend and a good man. My weaknesses aren't your fault. Accept my apology?"

The younger man waved, but Payne's remark disconcerted him. If only the editor knew how often he doubted his own abilities—and how inadequate and downright helpless he felt in certain areas of his life, notably his home life.

Still, he had never forgotten Payne's lecture about careless writing, and how it might fix some grammatical error in the mind of a man who trusted you to be correct. He thought a similar principle applied here. The *Union* would not promote sympathy for a thief.

"Of course I'll accept it, Theo. On one condition." Gideon smiled. "That you go over these, and if you agree with my thoughts on the Kansas City piece, ask Sal Brown to take another crack."

"I certainly shall."

Back at the paper, Gideon went into a long session with the circulation manager. When the meeting ended, his watch showed three o'clock. Dawes should be coming in soon.

He wanted to ask the drama critic a question about George Aiken's dramatization of *Uncle Tom's Cabin*. The play had first been produced by the resident acting company at the Troy Museum upstate, shortly after Mrs. Stowe's influential novel was published. A year later, in 1853, Aiken's revised six-act version had been brought to New York City—again with not one penny of royalty going to Mrs. Stowe. Loosely drawn copyright legislation permitted playwrights to pilfer any published work they chose.

Since '53, the Aiken play had been staged hundreds of times. The productions ranged from spartan to opulent. After the war the play's popularity had remained undiminished. Even today scores of companies were always out in the provinces playing Tom shows, as productions were called.

Gideon had only seen one version, but it had been a lavish one. Julia had taken him to it in Cleveland. He could never forget the scenic effects, especially Uncle Tom's ascension to Heaven in a gilded car at the final curtain, and the thrilling picture created by live bloodhounds pursuing Eliza across the ice in the Ohio River scene. The bloodhounds were an interpolation by the producers, Julia said. She'd seen two other versions which didn't use dogs, and thus assumed they weren't specified in the text.

Although the play, like the novel, was fundamentally an abolitionist tract, it was nearly as popular in the South as in the North. Gideon supposed it was because in some respects, the drama pandered to, and even reinforced, stereotyped ideas about nigras. Audiences tended to ignore the fiercely militant and freedom-loving George Harris, Eliza's husband, and fix on the other black characters. But even the resigned and deeply religious Uncle Tom would probably not be so objectionable to newly freed blacks as would Topsy, Gideon supposed. Topsy was a thoroughly shiftless and treacherous girl who delighted in tricking whites. Of course audiences found her grotesque misunderstandings of proper English to be hilarious—as the author intended.

Still, there was no getting around one fact. The play was undoubtedly the single most important social drama created in America so far in this century. At the same time, Gideon had found it a thunderingly good melodrama. Any girl interested in the literature of the theater ought to own a copy of Aiken's work—even if it did come to her from a former Confederate. That was the conclusion he'd reached when the idea popped into his head earlier. He couldn't imagine that Margaret would object. The play was on its way to becoming a classic.

He saw Billy Dawes come up the stairs from the street, and went to meet him at his desk.

"Hello, Gideon. What can I do for you?"

"Answer a question, Billy. Are there any printed texts of Aiken's Tom show available?"

"I could be wrong, but I don't think so. Nothing but prompt scripts for the actors."

"Could you get hold of one? In time for me to put it on a late train to Boston?"

"You mean a late train tonight?"

"Yes."

"That's a tall order."

"Draw any amount of money you need."

Dawes grinned. "You just shortened the order considerably. I have friends in most of the playhouses. I'll see what I can do. Will Mr. Payne think I'm malingering?"

He glanced toward the cubicle in which Payne could be heard chastising Staniels, the city editor, for what Payne considered poor opening paragraphs on several recent stories.

"I'll keep him occupied," Gideon promised. "Will you get started?"

"Right away."

Gideon next wrote his telegraph message to Kent and Son, Boston. Dana Hughes wired back that it was a difficult assignment, but if Gideon could put the prompt script on a midnight express, a representative of the publishing house would meet the train, all regular work would be set aside in the type shop, pressroom and bindery, and the special order would be delivered by the requested date.

Hughes' message concluded by asking what Gideon had heard about Mr. Matthew Kent's participation in the historical project.

Nothing, Gideon realized with a glance at a calendar. Another day had gone by without a letter or cable. Where the hell was his brother? In hiding in order to finish some important piece of work?

Gideon decided he was either growing old, or growing

conservative, or both, because he certainly didn't understand the mind of someone like Matt any longer. He didn't
even have much of a desire to try.

iv

True to his word, Hughes had the finished, one-of-a-kind
book in Gideon's hands by three o'clock on the afternoon
of Eleanor's birthday.

Gideon had been warned that the special edition might
cost as much as a thousand dollars by the time all charges
were in. But he thought the price was worth it—especially
when he unwrapped the layers of paper and protective wad-
ding and examined the finished volume.

It was an oversized edition, bound in rich, maroon-dyed
leather and elegantly stamped in gold. The title of the work
as well as Aiken's name and that of Mrs. Stowe glittered
on the spine together with the Kent and Son colophon,
the half-filled tea bottle. The vellum smelled new. So did
the leather.

The text had been set with a ragged right margin, in
twelve-point type, generously leaded. It made for a bulky
book but Gideon liked the effect. He immediately sent
Hughes a telegraph message expressing his pleasure and
his thanks.

He left the *Union* at six, over the protests of Payne, who
wanted to have supper at the tavern and discuss a series of
forthcoming articles on the country's continuing economic
woes. "Tomorrow night," Gideon promised, and scooted
for the staircase with the gift tucked under his arm.

The gift looked beautiful. One of the copy boys who
aspired to be an editorial artist had claimed he was good
at fixing up fancy presents. The beribboned package which
he'd returned to Gideon's desk had proved it. And earned
the boy five dollars on top of the cost of the wrapping
materials.

Gideon's carriage clipped north along Fifth Avenue. He
was genuinely excited about the evening ahead. With luck
it might be one of the happiest in the household in years.

Again he blessed Julia for urging him to make the effort
to create that happiness. She was far wiser than he, but he

was beginning to learn again that kindness and patience brought greater rewards than anger.

A spring sky of pale yellow spread above Central Park. Black thunderclouds were rolling in from the northwest. Through the open window of the carriage he felt the chilly brush of an approaching storm wind. Soon the first drops of what might be a downpour thumped the carriage roof. But no storm could dampen his enthusiasm for the coming celebration—or the sheer joy of being able to go home to children he loved.

The carriage swung into Sixty-first Street, then into the yard at the rear of the mansion. He said a cheerful goodbye to Mills and, with the package tucked under the left side of his coat, started inside. At the back door he remembered something, turned and called, "Was the train on time?"

The coachman booted the brake, shouted back through the rain and noisy gusts of wind, "What train, sir?"

"The train my wife sent you to meet this afternoon. Mrs. Kent's train from the Jersey shore." Raindrops splashed his forehead, oddly chill. "Didn't you go down to the ferry station where the passengers arrive?"

"No, sir, I didn't."

Ah God, Gideon thought as the rain trickled down his neck and dampened his collar. *She forgot again. Molly probably had to take a hack from the North River piers.*

Well, if that was the evening's only mishap, nothing would be lost. He composed himself and went inside. He took off his light checked MacFarlan with its separate sleeve capes and his matching brown beaver hat. The butler, Samuel, juggled those and the wrapped package as Gideon rubbed a palm over his hair, which he now parted in the middle and groomed with Macassar oil, as most men did.

"I suppose Mrs. Kent arrived from Jersey in good order?" he said with a smile.

"The elder Mrs. Kent, sir?"

Gideon nodded.

"Is she supposed to attend the celebration?" Samuel asked.

"She is."

"Then I'm sorry to report that she's late."

"You mean to say she isn't here?"

"No, sir. I wasn't even aware she was expected."

"My wife didn't inform you?"

"No, nor cook either. Only four places are set in the dining room, not five—" Samuel's voice trailed off. He was addressing the master's retreating back.

Gideon went up the staircase two steps at a time, heading straight for Margaret's room. A scowl marred his face. His earlier mood of anticipation was gone.

CHAPTER XVI

HOUSE OF MADNESS

i

GIDEON KNOCKED ON Margaret's door. She refused to let him in. Instead, she opened the door and quickly slipped outside. Their reflections were dim and distorted in the rain-speckled window at the end of the corridor.

At least she'd remembered to dress properly. In fact she looked quite pretty in a gown of tan faille silk with a white taffeta drapery. The dress had a pointed train decorated with bow knots from the peak of the bustle downward. She'd completed the ensemble with white slippers and an arrangement of aigrettes and white ostrich tips in her hair.

"What did you want, Gideon?"

For a moment he saw the woman he'd once loved so fiercely. All the old memories helped him speak with a degree of control.

"I wanted to ask about Molly. Where is she?"

"Why, I have no idea. Down at Long Branch, I suppose."

"She was planning to join us this evening."

Margaret looked puzzled. "Are you sure?"

His stomach began to ache. "You were the one who suggested it, Margaret."

Her confusion deepened. "I? Gideon, I'm very sorry, but I have no recollection of that."

She blinked once, then again. Through the mask of her perfume he whiffed whiskey all at once.

He continued to study her by the light of the hissing gas fixtures. Continued to search for signs of the lie that was always so easy to detect in Eleanor. God help him, Margaret seemed *sincere*.

"You don't recall saying you'd send Molly a note of invitation?"

"No, because I never said it," she answered in an ingenuous voice. One plump white hand plucked at the décolletage of the gown. She seldom dressed so finely any more; she was ill at ease.

"I'm sure I didn't," she said, smiling at him in an almost infantile way. A stir of air moved the bedroom door. The latch clicked and the door opened an inch or so. She reached behind her to close it, but not before she smelled the staleness. Didn't she ever ventilate the place?

He forced himself to speak softly. "I see. I must have misunderstood."

"I hope you're not accusing me of another lapse—"

"No, no." He touched her arm to reassure her. She jerked away. His jaw whitened a moment. Then: "It's my fault. Entirely mine. Now if you'll excuse me, I must change. I'll join you downstairs."

He turned and hurried away, no longer angry but alarmed. He kept seeing her forlorn, vacant eyes. She'd forgotten again!

He shut the door of his room and leaned against it. For a moment he felt a remarkable kinship with Thomas Courtleigh. Kinship, and sympathy for him as well. He understood the agony Courtleigh must have gone through because of his wife—the agony of wanting to help and being unable.

What was wrong inside that poor head of Margaret's? Was it the frustration of not being able to control him? The damaging effects of the drinking? Some unknown flaw inherited from her father? Was it one cause, or several? Who could explain? Who could help?

He shook his head in despair. There were no answers.

ii

Silver candelabra all along the table lent the dining room a festive air. Yet somehow Gideon knew the evening was foredoomed.

Margaret was the last to arrive. She swept through the entrance and flung a pettish look in his direction. His inquiry about Molly, and the implied accusation of faulty memory, had obviously put her in a bad mood.

He had an impulse to flee and seek sanctuary in the parlor, where the servants were kindling a fire now that the spring air had turned sharply cooler with the coming of rain. He would have done that, except for Eleanor.

She, too, was wearing her best dress, a gown of velvet. She looked radiant, and far older than the fourteen years they were celebrating.

Both children sensed the tension between their parents. Eleanor tried to keep the conversation lively and inconsequential, chattering about events at Miss Holsham's while the soup course was served. Will wiggled in his chair, repeatedly pulling at the tight, high-standing collar and scarf cravat he'd been forced to wear. When he picked up his spoon to dip into the turtle soup, he was so nervous the spoon fell and clanged against the silver tureen. Margaret gave him a withering look. Despite encouragement from Gideon, he didn't try to taste the soup again. He sat rigid, darting apprehensive glances at his mother.

She didn't taste the soup either. When the serving girls came to clear away the tureens, Margaret pushed hers away so sharply, soup splattered all over the spotless tablecloth. Eleanor kept her gaze confined to her own place.

As the next course arrived, Will screwed up courage to ask his father if the paper had received any new dispatches from the Dakota Territory, where the army was mounting a punitive expedition against the Sioux. Thoughts of soldiers and Indians could always overcome Will's fear and put a sparkle back in his eyes—but Margaret quickly took care of that by slapping the table.

"Kindly do not bring up such distasteful subjects at this table!"

Gently, Gideon said, "He didn't mean any harm, Margaret." She just glared.

Will had already shrunk back against his chair. Reluctantly Gideon turned to him. "Let's try to honor your mother's wishes." The boy was almost pathetic in his haste to nod. *God,* Gideon thought, *how many more times can he be defeated without being ruined for life? Not many, I fear.*

Mercifully, the meal was quickly eaten. They reached the sherbet and the plates of fruit and cheese in thirty minutes. Gideon sensed that Eleanor had hurried deliberately, perhaps wanting to get them to what might be happier surroundings. But for all its warmth, and for all the cheerful light generated by the gas and the flickering wood fire, the parlor too seemed to lie under a pall—the pall of Margaret's dour and volatile presence.

Gideon strode to the mantel where the important family keepsakes were displayed: the small, stoppered green bottle containing an eighth of an inch of dried tea and, hanging on pegs above, the French infantry sword and the Kentucky long rifle. The portrait of the man who had collected the mementoes hung on the opposite wall.

Philip Kent's picture had been commissioned after the Revolution. By then he'd been in his late thirties, affluent and conservative. Yet the painted image had a youthful vitality, as if a pugnacious street urchin was hiding just behind the face of the splendidly dressed adult.

Gideon stared at the portrait a moment. He was Philip Kent's heir—and that meant being spiritual heir to some of the strength which seemed to radiate from the canvas. He drew a breath, resolving again to make the evening a good one.

Eleanor settled herself, arranging her skirts. Will ran in, then skidded to a stop when he saw Margaret's reproving eyes. Very cautiously, he advanced to stand beside his sister. He pulled his hand from behind his back, thrust something at Eleanor and blurted, "I-hope-you-like-it-I-know-you-won't-but-you-know-I-don't-have-a-big-allowance."

Gideon laughed at the breathless words. Sheepish, Will looked at his father. Gideon summoned him to his side with a smile and the boy gratefully went. Gideon slid his hand around Will's shoulder as Eleanor examined her brother's gift—a clear jar containing a dead frog afloat in brine.

From the protection of his father's side, Will added, "I caught him over in the Park. Gigged him to death myself."

"How repulsive," Margaret said. "Don't ever bring such a thing into this house again."

"Please, Mama," Eleanor whispered, sounding almost desperate. "It's a—very interesting present. I'll treasure it, Will."

Her cheeks were the color Gideon had mentally dubbed Fibbing Pink. Eleanor's kindness shamed Margaret. The older woman said in a lame way, "Yes, I must remember that the intent always counts more than the gift itself—"

No one commented. Will looked relieved. He didn't realize his sister had been employing her acting talent. Thank goodness for that, Gideon thought.

An instantaneous change took place when Margaret became the center of attention. She was cheerful, almost jolly. She made an elaborate show of stealing out to a foyer closet and returning with several beautifully wrapped boxes. The boxes contained an assortment of scarves and two dressy hats, one of which was decorated with artificial flowers and a long plume dyed brilliant blue. She proudly announced that the gifts were imported from Paris. They pleased Eleanor.

Then it was Gideon's turn. He reached under a divan and pulled out the package. Eleanor unwrapped it, glanced at the gilt lettering and caught her breath in surprise and delight.

Margaret leaned forward in her chair. "What is it, dear? It looks frightfully expensive."

"Yes, Mama, indeed it does."

"Don't worry. We got a special discount," Gideon said with a nervous smile. "I had it printed and bound at the firm in Boston."

Eleanor added, "It's a deluxe edition of *Uncle Tom's Cabin,* Mama."

Gideon hoped that would end it. If Margaret had taken a stiff dose of her tonic after dinner, it might have. But she was sober—and curious. She picked up her train and walked to where her daughter was seated. Gideon held his breath.

Margaret bent forward. "The Stowe woman's novel?

Why would you give her that, Gideon? Why on earth would you spend money to bind up that piece of Yankee trash?"

Even as her mother was speaking, Eleanor was closing the book to conceal the text. But she wasn't fast enough. The arrangement of the page finally registered on Margaret. "Let me see that." She snatched the book and tore it open. "It's a play. It's the play version."

Silence. A small log broke in the grate. Rain pelted the windows.

"I saw no harm—" Gideon began.

"You did this to defy me."

"Please control yourself. I did it because Eleanor is interested in—"

"To *defy* me!" Margaret repeated, shaking the book at him. Eleanor reached for her mother, perhaps hoping to calm things with a touch. Margaret saw the outstretched hand and slashed downward with her right arm, nearly striking her daughter. Eleanor drew her hand back and covered her mouth.

Gideon was desperately struggling for patience. "There is no harm in books, Margaret. Not in any book, whether it be a play or—"

"But you know I won't permit this kind of thing in my home, this"—her voice was growing steadily shriller—"this kind of filth. Anything connected with the theater is filthy. Obscene and filthy!" She flung the book into the fireplace.

Eleanor uttered a cry and leaped to retrieve the book. Gideon shot out his hand to bar her. "Please don't."

"But, Papa!" She slipped under his arm and knelt on the hearth.

"Don't, Eleanor." With effort he lowered his voice. "Let it burn. I'll buy you something more acceptable."

She looked at him, then at the book. The paper was charring, the leather wrinkling. Bright flames surrounding it made the tears in her eyes sparkle.

"Papa, I don't see anything wrong with owning a dramatization of a famous—"

"Let it burn!"

Quite without wanting to, he had shouted at her. She showed greater self-restraint. She rose, smoothed her skirt and stepped back from a sudden eruption of fire. The paper in the open book ignited and quickly disappeared into curls of black ash. The leather darkened. Gideon wiped his perspiring upper lip and said, "I really thought there was no harm in a book, no matter what its origins. I was in error. I'm sorry." It took immense effort to add, "I also apologize to you, Margaret."

She sneered. "Why do you bother? You did exactly what you wanted and you'll do the same thing again. You always do whatever you want."

With a thin smile distorting her mouth, she marched back to her chair. Will had ducked behind a divan when the book was thrown. Now he reappeared, returned to Gideon's side and clasped his hand.

"Don't feel bad, Papa. Maybe you can buy Eleanor a present in Philadelphia if we ever go there. We're all really sorry we can't go next month because you have to work so hard writing up those political meetings."

"Can't go?" Gideon blinked. He turned and looked at Margaret, who was gazing at her son as if she wanted to wipe him off the earth. "But it's your mother's illness that—"

He bit off the sentence. He was beginning to understand. At first it frightened him. Then it made him pale with fury.

"Children—Eleanor—" His voice was barely controlled. "I'm sorry to spoil the party, but I must speak to your mother alone. Please leave us."

Eleanor and her brother exchanged hesitant looks.

"I said please leave!"

For a second Eleanor seemed ready to protest. But she herded Will out ahead of her and, with her head bowed, closed the parlor doors. Instantly, Gideon stormed toward his wife.

"What have you been saying to those children behind my back? You—and Dr. Melton's advice—forced the cancellation of the trip." He grabbed her wrist. "Have you been saying otherwise, Margaret?" He shook the flabby white arm. *"Have you?"*

She struggled. "Don't do that. Let me go—"

His voice overlapped hers. "What else have you been telling them? I should have guessed long ago that you were up to something like this. Will's always looking hurt—Eleanor's always angry with me—"

Able to contain his rage at last, he released her and

stepped away. Something turned in his mind like a key turning in a lock. The drinking hadn't affected her as much as he'd thought. Her lapses of memory were cold-blooded shams designed to annoy and harass him. She might go to the liquor cabinet too often, but she was more scheming than sick—and far more bloated with the pus of hate than he'd ever suspected.

"I'd like to know," he said, "just how many lies you've put into their heads."

The pudgy white fingers of her left hand trembled as they rose to her other arm, and massaged it. "You hurt me."

"And what have you been trying to do to me with your falsehoods, your deceptions? You've used my own children—and yours—as the instruments of your animosity. My God, what a wretched creature you've become."

His voice dropped, hoarse with pain. "You'll find it understandable if I'm no longer able to stay in this house with you."

He trembled, because he understood the enormous significance of what he'd just said. He had severed all but the last tie binding them together.

Well, so be it. Painful as it was, he'd endure it. Anything was preferable to trying to live in a house ruled by a mind as sick and twisted as hers.

He started for the doors. He heard a faint creak. Someone was outside, leaning against one of the panels and listening. "You hurt me," Margaret repeated as he rattled the handles to warn the eavesdropper. A moment later he opened the doors.

Although the gas was lit in the foyer, it was trimmed low, and shadows clotted the corners, Eleanor stood two paces from the doorway. Her face showed confusion.

Behind Gideon, Margaret rubbed her arm so her daughter would be sure to see. This time she shrieked, "You hurt me, damn you!"

"She's tricked you, Eleanor," he said. It almost tore him apart to say that about the woman he'd once loved. The sound of his own voice was a roar in his ears, as though winds of unbelievable force were rending the earth. "She's lied about me. Repeatedly, it seems."

"Papa, be kind," Eleanor whispered. "She isn't herself tonight."

"She hasn't been herself for years. She's beyond help. I can't stay here any longer, Eleanor. She despises my work and she despises me. She's been determined to penalize me ever since I made it clear I wouldn't give in to her every whim." He extended his hand. "Please try to see my side for a change—"

Eleanor dashed tears away and stepped out of reach. Gideon felt as if his outstretched hand was covered with filth.

"I see a woman who needs support and love," Eleanor said. "And I see you walking out on her."

"I can do her no good at all. If anyone can—if it isn't already too late—it's a doctor in some sanitarium for—"

"I'm not going anywhere!" Margaret screamed at him. "I'm perfectly fine. I don't need a doctor, as you so snidely declare all the time!"

Gideon kept his eye on his daughter. She was the one most urgently in need of saving: she and her brother.

"I can't let you and Will stay here. I'll consult a lawyer. We'll find a way to get you both out of—"

"I'm staying, Papa. No matter what else has happened, she needs us."

He wasn't strong enough, or, God help him, compassionate enough just then to respond to Eleanor's plea. A part of his mind acknowledged the rightness of her words. But he was much too angry to let that part have any influence. Too angry, humiliated and worn-out.

It all burst forth in another shout, "She doesn't need me!"

"She does."

"No!"

"Well, she must have once—were you here then?"

I was with Julia.

"Goddamn it, she drove me out! She hates me!"

"And can you say you've never given her cause, Papa? Can you say that?"

The blazing accusation made him recall how Julia had pointed out his own unconscious withdrawal from the family. He thought of how he'd increasingly come to depend on the *Union* as a refuge without even being aware of it. His daughter's scornful eyes were like mirrors showing him all his flaws, and there was no way on God's earth he could in conscience answer, "No." He could only say in a shaken voice, "I'm sorry I ruined your birthday."

He ran up the stairs two at a time. In his room he collected a hat, outercoat and valise, and a few moments later walked out the front door into the darkness of Fifth Avenue.

By then Margaret had undergone a remarkable transformation. She was composed, with no trace of her earlier hysteria showing save some redness around her eyes.

She took Will into the protective curve of her left arm. He stood rigid, afraid to move. Eleanor faced her mother, fighting back tears. None of them did more than start slightly when the front door slammed, and none of them moved to the windows to see which direction Gideon had taken in the rainstorm.

Will turned his head that way, but Margaret pulled him tight against her side and held him there. Eleanor covered her eyes and began to cry. With no one to see, Margaret permitted her mouth to set into a small, satisfied smile.

iii

From the night Gideon moved out, Margaret became the household's unquestioned ruler. That fact seemed to restore some clarity to her mind. Only forty-eight hours after her husband's departure, she spoke with the butler behind closed doors.

"I want to make doubly sure you bring me the mail as each post arrives, Samuel. Bring it to my room. If there's no answer when you knock, slip everything under the door. I want to see it all before anyone else does."

"Certainly, Mrs. Kent," the butler murmured.

"And don't mention this conversation to another person. If you should do so by accident, your job will be forfeit. Do you understand what I'm saying?"

"Perfectly, madam." His expression left some doubt that he really did, though. Nevertheless, he added, "There'll be no slips."

Margaret smiled. "For the sake of your seven children, I hope you're right."

She'd spoken to Samuel none too soon. Next day, the

afternoon delivery contained an envelope addressed to Eleanor in Gideon's handwriting. Margaret tore it open and went into a rage as she read her husband's blatant attempt to win Eleanor away from her. Gideon wanted his daughter to come down to the *Union* as soon as possible, so that he could speak with her and prove that it wasn't advisable for her or for Will to remain in the house. When the worst of Margaret's wrath had passed, she tucked the letter into a pigeonhole in the secretary in her bedroom. The pigeonhole was large, roomy enough for many more letters.

For a little while she felt very assured. Very much in control. But she had other moments when she didn't think she could remain conscious one second longer. During those moments she thought of her children and of how she'd manipulated their emotions in order to turn them against their father. Accompanying the recollections was a terrible guilt. She even had moments of total lucidity in which she was ashamed of what she'd done to Gideon himself. Those moments were rare, though.

As the days went by, her swings between euphoria and depression became more frequent and pronounced. She had a tonic bottle in her possession every waking hour. The damnable guilt began to pervade her mind so completely, sometimes she felt controlled by it.

On June 25 there occurred an event which did not help her mental balance, even though it had nothing to do with her personally. That day, out in the Dakota Territory along a river the Sioux called the Greasy Grass, the famed boy general of the Civil War, George A. Custer, led a Seventh Cavalry column to disaster. He and 265 of his men were massacred.

Two fundamental errors on Custer's part were responsible for the slaughter. One was his decision to fight when he was under orders to await the main army force moving up to join him. The other was his decision to divide his single column into two. Part of his command survived, but not Custer and those with him. They were surrounded and killed by two thousand or more Sioux under their battle leader, Chief Crazy Horse. The Indians wanted revenge for the invasion of their tribal lands by the white gold hunters. They found that revenge when they found the blue-clad soldiers who had come to legalize the theft by force.

For days, no one in the East spoke of anything but what the press christened the Little Big Horn massacre. All the papers were filled with long dispatches about it. In secret, Will read every account he could get his hands on. So did Margaret. She went over and over the ghastly details in her mind without understanding why.

The news stories produced a strange new anxiety within her. At night, as she fell into the alcoholic stupor which now passed for sleep, the last images in her mind were war-painted faces and shiny scalp knives wet with blood.

Certain passages in her diary began to reflect her disturbed condition. Five days after the Custer massacre was front-page news, she wrote:

> —*I do not know why I must feel so terrible all the time. HE is the one—*

She paused to ink her pen, then raked the nib horizontally beneath the capitalized word.

> —*who is guilty, HE, HE, HE, HE, HE—*

Even as she printed the word over and over, the guilt battered her. It wasn't true. She knew it wasn't true. She was the guilty one. She drank more tonic. It didn't help.

She wanted to cry out, scream. Instead, she wrote faster and faster, as if some exterior force had taken possession of her hand and was operating it like a piece of machinery. She lifted the pen and began to slash more lines beneath the fourteen repetitions of the word *HE*.

She stumbled to her feet, slashing so hard she tore the paper. Her chair crashed over, then the brown bottle. Loose hair tumbled into her eyes. Her face contorted, sweaty and anguished as she raked the pen back and forth, back and forth.

Like a dagger. Like a sword. Trying to obliterate. Trying to destroy.

Inside her head, a voice said, *You are the guilty one.*

With a cry she fell backward, fainting.

When she awoke hours later, she was amazed and frightened to discover her dress was spotted with ink. The tonic bottle lay on its side on the carpet, in the center of a soaked place two feet wide. Her diary was open to pages that were now nothing but shreds of paper. Shreds stained with crude, fantastically shaped blots of ink that had flown from the slashing pen.

She had no recollection of how any of that disorder had come about.

iv

A few nights later, about one in the morning, Eleanor heard an outcry from the stairway landing.

She jumped out of bed, hurried along the hall and stopped short at the head of the stairs. Then, uttering a soft "Oh," she rushed down to the source of the cry.

In her nightdress, Margaret was crouched by the leaded window on the landing. The window overlooked Fifth Avenue and Central Park. From high above the Park, the moon bleached the tops of black trees.

Margaret turned and peered at her daughter. For a moment her eyes showed no recognition. Eleanor almost gagged at the cloying odor of the tonic. Margaret raised a cautioning finger.

"Sssh. They're watching the house."

Eleanor felt icy. "Watching?"

"Yes. They're over in those trees."

"Who, Mama?"

"Men. I don't know their names. They've been put there for an hour. I heard them calling my name and came to look. Keep your eyes open and you'll see the men dart between the tree trunks."

"Mama, there's no one over in Central Park at this hou—"

"The men are *there,* Eleanor!" She gazed into her daughter's eyes, entreating her to believe. She acted afraid to speak above a whisper. "They were sent to hurt me."

Eleanor shivered. Despite all the things she'd said on the night her father left, she found herself wishing he were in the house. If there were a real emergency, she didn't even know where he was staying. He hadn't bothered to communicate with her, or with Will. Not so much as a note.

"Who sent them, Mama?"

"I don't know, but they've come to punish me, just the way the Indians punished poor General Custer."

Eleanor couldn't believe what she was hearing. "Punish you like—? What makes you say such things? Who would come here wanting to punish you? No one."

"You're wrong. They're over there. I swear they are. I've seen them. I heard them mocking my name. Daring me to come out, but I won't. I won't."

She turned huge, horrified eyes toward the moon-drenched Park. There in the peaceful silver and shadow of the landing, Eleanor at last realized Gideon had been right about one thing. All the stimulants her mother consumed were hurting her. For the first time, she began to fear for her mother's sanity.

CHAPTER XVII

VOYAGER

i

TOWARD THE END, she always began to swear like a slut from one of the London rookeries. But they were seventy-odd miles from that sort of squalor, sporting in a moon-dappled bed on sheets of satin.

She squeezed him with her plump pink legs like a rider clinging to a horse. Her name was Armina, Duchess of Tichfield. She was seven years older than he, with practiced hands and big, soft breasts—altogether one of the most blithely amoral women he'd ever met. Sometimes that shocked a part of him that had never quite grown out of a Virginia boyhood centered around Sunday church and daily devotions.

He should have enjoyed what they were doing. In terms of pure physical sensation, he did. Yet as he felt the end approaching, a sadness overcame him in that sumptuous bedroom above an English garden drowsing in the summer night. A sadness, and a sense of futility.

The Duchess had yellow curls, and blue eyes, and in certain lights a marked resemblance to Dolly.

"Matt, oh my God, love, go on, *go on, damn you*!" Then she became completely incoherent except for her cursing.

Her husband the Duke had had a foot blown away while serving with the artillery in the Crimea. She liked to tease Matt by forming a little circle with her thumb and forefinger, slipping it around one of his fingers and rubbing it back and forth while she winked and said the Duke had gone to the Crimea and lost his foot and the iron in his rammer, too. At the moment he was up in town, occupied with his endless speculation in consols, or with some business pertaining to his seat in the House of Lor—

No. That was wrong, a peripheral part of Matt's mind warned him suddenly. He stopped the lovemaking, bracing on his elbows with his rump cocked high in the air. The Duchess protested in purple language. For a moment all he could see, through his inner eye, was an image of himself poised above her with his fundament bare in the breeze. It was another splendid lesson on the unintentionally funny attitudes the pretentious human beast fell into. But he had no time to really savor the picture.

He twisted his head toward the foyer of the bedchamber. Was the bolt securely shot? Armina had been so warm to have him tear away her underskirts and corset, she'd said there was no need. But now he heard a fuss and clatter in the hall, and his quickening heartbeat told him there was.

"Matt, damn you, why have you left me in the absolute bloody middle of—?"

"Sssh!" He moved erratically, nearly jabbing his own eye when he jerked a finger to his lips. Perspiration beaded and cooled in his mustache. "Can't you hear all that?" He meant the servants chattering, trying to warn their mistress, and the *frumph-frumph* of a man repeatedly clearing his throat.

"God save us, it's the old bugger himself," the Duchess whispered. She giggled.

"I'm glad you find it so amusing," Matt snapped as he disengaged and started to slide off the bed on the side where he thought his pants and smallclothes lay. His bare foot slipped. He landed on his rump. The hall door, unbolted, smashed open. A huge shadow—a beaky head, an arm, a jutting pistol—was flung across the bedroom wall by a multitude of lights in jiggling candle-brackets.

"Show your face, you cuckolding bastard!" the Duke of

Tichfield shouted in his phlegmy voice, and things were comical no longer.

Matt didn't bother with his drawers. He jumped to his feet, jerked on his pants and flung a glance toward the open French windows overlooking the garden perfumed with roses. Some instinct said that if he ran that way, a bullet would find his back.

In desperation, he chose the surprise of a frontal assault. He doubled his shoulder as one barrel of the old-fashioned pistol discharged, spitting smoke and sparks. The Duchess shrieked and slid down in bed and yanked a sheet over her face. The ball whistled over Matt's lowered head and thunked into the wall. The Duke took more careful aim.

Matt ran like a demon, outraged by circumstances. *A promising career may be cut short here, damn it!*

He charged in beneath the muzzle the Duke was attempting to reposition for a close-range shot. His bare shoulder hit the Duke's waistcoated paunch. The pistol thundered. Something—powder?—stung his cheek, and he actually felt the bullet or ball scorch past his ear as he knocked his would-be murderer head over trousers into the wall. The Duke fell with a yelp of pain. Matt kicked the pistol away from the Duke's clutching fingers.

The Duke's right leg seemed bent at the knee, and his calf and boot folded beneath him in an unnatural way. That evidently accounted for the Duke's steerlike bellows. Matt had to shout to be heard.

"Toss me my shirt, Armina."

It came sailing from the far side of the bed. "I don't know why he came back unexpectedly—" The Duchess' apologetic cry was barely audible above the caterwauling. Matt shoved his shirt into his waistband and swung toward the blinding spread of candle-flame. Men in the dark behind the small haloed lights were voices without substance.

"Don't let him through, Alf!"

"Listen 'ere, Lysander, his lordship don't deserve no favors from me, the nasty old son of a bitch. This way, laddie—"

One of the candelabra appeared to float aside. A dark portal opened in the wall of light. Matt sprinted through it, and on to the staircase, and the main floor, and then the white and black of the moonlit summer midnight.

He ran so hard his chest hurt. He ran till he felt he couldn't run any more, but he did. A sudden cloud hid the moon and he didn't see the stable wall until he bounced off it like a ball of India rubber.

Inside, rubbing his dizzy head, he roused a stable boy and demanded a saddled horse. The boy had seen Matt around the estate on other occasions and knew he was the Duchess' current lover, so there was no quibble. But the boy's eyes rolled when he heard alarms from the great house. All at once he acted uncertain about releasing the horse.

"Sounds like 'is lordship's callin' for you to 'old up, sir."

"You're mistaken," Matt barked, shoved the boy backwards over a hay bale, and fairly leaped into the saddle.

He kicked the animal with his bare heels and went galloping away through a barricade of wildly swinging lanterns, a storm of oaths and the roar of an old fowling piece. If his head hadn't been down over the neck of the racing horse, it would have been shot away.

But desperation carried the evening, and Matt was soon clattering north through the Kentish countryside, wondering why he indulged in such stupid escapades. Affairs with married women were frequently dangerous and always futile.

The trouble was, whenever he met a woman who reminded him of Dolly, he wanted her. In fact the only women with whom he trifled were those who resembled Dolly in one way or another. He'd realized it consciously only a couple of years ago.

The realization hadn't put a stop to the behavior, though. He continued to chase women who were always Dolly and could never be Dolly. He did it, he supposed, because she was the only true love of his life, and because she was forever lost to him. He knew she was lost because, when she wrote to him, she refused to make reference to lines in his letters in which he begged her to come back.

Her letters were friendly, polite, full of news of India and her teaching and of their son. But they contained not so much as a grain of sentimentality. If she felt any, she hid it. So his pursuit went on.

With each woman, he hoped anew. With each he was disappointed and saddened. He supposed the pattern would keep repeating until he withered into senility or got shot to death by some outraged husband whose aim was better than the Duke's. What a damned depressing future, he thought as he jogged on through the moonlight toward London.

ii

Two nights later, Matt went to Jim Whistler's for supper. His friend was in a lather about a new commission he'd received. He was to redecorate part of the Hyde Park town house belonging to his patron Frederick Leyland.

Leyland was a self-made shipping tycoon from Liverpool. His mother had once hawked meat pies in the streets of that city, and the man was inordinately proud of his rise in the world. He threw fistfuls of money around to dramatize it—and as part of this largesse, he'd given Whistler permission to refurbish the town house dining room.

Whistler had known Mr. and Mrs. Leyland for some time. He'd painted stunning full-length portraits of the couple in '73. There were gossips who said the artist was more interested in Leyland's wife than in his money though.

The new commission had developed in an unusual way. Whistler's painting called *La Princess du Pays de la Porcelaine* already hung in the Leyland dining room. The artist had complained that the setting was all wrong for the picture. Very well, Leyland replied, create the right sort of setting.

Whistler had instantly accepted the offer. Perhaps for more than artistic reasons; Matt knew his friend was still seeing Mrs. Leyland. He didn't bring that up during supper, though. Whistler's newest mistress was also at the table.

Whistler enlivened the meal by showing and discoursing on his sketches for tall window shutters in the dining room. Great fan-tailed birds done in gilt would decorate each one. He'd already settled on a basic color scheme of blue and gold, and referred to the project as his "peacock room."

The new mistress seemed somewhat impatient with him, uninterested in peacocks or the Leylands. She tended to be haughtier than the departed Jo, but Matt had observed that she had Jo's reddish hair. Perhaps Whistler, too, pursued and loved only one woman.

The thoroughly enjoyable evening was spoiled when Matt got back to his quarters. His landlady presented him with a note that had arrived by messenger while he was out. He recognized Armina's handwriting. The landlady then said four gentlemen, well dressed but quite unfriendly, had called and asked for him. He didn't understand who they could be until he retired to his rooms and read the note from the Duchess. The essential passage said:

> *He is incapacitated with a broken bone, but rants that the moment he is up again, he will kill you. I think he is just enough of a silly fool to attempt it, my dearest— or to persuade some of his army cronies to do it for him. Britain is not safe for you for a few months, I think. Have no fear for my well being. As long as the old curmudgeon wants to keep me around him like an expensive watch fob ornament, he knows he daren't lift a hand near me—except, of course, to present me with some little bauble or other. Lovers, alas, are not so favored. Do be careful, and make haste to leave if you can possibly do so.*

He read the note twice more, thought of his landlady's description of the quartet of callers, and made up his mind. What the hell was there to keep him in England anyway? Nothing.

As he was packing a portmanteau and considering where he might take a holiday, his eye fell on Gideon's letter.

In it, his brother had described some nonsensical project involving a lot of quick sketches of Americans baking bread and threshing wheat and potting at the redcoats on Breed's Hill a hundred years ago. Patriotic twaddle. Or commercialism inspired by the American centennial, he didn't know which.

He had no intention of lending himself to such an infantile project. But, unexpectedly, he realized he had a strong desire to see his brother again. Talk with him. Find out how he was faring with his family, and with the newspaper. Perhaps it was because he felt rootless now that the affair with the Duchess was over. They'd enjoyed an intense

month and a half together—so intense, he hadn't had time
to answer Gideon's letter or do any work except for some
pornographic sketches of aspects of Armina's naked body.
He'd presented her with one of the sketches and locked
the rest in a closet.

He definitely had no desire to see America again. Still,
as long as it was advisable for him to get out of England
for six months, he might as well pay that visit Gideon was
always writing him about.

He didn't care for the circumstances attending the departure. He had to race back to Whistler's next day to make
arrangements for shipping certain of his belongings, and for
forwarding of mail. He had to confer with his landlady, and
book passage—and do it all while skulking through obscure
courtyards and dingy mews, in case anyone was watching.

"Just like Paris all over," he grumbled, but it was not.
Dolly was far away in Lahore with their son Thomas, who
would be seven at the end of the year. She'd sent Matt a
small daguerreotype he treasured. Tom was turning out to
be a sturdy, handsome boy who resembled his mother. Matt
hoped his son didn't waste his life on some dog's profession, as Paul Cézanne so aptly called theirs. Where did
being a painter get you?—except into a sooty compartment
aboard a late train for the Southampton docks. A compartment where you sat alone, skulking like a damned fugitive.

A dog's profession, by God. No doubt about it.

iii

July storms plagued the uphill passage of the Nord-
deutscher Lloyd steamship *New York*, which had called at
Southampton to take on passengers. The Germans were
giving the Americans as well as the Cunard Steamship
Company fierce competition on the transatlantic run. But
the bad weather restricted the *New York*'s speed this trip.
She was fourteen days en route to a North American
landfall—some kind of record for slowness in this age of
steam, Matt thought on the morning they were supposed
to sight the coast of Maine.

He stood forward on the boat deck, awaiting the first
glimpse of land. Leaning into the wind at the rail, he cut a

dashing figure despite his wretched internal state. It was a steamy day, with the sun hidden behind a thin haze. Yet the sun's light was painfully evident in the metallic highlights on the slopes of the high waves. The light hurt his eyes. His head throbbed and his stomach ached.

Matt's shipboard conquest, Miss Trautwein of Omaha, was still asleep in her suite. She claimed to be a stockyards heiress, but this morning she was also a disappointed lover. Last night, after kissing her long blond hair and embracing her pale body for the last time, Matt had told her he was a married man.

Miss Trautwein threw things, then cried and said it didn't matter. But they'd parted anyway, at Matt's insistence. He'd paid the man on duty in the saloon bar to keep it open, and keep the whiskey flowing, so he could watch the sunrise while drunk. The sun didn't rise—visibly, anyway— and the barman fell asleep and all he could think of was how idiotic it was for a man to forever search for the same woman within different ones.

Now, several hours later, a short sleep and a shave had restored him at least outwardly. He looked trim, even natty, as he peered toward the west. He'd thrown on an assortment of summer clothes, but they fitted him well. His summer outfit, of the latest English fashion, consisted of a navy blue flannel jacket with breast pocket handkerchief, white flannels and sporty shoes of sailcloth and leather. A straw boater with a striped band was tilted over his forehead to keep the light out of his eyes and prevent an intensification of the headache.

He pondered what he'd do when he reached New York. His chief objective when he boarded the steamship was to take himself out of the Duke's reach until the old idiot came to his senses. He wasn't going *toward* anything, he was running *from*—and as a consequence, he didn't know how he'd occupy his time for the next month or so. Oh well, he'd think about it in New York. Probably there were blond, blue-eyed women there, too.

Of course there was always that book of Gideon's, nonsensical as it sounded.

He went below to his outside stateroom and rummaged in his belongings till he found the letter. Back on deck, he reread it. He'd forgotten all the pressures Gideon had applied. He was half angry, half amused.

"Save the family farm. Save the family honor. Save the country and come home to your brother's arms. You dirty bastard."

Several promenading ladies eyed him with alarm as he uttered these remarks to the open sea. He crumpled the letter into a ball and consigned it to the wind. It was carried far off to port, and plummeted out of sight between tall whitecaps.

"Are there any other heart wringers you could have used, Gid? I don't think so."

Suddenly the ship's whistle sounded. The noise nearly blew his head apart. Passengers crowded up on either side of him, pointing and exclaiming in English and German and several other languages.

The steamship was swinging to run parallel with the coast. Thus the thin, dark line smudged the starboard horizon. How featureless the coastline was there in the haze. How unforbidding compared to the nights he'd searched for it with one eye, and for Federal gun ships with the other.

America. He almost felt sentimental for a moment.

Then he sniffed, brushed his nose with a knuckle, and called himself a fool.

iv

From high at the rail of the *New York*, Matt saw his brother down on the teeming North River pier. Gideon waved. Matt grinned and tipped his summer hat.

All of his uneasiness about getting along with someone he hadn't seen for years—all his carefully marshaled arguments against joining Gideon in the publishing project—faded the moment he saw how pale and emaciated his brother looked. What had happened to him? The mere passage of time didn't explain such strain.

In the arrivals shed, Matt unfolded his passport. The customs official compared the man he saw with the one described on the sheet of parchment. Satisfied, he returned the document. "You may pass."

Gideon was waiting by an iron pillar beyond the barrier. Matt went straight to him.

"Matt."

"Gideon—good God—"

Neither of them could think of anything original to say. They hugged one another with fierce masculine affection, then separated, Gideon the soberly dressed businessman and Matt the picture of a dashing young sportsman.

Matt fanned himself with his boater and tapped a toe on the ground. "The sod of my native land. The Yankee part of it, anyway. Never thought I'd tread on it again."

"I can't say how happy I am that you are. I didn't think *100 Years* would really excite you."

"A hundred—? Oh, the book. Well—" Matt hesitated, unwilling to bring up bad news immediately.

"I did wonder why you took so long to give me your answer," Gideon said. "You never really did, you know." He sounded just a shade sententious, Matt thought. Probably that came of running a newspaper, and bossing people.

"Got very busy all at once," Matt evaded. "But I did spend a bundle to cable you from Southampton and tell you I was on the way."

"That you did. By God it's good to see you after so many years."

"I'm sorry I wasn't here when Pa died."

Gideon waved. "He'd have been buried a good two weeks by the time you caught a ship and got home. I think his death was an easy one—if any of them are ever easy. It was certainly quick. But let's not be so blasted gloomy. I have some good news. The Wilmington picture's attracting a lot of favorable comment at the exhibition. I've saved some articles by two of the leading critics."

"I hope they had nothing kind to say. That's bad luck for a painter. Among my friends in Paris, I think the only ones who are certain of lasting fame are the ones the public hates and the critics devastate. Paul Cézanne. Manet—"

Gideon interrupted. "You didn't finish what you started to say about the book."

"Oh. Well, perhaps that can wait until we're at the house." The brothers were jostled forward into the claiming hall

where stevedores piled luggage in great teetering heaps
without much concern for order or damage. Even in the
confusion, Matt saw the unhappiness on Gideon's face.

"I'm not living at home, Matt."

"My God. Since when?"

"Since the first of June."

"Where are you living?"

"At a hotel downtown. I've reserved a suite for you
there—"

Suddenly he pivoted to face his younger brother. Passengers streamed by them, some cheerful, some complaining.
"I might as well give you the whole of it right now. Margaret and I are finished. I moved out. Things are in a complete mess. I don't seem able to control events any longer.
They control me."

"Sounds like an excuse for a good bender of two or three
days' duration—what do you say?"

His smile faded as Gideon gave him a piercing, almost
injured look. Matt didn't understand his offense. Why
should a reference to drinking upset his brother? Gideon
had never been an abstainer.

Confused, he covered it by hunting for a bill and flourishing it to summon a porter.

"That steamer trunk, my man. And that one. To a hack,
if you please."

For his part, Gideon was regretting that he'd been so
candid so soon. Somehow, though, just seeing his younger
brother had made him feel that here was the one other
human being besides Julia with whom he could share
everything.

There were changes in Matt, of course. He was thirty-
three now. Time was beginning to cut lines into his raffishly
handsome face. He acted as if he didn't have a care. For
that reason Gideon felt bad about pouring out his troubles.
He wouldn't reveal any more of them just now. He didn't
want to spoil Matt's homecoming by trying to explain things
like the three notes he'd sent to Eleanor since he'd
moved out.

All of the notes had gone unanswered. One Saturday
morning he'd driven up Fifth Avenue and asked for his
daughter, only to be told by Samuel that she refused to
come to the door and speak with him.

"All right," he replied in a tired way. "Just answer one question. I've sent her three letters. Have they arrived?"

Samuel said, "Yes, sir," and Gideon's world began to crumble in earnest.

The other man seemed on the point of amplifying his remark. His eyes darted to one side in a nervous way. Margaret's voice rang out, demanding to know who was at the door. The butler leaned forward and whispered, "Things aren't healthy here, Mr. Kent. Not healthy at all. Get the children out if you can."

Margaret screamed at him and he slammed the door in Gideon's face.

The warning left Gideon frustrated and frightened. Were Eleanor and Will in danger because of his wife's deteriorating mental state? No, he doubted that. Whatever else he was willing to believe about Margaret, he couldn't believe she'd physically hurt her children. He feared Samuel was referring to some subtler but no less terrible form of injury.

What could he do? Abduct the children? Nonsense. This was the nineteenth century, not the Middle Ages. He felt unbelievably frustrated, though. He was powerless if Eleanor refused to answer his letters or speak to him when he called.

Gideon had yet to solve that particular problem. But he couldn't burden Matt with it. In the hack, he raised a pleasanter subject.

"I've gotten you a guest card at Salmagundi. That's a very fine private club for artists and art patrons. It's on lower Fifth Avenue. Has very commodious rooms, and I think you'll like the crowd. I've also been searching for a studio."

"Wait a minute. Wait!" Matt held up a hand. "That's rushing things a bit."

"You'll need a place to do the sketches for the book, won't you?"

Matt opened his mouth to speak, having decided it would be far better to tell his brother right now that he wasn't interested in the project. Somehow, though, he just couldn't utter the words. Gideon's haggard face, slumped posture—and most especially his announcement that he'd left Margaret—made Matt reconsider.

If there was anything he loathed, it was responsibility for someone else. But here was a case that absolutely demanded he take responsibility. Damn if he liked the idea. But Gid had been the older brother all his life, and now he obviously needed someone to assume that role with him. Matt finally shrugged.

"Oh, I suppose—"

"That's wonderful!"

The instant Matt accepted the responsibility, he began his retreat from it. "I'm not sure how long I can stay here, though. And I'm certainly not sure this book you're proposing is my cup of tea."

Gideon was already growing more animated.

"Of course it is. There's no one who could do it half as well. It's also the one thing in my life that hasn't gone to pieces. Excepting my relationship with Julia."

Another shock. "Who's Julia?"

"You'll meet her."

"Gid, are your children all right?"

"Yes." He frowned. "They're with Margaret." That said a good deal.

A little more briskly, Gideon went on. "As soon as you're settled, I want to show you a list of proposed plates for *100 Years.* I also want to hear about your work. And about Dolly, and your son."

With a rueful grin, Matt said, "We seem to be a couple of homeless wanderers, don't we? Men without their women, hanging around some hotel with nothing better to do than plan a picture book—" The smile faded. "I'll tell you this. It isn't the splendid, footloose life I once thought it would be."

"You mean your career?"

Matt nodded.

Quietly: "I feel the same way about the paper. The book and Julia are damn near all I have left."

Again Matt looked into his brother's ashen face and saw the need visible there. Yet something within him bawled like an infant, and fought the yoke.

"I won't promise to do more than try a few sketches. You've got to remember this isn't my country anymore."

"Yes, it is. Only now you'll see it with the eyes of someone who's been away for a while. You'll see it with fresh vision. You'll see what I miss because I'm too accustomed to it."

The enthusiasm in his brother's voice bothered Matt. "Look, Gid, don't get your hopes up. I didn't like the idea when I first read about it and I still don't. If the first half dozen sketches are no good, I want to be free to quit. You've got to give me that much."

"Happily, happily!" Gideon exclaimed. "Once you get started, I know everything will work out."

In a cynical voice, Matt asked, "Have you gotten religion while I was gone? You certainly have an unwarranted amount of faith."

But it was obvious nothing would convince Gideon the project was foredoomed. Perhaps his was a confidence born of desperation.

"All right," Matt sighed. "Let's take a turn through the lower part of the island before we head for the hotel. I'd like to see some of the changes. I'd like to see whether I can rediscover even"—he held his right thumb and index finger a quarter inch apart—"that much interest in this damn country."

Gideon laughed. "Anything you say. I feel better just seeing you. When everything else seems to totter, at least we have family to hold on to—oh, Matt, I'm glad you're home."

The carriage bounced on through the traffic of Tenth Avenue. In the sunless light of the summer day, Matt thought he detected a touch of moisture in the corner of Gideon's good eye. He poked his own with the tip of his little finger. A speck of dust or perhaps a bit of cinder thrown up from the noisy West Side streets had gotten in his eye and started it watering.

"Damn if I don't feel the same way," he laughed. And then the humor took on a hard edge that reality demanded. "Just don't get your hopes up, hear?"

INTERLUDE

SUMMER LIGHTNING

i

ONE YEAR LATER, on a Wednesday evening in July of 1877, Thomas Courtleigh entertained at his home in Lake Forest, Illinois.

Courtleigh had built the mansion in 1874. After his wife's death, he'd stayed there because he preferred the suburbs over State Street or any of the other fashionable addresses in Chicago. On Prairie Avenue, for example, one could be a neighbor of the Armours, and the Palmers, and other leading families. But one paid a price, and was forced to live close to a swelling population of immigrants and niggers.

That didn't suit the president of the Wisconsin and Prairie. He'd chosen to stay twenty-five miles to the north, in the exclusive little village platted on 1,300 wooded acres beside Lake Michigan. An architect obtained through Frederick Olmstead's company in New York had laid out the winding streets. Courtleigh had chosen to situate his forty-room residence on, appropriately enough, Wisconsin Avenue.

This Wednesday evening he was entertaining two dozen couples. An elegant buffet had been served at twilight on the terrace of the great limestone house. Now, as the summer darkness deepened, some guests sat or stood on that terrace, chatting quietly. Others had retired to the sweeping green lawn where the host had provided croquet equipment imported from Europe. Croquet had become a national craze after the war. As Courtleigh moved from group to group on the terrace, excited cries and applause came drifting through the warm air. Soon small torches set in special brackets atop the wickets began to flicker out on the lawn. Servants were lighting the torches to permit night play.

"—still undersubscribed for the new stained glass," Courtleigh heard one of the men say as he joined two husbands and their wives. All the male guests were members of the vestry of St. Margaret's Protestant Episcopal Church, as was he. Courtleigh's long, patrician face remained composed as he moved close enough to make his presence known.

"Undersubscribed by how much, Dillard?"

"Why, hello, Tom." The man chuckled. "By twenty thousand dollars, that's all."

One of the women said, "Twenty thousand? A bagatelle."

Unsmiling, Courtleigh nodded. "Quite right. In the morning I'll prepare a draft for that amount."

There were gasps, and then Dillard's wife exclaimed, "Oh, Tom! That's so generous. Sometimes I think you're the finest Christian in the whole congregation."

"No," said the second man, "merely the richest." They all laughed, Courtleigh included.

Then Mrs. Dillard put in a final word. "Dear Gwen would be so proud of your devotion to the church."

Courtleigh's bland face concealed sudden rage. There were so many things she could have enjoyed if it hadn't been for that damned Kent. Now the wretch was attracting national attention with some illustrated book that was soon to be published.

The book had something to do with American history—as if a Marxian socialist knew anything about that, or even had a right to trifle with it. Kent had written the text for the volume. The illustrations were wood engravings based on sketches by his brother, an artist who evidently belonged to a crowd of crazy European daubers.

In addition to the book itself, a limited edition portfolio of twenty etchings based on the pictures was being sold by private letter of subscription. Each of the two hundred fifty portfolios cost $500. Courtleigh knew all about the project because one of his church friends had shown him the elaborate solicitation materials. They included a reproduction of a section of one of the etchings. It depicted Kansas wheat farmers stringing the new barbed wire which, at long last, was making farmland safe from trampling by cattle herds. But no one on God's earth had ever seen farmers of the kind Kent's mad brother drew—spineless, curving figures half finished and completely repulsive. If that was art, Courtleigh was John the Baptist. But of course one might expect such obscene insults to the intelligence from a clan like the Kents.

The subscription materials had exerted a kind of fascination, though. One sheet had listed twenty-three organizations and charitable institutions to which the profits from the portfolios would be donated. On that list Courtleigh saw the benefit funds of several enfeebled unions such as the printer's and the typographer's. That was enough to put him in a wretched mood for two days. At least Kent hadn't had the audacity to mail him one of the damned solicitations.

The press of business, as well as the ineptness of underlings, had kept Thomas Courtleigh from dealing with Gideon Kent as he deserved. But Kent's punishment had never been rescinded, only postponed. The subscription materials, and the list of charities, had so enraged Courtleigh, he'd decided to make a new effort to finally administer that punishment. Preferably before Kent had a chance to see the disgusting, overblown book published by his company in Boston.

Of course, if Lorenzo Hubble had done his job a year ago, Courtleigh wouldn't have been forced to suffer such feelings of frustration now.

Standing among his guests, he cocked his head suddenly. The others hadn't caught the sound, but he had been anticipating it, and heard it easily. In the drive on the far side of the mansion, a carriage was arriving.

He excused himself. A footman came onto the terrace and intercepted him, saying quietly, "He's here, sir."

Courtleigh started for the house, murmuring about an urgent business matter. A vestryman's wife broke away from a group and rushed to catch him.

"Tom dear, do set my mind at ease before you go. This urgent business has nothing to do with that railroad strike in the East, does it?"

He lied. "No, Lilly. That's a small, isolated affair in West Virginia. Of no consequence."

Actually West Virginia was the lightning heralding an almost certain storm—a storm that could conceivably spread over several states and buffet certain sectors of their economy quite severely. But he didn't let on. He continued to parrot the official line of the secret consortium to which he belonged.

"It's only the work of a very small number of Marxians desperate to disrupt the status quo."

She fanned her bosom with a kerchief. "Oh, thank heaven. Several of my friends have been saying those anarchists would cause riots out here."

"I sincerely hope not, Lilly. And I really doubt it. As I said, there are just a few radicals involved."

"Thank you, Tom. You've reassured me. I told my friends that if anyone knew, it would be you."

Courtleigh nodded and moved on. Actually, he believed there was a fifty-fifty chance of the strike reaching Illinois. He was preparing for the worst, and wished he could have given Lilly reassurances based on those secret plans.

If it does spread here—or anywhere—decent people needn't worry. The strike, and the strikers, are going to be crushed without mercy.

ii

Lorenzo Hubble was waiting in the library.

Hubble was a slovenly young man who weighed nearly two hundred and fifty pounds. He had a wispy goatee, a mustache, and a round head already devoid of hair. He wheezed when he spoke, and his clothes always fit badly; he was forced to buy for size rather than style.

Self-educated, Hubble had come out of Conley's Patch. He was one of nine attorneys in the Wisconsin and Prairie's legal department, and not even a senior member of the staff. But in some ways he was closer to the president than any other person in the organization. It wasn't entirely accidental.

Hubble had joined the line several years earlier. At that time, Courtleigh had been confronting a crisis. One of his vice presidents, an important man on the W & P, had been on the griddle because of charges brought privately by the father of a fourteen-year-old girl from one of the poor sections. The girl was expecting a child, the vice president was married, and the father wanted fifty thousand dollars—the first year.

Courtleigh called a meeting of the legal staff. He stated his position. The vice president had to be protected, but the payment was a precedent he didn't care to set. Were there suggestions?

To the distaste of less aggressive colleagues, Lorenzo Hubble immediately volunteered to assume the burden of handling the entire problem. He promised that Mr. Courtleigh would not be unhappy with the results of his action. Several days later, the Chicago newspapers published accounts of a curious and coincidental double death. On her way home from the office of a physician who had examined her and found her pregnant, a young girl had drowned in the Chicago River. Not an hour later, her father had been shot during an attempted holdup.

The police couldn't connect the crimes, nor locate the man who'd made the girl pregnant. The victims had no other living relatives, and the gentleman, who'd brought the girl to the doctor and paid spot cash for the examination to which she cheerfully submitted, had insisted the doctor turn down the gas in his waiting room. In that way the man's face was never seen. All the physician could say was that the man had a huge belly, and breathed with difficulty because of his weight—and heaven knew there were hundreds like that in Chicago.

Courtleigh's trust hadn't been misplaced. Hubble was not only ruthless beneath the bovine exterior; he was discreet. After that conference of the legal staff, he never again spoke to his employer about the girl. Courtleigh and the vice president had learned that the matter was settled only by reading the papers.

A few months later, all of Hubble's work was rendered worthless when a heart seizure killed the vice president. But at least Courtleigh had found a valuable aide. The railroad's general counsel and staff still handled all legal matters. The president and Lorenzo Hubble handled the illegal ones.

Hubble had come with a sheaf of papers. He began to sort various items while Courtleigh closed and locked the library's black walnut doors, then its leaded windows. Perspiration shone on Hubble's cheeks and upper lip as he squeezed himself into a chair. He pulled a large Havana from the inner pocket of his linen jacket. The jacket had sweat rings under the arms.

"Don't smoke in here," Courtleigh snapped. "You know I can't stand the fumes in hot weather."

Without a complaint or even a flicker of disappointment, Hubble broke the cigar and tossed it into the dark fireplace.

"What's happened in Martinsburg?"

In reply, the lawyer chose a handwritten sheet from the material he'd spread on a small table at his elbow. Courtleigh's eyes moved across the array of items. When he saw a folded copy of the *New York Union* with the tea bottle device on the masthead, he felt rage of the kind that had nearly overpowered him on the terrace.

Part of that rage was directed at Lorenzo Hubble. The attorney had botched only one major assignment since entering into his private relationship with the president of the W & P. After Courtleigh had seen Gideon Kent at the Philadelphia exhibition, Hubble had arranged the attempted murder on Walnut Street. Later Hubble claimed he'd hired the best men he could find. The bungler who'd driven the hack had vanished afterward without attempting to claim the second half of his fee. As a result of the fiasco, Hubble was still not fully back in Courtleigh's good graces. It was time he tried to get there.

"—I'm sorry," Courtleigh interrupted, aware that Hubble had been answering his question about events in Martinsburg. Firelight from the croquet court shimmered on the windowpanes. Full dark had fallen.

"This"—Hubble waved the handwritten sheet—"is the text of a telegraph message being sent tonight by Governor Mathews of West Virginia."

"Sent to whom?"

"To President Hayes. The men I've posted to Martinsburg spread a lot of money around just to obtain this copy." He extended the paper. Courtleigh gestured in an impatient way. Hubble understood that his employer wanted the message summarized. He said, "Mathews is requesting Federal troops to put down what he terms unlawful combinations and domestic violence along the Baltimore and Ohio. To quote him—*it is impossible with any force at my command to execute the laws of the state.*"

"Is it really that bad?"

"No, not yet. He's a calamity howler. The violence has been sporadic, and of a minor nature. However, large crowds are out supporting the strikers."

Sharply, Courtleigh said, "Let's begin to refer to them properly, Lorenzo. Not strikers. Revolutionaries. Communists."

"Yes, of course." The fat man smiled nervously in response to Courtleigh's cynical smirk.

"Is any freight moving around Martinsburg?"

"Not a car."

Courtleigh smacked his fist lightly on the mantel. "None of us wanted it to get this far. We feared it might but we hoped it wouldn't."

Hubble again understood perfectly. By using the plural, his employer meant the consortium. The small, informal and highly secret group of railroad presidents chaired by Tom Scott of the Pennsylvania and including Jay Gould of the Erie, John Garrett of the B & O, and several others. Courtleigh had been invited to represent lines based in the middle West.

The consortium met from time to time at Newport or White Sulphur Springs or Saratoga to decide policy matters pertaining to the welfare of all American railroads. No decisions were binding, yet the consortium's so-called guidelines had a way of being widely observed, first by lines that were represented within the group, then by lines that were not.

"No one thought that son of a bitch Ammon would be so successful," Courtleigh fumed. "Is he in Martinsburg?"

"Our operatives haven't seen him, sir."

"Then where is he?"

"Traveling, we presume."

It outraged Courtleigh that the current trouble had been caused not by some low-class Jew radical, but by the college-educated son of a prosperous insurance executive. God knew where Robert Ammon had acquired his dangerous views. But in just a little over a month, he'd caused unprecedented damage.

Since early June, he'd been traveling from state to state organizing what he called the Trainman's Union. It was something wholly new and very dangerous in the labor movement—an umbrella organization covering all railroad workers, from senior engineers with years of experience to the newest, lowliest switchman.

Courtleigh's agents said the T.U. was spreading like a lightning fire on a dry prairie. The union's actual size was very difficult to ascertain, however. The wily Ammon had taken note of how earlier brotherhoods had operated on a more or less public basis and thereby come under attack, their members threatened or harassed until the brotherhood collapsed. To prevent that, he'd instituted a policy of absolute secrecy in the T.U., complete with passwords, secret oaths and hand grips. Still, it was almost a certainty that radicals from the T.U. were behind the unlawful strike that had hit the B & O in West Virginia.

The strike had come about as a result of the implementation of a ten percent wage cut for all B & O employees earning more than a dollar a day. The cut had gone into effect the preceding Monday, July 16. Strangely, there had been no strike when Tom Scott had instituted the same sort of cut on the Pennsylvania back on June 1. Oh, there'd been complaints—even a grievance committee. But Scott had met with the committee and glibly talked away all of its objections.

Or so everyone in the consortium had thought, congratulating Scott on his victory.

The wage cut had been one of the agreed-upon strategies of the consortium. To offset shrinking profits caused by the nationwide depression, the cut was to be put into effect line by line all across the country. Courtleigh's chief bookkeeper had already drawn up confidential schedules which would reduce the pay of all W & P employees down to the brakemen who even now received only $1.15 for a twelve-

hour day—well below the brakemen's national average of
$1.75.

Obviously the Pennsylvania situation had been atypical.
This past Monday, some B & O workers had walked off
the job to protest the cuts. By midafternoon, however, less
militant workers had gotten a few trains running again.
Then, just during the past forty-eight hours, strike leaders
had reached and persuaded their more timid brethren and
the disruptions had begun to spread.

There were more and more walk-offs and resulting inter-
ruptions in service. Quarrelsome mobs of trainmen converged at Martinsburg, one of the B & O's main junction
points. Courtleigh believed that all the turmoil was a harbinger, the lightning visible before the storm. If matters
weren't brought under control, and quickly, Ammon's damnable new organization could well launch the first national
strike in American history.

And once there was that kind of precedent for other
unions to follow, the gates of hell were open.

The telegraph message from Governor Mathews to the
White House was encouraging, however. Courtleigh and his
fellow owners believed they had a friend in President
Hayes. The three-time Republican governor of Ohio had
in effect lost the '76 election to the former Democratic
governor of New York, Samuel Tilden, who had campaigned as a vigorous foe of corruption; he'd helped smash
the Tweed Ring.

Last November Tilden had piled up slightly more than
4,284,000 popular votes as opposed to a little over 4,036,000
for Hayes. But those totals didn't represent the end of the
story. While Grant was preparing to leave office and publicly apologizing for errors of judgment, four different
states—Oregon, Florida, Louisiana and South Carolina—
had come up with disputed sets of electoral ballots. If accepted, the ballots for Republican electors could overturn
the outcome of the popular vote.

The question of the contested ballots was thrown to Congress for resolution. Behind the scenes, the Republicans got
busy. Promises were quietly made to a number of Southern Democrats.

If the dispute broke in favor of the Republicans, they'd
see that the last Federal troops were withdrawn from the

South. There were other, less specific pledges, including one whose vague language seemed to hold out hope of Federal financing for a program of industrial improvements in Southern states. But Courtleigh knew it was Tom Scott's railroad lobby that had carried the day. Scott's men had swung the needed votes by persuading Southern Congressmen that approval of a proposed rail line from East Texas to the Pacific depended on their decision in the matter of the disputed ballots. And so, a special Electoral Commission chosen by Congress had certified election of a new president—Rutherford B. Hayes—on March 2. Tilden's followers cried fraud in vain.

There was no direct evidence that Hayes would be in sympathy with the railroad men, or would cooperate with them. The President had a reputation for integrity, and a spotless one. Still, he *was* a Republican—and so were Courtleigh and his colleagues. Most auspiciously of all, Hayes had received the news of his certification while a guest aboard Tom Scott's private railcar "Pennsylvania."

Hubble saw that his employer was agitated, and tried to calm him.

"Perhaps we'll locate Ammon in a day or two, Mr. Courtleigh."

It helped a little. The W & P president sat down opposite the lawyer. "All right, let's not worry about that. Let's look at the whole picture. You've a good feeling for the mood of the scum we hire to run our freight and passenger services. Where's this strike going? Will it spread?"

"I believe it will, sir."

"Will it go nationwide?"

Hubble hesitated only a moment. "If it isn't nipped, I think it may. First, the times are ripe because they're so bad. No man can afford a ten percent cut in his pay. Second, Ammon's caught us unprepared. He's built a secret brotherhood faster than anyone thought possible. I think he's incited the workers on almost every line from the Mississippi east—including ours. Those men are ready for violence. And there will be violence—perhaps a little, perhaps a lot—before this is all over. It's a watershed, Mr. Courtleigh. Laboring men want to test the feasibility of a national strike."

Courtleigh muttered an obscene word.

A sycophantic smile spread over the lawyer's suet-like face. "I'm happy we aren't living in the ancient world where they killed the messenger who brought bad news. You pay me for candor, however—"

"And for successful execution of important assignments," Courtleigh retorted. Hubble's grin disappeared. His employer never let him forget the Philadelphia failure for long.

The consortium had expected isolated protests over the wage cuts, but not anarchy—and certainly not the widespread support for the strike that was becoming evident on the B & O.

Depressed, Courtleigh said, "If those damned troublemakers are indeed looking at this as some kind of test, it's even more important to have it resolved in our favor. If this is the first national strike, it must also be the last. I'm sorry the issue must be decided in our industry, but I suppose it's a tribute to the importance of railroads—in any case, we'll deal with it. We must hasten our own preparations."

"I've already taken steps." Hubble nodded, anxious to please. "In fact, pursuant to our last chat, I've been out in the dives most of the day, with two assistants—"

"Hiring?"

"Yes. You were absolutely right, Mr. Courtleigh. There's no need to pay the Pinkerton mark-up. My helpers and I got all the men we needed. The W and P now has almost four dozen blacklegs on call, ready to go instantly if the trouble spreads to Chicago. Among those I myself interviewed—if you can call a conversation with a drunkard an interview—there was one real find."

"Oh?" Courtleigh clearly wasn't interested, but Hubble sat forward, eager to tell.

"Quite by chance, I hired a man who once had a pretty big reputation out west. His name's Jason Kane."

iii

Courtleigh replied with a shrug, "Never heard of him."

A tolerant smile. "No, sir, of course not. You don't read the *National Police Gazette*. He was famous for a year or two. Then he dropped out of sight. I can understand why. He's a sot. But he's tough. Killed nineteen men, they say."

Something in Courtleigh responded to that. Hubble took note and pressed on. "I think I can keep his drinking under control. He seems almost pathetically eager for a job."

"What's he doing in Chicago?"

"He was traveling as a supernumerary—you know, one of the Indians—in *The Red Right Hand.*"

Another blank stare. Courtleigh never attended popular entertainments.

"That's the new play Buffalo Bill's touring in, sir. This Kane used to know Bill Hickok. That's how he landed the job. Before Wild Bill got blown to hell in Deadwood last year, this Kane talked him out of a letter of introduction. Kane said Hickok owed it to him because of some trouble they had in Abilene. Kane booted around down South for a while before taking the letter to Cody. He worked for him for four or five months, fetching Cody's liquor and women. But he started fuc—" A withering stare from Courtleigh changed that word hastily. "Fooling with a wardrobe girl Cody liked, and Cody fired him. Stranded him in Chicago with just a week's wages. Kane drank and gambled that away in one night. I tell you, Mr. Courtleigh, I have a hunch about him. A hunch that we can use him. I gave him two dollars for a meal, a bath and a decent bed and he damn near promised to do anything I wanted. I think he's a little touched in the head. When I started talking to him, he was pretty drunk. He babbled that he was being hounded by some Sioux Indian curse—I didn't quite get all of it. But if I can use his drinking habit to control him—you know, give him a little money every day, but not too much—I'd like to try him on the staff. A guard for the office. I've wanted to hire someone for headquarters ever since that lunatic switchman showed up three weeks ago with those nonsensical grievances and that homemade infernal machine—"

Which, thankfully, had failed to detonate when the crazed man threw it into the working area outside Courtleigh's office. Chicago police had been paid to haul the anarchist away and break both his legs. The man was now in jail awaiting a trial that would send him to state prison for life.

But Courtleigh understood Hubble's point. "You're quite

right. We should have guards downtown. I'm not anxious to be blown up in my own office. There could be another attempt, especially these days. This man you described might be just the sort we need." Courtleigh gave the lawyer another piercing glance. "Perhaps he can also undertake the assignment you failed."

Hubble's cheeks darkened. "I'll take care of that, don't you worry, Mr. Courtleigh. As a matter of fact, I intended to bring it up later this—"

Courtleigh interrupted. "First let's concentrate on the strike."

"Yes, sir." Hubble's fat white hand fluttered over the various notes and documents he'd laid out. "In case of widespread violence, we'll have the newspapers on our side, of course—"

Courtleigh pointed to the copy of the *Union*. "With a few notable exceptions."

Hubble picked up the sheet with great delicacy. "Our New York informant telegraphed that Kent is still following his practice of covering certain stories himself. He's wired for his western correspondent to immediately come in to Chicago in case of trouble here. The paper's editor dispatched another of the regular reporters to Baltimore. But Kent himself went to Martinsburg."

"Are most of the Eastern dailies sending men there?"

"Yes, sir, nearly every one."

That was good. As a group, newspaper owners were generally opposed to unions and to strikes. They considered themselves owners first and newsmen second. Of course there was a dangerous and misguided minority that included such men as Gideon Kent and his editor, Payne, who had been caught in the Tompkins Square riot and been a labor partisan ever since.

Hubble held out the newspaper. "This contains a dispatch Kent sent from Martinsburg. But I thought you might be more interested in his editorial."

The W & P president stared at the proffered paper. "I'm not interested in any of the swill Mr. Kent spews forth. You should know that by now."

Hubble's pink tongue crept across his bow lips as if to lick away some unclean speck. "But the editorial is strongly pro-strike, sir—"

Courtleigh guffawed. "Well, of course. And the sun also rises in the east. Why the hell are you wasting my time, Lorenzo?"

"The editorial discusses the wages on several typical lines—including the W and P."

"*What?*" Courtleigh fairly leaped to grab the *Union.* Hubble sat back, vindicated.

"Yes, sir. As you'll see, it cites your estimated worth of thirty million, and notes that our average conductor's wage is twenty percent less than that received by an apprentice bricklayer."

Thomas Courtleigh said another filthy word he'd never used in front of any of the members of St. Margaret's. With shaking hands, he opened to the editorial. He grew livid when he saw the title.

A MATTER OF DIMES AND DECENCY

He read the paragraphs with mounting rage. Kent was attacking the Baltimore and Ohio wage rollback, and the one on the Pennsylvania before that. He was also lending his newspaper's endorsement to a peaceful strike by the members of the Trainman's Union who worked for the B & O. Their demands were fully justified, he said, because they were "wage slaves" of the men who had imprisoned them in what he floridly called "a cage without bars, a cage of poverty and injustice without hope of redress."

Logically, the editorial should have confined itself to affairs in the East, but it did not. Kent had chosen to vilify Scott and Garrett—but he'd also chosen to drag Courtleigh in. All three were characterized as "bloated profiteers" determined to profit even more by plucking dimes from the pockets of already desperate workingmen—thievery that was akin to snatching bread from a child's plate, he said.

"Jesus Christ," Courtleigh whispered. Hubble gaped. To his recollection he had never heard his employer utter blasphemy within his hearing.

Courtleigh's hands were shaking as he read the slanted, vitriolic prose to the finish. The owners of almost every other paper in America considered themselves capitalists, like Jay Gould or Tom Scott or Courtleigh himself. But

not this damned, insufferable bastard who'd helped destroy
Gwen's mind and sent her to an early death.

Why had he permitted business to distract him for so
long? *Why* had he permitted Kent to remain alive? He
redoubled his determination to see him dead—and soon.

iv

Hubble was almost afraid to speak. "Any instructions,
Mr. Courtleigh?"

Courtleigh flung the paper aside. He stood up and began
pacing, each long step testifying to his anger.

"Yes. Telegraph Scott in our regular cipher. Say I urge
an immediate implementation of the scare plan. Tell him I
believe the editors of all the friendly papers must be contacted at once. Use those words. *At once.* Say that if we
wait, most of the impact of the plan will be lost."

"I have that." Hubble nodded, scribbling rapid notes
with a pencil.

The plan to which his employer referred had been devised as a contingency, and had been developed and refined
during the last three meetings of the consortium. It played
on the fact that the average American was terrified of
Marxist socialism—or Communism, as it was now coming
to be called. The "Communards" of 1871 had become
"Communists" six years later.

Courtleigh knew full well that there were only a relatively few Communists within the ranks of railroad workers.
Yet he felt that, with the cooperation of the press, it could
be made to seem that virtually all the workers favored riot
and revolution for achieving their objectives.

So far as Courtleigh knew, never before in American
history had there been a planned campaign to frighten the
public with a straw man. He was convinced the plan could
work, given the mood of the times, the willingness of the
railroad owners to play on ignorance and fear, and the attitudes of those who owned American newspapers—Kent
and a few other lunatics excepted.

Hubble finished his note taking. Courtleigh checked what
the fat lawyer had written, nodded.

Hubble said, "If there's nothing else, I have something on my mind—"

"There is something else." Courtleigh was thinking of Gideon. "But go ahead."

"Thank you. I just wanted to make a suggestion regarding Gideon Kent."

Courtleigh burst out laughing again. Hubble grew worried until Courtleigh assured him nothing was wrong, and urged him to continue.

"Very well, sir. As you know the strike will probably intensify. Perhaps spread to major junction points such as Pittsburgh, Baltimore, Newark, Ohio, or even Chicago. I could have Kent followed. If he should chance to be close to even minor violence, a couple of trustworthy men could perform the job I failed to take care of in Philadelphia. During a melee, we could eliminate Kent quite—ah—naturally. And without a shred of suspicion."

The lawyer had grown enthusiastic. He was leaning forward so that his huge paunch pressed against his thighs. His coat fell away and Courtleigh glimpsed the concealed pistol the other man always wore in a sweat-blackened holster tucked near his right armpit.

Fine thing, a W & P attorney walking around armed. Hubble claimed he'd acquired his first gun at age eleven, when he was guarding carriages at a bordello and needed to protect the vehicles from neighborhood toughs. Perhaps he still wore a weapon to compensate for his soft, weak body. But if he wanted to climb higher, he'd have to polish off those rough edges. He'd have to learn that gentlemen never overcame opponents with fists or revolvers. At least not their own.

Sweat began to slick Hubble's face as he waited for a reaction. Courtleigh was moved to snicker and say, "Anxious for absolution, are you, Lorenzo?"

"Yes, sir, very. Philadelphia still weighs heavily on my mind."

"And on mine," was the unsmiling reply. "I laughed a moment ago because the matter I was going to raise with you was the very one you brought up. I was going to order you to see Kent was killed once and for all."

The fat man breathed noisily, relieved. "What a fine coincidence! In view of your wishes, may I make a second suggestion?"

"What is it?"

"That we not limit ourselves to reprisals against Mr. Kent. That we also consider his family."

Stillness then. From the lawn came the shouts and laughter of a boisterous croquet game. In the library, the air was stifling. Hubble's cheeks ran with shining sweat. Courtleigh sounded eager as he whispered, "Go on."

"Well, sir, Kent's editorial stand on the strike is bound to run counter to that of most of the other New York dailies. That could cause"—a fat hand tilted back and forth—"let's call it resentment. Now I've investigated, and I'm aware that Mr. Kent is no longer living at home. But that isn't widely known. Also, the mansion in which his wife and children reside is located in a sparsely populated section of upper Fifth Avenue. Certain groups angry over Mr. Kent's editorial policy, certain"—the hand waggled again—"patriotic citizens who believe he carries the Marxian taint, but who don't realize he's moved away—they might take it upon themselves to mob that house. My information says there's no longer any love lost between Kent and his wife. Not since he took the Sedgwick woman as his mistress. But his children are an altogether different matter. In such a demonstration as I've just described, those children might be injured."

Another silence, lengthening and lengthening—until Thomas Courtleigh smiled.

With an expression of false piety, Hubble went on. "We'd wish no harm to any man's loved ones. But mobs do get out of hand. Kent's children might even be killed."

Unblinking, Lorenzo Hubble stared at his employer. Courtleigh glanced at the red-lit windows. Laughter pealed in the summer dark.

He had to be returning to his guests. But he took time to step to Hubble's side and squeeze the lawyer's flaccid shoulder.

"Implement both suggestions, Lorenzo."

Hubble brightened. "Yes, sir. I'll go to New York personally to arrange for the—ah—visitors."

A warning glared in Courtleigh's eye.

"Being sure that you in no way implicate the railroad or me."

Almost as enthusiastically as a puppy, Hubble declared, "Oh, no, sir, you needn't fret about that, not for a minute."

"If both plans succeed"—Courtleigh tried to tease, but it came hard for a man of his turn of mind—"Pope Thomas shall grant the aforementioned absolution." With obvious mockery, he drew a cross in the air. "He'll give you an increase in your salary, too. A hundred a month."

"Thank you, sir—*thank* you." Hubble was very nearly fawning.

Courtleigh started out. "Oh—and you may hire that man you mentioned. Add another, if you wish. Two guards should be better than one. I want no more red-eyed radicals storming into the W and P building looking for my head."

"I'll take care of it, sir."

Thomas Courtleigh felt an almost sensual excitement as he left the library. The thought of finally obtaining his revenge against Gideon Kent—and Kent's family—was somehow more thrilling than intimate relations with his wife had ever been. Lorenzo Hubble was a crude, slovenly, deceitful young man, but he had his virtues. He wouldn't flinch from organizing a mob that would maim or kill a woman and a couple of children.

Courtleigh stepped out onto the terrace in the cool darkness. It was difficult to keep his face composed. Despite the spreading strike, he was in a state approaching euphoria. Then he recalled one thing he'd overlooked.

He was surprised by the glaring omission, but he supposed it was understandable given the breadth of the discussion with the attorney. Courtleigh's accounts with Kent wouldn't be settled until he'd dealt with that Sedgwick woman too.

Well, he'd take that up with Hubble tomorrow. He was feeling so fine he could even begin to appreciate the lawyer again. Lorenzo Hubble definitely knew how to redeem himself.

Lorenzo Hubble knew how you got ahead in America.

★ *Book Four* ★

ELEANOR'S WAY

CHAPTER I

100 YEARS

i

ON THE EVENING Thomas Courtleigh conferred with Lorenzo Hubble, Matthew Kent was again in the pressroom of Kent and Son, Boston.

The July night was boiling. The dingy neighborhood near the North End piers resounded with quarrelsome voices and the squalls of fretful children. Matt felt the temperature had to be better than a hundred inside. He'd removed his shirt to proof the last three etchings.

The work seemed interminable. He'd mixed the proper proportions of copperplate oil with french black and frankfort black ink powders, but because of the heat, the customary mixing techniques didn't produce the expected result. When he picked up some of the finished ink on a palette knife, it immediately dripped off the edge instead of hanging there, as it should have. So he'd mixed it again, increasing the quantity of both powders just a little.

Then something went wrong with one of the screws which adjusted the pressure of the top roller on the copperplate press, and that took another hour to correct. It was a quarter after three before he pulled a satisfactory print of the final etching, *The Guide,* and with more hope

than certainty, lightly marked one corner with the notation
1/250—the first print of two hundred and fifty. He hoped
this plate and all the others would last that long.

He was too worn-out to take time to dry, redampen and
flatten the print properly. He grasped the sheet by its edges,
yawned and carried it toward the stairway leading up to
the office of Dana Hughes. He couldn't quite believe his
part in the project was finished, and he still had trouble
believing that, toward the end, he'd actually generated
some enthusiasm for it.

He still considered *100 Years* a jingoistic book. But that
was immaterial. When he'd arrived in New York a year
ago, Gideon had been a man drowning. The book—and
Matt's participation in it—had been a sort of life preserver
for him.

Incredible that I've put so much time into it, he thought.
But how the hell did you walk away from your own brother's cry of help? The answer was the same as it had been
a year ago. You didn't.

Since the summer of '76, Matt had traveled more than
twenty thousand miles studying locales and sketching figures for the plates for *100 Years.* He'd crossed the Charles
River to Breed's Hill, where the family's founder had
fought, and he'd stood with a haunted feeling in the clump
of trees at which Pickett had aimed his splendid, futile
charge at Gettysburg. He'd fallen in love with San Francisco, and damned the dust of West Texas. He'd gotten
splattered with oil from a derrick in Pennsylvania, and
slogged around in water up to his hips in a South Carolina
rice field destroyed by a hurricane. He'd savored strong
cheese among shy Scandinavians in Wisconsin, and
scratched at hellish little insects that crawled under his balls
while he sketched a heron in the south of Florida. He'd
been on riverboats and ranches, entered cathedrals and cat-
houses, heard the dead murmuring in the winds that blew
over battlefields and burial grounds.

For every historical figure depicted in the plates, he'd
used a living American as an anatomical model. For the
plate of Martha Washington darning her husband's stocking
by candlelight at Valley Forge, he'd sketched a Quaker
farm woman in Ohio. A Baptist parson in Oregon had

posed for lanky, foulmouthed Andy Jackson, and a black sharecropper in Louisiana for Crispus Attucks.

And almost everywhere he went, if he grew discouraged because his hand wouldn't do what his mind knew it could, he would discard the unsatisfactory sketches for a while and find a baseball game. Sometimes he played; sometimes he umpired. Either way, a few innings always restored his spirits and renewed his determination. That was true in spite of his realization that age was catching up with him. He could no longer sprint between the bases as fast as he once had, or throw the ball as powerfully or as far.

At first he'd been contemptuous of the purpose behind all his work and travel. But then a peculiar thing had happened. He'd forgotten all about the purpose and lost himself in the fascination of the work itself. It was as if he'd gone to a banquet against his will, loathing the host but ultimately forgetting about that as his senses surrendered in delight to the incredible variety of courses set before him. Unexpectedly, America was a banquet for his eyes and mind and, sometimes, when a particular scene or face moved him, for his heart.

The etching he'd just proofed was a study of Sacajawea, the young Indian woman who had guided the Lewis and Clark party to the western sea. As his model he'd used a Sioux Indian girl eight months pregnant. He'd been led to her in Cheyenne, Wyoming, by Michael Boyle, the hardheaded Irishman to whom his father had willed Jeremiah's third of the inheritance.

After meeting Boyle, Matt understood why Jephtha Kent had taken that step. Damned if Matt hadn't taken to the Irishman and his straightforward manner. Boyle made no secret of his ambition to earn a lot of money from the retail stores he and his handsome wife Hannah operated, and from the cattle-feeding operation they'd started more recently. He didn't pretend he was watching his balance sheets for the sake of God, country, or "progress"—a puzzling term which seemed to be the mantle with which Americans cloaked an incredible number of stupid or dishonest acts.

Boyle's candid admission that he wanted to make money because he'd starved in the slums as a child was in refreshing contrast to the pious cant Matt had heard down in Washington. Tom Nast had taken him there for a week, and introduced him to a flock of politicians. He'd met Nast through a mutual acquaintance at the Salmagundi Club, and they'd hit it off immediately.

Matt admired the Dutchman's draftsmanship and imagination. Nast had invented marvelous animal symbols for political organizations—the Tammany tiger, the foolish Democratic jackass, the strong and likable elephant of Nast's own Republican party. Matt was less enthralled by the man's crusading nature, and by streaks of outright bigotry and cruelty in his cartoons. Nast loathed Catholics, and it showed. And in the '72 election, when old Horace Greeley had campaigned as a reform Republican, opposing Grant's bid for reelection, Nast's artwork had lampooned the famous publisher without mercy. Many said the cartoons were a major factor in Greeley dying three weeks after the election, a broken man.

Nast had also been violent in denouncing Southerners during the war. But in his eyes Matt was more expatriate than Southerner. Nast knew of Matt's work, especially the painting of Wilmington, for which a private collector had paid a handsome price the day the Centennial Exhibition closed.

Gideon was aware that his younger brother had poked around Washington with Tom Nast, but he knew nothing about Matt looking up the Boyles in Cheyenne and enjoying their fine hospitality—as when Michael took him to a private cattleman's club, and bought him a dinner of the finest beefsteak he'd ever tasted. Matt just didn't mention the visit because Gideon still disliked the Irishman and his wife.

Matt had gladly taken advantage of their knowledge of Wyoming, though. It was through Michael that he'd located the Indian girl.

He'd drawn her relatively small, laboring up the steep side of a low, round hill. A row of identical hills, each only half visible, diminished behind it like one of those visions of infinity you could create by arranging two mirrors face to face. The repetitive pattern of the hills was meant to suggest the distances Lewis and Clark had traversed. Sacajawea was walking up the hill rather than down because he was thereby able to portray physical strain.

He'd sketched his model in her pregnant state, intending to use only certain details of her face and costume. Then he'd discovered Sacajawea had delivered a child, little Pom, during the expedition. So the finished version showed her with a heavy belly, late in her term. Matt thought that made the plate much stronger.

Sacajawea's head was turned, and her arm upraised to urge the unseen party of men to hurry along. He meant to imply the men couldn't keep up with a pregnant but determined young woman. The touch amused him—not that anyone would catch it. Well, no matter. Gideon had agreed to let him handle each subject as he chose. And for him, it was a single strong young girl undaunted by a physical burden or by unexplored distances that symbolized the opening of the West.

He really liked the picture. He liked the work he'd done in America. That was the most amazing part of the year just past.

ii

Heat lightning flashed outside the window of Dana Hughes' dim, stuffy office. Matt's shoulders and forearms ached from working the copperplate press. A daub of ink smudged his nose. He stepped into the office and coughed to rouse the editor, who'd fallen asleep at his desk. They'd been working steadily for eight days and nights to meet the production deadline. Matt had taken all his meals at the publishing house and snatched a few hours' sleep on the floor at night.

Hughes blinked and knuckled his eyes. "All finished?"

Matt reversed the etching and laid it on the desk by way of an answer. The bland and phlegmatic editor clucked his tongue—for him, the equivalent of wild enthusiasm. He capped it by saying, "I like the work you did on the plate. The shadow on the skirt is much more natural now. This is one of my favorites."

"Well, you can wake Frank and get him to start printing the balance of these."

"Don't you want to do it? An etching's a delicate business—"

"And Frank's a very capable fellow. He knows the effects I'm after. Besides, I'm sick of the project. Run the prints and let's see what we have."

Hughes said nothing. What they would have were two hundred and fifty portfolios, most of which were unsold.

Matt knew the editor and Gideon were disappointed in the low returns from their mail solicitation. How many orders had come in? Twenty? They wouldn't even meet the cost of production, let alone achieve a surplus for charity.

Advance orders for the book itself were equally small. Perhaps the moment was wrong for a volume such as *100 Years*. The centennial was over; perhaps the book had come too late. Or it might be enthusiasm for the celebration had dimmed as people saw hard times still gripping the land.

Hard, violent times. There was new labor trouble in West Virginia. Gideon had rushed off from New York to write about it.

Poor Gid, Matt thought as Hughes continued to admire the etching. An honest man. An idealist—and what had they done to him? Long ago hung him up on a symbolic cross labeled *Radical*. He'd carry the stigma all his life, and live forever on the fringe of respectability. That always happened when you championed unpopular ideas. It frequently happened from the mere act of involving yourself in public affairs. Paul Cézanne had known that long before he was Gideon's age.

Matt jerked a grimy kerchief out of his back pocket and swabbed his itching nose. He discovered the ink, and got rid of most of it. He leaned on the windowsill; stuck his head out. There wasn't much relief to be had by doing that. The stifling air bore the smells of a seafaring town—salt and fish and tar and turpentine. Limpid white glares occasionally lit the chimney pots and roof tiles of the North End.

For his brother's sake, Matt hoped *100 Years* would eventually be a success. Or at least pay for itself. The four engravers who'd reproduced Matt's sketches on wood blocks had done a remarkably good job. Gideon had written a paragraph of text to appear opposite each plate. But Gideon's involvement went far beyond that. Far beyond even Matt's massive investment of effort and time. Gideon Kent, Matt knew very well, was counting on *100 Years* to succeed because so much else in his life was failing.

Gideon's daughter refused to answer the conciliatory letters he doggedly mailed to her every four or five weeks. Even Gideon's mistress, a woman Matt liked very much, was unable to minimize the pain caused by Eleanor's failure to reply. If *100 Years* failed, Kent and Son would survive and continue on its mediocre way. Gid would survive too—physically. But there were other ways a man could die, and over the past months Matt had watched his brother go through a slow erosion of hope and energy.

Several times Matt had been so upset by Gideon's state that he'd almost taken it on himself to drive to Sixty-first Street and confront Eleanor, whom he'd never had occasion to meet. He hadn't done it. His confidence always failed at the last moment because of his own sorry record as a family man. He was afraid he'd bungle a plea for reconciliation, and make the situation worse.

Hughes patted the margin of the print in a proprietary way. "Oh, I do like this one, Matt. The whole book is splendid. The illustrations, I mean."

Matt turned his back to the stormy night sky and perched on the sill. Sweat ran down his breastbone to his navel. "If you're going to commend the pictures, you have to commend the text as well. I think Gid packed a hell of a lot of information into very short blocks of space."

"Yes, a first-rate job given his state of mind lately. It's obvious the text and the illustrations were done by men who love this country."

"Nonsense, Dana. I don't love America. How can you love a nation of poltroons and parvenues? All I'll say is that, visually, it's an incredible place."

"You know, don't you, that the ancients believed love entered through the eye?"

Somehow the teasing infuriated Matt, but he said nothing. Hughes stood, stretched, and Matt heard one of the older man's knees pop.

"Did your brother say whether he'd be taking the train up here to supervise the press run?"

"I think he meant to do that, but that railroad strike heated up and he raced off to have a look."

Hughes shook his head. "Running about like one of his own news cubs—I've never thought that was advisable. For one thing it's undignified. For another, that's a very troubled situation in West Virginia. Your brother shouldn't thoughtlessly rush into danger. He's the head of two companies now. Quite a few people depend on him for decisions—and for jobs. He should think of that before he goes places where he might be accidentally injured or killed."

Perhaps it was exhaustion, or the fact that it was the end of the night, the time of sad thoughts and bad dreams, that suddenly put a terrible realization into Matt's head: *Maybe that's what he hopes for now. Maybe things have gone so wrong for him, he doesn't care about living.*

Somehow he found the idea loathsome—especially in connection with Gideon. It insulted him, turned him into a coward. Yet the thought persisted. Matt was scowling as Hughes said, "I think you should stay and supervise the running of—"

"*No.* Frank can do it. I'm going to wash my face, put on my shirt and boots, and go get drunk—in that order. When I see you again, I expect you to hand me a finished portfolio—as well as a finished copy of that book to which we now owe our souls. Good evening, Mr. Hughes."

CHAPTER II

IMPRISONED

i

IN NEW YORK City, Eleanor Kent began that same Wednesday evening in a mood of great excitement. An unidentified guest was to visit the Booth Association. The weekly meeting had been changed from Tuesday to accommodate the visitor's schedule.

Charlie Whittaker was in charge of the affair. The preceding week he'd announced in his usual portentous way that the visitor was someone important in the theater, and was coming to Hutter Hall specifically to look over the troupe. Though all the members including Leo Goldman pestered Charlie ferociously, and even subjected him to a few mild threats, he had refused to say anything else. Consequently Eleanor's anticipation had mounted steadily over the past few days. It was a joy to have something about which she could be genuinely excited for a change.

Who could the mysterious guest be? Some well-known actor? A producing manager? Why would either sort of person bother with an amateur club?

Well, she'd know soon enough.

She hurried with her preparations for the evening. The sweetly scented powder she dusted on her cheeks and the backs of her hands helped offset the dank smell the mansion acquired in the summer. She'd picked out her lightest frock, but she still felt uncomfortably warm as she started down the second-floor corridor. The house seemed to have that effect lately. It produced a sense of confinement, of stale air imprisoned in lightless rooms, and of unhappy people imprisoned by their circumstances or, in her case, by the lack of courage it took to escape.

She knocked softly at her brother's door, then went in. "Will? I'm leaving."

He looked up from his reading, his eyes lackluster. "Do you have to go again tonight?"

"Yes!" She felt guilty about her sharpness, then resentful of his dependence on her. *If only I could make myself stop caring about him—and about Mama—I could leave this wretched place.*

But that was impossible. She tried to go on more calmly. "Don't you remember? Tonight we're having our surprise visitor."

Will gave a small shrug, as if he couldn't comprehend the importance she placed on such things. He should be able to understand, she thought. Her refuge once a week was the Association, but he had his own, available every day. His room overflowed with stacks of books of all kinds and sizes. He read those books at the expense of everything else. Over the past year his marks had gone down at the private day school he attended. He'd lost twenty pounds, and was becoming more and more passive and withdrawn. Eleanor felt incompetent to take him in hand. She'd tried playing ball with him in Central Park, but it wasn't the same as the camaraderie two brothers would have enjoyed. She'd encouraged him to walk over to the Park when boys from downtown gathered to organize ball games. The noisy, working-class youngsters intimidated him. He wouldn't set foot across Fifth Avenue by himself even though his eyes said he'd clearly like to go.

How wretched and forlorn he looked as he laid his book aside and stood. *Papa caused this when he walked out,* she thought. No matter who had started all the arguments between her mother and father, she held Gideon responsible for the misery in the household ever since her birthday a year ago. He was the one who had chosen to desert his home and leave her trapped here by her conscience and her responsibilities.

"Eleanor?"

"What is it?"

Will's eyes darted past her, as if to make sure the door was shut. "What if—what if she starts seeing those people again? It's happened twice already this week."

Those people. The formless, faceless men who came stealing to surround the mansion when darkness fell. Only Margaret saw and heard them.

This evening Eleanor had tried to avoid thinking about her mother's condition. It was impossible. Resentment of her father burst forth again, almost as fierce as her resentment of the duties thrust on her by his departure.

Still, there was concern mingled with her anger. The concern won out. She drew Will's skinny body against her side and held him a moment, even as the resentment slewed in a new direction.

I can't stand the misery of this place. Dear God, I must get out or I'll die.

But of course she couldn't leave. Someone had to keep things running. Her mother was incapable. Margaret consumed tonics and spiritous liquors from the moment she rose in the morning until she retreated to her room at dusk to hide from the imaginary watchers. Fortunately she had hired an excellent staff in her more lucid days, and that staff required only minimum supervision from Eleanor.

Will, however, was another matter. He was a responsibility she was failing to handle adequately—though could anyone do it, given the atmosphere in which they lived? It was an atmosphere of fear, and now it turned his voice shrill and made him clutch her forearm.

"Tell me what to do if she says they're outside again. What if she screams, Eleanor? Tell me what to do then."

"Send Mills for Dr. Melton."

"But Mills will be driving you to the meeting."

"It doesn't take long to reach Irving Place"—early in the year the subterfuge of the Latin lessons at the Whittakers' had been abandoned with everyone but her mother—"and he'll be right back. I'll come home as early as I can, I promise."

Disconsolate, the boy retreated to the chair. She left him

with the book in his lap, his hands on the chair arms, and his eyes fixed on some point in space. As she went out the door, a puff of wind flared the curtains, and he started violently.

Poor Will—jumping at gusts of air. Cowering from the sight—the very thought of his own mother.

The blame all belonged to Gideon.

Eleanor had been hurt that he'd walked out. Hurt, but she'd understood after she calmed down. She could well believe that her mother might have lied about certain things. Margaret was unwell.

Her father, on the other hand, was fully in control of his faculties. He had no excuses. And so Eleanor's pain had slowly changed to outright animosity when Gideon didn't bother to communicate with her, or with his son.

His failure to send his children so much as a note of remembrance on their birthdays, or at Christmas, confirmed her fear that he no longer cared about either of them. Several times she'd asked Samuel whether the day's mail contained anything from her father, and he always said no in a strange, tense way that told her he, too, thought it was shameful that Gideon didn't write.

An occasional visit by a representative of the Rothman Bank served to remind everyone that Gideon had provided Margaret with a more than generous bank account. The last two times the banker had called, Eleanor had received him; her mother was in a stupor. Eleanor didn't understand much of what the man said, but evidently that didn't matter; on the essential point he was quite clear—there was money enough to meet expenses and always would be.

Money couldn't buy forgiveness for her father, though. If he thought it could, he was damnably mistaken.

Sometimes she did wish Margaret and Gideon would reconcile. For one thing, she would then have been able to meet Uncle Matthew, who'd been back in the United States for nearly a year.

Of course he'd been traveling a lot during that time, doing illustrations for some book Kent and Son was to publish. But his name had popped up in newspaper gossip columns, and she'd heard the servants clucking about his escapades. Diving into an ornamental fish pond filled with white Bordeaux wine during a weekend party thrown by one of the rich, fast crowd up at Newport. Romancing some blond beauty at the Saratoga Springs racetrack. Visiting Cooper Union to speak with the evening art classes about trends in Britain and in France. He'd quoted the war cry of the painters called the French realists—*"Le soleil est dieu"*—and endorsed it, thereby touching off a small riot between sympathetic listeners and the more traditional students. Uncle Matt was Bohemian, highly advanced in his thinking, and famous in a disreputable sort of way. Of those few people she could count as family, he would have understood best her growing certainty that she would be an actress one day. Because her father was gone, she had no opportunity to tell Uncle Matt how she felt—and that was one more thing for which she blamed Gideon.

Still, some of her feelings about him conflicted with her anger. From time to time she wondered what he did with his free time after he left Printing House Square in the evening. Where did he live? With whom did he take his meals? Other newspapermen? Uncle Matt? That mistress whose existence she believed in, even though she had absolutely no evidence the woman existed?

Gideon's absence left an aching void in her life. It was more than just a sense of something being gone. Deep down, she cared about him, and worried about him. The servants still sneaked the family paper into the house, so she knew there was some sort of labor trouble on one of the railroads in West Virginia. And she'd heard cook say her father had gone to report on it firsthand, as he sometimes did with important stories.

Eleanor's instantaneous reaction had been a hope that he wouldn't be hurt. A few minutes later that reaction brought surprise, then disgust. How was it possible for her to love and hate a parent at the same time? Her inability to answer the question, or explain away her behavior, only deepened her confusion.

Going down the staircase, she saw her mother wandering aimlessly across the foyer. When Eleanor reached the bottom of the stairs, some three yards separated her from her mother. But she could smell the tonic. The odor of its alcohol base grew steadily stronger as she approached.

Margaret was slow to note that her daughter was dressed for the street. When she did, she asked, "Where are you going?"

"To the Whittakers', Mama. The tutor could only come on Wednesday this week."

Her cheeks were pink as she said it. She disliked having to lie to her mother when everyone else in the house knew she attended Association meetings. She lied because references to the theater still agitated Margaret—although not as much as something else she now touched on indirectly.

"That's all right"—Margaret's hand brushed at a loose strand of hair but somehow failed to touch it—"so long as you're not going to see your father."

"Never," Eleanor declared. It had become a ritual, that question and her answer. So long as she promised not to see Gideon—as if she would—Margaret was relatively lax in keeping track of her whereabouts. It was about the only real benefit she'd derived from her father's departure.

With careful contrivance, she could even arrange for Mills to drive her to an occasional matinee, and pick her up afterward. Inevitably, she drew stares and comments when she entered a playhouse without an escort. And she needn't have done it. There was a young man who would gladly have accompanied her. But his constant attention had created a whole new set of potential problems, and she had enough already.

Actually, she didn't mind going alone and causing comment. She knew most people thought she was a prostitute, but she didn't care a snap about that. Respectability was the last thing professional actors and actresses worried about.

Of course there was some risk when a girl sat down by herself amidst some of the riffraff in playhouse galleries. But so far, by keeping a parasol with a sharp ferrule handy, she'd avoided serious trouble. Her acting ability helped, too. On one occasion when she'd been accosted by a heavy-handed lout, she'd scowled at him and ordered him to leave her alone—threatening a long and loud scream for the police if he didn't. Her threat had been convincing; he left her alone.

She had to keep her wits about her during those excursions. And she was disgusted and frightened by the expressions of some men who let their eyes rove over her face and her body. But the rewards were more than worth the unpleasantries. Already this year she'd seen Junius B. Booth, Junior's wife Agnes in *Sardanapulus,* Adelaide Neilson charming the audience in *Twelfth Night,* and the team of Ned Harrigan and Tony Hart displaying their wonderful sense of comedy timing. She'd studied the technique of major performers such as the gorgeous Helana Modjeska and the handsome George Rignold, and even that of the pert little child actress, Bijou Fernandez.

This evening Margaret seemed particularly upset by thoughts of Gideon. She seized Eleanor's arm.

"You're positive you don't plan to see your father?"

"Why would I, Mama? He left us. He hasn't written, and he's only come to the house that one time—"

Margaret's mouth curved in a curious smile. "When you very properly refused to speak with him. You haven't changed your mind?"

"You just heard me say I hadn't."

"Swear it."

"Mama—"

"Swear it, Eleanor. I insist."

A pain spread in her midsection as she said, "I swear." Dear God, what a wretched game. But she knew the alternative—severe agitation on Margaret's part, even screaming or weeping. Twice through that kind of harrowing experience had taught Eleanor to humor her mother's demands for promises like the one she'd just extracted.

Margaret's smile disappeared as she crept to the front door. She peered through one of the narrow windowpanes flanking it, and it nearly broke Eleanor's heart to hear her say, "Oh, good. They're not in the Park yet. Perhaps they won't come tonight. Perhaps they'll leave me alone, and I can get some sleep."

Eleanor wanted to cry, *There's no one there.* She didn't because she knew Margaret wouldn't believe her. Would, in fact, turn on her with wild assertions that Eleanor just couldn't see the men who came back almost every evening as soon as the sun went down.

"Good night, Mama," Eleanor called as she started

toward the kitchen. Margaret didn't acknowledge her, muttering monosyllables while she continued to peer through the glass.

Eleanor dashed down the back steps and in a moment was on her way to Hutter Hall in the calash. The July evening was hot. The wind quickly dried the tears of frustration that formed in her eyes.

I wish I didn't worry about Will or feel sorry for Mama. I wish I could just pack a valise and run away from that God-awful place. I don't know how much longer I can stand it there. Lying to Mama. Not able to do anything to help her, or Will either.

If I stay there, it will be the end of me. I have to get out of that house or I'll die.

ii

When she reached Hutter Hall, all the members were in confusion, arranging and rearranging chairs and dithering even more than actors usually did.

All but one, that is: Leo Goldman.

Leo was tolerated by the other members of the Booth Association, but none of them really liked him. Most of the boys secretly envied his good looks and voice.

The female guests all chased Leo—with one notable exception. She was the only one in whom he was interested.

"Eleanor, may I speak to you?" He'd intercepted her the moment she walked in, and was keeping pace as she went to hang up her bonnet.

She didn't know what to make of Leo—or her reactions to him. She liked his cheerful and confident manner. And she positively turned to jelly when he read certain passages of dialogue or dramatic verse in that beautiful baritone. Since that first evening in the cloak room they'd gradually become more friendly. She'd never seen him anywhere except meetings, however, and that was a barrier he was constantly struggling to overcome.

Occasionally she was tempted to help him. But then fear and good sense always intervened—as they did now, behind her tart smile.

"You don't usually ask permission. Why should this week be any different?"

He took her hand and drew her into the cloak room. Quickly she pulled her hand away, fearful of how she felt. Too warm. Too eager for him to squeeze her fingers between his larger, stronger ones.

Love hurts you. Affection hurts you. Why was she so often in danger of forgetting that?

She knew. Leo was fearfully handsome, with those coal black eyes and that imp's grin.

And tonight he was as determined as ever. "How long are you going to hold out on me, Eleanor? By working extra at the Academy, I've saved enough to buy two gallery seats at any playhouse in town. When are you going to say yes and let me take you to a show? I'll go any afternoon you want. Any Saturday—"

She used the first argument that came to mind:

"You keep telling me that, Leo. But Saturday's your Sabbath."

"As far as religion goes, my father's given up on me," he said with a shrug. "My mother, too. They lost hope when I sneaked out of Hebrew school to sell papers. I'll never be able to read the Talmud, or keep all the six hundred thirteen commandments a pious man like my father tries to store in his head or, worse, observe. Why, if Hester Street went up in flames tonight, I'm afraid my father would first concern himself with the Orthodox way to fight fires—if there is any—and only think of the family later. Don't worry about my Sabbath. I figured out a long time ago that I couldn't be an actor if I began by asking to miss Saturday matinees. If I'm to be a good actor, I'll have to be a bad Jew for a while and hope I'll be forgiven."

He glanced quickly at the ceiling, miming supplication with clasped hands. Eleanor laughed.

"Sometimes I don't know what to think of you—"

"Think that I have all this money for tickets and carfare, and that I'll perish of misery if you don't say yes and go to the theater."

"You won't perish." She tried another excuse. "Besides, I don't think my mother would allow it."

"Pshaw, Eleanor. You tell everybody around here that you do as you please."

Her cheeks pinked; she'd been caught.

He stepped closer, his forearm accidentally brushing the tip of her breast as she turned away. The sensation melted her for a moment, then terrified her. In a sympathetic voice, Leo said, "I can guess one thing that might be worrying you. If you let me take you out, I promise I'll be polite. I know you don't like boys to touch you."

The startling statement made her whirl back to him.

"How do you know that?"

Her voice was so loud, one of the members passing the cloak room paused to glance in. Leo scowled at him and he went on.

"I didn't mean to make you mad. But I've seen how you react when you're performing a scene and the script says you're supposed to touch a boy, or let him touch you. You hesitate for a minute before you go ahead. Maybe none of the rest of them notice, but I do."

He grinned to relieve her embarrassment. "That's because I watch you twice as hard as anyone else. Let me take you to a matinee and I promise you won't have to worry about me getting fresh."

Again he stepped close. "You just *have* to say yes, Eleanor. I can't eat anymore, I can't sleep. I'm about to lose my job because of you—"

"Oh, Leo, no—"

"It's true. I can't keep the Academy's lobby swept or the refreshment booth spiced up because I'm so busy wondering when you'll give in."

"You mean if."

"When. I know you want me to take you out."

"Oh, you do? Of all the conceited, big-headed—"

"Now, now," he interrupted. "You know it's true." He looked straight into her dark eyes. "I see it and you can't hide it no matter how hard you try. So you might as well quit resisting me, and name the date. I've told you before, Miss Kent—Leo Goldman of Hester Street didn't come to America to wallow around being a failure. I intend to get everything I want. A famous name in the theater. Lots of money. And you."

He was still smiling in a mischievous way. But those dark eyes bored into her, seeing emotions she wanted to conceal.

Everything he said about her feelings was true. She wanted to say yes to him—

Suddenly cold, sharp images came stabbing into her mind.

Images of the ruined birthday.

Of the Christmas Eve when she'd peered through the steamy window on the Yorkville veranda.

Of the night she'd broken the Rogers group, and crouched on the stairway afterward.

"Well, Leo"—her face took on a stiff look that marred her beauty—"I'm afraid you won't get everything you want. Not this year. I won't go to the theater with you."

"That's crazy. I can tell you like me."

Exactly why I have to refuse you.

"Damn it, Eleanor, you've got to give me a better explanation than—"

"Say, what *is* this, a private rehearsal?" Quite unnoticed, Charlie Whittaker had poked his head into the cloak room.

For the first time, Eleanor heard a hubbub in the hall. She was furious when Charlie raked her up and down, hunting for signs of mussed clothing. Then, with an annoyed look at Leo, he went on. "If you can tear yourselves away from whatever intimate little things you're *doing*, our guest has arrived—my God, Goldman, what's the matter?"

Eleanor was afraid poor, soft Charlie was about to be felled by one of Leo's fists. But Leo kept his hands at his sides—for the moment, anyway—and shoved his face close to the other boy's.

"Get this straight. If you ever say another word to suggest Eleanor isn't a lady—or that she'd permit herself to behave in an unladylike way—I'll knock you from here to the East River." Giving Charlie a push, he stalked out.

Charlie pursed his lips. Planted his fists on his hips. "Ooo, that arrogant little *sheeny.* I rue the *day* he browbeat his way into this organization."

But he didn't say it loudly.

CHAPTER III

THE TOMMER

i

CHARLIE WHITTAKER TOOK the platform to introduce the visitor. He hooked his thumbs under the lapels of his frock coat and drummed his fingers on the outside as he spoke. Eleanor sat in the third row. Leo was in the row ahead, on the extreme right. He leaned forward, his elbows on his knees and his fingers laced beneath his chin. He was scowling.

The incident in the cloak room had unsettled Eleanor. She did like Leo, but she knew that if she admitted it, she was courting disaster. She was in such a state, she barely heard the first part of the introduction.

A freckled Irish boy named Shad Conway was seated next to her. When he let out a barely audible groan, she realized Charlie was still droning on.

"—and so we are indeed fortunate to have with us the proprietor and featured player of Bascom's Original Ideal Uncle Tom Combination."

Shoot, Eleanor thought as she took her first good look at the man Charlie was introducing. She might as well have stayed home. The visitor wasn't anyone famous, just a Tommer.

Still, she was curious as to why any professional, even a lowly Tom show actor, would seek out a group of young amateurs.

Charlie shot his hands high above his head. "—an actor who has traveled the length and breadth of the American continent in pursuit of his art, and now graces our humble stage with his august presence."

On Eleanor's left, the Conway boy whispered, "Jaysus, Charlie, calm down. It isn't the Second Coming."

Eleanor giggled behind her hand. A year ago, such a remark would have stunned her speechless. Now she took it entirely in stride; one of the first discoveries she'd made at the Association was that very few things were sacred to actors.

"And so, devoted fellow worshipers of Thespis, it is my high privilege and signal honor to present the celebrated and distinguished actor-manager, Mr. Jefferson—J.— *Bascom!*"

ii

The membership of the Booth Association and a half dozen female guests stood and applauded. Leo's clapping was perfunctory. As everyone sat down, he shot a wounded look at Eleanor. His mouth set as if to say he'd overcome her resistance yet.

The visitor took the platform. Eleanor gave the actor close scrutiny. Mr. Jefferson Bascom had a hooked nose, a large mustache, and wrinkled skin. He wasn't unhandsome, but his best years were behind him. He was sixty if he was a day.

She took note of the lack of any gray in his shoulder-length black hair. A wig, she decided. That was a clue to his character. She could think of several vain members of the Association who were always primping or displaying themselves in faddish clothes. Were all actors obsessed by their own images, like that man in the legend, Narcissus? She didn't think Leo was. He just knew what the Almighty had given him, and was determined to use it to advantage.

Shad Conway leaned close and touched her arm. She went rigid. Shad whispered, "Want to bet Jefferson J. Bas-

com's a false name? Little too close to Joe Jefferson to be
anything else."

She nodded and edged sideways on her chair, away from
Shad, while Mr. Bascom focused attention on himself by
glancing from face to face. His gaze lingered on Eleanor's
a bit longer than necessary. She was thankful the shoulders
of two members in the row ahead blocked Bascom's line of
sight when he tried to peer at the curve of her full bosom.

The actor spoke in what she had to admit was a mel-
lifluous voice—almost as rich as Leo's. "My young friends,
thank you indeed for allowing me to visit your meeting. I
am humbly grateful for that most flattering introduction by
Mr.—ah—"

"Whittaker," someone hissed.

"Whittaker," Bascom repeated without a blink. "Mod-
esty would force me to deny a great part of it, were it not
for one fact. The members of my troupe have made Bascom's Original Ideal Uncle Tom Combination unequivo-
cally the finest Tom show on tour anywhere. Further, it
is undeniable"—a self-effacing smile, and an index finger
pointed upward for emphasis—"undeniable that my Legree
has become the standard by which other interpretations of
the role are judged."

Shad Conway made a rude noise and muttered, "I never
heard of J. J. Bascom before tonight." Eleanor shushed
him.

"However"—Bascom began to strut back and forth
across the platform, pausing occasionally to point up this
or that word with a broad gesture—"personal problems on
the part of several members of the company necessitate my
replacing them before Bascom's Combination undertakes
its grand two-year Western tour just a few short days from
now. Hence my interest in this group—and my presence
among you."

A buzz of excitement traveled through the audience.
They understood. She noticed that Leo had lost his angry
expression and was looking interested. Even Eleanor felt a
little thrill. Never mind Bascom's age or his ridiculous wig.
He had the power to hire someone in Hutter Hall for a
professional engagement.

What was his company like? she wondered. There were

dozens of undistinguished if hardworking Tom troupes constantly crisscrossing the nation and playing one-night engagements in towns and smaller cities. The skimpiest company she'd ever heard about supposedly performed the play's twenty-nine male and female roles with a troupe of three, and no scenery. Despite Bascom's wrinkles and his hyperbole, his troupe surely had to be better than that. She sat forward on the edge of her chair, fascinated.

"—have positions on the extended tour for three new gentlemen and one new lady."

Bascom's eyes darted to Eleanor as he said that. He'd shifted to the left on the platform. The shoulders of the boys in the row ahead no longer protected her. She turned red as the actor's distinctly unpaternal gaze traveled up from her breasts to her throat and lingered on her lips. Leo looked as though he might lunge at the older man.

"Those selected shall receive handsome wages," Bascom boomed. Eleanor doubted it. "As well as full traveling expenses. More important, they shall have the privilege of joining a company that already includes eleven fine actors and actresses, including myself"—fifteen people counting the replacements; respectable—"and the distinguished American tragedian, Mr. Daniel Prince, who is our Uncle Tom."

When Shad nudged her shoulder, she was in better control, and didn't start. The boy whispered, "Aha! That fellow, I've heard of."

Charlie Whittaker turned and glowered. Shad ignored him.

"Prince drinks so much, no playhouse in town will hire him any longer. I'll bet he took this part out of desperation."

"Now," Bascom said, beginning to bounce on the toes of his cracked boots, "if there are any here who might be inclined to read for possible inclusion in the company—"

His gaze returned to Eleanor. Quickly she glanced into her lap so he wouldn't think she was a candidate. But she wished she could be. Going with Bascom's troupe, she'd be free of that cursed house forever.

"I have brought a prompter's script of the play. Do I have any applicants?"

Shad Conway's hand shot up. So did the hands of a number of others—including Leo's, Eleanor was surprised to see.

"What, no female candidates?" Bascom again let his eye rove until it came to rest on her. She couldn't help being flattered that he'd singled her out, but she doubted he was interested in her acting ability. She shook her head. His face fell. With less enthusiasm, he waved at one of the hand raisers in the front row.

"All right, sir, you first. We'll be reading from the opening scene in act one. Dialogue between Eliza and her husband George."

There were some groans. They elicited a sharp glance from Bascom. "Anyone unwilling to double in brass and appear in darkie roles need not bother to audition. I should point out that a player of Mr. Prince's stature does not consider it beneath him to don blackface and portray Uncle Tom."

"No, not when he can't get a part anywhere else," Shad laughed under his breath.

"And further, his talented wife delights audiences with her interpretation of Topsy. Now, young sir, you and one of your lady friends step up here."

One by one, three young men read the scene, each choosing one of the girls for a partner. Then came Leo's turn. His glance slid to Eleanor before he made his choice—the girl who'd just read. Eleanor knew the slight was deliberate, but she supposed she deserved it.

Leo's audition drew a favorable comment from Bascom, and some applause. Eleanor joined in. Leo noticed; when he looked at her, his face had an almost lovelorn expression for a moment.

When Shad was called forward, he grabbed Eleanor's hand. "Come along and read Eliza with me."

Before she was half out of her seat, Bascom exclaimed, "Yes, bring that young woman up here! Seldom have I seen feminine physiognomy more suited to gladdening the eye of provincial playgoers."

"I'm not a candidate, sir."

"I am crestfallen. No, I am devastated. I very much wanted to hear you read."

"I'll be glad to read with Shad so long as you know ahead of time that I'm not trying out for the troupe."

"Capital!" Bascom rushed down the steps; he couldn't wait to get his hand on her arm and assist her to the platform. Leo followed the actor's every move.

Bascom took hold of Eleanor's upper left arm. The back of his hand bumped her breast when he pretended to slip.

"Oh, my fault. Forgive me, Miss—?"

"Kent. Eleanor Kent."

"What a fetching creature you are," he murmured, almost dropping the prompt script. Shad caught it. A vein started to jump in Leo's neck.

"All right," Bascom said, hardly giving Shad a glance. "As I told the others, never mind the dialect at this stage. I only want your feeling for the material."

She and Shad got through just fourteen speeches before Bascom stopped them and snatched the script away. Eleanor was disappointed for Shad's sake. The others had been permitted to finish the scene.

Then, to her astonishment, Bascom started turning the pages of the script. "I'd like you to read a very short passage we haven't done before. Third act, fourth scene. Little Eva's chamber. Eva is dying. That's you, Miss Kent."

He thrust the script at her. "You don't have much dialogue. But it's an unparalleled opportunity to emote. As for you, Mr.—ah, ah—"

"Conway."

"Quite so. You read St. Clare's dialogue. I suppose I needn't tell you St. Clare is Eva's father?"

"No, sir, you need not. I have seen the play four times."

Shad was understandably miffed. Bascom had been looking at Eleanor while he addressed the boy.

Still with eyes fastened on her, the aging actor said, "I shall read Tom, and Marie's one line. You two give me as much business as you can, consistent with handling the script. All right, here we go. And, Miss Kent—"

His scrutiny made her squirm. "Yes, sir?"

"Kindly don't hold back a thing."

She had an uneasy feeling he was trying to put more into the plea than a reference to acting. But she pretended to be unaware.

"Begin with St. Clare's first speech, Mr.—ah—"

"Conway, Conway! Jaysus."

"Yes, yes, to be sure. Go ahead."

Shad cleared his throat, then practically bowled Eleanor over with his first line: "*Hush! She is dying!*"

Bascom spoke in a falsetto—as the white man's cousin, Marie. "*Dying!*"

Someone giggled. A glare from the actor silenced whoever it was.

Shad peered at the stage directions, then quickly picked up his cue. "*Oh! If she would only wake and speak once more—*"

He bent his head till his face was uncomfortably close to Eleanor's. From the corner of her eye she saw Leo watching. There was no question that he was jealous. Good.

Then Shad slid his arm around her waist. She stiffened. The reaction made him noticeably delay his next line. "*Eva darling!*"

She fought to control her unreasonable fear. He was holding her only because the script made it justifiable. She concentrated on the reading; she had no dialogue, but she did have a stage direction. She opened her eyes, then slowly let a smile form.

She raised her chin and opened her mouth as if about to speak. She thought she was prolonging the whole piece of business horribly. Shad's eyes were impatient. But Bascom seemed transported. He breathed a word not in the script.

"*Beautiful.*"

"Do you know me, Eva?" Shad exclaimed, sounding as if he didn't much care. She was reluctant to follow her next direction. Was Leo watching and noticing her hesitation? It took all of the nerve she had for her to throw her arms around Shad's neck.

"Lord God, what a face," Bascom murmured, just before Eleanor delivered her line in an intense stage whisper, "Dear—*Papa!*"

Flinging her arms wide, then letting them drop, she collapsed in Shad's arms.

He practically foamed with emotion as he spoke his line.

"Oh, heaven! This is dreadful! Oh! Tom my boy, it is killing me!"

In character as the old black, Bascom pointed at Eleanor. "Look at her, mas'r."

"Eva!" Shad paused for effect "She does not hear. Oh, Eva. Tell us what you see. What is it?"

Eleanor opened her eyes and smiled.

"Oh! Love! Joy! *Peace!"*

She collapsed again, even limper than before. It was the best she could do to follow her final stage direction—*Dies.*

She heard clapping. Bascom said in dialect, "Oh! Bless the Lord! It's over." Then he abandoned the accent. "That's fine."

Shad purpled. "But I have one more long speech."

"Not important. I have an idea of what you can do." He seized Eleanor's hand. "Miss Kent, you were highly impressive. Highly! Are you certain you can't consider yourself a candidate?"

She was surprised at how reluctant she felt when she replied, "No, sir, I have responsibilities at home."

"Oh." He glanced at her left hand. "Already married, are you?"

"Heavens no," she began, but Shad interrupted.

"She's hardly of marriageable age, Bascom. She just turned fifteen."

She knew Shad said that because he was hurt by the older man's indifference to his reading, and because he wanted to undermine her success if he could. Actors were warm, generous people, but she'd found they could also be supremely vindictive when professional success was at stake.

Bascom, however, wasn't the least put off.

"Fifteen? I'd swear she's three to five years older. So would every man, woman and child in our audience, I'll wager."

"Well, be that as it may"—gracefully Eleanor side-stepped his attempt to draw her into the curve of his arm—"I'm not free to leave New York just now."

Bascom shook his head. "Too bad. You read well and move nicely and I'd love to get you under—ah—" He coughed. "That is, with proper tutelage and in a company as distinguished as ours, your talent would surely flower. Well"—he fished in a food-spotted waistcoat, produced a soiled card—"as I said, we won't be leaving for some days yet. My office is my suite at the Paramount Hotel in lower Broadway. That's jotted on the reverse of the card. If you should change your mind, please come see me."

He gave her a last, imploring glance that seemed a trifle sad. Eleanor had quite lost her fear of him. He was just a harmless old man in seedy clothes and a wig that didn't fit very well. Yet, he had a certain avuncular quality that she liked.

"Thank you, Mr. Bascom," she said, meaning it.

There were two more auditions. When they were over, Bascom again addressed the group.

"I have been very impressed by what I have seen here this evening. Now I shall have to mull over my conclusions. Should I wish to call any of you back for a second reading, I shall be in touch on a personal basis, providing you have correctly listed your address on the sheet which Mr.—ah—"

"Whittaker," Charlie said.

"—which Mr. Whittaker provided. Thank you again, one and all."

Once more the members and their guests rose to give him a round of applause. Eleanor suddenly saw that Leo was missing. She discovered him by the door leading to the stairs. He was clapping for Bascom but watching her. She couldn't decipher the look in his dark eyes just before he turned and disappeared.

Was he still hurt about the way she'd rejected his invitation? Or was he disappointed by the inconclusive audition? She had a strange feeling she wouldn't be seeing him any more, and that made her sad.

As the clapping faded, she realized she'd dropped Bascom's card. She searched the floor until she found it.

iii

About four the next afternoon, Charlie Whittaker rang the mansion bell and asked for her. She met him in the library. He was out of breath.

"Eleanor, he *hired* him. Bascom hired that little Jew!"

"He hired *Leo*?"

Pouting, Charlie nodded.

She didn't know what to think—or how she should feel. Pleased? Sorrowful? There was no doubt about Charlie's feelings.

"To think a sheeny would win out over Christian actors—"

"Charlie, you mustn't keep making derogatory remarks about Leo's religion. You're only doing it because you're mad. We both know he's the best actor in the club. I can just see women fainting away when he emotes with that beautiful voice of his."

"How'd he get a voice like that? I suppose he thinks it's some sign God has *blessed* him!"

"Do sit down and get over your jealousy. The things you're saying are very unkind. It isn't at all like you."

He sank into a chair. "Guess it isn't. Don't know why I should be jealous, really. Pater and Mater wouldn't let me go on a long tour. Not yet. That's why I didn't even audition."

"How'd you find out about Leo?"

"Bascom came to the house." Charlie studied the carpet a while, then finally mumbled, "Leo's name and address were omitted from the list I gave him."

"Leo's too bright to accidentally leave—oh, Charlie. You didn't erase them?"

He transferred his attention to his kneecap. "Well, damn it, yes, I did. Nobody has a right to be that handsome. Besides, no harm was done in the long run. I couldn't keep up the pretense. I gave Bascom the address the minute he asked. I heard him tell his hack driver to go straight to Hester Street."

Strangely melancholy all at once, Eleanor sat down opposite her friend. "That's grand for Leo. Just grand. I know he'll go on the tour. He needs the money, and there's hardly room for him in that tenement where he lives."

Charlie shot her a sharp glance. "You know quite a bit about him, don't you? I've observed that you two are very friendly—"

"There's nothing wrong with being friendly to anyone! And that's all we are—friends."

He looked unconvinced. In a moment he went on.

"I wouldn't count on Leo getting rich. Before the meeting last night, Bascom told me he can't pay his other people very much due to Mr. Prince's high salary. Why do you think he came around to an amateur club?"

"Oh, that's it, then." She felt naive. "Cheap talent."

"Exactly."

"Still, Charlie, it's wonderful experience."

"I suppose. They are going all the way to California eventually. I wouldn't mind that part of it, I confess. I wouldn't mind being paid to travel and do work that's essentially enjoy—" He stopped. "What's wrong?"

I must leave this house.

But I can't.

And I may not even get to see him before he leaves.

Charlie could tell she was troubled. With genuine sympathy, he said, "Eleanor, please tell me what's wrong. Did I say something I shouldn't have?"

She shook her head, then fabricated a flimsy excuse about not being herself because of some trouble among the servants. Charlie didn't understand the reason her cheeks were red.

"You needn't feel bad about the readings," he said. "You did splendidly. Bascom would have hired you in a trice—he told me so when he picked up Leo's address. He wasn't interested in you merely because of your looks, either."

"Yes—well—I wouldn't be interested in two or three years of wandering back and forth over the prairies and mountains with Mr. Bascom's Tom troupe, thank you. I realize it's professional training, but I prefer to take mine here in New York."

Her face was red again. *Liar,* she thought. She was in a state of complete confusion. She knew it was dangerous to care for a boy, yet now that Leo Goldman was leaving, she discovered she cared for him.

And she desperately wanted to go with Bascom. But her responsibilities to Will and to her mother prevented it—

"Charlie," she said abruptly, "I must get back to the kitchen. Thank you for coming all the way up here with the news."

"Why, certainly. I had some errands with the carriage, and I thought you'd want to know."

She wasted no time ushering him to the door. When he was gone, she walked slowly up the stairs to her room. There she gazed at the smudged card tucked into the frame of her pier glass.

Jefferson J. Bascom's
ORIGINAL IDEAL UNCLE TOM
COMBINATION

featuring
Mr. Bascom's
world-renowned personification of
Legree

"Finest Tom Troupe
Traveling the Nation!"

The musty, humid house seemed to close in around her—lightless, cheerless. Tears ran down her cheeks. She snatched the card from the frame, tore it and flung the pieces at her feet.

CHAPTER IV

"HELL WITH THE LID OFF"

i

THE CITY OF Pittsburgh rose on a triangle of land whose western apex was the junction of the Allegheny and Monongahela Rivers. Eastward from the point to about Eleventh Street, the site of the Union Depot, the land was fairly level. Near Eleventh a hill rose to divide the triangular land mass.

The hill resembled a kind of fish fin running eastward to Twenty-eighth Street and beyond. It was a steep and formidable barrier to easy passage between the Allegheny and Monongahela sides although at Twenty-eighth it dipped down sufficiently to permit the cross street to straggle over the summit. The principal east-west railroad tracks lay at the base of the hill's north slope. There was a major crossing where Twenty-eighth intersected the tracks.

It was late Saturday afternoon following the start of the strike in Martinsburg. For several hours, individuals and families had been gathering on the north side of the hill directly above the Twenty-eighth Street crossing, as well as to the east and west. Now the hillside teemed with five to seven thousand observers, by Gideon's best guess. Most of them had come anticipating the arrival of the Philadelphia militia. And not a few of them had come in anticipation of bloodshed.

He really had no call to be superior, though. As a newsman, he was present for essentially the same reason.

Commanded by General Robert Brinton, the militiamen had arrived a short time ago. Six hundred of them—about half the number placed on active duty in response to the deteriorating situation in Pittsburgh.

The railroad strike had spread from West Virginia. Trainmen who worked for the Pennsylvania in Pittsburgh had refused to operate the line's engines, thereby idling nearly two thousand freight cars containing durable goods as well as perishables. All of those cars stood in the yards that stretched out below the north face of the hill. The durables would come to no harm, but thousands of dollars' worth of fruit and vegetables were rotting.

Since Thursday, relatively few freight or passenger trains had moved in or out of the city. Crowds of striking railroaders, their families, and those of sympathetic steelworkers had joined together to swarm through the yards and prevent it. Once in a while the strikers would allow a freight with livestock to pass so the animals wouldn't die. Everything else came to a standstill, the steelworkers swearing solidarity with the railroad men until the Pennsylvania canceled its wage cuts.

There had been occasional outbreaks of violence when the strikers came in contact with yard officials. Local militia and the Pittsburgh police had been unwilling or unable to stop the trouble. So finally, on this Saturday afternoon, July 21, a desperate telegraph appeal had been answered. The six hundred Philadelphia militia had arrived on a train whose cars had been struck and damaged by rocks and bricks thrown by mobs at Harrisburg and other points along the line.

Now, below the hill where the people stood or sat like spectators in a Roman arena, an officer of the militia shouted an order, *"The tracks must be cleared."*

A stir of excitement rippled along the hillside. In the crowd, Gideon noticed some members of the Pittsburgh militia. They had retired to rest and observe their fellow soldiers from the east. The Philadelphians, some in smart red blouses and some in blue, were formed up to the east

of the Twenty-eighth Street crossing. The militiamen nearest the crossing had shifted into a formation Gideon hadn't
seen since the war—the hollow square.

Those in the square faced hundreds of roughly dressed
civilians massed at the crossing and around it. Gideon's
vantage point for all this was just about halfway up the hill,
a few steps west of the rutted track of Twenty-eighth Street.

On command, the militiamen began to advance slowly
toward the crossing. There were a few curses, then some
shouted taunts; those at the crossing were in an ugly mood.

So were most of their supporters watching from above.
Soon a chant began on the hill. Though it was barely audible at first, Gideon had no trouble distinguishing the words.
Ever since his arrival late last night, he'd been hearing the
same words growled in ale houses and shouted by bands
of men roaming the yards.

"Bread or blood! Bread or blood! *Bread or blood!*"

Trouble was coming, serious trouble. He had no doubt
of it any longer.

The mob on the hillside contained some odd elements. Gideon had encountered several groups of well-dressed people
who'd brought picnic hampers. That reminded him of First
Manassas, when great crowds of Yankees had driven out from
Washington to watch the carnage. He'd briefly interviewed
one dentist who had come out because he'd heard there was
going to be "a good big fuss." Why in the world was the
viewing of violence so popular in America?

Most of the men and women on the hillside weren't pic-
nickers, but poorly dressed working people. Mill hands,
with their wives and their children. They'd come to show
support for the Pennsylvania crews.

On a spur track parallel with the main lines, Gideon suddenly saw dozens of men climbing up the sides of four
coupled coal cars. The men scrambled into the coal, laughing and jostling one another, then dabbing each other's
faces with sooty thumbs. Soon several picked up lumps of
coal—weapons inadvertently provided by the line that
couldn't meet its shipping commitments.

The spread of the strike had been swift and unpredict-
able. President Hayes had sent the requested troops to
Martinsburg, only to receive another message saying that
violence there had stopped. Meanwhile a confrontation was

taking place in Baltimore. State troops called out for the emergency fired into a mob and killed at least ten civilians, perhaps more.

That had happened last night, while Gideon was aboard one of the few passenger trains permitted to enter the city. When he stepped off and heard about it, he was glad one of the *Union's* men was in Baltimore.

He'd boarded the train for Pittsburgh on a hunch the city would be a major flashpoint. When he'd come in, there had already been crowds at the crossing, which was now completely blocked. But the train had gotten through to the depot. And during the night there had only been small and isolated outbreaks of violence.

This afternoon, however, the situation was entirely different. Moving through the crowd and making rapid notes—phrases that described what he was seeing and hearing—he still felt like a ghoul. His hunch had paid off, and here he was, just waiting for trouble to start. When it did, lives might be lost. The railroad strike was a perfect symbol of the tormenting paradox of his profession—human suffering sold more newspapers than happiness did.

He drifted on, all but unnoticed. He was dressed in a shabby jacket and old trousers with a dark blue scarf tied around his neck and a peaked cap on his head.

He paused to introduce himself to a weary-looking woman of middle age. "Is your husband a railroad man?"

After regarding him suspiciously for a moment, she answered, "No, but he's down there at the crossing because he's a workingman. It's all the same cause."

A cloud passed in front of the sun. The hillside darkened. The woman glanced at Gideon's pad and busy pencil. "You sure you aren't an eye?"

"What?" He touched the leather patch. "Do you mean this?"

She shook her head. "I mean, are you a Pinkerton?"

He understood then. Allan Pinkerton's National Detective Agency employed a wide-open eye as its symbol, along with the motto "We Never Sleep." Once or twice before he'd heard the agency's operatives referred to as "eyes"—either sarcastically or nervously, depending upon the speaker.

The woman went on. "You sure you aren't taking down names? You ain't gettin' mine."

"Ma'am, I told you I'm with the New York *Union.* Our paper supports the strike, provided no one starts destroying property or taking lives—"

"Hah! Then you don't really support the strike at all. You think Tom Scott and the rest of them rich bastards will give us bread just because we ask? Devil they will. We got to take it. Scrap for it. Bleed for it."

Sadly, he realized he might have been listening to Sime Strelnik. The woman scanned his face, contemptuous.

"Your newspaper's probably like all the rest of them. Your bosses don't really give a damn if people like us starve by the thousands."

Before he could argue, she turned her back on him. He watched her walk to another worker hunkered down a few feet away. The man was fingering a melon-sized rock.

The woman said, "Beg pardon, mister. Have you seen two youngsters with their hands full of leftover Fourth of July torpedoes?" When the man shook his head, she moved on down the hill, calling, "Lindsey? Verne? Where'd you boys get to?"

Gideon was suddenly diverted by a flash of color higher on the hillside. He turned, focused his good eye, and frowned at the sight of a man with a nondescript face and equally drab clothing. What distinguished the man was the neckerchief he wore. A railroader's neckerchief, like Gideon's, except that it was an unusual color—bright yellow. Most were dark blue or dark red, to absorb sweat and hide dirt.

But even at that, the yellow neckerchief would have been unremarkable except for one fact. Not ten minutes ago, back near the Union Depot, he'd seen a different man wearing one exactly like it.

On a chance, he gazed west along the side of the hill. Sure enough, there was the man from the depot. All at once Gideon felt uneasy.

The man from the depot was making his way in Gideon's direction, moving steadily but with no apparent haste. Gideon checked the second man again. He was coming down the hillside to intersect the path of the first. As the two appeared and disappeared behind shifting groups of people, Gideon understood the reason for the yellow bandannas.

Easy identification in what could become a very confused situation.

The men were searching for someone; their movements were too deliberate for it to be otherwise. They studied faces as they walked, and they didn't do it casually. For a moment he thought the men might be after him, but that was ridiculous. Even though his editorials had repeatedly criticized the Pennsylvania Railroad and its tame legislators in Harrisburg, right now Tom Scott had more important things to worry about than trailing an unfriendly journalist. Gideon could only conclude the two men were detectives sent to the hill to spot those fomenting violence. Spot them and, later, testify against them in a trial.

"Bread or blood! BREAD OR BLOOD!"

The continuous chanting had grown louder. The Philadelphia militiamen had fixed their bayonets and were advancing slowly toward the mob blocking the crossing. Gideon glanced over his shoulder. The men in yellow bandannas were still drifting his way, but paying no attention to him.

In the midst of all the noise, he suddenly had a good thought for the opening of the dispatch he'd write when the day was over. He flipped to a new page on his pad and scribbled:

> *Citizens of Pittsburgh sometimes call their city hell with the lid off, and not always in jest. When the fires of the steel mills light the evening sky, the metaphor is seen to be an apt one. Today, the widening railroad strike gave the phrase a new, grimmer meaning—*

He put a squiggle beneath the last word, then made a face. He was as shameless as any ambulance-chasing cub on the *Union* staff. Writing of disaster before it happened, as if it were *certain* to happen.

But it was. An angry roar came from those blocking the crossing, and from the thousands on the hillside. He had a feeling some of them weren't sure why they were shouting—or even why they were present. He passed three such men, all drunk as owls and stumbling against one another. One of the men had a pistol in his belt.

The Philadelphia militiamen at the front of the hollow

square had reached the crossing. They began to poke at the nearest civilians with their bayonets. Very lightly—very cautiously—barely touching an arm here, a shoulder there. But probing, jabbing, nonetheless.

An officer again ordered the civilians to clear the crossing. The bayonets thrust and jabbed. Some of the workers fell back. The men who'd climbed atop the four coal cars watched the bayonets flashing and grew angry. One of them threw a lump of coal.

The coal struck a militiaman's head, knocking his black-plumed hat off. The soldiers on either side of him spun and glared at the men on the four coal cars. Somehow, just that attention incited the men. From the cars there suddenly came a barrage of coal.

This is the start, Gideon thought. He saw it in almost every sunlit face, and heard it in the chant for bread or blood. The militiamen dodged the chunks of coal. Their officers bawled orders to keep them from firing at their attackers.

While Gideon was gloomily studying the scene, his eye was drawn to a slab-jawed fellow at the bottom of the slope. The man was gazing up at him. Just as Gideon noticed him, he started to climb a footpath, heading in Gideon's direction.

Gideon's heart pounded. Exactly like the two who had again vanished in the hillside crowds, the man wore a bright yellow bandanna.

ii

There was a great deal to keep track of simultaneously, and Gideon's glance kept flying from one spot to another—first to the crossing, then to the man climbing the footpath, then to someone yelling a taunt from higher on the hill, then to a couple of giggling boys who dodged behind a wooden watchman's shanty near the crossing.

The shack screened the boys from the civilians and soldiers just below. The boys began to pick up rocks. Grinning adults nearby tossed them extra stones, sticks, and even a couple of old shoes. When the boys had their arms full, they jumped into the open on the east side of the shanty and started throwing the objects at the militiamen.

None of the objects was large enough to do serious damage. But the harassment drew more glares from the soldiers. A rifle or two swung toward the shanty. Several people shrieked and ducked. The boys scampered behind the shanty again, pleased with themselves, and that might have been the end of it if those on the hillside hadn't begun doing what the boys had done.

Throwing shoes.

Rocks.

Broken pieces of brick.

Anything available.

One militiaman went to his knees, a bloody gash opened in his temple by a chunk of brick. He had his rifle halfway to his shoulder before an officer seized his arm to restrain him.

But hundreds saw the young man start to take aim. Defiant cries rose all over the hillside.

"Shoot!"

"Shoot, you sons of bitches!"

"YAH, YAH, YAH—WHY DON'T YOU SHOOT?"

The slab-jawed man was still working his way upward on the congested footpath. His coat flapped and Gideon glimpsed a pistol. Again he tried to tell himself the man wasn't after him. Perhaps the trio in yellow bandannas didn't even work for the railroad. They might be agitators acting on behalf of the International. Informants had told him Marxists were definitely operating within the strike movement, hoping to increase the ferocity of any confrontation.

Suddenly there were loud cracklings, like gunshots. People screamed and scattered. Gideon held his place and saw two boys being collared by the woman to whom he'd spoken earlier. Spurts of blue smoke on the ground behind them told him the boys had ignited some of their Fourth of July torpedoes. No one down at the crossing seemed to realize they were hearing firecrackers.

The loud reports, the missiles raining from the hillside, the bloodythirsty yells of the civilians—all combined to spread panic among the Philadelphians. Nearly every man in uniform was bellowing something at the civilians—

profanity, commands, pleas for reason—God alone knew what all. In the midst of all that noise, Gideon didn't hear the shot that touched off the carnage. Nor did he see who fired it. He couldn't tell whether it had come from the hillside or the crossing. All he knew was that, without warning, the militiamen knelt or stood and began shooting in all directions.

A man screamed and pitched off one of the coal cars. Another civilian fell at the crossing, hit in the chest. Ten feet to Gideon's right, a girl of three or four dropped her rag doll and screamed. A man bent over her, pulled her bloodied skirt away, and Gideon heard him cry, "My God, half her knee's gone."

He started toward the distraught father to see if he could help. He'd taken just two long steps in the chaos of exploding firearms, running civilians, thickening smoke when two men seized his arms from behind.

He writhed, lunged, tried to pull and kick his way free but the two were strong. A well-dressed civilian went fleeing by, holding his top hat in place with both hands. As soon as he was out of the way, Gideon saw the slab-jawed man approaching from the footpath.

He wrenched his head around. Glimpsed exactly what he expected to see—a yellow bandanna knotted at the throat of the man holding his right arm. He was sure the man on the left wore one as well.

Members of the Pittsburgh militia who'd withdrawn to the hillside were up and running now, driven by conscience to help their fellow soldiers. Half a dozen of them were coming from the west, on a path that would bring them right to Gideon—but probably not fast enough to be of help.

The slab-jawed man crowded in close. Drew out his pistol. One of the others grabbed Gideon's hair. The three pressed around him, making it virtually impossible for the gun to be seen.

Rifles roared at the crossing. Hand weapons began to answer from the hillside. Some of the spectators were gleefully potting at the militiamen, scattering scores of others around them. In the confusion, these three who had obviously been following him for some time would do what they'd been hired to do.

"Who sent you?" Gideon gasped at the slab-jawed man. "Tom Courtleigh?"

"Smart bugger, ain't he?" said the unseen man at Gideon's left. The slab-jawed man snickered, his smile revealing brown teeth.

"Why, Mr. Kent," he said, "we ain't s'posed to use any names. 'Cept yours, of course." The muzzle of the pistol jabbed Gideon's belly. "Let's just say we're bringin' regards from a friend in Chicago."

Gideon wrenched to the left. The man holding his right arm exclaimed, "Hurry it up, Jim. Them Pittsburgh sojers are comin' right this way."

The slab-jawed man took time to glance over Gideon's shoulder and verify the warning. Again Gideon lunged. He couldn't free himself. The slab-jawed man retreated one step. He took aim. The pistol cracked, the noise all but unnoticed in the pandemonium.

At first Gideon felt no more than a sting in his left side. Then, rapidly, dizziness and pain swept over him. His knees buckled. The two men continued to prop him up while they and their leader tore off the yellow bandannas. Then they let go and scrambled out of the way of the Pittsburgh militiamen.

Gideon tumbled sideways down the hill. He dug his hands in the dirt and stopped rolling as one militiaman yelled, "Francis, we should help that fella. He's bleedin'—"

"I wouldn't lift a hand to help any of these civilians. They get hurt, it's their own damn fault for comin' out here to cause trouble."

The voice faded. Gideon lay on his belly, gazing at the summit of the hill. Between the flickering figures of the Pittsburgh men running by, he saw the three thugs climbing Twenty-eighth Street and disappearing over the top of the ridge.

All around he heard guns volleying. Men cursing or yelling in pain. Women shrieking. Children wailing or calling for their parents.

Someone stumbled into him. His hands lost their hold and he started rolling again, over and over down the hillside. The cindery soil tore his face open. He crashed against the watchman's shanty, his descent arrested. He could feel blood sopping his left side.

How badly was he hurt? No way to tell. He shouted. No one heard. Or if they did, they refused to come to his aid.

He thought of Courtleigh. So full of hatred, he'd had to pay men to balance his accounts—and in such a way that he could never be held responsible. Gideon didn't like to believe Sime Strelnik had been right, and that the Courtleighs of the world were beyond the reach of justice. But because they could hire others to kill for them, perhaps they were.

How had the three men found him? Followed him on the train to Pittsburgh? Or had they been watching at the depot, just like the old woman in Chicago six years ago?

He'd never know the answer. It made little difference anyway. He was frightened of the blurred quality of his right eye, and of an uncontrollable heaviness of his eyelid.

Julia's dear face flashed into his mind.

Then poor Margaret's.

Will's.

Eleanor's—God, why hadn't she answered his letters, so that he could have seen her one time before he died?

You aren't going to die, he told himself. But he feared it was empty confidence. The left side of his chest felt as if it had been set afire.

He thought of Matt. The book they'd done together. He was furious and sad that he might never see a copy of *100 Years.* He no longer cared whether it succeeded or failed. It was a good work, it said what he wanted to say, and Matt's illustrations were genius. That was enough.

The thunder of firearms had become almost continuous. His left shoulder was wedged between the ground and the wall of the watchman's shanty. He saw distorted images of people racing by—grotesque shapes against the ridge and the summer sky.

"Wrong," he said, growing delirious. "Wrong—all this. Bread, but—not at—this price—"

The almost incoherent whisper faded. He braced a palm beneath his body, vainly tried to lift himself. "Jesus Christ," he gasped, more as a prayer than an oath. In pain, he fell back, his head slamming the side of the shanty.

He fought the weight of his right eyelid. He couldn't keep it open. He slipped away to darkness, terrified that he'd never wake again.

CHAPTER V

THE PUNISHERS

i

LIKE A GREAT many theatrical people, Eleanor preferred the fantasy of the stage to the reality of the everyday world. Consequently she had little interest in major news events, and seldom let them intrude into her thinking. That weekend, though, such intrusion couldn't be avoided. With one exception—Margaret—everyone in the household, even Will, was talking about the strike and the frightful headlines it had generated:

Bloodshed in Baltimore!
———o———
Looters Threaten Pittsburgh!
———o———
The Great Strike Spreads!

When Eleanor went downstairs for Sunday breakfast, the serving girls had a nervous, fluttery air. All of them seemed in a hurry to rush back to the kitchen. Eleanor said to one of them, "What on earth's making you so jumpy, Bridgit?"

"Why, I'm anxious to keep up with the latest about the

577

strike, mum. Most of the papers are puttin' out special Sunday extras."

Eleanor nearly dropped her coffee cup. The trend toward regular Sunday editions was accelerating, but still met resistance from some clerics and their conservative congregations. The *Union* wasn't yet publishing on the Sabbath. A few months before Gideon had moved out, she recalled him saying it was probably inevitable, though. The strike was truly an event of apocalyptic importance if the New York dailies were rushing extras onto the streets today.

She followed Bridgit toward the kitchen. "Has the *Union* put out an extra?"

"We understand it will, mum. The *Union* and several others that are a wee bit behind the rest. Mills has gone to fetch the latest batch. He should be back soon."

Growing more and more curious, Eleanor walked into the kitchen. All the servants were gathered around cook, who was reading from a paper Eleanor identified as the *National Republican,* published in Washington. Tense faces turned Eleanor's way as she walked in. Normally she would have been greeted as befitted the mistress of the house. Today, with the world in turmoil, only nods or strained smiles acknowledged her arrival.

"—an' the fact is clearly manifest," cook read in her resonant voice, "that communistic ideas are very widely entertained in America by the workmen employed in mines and factories and by the railroads. This poison was introduced into our social system by European laborers. Now it is true that postwar prosperity has fa—fa—"

Bridgit glanced over her shoulder to help her with the word: "Facilitated."

"Just what I was about to say." Cook let the younger girl see her displeasure. She rattled the paper, cleared her throat and resumed, "Facilitated the sudden"—another pause; this time Bridget kept quiet and cook was forced to stumble through on her own—"acquisition of wealth through dubious and unscrupulous means—Lord, why can't they use plain words ordinary folk can understand? Where was I—ah. It is also true that the crimes of certain men who made haste to grow rich are—oh, you take over." She thrust the newspaper at the butler, who finished the sentence:

"Are reprehensible." Samuel scowled. "Since when is it a crime to grow rich?" he asked rhetorically. Then he went on, "Nevertheless, the rail strike is nothing less than communism in its worst and most poisonous form—not only unlawful and revolutionary but anti-American. It is the dread Commune of 1871 reborn on our very soil!"

He ended the reading dramatically. Reaction ranged from ashen faces to a breathy "Amen." Eleanor was about to ask a question when Mills tromped in, carrying more papers.

"The *Union*'s out." His voice was strangely hoarse. "It contains Mr. Kent's final dispatch from Pittsburgh."

Eleanor rushed to his side. "What do you mean, final?"

He was careful to avoid her eyes. "During yesterday's violence, he was shot."

ii

She could hardly believe it. But the black-bordered box on page one was indeed headed OUR PUBLISHER INJURED.

Quickly she read the special bulletin copy. Her father had been shot during mob violence at the Twenty-eighth Street crossing of the Pennsylvania Railroad. He'd been taken to a hospital and, following removal of the bullet from his left side, his condition had stabilized.

Eleanor was conscious of the servants pressing in around her, as anxious as she was to learn what had happened. A part of her hated Gideon—and with justification, she believed—but at a time like this, he remained her father. Blood ties were stronger than any other, she was forced to admit.

"My Lord, they burned boxcars and rolled 'em into the depot where the Philly militia spent the night!" Bridgit exclaimed, pointing to the ten-deck headline of the main story. But Eleanor was scanning Theo Payne's signed editorial statement below the boxed bulletin.

—and while the arson, bloodshed and looting in Pittsburgh cannot be condoned in the name of the struggle for workingmen's rights, neither can we condone what

is being done in other quarters. We refer to the widely
published accusations against the strikers.

It is alleged that, to the last man, the participants
in the strike are Marxists. Such statements are not
only false and dishonorable; they are dangerous. Society must rigorously punish lawbreakers, but just as
rigorously protect the right of legitimate protest. It is
the opinion of this journal, and this writer, that a
peaceful strike falls under the last heading.

We want no part of Communism in America. But
neither do we want it used as an all too convenient
tar brush with which the illiterate, the gullible and the
unscrupulous alike may attempt to ruin reputations
and eliminate honest dissent.

Reactions were quick and varied. Eleanor admired what
Payne had written. But one of the other girls who'd been
reading along with her exclaimed, "Why, he's as much as
standing up for them Communards."

Eleanor frowned. "Surely you don't get that out of it,
Martha."

"Indeed I do, ma'am." Others nodded vigorously.

"But Payne says Communism isn't wanted in America.
Look—it's right there."

"I'm reading between the lines, ma'am. I won't say any
more."

"Yes! Explain what you mean."

"Well, ma'am—I beg your pardon, since your father is
the publisher, and he's just been hurt, but—the truth is, I
trust other papers more than I trust the *Union*. Other papers are more patriotic. That one, for instance."

She pointed to another edition Cook had picked up from
the stack Mills had brought in. One of the main headlines
was clearly visible:

COMMUNISTS LEAD PITTSBURGH RAMPAGE!

Eleanor realized what the young girl was saying. The
Union had been misread, misjudged, and found guilty of
standing for something other than the best interests of the
country—at least as most of the people in the kitchen perceived them. She was appalled that anyone with half a brain

could be taken in by sweeping allegations and at the same time distort or actually ignore the exact words Payne had used to explain the *Union*'s position. She didn't know who was right or wrong in the debate over the strike, but she was learning some unpleasant lessons about human fear and fallibility.

The butler summed it up. "If this is an example of how trade unions work to improve the lot of their members, I say hang every man who belongs to one!"

No one in the kitchen disagreed, not even Eleanor—she was too stunned by the ferocity of Samuel's statement.

iii

Around dusk it began to drizzle. Margaret had stayed in her bedroom throughout most of the weekend. But she lurched to Eleanor's room around nine o'clock.

Eleanor hadn't told her mother about Gideon's injury. She doubted Margaret would have understood what she was trying to say, and she knew the mere mention of her father would probably send her mother into a spell of incoherent fury. It always did.

She'd shared the news only with Will. His face showed barely a glimmer of reaction. When she told him Gideon would pull through, he murmured, "Good," and walked off. It was typical of his listless behavior of late.

A moment after Margaret entered their room, Eleanor thought her mother must have heard the bad news from one of the servants. She'd seldom seen the older woman so wild-eyed.

"The men are in the Park again. I opened the window and I could hear their voices."

"Oh, Mama, please don't start—" Eleanor bit her lip.

There was no point in arguing with someone so disturbed.

"Please don't worry," she resumed, as patiently as she could. "I'll inspect the downstairs to make sure everything's locked."

Margaret's pale hand quivered near her chin. "You've seen them too?"

"No, Mama. I'm just trying to set your mind at ease."

"I tell you they're watching this house!"

Gently, Eleanor patted her mother until she calmed a little. Then she took Margaret's hand and led her back down the hall. "I'll make certain we're safe. Leave everything to me. Here's your room—why don't you lie down and rest if you can?"

Margaret peered at her in a vacant way, as if she didn't recognize her daughter. The whiskey stench was stronger than ever. For a moment Eleanor understood why her father had found living with Margaret impossible.

It took the older woman almost a minute to fumble the bedroom key out of her pocket, then insert it in the lock. She seemed alarmed by Eleanor's attempts to help, as though her daughter's presence somehow threatened the sanctity of the room. Finally she got the door open and disappeared inside without a word.

Eleanor heard her relock the door. Wearily, she turned and walked down the front stairs. Because the evening was sultry, the window on the landing was open. As Eleanor walked by, she glanced outside. She stopped, her heart suddenly beating fast.

Was her mind playing tricks too? Against the darker background of the trees in Central Park, other shadows seemed to be stirring. Stirring and flowing across Fifth Avenue.

Then, distinctly, she heard a man's voice. He was calling something—an order, a question—to someone else. The shadow figures flowed on, not fully visible or even clearly defined as yet, but unmistakably *there,* a tide flooding toward the mansion.

She glanced over her shoulder. Where was Will? Reading in his room. The servants? Mills had the evening off. That left Samuel, plus one footman and the women.

And she could think of no weapons in the house except for the antique sword hanging in the parlor.

Picking up her skirts, she raced down the last flight just as the unlocked front door burst open. The first of the shabbily dressed men lumbered in, a billy in his fist.

iv

The man shouted to others crowding in behind him.

"There's one!" He peered at Eleanor. "You be Kent's daughter, girl? You're too finely dressed for one of the kitchen sculls."

She counted at least six in addition to the man with the billy. He was middle-aged, paunchy, and smelled of sweat and tobacco. A sore glistened on the stubble of his right cheek. Trembling but trying not to show it, she said to him, "Get out of this house."

The leader snickered. "What? You're givin' orders to us? We're the ones doin' the dishin' out, missy. We don't care for your dirty Comminist father, his Comminist paper nor his Comminist family, either."

He stuck the billy in his rope belt and reached behind him. One of the others handed him a bucket of red paint. He flung the contents over the wall to his left.

At the side of the house, glass broke. A dining room window. Footsteps pounded along Sixty-first Street.

Eleanor glanced anxiously at the staircase. The running footsteps faded, then they grew loud again. The men at the rear were inside the house. Cook screamed.

"Will, lock your door!" Eleanor cried. She spun and raced for the parlor. Laughing, the thug with the billy came after her. So did two of his companions.

Glancing over her shoulder, she saw a man with his pants open, and something white in his hand. The sight of it turned her cheeks scarlet. The man hummed and danced a clumsy jig as urine ran down the foyer wall.

"I don't think she liked the looks of Sharkey's machine," said one of the men crowding the parlor door. Deep in the lightless room, she dashed for the mantel. She wrenched the French infantry sword from its pegs. Yanked the scabbard off and cast it aside. Shrieks and the sounds of breaking furniture and glass grew steadily louder at the back of the house.

Standing in darkness with her three pursuers silhouetted against the glow of gaslight in the foyer, Eleanor had a slight advantage. If only she had the nerve to use it.

The man who'd spoken touched his crotch. "Maybe she'll like mine a little bet—"

Eleanor ran at him. The sword would have pierced his groin if he hadn't pivoted to the left, taking the blade in his right thigh. His trousers tore. He yelled but he didn't fall. He pulled a shot-loaded stocking from his rear pocket and whipped it against her temple.

The blow drove her all the way back to the mantel. She struck her head, grew momentarily dizzy. A second man leaped at her.

Hard, rough nails dug the inside of her wrist. Try as she would, she couldn't hold on to the sword. The man grabbed it.

"I got the sticker, Freddie." The man's labored breathing slowed as he spoke to the leader. "Hubble didn't tell us the gal was a looker."

Hubble? Who was that?

The man yanked her arm. "Let's get them clothes off, gal. We're going to give you what for—"

"I'm first." The leader shoved the other man aside. The wounded one had collapsed into a chair, his stabbed leg stuck out in front of him. The foyer gaslight gleamed on the blood staining his pants.

"First," the leader repeated. "Come on, dear. Come on, you comminist bitch. Don't be shy. Show Freddie your tits an' your other treasures—what d'you say?"

And then two of them were all over her with strong hands she couldn't turn aside.

They pressed her against the mantel. Her bodice tore. She writhed, kicked, bit at the hands groping over her body. Her struggle only seemed to excite them further. They got through to her undergarments, ripped them and flung her down on the uncarpeted hearth.

Her ruined dress bunched into a hard, hurtful knot beneath her. The hearthstone was unbearably cold on the backs of her thighs. Freddie knelt and worked a finger, then a thumb between her legs.

Pushing.

Twisting.

Hurting—

Her heart began to pound in her bare breast. She felt sick at her stomach as Freddie touched her—thrust at her— but not with his hand any longer. She bit down on her lower lip while he grunted.

God, it was painful. She squeezed her eyes shut. She couldn't move beneath Freddie's heaving body. The second man was behind her, holding her wrists up over her head. There was no appeal. No reprieve. And nothing but her will to prevent them from knowing how much they were hurting and humiliating her.

I will not scream.

She said it over and over, in silence, her eyes closed, her cheeks wet with tears, as Freddie jerked and gasped.

I will not let such animals hear me scream.

Animals.

Men.

The same thing.

All the same thing.

Leo Goldman might never have existed.

V

When the sounds of the destruction reached the second floor, Margaret Kent dropped the bottle from which she'd been sipping, unbolted her door and stumbled out of her room.

She brushed away the loose hair that blurred her vision like a veil. Two men—two strangers—appeared at the head of the stairs. One of them emptied a bucket of red paint on a wall. Then they saw her.

There was danger here. *Danger.* All at once she was lucid, and in charge of herself. She calmly locked her door from the outside. Then she glanced across the hall, to where she thought she'd heard a whisper.

Sure enough, she saw part of Will's white face—half a nose, a frightened eye—beyond the narrow opening of his door. Behind her, she heard the men advancing. She knew who they were, of course. She wanted to howl with fright. But she fought the impulse long enough to say, "Will, bolt your door and pile furniture in front of it. Don't open the door unless you're told to do so by Eleanor or cook or Samuel or someone else whose voice you recognize."

She heard one of the men say, "Must be old lady Kent."

"Will, *do it!*"

He obeyed, shutting the door. Then she turned to confront them.

Her mind gave way.

They've come for me. Come to punish me, just as I knew they would.

Eleanor had secretly laughed at her fears. Margaret had sensed the disbelief a dozen times. But the men were real. They'd been biding their time in the Park. Waiting all through the autumn. The winter. The spring.

Now they'd come. Now Eleanor would *believe.*

Screaming in a wild way that made the two roughly clad men exchange hesitant looks, Margaret ran from them. She couldn't flee past them, so it was logical to flee in the other direction. *Punish,* the pumping of her heart seemed to murmur in her ear. *Punish* for hurting Gideon. *Punish* for deceiving Gideon. *Punish* for alienating Gideon's children.

Too late, she remembered there was no exit at the end of the corridor toward which she was running. She tried to check her forward momentum. Making a kind of mewing noise, she extended her hands toward the nearest wall. Then she stumbled. She saw a looming reflection of her own gaping mouth, immense eyes, unkempt hair in the glass of the tall window.

She fell against the window, and through it, and down. It was only a fall of a single story, but the lawn was hard despite its mat of trimmed grass. Had she fallen at a slightly different angle, she might have sustained only a broken bone or a few bruises. But she was howling and flailing, and her head rolled under her body just before the impact. Her neck broke and she died.

vi

Within fifteen minutes the house was quiet again. Only the weeping of one of the servant girls broke the silence. She staggered half-naked through the downstairs, repeatedly wiping parts of her body with a piece of towel. One of the men had assaulted her in an unspeakable way, and her voice was like some battered wind instrument wailing a distorted tune.

On the floor of the darkened parlor, Eleanor roused from

the half-conscious state into which she'd let herself escape after the men had used her. She lifted her head. Pushed with her hands. Retched when she grew aware of the wetness between her legs.

Finally she gained her feet and stayed upright by seizing the mantel and holding on. Her left hand accidentally knocked against the tea bottle. As it started to tip over the edge, she gasped and caught it. She was shaking as she set it back in place.

"Miss Eleanor? Where are you?"

It was Samuel. Frantically she tugged her skirt down over the tatters of underclothing. She covered her bare breasts with her forearms and turned sideways to the door as his shadow filled it.

"I'm"—*speak louder or he'll suspect*—"I'm in here, Samuel."

She edged toward the periphery of the gaslight. "Would you find a blanket for me, please? They tore my dress."

Blood shone in the hair above his left ear. "Is that all they did, Miss Eleanor?"

She almost told the truth. It would have been comforting to share the anguish. She couldn't.

Don't let anyone see what's been done to you. The filthy, humiliating thing that's fouled your body forever.

"Miss Eleanor?"

Bascom said you were an actress. ACT!

"Yes, Mills, that's all. I used the old Lafayette sword and frightened them off."

"Oh, that's a blessing. I'll fetch a blanket. Be right back."

His angular shadow followed him. Eleanor leaned her forehead against the mantel. Now she knew what men and women did together. It was hurtful, horrible, and it only strengthened her convictions about the pain love could cause.

Somewhere in the downstairs, the weeping of the serving girl went on and on. So did the silent screaming in Eleanor's head.

CHAPTER VI

HATRED

i

THE SANCTUARY WAS an airless oven. Gideon's tightly bandaged wound throbbed under the hot layers of his singlet, shirt, waistcoat and suit of mourning broadcloth. It was Monday afternoon, a full week after the invasion of the house.

The pastor was the one who'd taken over the pulpit of St. Mark's Methodist Episcopal Church following Jephtha's death. He moved down to the closed coffin. Elaborately scrolled and finished with an imitation silver patina, the coffin lay on trestles hidden by huge arrangements of roses and lilies. The heat had already wilted most of the flowers.

The pastor clasped his hands and began to pray for the soul of the departed, Margaret Marble Kent.

Gideon bowed his head. He closed his eye and used his right hand to conceal the upper part of his face. The grief grew steadily stronger.

The devastating news had reached him in the hospital in Pittsburgh. Since then, the strike violence had flickered out in the East, only to erupt elsewhere. The worst outbreaks had occurred in Chicago and St. Louis. Others on the *Union* would report what had happened. He'd put most of it out of his mind.

Most, but not all. He could never forget the men in the yellow bandannas. Or the words growled just before the gun blew a red hole in his left side.

He'd been wounded late on Saturday, over a week ago. He'd finally come back to his senses the following Monday afternoon. A doctor was waiting to say the bullet had been removed with no difficulty—and to hand him a telegraph message. Twenty minutes after he'd read the unbelievable words sent by Theo Payne, he was dressed and on his way out of the hospital.

He was pale and weak. Three doctors tried to stop him, using everything short of physical force. They said he was risking collapse if he left without at least a week's rest.

He left anyway. He telegraphed the grim news to Julia— she was lecturing in Macon, Georgia—then went to the burned-out shell of the Union Depot to catch a passenger train east.

In New York he'd gone neither to the *Union* nor to the hotel where he'd been living for the past year. He'd caught a hack directly to the house. When he arrived, he was astonished to see Eleanor out in front, shooing a carriage-load of gawkers away from the curb. Mills was hammering boards over broken windows.

Eleanor turned toward him just as he stepped unsteadily from the hack. It was early Wednesday morning, a cool, crisp day. Unusual weather for July. His daughter wore a black armband. Except for a small bruise on the left side of her jaw, she showed no aftereffects of the terror that had swept through the house the preceding Sunday night.

No, that wasn't quite correct, he realized a moment later. In her dark, oval eyes he detected a terrible anguish.

"Hello, Father."

That was all she said. She turned and preceded him into the house. There was no inquiry about his wound; nothing except that lifeless greeting. But contempt animated her face when Will ran across the paint-smeared foyer and threw himself into Gideon's arms.

Despite the pain Will inadvertently caused, Gideon hugged his son and was hugged in return. Dry-eyed, Eleanor marched up the staircase and disappeared.

Since that homecoming, Gideon's conversations with his daughter had been few and brief. On her part they were terse to the point of rudeness. But one exchange yielded a tantalizing fact pertaining to the invasion of the house.

Gideon's first theory about the invasion was that it was simply a spontaneous reaction to Payne's front-page statement in the Sunday extra. A second suspicion presented itself when Eleanor said one of the thugs had spoken a name: Hubble. No indication of how you spelled it.

Eleanor thought Hubble had given the men instructions about where to go and what to do. She couldn't recall exactly when the name had been used—she glanced away as she said that, and Gideon knew she was lying—but she'd swear on her grave it was spoken during the attack.

The resulting suspicion was far-fetched. Yet the moment it popped into his mind, he knew he couldn't rest until he proved or disproved it. An attack on a man was one thing, an attack on women and children quite another. The serving girl who'd been assaulted in such a foul way had been taken to her parents' home. Gideon had sent doctors to attend her. They reported the girl was out of her mind with shock and shame. She might never recover.

And Margaret was dead.

If Thomas Courtleigh was responsible for all those things—

The rage Gideon felt at the mere suspicion was so powerful, it left him shaken for an hour or more. He telegraphed the *Union*'s Western correspondent, Salathiel Brown, who was already in Chicago. He asked Brown to look into whether the Wisconsin and Prairie had anyone named Hubble on its payroll.

During the days of preparation for the funeral, Eleanor continued to concern him. She insisted she'd only been roughed up by the men who stormed the mansion. Her dress and chemise had been torn, and one of the men had hit her, but she claimed that was the extent of it.

Gideon found it illogical that the thugs would rape a serving girl and leave a mistress of the house untouched, particularly since it was quite clear from inscriptions painted on the walls that the Kent family had been the target of the attack. Eleanor refused to change her story, even though something flickering in her eyes from time to time hinted that there *was* another one.

On the same Wednesday night of Gideon's return, Dana Hughes had located Matt in Roxbury, Massachusetts, where

he was drunkenly playing the outfield in a baseball game
between two volunteer fire companies. The editor had sobered him up and put him aboard a southbound express
the next day. On Saturday morning, Julia and Carter had
arrived from the South. Carter's school was out for the
summer and he was accompanying his mother on the lecture circuit.

Julia and her son paid a courtesy call at the house late
that day. From the moment they walked in, Will was fascinated by the fifteen-year-old boy who had the same last
name he did. Carter had shot up over six feet, and was
astonishingly handsome—the one person in all the family
who looked as if he had Latin blood, which he did.

Julia chose to stay at a downtown hotel. But she brought
Carter back to the mansion on Sunday, to see whether she
could help with arrangements for the memorial service next
day. Again Gideon's eight-year-old son followed the older
boy everywhere. Carter didn't seem to mind. He appeared
to enjoy the adulation, in fact.

By that weekend, just prior to the funeral service, the
rail strike was all but over. Many newspapers had warned
of continued, Communist-inspired rioting, even of revolution. But much of the hysteria had been unexpectedly
dampened by an interview the *National Republican* obtained from none other than President Hayes. Only a day
after the start of the Pittsburgh violence, the President said
he didn't consider the looting and bloodshed to be evidence
of "the prevalence of a spirit of Communism, since the
acts were not primarily directed against property in general,
merely against that of the railroads with whom the strikers
had had difficulties."

The Marxist scare continued, of course. But the President's calm statement had undermined it. Gideon was too
wrung out to do more than take note.

So now it was Monday afternoon. Following the memorial service, he planned to travel to Massachusetts to see
Margaret's burial in the family plot in Watertown. Her remains were not actually in the coffin as yet. Because of the
season and the problem of deterioration, the body lay on
ice at the undertaker's.

About two dozen mourners were scattered in the pews
of the small church. They listened dutifully as the prayer

droned on. Molly was seated on Gideon's right, and Matt
to her right. Gideon's younger brother looked wretched, as
if he'd been working too hard on the book, or imbibing
too heavily, or both. Will leaned against his father's left
side. Just beyond, on the center aisle, sat Eleanor.

Gideon turned his head far enough to study her profile.
She was staring at the minister, not even bothering to slit
her eyes in a pretense of piety. He marveled that he and
Margaret had brought such a lovely creature into the world.

But there was still a secret grief lurking in her gaze. It
wasn't merely his opinion. Matt had sensed it. And Julia,
who was seated two rows back, with Carter. In private,
she'd told Gideon she thought Eleanor was suffering from
some deep inner wound about which she refused to speak.
Was it Margaret's death causing that? Julia wondered
aloud. Gideon doubted it. What, then? He didn't know.

Behind Julia sat a number of people from the *Union*,
including Theo Payne and his tiny, kindly-looking wife.
Most of the servants were back there, too. When the service finally ended a few minutes later, Gideon noticed a
late arrival he hadn't seen before—the impeccably dressed
Joshua Rothman.

As the organ pealed the postlude, Eleanor left the pew
without waiting for her father to usher her to the foyer.
Gideon frowned, then took Will's hand in his and started
down the aisle. As they passed Julia's pew, Will noticed
Carter watching him, and immediately pulled his hand
from Gideon's.

Molly walked out holding Matt's arm. Several steps
ahead, Gideon went to Rothman in the foyer.

"It was good of you to come, Joshua."

They shook hands. The banker was in his mid-fifties and
growing portly. "I apologize for disturbing the service—"

"You didn't."

"But my train was late. Miriam wanted to come with me,
but a"—he colored slightly—"a female complaint has kept
her indisposed for the past month."

"I hope she'll be all right."

"The doctor assures me she will. He says this is merely
a painful phase all women pass through." He laid a hand on
Gideon's shoulder. "You're the one I'm concerned about at
the moment. How are you bearing up?"

Gideon glanced toward the main doors; Eleanor had already gone out and down the steps to the line of waiting carriages. Her chin was raised and her back was stiff as a soldier's. *There's no love in her,* he thought suddenly. *Or if there is, she hides it. As if it somehow isn't proper to display affection for anyone.*

My God, have I caused that?

He realized Rothman was peering at him, awaiting an answer. Molly and Matt passed by. Molly clearly wanted to speak to the banker, but she walked on so as not to interrupt what had the look of a very private conversation.

"Bearing up? As well as can be expected, I suppose," Gideon said. He felt himself growing cross. His bandage itched, and the wound hurt. The heat of the foyer was making him dizzy. His voice was sharp as he added, "Let's go outside, shall we?"

At the door, there was the obligatory handshake and a murmur of condolences by the pastor. Three burly young men in cheap suits and derbies came up the steps and entered the sanctuary; they had come with the black-lacquered, glass-sided hearse which was standing near the corner at the head of the carriage line.

Gideon accompanied Rothman down the steps. A few spatters of rain dotted the wooden walk. Perhaps there'd be some relief from the heat. He found no relief from his bad temper when he glanced to his left and saw Eleanor smiling and chatting with Matt. With her own father, she was barely polite.

Coming right on top of the heat and the pain and the strain of the memorial service, that made him unreasonably angry.

ii

Eleanor was enthralled by Papa's brother. Even in a suitably sober suit, Uncle Matt was a dashing figure with his hair curling over his collar, and his mustache drooping past the corners of his mouth. He fanned both of them with his straw boater, then lit a cigar as she said, "I know this isn't the time or place, Uncle Matt. But sometime I hope you'll talk to me about the theater."

"I confess I don't know much about it, Eleanor."

"Yes, but you're a painter, and I've read that painters suffer just the way actors and actresses do."

She was so fervent, she completely overlooked the wryness of his smile as he answered, "Well, I suppose I can give a little expert testimony in that department. Your father's told me about your interest in acting. I'm not sure he approves."

Her eyes glinted. "He's the one who first took me to a play."

"Watching them isn't the same as spending your life performing them. Besides, you're older now. You're a daughter, and he's a father—" He stirred the humid air with his cigar, as if stirring a cauldron. "That creates a special family brew. I'm told fathers become highly protective when daughters reach your age."

"I can take care of myself," she retorted. "And I don't think he cares two pins about protecting me. I don't think he cares about anything I do."

"Eleanor, you're wrong—"

She rushed on. "But I knew you'd understand what I want. You of all people in this family must know what it's like to feel a terrible craving to be a dedicated artist."

Matt was amused by the passion of her words, and by the words themselves. But he didn't let on. That would have hurt her. It struck him that he must be getting old, because he was beginning to take cynical note of how intense, idealistic and optimistic young people were. There were apprentices up at Kent and Son, Boston, who were sure they'd own the biggest printing house in the land by the time they were thirty.

"I'll be glad to talk with you any time you want," he said, fully matching her seriousness. "I can tell you this much right now, though. I have a friend in Paris, a very fine painter named Paul Cézanne, who's going to be well thought of one day. He once called painting a dog's profession. He meant it was lonely, frustrating, unsatisfying for long periods of time—and that there was no guarantee of success. I imagine the same can be said of acting. To be very good at something, you usually have to give up something else. Peace of mind, perhaps. Or a normal life. Sometimes the choice is unappealing and damn—uh, very painful."

"I'd give up anything to do what I want, Uncle Matt."

"Sure you mean that?"

"Absolutely."

How fiery she was, and how cheerless. He tested her a little further.

"Most girls your age are envisioning a marriage, babies—"

"I'm not. I never want to get married. I'm not even going to let myself be interested in a boy; that just—distracts a person."

He had the feeling she finished the sentence in a way that concealed what she'd really started to say. Again he was troubled by the intensity of her statements. They were born of deep conviction—and perhaps of more than a little pain. But she hid that. There was a quality about her some would call strength and others hardness. It was difficult to tell at this stage whether it would help or harm her.

He tried teasing her. "The gain of the theater will be the loss of the male population, I'm afraid. I guess it isn't amiss to pay a compliment to a niece and say she's a very pretty young woman."

Eleanor's cheeks pinked. She wasn't completely lacking in human feeling.

"Also a very determined one," he added. "I have a notion you'll be a success at anything you choose to do."

"I'm glad someone thinks so." She directed an unfriendly glance at her father, who was standing with a stranger a short distance down the walk. Then she gave Matt a warm, almost worshipful smile and murmured, "Thank you. We'll talk sometime when Papa's not around. I'd better go to the carriage now. I suppose they're all gossiping because I'm not wailing and sobbing like an infant."

What a curious girl, Matt thought as he puffed his cigar and watched her enter the carriage in which Molly was already seated. Fiery about certain things, cold about others. Didn't she mourn for her poor mother? Or did she keep her sorrow buried inside?

And why had she looked at her father with something close to loathing? Gid had said long ago that his relations with his daughter were strained, but that seemed to be understating it.

As far as Matt could tell, Margaret's death hadn't brought father and daughter closer together, as family grief sometimes did. Disturbing, he thought as he finished his smoke. Damned disturbing.

iii

At that moment Joshua Rothman was saying to Gideon, "Did you know your father's second cousin, Amanda Kent, had her mansion in Madison Square mobbed too? Just about twenty-five years ago, it was."

Gideon wrenched his glance from Eleanor, who was getting into the family carriage. She'd obviously enjoyed speaking with his brother as much as she disliked speaking with him.

Once Theo Payne had told him adolescents went through a normal period of disagreeing and even quarreling violently with their parents. At the same time, Payne said, they frequently chose other adults as idealized mothers or fathers. Maybe that was happening with Matt. If so, it was wrong for him to be angry with his daughter.

In response to Rothman's remark, he nodded and said, "Yes, I did hear my father mention that once or twice."

In a thoughtful way, the banker continued. "Amanda died as a result of the attack. It's a sad and interesting parallel. In 1852 the trouble came about because Amanda protected a runaway slave. Runaways, or contrabands as they came to be called, were one of the hottest issues then. I mean the question of whether they should be given sanctuary, or returned to their masters. Amanda took a stand on behalf of a poor black's freedom, and she died for it. Your home was ransacked and Margaret lost her life because of your concern with another downtrodden class. It's curious how idealism leads the Kents back over the same ground—"

Gideon's accumulating tension made him snappish.

"I fail to see much of a comparison, Joshua. Amanda was shot defending her house. I brought the trouble down on Margaret and the children, but I wasn't here to help them deal with it."

"Gideon, you mustn't blame yourself for your wife's death."

"Why not? Everyone else does." Instantly, he realized how self-pitying that was, and apologized.

"Have the police located the men responsible?" Rothman wanted to know.

Gideon shook his head. "Eleanor and the servants were only able to provide very sketchy descriptions."

"Then you have no hope of finding and punishing the ringleaders?"

One, he thought. In Chicago. But Rothman wouldn't have understood, so he simply shook his head again and murmured, "Very little." He took hold of the banker's arm. "Come to the house for a while, Joshua."

"Certainly—if I won't be disturbing you."

Gideon assured him he wouldn't. "Will you stay to supper?"

"I'm afraid I can't do that. My train leaves at six forty-five."

Gideon handed Rothman into his hired carriage. Next he went to see Julia off. As Matt approached, she declined the same invitation Gideon had given the banker.

"I think it's best you devote your attention to Molly and Mr. Rothman and the children."

"I agree," Matt put in. "I'll see Julia and Carter back to their hotel." He grinned. "May even steal her away from you, Gid."

Gideon didn't smile. Julia noted the tension on his face. She laid a gentle hand on his arm.

"If you have time, come by this evening before you take the train for Boston." Matt drifted away again, to corral Carter. Julia stepped closer. "Above all, try to heal the rift with Eleanor."

"It's that apparent, eh?"

"Yes."

"All right, I'll do what I can."

But he was beginning to believe the gulf was already far too wide. His own ill humor wasn't helping to narrow it.

Matt returned with Will and Carter. Julia's son had his arm around the younger boy's shoulders. Will's eyes were still red from the crying he'd done early in the service. Carter was speaking to him in a low, comforting voice.

"I'll be up to see you soon, Will," Carter called as he and Matt climbed into Julia's carriage. Will gave the older boy a grateful glance, then preceded Gideon into the Kent carriage. Eleanor sat against the far wall, rigid. She barely turned her head to acknowledge her father's presence.

Gideon squeezed in beside his stepmother. He shut the door and thumped the roof. The carriage rolled forward past the hearse into which the empty coffin was being loaded by the three young men wearing derbies. Gideon heard them cracking jokes. He bowed his head, controlled his temper, and began speaking in a moderate voice.

"Eleanor, I believe that you and I—"

"Papa," she broke in, "we have nothing to say to each other."

All his resolve vanished in a renewed rush of anger.

iv

"Molly," he growled, "you must forgive me, but it's time Eleanor and I settled a few things. The conversation may not be pleasant."

His stepmother frowned. "I think it would be more appropriate if you waited until we arrived home."

"Indeed it would be," he shot back, struck by another spell of dizziness. He gripped the edge of the open window to steady himself. "But I refuse to wait that long. Eleanor, I'm sick of your disrespectful ways and your accusing looks. There is no reason for either."

She acted incredulous. "No reason? Papa, she might be alive right now if you'd been here to protect her."

"Do you think I don't know that? Do you think I haven't thought of that every minute since I heard she was dead?"

"Will," Molly whispered, "come sit by me." The wide-eyed boy squeezed against her side.

"Even when she was alive," Eleanor went on, "you never thought of what she was going through."

"That isn't true. I did."

Contempt then: "Did you really see the words that the

painters had to cover up? 'Communist' spelled out in red
letters three feet high? The other filthy things?"

"Of course I saw them. What are you trying to say?"

"That Mama was always terrified of the very thing that
happened—people attacking the house. She must have understood your work better than I did. But you kept on with
your—your *causes* and never made it easy for her to forget
her fear. You kept so busy at that blasted paper, you never
made it possible for us to live like an ordinary family."

"Now see here!" he said, his voice shaking. "You have
to understand my side of it. She demanded that I give up
my work. She wanted me to be something I couldn't be—
a drone in some safe, secure job. She wanted everyone to
obey her, but especially me. I wouldn't, and it was wrong
of her to ask—"

"So you did exactly as you please, and now she's dead."

"Damn it. Don't twist everything!"

"Gideon." Molly's lips were all but colorless. "Don't
curse, and for the love of God, don't keep up this wran-
gling. The poor woman isn't even buried." She stabbed a
look at Eleanor. "Both of you show a little restraint."

He shook his head. "We're going to settle it, Molly.
Somehow my own children have been turned against me
with insinuations and outright lies. I'll never know what
Margaret said to either of you—" A glance at Will, cringing
at Molly's side. "I'll never know how she worked on your
imaginations. But I know she did it. She lost her sense of
what was right and wrong. I could see it happening before
I left. The alcohol affected her mind, just as it affected her
father's. She was a sick woman—"

"Did you make things easier by staying with her, Papa?"

In answer to the scorn, he shouted, "She made it impossible for me to stay! She—"

Suddenly he stopped. The carriage swung around a corner. He was only alienating Eleanor all the more. He had
to change direction.

"All right." His voice was much softer. "Will it calm
things and help us start on a better footing if I admit I
made many, many mistakes? If I accept my share of the
blame for all that happened?"

"You deserve *all* the blame! You were the one who
walked out—" She rubbed her eye, then shook her head

as if annoyed with herself. "You were the one who never even wrote a line to find out whether we were still alive."

"Eleanor, what are you saying?"

"That you never cared enough to write so much as a single line after you left."

"But I did. I must have sent you a dozen letters. Begging you to come down to the *Union*—I was willing to meet you anywhere, so we could patch up our differences—"

"That's a convenient lie now that she's gone," Eleanor scoffed.

"I swear to God I wrote to you! Surely someone in the house saw the letters—"

She shook her head. "I kept asking Samuel, but there weren't any."

"Then somehow your mother must have intercepted them. It's the only explanation. She must have destroyed them."

Eleanor looked close to tears again. "Oh, Papa, that's cruel. There's no end to your cruelty. First you desert your wife and then you bring your mistress to New York and flaunt her in front of—"

"Don't speak about Julia!" Gideon roared. "By God your disrespect is unbelievable. You're not old enough to—"

"I was old enough to care for Will when you abandoned us! Old enough to care for Mama and run the house!"

"Eleanor—stop!" Will screamed. "Stop, stop, *stop it*!"

Molly's eyes accused both Gideon and his daughter. "I told you that you were going too far." She turned and comforted the crying boy. Gideon felt bludgeoned. There was a defeated tone in his voice as he made his last, desperate appeal to Eleanor's reason.

"You mustn't vilify Julia. She wanted to come to New York to pay her respects. She's a fine woman. You may not believe it, but she's been a strong partisan of you and Will for as long as I've known—"

"Gideon," Molly whispered, "that will be *all*. Can't you see the damage you've already done?"

He could, and it broke his heart.

Will's face was buried in Molly's skirt. Eleanor stared out the window at passing rooftops sprinkled by the rain that hadn't even dampened the pavements.

He'd failed.

Exhausted, he leaned back against the cushion. She blamed him. She hated him. She always would. The family was sundered, and in the carriage he'd finally faced the truth of his own role in that destruction.

Something unexpected had happened during the ferocious, enervating argument. By admitting his culpability to his daughter, he'd also admitted it to himself, and done so without reservation, for the very first time. He could no longer put all the guilt on Margaret. He must shoulder his share, because it was deserved.

In one way poor Margaret was better off. She no longer had to carry that guilt. He'd bear his till the hour of his death, never forgetting that he was the sole living engineer of the Kent family's ruin.

The pain of it made the wound in his side a scratch, a trifle, nothing.

V

An hour later, while he was talking with Joshua Rothman in the Fifth Avenue study, Samuel brought in a telegraph message that had just been delivered. Gideon tore it open. Rothman noted the younger man's harsh expression as he read the one-line report from Sal Brown:

LORENZO HUBBLE A STAFF ATTORNEY FOR
WISCONSIN PRAIRIE.

After a moment the butler murmured, "The boy is waiting, sir. Is there to be any reply?"

"Yes, Samuel."

Pale, Gideon strode to his desk and wrote a message asking his reporter to investigate Hubble's whereabouts on Sunday, July 22, as well as the day before and the day after. No expense was to be spared.

Samuel took the message and started to leave. At the last moment Gideon called him back. He watched the butler closely as he said, "During the past year, I mailed a number of letters to Eleanor. Evidently they didn't arrive. At least she says they didn't."

Samuel frowned slightly. Gideon concluded he was trying to flog his memory. At last, looking his employer in the eye, he said, "No, sir, I don't remember any letters in your handwriting."

"Did Mrs. Kent ever collect the morning or afternoon deliveries herself?"

"Yes, sir, frequently, when I was busy at some chore. She liked to do it, she said."

"I'm sure she did." Both the butler and Joshua Rothman looked mystified by Gideon's extreme bitterness.

Samuel hesitated, then said, "You sound upset, sir. Did I say something wrong?"

"No, Samuel. You didn't give me the answer I hoped for, but you gave me the one I expected. That's all. Thank you."

CHAPTER VII

CALL TO FORGIVENESS

i

BY EVENING, RAIN was drenching the city. Water cascaded from the eaves of the roof of the train platform. The sight and sound of it carried Gideon back nearly six years, to another rainy platform where he'd discovered he couldn't leave the woman who was still at his side this evening.

The intervening years had brought almost continuous and sometimes shattering change. Through it all, only Julia, his children and his work had sustained him. His work had finally brought down the vengeance Courtleigh had promised. His oldest child was his enemy. Only Julia remained a constant. Thank God she did, or he'd never have been able to go on.

Impatiently, he took out his pocket watch. "Twenty after already." The Boston express left at half past the hour. The wagon bringing the coffin was nowhere to be seen.

A few latecomers were hurrying to board the passenger coaches. Gideon had arranged to accompany the coffin in the express car, whose open door was just to his left. He didn't know precisely why he'd decided to do that, unless it was because he no longer had anything to offer Margaret except his presence on the final stage of her journey. *A*

603

memorial of dubious value, he thought with the bitterness that had infected his thoughts ever since the quarrel with Eleanor.

He peered along the platform. The lanterns hanging from the platform roof were dim. Blowing steam hampered visibility even further. Rain pelted his face. He wiped it away with his cuff. "What have they done with the damned thing?"

Julia laid a gray-gloved hand on his arm. "Don't fret. It'll be here." The sympathy and patience in her voice calmed him a little. The calm was superficial, though. Inside, he felt like a baffled, frightened child.

Julia had sensed it when he'd stopped by her hotel. It was she who'd suggested she keep him company on the melancholy ride to the terminal. In the hack, they'd embraced with an unexpected ardor. They didn't kiss, merely put their arms around one another and held each other tightly, as if each needed comforting after a day too full of rancor and reminders of their own mortality.

Now Julia said, "You didn't finish telling me how things went after you got home."

He shrugged, his mouth setting in a bitter line. "Eleanor refused to speak to me. It was more peaceful than the carriage ride, but hardly more cordial. Will said she's happy that Matt's moving from his hotel to the house to look after things while I'm in Boston."

"I've been thinking about that house, Gideon."

"You're still planning to come live there, aren't you?"

She said softly, "No, I don't think I should."

"Julia, we agreed—"

"I know what we agreed, darling. But just this evening, I changed my mind. What you told me about the conversation with Eleanor convinced me I'm right. You built that house with a great deal of hope. But it's become a mausoleum for bad memories. Memories of arguments, violence, lives half lived and half fulfilled—but discounting all that, it remains your wife's house, not mine. For me to move in even temporarily would be a kind of desecration of Margaret's memory. Just as important, I want our house to be a loving house. Yours isn't, not any more. I'm sorry, my dear, but that's the way I feel."

He respected her conviction, but he felt adrift again. "Then where will we live?"

"Anywhere else you choose. Perhaps we should go to another city for a while. Boston, if you'd care to involve yourself in the affairs of Kent and Son for a while. The change of scene might be beneficial, and the firm will need guidance to capitalize on the success of *100 Years*."

"I'm not that confident the book will succeed."

"I am. In any case, it doesn't really matter where we go if we're together and have work that satisfies us."

He was about to object, then thought of something he'd done earlier in the evening. It prompted him to say: "You could be right about the house. After supper I went up to Margaret's room. The mob never got into it. I stood outside for ten minutes, wanting to unlock the door. I didn't have the courage."

"That's perfectly understandable."

His eye fixed on the terminal at the end of the platform. "Before we move out permanently—if we do—that room must be opened. Everything in it must be taken out and disposed of."

"Don't you think you should examine the things first? There might be some items the children would find valuable. Some keepsakes—"

His reply was abrupt and vehement. "There's nothing in there but grimy furniture and old clothing. Nothing worth saving. If there are memories in the house like the ones you described, that room's the chief source. Just as a practical matter, it has to be cleaned out before any prospective buyer looks at the property."

"I still think someone should examine Margaret's effects. I can understand why you don't want to do it. I'd be willing to take on the chore—"

"No!" His blue eye shone bright as a gas flame, reflecting one of the lamps inside the express car. "Everything will be burned."

She sighed. "I can't agree with your decision. But—"

An expressman appeared in the open door of the car. "That box here yet, Mr. Gray?"

Gideon had filled out the shipping papers under the assumed name, and spread some money around to assure silence on the part of the terminal superintendent and his staff. Passengers weren't usually allowed to ride in express cars. If higher-ups ever found out that permission had been given to Gideon Kent, the radical newspaperman who regularly attacked railroad owners, someone could lose a job. It was better to travel anonymously.

"Not yet," Gideon answered. "I'll go check on—wait, here it comes."

A four-wheeled wagon pulled by two freight handlers appeared at the terminal doors. Like an image in a dream, it seemed to float along in the billowing steam. The iron wagon wheels rumbled. Rain slanting through the lamplight glowed and splattered on the lid of the coffin.

Julia saw how pale he'd grown. She slipped her hand in his. He didn't turn. His eye remained fixed on the silver box.

The freight handlers rolled the wagon up beside the wide door of the express car. They lifted the coffin and maneuvered it inside. Only then did Julia say, "Did you decide to tell the children you and I had discussed marriage after a suitable mourning period?"

He pulled his gaze from the rain-speckled coffin. "Yes. I brought it up at the supper table. I didn't know whether they'd think me callous with Margaret not yet buried. On the other hand, even Will knew she and I weren't getting along. And Will has really taken to your son. All in all, I saw nothing to be gained by a delay. Will was excited. Not so much about you and me as about the possibility of having Carter around all the time."

"And Eleanor?"

"You don't really want to hear—"

"Yes, I do."

He hesitated. "The first time I spoke your name, she left the dining room."

Julia sighed again. "I know she's bound to resent me for a while. I only pray it won't be permanent. I'll do my best to see that it isn't. I've already written Lucy to say I want to curtail my travel for six months to a year. With a little luck and some help from the Almighty, perhaps we can give your children the kind of home they haven't had for too long a time. Here in New York, or in Boston—"

Glum, he said, "I don't know how Eleanor will accept

that intention. I'm just coming to realize my daughter isn't a child any longer. My God, she isn't even sixteen and strangers think she's nineteen or twenty. And she certainly has no qualms about addressing her own father in the most disrespectful way imaginable. I'm damned if I know what's happening to the younger genera—may I ask what's so funny?"

Her smile was gentle, not meant to hurt. "You, my darling. You're sounding like an old fuss-budget. Or should I say a typically conservative parent?"

"Conservative? Me? Nonsense."

"Don't bristle so. I think it's a healthy sign."

He refused to smile. "The hell it is. I'll never be a good father, Julia. I've come to the conclusion I never had it in me."

"You mustn't say that just because of Eleanor. Regardless of how old she looks, she's young, emotional. Passion is characteristic of girls her age, but clear thinking isn't." A rueful smile. "I recall that very vividly, and with embarrassment."

No amount of banter seemed able to break his grim mood. He turned toward the express car where the casket lay glistening. The expressman bent over it and began to wipe the water away with a clean rag.

"Over and over," Gideon said, "I tried to make things go smoothly at home. I tried to persuade Margaret that we could have a happy family even though I gave a great deal of time and energy to the newspaper. She wouldn't accept that. Then she started to make my work—and my unwillingness to give it up—a register of how I felt about her. From then on everything went to hell. 'Smite the Midianites.' Remember that? The passage my father picked from the Bible?" His tone grew steadily more bitter. "I'm glad he never lived to see that in doing what he thought I should, I destroyed my family."

"All right," she said, softly yet with great intensity. "There were mistakes. Imbalances. But there comes a time when you have to forgive yourself."

Again his attention seemed to wander. "Destroyed my family and killed my wife in the process—"

"Gideon, listen to me! Newsmen are so anxious to perfect the world, they forget it can't be done with human beings. Accept that fact. Forgive yourself and—"

"I *can't.*"

His anguished cry made the expressman glance up. Gideon turned his back on the car. Up and down the train, brakemen began signaling with their lanterns, streaks of light in the spectral steam.

A last passenger scrambled up the steps two cars behind. A conductor at the end of the train called, *"All aboaaard!"*

Julia looked dismayed by Gideon's reaction. She marshaled her thoughts and said, "Very well, if that's impossible, at least don't speak of your wife with such bitterness. Be kind to her memory. She helped you learn, and grow. That took you out into the world, away from her. Resentment on her part was only natural. You had your work, but what did she have except tending her home and her children? What else was she prepared to do? *Permitted* to do—by you and by society? If you can't forgive yourself, at least forgive her. No matter what you think she did, she's gone. So be kind—"

"Mr. Gray, you'd better get aboard," the expressman warned. In the dark at the head of the train, the beam of the oil lantern speared out. Gideon was somewhere else; in memory he'd returned to Richmond. To a footpath beside the canal in the desperate, bittersweet weeks just before First Manassas. Weeks in which he'd worn a splendid, spotless uniform and whispered endearments to a pretty, dark-haired girl.

"I loved her so," he whispered. "Where did it go?"

Julia slipped her arms around his neck and drew his head down. "It's futile to think of that now. We must only make sure our love doesn't vanish the same way. We must work to keep it strong. And make sure your children are warmed by it, too. Both your children—"

At first he thought raindrops had splattered her cheeks. But he was wrong. She was weeping.

"Forgive yourself. The past is gone. All that matters is what's ahead. If we make the future good for Will and Eleanor, it will be good for us too. Now kiss me goodbye."

His mouth pressed hers with aching hunger.

Clanking and lurching, the train began to move. The expressman called to him a second time. He broke the embrace and ran up beside the slow-moving car. He seized a handrail to the left of the door and vaulted up to the opening as the car gathered speed.

Getting drenched as he had on that long-ago afternoon, he hung in the open door and watched Julia's figure diminish. Dear Lord, how he loved her. How sane and compassionate she was!

And she was right. He'd already accepted his share of the blame for the failure of the marriage; it was he who had gone to Julia's arms, after all. He had to find absolution, and get on with the task of making a new home, a new life.

But not on Fifth Avenue. She was right about that too. Perhaps Boston would be the ideal place. If *100 Years* was even moderately successful, Kent and Son would need good management. Theo Payne had run the *Union* before he got there, and the editor could do it again. Payne would keep the paper flourishing forever. He'd never die; the alcohol flowing in his system would make him immortal.

Yes, Gideon thought, Julia was altogether right. He must look forward, not back. Forgive himself, and get on with rebuilding the Kent family.

ii

In the little Watertown cemetery, four workmen put the coffin into the ground.

It was a warm, clear day. All the rain had passed on to the south. The brilliant blue of the sky and the sweet odors of damp grass and loam refreshed his spirit.

Oddly enough, so did the large square of ground surrounded by the low fence of ornamental black iron. Here the Kents lay. Here there existed a sense of belonging, and of purpose. Standing near his father's headstone, he knew he hadn't been wrong to print the *Beacon* or go to the *Union* and do what he'd done with each of them. Those things had been wrong for his marriage, but he would never be ashamed of them in principle. He was proud of his work, flawed as it was and negligible as the results sometimes seemed.

There was renewal in this balmy midsummer day, and in

this Massachusetts earth. It was time he stopped pitying himself. He wasn't the first Kent who had suffered. One way or another, all of them had.

Philip.

Anne Ware Kent.

Philip's second wife, Peggy.

Gilbert Kent.

Amanda.

His father.

They had known defeats, but they had persevered and conquered in the end.

As he must with Eleanor.

She was the primary challenge now. He admitted he'd neglected their relationship because of his anger with Margaret. He must break through her resentment somehow, *somehow*.

Realistically, he supposed Eleanor blamed him too much ever to wholeheartedly love him as most daughters loved their fathers. He'd be content if he could just restore her life to something close to normalcy. The first step was to try to overcome her hostility.

A formidable task. Yet here among his own people, he didn't feel helpless about it. To the contrary. For the first time since the memorial service, his face was composed. The wind blew his hair as he held his hat in his hands and watched the coffin being lowered slowly into the freshly dug hole.

Soon the workmen began throwing earth down into the opening, their spades glinting in the sun. A little longer to mourn the dead, and then he must get on with the task of restoring a decent life to the living. Thank God for Julia. She was his anchor and his hope. He couldn't imagine how he could have come through this difficult period without her—or, for that matter, how he could face the months ahead if she weren't with him.

He bowed his head as the gentle mound was tamped by the graveyard workmen. "Forgive me if you can, Margaret," he whispered in the windy silence. A bird began to sing as he turned and slowly walked away.

Chapter VIII

Call to Courage

i

DURING THE NIGHT that Gideon was en route to Boston
with the casket, Eleanor had difficulty sleeping. She was
still upset by the shameless way her father's mistress had
appeared at the church. Then he'd had the audacity to try
to effect a reconciliation in the carriage. And at supper,
according to what Will had told her afterward, he'd announced that he intended to marry that Sedgwick woman
and move her into this very house.

That and all the other events of the day had completely
shattered the facade she'd worked so hard to maintain ever
since those men had invaded the mansion and—

And—

Her mind refused to put words to what had happened in
the parlor.

Though she couldn't verbalize it, she could never forget
it. She had nightmares in which it was repeated again and
again. Sometimes, quite without realizing it, she'd even slip
into a daydream in which she was lying on her back on the
hearthstone, feeling the terrible thrust of—

Again her mind veered away from the memory of the

611

frantic pushing. The pain. The sudden wet mingling of her
blood and—

"Stop!"

Crying out softly, she wrenched over onto her side,
seized her pillow and hugged it between her breasts. Lying
that way, her eyes shut, she shuddered for several minutes,
making small, whimpering noises.

Finally the terror began to pass. Shame crept in. When
that happened, she was able to assert self-control again.

She released the damp pillow. Sat up in the dark and
breathed deeply until she could think of other things. She
was hardly aware of a slight paling at the edges of the
bedroom curtains. A picture of her father's mistress was
forming in her mind.

Eleanor had to admit Julia Sedgwick was lovely. Independent and tough-minded, too, she supposed. Undoubtedly someone who lectured for the suffragists had to have
those qualities to be successful. Eleanor could almost see
what her father admired in the petite, dark-haired woman.

But she knew she could never accept the woman moving
into her mother's house. No matter how kind or considerate Julia was, Eleanor just couldn't give Papa's mistress
any affection.

Affection. Her mouth twisted. No one would get that
from her. She was more convinced than ever that
affection—love—only led to the kind of suffering she'd endured in the past year. And the way in which men and
women expressed their love physically—that was agony.
She knew from personal experience now.

What if her father did move Julia into the house? Will
would like it. He was taken with that swaggering lout Julia
hauled around with her. Carter Kent had tried to make one
friendly overture to Eleanor, but she'd rebuffed him
quickly and unmistakably.

What could she hope to do about Julia? The answer was,
nothing. The realization came as a jolt, and compelled her
to do some serious thinking about her future.

One possibility lay open to her. One avenue of escape.
The thought of taking it frightened her a little, but at least
she could accept it. She couldn't accept living in the same
house with Papa's mistress. Not even if he married her.

She was still mulling the risky plan when she realized it

must be close to six o'clock. A cool breeze belled the curtains, and the light around the edges was stronger. She heard a door open somewhere along the second-floor hall. Then footsteps passed, creaking a floorboard here and there.

Too heavy for Will's tread.

Uncle Matt!

This was her chance. She leaped from bed, found her robe, and a moment later slipped down the staircase to the library, where she heard him stirring.

ii

She knocked softly at the open door. "Uncle Matt?"

He turned from the curtains he'd been pulling back and fastening with their velvet ties. The sunlight of a summer dawn was brightening Fifth Avenue. Birds warbled in the Park.

Her uncle looked sleepy but handsome as ever, wrapped up in an old velvet dressing gown, an unlit cigar stuck in the breast pocket.

He smiled. "Good morning, Eleanor. You're up early."

She brushed hair from her eyes and smiled in return. "I didn't sleep very well."

"Nor I. Yesterday was pretty miserable for everyone."

"Could we talk a little now?"

"Oh, yes, we're supposed to have a chat, aren't we?" The hair straggling over his forehead had some gray in it, she noticed. He took out the cigar and waved it. "By all means, let's do."

He fished in his pockets for a match, found one, and puffed clouds of harsh-smelling blue smoke as he sat down. Nervously, Eleanor took a chair nearby.

How should she begin? Certainly she didn't want to reveal everything she'd been thinking. He might tell Papa, and spoil it if she decided to go ahead. She noted his attentive expression, blushed and made a start.

"I guess—that is—oh, I'm afraid I don't know how to say it right—"

"The best line is a clean line. Just say it."

His kind expression put her at ease. "All right. I guess I need encouragement, Uncle Matt."

"About becoming an actress?"

"Yes."

A slow puff of the cigar. "Sure that's what you want to do?"

Careful. Don't let on.

"I think so. Eventually."

A haze of smoke thickened around him. "We butted heads with this same problem yesterday. You won't like my first piece of advice. Before you do anything, you should get your father's approval."

She reacted with a vigorous shake of her head. "No, that's impossible now."

"I see. Is that why you're asking me instead?"

She faltered a little. "I—I just wanted to know whether you thought it was a good idea."

"No," he replied at once. She was startled and hurt.

"Eleanor," he went on, "you're a grown-up young lady. Practically a woman. You look five years older than most girls your age. I want to be honest with you because you're my niece, and because acting is obviously important to you. First of all, I'll say again that I don't know much about the theater, except that I enjoy a good show from time to time. But I suppose the theater has certain things in common with all the arts. I know you've had some acting experience."

"How do you know that?"

"After I brought my bag from the hotel last night, Will and I spent almost two hours talking. I heard all about the Booth Association."

"That blabbing little brat!"

He chuckled. "You mustn't blame Will. Sounded to me like nobody had been around to listen to him for a month of Sundays—not even my own brother," he added after a moment.

She was quick to nod. "That's true."

"You certainly have the beauty to be an actress. You could carry a whole first act with your eyes alone."

She reddened again, and fixed her gaze on her folded hands.

"I'm not teasing, Eleanor. You're prettier than nine tenths of the female performers I've ever seen. If you have ability on top of that, I'd say you have a fine start. The question is the same one I asked a while ago—"

Matt's eyes clouded as he examined his cigar. He flicked ash into a porcelain dish beside him. "Are you really sure you want a start in that business?"

"And I said I thought so. Then you said it wasn't a good idea."

"No, not unless you're willing to give up a devil of a lot."

"I told you yesterday that I was."

"Be very sure. If you become an actress, there are some homes where you'll never be welcome. You won't be respectable. And you must remember that a lot of people dislike the arts because they don't understand them. What people don't understand, they fear."

"Then you think the stage would be a miserable life?"

"At times."

"Is being a painter miserable?"

"Compared to being a lawyer or a ribbon clerk? Absolutely."

"Do you mean that? It's truly miserable?"

"Often, yes."

"Why don't you quit?"

"I can't do anything else."

"I don't think I can either."

"Ah." He smiled again. "That's what I was waiting to hear. It makes all the difference. Those who can do something else should do it. They'd be fools to pay the price. Those who can't do anything else need no advice from me, or anyone."

"But I want advice, Uncle Matt."

"All right—but take warning. I may get a little smarmy, as my friend Jim Whistler would say."

He drew on the cigar, exhaled a thin blue plume.

"There's no lower, more frustrating, idiotic or misunderstood calling than being an artist. Any kind of artist. Pots of pigment or pots of rouge. I don't suppose it makes any difference. It's a solitary business. A business in which you're supposed to create something. A little sketch of a washerwoman, or a believable stage portrayal of a young

lady in love. Some days, you just can't. But you do it anyway. For that reason and a lot of others, there's no harder
life. Trouble is, there's also no higher calling."

His voice had fallen to a low pitch. She sat forward,
mesmerized. She didn't know whether he was really speaking to her, or to some ghost he saw in the smoke of his
cigar.

"As my old tutor Fochet used to tell me, an artist lifts
people out of themselves for a few minutes and says to
them, See here. We all share the same misery, but we share
the same beauty, too. Behold a small piece of it."

A supple gesture left smoke traceries in the air. There
were no sounds in the house. The birds had hushed their
singing over in the Park. All the world seemed to be holding still for one momentous instant.

With a rather bemused expression, he said, "I even found
there was beauty in this crass country. Much to my surprise.
I owe your father a lot for making me search for it. In any
case, Eleanor, I've probably confused you more than I've
helped. I can't tell you anything about being in the theater,
only about being a painter. It can be stinking. Because of
what I wanted to do with my life, I lost the one woman I
ever loved. You give up so much—"

Nothing that I don't want to give up.

She didn't say it. She didn't dare disturb his train of
thought. She wanted to weep for him, his face had been so
sad a moment ago.

Then all at once, his shining grin returned. "But there
are a few rare moments when you get back more than I
think even God planned for. We're a pretty wretched
bunch, Eleanor. I mean human beings. We say we're modern, enlightened, but I don't see much evidence. We seem
to be just about as foolish and stupid as we were a couple
of years after the Creation. But the artists, now—the artists
help us get along. They shine a little light in the darkness,
and help the whole cantankerous, benighted race survive
the mess it keeps making every generation. Survive and
endure—"

He took a puff but the cigar had gone out. "To be a
successful actress will take every bit of courage that's in
you. You'll survive on that courage when there isn't any
logical reason for hope. I know, I've done it. A while ago,

I was being the good and responsible uncle and urging you to square things with your father. Forget that. If you want to go into the theater, you won't ask anyone's permission. As I said before, you won't be able to do anything else with your life. Just grant me one favor, my dear. For God's sake don't tell my brother I told you."

She erupted from the chair, ran to him and flung her arms around him.

"Thank you, Uncle Matt. Thank you!"

He stepped back from the embrace, shaking his head.

"I don't think I spoke one coherent, worthwhile sentence."

"Yes, you did. You helped me decide something very important."

His wry humor took over. "Well, I hope so. It's too damn early in the day to discuss the insignificant. Wonder if I could be excused a minute? I'd like to stroll out to the kitchen and put a match to the stove for some—"

By the time he was that far, she'd left in a rush, her face joyous for no reason he could readily understand.

Just another of the mysteries that dwelled in the unfathomable hearts and minds of young girls, he thought as he relit his cold cigar and went in search of tea.

iii

Eleanor was dressed by eight o'clock. At fifteen past, Uncle Matt went into the dining room with Will to have breakfast. As soon as she heard conversation and the clink of dishes, she slipped out the front door.

She'd be forever thankful that she'd worked up enough nerve to speak to her uncle when she did. She hadn't understood some of what he'd said about an artist's life. Yet the eloquence of it had thrilled her, and set her onto a path to a final decision.

One thing he'd said was very clear. She needed courage to implement her decision. She summoned all she had as she left the house and started downtown.

She had a long way to go. She ran until she was out of breath, then slowed her pace for several blocks. When she'd recovered her wind, she started running again. People gave her peculiar looks. One didn't usually see well-dressed young ladies dashing down Fifth Avenue by themselves at this hour of the morning. Or any hour, for that matter.

She reached the Paramount Hotel just after nine forty-five. When she asked for Mr. Jefferson J. Bascom, the desk clerk gave her a dirty smile. His eye swept along the curve of her breast.

"Room three-sixteen." The clerk must have disliked Bascom because he added, "Smallest and cheapest in the house."

As she left the desk, the clerk turned and whispered to someone behind a partition. Eleanor was sure they were discussing her. What did they think she was, a prostitute come at Mr. Bascom's bidding? Her face grew red and her back stiffened as she waited for the slow-moving elevator cage to descend. Then she remembered one of the words Uncle Matt had used. *Misunderstood.* And suddenly, she no longer cared a whit for anything the greasy clerk might say or think. Courage would help her endure that and a thousand other insults.

Presently the car arrived. Several male guests got off and she got on. As the car began to rise in the barred shaft, the operator studied her from the corner of his eye. Eleanor glared right back. He looked down at his unpolished shoes.

Odors of stale smoke and dust suffused the dim third floor. Halfway to Bascom's room, she almost turned back. But she thought of Julia Sedgwick moving into the mansion—and again of Uncle Matt's words—and she walked on. Her legs stopped wobbling.

Actually, Papa's mistress had helped make her decision easier. She knew Julia Sedgwick had traveled all over the country, by herself, and never come to harm. Certainly Eleanor felt every bit as resourceful. Besides, she wouldn't be traveling alone—

If she wasn't too late.

Anxious now, she ran the rest of the way.

Bascom's room was at the rear corner of the third floor. She knocked. There was no response. She held her breath, knocked again.

Again no response. He'd already gone out! She'd come

blocks and blocks for nothing. She'd probably never find him.

Then she realized she was giving up too easily. She knocked a third time, much louder. Miraculously, she heard shuffling feet, then a wordless grumbling.

The door opened. She didn't know whether to giggle or gasp in horror. There stood Bascom with his paunch ballooning the front of his faded nightshirt, and his jet black wig tilted down over his left ear.

Still, he was an intimidating sight, somehow. Before he had a chance to say anything, she screwed up her nerve and blurted, "Mr. Bascom, I'm here about the position with the troupe. Is it still open?"

Recognition finally erased his sleepy look. He realized his locks were canted and hurriedly straightened them. "Miss Kent!" he exclaimed. At least he recalled her name.

He opened the door wider as if to invite her in. Then he thought better of it. Eleanor glimpsed a cluttered room not much bigger than a spacious closet. It bore out one of Uncle Matt's statements about the artistic life. Mr. Bascom's quarters were about as low as you could get.

His red-rimmed eyes darted toward the curve of her hips. "Yes, I can still use you—" She didn't like the suggestive undertone, but said nothing. She'd get the job first and worry about handling his advances later.

"It *is* Miss Kent, isn't it?"

"That's right, sir. It's kind of you to remember."

"Kind? Balderdash. I've a memory for a provocative— ah—" He stifled a belch. "Talent."

One hand pressed his side as if he were in pain. His expression grew a trifle bilious as he added, "I'll meet you down in the dining room in ten minutes. Meantime, you may begin your apprenticeship under J. J. Bascom by fixing one thought firmly in mind. Unless you are specifically instructed to do so, never, never, *never* wake a fellow thespian before ten in the morning."

He slammed the door.

iv

Buoyed by excitement, she rushed back to the elevator. She was too breathless to wait for the cage and instead ran down the three flights to the lobby. Before another hour had gone by, Jefferson J. Bascom had hired her for his Tom show.

Then he went through an elaborate ritual of patting and searching his patched frock coat. "Dear me, I came down in such haste. I do seem to have forgotten my money clip." He passed her the bill for his enormous breakfast.

She was elated to have the opportunity to pay it. Uncle Matt was right. A little courage worked miracles.

Chapter IX

From out of the Fire

i

CARTER AND WILL slipped out the front door after breakfast. It was the second Saturday in August, a mild, bright morning fragrant with the odors of newly scythed grass in Central Park, and of fresh paint throughout the mansion.

Both boys wore old clothes. Will's face had a sleepy look because he and Carter had stayed up till well after one o'clock, talking. At Will's request, Carter had moved into the house, even though his mother insisted on remaining at her hotel and traveling back and forth to upper Fifth Avenue in a hack.

At night the older boy regaled the younger with lurid descriptions of his adventures with tobacco, alcohol, and willing, not to say eager, members of the opposite sex. About ninety percent of the stories were invented, but each boy gained something from them—Carter the sense of pride and burgeoning manhood that was important to someone his age, and Will the sense of great adventures that could be his when he was as old as his newfound friend.

Carter was halfway down the front steps when Will hesitated, looking across to the park. Behind some trees, boys could be heard yelling.

"What's holding you, Will? You said you want to go."

"I know, but I changed my mind."

"None of that, now. Come on."

"Carter, I've gone over there before. They never let me play."

"I've told you it's probably because of the way you ask. As if you expect them to say no. You've got to take charge and tell them what to do. But you have to be sly about it, so they don't realize they're being bossed." He climbed back to the top of the stoop and grasped the younger boy's hand. "I'll show you how it's done. You've got to learn to make your way, Will. If you don't, you'll be stuck in a house reading books all your life. Then you'll be white as paste and no girl will want to look at you. You don't want that, do you?"

"Hell no," the small boy declared in a squeaky attempt to imitate Carter's occasional profanity. The older boy suppressed a smile.

They crossed the Avenue, dodged through the sun and shadow of the trees and emerged in a fragrant meadow. On the far side, two teams were being organized by thirteen or fourteen boys about Carter's age. Again Will hung back. Carter yanked the bill of his cap down over his forehead and hissed from the side of his mouth.

"Keep up with me. They'll think you're a sissy if I pull you along by the hand."

As the two approached, the other boys fell silent and turned to stare. The boys were a rough-looking lot, most of them shabbily dressed and none too clean. One or two grinned, but not in a very cordial way. Carter sauntered up to a tall, emaciated youth who seemed to be the leader.

"Got two more players for you."

A boy with a blemished face came from the back of the group to assume the role of spokesman. He jabbed a finger at Will. "That's the rich little twit from across the Avenue. He's tried to butt into our games before."

"You should have let him," Carter purred. His chilling smile made the pimply boy blink. "He wants to learn the game. I hope you don't hold it against him that he's a beginner. Or that his pa's a rich newspaper publisher. I hope you don't hold it against *me* that I smoke—"

With a flourish, Carter plucked a long black cigar from the breast pocket of his shirt. Where he'd gotten the cigar, Will had no idea.

"Not cheap ones, either. Genuine Havanas." By then, a couple of the boys were looking impressed. He went on, "And I hope you don't hold it against me that up at Dartmouth"—faint condescension—"that's a college—I've studied scientific grappling—"

Will was stunned by Carter's audacity in making up such tales. But the pimply boy lost patience and started to swear. Carter bit down on the cigar, grabbed the boy, whirled him around and demonstrated his mastery of scientific grappling by bending the boy's left arm up behind his spine. Carter's other elbow crooked around to crush the boy's Adam's apple.

He grinned and chewed his cigar while the pimply boy made gagging noises. But Carter didn't really hurt his victim, and in a moment he let go. He dusted his hands, then struck a match on the sole of his shoe.

He puffed his cigar in a nonchalant way. The others didn't know what to make of him. Finally he said, "Did you choose up yet?"

The tall boy muttered, "We were just starting."

Carter rubbed his hands. "All right, let's go. My cousin here—"

"That's your cousin?" another boy jeered. "He don't look like no greaser. You do, though."

Carter didn't turn a hair. "You've got a quick eye. My great-grandfather was Alphonsus the Mighty, eighty-seventh king of Spain. But he never married my great-grandmother, so I'm part Spanish and part bastard." He said it so casually, yet with such conviction, that the only reaction was speechless surprise. "Now, my cousin here—his name's Will—he hasn't played ball as much as I have. He's going to make mistakes. But it looks like we've got some pretty fair teachers in this crowd."

Will was in awe. Carter's combination of bluster and outrageous lying had completely overwhelmed them, and had kept them so busy, they forgot to be hostile. If ever there was a Kent born to sway and lead others, it was Carter.

"And good teachers don't get sore when their pupils mess up," Carter went on. "They show 'em how to do things right because the teacher is the older, smarter one, and how's anybody going to learn if the teacher won't take time to teach?"

The tall boy grinned. "All right, we'll show your cousin how it's done." He turned toward his friends. "I say these two can play. That okay with everybody?"

The pimply boy stared at the ground and grumbled. Another of the group said, "Sure, let 'em play. It's better than having your arm busted."

"Knew you'd see it my way." Carter nodded with a quick smile at Will.

"Let's quit messing around and choose up," a third boy said. There were enthusiastic yells, and some clapping. Will was ecstatic. If Papa and Julia got married eventually, and they all lived together in another house, maybe Carter would teach him more about getting along in the outside world. It wasn't such a frightening place after all, provided you had a little nerve.

He was so excited about the coming game, he didn't notice the plume of smoke from the vacant lot on the south side of Sixty-first. There, hired workmen were starting to burn his mother's belongings.

ii

"Leaving?"

Gideon's voice mingled consternation with disbelief. His ears had tricked him. She couldn't have said she was joining a theatrical troupe.

He rose so hastily from his study chair, a taboret beside it overturned, spilling the copy of *100 Years* which Matt had picked up at the express office and brought to the house the night before. After delivering the book, Matt had told Gideon that because the project was finished, he wanted to go back to England. He'd booked a cabin on a Cunard steamship. The vessel sailed for Southampton on Monday evening.

The book had fallen open at the engraving which depicted Matt's favorite baseball team, the Cincinnati Red Stockings. *100 Years* was a handsome volume, printed on better than average paper and bound in good-quality cloth.

But the book was forgotten as father and daughter stared at one another. Eleanor stood just inside the double doors of the library. She'd put on her best summer frock and a flowered hat. A bulging valise rested on the floor beside her.

"Yes, Papa, leaving," she said. "I decided it was best for all of us."

The smell of smoke filled the house. Out in the foyer, one of the workmen appeared, draperies from Margaret's room folded over his arms. Two lacquered boxes rested on top of the drapes. Gideon had retreated to the library after breakfast because he couldn't bear to watch the removal of Margaret's things. Nearly every item brought back some special memory. He'd given her the lacquered boxes as an anniversary gift.

A breeze stirred the library curtains. A large wagon went rattling north on Fifth Avenue carrying fifteen or twenty young people on an excursion into the country. From the Park came the cheers and catcalls of a lively ball game.

Gideon was hardly aware of any of it. He felt as if someone had bludgeoned him. He raked a hand through his hair. Jerked the belt of his morning robe tighter. Finally, he erupted, "I don't know what you mean, best for all of us. It certainly isn't best for you. Girls your age don't just walk in one morning and announce that they're leaving home."

"I'm sorry, Papa, but this could never be my home now. Not with Julia here most of the time."

"I told you we weren't going to stay in this house—" He was floundering.

"It would be the same no matter where we moved."

"Eleanor—" He took a step forward, saw her go tense, and stayed where he was. He held out his hand. "Please. Come in. Close the door and let's talk."

Two more workmen grunted their way down the staircase with the secretary from Margaret's room resting on their thighs. The desk had remained locked since her death.

When the workmen were out of sight, Eleanor shook her head.

"There isn't any point. I'm going."

"You are not of legal age! You don't have permission to leave!"

She flared suddenly. "I don't want or need your permission. I could have run away without telling you! I looked for Will but he and Carter must have gone to the Park. I left a note for him."

Desperate now, he pointed to a chair. "Eleanor, sit down. I beg you. Tell me what brought this about. That blasted theatrical club you mentioned a few days ago?"

"I have no time to visit, Papa. I'm due at the New York Central depot in half an hour. There's a hack coming for me. The manager of the troupe arranged for it."

"*Depot?* When you said you were joining a theatrical company, I thought you meant here in the city."

"No, it's a traveling troupe."

"Good Lord."

"I don't understand why that upsets you so much. You gave me scripts to read. You took me to see my very first play at Booth's—"

"Taking you to Booth's isn't the same as encouraging you to run around the country with a bunch of immoral—what's so funny? *Damn it, Eleanor, answer me!*"

"I'm sorry, Papa. I don't mean to laugh. I can't help it. Because of all the things you publish in the paper, everyone thinks of you as a radical. But here you are ranting against the immoral theater. Almost like Mama used to do—"

"My liberality doesn't extend to allowing my fifteen-year-old daughter to travel with a pack of godless wastrels."

She shrugged. "I'm going, though."

How assured she sounded, in contrast to his own confusion.

"What—what's the name of this troupe?"

"Bascom's Original Ideal Uncle Tom Combination."

"God in heaven—a Tom show? That's even worse."

"You're making this very unpleasant." She was beginning to anger. "It's a grand opportunity. I'm to play one and perhaps two parts, and help backstage with the wardrobe. I couldn't find better preparation for a career as an actress."

"Who's been encouraging you? My brother? Has he been filling your head about how fine it is to be a free-spirited artist?"

"No, Papa. Uncle Matt had nothing to do with my decision." But the pink in her cheeks gave her away.

"I don't believe you," he shot back. "Whatever Matt said, it was nonsense. A painter's existence—or an actor's—isn't glorious or noble. I know. My own mother tramped around the country with her second husband. She was miserable because Lamont was a typical actor. No sense of reality, or of responsibility—it's a wretched, disorderly life."

Very quietly, she replied, "It can't be any more wretched or disorderly than the life in this house."

"Eleanor, I don't want to hear that again."

She paid no attention, answering his anger with her own. "But of course you wouldn't know anything about that. You were always too busy to care about your wife and your family. I don't see why you're suddenly doing a turnabout now."

The familiar accusation defeated him for a moment. He lowered his head, covered his eye with his right hand.

He couldn't let her go. Despite the flip way she brushed his arguments aside, actors were amoral people. And what did she know about men's desires at her age—or how to deal with them? She knew nothing.

Unless—

Oh, good God. Had someone already—?

He could barely stand to think about it. If he ever discovered that some middle-aged man had sullied his daughter, he'd turn into a Tom Courtleigh himself, and do murder. Only he'd do it personally. He'd horsewhip the damned lecher to death.

Despite his panic, he tried to speak calmly. "All right. It appears your decision's final. But you can give me a few more facts, can't you? How long will this junket last? A couple of weeks? A month?"

"Two years."

"*Two years?*"

"Three if we're successful. Mr. Bascom, the proprietor of the company, wants to take the production all the way to California."

He had a notion that he must look like an idiot, his mouth open and consternation on his face. And was that the hack clattering up Fifth Avenue this very moment?

"Where did you meet these people? What do you know about them?"

"I met Mr. Bascom at the theatrical club, just as you guessed. We'll be traveling together like a big family. There's even a boy in the company whom you met once. Remember Leo Goldman?"

With a blank look, Gideon shook his head.

"In any case, trouping's nothing new for most of them. They're quite experienced."

"And I don't doubt they'll use *you* to enhance that reputation."

"That's indecent, Papa."

"It's a matter of fact. A girl your age doesn't know how to take care of herself. How to guard against—against—"

"I know what you're trying to say and I want no part of it. Ever."

There was such pain in her eyes, and such venom in her tone, that he was taken aback. What had happened to her? Had she been attacked when the house was invaded? Julia spoke of the secret grief she sensed in Eleanor. Was the cause something she dared not reveal to anyone?

He shot a frantic glance at the window. The hoofbeats of the hack horses sounded loudly outside, slowing down.

"Do you have an itinerary? At least tell me where you're going—"

She reached for the valise. "Medium-sized cities and small towns, mostly. Our first three engagements are upstate."

His helplessness finally overcame his rage, and he was no longer a father berating a child, but an adult pleading with another adult. "Will you write us, then?"

She broke his heart when she smiled and said, "Of course, Papa, just as often as you wrote to me after you left."

And then she whirled and ran, one hand clutching the valise, the other holding her bonnet.

He rushed to the window as she dashed down the steps to the waiting hack. He watched the hack turn on Fifth and clip south again. After it was out of sight, he remained motionless at the window, a man who realized he'd grown old in an instant. Old, confused, and unexpectedly full of a sense of his eventual death.

Old. His child was gone from him. As all children left their parents.

No, that was wrong. Eleanor was different. She'd left with a heart brimming with hate that he hadn't been able to overcome.

He heard workmen complaining out in the foyer. The smell of smoke hung everywhere. The breeze fluttered the pages of the fallen copy of *100 Years.* Sunlight drenched Fifth Avenue, and the dust raised by the hack drifted away and dispersed.

iii

"Julia? Julia!" He stormed through the main floor, searching for her. Cook hurried from the kitchen.

"She's across the street, sir."

He didn't understand. "You mean in the Park?"

"No, sir. The vacant lot where they're burning Mrs. Kent's effects."

Cook's gray eyes hinted at disapproval. Julia had been spending almost every day at the house, but none of the servants was as yet fully accustomed to her presence.

"She went to see to their disposition," Cook added.

"God*damn* it!"

Cook stepped back as he stalked by.

"I told her to leave all those things alone—" he said under his breath as he rushed to the rear stairs and into the coach yard. One of the hired men was dippering water from a bucket. He started to wave, but saw Gideon's face and thought better of it.

"Julia?"

On the other side of Sixty-first, she turned and came toward him through knee-high weeds. The workmen had cleared a sizable area and trenched its perimeter to a depth of a foot and a half before igniting the fire. Gideon waited in the coach yard, his face thunderous, as Julia picked up her skirts with one hand and crossed the street. There was something black and square in her right hand. He paid no attention. He spoke before she was halfway to the curbstone.

"Julia, I specifically asked you to have nothing to do with the disposal of Margaret's—"

"Asked?" she broke in. "You ordered me."

He seized her wrist. "Whatever verb you care to use, you chose to disregard—"

"Of course I did." She wrenched away. "What's come over you, Gideon? I'm not some slavey, to be given orders and abused at your pleasure. If you think I am, I'll be happy to go back to the hotel, pack my things, and leave New York before the day's over."

Trembling, she gazed up at him. His blustery wrath faded. He realized she was carrying some sort of charred book, and a packet of letters whose edges were burned. She went on in a firm tone.

"But as long as I'm here, I'll continue to inspect everything before it's consigned to that fire. Most of Margaret's clothing is in perfect condition. It only wants a little cleaning, and it can be given to the poor. I'm sorry to hurt your feelings, but I can't stand unnecessary waste. And it's a good thing, because I found something important. That is, one of the workmen found it after I asked him to break the lock on Margaret's—"

"Julia, Eleanor's gone."

"What's that?"

"I said Eleanor's left. For good. Didn't you see the hack?"

"I noticed it, but I paid no attention. I thought the driver had gotten the wrong address."

"Eleanor took it. She's leaving the city. Going on tour with a Tom troupe."

She understood, but it was clearly difficult for her to believe the news. She shook her head and uttered a low, ragged sort of laugh. Then she leaned against Gideon's side.

"Dear God. Two such shocks in one morning is one too many."

"I don't know what you mean."

She showed him the book, and the envelopes with blackened edges. The envelopes were bound in a piece of old twine that had somehow survived the fire.

Astonished, he recognized the handwriting on the top
envelope. Then he saw the address. He snatched the packet
and riffled through it.

"These are letters to Eleanor that I wrote after I
moved out."

"So I assumed." Julia nodded. "We didn't discover them
until the desk was in the flames. As you can see, they
haven't been too badly damaged. Or this either." She held
out the blackened book.

He'd never seen it before. He returned his attention to
the letters, speaking his thoughts aloud. "She must have
intercepted them. Hidden them. But Samuel said—" He
stopped.

"Said what?" she prompted.

"The day of the funeral, the subject of these letters came
up with Eleanor. She denied ever seeing them. I questioned
Samuel and he told me Margaret had frequently picked up
the mail. He also said he'd never seen any letters like this.
Not one." He shook the packet. "But she couldn't have
intercepted this many without his cooperation—or without
attracting his attention, at the very least."

"You mean to say he lied to you?"

"Evidently."

"But why?"

Gideon spun toward the house. "We'll soon find out."

She caught his arm.

"Take the book too.

He turned back. He didn't understand why her eyes were
so apprehensive.

She continued. "It's a diary, Gideon—one which your
wife must have begun several years ago. I—"

She dabbed at her upper lip with a sleeve kerchief. From
across the street, the bite of a workman's ax sounded, tearing into wood which another man proceeded to pitch into
the translucent flames. A plume of inky smoke rose and
drifted away.

"I only glanced at a few entries. I think it will require a
good deal of courage for you to read the whole thing."

He tucked the blackened volume under one arm. Then
he stalked into the house. Julia followed.

They cleared the kitchen and confronted Samuel. Accused and confronted with evidence, he broke down almost

at once. Yes, he'd lied to Gideon. Of course he'd seen some of the letters to Eleanor.

Looking miserable and speaking in a halting voice, he described how Margaret had informed him over a year ago that she wanted to see all the mail before anyone else did. He said she'd warned him against mistakes; threatened him with firing if so much as one letter slipped by. He'd weighed the ultimatum—it *was* from the mistress, after all, and Gideon was gone—and from then on had made sure the postman put all deliveries into his hand and no other.

"But I didn't realize she was holding back certain letters, Mr. Kent. I thought it was just another of her—peculiar whims," he finished in a lame voice.

By then Gideon was almost drained of emotion. It was Julia who asked, "Why on earth did you lie to Mr. Kent the day of the funeral?"

Samuel shifted from foot to foot. "All at once I realized I'd gotten in too deep. I was afraid that if I confessed, I'd be sacked. I have a very large family—seven children. Jobs that pay as well as this one aren't easy to find."

Too weary for retribution, Gideon said, "All right, Samuel. I'm glad it's cleared up. Perhaps I should discharge you, but I won't. Just get out of here."

The butler vanished without questioning his good fortune.

Gideon carried the letters and the book into the library. Julia closed the doors. She picked up the fallen copy of *100 Years* and placed it on a side table as Gideon opened the book's browned pages. He read one short entry.

"Oh my God." He sank into his chair, read another, a third.

As Julia had said, coming right on top of Eleanor's departure, the shock was almost too much for a single human being to bear in a single morning.

iv

Julia asked a question about his daughter. He looked up and briefly told her what Eleanor had said. Then he returned to the book.

He discovered some of its pages were splattered with

curiously sinister inkblots. Others had holes or rips in them, as though damaged by the nib of a pen. Those were the pages on which she'd referred to Gideon as *him*. The pages conveyed her hatred, her deceit, and the steady deterioration of her mind in a way that left him openmouthed and made his belly hurt.

"She did lie to them, Julia. Deliberately. I wasn't wrong."

"No, my darling, you weren't." There was grief in her voice, pity, too.

Suddenly he stood up, slapping the book against his thigh. A corner of the cover broke away. Black flakes fell to the carpet. "I'm going to throw this back in the fire—"

He saw Julia shaking her head.

"Why the hell not?" With a trembling hand, he shook the book again. "No one's going to see this sad, filthy thing. It deserves to be forgotten."

"By everyone except one person. Eleanor."

"What?"

"You must get the book to her, Gideon—the book and the letters. Let her read them. Let her be the one to destroy them."

"Do you know what you're saying? You want me to show Eleanor this—this testament to her mother's deranged state?" He uttered a short, bleak laugh. "She already thinks I'm a monster. Now you want to confirm it."

"I want your daughter to know she was manipulated—just as you said she was. I want her to know it so she won't hate you for the rest of her life."

He understood. Pondered. Hesitated.

"It would only defame Margaret's memory—"

Julia seized his arms and shook him. "Margaret is *dead*! She can't be hurt any further. The living members of this family are the only ones who count now. If you want Eleanor to be your daughter in more than name—"

"You know I do."

"Then what's wrong? Are you afraid she'll reject you again?"

His blue eye brimmed with pain. His voice was barely audible.

"Yes."

"Could she dislike you any more than she already does?"

A pause. "No."

"Then you must show her the diary and the letters."

Still uncertain, he stared at her.

"You must, Gideon!"

Ten minutes later, dressed and lashing the buggy nag furiously, he went racing down Fifth Avenue in the calash, hoping he wasn't too late to catch her, find her, make her listen.

CHAPTER X

TWO FAREWELLS

i

THE SCHEDULE BOARD showed only one train for upstate New York during the rest of the day—a noon local which terminated at Albany. An express for Buffalo, Cleveland, and points west had departed at ten after eleven. Eleanor might have boarded that one at the last moment, Gideon thought as he hurried from the station into the train shed, the letters and the diary clutched in one hand.

The local had only three second-class passenger coaches. He sprinted past the rear one, then the second. There was a severe and steadily worsening ache all across his chest—his age showing.

A puff of steam obscured his vision a moment. When the steam cleared, he saw people milling up near the express car. Since most of them were shouting and gesturing, he presumed he'd found the troupe of actors. One of the men, a rascally-looking old fellow with a black wig, was waving a paper at someone inside the express car.

"Your loutish helpers dropped three different pieces of our scenery. The wings for Little Eva's dove, the ice floes, and the heavenly gates. If there's so much as one scrape or tear on any of them, this line will pay!"

635

Gideon shifted his attention to the dirt-streaked windows of the front passenger car. No sign of Eleanor there. He needed to go inside and look for—

He was distracted by a ferocious yapping. Again he looked toward the front of the train. He saw a man with two magnificently proportioned but carelessly groomed dogs on long chains. Apparently the man had been exercising the dogs on the empty track next to the platform on which Gideon was standing, and somehow the animals had gotten excited.

As the companions of the man in the wig closed around him to second his protests to the invisible expressman, the other man's dogs gave a lunge against their chains. The man nearly pitched on his face on the empty track.

Just in time, he righted himself. The dogs kept dragging him forward. He jumped up and landed on the platform with a thump, one hand clutching his wide-brimmed hat while the other, with the chains wrapped around it, was repeatedly yanked.

All the commotion around the express car merely incited the animals. One of them gave another lunge and tried to climb the front steps of the first passenger car.

By then the owner of the dogs was only a few feet from Gideon. The man wore clothes several years out of date, but they still had a costly look. Although the man was short—the crown of his hat was level with Gideon's shoulders—he carried himself with authority. He was slim, in his middle forties, with lively gray eyes and wavy dark hair streaked with white.

He gave Gideon an imperious look, as if questioning his right to be on the same platform. Then he swung toward a portly conductor who had appeared in the vestibule above the steps the dog was trying to ascend. While the other dog yapped and turned in a circle, the first kept its paws on the lowest step. The conductor's path down to the platform was blocked.

"Animals in the baggage car!" he exclaimed. He aimed a kick at the dog but missed. Fangs snapped together, inches from his shoe.

The small man might have been handsome except for a tomato-colored nose that had grown too large for his face. His cheeks turned the same color as he yelled, "Don't do that again, sir, or you'll face a lawsuit. Nicolai and Nicolette are not mongrels to be abused. They are full-blooded Borzois."

To add to the confusion, someone began yelling, "Daniel? Daniel, why don't you ever wait for me?" A tall, skinny, drably dressed woman emerged from the crowd still hectoring the expressman. Although the woman was as old as the man with the dogs, girlish ringlets dangled below the brim of her hat, and she'd blacked her eyes and rouged her face like a woman half her age. Her jaw was long, her face more than a little horselike. But she had large, vivid dark eyes, and a voice as mellow as a French horn.

"Daniel, you're a rude boy." She came hurrying toward him, hiking up her skirts so anyone could see her pantaloons. No one was interested.

"I don't give a hang if they're the Czar's children," the conductor snarled. "Pets don't ride with the passengers."

The small man took a long, deep breath and drew himself up while the wolfhounds snapped and pranced around his legs, winding him in their chains. All at once a little breeze carried an odd aroma to Gideon's nose. He identified it as hair dressing or cologne, mixed with another scent that had a sad familiarity. Whiskey.

"Daniel Prince's dogs do not ride anywhere but in the passenger section!" the actor shrieked. The ringleted woman tried to reach his side but was prevented by the wolfhounds still racing in circles. Wrapped in chain, the actor started to topple.

Gideon jumped forward and propped the man up. In the process he got a blast of whiskey breath. He backed away quickly to avoid being bitten by one of the wolfhounds. It was snapping at him while the other one tried to jump up and lick his face.

"Thank you, sir, thank you," Prince panted as he struggled to extricate himself from the chains. Gideon was impatient now.

"Is the Bascom Tom Company aboard this train?"

The small man couldn't answer. The Borzois were yanking him toward the empty track again.

The conductor said, "Yes, the troupe's on board and I wish it weren't. Theater folks are nothing but trouble. Noisy show-offs, the lot of them."

Less than cordial, Gideon said, "My daughter's with the company. I'm trying to find her. Miss Kent is her name—"

The conductor shrugged. "Believe me, I don't introduce myself to any of them." He jumped from the bottom step, avoided the entangled actor and rushed to the assistance of the expressman, who was now rolling on the platform, locked in a tussle with Bascom. The latter's black wig had fallen off, revealing a totally bald head. The members of the troupe were yelling encouragement to both combatants, much to the annoyance of their employer.

Other passengers began to raise the car windows and poke their heads out. Gideon was nearly beside himself with impatience. He'd only been on the platform two or three minutes, but what he'd seen in that short time renewed his fears for Eleanor's safety and sanity.

He grabbed the handrail beside the steps and started to climb up. A hand touched his sleeve. He spun and found himself facing the woman with the ringlets.

"I bed your pardon, sir. Did I hear you say you are Eleanor's father?"

"That's right."

"I am Mrs. Prince." She indicated the small man, who was still uttering feeble pleas for help with the chains. The Borzois had worn themselves out. One flopped at Prince's feet, tongue lolling. "I am indeed happy to meet you, Mr. Kent. We weren't aware anyone would be seeing Eleanor off. She's our new Little Eva, you know. A charming girl. Bascom raves about her talent."

"Bascom raves about anything which moves and wears petticoats," Prince said. He studied Gideon's shoulders, then his legs. Someone at an open window snickered. Prince glared.

"My name is Martha," the woman said, extending her hand. Gideon shook it. Time had marked Mrs. Prince's face with deep lines, and there was a certain sad quality about her arresting eyes. But she seemed a kind and essentially cheerful woman. She went on, "I've only chatted briefly with your daughter, but in that time I discovered she's quite young. Much younger than she looks, most assuredly. In a group like this, she will need someone to look after her. She has a young gentleman who seems willing to undertake part of the responsibility—"

"A gentleman? Who is he?"

"Mr. Goldman. Another new member of the company."
The name had a familiar sound, but Gideon couldn't put a
face with it. "Daniel and I shall look after her, too. We
have no children. We'll be glad to watch over her as if she
were our very own."

"Very kind of you, Mrs. Prince," Gideon said, though he
wasn't so sure the actor's attention would be any great
blessing. "It's quite important that I see Eleanor for a moment. Do you know which car she's in?"

"Certainly. This one. The third or fourth seat on the
other side."

"Thank you very much." He raced up the steps.

ii

All at once he was terrified of failure. His heart lubbed
so hard, it seemed to drown out the murmur of conversation in the second-class car. The car swarmed with flies,
and smelled stale and unclean.

Eleanor didn't seem to mind. She was seated beside an
open window, maintaining a distance of two or three inches
between herself and her companion, a young man with a
great deal of dark hair. She appeared to be enjoying an
animated conversation with the young chap. For a moment
Gideon hated a world that made a man and his children
grow old and apart.

Heads turned because he was standing motionless, just
to the rear of her seat. Her head moved last of all. She
glanced over her left shoulder. "Papa!"

She seemed too astonished for anger. Her exclamation
brought her companion bounding up. When he swung
around, Gideon recognized him at once, although the boy
had shot up and filled out since that night in Printing House
Square. The boy's pleased expression showed he remembered Gideon, too.

Eleanor said, "Papa, may I present Mr. Leo Goldman?
Leo, my father, Mr. Kent. I think you two met years ago—"

"We certainly did," Gideon said as they shook hands.
"Every man his own king—every man his own priest."

"That's right!" The boy had an incredibly rich baritone

voice. "I'm truly astonished that a man as busy as you would remember something I said."

Gideon managed to smile. "Yours was a much better definition of America than many I've heard."

"Leo's a member of the troupe." Eleanor's tone was neither friendly nor unfriendly.

"Yes, you did mention that this morning." He noticed she was looking at the book and letters under his arm. Then she searched his face, as if to find some clue to his state of mind.

"Leo and I met at the Booth Association," she explained.

"And you're on your way to make your fortune, eh, Mr. Goldman?"

"I certainly think so, sir."

"Splendid," Gideon replied, not intending it to sound as caustic as it did. "I don't want to be rude, but time's extremely short. I must speak to Eleanor privately."

"Of course, sir." Leo stepped aside so she could reach the aisle.

Gideon saw Eleanor's defenses rise as she murmured, "Speak to me about what, Papa?"

His fear worsened. He shouldn't have come. Even though the book's authenticity could hardly be questioned, she'd find some way to reject it—or cast the blame for its contents squarely back on him. He almost turned and fled. He'd never been more frightened of losing anything than he was of losing her affection for the rest of his life.

But she's already lost. That's why you're here.

"About what, Papa?" she repeated.

"About these."

He showed her the handwriting on the letters.

"If you'll examine the dates, you'll notice that I wrote you the first of these letters a few days after I moved out. All of them were found in your mother's desk."

iii

Her face lost color. Leo craned his head so he could see the letters. Gideon withdrew them. "If you'll excuse us— may we go outside, Eleanor?"

All the passengers were staring, but he didn't give a damn. All he cared about was her nod as she preceded him down the aisle. His heart was still beating hard as he opened the door for her.

Fortunately the platform near the foot of the steps was deserted. Daniel and Martha Prince and the Borzois had returned to the express car, where a rumpled Bascom was gesturing with his wig and haranguing a railroad official. One of the other actors was offering the expressman a bandanna for his bloody nose.

It all faded into insignificance as he said, "After you left this morning, I happened to open your mother's desk just before it was burned." The lie was spoken to spare Julia any further ill will. "My letters were in it, wrapped in cord just as you see them. I then questioned Samuel and he confessed he helped her confiscate the letters as they arrived. She ordered him to help her. All of that's in here—"

He opened to one of the diary's blotted pages. "And a good deal more that isn't very pleasant. I just want you to read a little of it."

He located the passage describing the start of Margaret's scheming.

"Start at the sentence that reads 'I shall never do anything so lacking in subtlety.' Read from there to the end of the page."

Her head bent over the book. In a moment her hands began to shake. He wanted to touch her but feared that if he did, she might fling the diary in his face.

He started at another outburst further up the platform. It was Prince, marching angrily in their direction. The actor had lost the battle of the Borzois. Their plaintive yelps sounded from the express car.

Prince's wife clung to his left arm, trying to soothe him. Still clutching his wig, Bascom was doing the same from Prince's right. The other actors trooped along behind as Prince exclaimed, "No, no, no! Explanations and apologies are useless, Bascom. You guaranteed the dogs would ride as passengers. The gold of your word has proved itself mere dross."

"Listen, I damned near got walloped to pieces for those goddamn mongrels!" Bascom retorted. "Your pardon, Martha."

Some of the actors laughed. Several passengers leaning out the windows gasped and slammed the windows shut. Out of sight inside, the conductor shouted a warning about foul language on New York Central property.

Prince ascended the steps, the perfect, and perfectly exaggerated, picture of a wounded man.

"In view of your insults, Bascom, I don't know whether I shall be able to perform in Albany."

"You better or I'll sue you from here to the Canadian border. Martha, give him his flask for God's sake."

The actors vanished. The whistle blew. Gideon turned back to his daughter—

To find her oval eyes bright with tears.

"I never believed you," she whispered. "I never believed she lied to us on purpose."

A weary smile. "I tried to convince you. But I had no evidence. Anytime you wish, you can write Samuel and he'll confirm what I said about the letters."

How he hated to see the vulnerability on her face. She was young again—young and hurt. He wasn't sure she'd forgive him for this pain, either.

She tried to hand him the diary and the packet of envelopes. He blocked them gently with one palm.

"They're yours. Destroy them if you want. It's up to you. I only ask you to read the letters, and some of the diary. I've come to realize belatedly that I caused a great deal of the trouble that beset our household. I could have gone much further than I did to smooth over the difficulties, but I didn't do it because—well, because I'd fallen in love with Julia. No human being is perfect, as you've discovered too early in life."

The whistle howled.

Haltingly, he began again. "I used both Julia and the *Union* as excuses to keep me away from an unpleasant situation at home. By doing that, I also neglected you and Will. To all that, I plead guilty. But—"

The conductor leaned down from the vestibule, a ghostly figure surrounded by billowing steam. "Miss? Get aboard, please."

"Papa, can you ever forgive me?"

The very sound of it was balm to his soul. "Of course. I already have. You're my daughter. The question is, can you forgive me? Because of all that I did, I don't suppose it's possible for you to love me. But certain things can't be changed. I *am* your father. I love you. I may have failed you, but I love you."

She was too overcome to speak.

"I only ask that you don't push us out of your life. Julia and Will and I are all the family you have now. I don't want you to go on this damned trip, but if you must, then remember we're here waiting for you to come home."

"Yes, Papa. I will."

He almost dropped to his knees to thank a God with whom he was on less than familiar terms. She darted another swift look at the passenger cars beginning to move slowly toward the flare of sunlight at the end of the shed. All at once she was crying.

"I'm so sorry for what I did, Papa, for all the cruel things I said—"

"It's over! Only the future counts. Write us. Tell us what you're doing. Whether you're safe, and well. Write to the *Union* because we may be moving soon. Wherever we go, will you come home when you can?"

"Yes. *Yes.*"

"Oh, Eleanor—" He took hold of her free hand. He could feel the sudden tension in her fingers. Had he hurt her so deeply over the past year or so that she recoiled from the touch of another human being? He only hoped it was his touch, and not every man's, or she was truly a wounded creature.

"Papa, I love you!"

The cry seemed torn from her. Tears streaming on her face, she flung her arms around his neck and hugged him hard for one supremely joyous instant.

Then she turned and ran along beside the passenger car and reached up to grasp the conductor's hand. Once aboard, she gripped the vestibule rail and looked back at him. She began to wave, her face and form dwindling in the blaze of summer light outside the station.

Why did she have to go? She was too young. Too inexperienced. He was afraid for her to be alone with those people. The Goldman boy and Mrs. Prince seemed kindly, but what about the rest? He was afraid for her to travel to strange places among such a raffish crowd.

He was afraid just as any father would be.

He *was* her father again, he realized. Happiness overwhelmed him, and he stood waving until the last passenger car shrank away to nothing out there in the August light.

He was her father again!

iv

Late that afternoon Gideon fell ill with violent stomach pains. On the advice of his doctor, and over his protests, Julia put him to bed. By nine that night he was running a high fever.

Dr. Melton lanced the sutured bullet wound, relieving a buildup of pus, and prescribed a heavy draft of whiskey for sleep. As Julia ushered the doctor out, he gave his professional opinion.

"All the events you've mentioned have undoubtedly been extremely aggravating to his weakened condition. I should imagine that if I were shot in the midst of a riot, lost my wife and then had my daughter decamp with a pack of actors, my sanity would be gone right along with my health. I can't understand how the man keeps going—"

She smiled. "The Kents seem to be a hardy breed."

"Hardy but not indestructible. Keep him in bed for the next three or four days. Even if you have to use ropes."

v

Gideon was awake at four on Sunday when a man from the *Union* brought him a long telegraph message just in over the newspaper's leased wires. Out in Chicago, Salathiel Brown had reached a dead end.

In circumspect phrases, Brown reported that he'd spread his *fund*—he meant bribe money—among three guards the Wisconsin and Prairie now employed at its headquarters. The guards had been quite happy to give him the company version of what had happened the weekend of the railroad strike. Lorenzo Hubble had been in Chicago the entire time, and the guards were prepared to swear to it if necessary.

Brown had interviewed each man separately, in a saloon. One of the three, a consumptive roughneck named Kane, had gotten drunk enough to let a damaging fact slip. In between swallows of gin and spells of coughing, Kane said he and the others had been paid a hundred dollars apiece, in advance, in case it became necessary to testify to Hubble's presence. Kane knew Brown could never prove what he'd just heard by accident, but he threatened Brown anyway, saying he'd do Brown serious injury if the reporter repeated the slip to anyone. The man seemed to enjoy that sort of bullying, Brown noted.

Finally, Brown had done some further checking, and discovered that no reliable witnesses could actually place Hubble in Chicago during the weekend in question. In other words, the report concluded, it appeared that Hubble had been out of town, and that for some reason, the W & P was prepared to prove otherwise.

Gideon flung the crumpled message on the floor beside his bed. Courtleigh's guilt was unmistakable. But what the hell could he do about it? He could think of nothing except the kind of unthinkable act to which Sime Strelnik had predicted he'd be driven to by this sort of frustration.

He was sorely tempted. Only after an hour of reflection, and a conversation with Julia, did good sense prevail.

vi

Late on Monday, dressed for traveling, Matt came to his brother's bedside. Hot sunlight blazed in the room, slanting from the west above the park. Gideon felt much better. He insisted he'd accompany Matt to the Cunard pier.

"I won't hear of it," Matt said. "Julia's going with me. I'm only sorry the trip to the West Side won't be longer. There isn't time for me to take her away from you."

Gideon laughed, then sobered. "I'm sorry you won't stay."

"I stayed much longer than I ever expected to, Gid." Matt pulled up a chair. "There's too much of me still in England, and not enough of me here."

"There's a lot of you here now that the book's published."

"Maybe." A shrug. "By the way, I was in that palace of a bookstore on Union Square this morning—what's the name of it?"

"Brentano's. August Brentano opened it last year. It's already the best store of its kind on the East Coast. For an immigrant who used to peddle newspapers and magazines in the streets, August is doing very well."

"They told me *100 Years* is selling briskly. If the trend continues, maybe the fortunes of Kent and Son have finally been reversed. I'm afraid the etchings are a disaster. There'll be precious little money for charity—"

"Matt, in a few years one of those sets will be priceless."

The younger brother studied the older with affection. "I don't know which of us is the biggest bull thrower."

"Before you go"—Gideon coughed, then winced; the wound was hurting like fury and leaking pus again— "there's something I need to ask you."

Matt pulled out a cigar. "Ask away."

"Did you speak to Eleanor about an acting career?"

Matt strode to an open window and gazed across at the Park, trying to sound offhand. "Yes, we had a conversation. She asked my opinion on some things."

"Such as whether she should leave home?"

Matt pivoted. "That question didn't come up specifically."

"By implication, then?"

Matt slipped his cigar back in his pocket. He didn't avoid his brother's gaze. "I suppose you might say so."

"Did you encourage her to go?"

He sighed. "Does it really matter? I think she'd have gone whether I encouraged her or not. Or whether or not you approved. I got the very clear impression that she couldn't do anything else with her life. When that happens to someone, you just have to accept it."

"*I* don't have to accept it!"

Quietly: "Gid, your age is showing."

"What the hell does that mean?"

"You're a very liberal thinker in some ways. But you'll never understand the kind of life I lead—or the kind Eleanor wants to lead, either. Never understand it fully, I mean. Hell, I don't myself, or I'd have never let Dolly walk out on me and travel halfway round the world to have our son. In any case, I think I know what's worrying you. Her age, and her virtue." Gideon reddened as he went on. "Contrary to what you may think, artists are not all ravening lechers. Some of them are the kindest people on earth. Crazy, but kind. I'll tell you this. I'd sooner see your daughter in an acting troupe than cast adrift in a room full of politicians. Those bastards would have her compromised in ten minutes."

"You're saying actors won't?"

"Of course I'm not saying that. People are people. But you need to have more faith in your own child. Eleanor's a strong, capable young woman. I suspect she can take care of herself. She did while you weren't living here, didn't she?"

Propped against damp pillows, Gideon grimaced and murmured, "Point scored."

Matt came to the bedside and embraced him. "Look, my esteemed older brother, it's too late to change what Eleanor's done. You said she softened her feelings toward you when you proved Margaret had been deceiving her. Be thankful for that. Be proud of her ambition and her spunk. She'll probably turn into a Kent we can all admire. I know newspapermen are professional scolds. But don't let it carry over to your family. Don't find fault with Eleanor. Enjoy her! We forget how little time we really have to enjoy each other. You're a damn lucky man, Gideon. You have a fine son and daughter, and a fine lady who loves you—"

"Julia?" He smiled. "I couldn't survive without her."

"Don't try. I swear, if she had yellow hair and blue eyes, I'd abduct her. By the way, do you know how late it is?"

"See here," Gideon teased, "you're prosperous enough to afford a watch. If I'm wrong, I'll buy you one."

Matt grinned. "No, thanks. I don't like being reminded of how little time I have left." He glanced out the window toward the sun-drenched Park. "To judge by the light, I'd better be going along or I'll miss the ship."

"Next time don't make it so long between visits."

"Listen," Matt said with his old, sardonic grin, "working on that book, I sucked out the meat of this country, just as if was a ripe orange. There's nothing left. I'll come home again when I think something else might interest me. Such as the christening of a new nephew, maybe—?"

"I'm too old for fatherhood!"

"And for all that goes with it?" Matt said with a straight face. "For Julia's sake, I sincerely hope not." He picked up his boater, waved and left his brother musing in a dazzle of sunlight.

No, Gideon thought, he would never understand all of Eleanor's motives, nor what deep need drove her to perform in front of an audience. But Matt seemed to understand, and to think it was an acceptable life. Uneasily, he decided to trust his brother's judgment.

Was his daughter talented? She'd always shown off at home—and sometimes in public, when she shouldn't have. Much to his surprise, he found himself conjuring an imaginary scene in which he and Julia sat in the front row of a great playhouse and watched an immense red velvet curtain descend. Then it rose again, and Eleanor stepped to the footlights to receive an ovation.

With his eye closed, he saw it like a painting in his mind. The image was unexpectedly a very pleasing one.

vii

Julia accompanied Matt aboard the Cunard Steamship *Persia*, kissed his cheek fondly, and left the ship as stewards hurried around the decks, ringing gongs to send all visitors ashore. She waved at Matt from the pier, then turned and walked toward Tenth Avenue. Mills was waiting with the calash on the other side of Tenth, unable to get closer because of the usual congestion.

Even though it was already sunset, a time of shadow and deceptive red light, this part of the West Side still swarmed with people and vehicles. Every half block or so, piers jutted into the river—ferry piers serving the rail lines operating from New Jersey, and shipping piers where the Cunarders and other seagoing vessels docked. The Jersey bluffs were all but hidden by hulls and masts. There were paddle steamers, screw steamers, even some beautiful clippers still traveling the tea routes to India and China.

Tenth Avenue was clogged with freight wagons, drays, hacks and private carriages. Passengers, seamen and longshoremen hurried past Julia as she waited for an opportunity to cross.

She was thankful Gideon had stayed behind, in bed. He desperately needed rest, and a time of peace, after the stress of the past few weeks.

Perhaps their lives were smoothing out at last. Gideon and Eleanor might never come to a complete and harmonious understanding of one another—that was almost too much to ask—but at least there'd been an armistice, and some sign of affection on Eleanor's part, a sign Gideon had desperately needed for a long time. Now if they could only locate a suitable house—Boston looked more and more like a possibility because of Gideon's expressed desire to delve into the affairs of Kent and Son—they might be able to look forward to a period that was free of turmoil and unhappiness.

All in all, she felt quite fine on this warm summer evening as the shadows of hurrying men lengthened around her. One halted just to her left. She glanced back from the traffic she'd been watching and saw that the man was wearing a heavy coat. Odd garb for August. The coat didn't even fit. The sleeves were too long, and concealed the man's hands, just as an old hat concealed most of his face.

He was one of the army of beggars still tramping the streets, she supposed. Because she felt at peace with the whole human race this evening, she started to open her reticule even before the man made his plea.

But the beggar said nothing. Her eyes opened wide as the man's right hand rose. The cuff of the coat fell back. A sliver of metal flashed in the sunset.

He rammed the knife through Julia's dress into her stomach, released the handle, whirled and ran before anyone moved to stop him. By then Julia had fallen to the ground.

CHAPTER XI

SKY FULL OF STARS

i

A FEW HOURS after Julia was struck down, a train carrying the Bascom troupe sped westward through the darkness and solitude of the Mohawk Valley.

Eleanor dozed awhile, then woke abruptly. She didn't know the exact hour, but she was sure it was somewhere in the middle of the night. She just couldn't make herself comfortable in the unfamiliar confines of an upper berth. Her restlessness was heightened by all the confusing and disappointing things that had happened in the past twenty-four hours.

She put on her robe. Carefully, she poked her legs out between the curtains. She wiggled around until she was on her stomach, then stepped down, making sure her bare toes didn't press too hard on the curtain of Miss Ruthven's lower berth. If she didn't cut her own career short with wretched acting, Miss Adelaide Ruthven would try to cut it short for her, that much she knew after only one performance.

Adelaide Ruthven was a good fifteen years older than Eleanor. She was a talented and experienced actress, with a face that resembled the blade of an ax. That was fine for character roles. For Bascom, however, she played Eliza.

The troupe's first audience had had some difficulty accepting Miss Ruthven as a mulatto. In fact there was a great deal about Bascom's Original Ideal Uncle Tom Combination that audiences would have difficulty accepting, Eleanor now believed.

Safely down in the aisle, she tiptoed through the swaying, clacking Pullman. The car was dimly illuminated by small, metal-shaped lamps at either end. She passed Leo's berth. His presence was something else that troubled her. She felt the same strong attraction for him that she'd felt at the Booth Association. She was still afraid to admit it, though. Thank heavens the troupe had kept busy preparing for and playing the opening performance. She hadn't had to deal with Leo yet. But occasionally he gave her an intense glance that said she'd have to do so soon.

Perhaps she'd be sent back to New York, and that would solve it.

She opened the door and stepped out on the platform between her car and the next. Chilly wind gusted against her cheeks and set her hair streaming behind her. The weather had turned unexpectedly cool. Dark hills went slipping by on either side of the train. Above, between the cars, she saw one of the most dazzling and breathtaking displays of stars she'd ever set eyes on.

For a moment the sight of the sky took her mind off of her miserable opening night performance, and all the other attendant difficulties. How clear the stars were! Hundreds of them, thousands—a shimmering canopy stretching from horizon to horizon. Some of the stars were brilliant white, some bluish, and a few had a red cast. Individual stars brightened or dimmed as the train kept moving and changing her perspective.

The berth had been stuffy. She welcomed the bite of the night air, even though her bare feet were cold. She clung to the platform rail, savoring the wind's sweetness as it blew her hair against her cheek one moment, snapped it out behind her the next. She closed her eyes and raised her face to the stars. Her feelings overwhelmed her.

Feelings of shame at having accused her father of being responsible for all the trouble in the household. That terrible book she could barely stand to read had proved how mistaken she'd been.

To be sure, Gideon would always bear some of the blame. He'd said as much himself. But he hadn't abandoned the family entirely by choice. Margaret's schemes, the products of her sick mind, had driven him out by making it intolerable for him to stay—just as he'd told her. She hadn't believed him then. She'd played into her mother's hands, and unwittingly behaved exactly as Margaret wanted her to behave.

She was beset by feelings of failure, too. Feelings of having made a dreadful mistake.

And feelings of homesickness.

She'd expected to miss Will, but she hadn't expected to miss the Fifth Avenue house with all its unhappy associations. She even found herself missing her father. The strange new longing had been with her ever since she'd impulsively embraced him on the depot platform.

She found herself a little more tolerant of his relationship with Julia Sedgwick, too. She could never condone the relationship—that would be a kind of betrayal of her mother—but at least she understood why some such relationship had been necessary for her father.

The whole sorry business merely proved again that love was hurtful, and that she'd best dampen her feelings for Leo Goldman. Besides, she'd probably have no opportunity to indulge them. Considering the show in Albany earlier tonight, she'd be lucky to be with the troupe one more day.

ii

The company had arrived in Albany late on Saturday. They were to play the New Novelty Theater on Monday evening. In violation of local ordinances, the theater was surreptitiously unlocked on Sunday afternoon so Bascom could conduct a rehearsal for the benefit of the new players—Eleanor, Leo, and two older men who seemed chiefly interested in their friendship with one another.

To Eleanor's disappointment, only she and the three new men were present for the rehearsal. And rather than walking them through the entire show, Bascom sat them in chairs and supervised a swift reading of the dialogue. He only made one or two comments to each person. Eleanor had hoped for intensive discussion of character motivation. Instead, she was given a curt "Louder there." Or "That's where you roll your eyes. By God, they'll cry buckets."

The session lasted about two hours. Then they spent another hour following Bascom around while he showed them where the various flats, flown backdrops, and pieces of special machinery would be positioned for each scene. Eleanor made frantic notes on her sides of dialogue. So did Leo. The older men didn't bother.

She had already been warned that Bascom never arranged stage pictures, or directed entrances and exits, let alone whole scenes. If the actors formed a pleasing picture, or played a scene with special skill, it was solely by accident—and if the picture or the performance was duplicated on another evening, it was due solely to the effort of the cast.

Late on Monday, Bascom did call the whole company together for another line rehearsal, this one with the actors and actresses sitting or lounging around the stage wherever they wished while they clipped off the dialogue at top speed. Even reciting that way, Eleanor drew spontaneous applause for Eva's death scene—and her first looks of animosity from Miss Ruthven. What a pity Monday night's show hadn't matched the intensity, or the success, of the rehearsal.

In addition to playing St. Clare's daughter, Eleanor doubled in brass as a female spectator at the slave auction in act five. And, wearing men's clothing, she was a supernumerary patron in the tavern scenes, including that in the first act in which Eliza appeared with her young son Harry. The role of Harry was unrealistically played by a midget named Elmer Fiddler. During the rest of the show, Fiddler, who was thirty or so, supervised the movement of scenery. A white midget made up as a mulatto boy was only one of many anomalies in Mr. J. J. Bascom's tawdry and slapdash production.

Before Eliza—Miss Ruthven—escaped from the riverside tavern, Eleanor was already drawing glares from the older actress. She had to suffer through the rest of the show before she found out why. And "suffer" was none too extreme a word. The evening quickly became a disaster for everyone.

The first trouble came during the pursuit of Eliza across the painted ice floes. Dan Prince's two Borzois had been off the boards for about six weeks. They were not yet reaccustomed to the stage lights. While the piano in the orchestra pit thundered out its menacing music, Nicolette jerked on her leash and began barking. She wouldn't stop. Then Nicolai looked stage left, instead of stage right at the fleeing Eliza, and relieved himself.

The audience howled. But worse was in store.

Leo Goldman was far too young to play Eleanor's father, St. Clare. Even with his stirring voice, he couldn't carry it off, and the audience let the players know it. Loudly. Eleanor was so unnerved, her opening scene as Eva totally lacked the conviction she'd given the part in rehearsal. She knew she was floundering and doing a lackluster job, and the more she fretted while she was onstage, the more nervous she became.

Then, behind the scenes, she found herself cornered in semidarkness by J. J. Bascom. He insisted he needed help getting into his Legree coat. That turned out to be a pretext for pawing her. She made him cross by repeatedly pulling away.

"Your coat fits perfectly, Mr. Bascom." She yanked it smooth around his collar, again dodged his groping hand and hurried off.

Either Bascom was still angry with her when he made his first entrance, or bombast was his regular style. Whatever the reason, he roared and foamed and overacted dreadfully in the part of the overseer. Dan Prince, on the other hand, was surprisingly good as Tom, even though he reeked of whiskey during the entire six acts—something that reminded Eleanor of her late mother, and further unsettled her.

One of the other actors derisively told Eleanor that Prince drank to make his slurred dialect that much more realistic. She thought it was a nasty, vindictive thing for an actor to say about a member of his own company. Probably the man was just jealous of Prince's talent. It was another jolting lesson. The theater certainly wasn't the glamorous and idealistic place she'd imagined.

Drunk or not, Prince drew loud and spontaneous applause when he ascended to heaven in the final tableau.

The applause might have lasted longer but for another mishap. Eva—Eleanor—was seated on a cutout dove hung beside the gates of heaven. One of the wires supporting the dove suddenly broke. With a surprised screech, Eleanor fell to the stage. She landed in a graceless sprawl, discovering a moment later that her wig of yellow curls had tumbled off. Dazed, she thought she should retrieve it as fast as possible. She started crawling toward it but was frozen in place by the booming sound of laughter.

Considering all the flaws in the show, the audience was surprisingly generous with its applause at the final curtain. Prince took the last bow, Bascom the penultimate one, and Martha Prince the one before his. Despite her age, the actor's wife was marvelous as Topsy. She'd danced the character's breakdowns with a liveliness that startled and enthralled Eleanor as she watched from the wings.

While the sets were struck and crated under the profane supervision of the midget stage manager, ladies of the town came in with hampers containing a cold supper for the company. Several adolescents—so Eleanor thought of them, having gotten through one complete professional engagement, albeit wretchedly—lingered on the sidelines. The young people watched the actors enviously, but were too shy to speak to them. For a brief moment she felt vastly superior. Then she remembered her poor performance and decided she was being an arrogant ninny.

On top of that, she noticed Miss Ruthven staring at her in a hostile way. After that, Eleanor couldn't eat so much as one piece of cold chicken.

The moment the townspeople left, Miss Ruthven again collared Bascom and yelled her complaint. In the first tavern scene, Eleanor had been sitting upstage near a cutout window. She'd done her best to pantomime the part of a lively, convivial rustic. Too convivial! Miss Ruthven screamed to the manager. Eleanor had deliberately upstaged her—and then done miserably in her own part.

Eleanor tried to apologize and tell Miss Ruthven the first crime was unintentional. The actress turned her back. She threatened to quit the company and return to New York to accept an ingenue role unless Bascom discharged Eleanor, who by then was ready to burst into tears.

Abruptly, Dan Prince came lurching onstage, his neck

still stained by his blackface makeup. Rings of it surrounded his red-rimmed eyes as well. He could barely stand
upright as he passed Leo Goldman. He gave the young
man an affectionate pat, then moved on to Eleanor and put
his arm around her. He acted drunk but he sounded sober.

"Addie, shut your mouth. We all know—that is, those of
us who are experienced in this troupe know—that you insist
on initiating all newcomers. Very well, you've done it. Miss
Kent was brilliant in rehearsal and rotten onstage. You've
had the same experience a hundred times, I'll wager. So let
her alone and stop those silly threats. You know full well
that no New York manager is going to hire you to play an
ingenue any more than he's going to hire me to play a
romantic lead."

He glowered. So did she. Then Miss Ruthven whirled
and stamped offstage. Prince squeezed Eleanor again,
belched softly, and staggered away. That ended the battle,
but she suspected the war would continue.

There on the swaying platform, Eleanor asked herself
whether it was worth staying in the company and struggling
against Miss Ruthven's obvious enmity. She just didn't
know. In one evening, she'd lost her enthusiasm for trouping. The applause from the audience seemed ludicrous in
view of the production's excesses, miscastings, and mistakes. The scenery showed its age. So did the costumes.
Altogether, Bascom's was a third-rate troupe. No, tenth-
rate—or worse.

She gazed at the starry arch of sky in a forlorn way,
letting the night wind spread her hair like a dark flag again.
She felt small. Frightened. She wanted to go home—

The door of her car crashed open. In terror, she pressed
against the rail. For a moment she saw no one in the dark
rectangle. But she was certain it was the troupe's proprietor, come to find and discharge her.

A cloud of whiskey fumes floated out, followed by Daniel
Prince in a quilted dressing gown with a large hole in one
elbow.

He shut the door behind him. A sudden sway of the train
hurled him sideways. Eleanor shrieked softly, grabbed the
dressing gown and kept Prince from tumbling down the
steps and over the chain to the rocky embankment.

"Mmm," Prince muttered. "Damn rough roadbed. Guess I'd better hang on."

He reached for the rail and missed. On the next attempt, Eleanor guided his hand.

"Thank you," he said, using the words as the cue for sliding his left arm around her shoulders. He felt her stiffen. "Martha woke me. She heard you leave the car and thought I should see whether you were all right." He was sounding surprisingly sober all at once. "Care to tell me your troubles?"

"I was awful in the play, Mr. Prince."

He thought a moment. "I couldn't agree more. But as I told Addie, it's happened to every actor. As you gain experience, you'll learn to save yourself in rehearsal so there'll be energy left for the performance. You shouldn't worry too much. The audience didn't go so far as to throw things. Only your colleagues knew how really bad you were," he finished with a chuckle that took the sting from the remark.

"Well," Eleanor replied, "I don't know whether I'll be around long enough to learn from my mistakes."

"Mmm," he said again. "Are you homesick?"

"Very."

"So Martha and I suspected. I hope that will pass. After a night or two, you'll be splendid as Little Eva, take my word. Even Goldman won't be half bad once he learns how to use makeup to age himself. Handsome boy, Goldman."

"Mr. Prince, I don't mean to offend you, but except for the scenes when you or your wife were onstage, the whole show was terrible. The audience knew it, too."

He digested that. "Of course they did. But they still enjoyed themselves. They helped create the illusion that they were witnessing a passable performance. We created the illusion that we were presenting one—and more important, we sustained it afterward. You'll find that actors are superb at convincing themselves they were grand when they weren't at all. You have a candor that's refreshing, Eleanor"—he squeezed her shoulder—"and you do have talent. I, by contrast, shall never be a performer of the first magnitude. I might have had some chance at one time, before certain—appetites of mine got the better—well, never mind that. Merely let it be said that I do have an eye for spotting talent in others. Even more of an eye than old Horace."

"Who?"

"Horace. Bascom. That's his real name."

It struck her as funny, somehow. She laughed, and Prince went on. "When Horace auditions females, he tends to be mesmerized by bustlines and speculations about who might be willing to warm his bed." There was an odd undertone of disgust in the actor's voice. His eyes drifted to the passing hills. "This time Horace chose wisely—as regards ability, I mean to say. I was genuinely impressed by your reading at the rehearsal. I do believe that with the proper guidance and a few strokes of good fortune, within ten or twelve years you can be an actress who is respected and sought after by the leading producers and managers. I'd even go so far as to say you might well be one of the reigning ladies of the American stage."

For several moments she couldn't speak. And then she could only think of something hopelessly inane. "That's very kind of you, Mr. Prince."

"Kindness has nothing to do with it, my dear. I told you the truth. If you do achieve what I think you can achieve, limitless possibilities will be open to you. The most important, I suppose, would be in connection with a marriage partner."

She wanted to tell him she had no interest in that sort of thing. But she didn't want to interrupt and perhaps hurt his feelings.

"You'll be able to do much more than select from one or two gentlemen of promising but unrealized potential. You'll have a flock of 'em after you. Men who've already made their marks. Piled up fortunes, or gotten hold of the reins of political power. It won't be a case of too narrow a choice, but too wide a one. And it all comes from making the stage your conquered province. You can do it. You have the beauty. I am now satisfied that you have the talent. The only thing lacking—indeed, the ingredient even more essential than natural ability—is ambition. Without it, you'll never reach the pinnacle. With it, you'll be there while you're still young and vigorous enough to enjoy it."

It was a dazzling prospect, and his sincerity almost convinced her it was a realistic one. But she didn't want a husband, ever. She especially didn't want a husband who was a Congressman or a stockbroker. She only cared about one person, and she hardly dared admit that to herself—

Prince took her silence for suspicion.

"Believe me, there's no ulterior motive behind all I've said. Indeed, I shall be happy to look after you in a most fatherly fashion, and see that Bascom doesn't drive you wild with his pawings and slaverings. Has he started?"

"Oh, just a bit. I fended him off, though."

"Good. It isn't hard."

"No, it isn't."

"Horace is really quite a decent fellow. God-awful actor, but a decent fellow. As soon as you've discouraged him once or twice, he'll be off chasing some skirt he's spied in the audience. How he keeps it up at his age is beyond me. Just be assured, my dear—I have no interest in you as a bed warmer."

"I've never worried about that," she told him truthfully. "You and Mrs. Prince seem very happily married."

His laugh was touched with cynicism. "We are. In our profession, marriage is a great convenience. Two can eat more cheaply than one. Martha and I constantly help one another with lines, and with interpretations—we fix each other's costumes—it's an ideal arrangement. As for romantic inclinations"—he shrugged—"mine do not lie in the direction of the female sex."

The statement had an aggressive ring to it, as if he were deliberately defying her conventional notions of morality. And in truth, she was shocked. She'd heard of men who felt as he did. His thoroughly masculine manner had deceived her—though come to think of it, she'd noticed him being almost excessively cordial to Leo ever since the troupe left New York. She hid her feelings. The tension went out of the moment.

Musing, he went on. "But if I have any suspense passion, it's for the applause. I see the same worn, shabby backdrops that you do. I stand in the wings and watch Nicolai misbehave in front of several hundred people and I think, my God, this is a profession for madmen, and the people are equally mad to pay fifty cents to view such a debacle. But then the final curtain approaches, and I ride to heaven in my gold car, and the sound that comes swelling up from the house makes me quite willing to deceive myself for the rest of my life. Deceive myself into believing this tawdry existence is beautiful. That it's art. That it matters. You, though—"

Another squeeze. This time she managed to stay relaxed.

"You won't have to practice that kind of deception when you're my age. Before long, you'll leave Horace and Addie and the rest of us far behind."

Suddenly the door opened. Prince quickly lowered his arm. "Oh, Goldman. Good evening," he said rather stiffly.

Eleanor was embarrassed. So was Leo. "Good evening— ah—I was only looking for Eleanor—excuse me—"

Prince waved. "No, come out, come out. I'm just leaving."

Leo hesitated, then moved past him to stand near Eleanor. The older man added, "Make sure she doesn't stay out here too long, my boy. We don't want her coming down with a sore throat or chilblains."

Eleanor leaned forward and planted a kiss on his cheek. "Thank you," she whispered.

He blinked and reached for the handle of the door. The train swayed on its way around a long curve. Prince lost his balance. Leo grabbed his arm.

"Don't fall, sir."

With a look so intense, it made Leo glance away, Prince patted his hand and then disengaged. "Oh, no, my dear boy," he said with a little smile. "That happened many years ago."

He touched two fingers to his brow—a salute that somehow had great panache despite the hour and the setting. Then he turned, opened the door, and stumbled as he went inside. "Goddamn it," they heard him mutter as he disappeared, "I hate spoiling an exit."

iii

"Are you all right, Eleanor?"

"My," she said, "I seem to have my share of guardians this evening."

"It's very late. Almost dawn, I'll bet. Prince wasn't— bothering you, was he?"

"I think he's the last person who'd ever try that."

"I'm not so sure." Leo rubbed his upper arms slowly; he'd donned an old, faded overcoat on top of his nightshirt. His feet were bare, like hers. "I was worried when you came out here by yourself. Then Prince trailed you and I got even more worried."

"Were you lying in your berth listening?"

A nod, a rueful smile. "I couldn't sleep either. I was thinking."

"About what?"

"You."

She tingled, hearing that word—and suddenly she realized her fear of affection had weakened ever since her reconciliation with her father. It was as if that moment had shattered some invisible chain. Just a moment ago, she'd kissed Dan Prince and not even thought twice.

Still, she remembered how the men who'd come to the house had hurt her. A tightness spread through her loins and up into her breasts. She sensed that a crisis had come— one that Leo could know nothing about.

Nor did she dare tell him. Instead, she said, "I was doing some thinking too. I played my part so badly in Albany, I was actually thinking of resigning from the troupe and going home. Mr. Prince encouraged me to stay—"

"Good!"

"—and I decided I had to because it's wrong to be a quitter. People in our family just don't do it." All at once she felt incredibly tired. "We'd better get some rest, Leo. We have to play Syracuse tomorrow nigh—no, tonight. It's already Tuesday, isn't it?"

She started to move by him to the door. She didn't trust herself out here alone with Leo. She knew how he felt, and if she broke down, it would only lead to—

His hand closed gently on her forearm. She started to protest, then saw by starlight that his mouth had set in that determined way.

He said softly, "Before you go, I want to tell you one thing. I thought you were wonderful tonight."

"Oh, Leo, I wasn't."

"Then we disagree."

"I was so afraid—"

"Of what?"

"Everything."

His face was suddenly very close. And there were delicious feelings in her arm where he held her. The tightness was melting, and no matter how she warned herself about the danger, she didn't seem to care about it. The starlight, Prince's reassuring words, Leo standing so close and touching her so tenderly—all conspired to allay her fears and leave her open to a flood of wondrously new emotions.

"You mustn't be afraid of anything, Eleanor," he said. "Not of yourself, and not of me. I know things have hurt you in the past. I don't know what they are, I just see it in your eyes sometimes. But you mustn't be afraid of me, because I love you, and I have since that day I saw you at the Academy. I'd die before I'd hurt you intentionally—I'd die if I hurt you accidentally, too. I'm going to make you love me. I never thought we'd be together on this tour, but now that we are, I swear I'm going to make you love me as much as I love you."

Then his head blocked the stars as he bent to kiss her.

For the first few seconds she was terrified. She tasted the warmth of his lips, and felt their gentleness; felt how lightly, almost respectfully he held her with just one arm resting over her shoulder. The fear faded.

She slid her arm around him, drew away just a little and said in a hushed voice, "Do you know, I think you might."

Then she kissed his mouth with the ardor she'd denied far too long.

iv

After the kiss, he was the soul of courtesy. He continued to hold her, but he sensed the lingering tension in her and went no further. He put his old overcoat around her. Miraculously, both her chilliness and her tiredness vanished in an instant.

They stood talking in that shy, excited way lovers have, speaking of where they were going—far out beyond the Mississippi—to places they had only read about. She was unexpectedly, unbelievably happy. She could look forward to working. To perfecting her craft. And to being with Leo.

Perhaps Prince's prediction would come true, and Leo's as well.

Finally they fell silent, and she nestled against Leo's chest. He stood behind her, his arms around her and very lightly touching the undersides of her breasts through her robe. With his lips close to her ear, kissing gently every moment or so, they watched the immense banners of stars the night had unfurled.

The sky made her think of the flag. How many states had she seen in her lifetime? Only Virginia, New York, and those between. But the flag had thirty-eight stars now—Colorado had come in during the centennial year—and a population of nearly fifty million people.

Fifty million! So many—and so much country, westward beneath the arch of stars.

How wonderful to see it with someone like Leo. The prospect thrilled her. She'd write Papa and tell him everything she was doing—

Well, almost everything.

"Leo?" She covered her mouth to hide a yawn she couldn't hold back.

"Yes."

"I have to go to bed."

He cleared his throat in an exaggerated way. "At your service, madam."

To her astonishment, she found she could make light of something terrifying. Perhaps it would always be terrifying; perhaps the shame and the pain could never be expunged. Yet she took it as a hopeful sign that she was able to tease him.

"By myself, Leo Goldman. We aren't married yet."

"We will be."

She laughed. "You're impossible."

"And patient. Very, very patient."

On tiptoe, she kissed him, then took his hand and led him into the darkness, her fingers twined with his in perfect trust.

Chapter XII

Julia's Fate

i

ORDERLIES IN BLOOD-SPECKLED white aprons moved up and down the hallway where Carter and Will waited. The boys sat on a bench whose old wood was nearly as bleached and pale as their faces. It was three in the morning, Tuesday. From time to time Will reached out to pat Carter's hand.

The second floor of the New York Hospital at Duane and Broadway reeked of strong soap and other, less appetizing substances. Julia had been rushed to the hospital by ambulance, while Mills had taken the calash to upper Fifth Avenue to summon Gideon.

Carter and Will had said they wanted to accompany Gideon to the hospital. The boys had been waiting on the bench for nearly five hours. Carter sat motionless, staring at the old, worn flooring. The gas jet above the bench cast a sickly, wavering light on his face, and on Will's sagging head and drooping eyelids. Will jerked upright when a woman screamed in the distant reaches of the hospital.

He shuddered. Carter put his arm around the smaller boy and held him.

Some five minutes later, Gideon emerged from the nearby ward. His step was unsteady, his face pale and perspiring from the fever that still plagued him. Both boys watched Gideon. His expression quickly dulled the hopeful light in their eyes.

Carter's voice was barely audible as he asked, "Any change, sir?"

Gideon shook his head. He sank down on the bench next to Julia's son. "It may be hours, or days, before there's a change one way or another. You're too old for me to lie to you, Carter. Her condition is extremely serious. In the war, the surgeons always despaired when an ambulance brought in a man who had a stomach wound. The consultant I called in, Dr. Bradwell, is one of the best in the city. But even he's almost helpless. There just are no techniques for treating a wound like your mother's."

"Then will she—will she die?"

Gideon seemed stricken hoarse. "As I told you, we may not know until tomorrow, or for several days."

"What are her chances?"

Will couldn't tell whether his father was overcome with sorrow, or with anger. A little of both, he thought as Gideon said, "Very slim."

ii

At sunrise, Gideon persuaded the boys to go home with Mills while he kept the vigil. Shortly after eight, he was called from Julia's bedside to speak with a police inspector in the hallway.

The inspector reluctantly informed him that a sweep of Tenth Avenue had turned up no reliable witnesses to the stabbing. Several people had seen it, but most recalled the attacker only as a poorly dressed tramp. No one could remember a face, or a voice. The witnesses even disagreed on what the attacker was wearing. The inspector had three descriptions, no two of which matched.

Gideon had suspected it would come out that way. He simply stared at the inspector until the man doffed his derby and mumbled that he'd keep Mr. Kent apprised of any new developments. Then he put on his hat and shuffled toward the stairs.

Gideon went back into the ward and presently fell asleep

in the chair beside Julia's bed. When Dr. Bradwell woke him, afternoon sunlight was streaming in. In the bed beyond, a young man who'd lost a leg in a street railway accident moaned in pained slumber.

Bradwell surveyed Julia's still hands resting on the sheet. The backs of her hands were so white, her veins were clearly visible.

"You'd better go home and rest a while," the doctor advised him.

The pain beat like red waves in Gideon's mind. "I have to wait until I know whether she'll make it." He had never experienced such pain before—not with Margaret, not with his own father—never.

"Mr. Kent, I've told you before"—Bradwell sounded a trifle impatient—"it may be days. There is nothing you can do."

He saw Thomas Courtleigh's face. *Yes, there is.*

"All right. I'll go home."

iii

Two days later, Julia rallied for a few hours, then began sinking again. Gideon sat with her all Thursday night and into Friday morning, listening to her shallow breathing and saying to himself that he had to go on alone even if she died. The trouble was, he knew he couldn't.

Perhaps because he was exhausted and still sick, sometime during that long night something seemed to click over in his mind, just as it had the night he walked out on Margaret. Around seven, he kissed Julia's chilly forehead. Her lids barely stirred. An hour later, up on Fifth Avenue, Carter discovered him packing a valise.

The boy thought Gideon looked strange and wild. He spoke almost incoherently, as if he'd lost his mind. In a way, he had.

iv

"Out of town?" Theo Payne exclaimed later that morning. "At a time like this?"

Gideon stood beside Payne's desk at the *Union*. "I'll keep in touch by telegraph. Bradwell said there is absolutely nothing I can do here."

The editor's eyes narrowed. "You're going to Chicago, aren't you?"

Gideon didn't answer.

"There's nothing you can do out there, either. I've followed the dispatches Sal Brown sent back. I know you think that bastard on the W and P was responsible for wrecking your house—"

"And for Margaret. And now Julia. And for the death of a boy named Torvald Ericsson. And for God knows how many more that he's starved or cheated into ruin. Competitors, employees—"

"You thought you could get at him through that name your daughter heard. What was it? Huxtable?"

"Hubble. One of his attorneys."

"It hasn't proved out, has it?"

Gideon shook his head.

"You've got to be realistic, Gideon. In this country— in every country and every era—certain men are virtually untouchable. Their power, or their money and those they can hire with it, put them above the law. It shouldn't be so, but it is. It's the way of the world. In the United States we seem to be going through a long period of just that sort of thing. We'll either rise up against it, and curb it as best we can, or the rot that it's generating will spread and destroy everything that's admirable about this country. In any case, it isn't just your crusade."

Gideon didn't say anything.

"Look," Payne exclaimed, "you've run into a man who's above the law! Why waste your time with him? You'll only make yourself feel worse. You'll find the lawyers are no better in Chicago, and can do no more than lawyers right here. Courtleigh probably owns or can buy most of the Chicago police department, too. What can you possibly do?"

"I don't know," Gideon lied. "Search for new evidence, maybe—"

Payne shivered. "That isn't what you plan at all."

Gideon looked away. The little man began to plead.

"For God's sake listen to me, Gideon. Don't let one rash

act eradicate everything you've become. Don't reduce your-self to his level. Remember who you are. Remember the family you represent. Don't let the Kents be accused of conducting their affairs the way Courtleigh conducts his."

Gideon seemed oblivious. "Take care of the paper, Theo. You don't need me to run it. You never did. But I do thank you for all you taught me. Maybe I've done a little good in the last few years."

"And you can do a great deal more if you don't allow yourself to be driven into—"

Gideon had already turned and walked out.

Payne shivered a second time, upset by the rage he'd sensed in the younger man, and by the finality of his re-marks. It all implied something he didn't want to think about, but found he couldn't avoid.

At least not until he yanked the drawer of his desk open and reached inside.

V

In a dingy little gun shop on the Bowery, Gideon stood for a long time studying the contents of the fly-specked display case. Finally he pointed.

"I'd like to see that one."

The shopkeeper opened the back of the case. "Are you sure? This is a LeMat. It's twelve to fifteen years old, manu-factured in France, and imported mostly by the Rebs during—"

"I know what it is and who used it."

"Yes, sir, all right—anything you say."

Gideon examined the mechanism. Despite the revolver's age, it was in excellent working order. He laid it on the glass. "I want two dozen rounds of ammunition to go with it."

"Right away."

The revolver seemed the natural choice since the last handgun he'd owned had been the LeMat he lost the night of the Chicago fire. A LeMat went all the way back to the very beginning of his trouble with Tom Courtleigh.

Gideon put the box of ammunition in his valise, laid the wrapped revolver on top and secured the clasps. He had a sad, sinking feeling as he paid for his purchases. He was sorry it had come to this. But Sime Strelnik had been more realistic than he. Strelnik had predicted long ago that he would deal with the bosses this way, out of frustration and despair—even though Strelnik had never guessed Gideon's motive would be so personal.

He ordered the driver of his waiting hack to stop by the hospital. The hack stayed at the curb while he went inside. There was no change in Julia's condition. He knew from the eyes of the orderly to whom he spoke that those working on the ward expected her to die.

So nothing mattered any longer. Nothing but settling accounts the only way left to him—the way Courtleigh had always settled his. What happened afterward—arrest, trial, imprisonment, execution—was of no importance.

He climbed back into the hack and two hours later was aboard a westbound train.

CHAPTER XIII

THE LAW AND THE LAWLESS

i

AT A STATION midway across Indiana, Gideon left the train and sent a telegraph message to the *Union*. He asked that someone learn Julia's condition and wire the information to him in care of the central Western Union office in Chicago.

The train pulled into the city an hour and a half later. Gideon checked into the new Palmer House, flung his valise on the bed and washed his haggard face. He was exhausted. He'd spent the entire journey wide awake. He just couldn't sleep when he was traveling. Someday he should try to teach himself to—

Someday? A humorless smile wrenched his mouth. There weren't any more *somedays*.

He unpacked and loaded the LeMat. He studied the revolver for several minutes, turning it one way and then another in his hand so as to see it from different perspectives. What he planned to do was wrong. Absolutely wrong. It made him no better than Courtleigh. But he had no intention of canceling his plans.

He shoved the LeMat into the waistband of his trousers, between his shirt and waistcoat, and buttoned the latter.

With his frock coat on, there was a detectable bulge, but only a very slight one.

It was a mild August morning. With an unsmiling face, he moved through the pleasant bustle of the rebuilt downtown to the telegraph office. He stopped outside. He almost didn't want to receive a message. He knew what it would say.

Finally he went in. The clerk at the counter said, "No, Mr. Kent, nothing for you. But we've received no messages from the East for the last three or four hours. Sometimes storms knock down the wires and cause delays in transmission."

For an instant Gideon was both disappointed and relieved. The clerk went on, "The trouble's usually located and repaired fairly quickly. Perhaps if you drop back in an hour or so—"

"No," Gideon said with a slight shake of his head, "that will be too late."

ii

Thomas Courtleigh's office was located on the top floor of the new Wisconsin and Prairie Building two blocks below the river on Michigan Avenue. Gideon rode up in an ornate elevator cage and stepped off in a gloomy corridor.

To his left, at the corridor's end, he saw heavy doors with elaborately etched inserts of frosted glass. One door carried the word GENERAL in gold leaf. The other said OFFICES.

He walked slowly, passing the closed door of what appeared to be a service closet or work room. On the other side of the door, a man was coughing. It had a consumptive sound.

He passed through the main doors to a reception area and was directed down a hall to a similar but smaller area which could only be reached by the route he was taking; thus it had a certain privacy. The small anteroom held two cluttered desks at which a pair of clerks—one in his thirties, one bald and much older—faced one another. On a bench against the far wall lounged a burly young fellow in a garish plaid suit. He had a derby perched on his knee and a *Police*

Gazette in hands covered with an assortment of cheap, bright rings. The lump of a bolstered pistol was unmistakable on his left side.

Gideon gave his name to the senior clerk. He said he wished to see the president.

There was no response to the name, and a dubious one to his request. Would Mr. Kent state his business? He would not. Well, the bald man would take a card into the sanctum—he pointed to the heavy scrolled doors of dark wood—but he didn't hold out much hope.

Gideon produced a card, and the clerk's reaction was pronounced. Evidently the New York *Union* was well known at W & P headquarters, even if Gideon was not.

The clerk handled the card as if it were soiled. "You'll have to allow Mr. Freeman to search you," he told Gideon while starting for the double doors. "It's a policy we have been forced to institute since demonstrators broke in here—no doubt encouraged by radicals like you."

With that parting shot, the clerk vanished. The burly young man stepped to Gideon's side. "Raise your arms over your head."

Growing tense, Gideon obeyed. The bodyguard patted him here and there while speaking to the other clerk. "When's Kane coming back? I haven't had breakfast yet."

"He'll be back soon, I'm sure."

"Where the hell is he, coughing his guts out again? I don't like working around a man who's that sick." He finished the search and stepped back. "Nothing on him."

Gideon made an effort to keep his breathing calm. One of the heavy doors opened. The bald clerk emerged, looking astonished.

"Mr. Courtleigh will see you immediately."

Gideon smiled, but there was no mirth in the bright blue eye. Its cool ferocity made the bald clerk step aside.

"I thought he would," Gideon murmured, and reached for the ornate gold doorknob.

iii

The office was huge and impressive. It occupied more than half of the frontage of the top floor. The view was splendid from the row of tall windows to the left of the massive walnut desk where Thomas Courtleigh sat. The sun sparkled on the whitecapped lake. There were scraps of sail visible near the shore—pleasure craft—and a dozen or more lake steamers spread out from the mouth of the Chicago River to the horizon.

Yet the office itself seemed incapable of absorbing much of the outside light, and the moment Gideon heard the doors click shut behind him, the subterranean feeling only increased. The place was joyless and dark. Perhaps because of the heavy wood tones of the ponderous furniture, the wainscoting, the ornately carved fireplace and the chimney piece. The walls were hung with idealized oil paintings of W & P rolling stock, and with trophies of hunting expeditions. Directly behind Courtleigh, huge stuffed heads of a bison and a big-horned buck deer jutted put. Glassy eyes lent the heads an aura of sinister life.

The furnishings definitely contributed to the cheerless atmosphere but so did the two unsmiling men staring at Gideon. One was an obese young fellow, a stranger. Gideon had anticipated at least one bodyguard outside, but he'd hoped the president would be alone in his private office, though of course he'd known there was no way to assure it.

Well, even with all the restrictions, he would do what he'd planned. The fat employee would be no problem. He looked soft and weak.

Thomas Courtleigh tented his fingers. "I'm genuinely astonished, Kent. I never imagined you'd have the audacity to call here."

Courtleigh's auburn hair showed gray streaks now. Wrinkles radiated from the corners of his eyes. A pronounced paunch bulged the front of his waistcoat and trousers. He'd been working in his shirtsleeves when Gideon came in, and somehow he looked as old and tired as Gideon felt.

"To what do I owe this dubious pleasure?" Courtleigh's hazel eyes were unreadable. "Surely you didn't travel all the way to Chicago merely to speak to me."

"But I did."

"Oh?" That one syllable carried an edge of mild surprise, the beginnings of worry, alarm. Gideon laughed silently as he stood before the desk strewn with ledgers and memoranda.

"I'm a little surprised you'd admit me to this office, Courtleigh."

"Mr. Courtleigh thought it might be amusing."

The wheezy voice brought Gideon's head around. He'd turned his back on the obese young man who overflowed a chair between two windows. Now he gave the man a closer inspection.

The man's clothing was rumpled and duty. His left lapel bore specks of food, and one or two were tangled in his silky mustache. His goatee needed combing. All the hair on the lower part of his face heightened the nakedness of his skull.

Though the young man had truculent eyes, Gideon still didn't think he'd cause much trouble. The guard was the problem. He'd have to strike quickly, before the man could be summoned.

Sure enough, what he'd hoped for was right in front of him. A blade for opening correspondence. It lay within easy reach. The point wasn't as sharp as that of a regular knife. But if driven with sufficient force, Gideon was sure it could pierce the skin, and kill.

Sweat began to gather on Gideon's forehead. Courtleigh raised a hand. "No, no, Lorenzo—"

Lorenzo? Lorenzo Hubble?

"Those who oppose the formation of capital and the rights of property owners—the very foundations of this country—can't be considered even remotely amusing. They're dangerous. Mr. Kent is dangerous. He's a radical. A Marxist—"

"Or so you'd like everyone to believe," Gideon said.

"Yes, there you've hit it." Courtleigh smiled. "It doesn't really matter whether you are a Marxist—it only matters that the public is convinced you are. If the allegation's repeated often enough, the public will eventually believe it. As you may have guessed, I and certain of my friends are dedicated to that process of repetition—"

He frowned because Gideon was ignoring his little speech, and staring at the obese man. Sounding pettish all at once, Courtleigh said, "Mr. Kent, Mr. Hubble. One of our attorneys." Another smile, nasty. "And not in great favor around here at the moment."

Gideon nodded. "I know the name."

Hubble's tiny eyes blinked. "You do?"

"My daughter heard it the night of July twenty-second. From one of the men who broke into my house and killed my wife. The man said he'd received his instructions from someone named Hubble."

The obese man shot a worried look at his employer, then blustered, "What kind of ridiculous charge are you making, Kent? Do you think I'm the only man in America with that name? You said July twenty-second? The weekend of the strike? I was right here in—"

"Chicago," Gideon finished. "I've already checked into that story. But I don't believe it." He swung back to the desk. "Because I know how Mr. Courtleigh has felt about me all these years. He destroyed my house. Endangered my children. Caused my wife's death and probably the death of another mutual acquaintance who's lying in a hospital in mortal danger right this moment. Oh—and we mustn't forget the thugs sent to Pittsburgh. That's quite a list, isn't it? But it's nothing more or less than what you promised six years ago. I never thought you'd carry through on those promises, but you did. Sick man that you are, you did—and you've covered your tracks so you can't be touched. Not unless someone's willing to settle with you on a personal basis."

"Settle?" The word had a dry, papery sound.

"Settle," Gideon said, pronouncing it very clearly. He was trembling now. "And pay the consequences afterward. I'm willing."

Courtleigh seemed to lose confidence and shrink back against his chair. He tried to smile, but it was a mere twitching of the lips. "Surely this is a joke—"

"After all those things you did to me and my loved ones? Hardly."

"Lorenzo, you'd better get Freeman or Kane—"

The fat man struggled out of his chair, took a step. "He can't be armed, Mr. Courtleigh. They wouldn't have permitted him to come in if—"

"That's right," Gideon broke in. "I'm not armed. I had a gun when I started out this morning. I took it back to my hotel and left it there. I wish I could say I did it because I was high minded. I wish I could say I did it because I came to my senses and realized violence only begets more

of the same. Unfortunately none of that's true. I just recalled that I'd heard you employ guards here, and I knew
I'd never be allowed in this office if they discovered the
revolver."

He fought to keep his glance off the filigreed hilt of the
letter opener. He judged the distance. If Courtleigh remained in his chair for a few seconds, he could reach him,
drive that dull point into his throat.

Gideon's head hurt. His right eye was blurring a little.
He felt he was being swept down some long chute and
couldn't stop himself.

Hubble took another step. His left hand slipped up over
his paunch to unbutton his stained coat. Gideon saw Courtleigh glance toward the lawyer, but because of the eye
patch, he couldn't see Hubble himself.

"And I wanted very much to meet you face-to-face," he
went on. "I wanted to see whether you'd hide behind your
money and your authority even here, and deny you were
responsible for all those things."

"Deny it?" *Slam.* Courtleigh's fist struck the desk suddenly. Papers slipped to the carpet; a ledger thumped. He
jumped to his feet. "I would never deny that in this office.
You and I go all the way back to Sidney Florian. You cost
me the life of a valuable man, and then you cost me the
health and sanity of the woman I married, and finally you
cost me Gwen herself. Deny what I did? Of course I won't,
you bastard. You deserved every bit of it. And more!"

The words hung echoing between them. Gideon dared
not glance down at the letter opener for fear Courtleigh
would sense his purpose, and snatch the weapon out of his
reach. But pressure was building a terrible ache in his forehead. In his imagination he saw Theo Payne accusing him
with his eyes.

Gideon tried to concentrate on his surroundings. Hubble
was somewhere behind him—out of sight.

Courtleigh seemed to sense an advantage. He smoothed
his hair with a palm, brought his strident breathing under
control, continued.

"But of course, what you said earlier was entirely correct.
You can't touch me, or prove a single one of your allegations. Should you be foolish enough to print any of them

in that rag you publish, no one would believe them—least of all anyone charged with enforcing the law."

"Because you're above it, aren't you?"

Courtleigh smiled again. "So I like to think. I take your remark as a compliment, Kent. Since we're being so frank, let me tell you one more thing. Hubble has botched several assignments for me, and he'll be a long while regaining my full favor. One of the botches involved Miss Sedgwick. On my instructions, Mr. Hubble sent a man after her. The man followed her for several days before he found his opportunity. Now I understand she's still alive. I presume she was the mutual acquaintance to whom you referred?"

No answer. Courtleigh shrugged. "It doesn't matter. I hope she dies. But if she doesn't, be assured of this. The next man I send will succeed."

Gideon's control broke. He shot his left hand out and caught Courtleigh's throat, and with his right hand seized the blade on the desk.

iv

Courtleigh was soft. Gideon had no trouble dragging him forward with one hand. Or perhaps the rage that he finally released lent him unexpected strength. Courtleigh's thighs struck the edge of his desk. Gideon kept pulling, his face red. As he pulled, he pressed the point of the opener against Courtleigh's neck and watched the man's expression.

"Hubble!" That was the one word Courtleigh managed to squeal as Gideon dragged him across the desk, spilling more papers and ledgers. With his right hand he dug the opener deeper into the skin. Another moment and he'd pierce it, draw the first blood. He'd keep pulling and pulling until he'd impaled Courtleigh's throat on—

Remember the family you represent.

Don't let one rash act eradicate everything—

"Help! Someone help in here!" Hubble was shouting while Gideon silently cried out for Payne to leave him alone and let him do what was deserved and long past due.

Hubble's voice seemed far away: "Let go of him, Kent!
I have a gun—"

It didn't matter. Only Courtleigh's huge, horrified eyes
mattered, and his face bloating under Gideon's constricting
hand. The metal point went deeper.

Deeper—

Don't let the Kents be accused—

Bellowing like some gored animal, Gideon jerked the
opener back and flung it behind him. With the frustration
pouring through him, he doubled his right hand and
smashed it into Courtleigh's face, which had somehow become his own.

All of it had taken no more than a few seconds. Hubble
leaped forward to grab Gideon's shoulder—*"Stop it,
Kent!"*—as Courtleigh's nose exploded with blood. Hubble's fingers tore Gideon's coat. He twisted his head to the
left and saw a pistol in the lawyer's hand, evidently drawn
from a concealed holster.

Hubble's face contorted as he aimed at point-blank
range. Gideon released Courtleigh and flung himself to the
right. He heard the office doors crash open an instant before the pistol thundered.

The bullet grazed the side of Gideon's neck, or at least
he thought so as he fell. His back was toward the desk and
the reception area. He broke his fall with his hands. Dragging himself to his knees, he shook his head to try to clear
it. He heard a pained cry.

Courtleigh was bracing himself on the desk with one
hand. He had a sick, disbelieving expression on his face.
So did the lawyer. Hubble's fat fist all but hid the mechanism of his pistol. A curl of smoke climbed from the barrel.

"You stupid—*stupid*—" Courtleigh gasped. He couldn't
go on. There were tears in his eyes as he fell forward, his
face striking the desk and sliding off. He struck the carpet
and lay still. Hubble's bullet had found the wrong victim.

Frantic, Hubble glanced at the gun. Gideon was vaguely
aware of voices behind him. People in the doorway. Two or
three of them. One—it might have been one of the clerks—
exclaimed, "Don't let anyone else in here! Block the
corridor—"

All at once a sly glint showed under Hubble's half-closed
lids. He looked at Gideon, then flung the pistol. It hit the

carpet and skidded up near Gideon's braced left hand. Hubble spun toward the people in the doorway.

"Get the police. He killed Mr. Courtleigh. You saw it. You all saw it and you'll testify to it, won't you?"

The bald clerk nodded quickly. "I saw it, Hubble. I'll swear to it."

And then someone else spoke—the cheaply dressed guard who'd replaced Freeman in the outer office. "I won't testify to that, Hubble. *You* shot him. I watched you do it right after I opened the door, you dishonorable son of a bitch."

Slowly, Gideon raised his head. He knew he had gone insane. The deterioration of his mind must have started when he let grief persuade him to put all his principles aside and plan Courtleigh's death. It had started then and culminated in this—mirage, this—hallucination of a damned, deranged man . . . who heard his dead brother's voice . . . *who saw his dead brother's face.*

V

The guard was looking at Gideon with disbelief and something akin to agony. Gideon staggered to his feet. In a barely audible voice, he said, "Jeremiah?"

The bald clerk glowered. "What the hell's he saying, Kane?"

"Jeremiah, it's impossible that—" Gideon began.

Hubble didn't understand either. But he had more pressing worries. "For Christ's sake, Kane, how much do you want? Five thousand dollars? Ten?"

"I won't take a penny," Jeremiah said. "You killed him."

"Nobody'll accept the word of a known killer!" Hubble shrieked.

"Maybe not, but after I tell my story, they'll break down these other witnesses and get the truth. You're not going to send this man to prison on my say-so."

"Why do you care about him?" Hubble screamed. "He's a radical! A Communist! Courtleigh hated him!"

"Never mind," Jeremiah said, gazing at Gideon. "I won't lie."

Hubble yelled a wordless syllable of rage. Gideon

couldn't believe the incredible ruin he saw in his brother's face. Jeremiah was a young man. A *young man.* Born when? Forty-six? That made him thirty-one. He had the look of middle age. His upper lip puffed as if he wore false teeth that fit badly. A pair of spectacles stuck from the breast pocket of his jacket. There was a white streak in his hair. Phlegm rasped in his voice; it had the sound of diseased lungs.

But he was alive. How? *How?*

Suddenly Hubble came lumbering at Gideon, who was too startled to do more than sidestep and push him away. Hubble ducked for the floor. Gideon shouted, "He's going for his gun!"

But Jeremiah saw. His lips compressed and he reached under his coat with his right hand. Hubble snatched up his own revolver.

Jeremiah's gun tangled in the lining of his coat. Hubble fired. Jeremiah stepped backward, hit in the middle. But he got his revolver loose at last. Hubble saw that and tried to aim a second shot.

Jeremiah's gun boomed. Hubble shrieked, in genuine pain this time. He staggered backward, spun and crashed against one of the tall windows. He broke it and fell over the shards still in the frame.

Pedestrians below saw the revolver from Hubble's hand land in the street, frightening a dray horse. A wagon driver shouted and pointed upward at the grisly sight of a man slumped over the sill of a broken window on the top floor. From beneath the man's head, streams of blood began to flow down the face of the building.

vi

Jeremiah lay on the anteroom carpet. It was wonderful and peaceful to know that it was all finished, and that he'd never again need to fear Kola's prophecy or the irreversible disease eating in his lungs. He'd never again suffer the torment of having others fail to recognize his name or have to endure the misery of the animal teeth wired to metal rods and badly fitted into his mouth to replace all the teeth that had rotted.

He couldn't believe he'd found his brother here in Chicago. He'd had no time to wonder how it came about. But the attempt to ramrod Gideon into the hands of the police had been all too clear, and he'd done what he had to, and now there was a bullet in him and he could rest.

He felt cool and comfortable as Gideon knelt beside him. How had Gideon lost an eye? In the war? If Michael Boyle had ever informed him about that loss, he couldn't remember.

Gideon looked well for his age. Jeremiah hadn't seen him enter the W & P offices. It must have happened in those moments he was away, racked by another fit of coughing.

Someone said, "The police are coming."

Someone else said, "Yes, Hubble's dead. I looked at him."

"Jeremiah—Jeremiah—how did you get here?" Gideon said in a hoarse voice, touching his brother's face. "We thought that after Atlanta—we thought—"

"Oh," Jeremiah said, "that's a long story, as they say."

And one I'd be ashamed to have you hear.

"Why does he keep calling him Jeremiah?" a distant voice put in. "His name's Jason Kane."

"What are they talking about?" Gideon asked.

"I had some—different names—because—it was necessary."

Someone said, "He's Jason Kane around here. He was a famous trigger artist once, before the liquor got him."

And a lot of other things.

"Jason Kane," his brother said. "My God, Jeremiah, my newspaper almost ran a piece about a gambler named Jason Kane who was tarred and feathered in Kansas City."

"Same customer, I'm"—violent coughing—"sorry to say."

"My God," Gideon said again. "Out of nowhere, you saved me from prison or worse—Jeremiah, can you hear me?"

"Just—fine."

"They say there's an ambulance on the way. We'll get you fixed good as new. Then there are a hundred things I have to ask you—"

He felt the cold sweeping up through his limbs. In panic,

he thought, *Jason Kane made a mark. Not a good one. Not till the end.* Maybe what he'd done for Gideon would balance a little of the rest.

"Lots—of things—I want to ask—you—too—"

His voice was weakening. He felt tears, just like the ones he saw on Gideon's face.

Suddenly the pain pierced him. He groped out with his right hand. "Oh, Gid—hold on to me."

His eyes widened. Gideon closed his fingers around Jeremiah's, cradling one hand in both of his and crying as his brother's pain-racked face smoothed abruptly.

A strange half smile quirked Jeremiah's mouth. His eyes cleared for a moment. He looked at Gideon with absolute lucidity.

"I just—realized—it was—you who did this. Hubble—shot me but it—was because of you."

Gideon knew his brother was out of his head because he was saying something that sounded like an accusation. Yet he was smiling.

"So—everything happened as it was supposed to. Just as it was supposed—"

His head fell over.

Gideon spoke his brother's name twice, then picked him up in his arms. Kneeling there, he held Jeremiah while the warmth drained out of the body. All the questions would be forever unanswered.

vii

With Thomas Courtleigh and Lorenzo Hubble dead, the office clerks had no reason to risk perjury. They told a straightforward story to the Chicago police. Gideon was ordered to come to headquarters to give a statement, and to attempt to clarify the puzzling matter of the identity of the dead guard, whom the clerks said was named Jason Kane. That sure had a familiar sound, one of the policemen thought. He couldn't place it, though.

Gideon continued to insist the man known as Kane was also his brother. It confused the police. It would take some sorting out. Meanwhile, one of the policemen was dispatched to get an undertaker.

Gideon's engraved card earned him polite treatment from the police despite the way he kept confusing them on the matter of names. When he insisted he wanted to telegraph New York for his attorney, the policemen saw no reason to deny the request. He was, after all, a newspaper publisher. One of the clerks verified that.

He was too numb to feel much of anything as they escorted him out of the building and into a police wagon. One of the officers even apologized for the shabbiness of the transportation. He wasn't a prisoner, but they wanted to accompany him to the station and had no other vehicles available.

He didn't care. He felt dead inside, condemned to a life without Julia.

And Jeremiah, who had been alive, after all, was dead.

God help him, he'd never forget the sight of that ravaged face. Nor would he ever be able to unravel the riddle of his younger brother's strange words there at the end.

Well, what did it matter, any of it? The world belonged to his children: to Eleanor and Will, and to Louis' son. There was nothing left in it that he wanted or cared about.

A police inspector accompanied him into the Western Union office where he wrote a telegraph message to the law firm that represented the *Union*. He asked one of the firm's senior men to board the first express for Chicago, to help him clear up certain difficulties with the police. He said he didn't believe he was being charged, but that a lawyer's presence was probably advisable.

As he started to leave, the clerk held out a sheet on which a message had been penciled.

"Your reply came in about forty minutes ago, Mr. Kent."

He didn't want to take it. The clerk forced it on him.

Gideon glanced at the four words. New tears sprang to his eye.

The message was signed *PAYNE*. It said *SHE WILL LIVE*.

The epic story of the proud, passionate men and women who made our nation...

The Bestselling
Kent Family Chronicles

by John Jakes

"John Jakes makes history come alive."
—*Washington Post*

The Bastard	0-451-21103-0
The Rebels	0-451-21172-3
The Seekers	0-451-21249-5
The Furies	0-451-21283-5
The Titans	0-451-21347-5
The Warriors	0-451-21381-5
The Americans	0-515-09133-2

S471/Jakes